Revolutionary Fires

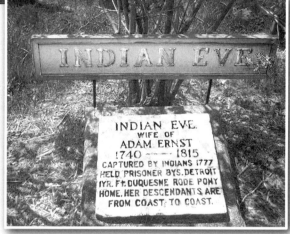

Photographs of the Messiah Lutheran Church and gravesite courtesy of Jessie Pruszynski and Ruby Lough

Across our country, isolated sites where founding mothers and fathers are buried need your support. To assist the Messiah Church Cemetery Association please send your donation to:

> Messiah Church Cemetery Association
> P.O. Box 488
> Osterburg, Pennsylvania 16667

> Your support will be greatly appreciated.

Revolutionary Fires:
A Tale of Indian Eve
Vol. I 1777 – 1779

Phyllis —
Life's journey is only as
rich as the friends & family
that we love.

Moira Z. Wilson
MZW Ink

Moira Z Wilson
November 19, 2005

Permissions: This small independent press has sincerely tried to secure permission to use quotes from materials originally printed after 1923. Houghton Library of Harvard University, University of Toronto Press, Indiana Historical Bureau, Burton Historical Collection of the Detroit Library, Wayne State University Press, Carleton College, the American Folklore Society, and the Messiah Lutheran Church of Bedford County, Pennsylvania are among those we were able to reach, who assisted us and who supported this endeavor. Some we approached never responded. Some efforts led to dead ends. While we live in times where much is available, we also live in times where tracking down sources can be difficult under the specifications of the new copyright laws. Without the assistance, support, and encouragement of those listed above, this book could not have come to print.

Please, be sure to take the time to appreciate the wonderful sketches drawn by British Officer Lieutenant Governor Henry Hamilton during his tenure at Fort Detroit or traveling the Wabash River. These are just a few of the sketches that have been preserved at the Houghton Library at Harvard University and represent yet another facet of a very complex man. [pfMS Eng. 509.2 (4)(7)(8)(11)(32) *by Permission of the Houghton Library, Harvard University*]

My deepest thanks to all these folks and many, many more unmentioned here!!
Thank you also for being a reader.
Enjoy!!

Know someone else who desires a copy of this book? Please contact
MZW Ink, % Moira Z. Wilson
PO Box 484, Hessel, MI   49745-0484

This book has been independently published. No copies may be made without
the permission of the author and MZW Ink.
Printer for this publication: McNaughton & Gunn
960 Woodland Drive
Saline, Michigan 48176-0010

This is a book of Historically Based Fiction.
Many of the characters are grounded on real people and real events but
it is still fiction in the fullest sense of the word.
One begins to realize that even history books may
Qualify to be fiction as well.
Over time,
Who
Is
To
Say
What
Is
Real
Or
What
Is
Truth?
Perhaps,
Only
The
Human
Heart
Knows
For
Sure.

Moira Z. Wilson
MZW Ink

Table of Contents

Sketches of Lieutenant Governor Henry Hamilton
Insert after page 310
  pfMS Eng 509.2 (4)(7)(8)(11) and (32)
by permission of the Houghton Library, Harvard University

Maps
    Major Tribes of the Northwest Territory
    Quebec Province
    Fort Detroit
    Forts of the Heartland and Ohio River Valley
    Major Treaty Lines (1682-1795)
    Major Treaty Lines (1807-1842)

Acknowledgements, Advice, and Dedications

For over thirty-five years, my family and friends supported this project. My husband Paul, from the first electric typewriter to a second go at college and four computers later, has offered encouragement to the woman who was told in her late teens, "you are totally incapable" referring to my English skills. To the hordes of librarians starting with the late Janus Storey and ending with Chris Roll, I have received monumental support. To the English Department of Lake Superior State University and to the Ken Shouldice Library, I owe unending thanks. Along the way, one cannot forget a first floor Librarian in Altoona, Pennsylvania who soothed an elderly patron when our sons dropped their rubber snake from the balcony while their distracted mother researched the Pennsylvania Archives. For those who love research, Inter Library Loans and the Internet have made this the best of times. I am amazed at the availability of information now, compared to thirty-five years ago when I first began. In addition, I have been blessed with the serendipity of chance acquaintances who have given me enormous amounts of information along the way including Sally Eustice and Ray Lozon (a relative of John Montour).

I am deeply indebted to the Messiah Lutheran Church near Bedford, where one can visit the gravesite of Eve Earnest (Erndst) Samuels. Because of their generosity and loving spirit, I am able to use the work of Emma A. M. Replogle. It is my hope that the people of our nation will honor the early founding women of this country as well as the founding fathers. I beg you to support this gravesite and others like it across our land. Glenna Fisher, Allan E. Semanek, Frank and Jane Antonson, and the late Thomas Imler of Bedford and Osterberg, Pennsylvania made tremendous contributions to this effort.

I am awed by the patience and by the commitment of my friends. They acted as editors and critics for me: Anne Westlund, Judy Hamel, Sandi Spieles, Janet Sitz, Dorothy Soudakoff, the late Kathy Hill and last, but far from least, Kim Dunn. These women (exercising the patience of Job) helped a dyslexic writer go beyond spell check and grammar check to a finished product. Hopefully, we caught all my errors, and I did not add others in the process. If you find more, let me know with my thanks. Number two son, Brian, prepared the cover, illustrations, and maps. As always, the support and inspiration of the Upper Peninsula Authors and Publishers sustains me. See: www.findingmichigan.com/uppaa for other Upper Michigan Authors.

This book is dedicated to my husband Paul, our children and grandchildren, my father, Fred Dibert, and my maternal Grandfather, Pah Pap, also known as David Malachi Mock, son of Henry Harrison Clay Mock and Matilda Imler. It is also dedicated to all the survivors in this world, which includes each and every one of you. We stand on the pluck of every single generation before us. Everyone has stories of survival because of the humanity and sadly, the inhumanity of mankind.

Support those who foster understanding and love. Fight intolerance, religious bigotry, and the restriction of liberty by those whose only motivation is greed and power. Pray that the noble experiment, begun by our forefathers and foremothers, helps to bring liberty to the world by example. Every single act of kindness creates another, as does aggression and hate. The choice is ours.

Apologies to anyone offended by my portrayals. I confess that I am a total romantic. I elected to use fiction rather than non-fiction with the hope that this will allow the reader to come much closer to the fantastic individuals that emerged from the research. As you can see from the character listing, most characters in this novel are based on real people or a composite. A hint, if the footnotes pop you out, read them later. You are seeing a pet peeve at work here, as I prefer to know what is factual in historical fiction. Another pet peeve includes the refusal in the "American Literature" canon to acknowledge American writers who spoke and wrote in languages other than English as part of our amazing birthright. Recognize as did the early Colonial leaders that we need a common language to truly communicate with each other, but we must also treasure our wonderful diversity...both constitute our national heritage.

Remember Benjamin Franklin once argued brilliantly for German to be our common language, as a final rebuff to England. As I understand it, they lacked one vote. Old Ben could be pretty persuasive.

Eve in Heaven

Eve, the mother of us all,
Walks in Heaven alone,
Jostled towards the outer wall,
Shouldered from the Throne,
Souls remembering her fall
Think upon their own.

Angels multitudinous
Shun her steps, and so
Saints and Martyrs scorn her thus
Praying as they go;
And "The woman tempted us."

From her side the seraphs start,
Lest her touch defile;
Modestly she goes apart,
Silent all the while.
What has she within her heart
Telling her to smile?

Still she smiles, nor envies yet
Crowns nor grace thereof
No—nor Saintly Mary set
All the saint above,
Never shall her heart forget
Eden and her love.

Sometimes even she will stare—
While the paeans roll—
At the Virgin crowned and fair
Whom the heavens extol,
Thinking, "She was never there—
Ah — poor soul, poor soul!"

Elinor Wylie, 1911

Prologue

September 1776

"These people from whom you receive this message are
enemies and traitors to my king, and before I would take
one of them by the hand I would suffer my right hand to be
cut off."

Lieutenant Governor Henry Hamilton to William Wilson, John Montour, and
White Eyes of the Delaware, September 1776 as quoted by Edgar W. Hasler,
Old Westmoreland: A History of Western Pennsylvania during the Revolution
(Pittsburgh, PA: J. R. Welden & Co., 1900), p. 22.

Betrayed by the Wyandot, William Wilson, John Montour and White
Eyes of the Delaware braced themselves against the open wrath of
Lieutenant Governor Henry Hamilton as they stood mute before the
council house in Fort Detroit. The beautifully woven belt, a beaded, peace
wampum, lay in scattered pieces about the ground at Hamilton's feet, along
with the shredded letter of George Morgan, newly appointed by the
rebellious Congress as the Indian agency's new leader. The three men had
been appointed ambassadors to extend an invitation to the Indian leaders
west of the Ohio River to meet in October at Fort Pitt to seek peace with
Congress and the new government. Their offer rolled like the beads in the
dust.

Hamilton's face appeared nearly as red as his British uniform as he
conferred and argued in French with Detroit's militia officers, many of
whom were once civilian leaders in New France. Rank, class, and
privilege, hallmarks of the old world, still held absolute sway under British
rule. Wilson, Montour and White Eyes had not planned to confront the
British so brazenly, but the Wyandot had left them no choice. Wilson,
unable to understand the heated French dialogue of the British commander,
felt uneasy, but far from terrified. Had he truly known the substance of
their conversation, he might have quaked in his boots. Ignorance spared
him, giving him the advantage of appearing fearless before the many
sachems assembled from the different tribes. He did not, however, miss
for a moment the lavish British gifts to the sachems about him nor the
undercurrents of mounting hostility.

Montour still smarted from the Lieutenant's raging fire. He felt as if
he had fallen from grace for not having followed the illustrious example of
his father, translator Andrew Montour, who had given remarkable service to
the Crown and Sir William Johnson. Unlike Wilson, he understood every
word, measuring the intensity of the hatred towards the three men by those
who spoke French, the British's Indian Allies, and their translators. The
desire to snuff out White Eyes' strong and persuasive voice for neutrality

burned pointedly in their dialogue. Having no wish to murder ambassadors, even those of questionable authority, Hamilton sued for civility and ordered compliance. His militia and the tribes assembled reluctantly complied, but not without loud verbal protests.

Ordered to leave Detroit before the sun rose, White Eyes endured the greatest humiliation of the three before his peers. If Hamilton had not guaranteed them safe passage, none would have lived to tell of their audacity.

Early Summer to Fall 1777 - Fort Detroit

"It is His Majesty's resolution that the most vigorous efforts should be made, and every means employed that Providence has put into His Majesty's hands for crushing the rebellion and restoring the constitution. It is the King's command that you should direct Lieutenant Governor Hamilton to assemble as many of the Indians of his district as he conveniently can, and placing proper persons at their head to whom he is to make suitable allowances, to conduct their parties and restrain them from committing violence on the well-affected and inoffensive inhabitants, employ them in making a diversion and exciting alarm on the frontiers of Virginia and Pennsylvania."

Lord George Germain to Governor Cramahe, March 26, 1777
as quoted by Silas Farmer in *History of Detroit and Wayne County and Early Michigan, 1890* (Silas Farmer and Co. Republished by Gale Research, 1969), p. 245.

Gargling daily with fresh urine could not remove the foul stench that issued from his mouth caused by his rotting teeth, although he tried. His diet laden with sweets had taken its toll, but no amount of sweets could alter the disposition of Philip DeJean, Minister of Justice. Close-set squinty eyes, hawk-like nose, black receding hair, he moved like a dark-pelted summer mink hunting in tall grass as he gathered his paint pot and regalia. His cold black eyes reflected the light from the candles which radiated golden light and warmth in the well-appointed room. Darkness and light contrasted.

"Is the great fire ready?"

"Yes, Governor Hamilton. The spitted ox near cooked. The rum has readied them for you, sir." DeJean's English was only mildly accented with his native French.

"And you have the tomahawks and the scalping knives ready for my signal."

"Yes, sir."

German=this font   English=this font   *French=this font*   *Delaware=this font*

"Did the fusils, lead, and powder arrive?"

"Yes, sir."

"Then it would appear that we are ready."

Lieutenant Governor George Henry Hamilton, British Superintendent of Indian Affairs, plucked a speck of dust from his red coat and polished one button with his coat sleeve before turning to face his inferior. The tall blond commander towered over DeJean. Hamilton's height gave him an advantage over men who deferred to stature. Young to have achieved his commission, he looked haughtily down at the shorter man who scurried before him.

"DeJean, is this absolutely necessary? I do not wish to play the fool."

"Sir, if you wish to win their savage hearts to his Majesty's alliance against the rebels as Lord Germain and his Majesty have ordered, there is no other course. Jehu Hay knows their ways."

"And you both feel that I must dance."

"It would be advisable. As they say, when in court…do as the King would do."

Over Hamilton's arm, DeJean slipped a wide wampum belt smeared with vermilion and covered with many miniature iron tomahawks. Through Hamilton's own belt, he slipped another wampum belt from the Mingos, before lifting the black paint pot off the desk to begin the final task. The flatness of the black paint contrasted with the spit and polish of the commandant's tall boots as DeJean drew strong black streaks on each side of Hamilton's long patrician nose. Two more black streaks were struck diagonally from the crest of his high cheek bones down nearly to his mouth. A final thumb-full was placed in the cleft of his aristocratic, well shaved, and well-defined chin. Hamilton turned his head quickly away from DeJean after the last stroke of paint, feigning a desire to see his image in the small silver-mirror that he clutched in his free hand. He stifled a cough.

"That will do. Enough!" Hamilton waved DeJean aside abruptly. Before replacing the mirror to the side-bar, Hamilton straightened his coat to his satisfaction, donned his hat to cover the plain tailored powdered-white wig, and turned to exit his quarters. Realizing that he had nearly forgotten his white leather gloves, he turned just in time to grab them.

Immediately, DeJean set the paint pot aside, wiped the last of the paint on his dark pants, grabbed his own hat, and followed the Lieutenant Governor. Major Jehu Hay stood waiting at the door and fell in behind Hamilton, keeping a tolerable distance from DeJean. They turned down toward the river and approached the sounds of revelry that filtered up the hill.

The fort streets lay comparatively quiet with only a few Rangers posted guard by Captain Mompesson. The deal struck earlier meant Mompesson's Rangers would be present at the fire to give an impression of unity between the civilian and military British authorities at the fort.

German=this font   English=this font   *French=this font*   *Delaware=this font*

However, in reality, Mompesson and Hamilton had difficulty being civil with each other.

Balmy and still intensely warm from the heavy heat of the day, the mugginess brought perspiration to the surface of each man's face as they turned toward the sound of the drums and the light of the fire. In the distance heat lightning flickered, backlighting the mounds of cumulous clouds. The soft roll of thunder kept in rhythm with the night's events.

"Major, did your men find a few who will remove the dead?" The officers knew that too much rum and the inevitable fights would take their toll.

"Yes, sir."

"It is very untidy in the morning to the locals when they find the dead ones. James Sterling and his reluctant militia men need no additional excuses for their lack of participation."

"No problem, sir. John Montour and Stalking Wolf assure me that Stalking Wolf's band of Wolf Delaware will help keep the peace and clear the area."

"Their price?"

"Double rations of rum, lead, and powder tomorrow, sir."

"They will do anything for rum, it seems."

"Just about, sir."

Their presence had not gone unnoticed. Outside the walls of the fort, a pathway magically appeared in a huge sea of red humanity. The men, militia members, warriors, and British Rangers alike, formed two great long lines from the river to the edge of the cedar woods. Near the middle, a great fire illuminated those who stood about a large drum which they continued to beat. Heart-like sounds pulsed in repetition. The voices of the encircled chanters slipped up and down from one octave to another.

The dancers and lesser drums stopped. Those who had dipped their cups and spoons into the pots of watered-down-rum strategically placed at intervals about the great fire stood expectantly. Behind the column of warriors, the women of the Ottawa, Potowatomi, Chippewa, Miami, Shawnee, Wyandot and a small delegation of Delaware from the Wolf clan lent support. All stood weaving and bobbing from the effects of rhythm and rum. A few women and warriors communed totally with the spirit waters. These had crumpled in place or dozed behind the line.

The smells of the great ox turning on the spit before them heralded the coming feast. Imbedded in the head of the ox, a large metal tomahawk with an incorporated pipe gleamed in the firelight. These special tomahawk pipes were developed by the British and French. Cleverly, the designers had integrated a pipe at the head and a stem within the handle of the cast tomahawk, making a highly desired trade item.

For weeks, Hamilton and Hay had met both to speak with and to listen to great and minor chieftains and their war lieutenants who could account for three-hundred warriors among them. The meetings had resulted in putting aside most of the old animosities and in creating new alliances.

German=this font   English=this font   *French=this font*   *Delaware=this font*

This event, choreographed skillfully after so many days of talks and diplomacy, built to an epiphany.**

Hamilton flicked his gloves at the temporary interpreter, John Coutincinau, who strolled casually to Hamilton's side. The Lieutenant Governor preferred that his department's interpreters, Jacques Duperon Baby, William Tucker, Pierre Drouillard, Joseph Martin and others stay with their respective tribes (the same tribes that these interpreters would lead to attack and to terrorize the Rebel's western flank). As a result, Hamilton condescended to accept the temporary services of John Coutincinau. The French trader had a reputation for a trumpeting voice, drunk or sober. His talents could be well used on this occasion. Besides, DeJean had recommended him.

"Eff we speak in French, Governor, most will understand your message from your English King." Coutincinau's tone smacked of superiority.

John Coutincinau, much shorter than Hamilton, burly, with his colorful centure fleche waistband tied tightly about his midsection, stood bareheaded and bare-chested. The perspiration exuding from his broad muscular chest covered with thick black hair plastered his curls against his tanned skin. The wisps of hair, curled in sweat which adhered to the sides of his smoothly shaven face, testified to his intake of rum and to his previous participation in the dances. Strong, virile, and ruggedly handsome, his long black curly hair was tied loosely behind his head. His manner revealed his adaptation to savage ways. A typical coureurs de bois, he walked with as much authority as Hamilton, which irked Hamilton, Hay, and DeJean alike.

"Do you speak fluent French, sire?"

Hamilton, the younger of two sons to Scotch-Irish parents, had rarely spoken cultured French in his home or within his intimate circle of friends. Educated well, his French, though fluent, lacked the accents and altered vocabulary of New France. The astute Coutincinau sensed that Hamilton, a veteran of the French and Indian War, felt a deep underlying animosity towards speaking in French, which gave Hamilton even less inclination to speak publicly. He also recognized from the governor's demeanor that this man did not like to trumpet his words.

Coutincinau, typical of those born in the new world, could care less about the achievements of the Lieutenant Governor's great grandfather, Sir Frederick Hamilton. His great grandfather, the Baron of Paisley and Governor of Ulster had migrated from Scotland. In the process, Frederick had amassed considerable land, money, and power in Ireland.

Of course, little of the inheritance fell to the Lieutenant Governor's own father, Henry, who was the third son born of his grandfather, Gustavas. With lineage practices under English law, although Hamilton's father held membership in the Irish Parliament and served as the tax collector for the port of Queenstown, he could pass little but name, prestige, connections, and a faint blood trace from Mary Queen of Scots to George Henry. So

German=this font   English=this font   **French=this font**   *Delaware=this font*

George Henry Hamilton had joined the military to seek his own fortune out of necessity. A true son of Cork, he quickly earned a commission in the 15th Regiment of Foot in the British Army, achieving distinction in the victory at Louisburg and Quebec during the Seven Year War (French and Indian War).

While in the colonies, George Henry Hamilton made two decisions, one minor, one major. First, Hamilton dropped his first name, becoming known simply as Henry Hamilton. Second, he understood that the military could only be a precarious and circuitous route at best to achieve his ambitions. Feeling the desire to be a civilian again with a capital "C", Henry Hamilton sold his commission. His love of luxury and his drive for political power combined with the Crown's discovery of his considerable flair for diplomacy after quelling the uprising in Terrebonne. As a result, Hamilton shared the power triad of Edward Abbott in Vincennes and Matthew Johnson, son of the late Sir William Johnson in Kaskaskia. They functioned as civilian governors for Quebec under vague orders and hazy lines of authority issued from the Crown through Lord Germain.

"Coutincinau, I prefer that you carry my words. Be sure your translation is correct!" Hamilton's disgust at even the presumption that he should lower himself to bellow loudly in French confirmed Coutincinau's earlier suspicions. *"As you may tell, my French is more than adequate to serve my needs."*

"Then first let us toast the King. No?" Coutincinau wisely changed subjects. After all, DeJean would pay him well for this night's work.

"Yes, of course. Toast the King."

"Brothers, join me in a toast to the king of England, King George the III."

Pandemonium reigned. Lines broke to push and to shove about the pots of spirits. More drums joined the main drum and dancing resumed with cups and spoons held high. Laughter and chants filled the air even louder than before.

"Drink, sire..." Coutincinau thrust a large pewter tankard into Hamilton's hand. Hamilton, sensing his role, raised the cup with great flourish. His chin thrust upward only to be greeted with a loud roar from the gyrating group before him. He drank to a chorus of cheers and then raised his cup once more as if to salute the dancers. Again the chorus sounded.

"Dance, sir." DeJean said under his breath to Hamilton.

Hamilton looked at DeJean as though he had suddenly gone totally daft.

"Now?"

"They expect you to dance, sir." DeJean whispered again before he began his own ridiculous shuffle about the fire. Major Hay nodded his encouragement and began his steps punctuated by small hops, jumps, and short yells.

Hamilton, seeing that he alone remained stick-like and straight as the

German=this font   English=this font   *French=this font*   *Delaware=this font*

walls of the fort, sensed correctly that he was out-of-step with the festivities. "When in Court..." he mumbled under his breath before breaking into an awkward, stiff dance to circle about the fire. The sweat building up under his heavy red woolen uniform caused him for one very fleeting moment to envy Coutincinau. He clutched his gloves tightly in one hand and his tankard in the other, being careful to show off the vermilion wampum belt without smudging his gloves.

"Brothers, another drink for the King, our father, who provides for us." Coutincinau improvised. DeJean frowned.

The crowd roared approval. They pushed and shoved around the pots, only relenting when a new pot replaced an empty one. In some instances, the new pot was drunk dry before it ever reached the intended spot.

Hamilton raised his tankard and pretended to take a hearty swig of the contents before raising the gleaming cup which reflected the fire light. Hamilton noted the head of the ox sagging. Obviously the great head, heavier still with the embedded tomahawk, was cooked through and could break free to tumble into the fire. The time approached for action. Calling forth one of Mompesson's Rangers, he directed him to gather others to remove the head and to bring it to him upon his signal. Snapping his fingers at Coutincinau, he whispered something in his ear.

Coutincinau raised his hands. Within moments, total quiet ensued.

Then began the verbal dance of Coutincinau, the interpreter; Hamilton, the superintendent; and the tribes assembled before them.

"Children, the great King of England knows of the pain you feel as the Rebels steal your Lands."

"Children, the great King of the English knows of the pain you feel as the Rebels steal your lands." When translated into French, a chorus rose like ash over a hot fire circling in the night air, flickering in the darkness, expanding with each ascending spiral.

"Your Father, King George, sees the Rebels cross the Alleghenies." Again the air filled with the translation answered by yells and drum-pounded accents. After each statement by Hamilton, Coutincinau, like a bandy rooster, translated the Lieutenant Governor's words into French.

"Your Father, King George, sees the Rebels stream North and West of the Ohio River." A cheer answered.

"Your Father, the King, understands the Rebels break their words to you." Drums and voices proclaimed agreement.

"His Royal Majesty grows angry at their surveyors who divide your lands before your very eyes." This time the response doubled in intensity.

"His Majesty is saddened that Rebels kill your beaver and stags, robbing food from your children's and your elders' mouths." Angry grumbles and a low consenting roar spun through the crowd.

German=this font   English=this font   **French=this font**   *Delaware=this font*

"Your Father sees the Rebels set up villages around the Great Salt Springs against their Father's wishes." The response from the Shawanese rose louder than all those assembled.

"Your Father sees the Rebels lay claim to the sacred Kentucky Lands."

The Shawanese response reverberated amongst a sea of red faces filled with anger again. Their loss of holy hunting grounds had built great resentment.

"The rebellious children have broken their word to their Father." Following each French translation, the crowd howled their agreement. The drums pounded, echoing the mounting excitement.

"These Rebels break his Majesty's treaties with you and turn against their Father and their brothers." This time the response nearly deafened the participants and those who listened.

"Your English Father sends many red-coated warriors across the sea to punish his rebellious children."

"Listen well to me, for I speak for the good English Father, who cares for you and your people."

"Who brings you blankets?" The drums answered. The people answered nearly in one voice at the urgings of Coutincinau.

Coutincinau relished his moment of importance. He crowed to and with the throngs, stirring up the frenzy like an over-boiled pot.

"The King of the English. The King of the English!"

"Who brings you kettles and cloth?" Again the drums sounded and the people screamed their answer.

"The King of the English. The King of the English!"

"Who brings you powder and flint to hunt for trade goods?" Each question brought the desired response.

"Who gives you fusils to protect your families?" The power of the rhetoric built.

"Who brings spirit waters to warm you around the winter fires?"

"The King of the English. The King of the English!" responded the fire watchers to each question as it was rephrased by Coutincinau into French. The spirited rendering excited the crowd with every statement as Coutincinau orchestrated their response.

"See how your Father, the Great King, provides for you." At that precise juncture and following Hamilton's preplanned signal, blankets, fusils, powder, and flints were brought forward. More rum, additional bolts of bright gingham cloth, kettles, and beads spilled before the women.

Immediately, the goods were greedily grabbed, hastily divided, and clutched up by those present. Squabbles broke out. Cloth ripped. Beads rolled in the dust again. Goods were claimed and counter-claimed. On one side of the crowd, a warrior fell as he was clubbed over a fusil. A squaw screamed in pain as another squaw's teeth sunk into her hand.

A hush fell over the assemblage. The Rangers marched forward with

German=this font   English=this font   *French=this font*   *Delaware=this font*

pageantry to the fire. The British Union Jack swung wildly over their heads. All eyes focused on the small troop. A young drummer drummed their steps. Soon the roll of their drum and the treads of their sliding march steps were echoed by Indian drumbeats. The Rangers cut the smoldering head of the ox free with flamboyant dispatch and brought the dripping head before Hamilton, who seemed now to be buoyed up by the heady response to his words and by Coutincinau's fiery translation and urging.

The rich smells of cooked tallow and blood filled the air. Blood and meat juices dripped in a narrow stream from the fire site across the well-trodden ground and pooled at Hamilton's feet as three Rangers held the great ox head before the Lieutenant Governor of Indian Affairs on their sabers.

Thrusting his cup and the vermilion wampum belt at DeJean, Hamilton pulled his white leather gloves onto his hands, seated each finger individually and tugged them perfectly into place. Each movement made dramatically unhurried. Grasping the hot tomahawk from the head of the ox, he brandished it in the air theatrically. Sighting the top chief of the Wyandot and wanting to use Half King's power for his own purposes, Hamilton walked forward with great presence, motioning to Coutincinau to follow him. Crying out at the top of his lungs, Hamilton thundered, "The King, your Father in England, sends his great armies to fight your enemies from across the immense salty sea!" Coutincinau thundered his words in French.

"Your Father will sever the heads of the Rebels in the East just like this ox!"

Half King looked fully into the eyes of Hamilton. Rage oozed from every pore of his muscular body. Both tall men faced each other. Each deliberately invaded the private space of the other with staunch purpose.

"Half King, I 'present you this ax to set against those people who want to possess themselves of your land. It is the King's command that I put this axe into your hands to act against his Majesty's enemies. I pray the Master of Life to give you success, as also your warriors, wherever you go with your Father's ax.'"**

Immediately, Coutincinau translated Hamilton's words into French to the captivated crowd. As he trumpeted Hamilton's words, Hamilton and Half King stood eye to eye, continuing to measure each other's strength and presence. Hamilton did not flinch. Neither did Half King.

Upon the last translated word, a tremendous cry broke forth from Half King, "'We take hold of the same tomahawk!!'"** Half King struck his war song, which soon began to spread across his fellow Wyandot. Other tribes began to raise their war songs. Half King covered the hands of Hamilton. Together, they held the tomahawk high into the flickering fire light. Then Half King took the tomahawk from Hamilton, turned, and lifted it high over his head with both hands as he cried with great passion in French, *"We take hold of the same tomahawk."* Then, in his own

German=this font   English=this font   *French=this font*   *Delaware=this font*

tongue, he bellowed the phrase for yet a third time. War songs and yelps from all present rippled back and forth across the seething mob. Screams of French and various native dialects mixed with English and crashed on the shore of the river banks like waves broken only by the rocks of Indian war cries and pierced by the wails of the women.

Hamilton seized yet another tomahawk from Major Hay's belt. He circled it above his head wildly. He yelled as he surrendered to the momentum of the event, any English reserve completely lost.

However, with some chagrin, Hamilton realized that he knew none of their war songs. He whispered a quick aside to Coutincinau, the interpreter, "What should I sing? What should I sing?"

Coutincinau sensed an amazing opportunity. What better time to play with the egotistical Lieutenant Governor. He slyly responded. *" 'Quand je vais a la guerre-ruh, J'emporterai ma grand cuillere-ruh.'"*** Clapping and singing aloud, he sang the words over and over. Laughing, he began leaping in the firelight, "'(When I go to war, I will bring my big spoon*), Quand je vais a la guerre-ruh, J'emporterai ma grand cuillere-ruh.'"***

Hamilton caught the music and rhythm of Coutincinau's words, punctuated by the drums. Ignoring the words, he began singing and yelling them just as loud as Coutincinau, if not louder. *" 'Quand je vais a la guerre-ruh, J'emporterai ma grand cuillere- ruh!'"*** Hamilton's voice rang. He danced and jumped as the tomahawks passed from one to another and then back to him. Staring back fully into each painted face that appeared almost magically before him, his blistering gaze added fuel to the enraged warriors. He repeated the chorus over and over as each man before him responded with a loud chorus of his own tribal war song.

DeJean receded into the shadows. He glared at Coutincinau. His lips silently spoke a threat. **"How dare you. You arrogant dog, how dare you ridicule me before Governor Hamilton! DeJean will not forget you, Coutincinau."** A drool escaped his notice as he mouthed the words once more before he drank from Hamilton's tankard.

At this moment, a principal civil chief of the Wyandot, Tscendattong, strode forward into the singing vortex. He nearly reached Hamilton before a Ranger barred his way. In distinct English, he made a verbal challenge which few of his tribal brothers heard as they took up their war songs and the tomahawk. But his words were absolutely clear to Lieutenant Governor Henry Hamilton. "Will your troops go before us? Who protects us from the Big Knives of the Virginians, the Rebellious Children of the British Father?"

Major Hay, standing near this chief, knew that he needed to drown out this dissenting voice. Realizing too well the tiff between Captain Mompesson and Hamilton, and the military's refusal to be part of the coming raids, Jehu Hay immediately broke into a raucous chorus of a children's rhyme that he heard the children sing-song daily near the fort gate. At the top of his lungs, he belted, *" 'j'ai le talon au bout due*

German=this font   English=this font   *French=this font*   *Delaware=this font*

*pied....(*My heel is at the end of my foot.*)'"*** Over and over, Hay sang his phrase as loud as he could to a makeshift tune. His words were slurred from the rum.

Tscendattong, sensing that his voice would not be heard over the spirits and the hatred, left the revelry to return to his camp. In his wake, Major Hay and the Rangers began to pass out the coveted tomahawk-pipes and red-handled scalping knives to the throbbing din.

Lightning and thunder spoke. But no one about the fire listened to it either.

**Closely paraphrased and some quotes from the text of Silas Farmer in *History of Detroit and Wayne County and Early Michigan, 1890* (Silas Farmer and Co. Republished by Gale Research, 1969), p. 246. Activities at the fire are a composite of more than one event.

Chapter 1   Home on Dunnings Creek

"I cannot conclude without expressing our earnest desire
that you will endeavor to discover & bring to justice the
perpetrators of the horrid murders committed on the
Indians at their late Treaty at Fort Pitt, which must
otherwise expose us to the shameful reproach of being
treacherous & perfidious as the worst of savages."

The letter of Governor John Page, Williamsburg, Virginia. In Council,
September 17th 1777 to General Edward Hand serving at Fort Pitt,
Pennsylvania. *Frontier Defense of the Upper Ohio, 1777-1778*, Edited by
Reuben Gold Thwaites and Louise Phelps Kellogg (Madison, WI: Wisconsin
Historical Society, 1912), p. 11-12.

October, 1777 Bedford, Pennsylvania

An involuntary shiver shimmered across Eve's broad shoulders,
prickling her back and erecting each and every hair follicle. The morning
sounds seemed diminished by the approaching winter, in spite of the sun's
promise of warmth. Even the freshly stoked fire behind her within the
cabin seemed insufficient to break her chill as she gazed through the sunny,
open cabin door down the slope to Dunnings Creek. Fog drifted in wisps
like tiny elfin creatures that tiptoed over the swollen creek filled with the
late fall rains. The cold air of the late October morning refreshed the
stale air that had been held all night within the cabin. Eve tucked the ends
of her woven shawl firmly into her thick apron-bound waist. Her braids
were already tightly coiled around her crown, preventing the ends from
getting in the porridge or slop water.

Winter soon enough would cast a gray and killing blow to the touches
of green which still remained amongst the fallen leaves and dried grasses.
The deep mahogany red of oak leaves edged to flat brown. The Sycamore's
tiny balls hung in the morning light, freed at last from interfering leaves to
dangle and dance in the wind. Eve monitored the sky and the beginnings of
the day. Not a single cloud. Full sun. Today would be warm. Indian
summer, she thought, filling momentarily with fear. Would the warmth
permit? Again an involuntary shiver shook her sturdy frame. Adam Henry
chided her for her foolish worries. "The war is far from us," he would
growl affectionately. "Besides, we have Fort Bedford near by."

But Eve could not fully repress the memories of the stories of the
Diberts' troubles. She could not forget the stark burned timbers about Fort
Bedford, nor ignore stories told by those who could read the chapbooks.
These stories told of terrible troubles, such as the tales of the Deerfield
folks up in the northern colonies.

1

Crisp pungent scents filled her nostrils. Apples, mounded in baskets behind her, were ready for apple schnitzing. Some would be made into crocks of dark, spicy apple-butter. She looked once more about her. Mornings held a special joy for her. She loved to see the low early sunlight dance across the grass, reflecting tiny rainbows within each dew drop. Each tiny glass sphere clung to its spear, longing for the warmth of the returning sun to sublimate its moisture. Today, however, the drops balanced lightly like miniature crystal balls, predicting a beautiful day. They were reluctant to evaporate.

Eve listened again to the various breathing patterns of each child as they filtered down the wooden stairway to mingle downstairs with the heavy, sated snore of their father. Adam Henry had returned to sleep after having awakened her earlier.

A slow easy smile inched broader as she identified the sounds of each sleeping child. The sound of sleeping children had to be one of the great earthly gifts a person could be granted to hear on this wicked earth, she thought. George could nearly echo his vater's heavy sounds. His patterns were slightly quicker and a bit higher in pitch. Their strapping fifteen year old with just a hint of beard would soon tower over her. Surely, he cannot be fifteen, Eve mused. Was it really sixteen summers ago that Adam Henry gave her vater a freshened cow to ease the loss of his favorite weaving assistant? Molly's little snorts gave her away, although muffled by her private blanketed corner. Her tiny snort, not a ladylike sound at all, reminded Eve of her sow, Minnie. Miss 'high-and-mighty' would wail with indignation if told of her signature sound. For a change, the baby breathed quietly with just a small rattle. For the first time in a week, Mikie had not greeted the early starlit morning with howls of pain. His ear-piercing outbursts hurt other ears in a vain attempt to share his pain.

In spite of Molly's doubts, Eve Dibert's Indian tea had worked well. Lil' Henry's temper would be less evident today after a good night's sleep. Jacob and Johannas, she could barely tell apart among the morning medley. Six children of nine had survived in sixteen years. "Enough foolish prattle. Far more survive here than in the old country!" her vater had snapped at her when she had mourned the loss of her second tochter (daughter) after a late spring fever had coursed through their community.

Always gifted with timing, Eve could still remember her vater's voice by the birthing chair for Michael as Adam Henry's strong arms encircled her contracting body.

"Time to quit the foolishness," he had admonished Adam Henry. "A man worth his salt can keep to himself." If it were not for persistent rumors of her vater's frequent visits to the backrooms in Chloe's Inn, Eve might have valued his opinion on the subject as she had pushed and strained to give birth to new life.

Eve paused, leaning against the jam. Tired already? The day had not begun. Then a quiet whispered prayer escaped her lips before she could stifle it. "Please dear God, I pray not another dear one. Mikie is not just two." As if to remind her of her wanton nature, a thin rivulet of semen ran down the inside of her right leg. Warmth continued to surround her, dispelling the earlier chills as she tucked her skirt quickly to soak up the sticky, musky liquid. Perhaps the fact that Mikie still nursed would keep another child at bay for a time. Her womanlies had not begun as yet.

So simply it had begun on this morning. Enveloped in the fresh scents of her mattress, filled with aromatic balsam and fresh hay, she had snuggled beneath the heavy quilts. At the first playful nudge, she awakened instantly and monitored her children's breathing. No one else was awake. She pretended to ignore the persistent surges by feigning sleep.

Adam Henry nudged her. Again. And still yet again. She could almost feel his gentle hardening as she remembered. The spot on her lower back where he had initially pressed still emitted his residual warmth. The memory of his touch lingered on her skin. Even now she could still feel his rough hands as he stroked the sides of her heavy breasts and brushed the tips of her hardening nipples under her flannel gown.

"Adam Henry..." she had whispered with a soft laugh. "Be careful, if I let down, you will get us both wet."

"Please Eve. Please..." So softly he had asked. Unlike many men, he never demanded his conjugal right.

Why could she not say no? Her mother told her "Lay duty at Satan's door. Say no. Enough is enough." Was it her namesake that made her so lustful? Was it that terrible Edenish hunger that made her long for him to touch her, to feel his beard prickle and tickle her skin, to have his hands explore her, to find his nose tracing patterns of delight on her moistening skin, to know the wetness of his tongue, and to hear his breath quicken to a deep sigh in her ear? And dear God, forgive her own wayward hands. Sometimes she felt that they moved of their own accord. They found a special joy navigating his muscles that soon moved in waves of pleasure and that quivered and tightened under her teasing touch. And the places she would put them to bring him pleasure. God forgive her.

"Enough, wicked woman of Eve. You will pay for your sins!" Voices from within whispered in her ears, sounding very much like Bruder Bergenfelder and her mutter.

But why must the pain of birth and a sweet child be biblically ordained as the punishment for loving another? Why did God return pain for pleasure? Why must loving be looked on as so indecent by many? Or worse yet considered simply a necessary duty to suffer and thereby earn redemption? Could one simply be close and loving without ever fearing pregnancy? Finding no answers to her outrageous questions, she broke her reverie, freeing her to begin the morning chores. Some inquiries must not be uttered aloud. The very fact that she questioned the order of life could lead to damnation. God forgive her foolish thoughts, she prayed.

Stooping over the small lidded pot by the door, she prepared to put the boys' night urine in her indigo vat. But there was no urine. Not again, she

German=this font   English=this font   *French=this font*   *Delaware=this font*

frowned. Lifting her skirts to clear the wet grass, her bare feet quickly treaded down the pathway that led to the house so that she could view the dormer first hand. Backing up and looking upward at the front of her home her eyes quickly found the telltale wet stain splashed against the house below the sill edge. Not even winter yet, and little ones will not patter down to use my pail she thought, shaking her head.

The cold wet grass caused Eve to return to the stoop. As she re-entered, the sunlight fell on the nearly completed coverlet on the loom within. Most of the fabric clung tightly around the breast beam, but the working surface still revealed a harvest of color. Too cold for her to work outside in the lean-to any longer, the loom had resumed its winter space. Nearly the whole family complained about its halving the living area. Molly particularly flounced about, wondering aloud why her Mother had to weave, when all her friend's mothers spun or knit. "Weaving should be a man's work," she stormed. Only her father Adam Henry's hot look had silenced Molly's faunching.

Eve's hand proudly ran over the surface of the overshot pattern. The bright orange-gold pattern threads, dyed with coreopsis and mordanted with tin, contrasted with the deep green brown-black made from the same dye when laced with rusty iron nails and copper salts.

Eve delighted in the dye pot. New colors filled her with excitement. She loved to experiment when she could find the time. Her vater had not discovered the rich dark color yet. He would never suspect that those gay yellow flowers, nodding in the wind up on the barren flats, could yield both these dye pots if one changed the mordant. Unfortunately, most of his colors were muddy and grayed from cooking in his iron pots.
Old man Broadhead, grumpy to most, had succumbed to her chicken pot pie. Over time, he had shared some special dyer's secrets with only one stipulation. Eve must never tell her vater, his rival. She found that an easy promise to keep. This permitted Eve one lone area where her vater's criticism could inflict no pain. She simply knew that her colors looked richer and brighter than his colors.

"Mutti, me catch. Mutti." Mikie's call from the loft opening immediately redirected Eve's attention. Turning quickly to the opening, she prepared to catch the warm bundle from above. She positioned herself just in time for the tiny creature, who trustingly hurled himself with reckless flight into her outstretched arms.

"You had best be sure Mutter's ready," Eve laughed, plunging her nose into the warmth of the child's clothing filled only with warm milk smells, before her hand stroked the mass of blond curls that surrounded the cherub face away from his blue sparkling eyes. Mikie squealed with glee, giggling as he tried to squirm down to the floor. "Come now, you pee pee in Mutter's pot." Positioning the child and lifting his skirt, Mikie soon obligingly tried to aim for the pot with only a few splashes on the stoop.

Lil' Henry crawled down the wall ladder from the loft.

German=this font   English=this font   **French=this font**   *Delaware=this font*

"And you, Henry, do you have anything left for Mutter's pot?"

Henry's chin dropped perceptively, but for only an instant before his dark brown eyes filled with devilment. "Yah, Mutter, I give you a little."

George and Lil' Henry, Jacob and Johannas, and Eve and Mike all shared trenchers. At the table, only Molly and her vater had their own separate trenchers.

"Mutti, Jacob is touching my meat again!" Molly sputtered as she tried to jab Jacob's hand with her fork, only to have Lil' Henry snitch her prize apple slice deeply covered with sugar and cinnamon.

"Mutti!" Molly's wail mixed with boyish laughter that bubbled around the table.

"What is all this unruly noise?" Erick Mens Emler, known by the English as George Imler, barked. Eve's father's short, stout silhouette filled the open cabin door. Quiet descended upon the room.

Unlike her vater's noiseless table, Eve and Adam Henry's table overflowed with banter, laughter, and chatter. The scraping of the sugar knife on the sugar block, milk, porridge in the trenchers, chunks of freshly pared-apple sectioned with the vater's knife for the younger Earnests and chunks of heavy grained bread loaded with freshly rendered lard filled the fall table. The harvest of seventy-seven had been good, even if it had been colder than usual.

"Good morning, Grossvater Emler," Adam Henry responded.

"I need help with the women." The curt order caused Adam Henry and George to leap to their feet, excusing themselves hastily from the brimming table to help the women outside from the wagon. The wagon's noisy approach had been unheard because of the morning's levity. The sharpness in Emler's voice had also silenced the affectionate squeals of "Opa" from Mikie and Lil' Henry which usually welcomed Eve's vater and their grandfather.

"You should be more watchful, Adam Henry," George Emler hissed under his breath to his schwiegersohn (son-in-law) as they approached the wagon. "It is warm today." He looked up at his bruder, Jac, who sat on his dark Bay, his double-barreled flint lock ready to fire, his murky eyes scanning the field surrounding the home. Jac gave a brief negative nod satisfying them both.

"You fear too much, sir. We are safe here." Adam Henry spoke quietly in response.

"Oma Emler, Schwagerin Jessie, Mrs. Samuels, Lizzie, Schwagerin Emily, welcome. Here, let me help you." Adam Henry reached for his mother-in-law, as George helped his Tante Jessie. Grossmutter Ester Ana Emler shook her tiny short frame free of wrinkles and reached to straighten Jessie's skirt.

"Mutter!" Jessie tried to stay her mother's hand. Unmarried and twenty-two, it was bad enough to be a spinster, let alone being treated as a child. "George, you grow strong."

"Yah, that is the way of it, Tante Jessie." But it was Lizzie's wide brown eyes burning holes in the back of his neck that made George most uncomfortable. This was a strange sensation for George. He turned to assist Mrs. Samuels, although Lizzie was next.

Adam Henry, sensing the source of his son's discomfort, assisted Elizabeth, better known as Lizzie, with a knowing grin. Emily Reighard, Eve's other schwester (sister), ambled down from the wagon with little assistance as usual.

"Adam Henry, our neighbor Isaac says he will help you with the fence rails come sun-up tomorrow. Is that good?" Emily Reighard spoke up quickly, for fear that once she began chattering with Eve, she would forget to ask.

"Yah, that is good. Is Joseph coming too?"

"Yah, I think so."

"Good, you tell Isaac that I will help him with his lean-to stalls when we finish."

Grossvater Emler groused about as he climbed aboard his wagon to reposition it where the horse's defecations would not fall in the pathway near the house. When satisfied with the new site, he carefully removed the long bore musket from its wooden hooks at the front of the wagon.

Adam Henry could hear the women's chatter funnel out the door behind him. He decided to leave behind what little was left of his breakfast. Two women in a house were bad enough...five more, a man would do well to exit.

Onkel Jac positioned himself on the porch with his feet spread slightly, ready to move quickly. His eyes repeatedly scanned the field and forest about them. His favorite double barreled flintlock lay cradled in his arms. He had placed wad, lead, and powder firmly. One flint was cocked and ready. An aura of darkness clamped around Jac like the dark shell of a great armored beetle, shielding him from any true human contact. Like the flint, he was poised to strike.

"I have better things to do than truck around with these women," Vater Emler snorted as Adam Henry approached him.

"You will eat the apple butter and the snitzings quick enough come winter fire," Adam Henry responded to his father-in-law's typical gruffness.

"Yah, but I have blankets to finish for the Blackburns." Vater Emler patted one of his prized paired blacks on the neck, straightened their manes, and waved off the deer fly intent on a bloody bite. "Humph, this weather brings the flies out. They smell blood, too."

Emler paused, looking around the small meadow adjoining the fields, scanning the tree line and the creek area. He placed his musket across his shoulders behind his head before he turned to Henry.

"I got to speak to you, Adam Henry." Emler quickly perused their surroundings, checking to see that the younger George and the other children were out of earshot. Satisfied that he and Adam Henry were quite alone, he prepared to speak.

"What news do you bring this time?" Adam Henry responded, trying to hide a trace of weariness in his voice. He tired of his father-in-law's constant litany of fear and unending rumors of horror. Yet out of respect for Eve, he prepared to listen.

"That bastard Hamilton, he is buying our hair now. That foul Englander!"

"Hair?"

"Yes, his filthy savages collect our scalps and then he pays them gold in Fort Detroit!"

"Oh, come now, Vater Emler. Surely..."

"Do not 'come now' me, Adam Henry. You listen to that Heckwelder and Zeisburger too much. I tell you since that shifty Shawnee, Cornstalk, and his son were killed at Fort Pitt in the spring," he paused to stress his point, "...those braves take up the hatchet again! The British egg them on, while your Quaker and Moravian friends drag their feet in Philadelphia and Bethlehem. And what do we get? We get no protection! That is what. They got money plenty to send to Washington's Rebel troops, but none for us. They want our men...our guns...and our money, just so Washington and his rich Virginians can wrest more land west of here from the British and from our commonwealth. That is what!" He paused again. "You listen to me, Adam Henry. Eve's Mutter say not to tell you, but two weeks ago, Eve's Onkel Jac was up near the nob hunting. He saw some of them savages. He bagged two of those bastards and a filthy squaw. Those two fell off their horses, in hell before they hit the ground already. Praise be to God."

A deep, deep shudder coursed through Adam Henry's broad frame. His short stubby fingers combed his coarse salt and pepper hair aside his head. He sighed.

"We are farmers, Vater. We do not make war. What good to kill us? What good to kill them? Let the soldiers do the fighting. That is why we came here to dis new land. Do you forget so soon?"

Emler scowled. His anger increased with the red of his face.

"You is a fool, Adam Henry! You is a fool to live so far from the town. Good God man, it is nine miles to der fort."

"Yah, may be so, Schwieger Vater Emler. But I am a blessed fool." With that formal address, Adam Henry turned abruptly from his father-in-law and trudged to the lean-to. His shoulders sagged. Minnie, the sow, needed to be restaked in a fresh area to forage for food. The cow, overdue for milking, lowed mournfully. Milk dripped from her teats. Her growing calf stretched its tether line tight trying to reach his share of the wasted bounty. The chickens feasted on the breakfast leavings. The rooster and prime hen squabbled over a tough crust.

German=this font   English=this font   *French=this font*   *Delaware=this font*

George Emler joined his bruder, Jac, to train his enkels (grandsons) in the way of arms. Best not to leave it up to Adam Henry, he thought.

"Eve, the coverlet," Jessie gushed, "bright orange gold and almost black. Will that clash with the blues and purples at the pillow edge and the pink, yellow, and gray in the middle? I think I remember blue, pink, and purple. Do I not?" Jessie covetously fingered the weaving peeking below the breast beam to see other colors soon to be wound in place over the earlier work.

"Yes, you remember well." Eve laughed as she handed Emily six newly dyed skeins in various shades. "I think of it as my Jacob's coat blanket."

"Oh, Eve. The colors. Wait 'til Isaac's wife sees these in my Christmas sweaters. Wool thread for you was a good trade."

"Foolishness. There is nothing wrong with the natural wool. God never made such colored sheep," Grossmatter Emler sputtered as she struggled to pull the bench from the table, only to bump into the leg of the loom. The grandmother juggled Mikie expertly within her free arm. "When is Adam Henry going to add onto this house? Eve, this place is like a pea pod."

"Yes, Mutter." Eve responded automatically as she set a large container of apples mid-table. "Molly, take Mikie outside and watch him."

Lizzie grasped Mikie's outstretched arms, handing him off to Molly, who stood with her arms folded defiantly. Her foot tapped as she stood by the door.

"Muuu tii," two descending notes of sass echoed through the cabin. "Can the boys watch him? Why me?" She finished on a whine.

"No sass now, Molly. The boys are shooting with Onkel Jac and Opa. You watch Mikie. Do not let him upwind of the target. You hear me girl?"

"Yes, Mutter." The descending notes rang of resignation as Molly accepted Mikie's plump form and scooted out the door, permitting a little additional space behind her. "I do not know why girls cannot shoot." She mumbled under her breath in Mikie's ear as she crossed the porch. She could see the menfolk setting up their target across the small meadow, so she headed down near the creek. Mikie would be happy there. Anywise, he could throw stones endlessly at the water and laugh at the ripples.

Jessie watched the girl's departure, and when sure that Molly was out of earshot, she spoke to the women of the table as their hands worked and the peelings flew.

"Eve, it is hard on Molly to be the only girl."

"How so?" growled Grossmutter. "How do you know with no children of your own, Jessie?"

"Mutti, please." Eve could sense her schwester's pain as Jessie's face blanched. "Jessie is right, you know. There are just two of us to fetch for Adam Henry and the boys. And with my weaving, Molly has more to do. Did you know that she pulled all the linen this fall? I have the floor above full of tow, thanks to her hard work. Besides helping me, she even cards wool for Emily and Eve Dibert."

German=this font English=this font **French=this font** *Delaware=this font*

"Eve Dibert, what you have to do with that breed, Eve?"

Emily amended Grossmutter Emler's remark, "Does not she have an evil eye?"

"Eve is a good woman," Eve retorted. She knew better than to tell her mother or her sister Emily of Eve Dibert's healing tea that had recently returned a smile to small Mikie's face. They would maintain that the tea could be the work of the devil. Just as she was sure that her mutter and Emily blamed every local woman's miscarriage on Eve Dibert's wandering eye since her misdirected gaze terrified them and others. No matter how terrified they were, however, if one travailed in childbirth, Eve Dibert would be among the first to be called.

"She is a strange woman," Jessie interjected.

"She is a widow. Her mann and one of her sohns were massacred before her eyes. Nothing more. You would be different, too, if that happened to you, all of you."

"I do not care what you say, Eve. I still say she is a strange woman. Her breed mann was murdered by the savages, yet she still grows and collects their savage medicines. Some say she has visitors in the night. She even chews Injun tobacco. Do not deny it, Eve...you know she chews."

"Yes, she chews, Jessie. We should all be perfect."

"No Eve is perfect. We women are all born sinners. Thanks to the first Eve, we suffer," Ester Ana spoke with absolute authority. "Enough tripe!"

Eve's mother had subtly reminded Eve again that Eve's untimely birth may have entrapped her mutter into marriage with her blustery vater. Eve did not miss the double entendre, even if the others failed or were too polite to wince or to look aside. Only Jessie flashed her sister a knowing glance and a quiet smile of sisterly support.

Quiet descended over the table, as the women focused on their paring and slicing. Each centered on her own thoughts. Lizzie gazed longingly out the door. She would much rather be watching George in the sunshine, than being in here with the womenfolk talking of dark subjects.

Outside, Molly turned her face up to the warm sun. Seated on the creek bank, her arms stretched in support behind her. Her hands anchored in the small stones, a mix of broken limestone and shale. She felt no pain from their hardness or sharp edges on her tow toughened hands. Mikie's giggles and splooshes faded from her thoughts as she imagined herself in the firing circle, with the gun stock placed firmly to her shoulder. Her bruders would look on with envy. Her shot would strike...

Mikie toddled and ambled through the tall grasses that waved over his head, moved by the soft breeze. Having slipped away from Molly, he found himself chuck-full of delight. He had seen something wiggle in the tall grass, askew from the mowed area and closer to the woods.

Something different.

Something strange.

He toddled forward. Fearless curiosity led the way. When he finally

German=this font   English=this font   *French=this font*   *Delaware=this font*

confronted that which he had seen move fleetingly, he was not as surprised as the warrior was to be found. Two deep brown eyes peered out of a mask of black that surrounded the eyes and extended into the coal black hair tied carelessly with a thong of rawhide. A white streak striped the chin, contrasting brightly with the deep mahogany flesh. The shirtless back absorbed the warm sun and leggings of buckskin brown blended with the grass where the creature stalked silently.

Mikie stopped. He cocked his head quizzically. His curls backlit by the sun haloed about his face in total contrast to the figure before him. What was this?

"Coon?"

It did not move.

"Coon?"

Cascading thoughts plagued Stalking Wolf. Now was not the time to kill the child. If this small one cried out, the cry would bring the men running with guns already loaded. Laughter would be the best weapon here. The black-faced figure slowly put his thumbs in his ears, spreading his fingers, stretched his tongue out to its fullest reach, and squinched his eyes shut. Wiggling all his appendages, the figure melted into the tall grass, leaving the giggling child behind.

A wave of terror swept through Molly as a sharp muzzle retort snapped her from her daydreams. Where was Mikie? Mikie where are you? Mikie? Her stomach lurched. Her eyes searched. Instantly, she realized that if she called out to Mikie, her own lack of responsibility would be clearly evident. The giggle reached her now hyper-attentive ears. Her feet quickly ran to the source. Thank goodness. Mikie was not in range of the muzzle loaders, but Molly sensed immediately that her vater would not be pleased to find him here in the tall grass unattended. As she approached, she lifted her forefinger to her lips.

"Funny coon," Mikie giggled, putting his thumbs in his ears, thrusting out his tongue, and squinching his eyes, only to be swatted in return. His long dress cushioned the impact to his bare behind. This was not funny? As he opened his mouth to loudly protest, his schwester quickly muffled his cry with her hand tightly clamped over his mouth.

"Shhh, Bruderlein. You get us in awful trouble with Opa and Vati," she whispered.

She removed her hand slowly from his mouth and then crouched before Mikie so that her own eyes were level with his.

"We must be very, very quiet. Do you want a big spanking?"

Mikie shook his head no very slowly.

"Quiet now, or Mutti and Vati will be very angry. Do you understand?" She whispered threateningly.

Cocking his head again, Mikie looked at her quizzically whispering, "Funny Coon-man?"

German=this font   English=this font   **French=this font**   *Delaware=this font*

"No more silly talk, Mikie." She shook his wee shoulder firmly but without hurting him. A yell of pain could still bring unwanted attention. "You understand? No more!" With finality, Molly arose and took Mikie's hand as they turned toward the creek bank and the stones.

Mikie glanced backward over his shoulder as he was drug forward. He wrinkled his forehead with questions none of his words could quite fit. Then a flying grasshopper diverted his attention before the creek beckoned to him once more. And as they neared the creek, Molly relaxed her grip on his hand, freeing him once more to throw stones under her watchful eyes.

Nighttime would come more quickly now with the approach of winter, so too soon Eve stood again by her door, waving reluctantly to her parting family and friends, who needed to depart to be home before dark. As much as she loved company, she felt an equal joy to return to her own. The cabin felt a bit stifling and muggy but filled with the rich spiciness of apple butter which simmered over the coals in the fireplace. Once more, laughter reverberated as the older boys no longer felt restrained by their stern grossvater and onkel's presence. Mikie squirmed on Eve's hip restlessly. He was overtired from playing outside nearly all the day. Having skipped his nap, he had become increasingly more ornery. He arched his back, thrusting his small body at an acute angle from his mutter. Then, as if invaded by some tiny demon, he put his thumbs in his ears, thrust out his tongue, squinched his eyes, and wiggled his fingers. Eve drew her head back quizzically, gazing at the little stranger in her arms. "What is this, little one? Who teach you this?"

Molly looked quickly away, turning her back to her mutter abruptly, so Eve could not see her face. Lil' Henry giggled first and that would be his mistake.

"You teach Mikie dis? Henry?" The question was pointed. Mikie, recognizing a new audience, twisted his torso, hanging still further from his mutter's arms to perform for the gathering siblings who came to see Mikie's latest trick. Squinching his eyes tightly shut and thrusting his tongue as far as he could, his face presented quite a sight among his dirty wiggling fingers.

Adam Henry had to forcibly restrain his smile and try to adopt a severe countenance. Clearly Eve's present state of fatigue would not abide this behavior for a single moment longer. He also sensed Eve's additional tenseness after having been around her mutter and vater the entire day.

"I did not do it," Lil' Henry protested between his giggles. Eve immediately pounced on both of the boys.

"This is no way to act, Mikie!" Her thumb, fastening on to the thrusting tongue, brought instant discomfort and a startled look. Mikie realized that his audience had been squelched considerably. "Henry Earnest, I am surprised at you! Why you teach your bruder this?"

"I did not, Mutti." Lil' Henry protested in vain once more.

"Enough of this foolishness, everyone! I take Mikie. Molly, help your Mutter spruce this area. I tell you a story. Then it is off to bed with all of

German=this font English=this font **French=this font** *Delaware=this font*

you. We have another busy day tomorrow. Isaac and Joseph will come early to help with the rails."

Mikie, sensing a time to tell stories, tried to gather his experiences of the day to tell his story to his family. Gathering his few words, he looked into his Vati's face. He began, "Funny coon?"

"Ah, so Mikie, you want a story about a Raccoon," his vater interrupted him. "Well, Vati does not know any coon story. What if I tell one about a golden lady?" Adam Henry knew Eve would have a fit if she knew the tale had come from an old Indian man who told stories at Garrett's for rum. But if he cleaned it up a little and if he did not murder the maiden at the end of the story to drain her blood over the fields,* Adam Henry knew that the children would enjoy it. Deflected from his own attempt, Mikie quieted as did the other boys about the fire, leaving the women to tidy up.

Adam Henry looked at the children's faces, a little wet from the cabin's heat but full of expectation. Even George, for all his years, loved a story. Adam Henry knew that Molly's ears would be listening hard, which meant she would not be stirring up trouble with Eve, who drooped with exhaustion.

"Well, this is an Indian story that I heard." Eve looked up sharply. Adam Henry smiled back at her. "It makes me think of our fairy tales from the old country, but this is a new country, so we borrow one of their stories tonight. Yah?" Mikie wiggled closer to his vater to snuggle nearer to the story voice that came softly from the chest near his ear. "Once upon a time," the magic words were spoken. An appreciative Eve flashed a broad smile and returned to her tasks. "There was a man who ate roots, nuts, and tree bark. He had no fire. He had no stories. He had no fine and loving wife. He had no strong sohns or beautiful tochters. He lived all by himself, far...far away from the Others. He was tired of digging roots. He was tired of gathering nuts. He was tired of stripping tree bark.* He did not eat good like we eat. He had no apple butter or bread with lard and schmierkase. He had no schnitz un knepp. He had no ham in the smokehouse. He had no chicken, eggs, or milk.

"One day he just did not eat anything at all. He lost his appetite. His life seemed not so good, so he just lay in the sun, dreaming and sleeping.*

"After he had been sleeping for many days and many nights, he awoke suddenly. Something or someone stood very near to him. At first he felt scared. What was this? Most importantly he realized—who was this? But when it spoke, he was very glad. There stood a young woman, just like our Molly with long blond hair."*

Adam Henry saw Molly smile and straighten. Lil' Henry thought of sticking out his tongue at Molly, but decided he better not. His mutti was not in a good mood. Although she did seem some better now. He refocused his attention on his vater's tale.

"This maiden lady was not like an Indian lady with dark eyes and the dark hair in long braids. Her hair hung loose like golden silk. He wanted her to come to him. But she shied away from him. He asked her to come

German=this font   English=this font   **French=this font**   *Delaware=this font*

close. But she refused him. If he tried to approach her, she seemed to go further away. Finally, he realized that he must find another way to speak to her. He cut a tiny stem from a bush. He made a flute of it. He sang to her of his loneliness. He played songs for her. He begged her not to leave him alone. At last, she told him that if he would do just what she said, he would always have her with him. He promised her that he would."*

"Where is this going, Vati?" Jacob interrupted Jacob as his vater made a pause for emphasis like any good story teller.

"Patience, Jacob...we will get to that. Now, where were we?" Adam Henry shifted a groggy Mikie in his arms so his arm did not go to sleep under Mikie's weight. "Now remember, the lonely Indian man wanted the company of this strange, lovely lady very much. So he promised the golden haired maiden that he would do whatever she asked."*

Adam Henry cast a loving glance at Eve's back. She asked so little, he thought.

"Well, the maiden led the Indian to a spot where there was dry grass. She told him to get two dry sticks and rub them together quickly. Soon a spark flew out and caught on the grass."*

"But Vati, would he not need steel and a flint?" asked Johannas.

"It takes longer son, but one can do it with sticks. I saw ol' Jasper do it once, but we digress. Now that spark burned as quick as an arrow. Soon the ground was completely burned over. Then the golden woman said, 'When the sun sets, take me by the hair and drag me over the burned ground.' The Indian man did not want to do that to the beautiful maiden. But she persisted. 'You promised me that you would do whatever I asked so that I could be with you always.' Still he refused. 'My friend, do as I say.' She told him that wherever he dragged her, something like grass would spring up, and between the leaves he would see her hair. When this happened, the seeds would be ready for him to use."*

George smiled to himself. He had solved the riddle and looked into the faces of his bruders to see if they had tripped to the tale yet. He smiled at his vater, who caught the knowing smile and nodded.

"The Indian man did not want to do this, but finally he did what he was asked. And to this day, when the Indians see the golden silk on the cornstalks, they know that the golden maiden has not forgotten them."*

"Vati, that is corny," chuckled Johannas, keeping his voice low as he could see Mikie was sound asleep and that Lil' Henry was not far from it. George rose, pulled Lil' Henry to his feet and walked him to chamber pot just outside the doorway. This pot was reserved for the collection of urine from only the youngest males in the family. This urine would be saved for his mother's indigo dye pot. George assisted in draining the small tyke before helping the groggy child up the steps to the loft. Pushing aside the strings of apples which now dangled like lumpy spider webs from the ceiling in between rows of senna and other herbs, he assisted Henry into his bed. Turning, he returned to the loft opening, knelt, and accepted Mikie from his father's outstretched arms. George gently settled Mikie in beside

German=this font   English=this font   *French=this font*   *Delaware=this font*

Lil' Henry. The younger child, although asleep, quickly cuddled up next to his older brother.

Returning to his place, George rejoined the circle of his older bruders. His vater pulled his long white-clay pipe down from above the fireplace to light a wee bit of tobacco as was his habit in the waning hours. George knew his mutter detested his vater's habit, but not the sweet smoke that filled the room. He had, however, overheard her remark once to her schwester, Jessie, that Vati tasted funny from the pipe. He wondered what his mutti tasted when he heard strange noises in the night.

"Vati?" George kept his voice low, so as not to wake his two younger bruders.

"Yah, George." Adam Henry visibly relaxed with the first puff of smoke which curled and mingled with the smells of apple butter and leftover supper.

"Does Onkel Jac still kill Indians?"

Eve nearly dropped an iron skillet.

Adam Henry drew hard on his pipe, clenching the tiny stem between his teeth set rigidly on the surface. He was no longer relaxed.

Jacob and Johannas' eyes riveted on their vater. They looked for all the world like two startled, wide-eyed spring peepers on a branch.

George stared down at his feet, unable to retract his words and devoutly wishing that he could.

"Yah, he still does." It was said very slowly and very quietly. Adam Henry decided that it was no sense lying to the boys. They would know soon enough. Gossip circled often in the small community.

"But Captain Jack died, and he does not need Onkel to kill any more."

"That is true." Adam Henry replied after a long delay and a third prolonged draw on the long clay pipe.

"Vati, why do you not kill Indians?" The question was so simply put. The silence stung. Everyone stood or sat stock still. The answer came very slowly.

"Never needed to."

Stillness filled the room, broken only once by the hoots of an owl without the glowing cabin as the sun dropped out of sight. Katie, the cow, seemed restless. Her mournful moo floated on the last of twilight, mingling with the owl's calls.

"Sounds like Katie wants Opa's Bull, Gregor, to come visit," Eve said in an attempt at humor that was gratefully received by Adam Henry, who adroitly changed the conversation's direction.

"How long before we take you to bundle with Lizzie, George?"

Finding himself now as uncomfortable as his vater had previously been, George flushed totally red, beginning at the spot where Elizabeth's eyes had fastened so intensely that morning. The redness spread entirely across his young face. The thought of lying next to Elizabeth with only the bundling board between them made him feel terribly embarrassed.

Quiet laughter filled the room as each acknowledged that it was time

German=this font   English=this font   **French=this font**   *Delaware=this font*

for bed. Each boy dutifully blessed the chamber pot before climbing the stairs.

Molly waited to be the last before her parents, desiring to avoid her brother's prying eyes before going outside to lift her skirts. Jacob and Johannas had become more curious of late. Evidently they had forgotten what they had learned about her in earlier years, and now she had absolutely no desire to refresh their memories. When she returned to the darkening cabin, she spoke under her breath. "Wish I had it as easy as the boys."

"Easy? You think they have it easy, my girl?" It was a soft question in response to the remark that Molly had made so quietly without realizing that her mutter had overheard her.

Molly's eyes flashed. "They get to shoot and everything, Mutti. Besides, they can stand up to do it. They do not get their skirts all wet in the grass or nothing. They do not even have to wipe. They just shake it."

A broad smile broke across Eve's full face. "Well, girl, you best had be to bed. Believe me, young woman; they pay a high price for their talents." With that remark, Eve took the small, wet hand towel from her tochter's hand to rinse and hang near the fire for the next use.

For the second time that evening, Adam Henry fought to keep a straight face when he would have preferred to laugh aloud. Poor jealous imp, he thought. Maybe I had best teach her to shoot. Would not that rake her Opa raw?

Eve noted the silent shake of his chest and his broad grin as he turned to dump his pipe into the ashes.

Eve crawled in bed last. Adam Henry still lay awake. She sensed his uneasiness in the darkness from the sound of his breathing and the position of his body. As the good book said, a man and woman should know each other. And this man, she felt she nearly knew; although he always had a few surprises left. Another dozen years and maybe she would know him fully. This was a desirable goal to be reached, she thought.

"Do you think that I should not have told them about your Onkel?" He asked quietly.

"No, truth is best, even when it hurts. The neighbors know. It would get back."

Neither spoke. Neither was ready to sleep.

Finally Eve spoke again, very softly. "I saw you and Vater speak."

"Yah, he is preaching fear and doom as usual."

"What fear?"

"Just more about dah savages."

"What about the savages?"

"Ack, Eve." Adam Henry rolled in place towards her, causing the ropes to creak.

"Truth is best, Adam Henry." She inclined her head so that their foreheads gently touched.

"Your Vater says the British are buying our scalps. The savages gather them."

German=this font   English=this font   **French=this font**   *Delaware=this font*

"You mean like those in Philadelphia who buy the heathen savage scalps?"

"Yah."

"He says we should move back to the fort, or at least nearer."

"But everyone gets sick there in the winter." The thought of losing still another child or perhaps each other posed the unthinkable.

"Yah, and where would Minnie and the cattle stay? They would die out here, if we leave dem, and the drunken folk's from Garrett's might kill them if we take them in the fort. Our chickens would be gone in a week, to be sure."

"I do not want to leave here, Adam Henry." A catch in Eve's voice spoke volumes in the darkness. "This is our home, Adam Henry."

"Yah, I know Eve. I know." His strong arms wrapped around her awkwardly. She said nothing more, but his arm felt wet where her cheek touched. And occasionally, a small shiver coursed through her body from top to bottom.

A troubled sleep fell upon them both as an owl called once more, breaking the stillness of the night. In time, they turned back to back, hip to hip, comfort to comfort, to sleep fully.

Mikie's first cry penetrated slowly into Eve's consciousness. The second louder and more penetrating wail indicated the ear pain had returned. Adam Henry's hand touched her hip gently. She acknowledged him by laying her hand upon his. Eve sat up slowly. She slipped on a pair of Adam Henry's heavy socks by the bed before padding across the rough hand-hewn floor. The fireplace, now full of low embers, gave little heat to the cool room. Reaching in the corner of the fireplace, she pulled the small container of medicinal tea that she had brewed in the event that Mikie began to experience pain again. A small pewter cup in hand, she scaled the loft ladder and soon settled beside Mikie, who was now sobbing and crying out with each wave of pain. He thrashed and struggled in Lil' Henry's arms.

Lil' Henry had tried to comfort him but to no avail. In the late hazy starlight, Eve could see Lil' Henry's look of vast relief when Mikie reached groggily for Eve, releasing his vice-tight grip on Lil' Henry.

"He is acting funny, Mutti. He keeps saying 'funny coon man' and then he sticks his fingers in his ears."

"Coon man, funny coon man." Mikie mumbled and then his fingers sought out his ears again before he began another loud wail.

"Mutti, make him be quiet." Johannas groaned from the corner.

"Be quiet, Johannas. He cannot help it," came from George's corner.

"Can you all be quiet!" sputtered Molly.

"Probably he was dreaming and his ears began hurting again, Henry. He will be all right once he gets some of Mere Eve's special tea," Eve said as she stroked Mikie's warm, sweaty face. As Eve placed the cup to the child's lips, he thrust out his tongue and closed his eyes more tightly than

German=this font   English=this font   *French=this font*   *Delaware=this font*

before. Obviously, the child was still not fully awake. Eve jiggled him gently until his eyes slowly opened again.

"Mikie, drink this. Mutti help."

"Coon man." Mikie started to reach for his ears again, but this time the bitter liquid in the metal cup began to trickle down his throat. He tried to turn away, but the gentleness of his Mutter's touch calmed him. Obediently, he swallowed the brew. Sitting cross-legged on the loft floor, Eve body-rocked Mikie between sips until slowly the special tea brought blessed relief. She nursed the child back to sleep and returned him to his place beside Lil' Henry. She descended from the loft. Upon reaching the floor, she stretched the painful crook in her back before she made her return to her bed.

Adam Henry's grunt acknowledged her return. She could hear a little shuffling upstairs. She heard the telltale dormer creak and knew that the urine dye-pot would be lacking again in the morning. She would have to have Adam Henry speak to the boys. If they were not stopped, the house would stink horribly by spring again. But for now, she felt just too tired to get up to address the problem. Precious time remained to sleep before the full sunrise. Isaac and Joseph would arrive shortly after dawn.

Her last groggy thoughts centered on Mikie. What gets into children? Always, something new challenged each day.

*Coffin, Tristram P., Ed. *Indian Tales of North America* (Philadelphia, PA: American Folklore Society, Inc., 1961), p. 80. "The origin of corn" A Wabanaki tale closely paraphrased and quoted for this chapter with permission of the American Folklore Society.

German=this font   English=this font   *French=this font*   *Delaware=this font*

Chapter 2   Indian Summer Closes

"I want to have you warriors come and see me, and help me fight the King's Regular Troops. You know they stand all along close together, rank and file, and my men fight as Indians do, and I want you warriors to join me and my warriors, like brothers, and ambush the Regulars; if you will, I will give you money, blankets, tomahawks, knives, paint, and anything that there is in the army, just like brothers, I will go with you into the woods to scout; and my men and your men will sleep together, and eat and drink together, and fight Regulars, because they first killed our brothers."

Revolutionary Rebel, Ethan Allen to Native Americans, May 24 , 1775 as quoted by Nelson Vance Russell in "The Indian Policy of Henry Hamilton," *The Canadian Historical Review, Volume 31(11)* (1930): p. 22.

Dunnings Creek Bedford, Pennsylvania

The children had not stirred noticeably. No doubt Eve Dibert's brew prolonged Mikie's sleep and so the others seemed to have joined him. Adam Henry had arisen earlier than usual to finish morning chores before Isaac and Joseph arrived to finish the rails for the expanded garden area. The area, now relatively free of rocks, had been plowed for the first time in September in anticipation of early spring planting.

Eve felt graced to have the hearth area to her and Adam Henry on yet another unexpectedly warm day. The moments that they could be quiet together alone were rare and therefore all the more precious. Once she thought that she heard a child giggle and shuffle about, but she dismissed the idea once the quiet returned.

Adam Henry held his cup of tea in both hands, allowing the heat to ease the increasing stiffness of morning and to dispel the chill that remained from having worked outside. He appreciated her quiet movements about the fire as he smelled the first few cinnamon-laden whiffs of schnecke. No almonds to be had here, only nanny berries, which tasted like raisins and hickory nuts, but they would taste fine enough. He wondered for a moment why the boys were not bounding down given their love of the small snail-like buns, but then with Mikie's middle of the night adventures and the busy day before, it would not hurt to let them sleep a little longer.

An owl hooted.

"Rain?" Eve asked questioningly of Adam Henry.

Adam Henry shrugged, shaking his head negatively.

Shortly thereafter, they heard Isaac's team and wagon.

Isaac loved to listen to the sound of bells. One Christmas he had been slow to remove them. After a number of his neighbors began a none-too-gentle razzing, Isaac stubbornly left the bells longer and longer. Now, he never took them off. Soon the jingling bells had become his trademark.

Adam Henry opened the cross bar and pulled the door open wide, letting the sun stream in. He resumed his seat at the table. A small low giggle trickled down from the loft, the sound of a few more soft shuffles, and then quiet returned once more. Reluctant to have the merry horde descend, neither Eve nor Adam Henry called out to them.

Adam Henry watched as Isaac and Joseph saw to their team at the side of the house. Isaac removed his long rifle and walked the path beside his son toward the cabin. Adam Henry glanced up just as the men paused to view the open cabin as they approached mid-path.

Suddenly, Joseph turned as cardinal red as George had the night before. He ripped off his flat black hat, working it nervously round and round by the brim in his hands. Then he stumbled directly behind his father, hiding his face as they continued to walk up to the door. Never once did he take his attention off the ground.

His father, Isaac, his eyes straight ahead, his Adam's apple at full attention as if he had swallowed a crane with a long beak, never wavered off the path, providing an impromptu shield for his son.

"Goodmorn' Frau Earnest." The formal greeting from Isaac caused Eve to quickly stop her tasks, pausing to wipe her hands on her apron.

"Frau Earnest? Now Isaac, what's come over you?"

At this point, Joseph turned an even deeper shade of red.

"I know **Thee** has a marriageable tochter, but **Thee** has a strange way of posting the news." Isaac had lapsed into bits of his mother's Quaker speech. The English '**Thee's**' had slipped in amongst the German which he did on rare, but more often than not, humorous occasions.

Eve looked at Adam Henry and then back to the two men before her.

Adam Henry began to suspect something was definitely amiss without, but Isaac's arm barred his way as he began getting up to exit his home.

"I think **Thy** wife should see to this, Adam Henry!" Isaac brimmed with repressed laughter. His eyes filled with tears. His cheeks fairly bunched like rosy apples full of good humor above his beard.

Eve looked quizzically at the two men and walked out on to the path. She stopped, turning to see the three men who peered foolishly out at her. But when she came to a halt, Isaac's waving fingers motioned to her to move further out into the middle of the path where he and Joseph had first glanced up. With each backward step Eve took, laughter inched closer and closer to brimming over for Isaac.

"Look up, Eve." Isaac turned a deep, deep red as he stifled a full guffaw before he turned his face away from Eve. He could not stand to

German=this font   English=this font   *French=this font*   *Delaware=this font*

watch her even a moment longer, or he would be rolling with laughter on the floor, and he knew it.

In the tiny dormer opening, two very female and very pink rear cheeks caught the morning light.

A hand flew to Eve's mouth. Oh dear, her Molly would never live this down. Her *bruders* were sure to tease her for a lifetime. Fixating on the path herself, she returned to the house mustering every force she had to repress the combination of her own laughter and to hide the embarrassment that she felt for her *tochter*.

Eve crossed the threshold, closing the door behind her.

No one bothered with the crossbar.

"Remember the discussion last evening just before Molly went to bed, Adam Henry?"

"Yes." Adam Henry answered slowly as he realized that his daughter had somehow found herself in a new amusing predicament.

"Watch the buns, Adam Henry. Someone is stuck in the dormer." Eve said.

Eve turned away from the three men.

Grasping the lard tub, a small towel, and a flat wooden paddle, Eve prepared to climb up into the loft, leaving three grinning men behind her.

As she crested the loft opening, she saw that her three eldest *sohns* stood like a great solid wall before their *schwester* and the dormer. At her left, Lil' Henry giggled softly by the loft opening, trying to help her up. Mikie still slept.

"Lil' Henry, go down and help your *vater*." Each word distinctly spoke had a deadly quietness to it. Eve had perfected an age old tone which fathers and mothers use to leave no wiggle room for the young.

Lil' Henry descended quickly.

Jacob and Johannas obviously wanted to escape too, but Eve spoke again.

"You three stay, I may need your help." At that, George stepped slowly aside to reveal the much tear stained face of Molly. Even in the shadows, one could make out her streaked ruddy face filled with shame.

"Molly and Jacob made a bet that she could not piddle from up here." George tried to explain, given that he was eldest. "And she is stuck."

"I see that." Eve answered. She sensed that her *tochter* would love to wail like a wounded pig; but given the recent arrival of Isaac and Joseph, she could not. Kneeling before her *tochter*, she took the tip of the towel, moistened it on her tongue, and wiped at the tear trails.

"You will survive, Molly. You will survive."

Prying her hands aside and lifting her nightgown, Eve saw that Molly was indeed stuck. Bent nearly in half, swelling had resulted from attempting to extricate herself. Each jab of the rough splinters firmly held her in place.

"George, open the roof hatch, so we get a bit more air and light in here." The men's voices softly chuckled and chatted below. Eve could

German=this font   English=this font   *French=this font*   *Delaware=this font*

hear the sounds of the pan of schnecke being pulled from the oven and trenchers being put on the table.

Using the paddle, she gently began to ladle lard around her tochter's swollen areas. Whenever possible the flat paddle edged between her tochter and the window jamb. When discomfort increased, Molly's sniffles grew louder. Jacob and Johannas each held tightly to one of their schwester's hands. Eve felt proud of them for rising to the occasion to give their schwester comfort. Meanwhile, George struggled a little with the hatch that his vater had wisely made to get to snow or chimney fires in winter. But when at last he could lift it with one straight arm, the hatch fell quietly open against the shingled roof. Eve proudly noticed that George had enough strength now to stop the hatch from falling with a resounding thud. Increasingly, he grew strong like his vater. Gratefully, she smiled. The rush of the fresh breeze circled the loft, refreshing Molly and Eve alike. Eve continued to ladle the lard in the attempt to help her tochter slip from the clutches of the dormer window. A wee smile soon came to everyone's face with the flood of light, even Molly's.

"George, come help pull Molly's shoulders. Jacob, Johannas, help her because this is going to hurt. Molly, I will pull your legs. Try not to scream, girl. You are going to get a few splinters. But, it cannot be helped."

Each positioned themselves for the pull. Molly took a deep breath. She fastened her front teeth over her lower lip firmly to muffle her cries.

"All together now, pull on the count of three."

"One…"

Molly clenched her eyes and her teeth, squeezing her bruders' hands almost to the point of pain.

"Two…"

As Eve continued to count slowly above, Isaac spoke to Adam Henry by the fire below as he bit into the warm schnecke with butter and sugar dripping down his whiskered chin.

"'We will not make many rails for it is going to rain soon—the owls are hooting.'"*

"Three!"

At the precise moment that Molly broke free, a deafening crash shook the entire front wall of the cabin. The door exploded open. Death followed two deafening volleys. Screams erupted from below.

Silence followed a whimper.

Molly looked dumbfounded at her mutter and bruders. She thought that she had bottled up her scream. Mikie sat up abruptly. His small body shook with terror. Then Joseph's cutting scream, gushing like the blood from his head surrounding the tomahawk, sliced into those in the attic, driving home a sense of gaping horror that invaded the center of their souls. Instinctively, Jacob and Johannas dove for the tow to hide, but George pulled them back abruptly.

German=this font   English=this font   *French=this font*   *Delaware=this font*

"No, they may fire us." All of them remembered the burned out ruins surrounding Fort Bedford and the scars on the Dibert home from the raids of earlier times. Brutal reality synchronized with the tales of horror whispered when the children were not supposed to hear.

"Dibert!" A word of instant communication sounded amongst Mutter and children. They had heard the tales of Indian troubles. Now they, too, must flee exactly as their neighbors had twice before them. Instantly, George began to stuff Jacob through the hatch. Johannas waited to follow. Molly, pulling her nightshift between her legs and stuffing it in at the neck, placed her foot shakily into George's hand, ready for his boost. Then George and Johannas pushed on her behind with little thought of their modesty or hers. For a fleeting moment, Molly looked back at her mother's sweaty face with tendrils stuck in tiny curving rivulets.

Eve mouthed to her, "You will survive, Molly. You will survive." Then she whispered very low to the boys, "Go with God. Go!"

Johannas climbed up next with a good shove from George. George turned to grasp his Mother. She pushed him away.

"German brooder bitch, descend with your chickens." The unmistakable English speech curtly demanded.

Eve turned for Mikie. If she and Mikie were to go with the other children, escape would be nigh impossible. Only one choice lay before her. She must stall to save the others. Never would she have ever considered leaving Lil' Henry and Mikie.

"Mutti," George whispered in a pleading voice to her. His hand reached out for her to grasp.

Her hand dropped to her side, pushing him symbolically away from her.

Eve never answered, nor did she look back. Pulling a terrified Mikie from his bed, she wrapped his small quivering arms about her neck and headed toward the loft opening.

"Ah, behold, brothers. The brood bitch and her brood come."

Realizing fully that no sounds came from her husband nor the other men below, Eve tried to move as slowly as possible without appearing to delay. The slower that she could descend the loft ladder, the more precious seconds would be left for her children to drop from the roof and to run from behind the cabin into the woods to hide. She prayed that the fact that there was no back door had not gone unnoticed by the savages and that their attention would be focused only at the front of the cabin. Minnie's dying squeal instantly confirmed that the attackers also had other interests. As the sound of the sow subsided, Eve's stomach lurched. She swallowed her gorge. Minnie and the promise of spring's piglets were gone.

Mikie hid his tiny face in his mother's neck as Eve began to descend through the loft opening. Brown arms reached for the child, but she swatted them away as Mikie clung tightly. Steady now. Slow now. Careful now.

Mein Gott in heaven give me strength, her unspoken prayer came as

German=this font   English=this font   *French=this font*   *Delaware=this font*

she deeply inhaled and viewed the unfolding horror beneath her. As she beheld her husband Adam Henry, Eve swayed against the loft ladder, clutching the loft edge. She paused. The bloody gleam of a major portion of his shiny white skull, the shredded gore of his chest exploded by the lead ball at close range, the bizarre tilt of his head, and the placement of his hands and legs quickly told her that Adam Henry was either dead or would be momentarily. He lay in a spreading pool of his own blood and urine. That same blood created an enveloping odor which reminded her momentarily of butchering the spring calf. Again her gorge rose, so she turned her head from Mikie and let the liquid spill below. The savage with half of his face blackened beside the ladder leapt back quickly. Eve clutched the ladder with white knuckles and again pushed away a savage hand. Slowly, choosing each rung with care, she made her descent. Each step brought her closer to the hell below.

Another brave stood with his back to the fire, nonchalantly munching on a schnecke with bloody hands. Behind him, Joseph lay haphazardly against the fireplace. Joseph's hand draped in the fire. A tiny trail of smoke arose as his sleeve and flesh burned slowly at the ember's edge. He had a large portion of his scalp missing which now hung loosely from the munching brave's belt beside a long, red-handled scalping knife. The stench of burning flesh mixed with the schneckes and blood filled Eve's nostrils. The necessity for air gave her no choice. She must breathe, bringing more horror deep within. She pressed Mikie's face to her shoulder in a vain attempt to shield him from the mayhem as she dropped from the final rung.

Isaac's partially bald head had not been spared the gross indignity of a scalping, either. Face down in another pool of blood, he sprawled in the mis-arrangement of death when muscles no longer needed to obey the needs of movement.

Lil' Henry stood stiffly like a clothes tree in the corner. His eyes resembled dark pits sightless with horror.

"Call down your other children, bitch!" The savage by the fireplace spoke as he pulled yet another bun from the pan. "We do not have all morning here!"

"George, Johannas, Jacob." Her voice quaked and broke.

"The young bitch too, trau bitch. She looks ripe even if she is stupid."

"Mary." Even Eve could hear the waver in her voice. Nothing she could do could control it.

At that precise moment she saw George out of the corner of her eye reach through the window to make a grab for the musket that still hung above the window. She heard Lil' Henry's yell as if it came from far distance.

All life slowed before her as she saw a musket rise in the arms of the savage beside her. She moved in the direction of the explosion of black

German=this font   English=this font   *French=this font*   *Delaware=this font*

powder thundering in her ears combining with Mikie's screams as George fell away from the window opening. She pushed against the hot barrel, hoping against hope that she had deflected the shot. Immediately, the savage turned towards the open door, so she threw herself and Mikie in his path. Her skirts blessedly entangled the breech-clothed bearer of horror. An arm thrust her roughly down to the wooden floor as the owner disentangled himself, swearing in French. Her diversion proved only momentary. Mikie began to bellow with pain as he was on the underside crushed by her weight. She rolled off of him and pulled him to a rocking position amid her legs. There she sat just as she had earlier trying to shush his screams of terror and pain.

Suddenly she was pulled to a stand. Mikie fell unceremoniously at her feet. A swift backhanded blow hit the side of her face. Lil' Henry, freed from his frozen state, leapt at the back of the man who had struck his mother.

"Ah, bear cub, so you want to be a hero." With a movement not unlike a horse sloughing off a pesky horsefly, Lil' Henry also fell to the floor with an ignominious thump.

"Try that again, cub, and I will kill your mother!"

"He does not fully understand der English."

"But you do, bitch. Don't you!"

"No more, no more Lil' Henry. Harm can come to all of us. You was brave, Henry, but do not do that again." Eve reached out to right Lil' Henry.

Henry hung his head.

Eve could hear the whopping and calls without. Mikie still screamed at her from the floor. Those who had escaped earlier were entirely in God's hands.

No longer could Eve ignore Adam Henry who sprawled beside her.

"May I go to my husband?"

"Why not? He's dead. Kaput as you say!"

Thrusting sniveling Mikie in Lil' Henry's arms, she turned her attention to Adam Henry. He had probably leapt for the gun, given his position. The shattered door hung askew on its hinges. She knelt beside the seated Adam Henry, smoothing what remained of his hair back from his blood-soaked face. She wiped the blood off on her skirt. A low moan came from his lips. Eve realized to her fullest depth of horror that a tiny flicker of life's pain still remained. Not wishing the villains behind her to have any realization of the fact, she protected Adam Henry's face from her captor's view. Bending very close to Adam Henry, she pressed her ear close to his lips.

A soft gush of air in a voice barely distinguishable from the sounds of her heart pounding in her ears came two words..."Bless...ed...fool," and then as if to make sure she heard them, the words repeated, "Bless...ed...fool...." His head fell forward onto her shoulder as his soul departed.

A single dry sob burst from Eve.

German=this font   English=this font   **French=this font**   *Delaware=this font*

Behind her, the attackers had returned empty handed. They watched her in silence. Finally fully cognizant of their presence, Eve arose from the floor to face her captors. The Indian with half of his face blackened had two scalps loosely attached to the rawhide thong that also held his tomahawk. The opposite side held his scalping knife. Both were covered with fresh blood. Splashes of blood streaked his chest. His bloody fingers curled around his long musket as he eyed Eve angrily.

Eve could not fathom his gaze. She recognized that the scalps belonged to Adam Henry and Isaac. The awareness brought a wrenching internal blow. Two others stood beside Stalking Wolf. The rangy one had a jagged lightning-like blue stripe aside his heavy face and enormous earrings hanging in large loops that once were the rims of his ears. The other stocky one wore a heavily soiled red British jacket and a stone gorget.

"Did you get them?" The leader, Blue Ice, asked.

"No they hide well. Not worth the time." The black-faced Delaware replied in his own tongue. *"Too many prisoners already."*

"What of the one you shot?"

"He is gone too."

"Too bad, we could have used his scalp. Now we go quickly."

"Not without the blanket. White Corn Woman loves color."

"We must not delay."

"What time does it take?"

"Those who escaped may bring others!" Blue Ice responded with a bit of sad resignation in his voice. He knew his men well. If there were no booty and no pillage, few would be eager for future raids.

As black-faced Stalking Wolf approached the loom, he withdrew his red-handled scalping knife. His first ripping slash of the warp brought a spontaneous shriek from Eve.

"Nein!"

Quizzically, Stalking Wolf looked at Eve, who walked boldly to his side to lift her long shears from the string where it dangled at the side of the loom. Out of fear for her sons' lives, she killed the impulse to drive the shears into his heart like a dagger. Mechanically, Eve lifted the shears to begin to free the coverlet from the loom. As each warp thread snapped before the shears, allowing the coverlet to drop in threaded sequence, a fiber of Eve's being snapped as well. Freeing the shuttle and its thread, Eve completed the task.

As the last few threads were severed, Stalking Wolf pushed Eve gruffly aside from his prize. Snatching the shears from her hands, ripping them free of the cord which held them, he stuffed them casually into his waist thong. In placing the shears, the drying scalps near his tomahawk attached to his belt dislodged slightly.

German=this font   English=this font   *French=this font*   *Delaware=this font*

White Corn Woman would like these twin cutting knives too, he thought, as he began to pull the coverlet from the breast beam. He yanked hard upon the cloth which stubbornly resisted his efforts.

Again Eve pushed him aside.

Stalking Wolf gave her room. This woman did not cower.

Her hands shook. Reaching under the breast beam to release the pawl which disengaged the clutch, Eve freed the breast beam from the tension. The tension released; a cascade of colors spilled to the floor as the coverlet unwound into a looped heap.

Immediately, interest in the coverlet increased around the room. The red-jacketed brave shouldered in for a closer view, jostling Eve into Stalking Wolf.

So intent was the brave on viewing the bounty of colors that had spilled before his eyes, Stalking Wolf failed to sense the hand that inadvertently touched the scalps held in his leather thong belt.

The touch went unnoticed.

At first, when Eve's hand became entangled in the scalps, a wave of revulsion filled her. But this immediately changed to steely anger and then to rage. The bastards would not have Adam Henry's scalp. Not if she could help it. Jostled by the braves, Eve began to gently tug the scalps free of Stalking Wolf's waist thong. Wet blood permitted easy slippage. His hand straightened his shifting tomahawk. In the process, his hand nearly collided with hers.

Her heart stopped. She began pulling once more. Her movements continued to go unnoticed as still another brave, Sitting Rabbit, jockeyed for position, ramming her into Stalking Wolf's side once more.

A wave of jealous competition arose. Sitting Rabbit and Stalking Wolf both pushed forward. Each tried to make a claim on the woven goods. Their movements proved totally providential for Eve, who pulled the scalps free with one last quick jerk and hid them in the folds of her skirt.

As the tenor of their voices rose, Eve could sense that a fight might ensue between her captors, who obviously appreciated color as much as she. Seeing their intense distraction with the coverlet, she continued to back slowly up to the bureau, moving behind Lil' Henry and Mikie. One hand rested on Henry. The other extended slowly behind her to reach across a drawer left open in the looting. Moving stealthily, so as not to draw anyone's attention including the boys, she slipped the clutched scalps over the back of the open drawer and dropped the bloody scalps deftly between the wooden bureau and the wall. Whispering some stupid nonsense syllables in Henry's ear, she tipped her body forward before withdrawing her hand just as carefully. Then she straightened up gradually, using her full hips to gently ease the drawer shut. For the second time that morning, the sound of her heart hammered in her ears with every beat as she wiped a bit of fresh blood within the folds of her skirt.

You *arsch pauker!* Her thoughts pounded in rhythm with her beating

German=this font   English=this font   **French=this font**   *Delaware=this font*

heart. You will not sell my Adam Henry's scalp. You will not sell him to the British dogs.

The leader, Blue Ice, standing by the fireplace, scowled before he wiped his face across his forearm to remove some of the melted butter.

"Brothers, divide the blanket later, or we may be divided from our lives!"

Immediately, the discord ceased. Stalking Wolf, using the shears, began to cut the coverlet free. His total focus remained only on the coverlet. Forcing Eve and the boys crudely aside, Sitting Rabbit pulled a quilt from the bed and began stuffing items into his makeshift bag.

"Silence the child, or he dies!" Blue Ice snapped at Eve.

Henry suddenly found his brother replaced by his mother's largest iron skillet. Then, the braves directed the threesome toward the open door. Sitting Rabbit slung the quilt filled with hastily grabbed booty over his shoulder. Blue Ice gathered up the two rifles, pouches, and their respective powder horns.

Stepping over Adam Henry's splayed feet, Eve moved numbly. Cradling Mikie against her and clutching Lil' Henry's night shirt with her dry but bloody hand, she led her two terrified children from the cabin. The light of the morning sun blinded her momentarily, but the warmth could not touch her. Prodded again, she fell in behind one brave. She did not look in the direction of those who might have escaped or who might have been killed. She must protect Mikie and Lil' Henry. She must keep them all together.

As Stalking Wolf finished his task at the loom, he threw the coverlet over his shoulder, covering the site of the missing scalps, and placed the shears in his traveling pouch. No points to jab his waist as he walked, he reasoned.

Laying aside the rifles for a moment, Blue Ice began to fish impatiently inside his pouch. The morning light for a moment played across the lines of flawless penmanship. The butter on his hands gave a transparency to one corner. He dipped the back side of the paper in the wettest blood very briefly and plastered it to the side of Adam Henry's face. The required deed done, both men nodded their accord. Gathering the last of the desired Earnest possessions, they withdrew from the cabin.

Prisoners presented such a bother, remained unspoken but felt by all.

Outside, another brave stood quietly with Isaac's team. One tethered to each hand. Both horses stood freed from bells and carriage; their hooves had been wrapped to prevent tracking. Minnie's freshly butchered haunches, a metal hoe, and wooden rake tied with rope straddled the dark bay. The hind legs of the cow hung over the other. The calf cried sadly over its half-butchered mother. Nudging the carcass, the perplexed calf could smell the milk but failed to understand why its mother refused to stand.

From behind, a gruff push sent Eve stumbling into Dunnings Creek.

German=this font English=this font **French=this font** *Delaware=this font*

Bits of slate gashed at her feet, tearing at her shoes. The cold clear water chilled her further and wicked up her woolen skirt.

Shock descended like the small wavelets that rolled over her feet. The dreaded Indian summer had struck another frontier home on the Rebel frontier in what would be known in time as the bloody winter of sevens.

Replogle, Emma. *Indian Eve and Her Descendants* (1911. Bedford, PA: Reprinted by Messiah Lutheran Church, 1990), p.15-20. This chapter inspired by Emma Replogle's account which related Eve hiding Adam Henry's scalp and the removal of the coverlet from her loom.
*as quoted in *Indian Eve and her Descendants*, Emma A. M. Replogle, p. 16.

German=this font   English=this font   *French=this font*   *Delaware=this font*

Chapter 3   The Journey Begins

"Since the closing of the council, I have been at the War
feast of each nation, and with the greatest decency and
alacrity has appeared. 30th of June most of the Nations
had brought in their Sticks for the number of warriors,
and in a Month I don't question one thousand Warriors
going against the Frontiers. At the same time I have
exhorted them to spare Old Age Women and children."

Henry Hamilton, Extract of June 1777 as quoted in *Frontier Defense on the
Upper Ohio, 1777-1778*. Edited by Reuben Gold Thwaites and Louise Phelps
Kellogg (Madison, WI: Wisconsin Historical Society, 1912), p. 13.

Near Dunnings Creek, Bedford, Pennsylvania

Molly lay shivering in the deep grass and nettles. Even with her eyes
scrunched tightly closed, she could not extinguish the image that played
before her. The face with black about its eyes haunted her. She knew that
he saw her. Their eyes had fully engaged. As the air rushed from her lungs
two words involuntarily joined the exhalation, "Coon man..."

Stalking Wolf had begun to reach toward her only to brush the nettles
that surrounded her. She had then crunched her eyes shut and covered her
head with her arms.

Molly heard a deep grunt, a rustle of grass, a warhoop, and then
stillness.

The quiet that surrounded her roared in her ears like the first wind of a
storm. Her heart sounds accompanied the terror. The sting of the nettles
brought less pain than the guilt hatchets that slashed at her from every
direction of her being.

Time crawled like a slug leaving an iridescent trail. The quiet
remained. Finally, the song of a meadow lark broke through the stillness.
A cricket warmed by the late fall sun joined the chorus which was answered
by still another across the field. Sound returned to the banks of Dunnings
Creek. The sun gradually invaded the shady spot where Molly lay and
began to flood her back with warmth. Had her bruders escaped? Where
would they have gone? Did they attempt to get to Wood's Stockade? Did
they go to the Diberts' cabin? Would they send help? What should she do?
She knew that her arms had welts where she and the nettles had kept close
company. The increasing sensation of pain urged her to move.

Deliberately, she struggled to a stand. Staggering momentarily, she
searched the area about her.

When she could not perceive any movement, she cautiously left her
painful thicket. Her bare feet stung with each step until she stood in a
neutral piece of grass.

Molly stared at her home that stood so horribly silent. No laughter rang from its rafters. An inner voice told her not to go within its silent walls. Seeing no one about her, she turned towards Mere Eve Dibert's home. The woman would know what to do. If nothing else, Molly could warn her and her son John's family. But what if she were too late?

Eve's Journey Begins En Route to Kittanning

Eve's feet slipped on the mossy rocks, causing her to fall gracelessly into the chilly water.

Mikie, who had fallen into a fitful sleep as he jiggled upon her sunny shoulder, awoke with a start as his mother's once comfortable shoulder failed to block a surge of cold water. A howl began to unwind only to be quickly silenced when Mikie found himself swinging by his feet. His head dangled over his own mother's head, his arms reaching, and his hands grabbing the air. His bare wet bottom gleamed as his infant gown fell in folds over his head.

"Keep him quiet," hissed the brave upon the horse beside her in the creek. Blue Ice had taken his turn upon the horse. "His blond curls would look strange filled with bloody tree bark. Do you understand woman?"

Eve nodded, struggled to her feet, and quickly gathered Mikie back into her arms.

"Why not just silence him? He could be trouble," asked Sitting Rabbit.

"He could also ease someone's loss. Or better yet, get us more goods at the fort for winter," Blue Ice responded.

"Silence, both of you! The child is quieter!" Stalking Wolf chided.

A frown cut deeply into Blue Ice's chiseled face. After all, was it not he, Blue Ice, who held their offerings which acknowledged his control over their actions? It was not Stalking Wolf, it was Blue Ice who was in charge. But even though Blue Ice knew that he could command their souls unto death, his leadership could always accept common sense. Stalking Wolf had spoken wisely. So he turned the horse away, taking up the rear of the small party. They continued in relative silence. Only the muffled sounds of the horse's wrapped hooves gave any indication of their presence.

Mikie, stunned by his latest rebuff, understood momentarily his predicament, and quietly settled on his mother's hip. The warmth, even with the dampness that emanated from his mother's body, felt welcome. In turn, Eve appreciated the small warmth from her son, who nestled in her arms. His hands tightly locked around her neck permitted her one free hand to maneuver the creek and grasp the willows to steady their passage. Whatever sense of direction Eve had trickled away and narrowed as did the stream they trod. She knew that they were climbing, for the temperature dropped with each passing hour. Her exertion increased inversely with the altitude. Having had no breakfast, her stomach growled so loudly that she was sure her captors must have heard it.

German=this font   English=this font   **French=this font**   *Delaware=this font*

Stalking Wolf stopped, listened, and raised his hand to stop the stumbling party. Then, after hand signaling the others, he pushed Eve up the stone embankment. Motioning her ahead, he directed her to continue up the slate wash. Earlier spring runoffs had left their mark. The dry bed provided a stone pathway, pleasantly warm to Eve's cold wet feet. Fleetingly, she rejoiced over her morning choice of the handspun wool skirt. The moisture would wick away with the warmth of her body over time. Wool, the blessed fiber, could help one be warm in cold and feel cool when hot, even when wet. Such a stupid thing to be thankful for, she mused, when all else seemed to be a ridiculous delusion with no apparent rational end or beginning. However, the sensation of a full bladder brought Eve closer to her stark reality.

Another hour passed. Stalking Wolf now walked ahead of Eve and the boys. With each and every step, Eve's bladder cramps intensified as did the cold with the increasingly higher elevation. Eve pondered her predicament. Mikie had already solved his need. Her hip had recently warmed and then chilled, leaving a distinct smell of urea in the air which clung to their bodies in a cloud as they walked. Finally, seeing no other recourse, she spoke.

"I need a moment for myself," Eve said.

Stalking Wolf frowned at her. His brow wrinkled. He did not answer her. Flicking his hand in the air, he turned instead and continued to walk the wash. She assumed that she should follow.

"I said I need a moment for myself." Her voice sounded firmer and just a little more distinct. Her English had a heavy German accent.

"Then take it." The reply stunned Eve. She had suspected that he understood English, during the interplay at the cabin. But that his first English words to her would be spoken so clearly with just a trace of French accent came as a complete surprise, given that earlier he had spoken only in his own language or French.

Eve, who had always displayed a modest side in the presence of her sons, simply could not conceive how she was to manage this small human need and continue to walk. She noticed that the men behind her had dropped back a small distance. Setting Mikie down, she motioned to Henry to walk ahead with him. She realized that she would not be permitted out of their area of surveillance. So hoisting her skirt and pulling her split petticoat aside, she let the liquid escape from her and watched the vapor cloud rise as the warm urine flowed across the cold stones beneath her. Then, straightening with as much dignity as she could muster, she dabbed the wetness that had splashed upon her thighs with her petticoat corner and caught up with her sons.

"Me too, Mutti," Henry said softly.

Remembering how Stalking Wolf had held his hand when he had motioned, she looked back at the men behind her. Motioning as he had, she made them understand. Soon the whole little entourage had drained themselves and once again trooped behind Stalking Wolf.

German=this font   English=this font   **French=this font**   *Delaware=this font*

As they walked, Eve had time to study him from behind. She could see that he was much taller than her husband, Adam Henry. Her coverlet, held in one hand, hung in folds over his left shoulder. Although his shoulders appeared nearly as broad as Henry's square heavy shoulders, she noticed a near absence of body hair. She could not see any curls across his chest or in the hollows across the muscles of his back. On his right shoulder a recessed, star-like patterned scar from an old wound sprawled and rippled as he moved to push an occasional bush aside using his long rifle like a staff. His skin, a rich acorn brown, blended with the lengthening shadows that skittered across him in the fading light. His faintly pocked face was painted black until it reached an imaginary line that connected slit ear to raven-like nose to slit ear. Each ear had a tarnished silver coin dangling from the loop slits. A thumb full of white accented the deep cleft of his chin. His hair, loosely tied with a leather thong, proved to be cleaner than she had expected. Somehow in her mind's eye, she expected all Indians to be like Old Joe who hung out at Garrett's Pub begging for rum and whose filthy, greasy, and stringy locks hung in disarray. This man walked so differently. Defiance, stealth, and pride accompanied each step, instead of shuffling on flattened feet and stumbling like Old Joe with his head bent forward, and his eyes downcast. Stalking Wolf's deep-set brown eyes constantly scanned and sought even the faintest movement. His ears keyed to the faintest rustle in the oak trees or to a skittering mole along the trail. Nothing failed to miss his attention. At that precise moment, he reminded her so much of her Onkel Jac that the uncanny resemblance shocked her. In the same breath, she sprang to his defense. Why would she think this heathen savage resembled her Onkel? After all, her Onkel came from civilized Christian people. Her Onkel should never be compared to a savage. Besides, savages like these had plundered his home, killing Jac's wife and children.

The thought brought back the last image of Adam Henry with flies crawling about his lips and face. Shaking her head and shivering from head to foot, she shook away the image.

Eve remembered how her mother had told her how Jac had gone nearly mad. He had stumbled about in the forests eating grass and moss for months until at last he strode into Lancaster. In Lancaster, he commissioned his rifle, a double-barreled long rifle. A double-barreled long rifle built especially for him to inflict the revenge her Onkel so deeply desired. Would she go mad as he? Would revenge strengthen her as it had him? What could sustain her now that Adam Henry no longer could? Would they attack her person? Would they separate or kill them?

Eve wondered how long little Mikie could totter along instead of being carried. She decided that every ten feet signified a milestone. A soft bird-like whistle caught her attention. Stalking Wolf, turning swiftly, pulled Mikie and her from the shale path. Glancing about, he espied a large fallen trunk and motioned to Eve to crawl into the open side that nestled against some low brush. Searching her eyes, he first held his forefinger to his mouth, then pointed to Mikie. He looked squarely at her again before taking his thumb to draw an imaginary arc beneath his chin and before he shoved Mikie into her arms. Shadows enveloped him as he disappeared. From her hollowed-out place, Eve could hear the group quickly disperse and then quiet. The remaining fall leaves suspended their rustle in an aura of suspense. She listened. Her ears strained for each and every sound. After many minutes, she thought that she heard voices. Not close. But she distinctly heard voices and the sounds of hounds. They are searching for us, she thought, also simultaneously realizing from the regularity of Mikie's breathing that blessedly he had fallen asleep.

Eve had been listening so intently that at first she had been unaware of the wood ants. Wood ants dismayed at her presence in their log. Soon the six legged creatures began to crawl and invade her skirt and legs. Paralyzed with fear for her sleeping child and terrified about the possible loss of Lil' Henry, Eve held her tongue. Her attention fluctuated between the sounds of the searchers, and the ants' bites. She feared that Mikie might wake any moment, endangering both of them. Her flesh crawled under their scaly feet.

Just as the sounds had come within hearing, they faded. Gritting her teeth, Eve drew a slow breath. If she could just concentrate on something, anything, she might keep herself from screaming. An ant ran across Mikie's face. She quickly dispatched it. He wiggled his nose a little. Then, making sucking motions, he wriggled closer to her. Concentrate on this child, she thought. The sweet life that she cradled in her arms held the only real promise that the life of Adam Henry would live on. She must survive.

As Eve struggled just to exist, she failed to sense time's passage. Exhaustion ruled. So when Stalking Wolf's hand shook Eve's shoulder, she jerked awake with a start. Darkness surrounded her. She surprised herself by handing Mikie to her captor before pulling herself slowly from the log. Excrement and urine had pooled about her within the folds of her skirt. Shamed, she knew that she reeked with Michael's and her own bodily discharges. Stiff and sore from her walk and then the long imprisoned position, she straightened with great difficulty. Even the ants had left her, she thought. They could not stand the stench, either. Trying to pick a few of their dead bodies from off her legs where she had pressed them senseless against the log's interior, she tried to stand with some trace of dignity. In the dark, she could not see Stalking Wolf's eyes, for which she felt strangely relieved. She wanted to look no one in the eyes now, not even a savage.

Eve felt a sense of gratitude as Stalking Wolf continued to carry the sleeping child. She followed him resolutely. Her head hung forward. Due to a starless night, her eyes strained to find any sense of the terrain. As she stumbled along, Eve realized that a cold mist had softened the leaves beneath her feet. Little sound came from either of the adult's footsteps as they rejoined to the original party.

German=this font   English=this font   **French=this font**   *Delaware=this font*

Stalking Wolf laid Mikie gently on the ground next to Henry. Lifting a corner of Eve's woven coverlet, he covered the sleeping child. Mikie snuggled up to his equally fatigued brother.

"I've smelled better skunks."

Stalking Wolf nodded in quiet agreement with Blue Ice. He motioned to Eve to sleep apart from them near a large tree trunk. Eve fell heavily against the tree. Drained of spirit, she fell into a fitful sleep. She clutched her arms about her legs and skirt to contain what little warmth she could. Her head rested on her knees. Stalking Wolf slipped in beside the sleeping boys.

Bedford, Pennsylvania

In their bed, Ester Emler turned slowly to her husband, George. She wanted to keep her voice low so that the children in the loft would not hear her. How could they possibly sleep at night, given the horrors of the preceding days?

"What did Jac say?" George had just rejoined their bed.

"Nothing."

"Jac and the men, they can find no trace?"

"No, darkness came too quick."

"But the horses?"

"They either pulled their shoes or they have covered their hooves."

For a few moments, quiet prevailed. When Ester spoke again, her voice quivered.

"George, I fear they—" she hesitated, trying to choose just the right word, "...touched Molly."

"What makes you think so?"

"There are marks around her buttocks, scratches on her sides."

"Does she say what they did?"

"Would any child talk of that?" Ester's voice trailed off at the end. "She says nothing," she continued, confiding to the silent man beside her.

"She says nothing?"

"Did the boys say anything?"

"No, she was not with them." The grossvater's primary concern revealed itself. "Is she spoilt?"

"I fear so."

Further Along the Path to Kittanning

Prying tiny fingers pulled at Eve's lashes, lifting her eyelid to expose the eyeball within. At first the eyeball did not focus, rolling around haphazardly.

German=this font   English=this font   *French=this font*   *Delaware=this font*

"Mutti? Home?" The tiny voice slowly pulled Eve to a conscious state. She rubbed her neck and swiveled her head. Then she rolled her shoulders. Rain fell softly around her but the tree had shielded her.

Mikie had crawled from the blanket's warmth to his mother.

"Hungry, Mutti."

Eve smiled and laughed very softly to herself. Mikie looked like a shaggy puppy on the ground beside her. He had crawled on all fours with his hair hanging down about his face. She knew that Stalking Wolf watched them both. "Of course you are hungry, little one." She reached out reassuringly, pushing his hair back from his eyes. Crossing her legs as was her habit, she pulled Mikie up onto her lap. Offering him her breast, she hoped to provide warmth and nourishment. With so little to eat or to drink, she wondered if there would be milk enough for Mikie. He had better have both breasts this morning, she decided. He had been eating more table foods of late, and she knew she was providing less nourishment than she had in the past as he weaned himself from her. Now with all this, would there be enough? She felt a soft letdown and a mild contraction of her uterus as the milk flowed. She leaned her head back against the tree trunk to relax.

One of life's sweetest moments sustained her. The suckling child blocked out momentarily the horrors of the recent past. She sighed with contentment. She closed her eyes, then opened them slowly as she sensed Stalking Wolf's fixed gaze.

She wakes with a smile, Stalking Wolf thought. Soon they would need to press on to Kittanning. Would she still smile? They were nearly to the waters' divide. The way would be rough until they reached the river. Scaling Blue Knob demanded strength. They should meet up with John Montour's party soon. He wondered if they would have captives as well. Scalps were so much easier to transport, but the live ones brought in more supplies and rum. His mouth watered briefly at the thought of the hot fiery liquid that burned his throat and made him touch the spirit world. As if to reassure himself of his impending bounty, his hand slipped to his side to confirm the presence of the two scalps which he had hung from the waist thong of his breech clout. He would have two to trade. What? Where are they? He felt again. He affirmed his scalping knife but not the trophies. He leapt to his feet. He wondered if when he lay on the ground, had they pulled free? His fingers raked the leaves on the ground where he had lain briefly. As he searched about, an uncanny feeling crept over him. Was the woman watching him? She seemed only to focus on the child. But why did he have this sensation? His skin prickled. Does she know what I am looking for?

Sitting Rabbit watched Stalking Wolf, attracted by his irregular movements. He had slept for a short period after Blue Ice assumed his lookout duty. Perplexed by Stalking Wolf's unusual behavior, he spoke.

"Did something bite you?"

"They are gone!"

"What are gone?"
"The scalps are gone."
"How can that be, the blanket covered them as you walked."
"I tell you they are gone."

Eve watched Stalking Wolf spin in his night nest. She watched him rake the leaves again with his fingers and then push the leaves with his foot, shaking leaves free that adhered to his moccasins. She could sense his mounting tension. She closed her eyes. A soft smile broke fleetingly across her face. Quickly she straightened her face. She must not show any interest or sense of the problem. Henry's squeal caused her eyes to snap open. Even Mikie became distracted, turning his head still firmly fastened and stretching the breast painfully to see his brother.

Stalking Wolf had gruffly pulled the coverlet from the sleeping child and inspected the ground where the children and the blanket had recently lain. He hauled Henry to his feet. He looked on the ground under Henry, turned him about, and roughly brushed leaves from his gown, grumbling aloud.

Blue Ice walked into the makeshift camp.

"Good thing no one is near. What is all the noise? Even rutting stags make less noise."

"Stalking Wolf has lost his scalps!" Sitting Rabbit reported much to the disdain of Stalking Wolf, who stood with his hands on his hips, staring intently at Eve.

She had slid her finger into the corner of Mikie's mouth to break the suction on her nipple which he had stretched beyond comfort. She looked up at Stalking Wolf as she shifted Mikie from one breast to the other before refocusing her attention to Mikie and offering him her second breast.

"When did you notice that they were gone?" asked Blue Ice.

"When I awoke."

Henry sensed that his captors were upset about something, but morning brought other demands, so he slipped behind a nearby tree.

"Is this a bad omen?" A note of fear entered Sitting Rabbit's question.

"More likely it is one who is foolish."

"Or one who is sly."

"What proof will I have for DeJean at the fort?"

"We can testify for you," Sitting Rabbit volunteered.

"Who believes an Indian?" Stalking Wolf retorted.

"It is easier to stretch and cut the young man's scalp to look like three. Forget it, Stalking Wolf. We must leave quickly. We have stayed too long. More parties will surely come." Blue Ice's curt suggestion expressed more concern for their lives than the missing scalps at this juncture.

"I think the woman knows."

German=this font   English=this font   **French=this font**   *Delaware=this font*

"What makes you think so? White women do not touch scalps. They are too weak."

"This one may not be too weak." Stalking Wolf turned to scoop up the coverlet from the ground. The edge snagged on a jutting branch, fraying a good bit of the cut margin. He pulled hard to free it.

Eve's face flooded with pain. Instinctively, she reached with one hand toward the torn and frayed edge, only to have her hand pushed away with disgust.

"Call your son. We must leave now."

"I need a moment in the morning."

"You reek already woman. Take your moments on the path!" Stalking Wolf snapped. Then, throwing Eve's woven coverlet over his shoulder on the side which once held the missing scalps, he stomped like a child out of the small clearing. Anger punctuated each step.

Inside, Eve grinned from ear to ear. She did not need to know the language to guess what had transpired. But outside, her face never changed. She simply struggled to a standing position, shook some of the night from her skirts, juggled Mikie, spread her legs, and urinated. Readjusting Mikie in her arms, she walked after the departing figure as Mikie continued to nurse.

Henry dutifully fell in line, clutching his mother's large iron skillet.

They continued to climb.   A new energy filled Eve; but hunger daunted them all.

Bedford, Pennsylvania

"Onkel Jac, I want to come."

Jac turned to the young man who walked behind him. "No son, you need to heal. You lost too much blood. Even if it was just a flesh wound, you must stay here. Besides, your schwester and bruders need you here for your vater's burial." With that, Jac swung into his saddle and adjusted the double-barrel long rifle in its sling across his back. He placed his bruder George's rifle in another by his saddle. Wood and other men from the stockade waited silently for Jac to join them.

"Believe me, young George, we will try to find your mutter. There may be others, too. We are not alone in this year of bloody sevens, I fear." Turning to Wood and the others, he stormed. "Damn the British. Damn the Tories. Damn the Rebels. They take our best men and arms to fight in the northeast, and we are left without protection. Meanwhile, those bloody Virginians continue to stir up things and steal our land. Wood, you best get a letter off to that damn excuse of a governor that you say you know so well and send him that stinking proclamation while you are at it."

Wood frowned. He understood most of Jac's outburst, even if it was heavily laced with his German accent. Jac tracked well, but the man was a

German=this font   English=this font   **French=this font**   *Delaware=this font*

powder keg. With Jac's angry retort still hanging in the air, the column of men departed.

Young George watched them leave. His anger and shame smoldered within because he had failed yet a second time. He did not hear his Tante Jessie who approached him from behind. She stood awkwardly. She ached to take this man-child in her arms to comfort him, but she feared that this would humiliate him further, rather than comfort him. So, encircled with indecision, she stood behind him. When she spoke, she selected her words carefully.

"Your mutter is a strong woman, George. She will fight to survive. She will protect your bruders with her life."

Opa Emler gruffly disagreed. "Do not give the child false expectations, Jessie. She is as good as dead. The boys lost."

Neither had heard him approach. His words slapped their spirits down as they both turned to face him. His words damped their weakly held hopes that fought to remain viable when all else seemed to fail them in the light of a harsh reality. "Get up to the house and help your mutter, Jessie. The mourners will be here soon enough to mourn that fool, Adam Henry." As Jessie turned to obey her vater, she distinctly heard him say under his breath. "Now I am stuck with two spoilt women."

Her vater's departing word venom bit into Jessie like a viper. She knew him well enough to know that when faced with emotional discomfort he would wallow in it and strike out at others. But why would he call poor Molly spoilt? She knew all too well the connotation of that word when her vater used it. She had endured his wrath on this subject far too often not to know.

Young George choked internally as his grossvater called his vater a fool. Schooled as he had been to respect his elders, he swallowed the full impact of the elder George's words. He struggled with his grief and his deep frustration at feeling so helpless. His love for his vater brought forth tears. These tears flooded his eyes, spilling over to his cheeks. No matter how he willed them to stop, the stopcock had opened.

"Be more a man, son. Strong men do not cry," Grossvater Emler strongly chided his enkel before he turned on his heel, leaving the younger George awash in emotions.

So utterly powerless, young George stood alone, watching the men ride away in the distance. One tear after another coursed down his cheeks as he tried to draw on some strength from his past. And then, inexplicably, George felt the reassuring pressure of his Vater's hand on his shoulder. The hand had often touched him there in trying moments. Comforted, he continued to stand alone until his tears subsided.

German=this font   English=this font   *French=this font*   *Delaware=this font*

Shipboard from Fort Detroit – En Route to Montreal

"'Would be to God, the storm that we have unleashed on the frontiers could be directed upon the guilty heads of the wretches who raised it and pass by the miserable many who must feel its fatal effects.'"** It was the second time that Hamilton had voiced this lament aloud. However, this time he stood on the foredeck of the *Angelica*. The first time had been when he had opened the directive from Lord Germain.

His secretary, Lieutenant Jacob Schieffelin, sensed the pensive mood of his superior. He stood quietly at his side. Jacob owed much to this man who had personally nursed him back to health after his bout of severe ague and chills. Hamilton convinced him to leave his business partners and to join Hamilton's vision of the victory to come. Jacob, a loyalist to the core, put his excellent writing and recording skills to the mounds of paperwork that seemed to plague the Lieutenant Governor. Whether endlessly rewriting Hamilton's proclamation to the Tories to incite them to defect, or writing letters to Hamilton's superiors, the industrious Schieffelin could be counted on. The pay for Jacob's personal allegiance and for the rank of Lieutenant proved more than adequate to Schieffelin. Considering his regard for Hamilton, just to associate with a man of his stature and class met a deep-seated need in Jacob. Born in Philadelphia, Schieffelin also brought valuable insights into the Rebel mindset which he knew his superior regarded highly.

Hamilton had come to appreciate Jacob's ability to prioritize. Jacob brought some semblance of order to the chaotic office which seemed to be the focus of a never-ending stream of lesser or greater tribal chieftains and war captains, who talked incessantly. Each native dignitary desired contact to seek special favors. The local merchants and leftover French gentry also felt that they, too, should voice opinions in petty or great affairs. Hamilton's inherent distrust of anything French or Catholic meant that while he tolerated DeJean, he felt no camaraderie. Lieutenant Jacob Schieffelin came about as close to a friend as Hamilton would accept, given Hamilton's strong belief that having authority permitted few friendships. Hamilton, well schooled by those of rank and privilege, maintained that one should not extend friendship to anyone below one's own rank. Class must always be considered if one wished to grow in the circles of power.

Jacob recognized that Hamilton grew increasingly enraged by the lack of military support, and at Mompesson, in particular. Hamilton also expressed his fury and his rancor concerning the merchant, James Sterling, and his reluctant militia. The feelings ran so deep that Hamilton had directed DeJean to confiscate much of Sterling's property and to pack him off to Montreal to be imprisoned. Sterling's very vocal refusal in public after the fire to go on the raids had snapped Hamilton's usual forbearance.

German=this font   English=this font   **French=this font**   *Delaware=this font*

Today, Hamilton felt it truly fitting to be on the *Angelica*, a vessel once owned by Sterling and his partners.

Finally, feeling no other recourse than to approach Governor Guy Carleton in person, Hamilton had left his post. Jacob understood that the ambiguous instructions and the lack of a clear chain of command deeply disturbed Hamilton. Even though Hamilton no longer served in the military, Hamilton desired the total authority, civil and military, which he felt he clearly deserved as the Lieutenant Governor at Fort Detroit.

Hamilton turned so that the stiff breeze felt from the broad reach could be better tolerated. The lake winds in fall could penetrate any garment. He stood for many minutes before he spoke again. His lips drew tight from the cold. Braced against a stay, he steadied himself as the boat rose and dropped with the swells. Flexing his fingers in an effort to keep circulation and warmth, he repositioned the drawing before him.

"Do you know what disturbs me most in this *petite guerre,* Jacob?" He added another line to his sketch. "The fools abroad and in Montreal cannot see that our true enemy is Spain. Yes, Spain, my good man." The emphasized words each time were spit defiantly in the wind. "Spain continues to supply the Rebel forces with gunpowder and supplies up the Mississippi. Spain supports the rebellion with letters of credit, so these pathetic fools try our patience. Spain continues to send in its papist teachers amongst the tribes, even along the Wabash, taking up where the foul French Recollects and Jesuits left off. Spain outbids our merchants and attempts to take over the eastern coastal trade. Spain makes inroads into the interior along the Mississippi from St. Louis and New Orleans.

"Why the English powers cannot see that Detroit should be the true center of English control for the province of Quebec dumbfounds me. Detroit will most certainly be the great city of the future. Why fight at the mere feet of this *petite guerre*, when you could sever the head and vanquish it?"

Lieutenant Jacob Schieffelin did not answer the questions posed to him and to the lake winds. He sensed his capacity for listening was needed more than any thoughts or opinions that he could possibly share on this icy cold deck. Schieffelin could do nothing more than to stand in awe of this great man's perceptive ability and to lay a reassuring hand on Hamilton's sleeve as they gazed out in silence at the steel gray water and the matching sky. Then Hamilton resumed sketching the billowed sails, attempting to catch the vessel's symmetry.

**Lt. Governor Henry Hamilton to Lord George Germain (Secretary of State for the colonies, 1775-1782) June 1777 as quoted by Nelson Vance Russell in "The Indian Policy of Henry Hamilton" *The Canadian Historical Review, Volume 31(11)* (1930):p. 25.

German=this font   English=this font   *French=this font*   *Delaware=this font*

Chapter 4   Kittanning on the Allegheny

"...to delegate to the merciless Indian the defense of
disputed rights, and to wage the horrors of his barbarous
war against our brethren? My lords, these enormities
call aloud for redress and punishment. Unless thoroughly
done away with it will be a stain on the national
character. It is a violation of the Constitution. I believe
it is against the law."

Lord Chatham to the Parliament of England, November 1777 as quoted by
Silas Farmer in *History of Detroit and Wayne County and Early Michigan.*
1890 (Silas Farmer and Co. Republished by Gale Research, 1969), p. 245

Dunnings Creek, near Bedford, Pennsylvania

In the fading light, four men stood guard outside Adam Henry
Earnest's busted door. The women within prepared the three men. Three
days had passed before the family and neighbors felt safe enough to return.
Torches lit the porch and rigs. Uneasy horses pawed the ground nervously.
The drivers clicked and clucked verbal reinforcements to hold their wagons
and teams in place. The loyal animals smelled fear and death in the crisp
autumn air.

"Do your duty child," Ester hid her own revulsion by chiding her
enkelin. Presiding as the directress of the proceedings, she marshaled the
women about their tasks. In particular, she admonished Molly at every
juncture as the women prepared Adam Henry's body and those of Isaac and
Joseph for burial. As usual, women were called to birth and death, the
horns of life. Ester had ruled against Jessie's persistent pleading that
Molly should be spared the full mantle of womanhood since she had been
so recently orphaned. Ester maintained staunchly that to coddle Molly
would make her weak. To do less, poor Molly might be led to the devil.

Molly's hands shook visibly as time and time again, she wiped the
blood and excrement from her father and rinsed the wash cloth in the cool,
water-filled basin. No amount of rosemary and lilac in the water could
mask the odors. Most of the bloody residue and flies had been washed free
now. With each cleansing effort, the pale specter lying on the kitchen table
distanced itself from the warmth of life that once filled it or surrounded it.
A large liver-colored splash covered her father's buttocks and thighs where
the blood had pooled as he sat facing death. Tiny lines of dehydration
around his eyes and lips gave his face a pursed appearance. The smell of

decaying flesh, the residual stiffness of the fading rigor mortis, and the slight bloating of the abdomen made it harder for the women to redress the body. Molly attempted to sweep a bit of leftover hair from her vater's forehead back to cover the marks of the tomahawk's rage. In desperation, ignoring her grossmutter's frown, she pulled down her vater's cap from the peg behind the broken door and placed it over her vater's bare skull. The cap cast a dark shadow over his blackening face.

"Your bruders could use dat cap," Ester scolded. "You are being wasteful. Your vater needs no cap where he is going."

A damp, warm hand covered Molly's as she began to reach to remove the cap. Tante Jessie gently stopped Molly.

"Mutter, the cap looks fine," Jessie flashed an enraged glance at her mutter. "The cap looks just fine," she repeated determinedly.

Ester felt the sting of the rebuff as both women turned toward her.

The child-woman's eyes appeared vacant. No tears. No emotion. Molly moved with stiff remote movements, as if the soul had been ripped away, much like the coverlet had been torn from the ravaged loom behind her.

Jessie helped Molly empty the basins, catching her as Molly swayed against the door frame. Finally, Jessie eased Molly with her hip into the chair by the table before calling the men without to pick up the three neatly scrubbed and dressed but ravaged corpses. Each was wrapped in the unusable cloth of the sacked household.

One by one, the men brought each victim outside to the wagons for their last, short ride down the hill to where the open earth awaited them. The three men would face the morning sun and the creek, side by side, in their final resting place.

Far West of the War Party
North of Warriors Trail, Pennsylvania

"Jac, for Christ's sake, are the dogs off trail again?" shouted Wood's indentured servant, Sill.

Jac hated traveling with this band of men. He could tell from the pack's bay that they were more than likely on track of deer or other game. If there were trail signs, these village idiots had obliterated them with their sluggish movements and their inept tracking skills. Jac felt that everything this group of men touched wiped out any sign of those who had previously gone before them. He chided himself for not having traveled alone. If he could just get shuck of them, he would. He cursed himself for following his brother George's admonition to wait and to take Wood and his men with him.

George had felt that Jac needed more guns in case of another fight.

German=this font   English=this font   *French=this font*   *Delaware=this font*

But Jac knew that of the lot of them, he alone stood the greatest chance of finding Eve. However, after these misfits had stamped in and out of the creeks, churning up the country side, Jac feared his chances had diminished considerably.

Sadly, Jac could not tell from the children's description if the attackers had been Shawnee, Delaware, Seneca, or Mingos. Could they have come from the lake country near Fort Detroit?

Jac sensed that Molly knew more than she told, but she simply would not describe her attackers. She had been the very last to arrive at the Dibert's homestead. Upon her arrival, John Dibert had escorted the grieving children to the Emler farm closer to the fort. When asked over and over again to describe her attackers, the girl maintained her silence. Jac knew that Indians rarely raped women when they ambushed. But more and more, he began reluctantly to accept George and Ester's fears. No doubt, the young woman was spoilt. Molly appeared shamed, which meant that she would not or could not share what happened. Her brothers added not a wit more.

The thought of his young niece attacked by a faceless enemy made Jac's hatred grow even stronger. Clutching his powder horn tightly, he pressed the point into his thumb until it bled. Jac stared and swore under his breath at those around him and at the approaching darkness. The pointless bay of the dogs in the distance meant that the men would have to call off this day's search. Minutes and hours delay meant certain failure. Three days delay and now, worse yet, four days delay meant that the effort to retrieve Eve and the boys would be nigh to impossible. The rain continued to destroy any signs of their route. Apparently, the raiding party had avoided the main paths and had walked the rocks. Rocks do not track easy, and they wash off even easier, Jac decided.

Kittanning Along the Allegheny River, Pennsylvania

Between the continuous drizzle, intermittent wind, and altitude, Eve's energy began to fail markedly on the fourth day. Slate had slashed open one knee during one fall and the palm of her hand on another. Yellow fat oozed from the palm cut. The constant throb stimulated her to watch her step with even greater care.

Mikie had cried himself hoarse the night before, so his voice had a raspy sound to it. His chest sounds wheezed. She found him warmer to her touch and could tell by the way that he tugged on his ear that the old pain had returned. Stalking Wolf offered to carry him, but Mikie had screamed so much that Eve assumed the burden once more, despite her own exhaustion. One crest after another seemed to come in monotonous succession.

German=this font   English=this font   **French=this font**   *Delaware=this font*

Blue Ice, Sitting Rabbit and Stalking Wolf felt slightly less guarded, of late. Although still obviously alert, they chatted quietly along the trail from time to time.

Henry seemed the most energetic of all of them. Earlier, Stalking Wolf had permitted him to ride the horse which plodded along quietly while Henry napped. The blankets about its hooves had begun to fray and tear and now left irregular prints. Sitting Rabbit had tied the large heavy skillet to the pack with the haunches of meat. Henry, freed from his weighty responsibility, ran eagerly ahead. He looked for curious rocks and sticks along the way. Like a squirrel, he scurried back and forth seeking tiny treasurers. Since the child obviously would not range far away from his mother, the braves allowed him some independence.

When the party walked in the creeks, Eve noticed that the water no longer rolled over her feet coming directly towards her and rushing past. Instead, the water welled up behind her and then broke over her heels before dashing in front of her. With each new bend, water gathered and widened until they were forced to walk the rock banks once more. Occasionally, the briefly emerging sun awakened a few water snakes, which flattened themselves in sunny, windless spots among the rocks. The men would flip them carelessly away from the path so as not to bar their way. Jumping about excitedly, Henry took particular delight in these flying reptiles, which slithered sluggishly for new cover.

When the ragtag group topped the next crest, Eve gasped quietly at the sight of the grandeur below her. Mahogany hills, reddish brown with the late oak leaves, lined the long valley. Far below, the deep burgundies and browns mingled with a few residual yellows of the shore trees along the hematite surface of the winding river. Intermittent silver gray trunks and crests contrasted with a rare deep green pine, where once the brilliant maples had hung heavy with color. Free of leaves, the silver-barked maples shimmered in the late afternoon sun. White and tan sycamores in other groves were sprinkled among the contrasting trees which resembled a crazy quilt.

High on the rock bluff, the party came to a halt.

"Do you see John Montour's men?" Blue Ice searched the ledges within view.

"No, and I think we would hear them. Or smell them if their prisoners are ripe as this one," Stalking Wolf responded.

"We must eat. The woman grows weak. The pale mongrel looks sick." Sitting Rabbit's own hunger wrenched him deeply. It was good to have a weak woman to blame it on.

Stalking Wolf chuckled softly to himself. He felt surprised that Sitting Rabbit had not spoken of food long before this. Sitting Rabbit loved to lurk about the pot at the village, fighting the pot lickers for the last leavings. He really had been on his leanest behavior.

Blue Ice looked at the tattered woman before him and the child with glazed eyes, dulled by fever. If they did not feed them soon, they would never make it to their village or the fort alive. No prisoner, no bounty received. Convinced that those who followed had lost their trail, he motioned Stalking Wolf toward the horse. Pulling the red-handled scalping knife from his waist thong, Stalking Wolf cut off narrow strips of raw pork from the haunches which had dried on the surface during the journey. He flicked off any imbedded debris and bugs. Then, pulling a pouch that had been tied to his side, he broke off a chuck of deer-tallow filled with dried strawberries, blueberries, and ground wild grain. Called pemmican, this food traveled well. Walking to Eve, he looked down at her. The stench that came from her repulsed him. His face filled with revulsion. Eve, abruptly reminded of her situation, looked down at the ground.

"Eat this, woman!" Stalking Wolf placed the fat and meat into her hand closing her fingers around it. "Be sure you give some to the child. Do not eat it all!"

Shame instantly turned to anger. To think this heathen murderer would accuse Eve of not feeding her child! Immediately, her head jerked up. Her shoulders squared.

"We do not eat raw pork!" She said and then threw the meat and pemmican back at Stalking Wolf's feet. She stood defiantly, staring up at Stalking Wolf, who smiled down at her smugly.

Deliberately, Stalking Wolf picked up the raw meat and pemmican covered with grit and dirt. He grasped her hand and again folded the meat and pemmican into her hand.

"Eat, woman, or you and the child will die," he advised Eve before turning away to rejoin the others.

"Hanu." Stalking Wolf motioned to Henry to come to him.

"Hanu." Henry, who had cornered an iridescent beetle at the base of a fuzzy mullein plant, frowned up at him, not pleased to be distracted. Childish curiosity had waylaid him again. Stalking Wolf motioned again to him. He pointed to his mouth, and then broke off another piece of pemmican from the pouch. Henry boldly went forward and took the piece of rich tallow offered to him. *"Eat."*

Henry looked quizzically at the piece. Stalking Wolf grabbed his hand and bit off a small chunk of Henry's portion of pemmican and pushed the leftover piece towards Henry's mouth. *"Hanu, eat."*

Hesitatingly, Henry bit into the tallow. Salty, sweet, and oily goodness filled his mouth. His tongue coated with the tallow. Although strange to him, Henry was so hungry that he swallowed it. Chewing and crunching the grains and savoring the dried strawberries, he grinned up into Stalking Wolf's face. In an unguarded moment, Stalking Wolf reached out and ruffled Henry's hair. When Sitting Rabbit glanced up, Stalking Wolf jerked his hand away.

"See, your son is not stupid, woman. Eat!" Stalking Wolf cut more strips of pork for those about him. The others had also taken pemmican from their pouches. Henry crouched with the men. They ate quietly.

German=this font   English=this font   **French=this font**   *Delaware=this font*

Stalking Wolf handed Henry strips of meat and additional pemmican when needed.

Ostracized, Eve looked at the food in her hand. The tallow had melted from the warmth of her hand mixing with the dirt and sandy clay that stuck to the surface. Picking a piece of strawberry with as little dirt as possible, she placed it in Mikie's mouth. A little dazed, he rolled it about his mouth and then started to chew and swallow it. He whimpered as the solid food slid down his sore throat. But like a bird, his mouth quickly opened for the next finger full of pemmican.

Then she lifted the dirty mass pemmican to her own mouth. Haltingly, she stopped and smelled it. Overruling her own revulsion to the fatty substance, she ate and shared pieces with Mikie. Taking the pork next, she chewed it until it became a brown ball of mush. She removed it with her finger to place it in Mikie's mouth. His baby teeth could not handle the tough raw pork. Blessedly, he did not refuse the nourishment. The saltiness of the pemmican now impacted on Eve. She saw Blue Ice go to a nearby rock outcrop and place his lips near the stone. Only then did she realize that a springlet rolled down the rock face. She watched as each man went forward to the rock to suck up the fresh springwater. Stalking Wolf lifted Henry, who was unable to reach the spot. He held the boy firmly while the child drank. As he stood Henry down, Stalking Wolf motioned Eve forward after all the men had drunk their fill.

Pressing her lips near the cold wet rock, Eve sucked in a reviving trickle. The biblical story of Christ shaming the wedding guests who wanted more wine, not water, flashed momentarily through her mind. Never had the stone wine pressed rich with minerals and icy from the depths of the mountain tasted so wonderful. Holding Mikie tightly to her side, she filled her mouth with the cool liquid and then transferred it to Mikie. The first sip startled him because it was so cold, then he simply could not get enough. Eagerly, he accepted the fluid from his mother's wet kiss, urging his mother to kiss the rock and kiss him again over and over, until they both giggled.

"Quiet!"

Startled, Eve looked up. The group quickly withdrew into the rock cleft. An owl hoot broke the silence. Eve remembered the call all too well. She never wanted to hear that sound of the owl again. For just a moment her recall flashed with her last backward glance of Adam Henry. Am I wrong to laugh? She reflected on her laughter with Mikie as they drank. May God forgive my laughter, she thought, as she hugged Mikie close to her breast.

Blue Ice returned the call. The call repeated.

"Montour." Blue Ice responded. The other men nodded agreement.

"We have company, woman," Blue Ice told Eve in an offhand way as he motioned her to move aside. "Bitch, you stink!"

Pulling Mikie close, Eve eased away from the men once more. The sun faded. She listened with the men as she heard the approach of others.

German=this font   English=this font   *French=this font*   *Delaware=this font*

The first figure that appeared startled Eve. Two wide white eyes appeared in the increasing darkness, framed in blackness as deep as the irises and pupils at their centers. These eyes snapped and sparkled in the fading light as if they contained a raging fire inside them.

"Keep your hands off me! I ain't no slave you can handle! I be free!" As the negress came around the cleft of the rock, she pushed Blue Ice away with disgust as he reached out to assist her. She stopped abruptly, looking at the figures before her, only to have the brave behind her push her forward, spilling her onto the ground.

"Quiet, bitch! The whole mountain can hear you," the brave hissed before pushing her. He kicked her rump with his heel, just hard enough to throw her ample chest to the ground a second time.

"How many do you bring?" Blue Ice queried.

"Four. Two women and two boys. The woman fell back aways. She walks slow. I think she thinks that if she is slow, they will find her. But we lost them quickly. This one has a big mouth, but she walks well."

Mikie's mouth dropped open with wonder at the woman before him on the ground.

"Bear?" Mikie asked.

"She looks like Chloe, Mutti, only she is prettier." Henry said softly.

"Yes, Henry, she is like Chloe. Here, hold Mikie." Eve set Mikie by Henry and then stepped forward to help the young woman stand as John Montour entered the clearing. He and Blue Ice immediately stood aside to continue a private conversation.

"Lady, you sure do smell bad. How long you been walking?" Her voice was husky and deep pitched. She stumbled but quickly regained her legs with little assistance from Eve. Brushing the soil from her dress, she peered down into Eve's face with no trace of deference.

"Four days, I think." Eve answered. Yes indeed, thought Eve, this woman definitely had spirit and gumption like Chloe.

"Me, too. I be Anne. Who be you?"

"I am Eve."

"Humph, like in the bible, but Dutchie by the sounds of yeh?"

"Quiet, bitches!" Blue Ice barked.

Eve nodded. Motioning Anne over to the boys, the four stood quietly.

"Anne..." Eve whispered, "Henry, Mikie." She pointed to each child respectively and then retrieved Mikie once more. The two women eased back against the dry rocks before sitting. Eve commenced to nurse Mikie. Neither spoke. Henry attempted once to crawl away to explore the outer perimeter of their spot, but Eve's swift hand quickly pulled his gown back to a sitting position. Rocking Mikie in her arms, he soon fell into a languorous stupor. Henry restrained from activity, rolled into a squirrel-like ball, tucked tail, and nested into a portion of his mother's skirt before he fell asleep. The women, sharing their warmth shoulder to shoulder, drifted off.

Anne awoke. Twice glancing around her, she noted that they were

German=this font   English=this font   *French=this font*   *Delaware=this font*

alone. Moving with deliberate stealth, she disengaged herself from Eve and the children without awakening them. Bending forward on all fours, she began to crawl from the site, only to come to an abrupt halt. An English boot held her skirt fast to the ground.

"Now, there, I wouldn't be leaving here if I were you." Anne rocked back on her haunches to look into the face of a British Redcoat who stood over her. His musket lay across his forearms. His face filled with amusement as she attempted to stand.

Eve groggily shook herself awake. Mikie moved restlessly. The earlier heat had increased to a full-blown fever. A practiced mother's hand touched his burning forehead accompanied by a frown. Henry curled and flexed.

"Mutti, is Mikie hot?"

"Yes, Henry, he is hot."

"Is he going to get sicker, Mutti?"

More to convince herself than Henry, Eve touched Henry's cheek tenderly. "He will be just fine, Henry. We will be just fine."

Eve struggled to a stand. Anne steadied her as she arose and stood beside her. It was then that Eve saw another woman standing in the shadow of the British soldier. Small dainty features, a bonnet shielded her face so her face was not raw with windburn or sunburn. A woolen shawl encircled her shoulders. Her dress appeared far less soiled and torn than either Eve's or Anne's. Clutched in her arms, she held a large skillet close to her body, reminding Eve of a knight with an ancient shield.

"Who be you, lady?" Anne looked the new woman over before shaking some of the leaves from her gray homespun.

"Mistress George Elder," the small woman responded quietly.

"I did not ask you who be your husband. I ask you; who be you, lady?

"Mind your mouth to your betters," the British officer snapped.

"Margaret Elder," the woman spoke as if the Redcoat had never uttered a sound. She extended her right hand to each woman, still clutching the heavy skillet with her left. "Sisters, may God preserve us in this time of peril."

Chagrined, the British soldier moved out of her way. Margaret knelt before Henry, touching his cheek briefly, and then she touched little Mikie with the back of her hand.

"He is with fever?" Margaret Elder caressed Mikie's hot flushed cheeks in a soothing manner.

Eve nodded affirmation.

"She be Eve. Them's her boys, Henry and Mikie." Margaret glanced up to acknowledge each woman again. She frowned as she touched Mikie's soaked hairline and forehead.

"I still have some fever salts in my pocket left from doctoring my neighbor. When there is water, perhaps Major Hay will permit enough time to allow him to drink."

The appearance of Stalking Wolf and Blue Ice drew the attention of the Major Hay and the motley group of prisoners. A young man stumbled between them. Blood trickled across his forehead and cheeks. His arms were tied behind his back. Tall, well built, a shock of blond hair hung across his bloody forehead and into his eyes.

Margaret Elder stood and spun quickly before marching without any fear up to the threesome. Her entire attention focused on the young man.

"Young Master Skelly, I pray you. Do not incite their wrath or it will not go well with you."

Felix Skelly dropped his gaze, as if to acknowledge the truth in her concern.

"Now remember, we gave our promise to Major Hay and Mr. Montour. We must abide by our word. Felix Skelly, remember the Lord is with us and will give us strength in our time of need."

With that, Margaret Elder looked into the face of each man beside Skelly.

"You will be kind to him? Please, he is young and inclined to be foolish." Then she took the corner of her shawl, spit on the tip, and wiped the blood from Skelly's face. Skelly tried to pull away, but Margaret prevailed.

The look on Stalking Wolf's and Blue Ice's faces filled with mutual amusement at the two men of the Indian Department. Both cowered in the presence of the commanding small woman before them.

"Are the canoes below?" the Major asked.

Stalking Wolf nodded.

"Then let us proceed quickly. Night will be upon us. Darkness should help cover our float past the settlements," Hay directed.

**Replogle, Emma. *Indian Eve and Her Descendants* (1911. Bedford, PA: Reprinted by Messiah Lutheran Church, 1990), p. 19-30. The account of the capture of Margaret Elder and Felix Skelly inspired this portion.

Emler's Farm, Bedford, Pennsylvania

Each of the four listeners stood entranced by Lizzie Samuels and caught up in the throes of her story. Jiggling her tiny schwester, Deede, in her arms for emphasis, Lizzie truly captivated her audience.

Touching the present for a change, even Molly listened intently with her bruders to Lizzie's wild tale.

"Everyone thought someone else had her. We just rode for our lives. There we were, all in the fort, when suddenly we saw no one had Deede. No one could believe that Deede got left behind. It was horrible. None of us could sleep. I was crying. My bruder rolled on the floor where they put us in. He barely slept.

"Poor Vati stayed up. I have never seen him so furious. He just paced

German=this font   English=this font   *French=this font*   *Delaware=this font*

back and forth, back and forth. Mutti kept crying. We just knew this little one was lost. Twice, the men stopped Vati from going back to the house. They even swore at him and threatened to tie him down. Twice! And," she jiggled her schwester twice again and then held up two fingers over the blanket for additional stress to make her point. "I thought Vati would go mad. When morning came, they could hold Vati back no longer. When he got to our cabin, praise be to God, he found Deede sleeping in the loft." Shifting her attention to her prized bundle, Lizzie cooed, "They did not find you, did they little one? You was a good baby. You was quiet."

A tear welled up in Molly's right eye and spilled down her cheek. At that point, a hand tugged at her elbow and attempted to pull her away from the circle.

"Your vater lays there and you foolish ones laugh and listen to stories." Ester tugged a little harder at Molly, who seemed to dip into her sightless trance once more. Lizzie looked up in shock.

Young George grasped his schwester's other elbow. Steadying her and looking severely at his grossmutter, he spoke. "Good schwester, Lizzie, has shared a miracle of God's love, Oma. We mean no disrespect." His deliberate use of his pet name for her softened the impact of his words. Ester Emler eased back in deference to his emerging strength and his impending manhood. Sensing that she spoke out of turn with these young people who stood quietly about her, she returned to the elder mourners.

"It is all right, Molly. Oma means no ill. She is just old country."

Lizzie looked fondly at George as the young people tightened their circle.

Apart from the others, John Dibert and his wife, Ene observed Ester Emler. John's mother, Mere Eve, had permitted the couple a rare outing. Clutching her husband's arm, Ene leaned in towards John, who inclined an ear.

"Can she not see the deepness of the child's wounds?" Ene whispered.

"No, her own pain prevents her," John responded.

**Replogle, Emma. *Indian Eve and Her Descendants* (1911. Bedford, PA: Reprinted by Messiah Lutheran Church, 1990), p. 39. The account of the survival of Samuel's Baby inspired this portion.

Along the Allegheny, Pennsylvania

Henry stumbled, falling on the large skillet that he carried before him. Stalking Wolf pulled him up by the seat of his pants. Setting him sharply upon his feet, he shoved the skillet back in his arms.

"Hanu, carry."

Henry choked back his tears. Looking up at the man at his side, he sensed what would please him. Burdened again with the skillet to make room for other looted goods, he smiled weakly and kept walking.

German=this font   English=this font   *French=this font*   *Delaware=this font*

The column of walkers could hear the river now. Blue Ice signaled a stop and whistled. A whistle returned.

The party commenced to the river banks. Major Hay and John Montour lowered two long birchbark canoes from two tall willows near the water's edge. Almost magically other bundles appeared from the trees. Bundles of loot and clothes were quickly piled on the river bank.

Eve stood holding Mikie close. He moved rarely and then only listlessly in her arms. The fever radiated from his small body. His lips cracked, dried, and bloodied in the crevices. Blood had trickled from one ear and dried on his cheek. When Margaret's hand touched her shoulder, she startled. But Mikie did not stir. Eve focused on the sick child. In the pit of her stomach, a gnawing fear clawed like a bear marking sign.

"If we separate, give this to the child. A little at a time in water. Too much can make him sicker." Margaret pressed a small container into her hand.

Eve nodded, but she felt enclosed within her own private world. When she was jerked by Blue Ice and motioned to climb into one of the canoes, she did so without thinking initially of her fear of deep water. Parcels and packs of loot were stuffed between her and the paddler. Pushed off, the rocking motion of the craft sent unexpected tremors of pure terror through her. Although she appreciated the opportunity to sit, the hard cedar slats on the bottom of the canoe offered little comfort, whereas the bundles behind her did. Mikie lay wedged in the cross of her legs. Her hands clutched the gunwales. Her knuckles turned white as she gripped them. She could see Henry in the other canoe between Stalking Wolf's legs, playing quietly. Margaret sat seated similarly to Eve ahead of Stalking Wolf. His body rocked forward and back in a seemingly effortless rhythm. The paddle dipped and pulled the craft through the water. She noted that for the first time, a soft linen shirt now covered his strong frame. Skelly and Anne would march with the other men, loot, and animals which remained ashore.

Eve realized she should be thankful for the opportunity to ride. She shifted her weight to be more comfortable and rocked the canoe precariously, sending another wave of terror through her. Water touched her right hand just moments before the paddle sharply rapped her shoulder. The canoe returned to horizontal.

"Sit still, woman!" Blue Ice snarled.

The glancing blow of the paddle stung. The pain shimmered through her. In reaching for her shoulder, the small forgotten vial that Margaret had given her rolled into her lap from her pocket. She had water. She had medicine. The realization pulled her attention to the needs of life and away from fear. Cupping her hand, she dipped a small amount of water as a wave rolled by. By being careful, the canoe did not alter its course, so the paddle did not lash out to strike her a second time. Eve wiped the water across Mikie's forehead and neck. Opening the vial carefully, she shook a tiny amount of the contents into her left hand. Again, dipping her right hand in the water without shifting her weight, she stirred the contents in the

German=this font   English=this font   **French=this font**   *Delaware=this font*

palm of her hand with her forefinger. Dipping her finger in the pasty mixture, she placed her finger in Mikie's mouth. He sucked it weakly. With repeated fingerfuls, most of her palm's contents trickled down Mikie's throat.

She wondered if Mikie would accept a breast. Moving with great care, she pulled Mikie to her breast. He nuzzled but did not clamp fast to the breast. Nestling his head in the crook of her leg, she squeezed the nipple until it protruded and a few drops fell onto his crusty lips. Whimpering, he licked off the pale blue-white liquid. Again, she drew his lips to her breast. With a weak thrust of his tongue, he pulled her expressed nipple into his mouth. She felt the release and prayed there would be enough milk to help the medication stay. Her back pained from the angle of her body. Her hips ached from the ribs of cedar. Cold mist clustered in tiny droplets over every hair on her body and Mikie's.

Eve's thoughts strayed to beg God's forgiveness for all her sins for which she paid an exacting price. Was death preferable to life? Then, she focused on the small, flushed and fevered face. No, life was infinitely better. This little life depended on her as never before…as did Henry's. She prayed for strength to meet the challenges that lay ahead. If she could just help keep the boys alive, perhaps the gift of life from Adam Henry would live on through the boys.

Chapter 5   Allegheny and to the Ohio

"There were no means which God and nature might have placed at the disposal of the governing powers to which they would not be justified in having recourse."

Lord Suffolk's reply to Lord Chatham as quoted by Silas Farmer in *History of Detroit and Wayne County and Early Michigan, 1890* (Silas Farmer and Co. Republished by Gale Research, 1969), p. 245.

Near Fort Pitt, a Disputed Territory Desired by Virginia, Connecticut, and Pennsylvania

A figure slipped stealthily through the forest near Fort Pitt. The bribe from McKee had done the trick. The guard at the jail had looked the other way and then agreed upon a short blow to the jaw to protect him from any Whig censure. The figure placed the correspondence in the appropriate tree trunk for the returning raiding parties. Looking about him very carefully to be sure he had not been followed, Simon Girty completed his task. Trained well by the Wyandot, Simon Girty knew the forest sounds well. Noting no change from the normal forest patter that would betray a follower, he slipped the oiled leather folder with its precious letters and maps into the hole that was just at the tip of his reach. Perusing his area again, he headed back to turn himself over to the Whig authorities. He would plead how horrid it was for him to be penned up inside the small cell and how he had just temporarily lost his mind. Girty would stress his importance to the Rebel cause. He had returned to show his loyalty. After all, why would one who was disloyal return? He would remind them that he had scouted in the Dunmore's war to protect their very homes. He would remind them that he had been taken prisoner with his brothers and saw both his father and step-father put to violent death at the hand of their enemies. He would remind them that his fluency in the tongue of the Wyandot could aid their cause in convincing the Wyandot to side with the Rebels against the British or remain neutral.

Rehearsing as he walked, Girty's figure merged into the shadows. He must return once more to Fort Pitt, earlier known as Duquesne under the French. The disputed fort nestled at the junction of the Ohio, the Allegheny, and the Monongahela Rivers. Because of its strategic location, both Pennsylvania and Virginia had clashed continuously for the ownership of this desirable outpost. Only their alliance to fight the British kept them from a bloody war with each other over the site.

Returning to Fort Detroit by Sail from Quebec

Jacob Schieffelin debated if Lieutenant Governor Hamilton would explode or implode. Lieutenant Governor Hamilton measured the Captain's quarters, three steps across, two back. The restrained loop connected and circled like a cat that had bit his own tail and refused to let go. Schieffelin sat apprehensively at the small ship's desk waiting for Hamilton to speak.

To see this great man demeaned and rebuffed by an obviously short-sighted and inept war department incensed Schieffelin as well. He could see the Furies whipping and building within Hamilton once more, just as it had in Carleton's office. The same anger that Hamilton had bottled up before Carleton's efficient but debasing sub-staff had nearly broken his commander's composure.

First, the war staff would neither confirm nor deny the rampant rumors of Burgoyne's surrender of over six-thousand fine troops at Saratoga to a ragtag army of Rebels. Their collective feigned ignorance raised Hamilton's ire. Second, there came the refusal to allow Hamilton to see Sir Guy Carleton after his long journey from Fort Detroit, which was accompanied with a mild reprimand from the staff (all of whom ranked below him) for DeJean and Hamilton's handling of civil matters. But the final humiliation contained the news that James Sterling had been released and that his confiscated property and goods were to be returned as soon as Hamilton returned to Fort Detroit.

Carleton's staff totally ignored Hamilton's demand to voice his displeasure with Captain Mompesson's arrogance and the lack of military troops to assist the Indian Affairs office in making the diversion along the Alleghenies. Carleton's staff rejected Hamilton's proposed plans to attack a weakened Fort Pitt in the spring. In addition, the staff totally refused to acknowledge Hamilton's strictly human needs, stating that there would be absolutely no time to rest, to sip brandy with friends, or to attend a dance or two in this outpost of civilization after his long trip. In fact, Carleton's office stressed that Hamilton should not tarry even one single day, demanding his return immediately to his post!

As if to further humiliate him, Carleton's staff heaped even more disrespect upon him. Hamilton found that Sterling, who had constituted a royal pain in his side and who had the gall to publicly challenge him, would sail on the same ship with Hamilton and his secretary back to Fort Detroit.

The total lack of support by his superior, the degrading response to his needs for clarification of his authority at the fort, and an avoidance of a clear order either to continue or to stop the western raids accompanied another discourteous demand of Hamilton. Carleton ordered Hamilton to write Lieutenant Governor Edward Abbott, a fellow in the triad of power, immediately upon his return. In this correspondence, Hamilton must inform Abbott, in no uncertain terms, that Abbott would receive no money from the crown for past or future debts. Hamilton realized instantly that

German=this font   English=this font   *French=this font*   *Delaware=this font*

this order could hamper his plan to strike against the Spanish with a united front, once the Long Knives were destroyed. This order would utterly destroy any rapport with Abbott. Hamilton felt overcome with disgust. He remained convinced that the entire Quebec office could not see a wick's length in front of their noses.

The only positive in the whole visit proved to be that the war office still paid and would continue to pay for Hamilton's office expenses, for war captains, and for supplies for the increasingly dependent Indian allies.

When Hamilton finally spoke, he spoke softly. Despite his rage, he knew the thinness of cabin walls loaned to him by the ship's Captain. Doubting Sterling's true loyalties and fearing that other unseen Rebel spies might lurk aboard, he vented his concerns to his secretary, who listened respectfully.

Near and Beyond Fort Pitt

Dawn and cold rain came simultaneously. Eve dozed fitfully, warmed by her fevered son. Mikie proved to be a strong child. She was not sure that Margaret's medicine had helped, but it had not harmed. Mikie clung to life tightly like a lichen to a rock. For over six days and nights, she had spent the majority of her time in the canoe. She felt convinced that she had permanent indentations on her thinning buttocks, which had molded themselves to the shape of the cedar ribs. With each passing day, her stench grew to become as much a part of her as the weariness that crept into every bone and fiber. A growing resignation that no one would come for her and the boys metastasized like a cancer within her. The parade of autumn colors and the breathtaking beauty of the river banks went virtually unnoticed by Eve. She did note, however, that her coverlet had been wrapped carefully in a hide to keep the water out.

Eve appreciated the deer hide that Blue Ice had given her the second day. She followed his directions. Fur turned out in the rain. Fur turned in when cold. She questioned the number of days that she had been gone now from the warmth of her own hearth and the comfort of her sweet-smelling bed. Had it been nine days now, or ten? Or was it eleven? She had lost count. She found the pain of remembering as painful as sitting folded and cramped. No matter how she forbade them, the memories were vivid. Sometimes she almost swore that she heard Adam Henry's voice, encouraging her just like he had during childbirth.

A silent debate raged within her. Should she try to remember or try to forget? The only certainty: whatever she and Adam Henry had known was gone. Or was it? Sometimes, when her back ached so badly that tears formed, she swore that she could feel his hands on her shoulders, massaging her just as he always had after many long hours at the loom. She vaguely remembered passing Fort Pitt. Their canoes had skirted the far shore in the small hours of morning when lax sentries slept. She

German=this font   English=this font   **French=this font**   *Delaware=this font*

remembered the hard slap with the strong admonition from Blue Ice that she and the child must be still or die. They had stopped only once down river of the fort to retrieve a small leather packet from the hollow tree. She sensed that they were going north again, not south, for the weather seemed chillier. The sun's position changed with each shortened day.

Ahead, the surface of the water churned. Eve had come to respect the craft that she rode in. In spite of sideswiping rocks and occasional rough water, the sturdy craft continued to slip through the water, propelled by its paddler. Often, when she espied recent tree falls with their bare branches jutting into the river amongst the white froth, she could sense Blue Ice's apprehension. Sometimes he stalled their forward motion in the currents as they approached. Other times he paddled or swerved quickly. Over the recent days, she had become aware of the rhythm of his paddling and felt a reluctant admiration for his skills and for Stalking Wolf, whom she observed from time to time, given their relative positions on the river. The cadence of their bodies moved in unison as they rocked forward from the waist and dipped the paddles. Unlike her, neither Stalking Wolf nor Blue Ice seemed stiff when they disembarked. Both men had remarkable stamina. She could hear Stalking Wolf and Henry, who answered easily to Hanu, chatting with their makeshift chatter across the water from time to time. He and the child had developed a language of their own.

More and more, Eve felt a growing resentment towards Stalking Wolf. His growing intrusion into Henry's life and Henry's withdrawal from Eve irritated her. Surely, she thought, Lil' Henry would not forget that this man had killed his father. At other times, she admired Henry's resiliency and his ability to find laughter and joy, regardless of their hardships. His little jokes and pranks helped her face each day.

Suddenly, an unseen, small, broken branch hidden just below the surface in the current ripples thrust up through the cedar strip flooring, interrupting her thoughts. The forward momentum of the craft broke off the branch quickly. Immediately, a gush of icy cold water rushed into the canoe's bow near the man-board. Instinctively, Eve thrust her foot forward. Her bare heel nested in the hole. While it cut down the volume of water entering the canoe, the icy coldness of the water on Eve's leg sent shivers through her. The wetness caused Mikie to howl.

"Why does that brat scream out?"

"We have a hole."

"Why did you not warn me, Bitch?"

Immediately the paddle struck Eve's shoulder, causing her foot to pull away. A small gusher shot up, getting Blue Ice's full attention.

Eve struggled to get her heel into the stopper position again. Pulling Mikie out of the water filling the bow, she tried to ignore the sting in her shoulder.

"I could not see it!"

"Stalking Wolf." Blue Ice's clear call resounded. *"We have a hole."*

"Pull ashore. There is a clearing ahead. We can patch it there."

With a grunt of acknowledgement, Blue Ice pulled his craft toward the quiet water ahead. Stalking Wolf's observation proved right. The spot made a good campsite. As they neared the shore, Blue Ice climbed out in the shallow area and pulled his craft ashore.

Grumbling to himself, Blue Ice reached out to Eve so that she and the child could come ashore. Her bare feet sunk in the cold clay mud. Accordingly, her dress drug in the water and soaked up water nearly to her knees.

"Put the child by the tree. Unload the canoe, sightless bitch."

Grabbing the deer skin from the canoe with a small move of defiance, Eve laid Mikie near the tree, tucking the skin about him. Since he was too sick to protest, Mikie lay curled quietly near the tree. Eve began her task. His blue eyes watched from tiny gray hollows as his mother trekked back-and-forth from the canoe to another spot in the clearing.

Stalking Wolf soon pulled his craft a short ways from Blue Ice. He lifted Henry, quickly set him ashore, and swatted him affectionately across the rump.

"Hanu, help mother." Henry looked quizzically at Stalking Wolf for just a short moment and then following his hand movements, he repeated the words softly and sprung to help his mother unload the canoe.

"Hanu help mother." Henry repeated as he ran up alongside of his mother.

"What did you say?"

"I said, Henry help, Mutti!" His eager little hands began digging in the piles of loot in the canoe. Then, he was off like a shot, before his mother could respond.

"Your son has a good ear for their tongue, Eve," Margaret said, as Stalking Wolf assisted her as she climbed from the craft. She kept her shoes strung around her neck, since Stalking Wolf would not let her wear them aboard. Seeing the need, she immediately pitched in to assist Eve and Henry. The shoes could wait.

Before long both canoes were unloaded and turned bottom up to dry.

"We will need fire," Blue Ice commented dryly.

"We will be safe enough here. We are far from the settlements. If the spirit of the river sees fit to poke its lance in our canoe, there must be a good reason."

Blue Ice smiled one of his rare smiles. *"There is good mud here. If we had a good hunter with us, we might eat well while we fix the canoe."*

"Well to be sure, we have one good hunter here."

"Only one?"

"Only one who does not have a hole in his canoe and no good women to fix it!"

"Take the little squirrel with you," Blue Ice sparred since it was obvious that Stalking Wolf would not do the mending chore for him.

German=this font   English=this font   **French=this font**   *Delaware=this font*

"Hanu, come," Stalking Wolf called. "Your son and I will go hunting. Do not fear for him, woman. I will watch him well."

Eve nodded as she watched Henry and Stalking Wolf leave the clearing.

"We need more wood, bitches."

Margaret and Eve, grateful to be able to walk without supervision, donned their shoes and began to scrounge for fallen branches close to the campsite.

"If the big one hunts, do you think they will get something to eat for all of us?" Margaret asked Eve.

"They have shared whatever they have had in the past. If I get hot meat, I think that my tongue will lick my tears of joy from my eyes right down to my chin."

Margaret chuckled. "How is the boy? He sleeps a lot."

"Too much, I fear. What a poor mother I am. I fuss when he cries. I fuss when he is quiet."

"God keeps your son alive, Eve. Be thankful. It could be worse."

Eve nodded in agreement.

"Bitches, talk less! Work your hands, not your mouths."

"Someone should work his mouth less too," Margaret muttered.

"Someone needs his mouth washed out with soap," Eve responded as quietly as she.

Smiling, both women resumed their task. Soon mounded with downed dry branches, the women returned to the campsite.

Upon their return, they stood watching Blue Ice, who removed a small frying pan and a roll of birchbark from his pack. In the pan, a black shiny substance reflected the firelight. A leather packet with a tiny woven basket filled with grease and an awl were laid upon the ground. The skillet placed over the small fire nestled in the hot coals. Soon the edges of the black shiny substance began to liquefy and melt. The thin cedar planking was slid away to expose the area about the hole and another piece of birchbark quickly cut and fitted over the offending area. Within the birchbark roll, strips of pre-split spruce root were withdrawn and placed to soak in the water near shore. In minutes, Blue Ice had made holes at regular intervals about the birch patch. A few sharp wooden pegs were cut to keep the patch in place. Going to the waters edge, he selected a soaked spruce root. Using the awl to aid him, he skillfully wove the root in-and-out through the layers of birchbark to begin stitching it in place.

"You, bitch, stir the pitch."

Margaret pulled her skirt away so as not to get in the fire and knelt to stir the pitch. Eve, totally fascinated by Blue Ice's activity, monitored his progress. Seeing that he neared the end of his first split root, Eve quickly selected one from the water near shore and returned to hand it to him just as he ran out. He cocked his head, looked at her quizzically, and then resumed his stitching.

German=this font   English=this font   **French=this font**   *Delaware=this font*

"They may not be totally useless after all," he mumbled to himself as he worked.

The stitching completed and any unused spruce root returned to the birchbark pack, Blue Ice took the skillet from Margaret. Taking a strip of birchbark, he dipped it in the hot brew, allowed it to cool, and bent it in a "u" shaped loop. Adding a bit more of the bear grease, he stirred the skillet. He repeated the process. Satisfied at the elasticity of his dipped bark the second time, he proceeded. He frayed the end of a green branch, filled it with the hot resinous mixture, and brushed the hot spruce gum around the edges of the patch and also on the stitches that he had made so neatly around the bark patch. Turning the canoe, he crouched and motioned for Margaret to hold the pan while he applied another coat to the inside where the stitches came through and also around the hole where the broken birchbark now lay flattened against the patch. Satisfied that he had enough resin applied to seal the patch, he straightened from his twisted position. As he did, so his breech clout slid slightly to the side, and he noticed that Margaret had seen his person before she looked quickly away.

The woman was not as ugly as the other one he noted. She did not smell as bad, either. Looking quite smug, he stood up to repack his patch kit and sat the resin pan aside to harden.

"May I look at your basket?" Eve found herself asking before she realized that she had spoken. Blue Ice shrugged and handed it to her. Eve looked with absolute wonder at what she held in her hand. Each layer was sewn together with a fine black thread. Turning it in her hand, she began to realize that the materials coiled, packed, and sewn so beautifully together were long pine needles. The maker had grouped the heads of the needles in a pleasing pattern which spun on the coil. The needles were not randomly placed. The maker had controlled the pattern so that the heads of the needles made diamond patterns on the side amongst an ascending spiral. She could not resist opening the tiny lid with its hinge and clasp of braided fiber, which circled a small reddish stone with a tiny hole in one side. On the lip of the small basket and the lid, the grass-like fiber was braided and then wound around the opening. To her amazement, she could see that the basket perfectly enclosed a small clay pot within. The top had concentric circles of braided grass and pine needles. Again, the placement of the pine needle heads made a pleasant design on the surface.

"What is this grass?" Eve asked as she looked very closely at the edge.

"We call it sweet grass. Smell!" Blue Ice said gruffly as he grabbed her hand and shoved the basket jar into her face.

"Indeed, it does smell sweet." Unable to resist the joy of her awareness, she handed the small vessel to Margaret, who smelled it tentatively. Unimpressed, Margaret quickly returned the jar to Eve.

Eve cradled the small container. She caressed the surface, rolled it carefully in her hands and smelled the sweet grass again. Reluctantly, she returned it to Blue Ice.

German=this font   English=this font   *French=this font*   *Delaware=this font*

"The maker of this has great skill," Eve said with a sense of awe, coveting the small container.

"Do you think only white people are skilled?" Blue Ice snapped.

Eve stepped back as if struck. She had not meant to offend him. She genuinely appreciated the small container. Hearing Mikie whimper, she spun quickly, returning to his side. Lifting Mikie into her arms, she cuddled him. Puzzling over what had angered Blue Ice so, she set to feeding Mikie. When she finished feeding the child and he had fallen asleep once more, she arose.

"Woman, we will be here for a while. You may wash yourself."

Eve looked at Margaret. Her faced mirrored more questions than answers.

"May we go a small piece from here?" Margaret asked.

"No."

Eve stood for a moment in a total quandary. Then she put her shoulders back and marched toward the river. Margaret watched in amazement as Eve took her shoes off and walked fully clothed into the river.

Standing on the bank, Margaret looked after her. "What are you doing? Eve, are you crazy?"

"Every thread I wear is filled with filth." Eve said simply. She began to rub the skirts of her dress and swish the water through it. Pulling her petticoat away from her body under her skirt, she contorted and moved until the water around her filled with the dried particles that had clung to the layers of material. The dirt accumulated over the last horrible days began to drift away. When the water around her clouded, she moved to another clearer spot to swish her garments again. Untying her waist and taking her petticoat and pocket from under her skirt, she rubbed the stained material, wrung it out and dipped and roughed it against her knuckles. Nearly blue with cold, her chin quivered, but she persisted in her task. Finally, dipping in the water up to her neck and rubbing her petticoat under the arms as well as cupping her hands to flush the water through the material there and across her breasts, she continued to wash the dirt and excrement from her person.

Margaret observed her actions from shore in total horror. "Dear God in Heaven! You will catch a death chill, Eve."

"I have been wet to the bone for days before, and God saw fit to spare me. Perhaps he will spare me one more time. At least this time there is a fire to stand by."

A splash startled Eve. She became discombobulated when she realized that Blue Ice had just dove in beside her and that he was totally naked. Seeing her discomfort, he splashed water in her face before gliding with absolute ease into the water like an eel. As he swam, his head never seemed to rise out of the water. Eve watched him with incredulous attention. She observed that as his arm raised and dipped reaching forward into the water before him, he drew a breath from under the arch of his

German=this font   English=this font   *French=this font*   *Delaware=this font*

armpit. Shivering from the intense cold of the water, she shook until her teeth rattled, but she could not take her eyes off of his swimming form. She had never in her entire life seen a man swim, and now to see one swim effortlessly as if one with the water, she felt in awe for the second time that day.

Finally, wringing her petticoat as dry as she could one last time, Eve waded from the water. She laid her petticoat over a nearby bush to dry. Margaret turned her eyes from the water. Modesty would not permit her to look at the swimming form that splashed about. She frowned at Eve. Taking wads of her skirt in hand, one after another, Eve wrung handful after handful before returning the limp mass to place. As she did so, she revealed her legs. Again, she could see from the expression on Margaret's face that her behavior was unacceptable. Her teeth chattered as she eased herself closer to the fire. She felt thoroughly frozen; but for the first time in days, she did not feel that she reeked from her own excrement. Warm tears of joy coursed down her face. Her nipples stood rock hard against the breast material of her dress as she continued to wring and re-wring her dress near the edge of the fire.

Eve heard footsteps behind her. She sensed that Blue Ice stood naked beside her. Grasping a blanket from the bundles of loot, he showed Eve how to funnel the heat from the small fire to warm and to dry her. In quiet appreciation, she followed his suggestions and tried not to look at his person, keeping her gaze above his shoulders. Laughing at her obvious discomfort, he deliberately used a corner of her blanket to towel himself off before donning his shirt, breech clout, and leggings. The whole time, the man proudly revealed himself to the women as much as possible to advertise his wares.

As Eve stood before the fire, she gratefully stepped aside as Blue Ice put a few more branches on the fire. As it flared up, she stepped back further, but once the flames died down, she returned again to funnel the warm smoke and heat to dry her clothes.

"You smell smoky, but some better," Blue Ice growled, before telling Margaret to gather more branches because her foolish friend had used all of them to dry herself. Even though his manners were gruff, Eve began to suspect that Blue Ice was not as savage as she initially thought. Not for a single moment did she doubt his ability to snuff out her life or the lives of her children; but paradoxically, she also realized that he was not totally cruel. Maybe something existed within him, something more than she had first suspected. She did not know whether her recognition of the craftsmanship of the tiny woven basket, the acknowledgement of the skills Blue Ice used when patching the canoe or her reluctant appreciation of his boating and swimming skills made any real difference. All she knew was that she saw more to this savage than she ever expected. Unlike David Zeisberger's description of them as unlearned children, she found this savage quite informed about what he needed to know.

Her teeth had stopped chattering. The warmth of the smoke and fire

German=this font   English=this font   *French=this font*   *Delaware=this font*

began to dry her out. The blessing of wool reasserted itself once more. Ripping a portion of her petticoat, she fashioned a cloth to clean Mikie. Smiling, she washed Mikie in small stages and uncovered only a small portion of his weakened body at a time. The fever that recurred at intervals would permit little else. Gradually, they both settled in the warm blanket. She wrapped Mikie in the folds of her arms and gathered him within the warmth of their mutual cocoon. They slept the afternoon away. Margaret also dozed. She had wrapped her shawl tightly about her and backed into the hollow of a large sycamore out of the wind.

"Mutti, Mutti, we have birdies." Henry's voice rang with excitement. He fairly danced around Stalking Wolf as they entered the fire area. Barely damp now, Eve stood and pulled the blanket about her and watched as Stalking Wolf walked up to the muddy shore. Even Blue Ice grinned at his return. Mikie, refreshed from his nap, sat quietly on the deer skin. Asking Henry to stomp his bare feet in the area near the river bank to make mud, Eve and Margaret watched as Stalking Wolf gutted the birds with his fingers and flung the offal into the water. Swishing the birds, he soaked the birds, feathers and all. Then, to the women's utter dismay, Stalking Wolf began to plaster the mud that squished about Henry's feet onto the feathers. In a few minutes, the birds were totally encased in a heavy layer of moist clay. Both Margaret and Eve looked on, filled with revulsion. What a total waste of good birds, they both thought.

Next, the mud-encased birds were placed within a nest of twisted sticks and suspended over the fire's coals, which Blue Ice had prepared as he muttered about useless women. Stalking Wolf instructed Henry how to turn the spit. Then the adults and Mikie huddled about the fireside, grateful for its heat. If the cage about the birds caught fire, one of the men would quickly swig a mouthful of water from their small drinking gourds. The spray from their mouth would put the fire out. Eve observed that the mud about the birds began to form a hard shell. Increasingly, when the men sprayed the limb cages with water, the splashes on the birds no longer dripped mud into the fire. Instead, the damp surface steamed. The smell of the cooking birds soon began to permeate the air.

Mikie began to salivate as the agreeable smell increased. Anticipation grew steadily for those huddled about the fire. Time tiptoed. Finally, Stalking Wolf took one of the encased birds from above the fire. He broke the encased creature against a rock like an egg. Both Margaret and Eve sighed aloud as it broke apart. Feathers and hide clung to the baked outer clay shell. Nestled within, rich moist meat glistened in the firelight. No one spoke. No one wanted anything more than the juicy, hot cooked meat within their mouths.

Eve could not help it. Saliva rolled down her chin as she had gratefully accepted her portion. She grinned broadly as she looked into Margaret's equally smiling face.

"Get that tongue out Eve," Margaret said as she primly tried to catch a drool which had escaped to run down her own face with the back of her hand.

German=this font   English=this font   *French=this font*   *Delaware=this font*

Grinning, the women gratefully accepted another helping from their captors. Henry smacked and munched with utter satisfaction. Mikie chewed on the juicy joints and sucked on the lightly-meated bones handed to him. Then he began to whimper and pull on his right ear.

Stalking Wolf took his tomahawk from his belt. Reaching behind him to pull a tiny pouch from his goods, he filled the pipe molded in the tomahawk. Pulling a brand from the fire, he lit his pipe. Puffing, he released the tobacco smoke in small circles above his head. He drew repeatedly on the pipe. The smoke streamed from his nostrils. Satisfaction filled his countenance. Laying the pipe across his lap, he motioned to Eve to pass Mikie to him.

A wave of fear shuddered through Eve's frame as she glanced down at the tomahawk.

Sensing her fear, Stalking Wolf frowned and reached out for the child again.

Eve reluctantly handed Mikie to Stalking Wolf. For a change, Mikie, logy from the first real food other than his mother's milk in many days, groggily accepted the hand-off.

Stalking Wolf laid the child on his shoulder with a practiced hand. Puffing once more on the pipe, Stalking Wolf cupped his hand over Mikie's ear, the same ear that Mikie had pulled on. Like a father, he gentled the child and proceeded to blow a thin stream of smoke into the child's ear. Instinctively, dubiously, Mikie pulled away. But, the warmth of the fire and the gentle handling caused Mikie to relax again. Repeatedly, Stalking Wolf blew a thin stream of smoke into the child's ear. With each puff, both women could see the pain in Mikie's face ease and then subside. After about ten puffs, Mikie drifted into a sound asleep. Laying the pipe aside, Stalking Wolf relaxed, still holding the sleeping child upon his shoulder. On his thigh, Henry had nodded off to sleep like a milk-sodden puppy, his arm draped casually across Stalking Wolf's legs.

Blue Ice rose and cut a few alder and willow branches from tags near the river. He returned to his spot.

Sunlight faded with deep reds and purples as night drained the last traces of twilight. Firelight danced on their faces, warming the lighted-side. The chill of the impending night invaded on the darkened side. Bending the willow into tiny loops about a palms width across, Blue Ice bound the crossing of the willow loop with reeds or grasses that he flattened between his teeth. Then, rustling in the pack behind him, he withdrew a scalp from among the packs. Both women blanched with horror, as he proceeded to begin to lace the scalp to the loop, using tiny stitches this time, not the larger stitches of the canoe patch. He bound the scalp to its tiny willow frame with studied precision. Bending the grasses and wetting them with his mouth, he passed them through the small holes made by the tip of his red-handled scalping knife as he laced the scalp neatly into place.

German=this font   English=this font   **French=this font**   *Delaware=this font*

A shudder passed through Eve as the man before her took many steps backward into savagery before her very eyes. Tears welled up.

Margaret looked toward the river. Her lips moved in silent prayer as she stared into the growing darkness.

Eve continued to watch him. Although repelled by her morbid fascination, she could not look away. Where recent tears of joy had fallen, tears of profound sadness fell in silent curtains.

The long locks of Isaac's son, Joseph, gleamed in the flickering light as Blue Ice finished his task.

German=this font   English=this font   *French=this font*   *Delaware=this font*

Chapter 6   About the Hearths

"What! to attribute the sanction of God and nature to the
massacres of the Indian scalping-knife? To the cannibal-
savage, torturing, murdering, roasting, and eating—
literally, my lords, eating—the mangled victims of his
barbarous battle? Such horrible notions shock every
precept of religion, divine, or natural, and every generous
feeling of humanity. They shock every sentiment of honor.
They shock me as a lover of honorable war, and a detester
of murderous barbarity."

Lord Chatham replies to Lord Suffolk as quoted by Silas Farmer in *History of
Detroit and Wayne County and Early Michigan, 1890* (Silas Farmer and Co.
Republished by Gale Research, 1969), p. 245.

Along the Ohio River

"You will wait here. If you attempt to leave, I will kill your son,"
Blue Ice said to Eve. "Do not interrupt us!"

Lil' Henry stood aside with Stalking Wolf. Eve nodded her
compliance as she watched Lil' Henry depart with the two men.

"What ungodly thing do they do now?" Margaret asked quietly as
she stood beside Eve and Mikie.

"I do not know," Eve answered.

The woman could hear bathing noises in the dark from the river before
a fire lit along the shore which filtered through the trees. Soft chants hung
on the crisp night air.

Margaret, Mikie, and Eve huddled together in the cold, sharing their
body warmth. When the men returned a few hours later, Eve and Margaret
both recognized immediately that the men had removed all war paint. If
they had clean garments, they were worn.

Another fire built for their mutual warmth made the cold easier to
tolerate.

The following day, when the canoes approached the Delaware village
on the banks of the Ohio, whoops from the canoes by Stalking Wolf and
Blue Ice alerted the encampment of their coming. As they pulled the
heavily laden canoes ashore, a small crowd began to grow about them
consisting of older men, women, children and dogs, which yelped nearly as
loud as their masters who greeted the returning men and their captives.

"Unload the canoes, bitches," Blue Ice growled to Margaret, jerking
Eve out of the canoe. He strutted proudly about as the women worked.
Stalking Wolf disappeared among the crowd with a fur bundle tucked under
his arm. Eve had devised a small sling to carry Mikie from her shredded

apron, which now left her hands free. She began to unload the packets of loot while Mikie clung to her neck, peering over her shoulder at the gathering crowd that pushed nearer and nearer to his mother. Margaret, her bare feet padding the well-trod ground, quietly toted her fair share.

"Ho, Red Jacket, have we beaten the others?" Blue Ice called to one of his countrymen.

"No others yet."

Pulling a long pole from the canoe, he held the staff high. Crying loudly into the wind, raising the staff above the heads of the milling crowd, he let the wind separate six willow hoops that dangled on their braided tethers.

"We will have many supplies from the British Fort for winter. Many more of our father's wayward children will soon let the wind blow through their hair."

Laughter and whoops rippled through the crowd. Raw hostility emanated from the faces that peered and sneered at Margaret, Eve and the boys. Henry, sensing the difference, clung tightly to his mother's skirt, while Mikie hid his face in his mother's neck. Now that their work had finished, Margaret held her iron skillet fast to her chest like a shield. The women stood back-to-back, sharing a mutual backbone of terror.

Eve noticed that the cabins that encircled the working area looked not too much different than her cabin. Their similarity surprised her. Instead of glass or greased papers over the window openings, she saw woven mats. Many of the cabins once had had flowers about their doors. Now, frostbitten or in full seed, their dry stalks mixed with a few green pot herbs and sage which Eve recognized. Stones for grinding corn stood vacant now as the Delaware women's attention had focused on the captives. The smells of stew kettles with meats and vegetables made her mouth water. Eve could see the stalks of corn in the distance. Though not in neat rows, she could see many ears still drying in the fields that surrounded the village. Squash and pumpkins skirted about the stalks recently made bare by the frost and gleamed golden in the afternoon light. Beans clung to the dry stalks, their full pods shrinking in the late autumn warmth. The smell of drying meat and a few fish from the drying racks also permeated the air. Chunks of pumpkin and squash dried on other racks. Harvest had been good to these people.

Suddenly, a sharp stick painfully poked Eve's thigh, diverting her attention from the fields. Looking down in the direction of the jab, she saw her small tormenter stood not much taller than Henry, who had wedged himself tightly between Eve's and Margaret's legs. Would they continue to be prisoners? Or not? Would they be killed now? Eve thought. New fears crawled over her, just as the ants once had within the log. The newer, more threatening possibilities presented a very strong case as she sensed the deep hatred of those swarming around her.

As Eve tried to comfort Henry, she observed a very ancient woman with a long staff approaching their huddle. The ancient one held fast to the

German=this font   English=this font   *French=this font*   *Delaware=this font*

arm of Stalking Wolf. Her face was not as dark as many who surrounded them. Deeply lined, as only time can cut, her face spoke of age, strength, and many life trials. Power radiated from her, which far exceeded the first impact of her general appearance. A mantle of regality clung to her shoulders. In deference, people parted to give way to her. Eve inhaled sharply. Something else also clung to her shoulders. Eve's woven coverlet torn from her loom surrounded the elder woman standing before her. Whispers of approval and envy sprang from many of the women's lips. Blue Ice frowned. The ownership of the many-colored quilt had been settled. The quilt would not be divided.

"You two will serve White Corn Woman until the others come," Stalking Wolf stated. "She needs wood for her fire and pumpkins cut for drying. Do this, so you may sleep in her cabin."

The angry crowd separated and allowed the prisoners to follow White Corn Woman, but not without other jabs and spit. Margaret fended off some of her attacks with the skillet. Mikie howled when one blow caught him in the ribs. Quickly, Eve swung him across her chest, shielding him from other blows as she curled about him. Taking the blows across their backs, the two women staggered after White Corn Woman. The sheer numbers of the onlookers extinguished any hope of escape for Margaret or Eve.

When they stopped before White Corn Woman's cabin, Stalking Wolf spoke and motioned. *"Hanu come."*   Henry looked first at his mother and then at Stalking Wolf. Something struck Eve. Eve sensed that she must not show her feelings. She pulled Henry's hand from her skirt, trying not to show her wrenching fears for her son. *"Hanu come."*   Stepping away from his mother hesitatingly, he began to run toward Stalking Wolf, only to have his mother's earlier tormenter try to trip him up with his stick. Henry's reflexes, honed by years of surviving big brothers, responded automatically with a well placed shove in return. When the other boy hit the ground with a resounding thud on his prat, a ripple of laughter sprung from some of the older men. Henry looked up to Stalking Wolf, seeking approval. An easy smile answered his unspoken question.

"Ho, Little Fox, Hanu can push back too!"   A voice in the crowd spoke.   The elder's approval of Henry's response and their amusement over Little Fox's fall smarted equally.

Stalking Wolf pulled Little Fox to his feet, dusting off his nephew's behind. *"Now you can help Hanu bring pumpkins to White Corn Woman. We shall see which of you can work harder."* A grunt of approval from the spectators meant that Little Fox must comply.

"Hanu, this is my nephew."   Sensing Hanu could not follow his train of thought, Stalking Wolf dropped the subject. His mother could not translate for him at this point, for she and Margaret had already moved out of earshot. Her boy seemed to know little English, so English would be useless. *"Little Fox, you will show Hanu what to do. Now do it."*

Following his uncle's directive, Little Fox headed out to the pumpkin

German=this font   English=this font   *French=this font*   *Delaware=this font*

patch. Little Fox tugged and jerked Henry's tattered sleeve to show him the way.

By the third day, blisters covered both Eve's and Margaret's palms. The blisters broke. In the tender flesh beneath, new blisters formed and were breaking and seeping. A large pile of pumpkin and squash had been placed on the drying racks and more waited to be placed. Even Mikie helped for short periods, stringing pre-pierced chunks of pumpkin. Both women strove to be industrious, sensing the need to be of some value to hold death at bay. Instinctively, both women realized that keeping busy kept their fears at a manageable level.

White Corn Woman spoke only once to her captives and that screech came when Eve had selected the wrong wood for her fire. Shaking her head and frowning at her captive's stupidity, she pointed her staff at the proper pile for Eve to use before striking her across her back.

Eve and Margaret had noticed early on that different woods were placed in different stacks. The bark proved to be the identifying key. Following the examples before them, the wood gathered on long, guarded walks was placed in its appropriate stack. The two women began to understand that the Indians preferred some woods for certain tasks. Some burned hotter. Some held their heat longer. Some made ash that the old woman considered dirty. Every day, others in the tribe provided a pot of mixed stew for White Corn Woman, which she reheated over her fire. Neither woman spoke back to their mistress, who allowed them and the children to eat from her pot after she had had her fill. Though the strange flavors proved different to the prisoners' palates, they felt thankful for the sustenance.

When White Corn Woman approached the two women and gruffly inspected each of their hands before grunting and returning to her cabin, both captives looked at each other quizzically. Moments later, White Corn Woman reappeared with a small red clay pot in her hand. Taking each woman's hand in turn, she applied yellow-green colored grease to each hand and then wrapped their palms with grasses and corn leaves which she had tucked at her waist. She then motioned them to sit and returned to her cabin.

"I guess that means the old crone will let us stop for a while," Margaret observed as she dropped on the sunny side of the cabin. She sat with her back to the wall and her feet spread before her like a discarded doll. She held up her hands wrapped neatly in the grasses. Already, the pain lessened.

Mikie, having improved with food and shelter, played near the cabin. He had learned painfully that he must not stray. A few times, when he ranged too far, he was quickly picked up and thrown at his mother's feet. Not a stupid child, he adapted to the boundaries set for him.

Henry, however, had run of the camp and did not seem to draw hostility like the smaller blond child. Little Fox and he became nearly inseparable.

Eve observed this, as did Margaret. Henry had stood up to his captors, and this seemed to be a trait they admired. As for the antagonism felt toward Mikie; both women simply could not explain the animosity. Eve particularly expressed her dismay given that before, one toss of his blond head and a cherub smile had charmed everyone he met.

The skin of Eve's face had burned, peeled, and burned again. Except for the pink patches that had peeled, she had developed a brown shell of tough skin that daily altered her pale complexion and bare arms. Since she had no comb, she finger-combed her hair and tied it back with another scrap from her apron. Tendrils had worked out and crawled around her face, giving her a Medusa look.

"My hands feel some better. Do yours?"

"Yes. God knows what devil's medicine she put on us. But I have to admit, they feel some better." Margaret leaned wearily back against the warm logs of the cabin. Her bonnet askew, her face had not become as weathered as Eve's.

Eve felt tempted to ask Margaret why she thought the healing ointment had to be the work of the devil, but thought better of it. For a moment, Margaret's pious attitude reminded Eve of her Mutter.

A loud whoop broke in the distance. This was followed by a voice that both women recognized immediately.

"Anne?"

"Sure sounds like her."

"Don't you push me, mister! I ain't no slave. I be freeborn."

Anne's mantra brought a smile to both women's faces as Anne stumbled into the clearing at the edge of the field. Her back bent nearly double with a heavy load of looted goods, she walked at the head of a long line of prisoners.

"Anne, hush, they'll hit you again." A higher clear voice could be heard to carry across the field. Behind Anne, a slightly built, fair young woman struggled with her own heavy pack. Behind the young woman, Skelly, the young man captured initially with Margaret, staggered under an enormous load. Major Hay, walking alongside, prodded him from time to time with his musket, grinning when Skelly stumbled.

Margaret and Eve sat watching the ragtag party's approach. The village, alerted to their presence, flooded the commons area to see the new captives. For the first time, Eve studied the appearance of the British Major as he approached with the war party and the prisoners. A handsome man, his demeanor spoke of training and education. However, she would never see a redcoat again without feeling a deep anger. This so-called civilized man had helped to bring down terror on her family and others. For the first time in her life, Eve filled with enormous contempt for the English crown; and, in particular, its representatives. She despised Hay. Once, Eve had been ambivalent, like many of those who lived away from the major communities; now she joined the Rebel cause with conviction born of experience.

German=this font   English=this font   *French=this font*   *Delaware=this font*

White Corn Woman stood near Eve and Margaret. The commotion had drawn her from her cabin. She squinted at the approaching party and frowned. "Humph, she black white one," she said softly.

Surprised and startled, Eve and Margaret could not believe at first that they even had heard her. Neither could recognize the accent, but they both felt White Corn Woman might know more English than they had suspected. Had she understood them when they spoke bitterly about her and their captors? Chagrined, the two captives realized that they had underestimated their enemy once more.

Mikie, hearing the approaching party and the angry shouts, ran to his mother and crawled into her lap. Pawing at her breast, he sought security.

Fort Detroit

John Leeth fidgeted with his felt hat, turning it first one direction and then back. The young man wore a breech-clout beneath his hip-length leather wamus with tall leather leggings tied just below the knee to keep them from dragging. Long fringes spoke of his ease with inclement weather and the woodlands that crowded about the fort. He stood shifting weight from one moccasin to the other and looking uneasily about the room. The room felt entirely too warm with the hearth blazing brightly behind him.

Lieutenant Governor Hamilton observed Leeth without seeming to look up from his writing. Hamilton recognized that this discomfort could be levered into an advantage as he pursued his needs and that of the crown.

DeJean had reported to Hamilton earlier saying that he felt that he had found another party leader. He related that the young trader spoke the Delaware tongue fluently because Leeth had been adopted a few years before by a Delaware named Standing Stone. Given Leeth's trading skills, he appeared to be on good terms with some of the savages. The young man had come to DeJean to secure a license and a pass to take goods to his employer in Sandusky. Martial law had many uses. Not the least of which, the misused law controlled the flow of individuals throughout the area north of the Ohio and fleeced the merchants and traders with added costs for the Crown. DeJean seized the opportunity and decided to send Leeth to Hamilton under the guise of receiving a pass.

"Now, what can I do for you?" Hamilton spoke after he felt the young man would not tolerate a moment more of waiting.

"Need a pass, sir. So I can join up with my employer, sir."

Hamilton looked the young man over, disguising his great interest and utilizing a practiced countenance that appeared on the surface to be mild disinterest. Although the young trader was slight of build, he appeared wiry.

"I see. And what do you do for this employer."

German=this font   English=this font   *French=this font*   *Delaware=this font*

"Ah, I help him with his fur tradin'. He left orders for me to bring the trade goods and 'follow after him.'"**

"I see, and just where do you follow him to?" Hamilton began to recognize that the young man would not volunteer any information unless asked directly. This could be a desirable quality for one of his party leaders. Given that the Delaware were the King's weakest allies, his Lenni Lenape language skills would be an even greater asset to the crown.

"Sandusky, sir." John Leeth did not like being dangled like a fish on a line. A creepy uneasiness began to further disturb him. Trying not to let his increased apprehension of the man become apparent, he inwardly warned himself not to let his gaze drop from the obviously clever man before him. John sensed correctly that there was more to asking for this pass than he initially had been led to believe. He chided himself for not being more alert to the undertones coming from the weasel that had referred him to this superior. This smacked of a definite set-up and a plan to trip him up, but for what end?

"Do you speak any of the native tongues?"

"Yes, sir."

"I see. And just what do you speak?"

John transferred his weight again; and without backing down, he held his ground. "Some Delaware, sir, and a bit of Wyandot."

"What does your employer in Sandusky pay you? By the way, what did you say your name was?"

"Leeth, sir. John Leeth. I 'receive seven pound, ten shillings per month, sir and my victuals and clothing.'"**

"Not nearly what you are worth, I am sure." Hamilton tried to appeal to his materialistic side. "Why not work for me? I will 'pay you two dollars per day and one and a half rations.'** A wage far more in keeping with your talents, to be sure, Master Leeth."

John knew instinctively that that much money did not come without a price. The use of "master" had a mocking tone beneath the feigned politeness. What exactly did the Lieutenant Governor want him to do? To John's credit, he did not flinch, nor did he shy from answering the question.

"That seems a might high, sir, given my age and never having been apprenticed 'n all. Just exactly what service would you want me to render for that wage, sir?"

Hamilton sensed shrewdness here and courage to be tested under fire. "You would be an interpreter for the Indian Department. Sometimes you might—'go to war' with them.** And given that you understand English and the native tongue, you would be of a—" Hamilton paused to select just the right word with just the right connotation, "of a 'particular service' to the crown."**

Immediately John Leeth looked away. Hamilton noted the rapid withdrawal of his heretofore steady gaze. The young man shifted his weight again, spun his hat, and then tightened his grip on the rim before fully engaging Hamilton's gaze again.

German=this font   English=this font   *French=this font*   *Delaware=this font*

"You know, sir, I am not a healthy man. And I perceive the rigors of being an interpreter for you would cause you more trouble than I am worth. Been sickly all of my growing years, sir. My paw and maw wast that a way too. Lost both of them before I was six, sir. I just don't think that I would be able to do you that service, sir, being that I am given to so many poor spells. I must decline your kind offer."**

Hamilton's eye twitched and his pupils narrowed perceptively. John did not look away. Recognizing a boldfaced lie laced with just a smattering of truth when he heard one, Hamilton relaxed back in his chair, raised his chin, and responded.

"John Leeth, think on the crown's offer this evening and return to me here tomorrow morning at nine o'clock. It would be advisable to think this over carefully. You are dismissed until then."

John turned, gratified not to have to spar directly any longer. At least for the moment, he was free to go.

John Leeth's restless and sleepless night came to an end. The more he thought about Hamilton's offer, the more he felt 'affrighted and confused.'** The man reminded him of a steely-eyed viper that liked to render its victims helpless with a mesmerizing stare, immobilizing them before the strike. He did not relish the thought of facing that man again, but he knew with a certainty that running would be even more dangerous.

Promptly, at nine o'clock, he stood before the Lieutenant Governor, clutching his hat once more. This time, his wait proved short.

"Now, Leeth, John Leeth. Do you accept the generous offer I have made you to be an interpreter for this department?" Hamilton assumed the offensive immediately.

"No sir, I must sadly express my regrets, sir. My poor health will not permit me to serve in the capacity that you desire, sir." John Leeth looked directly into Hamilton's eyes. He did not back down mentally or physically from the man before him. He fully realized that he might be thrown into the Yankee Hall gaol for his impudence or in one of the prison ships that floated in the bay, but the tales and rumors of horror told of the settlers to the east and to the south led him to accept imprisonment over this type of employment. Fogherty's Tavern was rife with tales of these excursions. He had seen more than enough with the entry of the prisoners. He just wanted to earn a decent man's wage and go his way, a free man.

"As I remember, you need a pass to deliver your trade goods to Sandusky.

John heard the strike in Hamilton's voice before his fangs struck.

"That is correct, sir."

Hamilton pretended to order the papers before him. And then a grin slithered across his freshly shaven face as he returned his gaze to Leeth. "Well, John Leeth, 'if you are not fit for service, you are not fit for Sandusky; and you will stay where you are.'"**

John Leeth remained quiet. His face revealed neither anger nor relief.

German=this font   English=this font   **French=this font**   *Delaware=this font*

He simply turned and left Hamilton's office. On his way out, he noted Hamilton's weasel, DeJean, waiting for an audience. He saw in the two men the traits that Standing Stone most disliked in what he called excuses for men. Standing Stone maintained that these "excuses for men" delighted in using their power to the detriment of others. And sadly, far too many men enjoyed controlling another man's life with evil intentions.

Jeffries, Ewel, *A Short Biography of John Leeth, Giving a Brief Account of His Travels and Sufferings Among the Indians for Eighteen Years Together With His Religious Exercises From His Own Relations.* **(Lancaster, Ohio: Gazette Office, 1891) as related by Thwaites, Ruben Gold, Ed. *A Short Biography of John Leeth with an account of his life among the Indians.* **(New York: Benjamin Blom, Inc., 1972). Closely paraphrased p. 29-31. Quotes p. 29-31.**

German=this font   English=this font   *French=this font*   *Delaware=this font*

Chapter 7   Letters and Pictures

"Honored Sir—I am Just Returned from Bedford with My family and find this Quarter of the Contry mutch Destressed, and in the greatest confusion..."

Col. John Proctor to Gen. Edward Hand at Fort Pitt on November 8, 1777 as quoted in *Frontier Defense of the Upper Ohio, 1777-1778*, Edited by Reuben Gold Thwaites and Louise Phelps Kellogg (Madison, WI: Wisconsin Historical Society, 1912), p. 51.

Bedford, Pennsylvania

The circle of men who stood around in George Wood's cabin smoldered like the fire in the hearth behind them. Wood's makeshift stockade offered a little protection to the men within. Sentinels had been posted. Tension hung like chimney smoke on a low day; and just like it, the sooty residue would not rise or dissipate but remained a heavy covering for everything and everyone in the room.

Jac and George Emler stood closest to Wood's desk. But it was Jac who spoke, not his older brother. Jac's disgust hung on every word.

"I do not give a goddamn, Wood. You can write those wealthy bastards, but mark my words, they will not cut loose with funds or men to help us out here." Some assenting murmurs agreed with Jac, for he spoke the words that few of them dared to express. "Instead, they will be coming to you for more money and more of us to fight on the coast and asking us to leave our homes even more unprotected. Bless their pious Quaker asses and their so-called noble Rebel intentions; unless there is a profit in it for them or a pat on the head from that damn Virginian, Washington, they will not budge."

"Now Jac, let us not sound radical here."

Brother Bergenfelder frowned most. "Jac! Your language does not befit a Christian," he chided in German.

The last comment inflamed the usually non-communicative Jac, who seldom spoke out in public. The depth of his anger freed his tongue. Given his own history, his frustration at the loss of his niece, her two boys, and his grandniece's condition, not to mention the inept rescue attempts of those about him, made him both furious and loud. All the contempt that he felt when they foolishly divided into two parties boiled to the surface. The bungling decision resulted in injury to one and death to seven others. He retaliated immediately.

"Christianity has nothing to do with this hell, brother. Tory be damned. Whig be damned. Rebellion be damned." Some of the listeners gasped as Jac stormed on. "It is all right for us to buy their property and line their bloody pockets. But it is not their friends and family that is dying and getting chopped up and burned like firewood to fuel the British fires. Hell, they cannot even send troops to Fort Pitt. The goddamned landgrabbing Virginians are taking over there, too."

Thomas Smith, a cooler head, spoke up. He had had enough of Jac's ranting. The men were emotionally and physically exhausted.

"Look, Jac, be sensible. If we do not ask for help, for damn sure, we will not get it. Wood, I can help you write the letter to President Wharton."

Jac sensed that the assembled men would not listen to common sense, just like when they had walked out rather than vote for or against the rebellion in Philadelphia. As a result, Bedford had lost many representatives, and with it many of their county's votes and much of their clout to the richer counties, who were more willing to side with the Rebel cause. While Jac sided with their stand against the loyalty oaths, he also realized that no one agreed with him about the futility of their situation and the need to form their own militia. He suspected that many of them might have Tory leanings, anyway. He doubted if any were truly eager to go to war against the British.

"Write your useless letter, you spineless bastards. You think if you piss into the wind, you won't get wet. Waste your time! I am going hunting!"

Every man in the room knew down deep exactly what Jac really meant. His bruder George's face remained expressionless, for he was totally embarrassed by his brother's unprecedented outburst. While he might have agreed with him, he would not show his feelings so openly before his friends and neighbors. Too old and too ill to assist Jac, he kept his face rock hard. Only the pulsing of a small vein on his temple gave any indication of his emotions.

George Sill, Wood's indentured servant, spoke under his breath to the man nearest to him; but in the quiet of the room, his words could be clearly heard over the crackle of the fire.

"The old savage, he's as uncivilized as them he hunts."

That did it! Jac's face turned ashen white and then flushed deep carmine. The throbbing veins on his neck swelled. Grabbing his coat, his double-barreled long rifle, and cap, he tore from the room, slamming the cabin door behind him.

The men in the room, shocked by the depth of his anger, looked to Wood and Smith for leadership.

At first no one spoke.

"Gentlemen, I suggest you get back to your families. Smith and I will draft the letter," Wood said.

The others filed silently from the room, leaving the two men to wrestle words for their thankless task. Someone would have to inform the new widows.

German=this font   English=this font   *French=this font*   *Delaware=this font*

Along the Ohio, Among the Wolf Delaware

The rains had fallen hard for three days. Eve felt melancholy. She had cabin fever which was made worse by unfamiliar smells and the heavy smoke that hung in the poorly vented cabin. She even missed going for wood and cutting pumpkin, which made her momentarily wonder if she was going totally daft. Exhausted, Margaret had curled in the corner on a mound of furs with Mikie enfolded in her arms. The two slept, their soft snores rising and falling with their chests. White Corn Woman had left the cabin earlier to see to her functions and visit another cabin.

In the hazy light of the fire-lit room, Eve found herself drawn to her coverlet. The edge had frayed where the weft had shifted in the warp, having been ripped as it had been from the loom. Standing indecisively at first, she surrendered to her inner demands and lowered herself to sit cross-legged on the floor at the edge of the coverlet. First she touched it, running her hands over the fibers. Unfolding it, refolding it, and running her fingers over the individual colors; she closed her eyes and held it to her cheek once to test the softness. Unable to resist any longer, she grasped three warp threads in her hand. Then she carefully slid the weft threads closer to the main body of the material and, with a deft motion, placed an overhand knot at the edge of the material. She snugged the strayed weft securely in place. Grasping another set of three warp threads, she soon established a rhythm that totally absorbed her, pulling her away from her surroundings and drawing her into a dream of the past. For a moment she returned to her own hearth. Adam Henry kneaded her shoulders, relieving the tension of the day. All her children clustered at or round their table as George stumbled over his words in an attempt to read psalms from the Psalter to the older ones. The two wee ones played on the floor. Eve, lost in her reverie, focused on her task. She did not realize that she was being watched suspiciously by dark eyes near the door. The person had entered the cabin nearly soundlessly, opening and closing the door mat. Even the cool moist breeze as the mat raised and lowered did not alert Eve to the figure's presence. Her moccasins made no sound as she crossed the room and stood over Eve, observing her every move.

"What you do?" White Corn Woman's question in halting English yanked Eve back to the present. Eve had been totally unaware of her presence until that very moment when her softly spoken question had jolted her back to her harsh reality.

"Knot. See it ...." Eve struggled to find the English words. Much of her mind lagged behind in another time, in another language. "It pulls apart. It frays," Eve's fingers explained, paralleling her words.

White Corn Woman clutched her staff tightly in both her hands. With dignity and difficulty, she lowered herself to sit beside Eve. She watched her as Eve continued to carefully knot.

German=this font   English=this font   *French=this font*   *Delaware=this font*

"You make dis?"

"Yah, I made this." Eve acknowledged her handiwork with great sadness. Never once did she raise her eyes, for fear of what she would see. She almost cowered, wondering when the blow from the staff would fall.

"You make...You spin thread?" Each word resembled a tooth, pulled slowly and painfully from a deep socket.

"Yah. Some of it."

"You make?" White Corn Woman paused, trying very hard to retrieve a word, a word rarely thought or spoken over the many years. A word tucked back in time. "You make?" Frustrated because it just would not come, she pointed to the dark yellow-green, then the bright yellow-orange, then the black, and then to the soft bluish-purple, yellow, and grayish-green on a woven basket that sat near them.

"Color?" Eve responded, recognizing the only thing the articles had in common.

"Yes, Col...Color.

"Yah."

"How?" The question was abrupt, quick, and shortened almost to a grunt.

Eve looked up into White Corn Woman's face. Her hands, automated now to the knotting, never halted.

"Wh...what use?"

Eve felt stunned by the question. The woman had become almost like her mother or her old aunt when asking her. The animosity had suddenly and mysteriously dissolved between them.

"Which color?"

White Corn Woman pointed slowly at the intensely bright yellow-orange. Then she looked back into Eve's face and every line and wrinkle spoke of curiosity and intelligence. The latter really took Eve back a little.

Eve responded slowly. Given the woman's poor English skills, how could she fully communicate with this old one? Eve responded slowly for a second reason, as well. She found herself wanting to share the knowledge with her and felt puzzled at her willingness to do so. Was this not a savage? Was this not her enemy?

Eve realized as thoughts cycled and swirled that she would need something other than words.

White Corn Woman grunted and frowned. Mistaking Eve's slow response as an unwillingness to answer her, she grasped her stick to rise. When she realized that Eve was tugging her down and restraining her gently, she stopped.

"Wait. Please. Finish this." She spoke slowly, quietly, but very distinctly, and then she added, "thinking," as she pointed to the side of her head three or four times quickly before resuming her knotting, barely breaking her rhythm.

"Ah..." Corn Woman settled down again, sitting patiently as Eve continued to knot.

German=this font   English=this font   *French=this font*   *Delaware=this font*

With the frayed edge secure, Eve turned toward White Corn Woman and dusted a bit of the earthen floor between them free of the lose debris. She motioned to White Corn Woman to give Eve the knife that she carried at her waist. White Corn Woman hesitated but then handed it to her. In the dirt, Eve drew a coreopsis flower, the shaggy petals, the bulbous buds, and the lancelet-shaped leaves. As it began to take shape in the dim light, a slow smile began to inch across the face of White Corn Woman, rearranging her wrinkles in a formation that Eve had not seen in all their encounters.

"Ah..." White Corn Woman nodded knowingly, and then taking her staff, she pointed at a bundle of dried flowers that Eve had not really noticed among the many that hung from the rafters.

"Yes." They both smiled, acknowledging their mutual understanding.

Then White Corn Woman pointed at the iron trade kettle that hung near the fire, a kettle that she owned with great pride.

"Cook?"

"No."

"No?" Now her face filled with puzzlement.

Eve motioned to her to give her the staff, so that she did not have to move either. She pointed to the recently looted tin pail that sat by the door.

"Cook slow, yes." Eve pointed to the tin pail and returned her staff.

"Not kettle?" White Corn Woman's puzzled frown and turned head registered some serious question of Eve's directions.

"No. Kettle iron."

"Yes, kettle iron. Kettle cook."

Eve wondered again how could she possibly tell her this subtle difference. Then it struck her, first, she pointed to the coreopsis on the floor. Second, she pointed to the dark black and deep green threads in her blanket and then to the flower again and then back to the iron kettle. "Color dark. Cook iron kettle."

She studied White Corn Woman's face. Next, she pointed to the brighter yellow-orange and the tin pail, "Color...bright. Cook pail. Same flower." And then she pointed to the coreopsis drawn on the floor.

"Ah...h...h...ha." This time White Corn Woman nodded with full understanding.

Then White Corn Woman sat back. She looked expectantly into Eve's face. She appeared to wait for something.

Eve was puzzled. Obviously, White Corn Woman expected some response. For the love of God, what did she want? Then she realized quite suddenly that it was her turn. She had given, now she was to receive.

Eve pointed to the soft bluish purple on the basket. A smile raced across White Corn Woman's face.

Asking by handsigns for the knife back, White Corn Woman erased the coreopsis and patted the surface flat. Then she proceeded to draw a cluster of tiny flowers that drooped from a stalk. Eve looked quizzically at her.

German=this font   English=this font   **French=this font**   *Delaware=this font*

Then she drew the easily recognized seed pod. Eve grinned, took a small stick, broke it with a snap, and said one word, "milk," before pointing to her breast.

"Yes!" Corn Woman nodded vigorously.

Eve then touched the wet moccasin that was before her to get her full attention. With her finger she drew the river that flowed by the village, making a few little houses.

"Water?"

"Yes."

"Which one?"

"Water is water!" White Corn Woman maintained.

"No."

"Water is water!" White Corn Woman asserted again.

"No, like kettle and pail!"

"Ah...h...h..." This time White Corn Woman's response pondered the thought. Both women sat quietly. Then she looked into Eve's face.

"Water..." and she pointed to the makeshift river on the floor, "No water," and she wiggled her fingers down on both hands in a makeshift rainfall.

"Not same."

"Not same."

"Mutti, potti." The child tugging at Eve's skirt broke the spell.

Both women snapped apart abruptly. Both stood up quickly, like mischievous children. Margaret sat up, frowning at the two women before her. Eve felt strangely guilty. She wondered what had been her transgression, but she definitely felt Margaret's displeasure. Grasping Mikie's tiny fingers, she headed towards the door. But this time, she was held back gently.

She turned to White Corn Woman, who was pointing to the bright orange-yellow again. "Water?"

Eve smiled in spite of herself. "Rain," she said, wiggling her fingers down with one hand as White Corn Woman had done moments ago. She turned towards the door, ignoring Margaret's deeper frown.

"Ri...river, mine," White Corn Women called to her softly.

Eve heard her and nodded. She saw to her son's needs, smiling.

Bedford, Pennsylvania

The men had worked for most of the afternoon and into the early evening. Wood's wife, concerned, had brought them a cup of tea and a dry biscuit. Neither man acknowledged her presence as she returned to her spinning.

Wood pulled up the last draft.

"Let me read it to you, Smith, and then we'll write her up proper. Paper is dear, but I hate to send the man a paper with scratching and

German=this font   English=this font   *French=this font*   *Delaware=this font*

scraping on it. They are inclined to think ill enough of us, as it is."

Smith nodded in tired agreement. He settled back in the seat beside Wood and prepared to listen.

"I am going to date this, November 27th. We need to send this rain or no rain."

"'GENTLEMEN: The present situation of this County is so truly deplorable that we should be inexcusable if we delayed a moment in acquainting you with it, an Indian War is now raging around us in its utmost fury. Before you went down they had killed one man at Stony Creek, since that time they have killed five on the Mountain, over against heads of Dunnings Creek, killed or taken three at the three springs, wounded one and kill'd some Children by Frankstown, and had they not providentially been discovered in the Night, & a party went out and fired on them, they would, in all probability, have destroyed a great part of that settlement in a few hours. A small party went out into Morrison's Cove Scouting, and unfortunately divided, the Indians discovered one division and out of eight killed seven & wounded the other. In short, a day hardly passes without our hearing of some new murder....

'It is not for us to dictate what steps ought to be taken, but some steps ought to be taken without the loss of an hour. The safety of your country, of your families, of your Property, will, we are convinced, urge you to do every thing in your Power to put the Frontiers in some state of defence. Suppose there were orders given to raise about 100 Rangers, under the Command of spirited officers who were well acquainted with the Wood and Indians and could take them in their own way.... About this place especially, and all the country near it, they are distressed for the want of Guns, for when the Men were raised for the army you know we procured every Gun that we could for their use,...[this] reflects hard on us.... We need not repeat our entreaties that whatever is done, may be done as soon as possible, as a day's delay may be the destruction of hundreds.

'We are in haste, Gentlemen,
'Your most obedient, humble servants,
George Wood,
Thomas Smith'"**

"Do you think it states our situation, Tom?"
"It is the best that we can do, George."
"I agree."
"Damn, I hope Jac is wrong."

Long into the night, Wood dutifully copied their letter. Finally, as Wood folded and prepared to seal their correspondence, Tom Smith spoke

German=this font   English=this font   **French=this font**   *Delaware=this font*

up once more. "Do not forget to send that damned proclamation along."

"I am sure they have seen others."

"I am sure they have, too, but Adam Henry Earnest's blood is shed upon this one. They need to see it again. Maybe his blood will speak more volumes than our letter."

On the reverse of the proclamation, Wood printed neatly…Found stuck in his life's blood upon the face of Adam Henry Earnest, died October 1777. Enfolding it neatly in a fresh piece of paper, Wood enclosed the bloody proclamation within their correspondence to President Wharton of Pennsylvania.

History of Bedford, Somerset and Fulton (Chicago: Waterman, Watkins and Co. , 1884), p. 88-89.

Fort Detroit

Across town, an uneasy young man stood before his employer's representative. His employer had instructed Leeth to contact this man in event of unforeseen problems.

"So you can see, sir, given that I have riled Governor Hamilton and his minister, I am prevented from honoring my contract with your partner. I am unable to leave the fort. So it appears I must return my advance and find a way to repay your partner for these clothes. You had best discharge me, sir."

Ezekiel Solomon scrutinized John Leeth, who stood before him. A tiny hint of a smile appeared and then disappeared. Already, he respected the young man who would put principle ahead of self. This man constituted a rare find. To lose him at this juncture and his valuable skills, not to mention his obvious integrity, would not be a sound business practice. No matter what circumstances presented themselves, Solomon, the Jewish merchant, measured men well. His shrewd and honest business practices, no matter who assumed power, kept him in good stead with many of the native born, as well as those from abroad who mistakenly felt they held the power in this new land. As a silent partner to many, even those who would not acknowledge their acquaintance with him in public, he and his cousin had won begrudging respect. In the new world, men could be respected by the fairness of their dealings, not just by the accident of their birth.

Solomon continued to evaluate the man as he spoke. "There is no reason yet for your discharge, John Leeth. There is a time for every purpose, my son. A time to keep and a time to cast away. Let us 'wait on the result of this matter.'** Until then, may I suggest that you accept board at Fogherty's* Tavern and Inn. As long as you continue to receive your wages, you need not care where you are. Here or Sandusky. Do you find that agreeable?"

German=this font   English=this font   *French=this font*   *Delaware=this font*

Unable to fully comprehend this positive turn of events, John felt humbly thankful for the unexpected good fortune. John shook on the agreement. Sleeping at Fogherty's sounded much better than the livery stable. Although it might not be as clean, it would certainly be drier if it rained.

"Yes, sir. I'll wait, sir." With that, John Leeth left the Solomon home.

Stepping into the muddy streets, John Leeth shivered from the updraft as he rounded the corner before heading directly to Fogherty's to settle in. Casting an eye at the gray sky and the cooler blues, he recognized the signs of impending rain. Uneasy accepting payment for no labor, but also glad not to spend another damp night in the livery, he turned in at the tavern's door.

Solomon pondered the closed door long after John left. Then he spoke aloud to the empty room. Sometimes just hearing the words helped him gather his courage. He touched the tefillin, one of the small black cubical boxes made of leather strapped to his upper forearm and discreetly hidden in the folds of his sleeve. Here on the fringes of commerce, unable to attend weekly Morning Prayer service within his synagogue, Shearith Israel, or to consult a minyan of his peers, Solomon occasionally wore the boxes filled with a small scroll upon which verses from the Torah were written. The second tefillin, worn about his head snuggled and hidden amongst his curls, served as a physical remembrance of his faith and of the Presence of God. In this way, when troubled, he sought to remind himself to seek unity and consistency in his thoughts and deeds. Feeling the turmoil about him and dismayed by current British policies which he found increasingly offensive, he inwardly longed for the day that he could return to his congregation in Montreal and wear them openly beneath his talis. "Mazel tov, my young friend. Blessed is the man that walketh not in the counsel of the wicked, nor standeth in the way of sinners." Ezekiel spoke the words first in Hebrew and then in English. He stopped, reflected on another individual that he held in disdain, and spoke aloud a second time as before, "For Thou art not a God that hath pleasure in wickedness: Evil shall not sojourn with Thee. The arrogant shall not stand in Thy sight: Thou hatest all workers of iniquity." Each word of the fifth Psalm testified to his opinion of the British Lieutenant Governor and his staff. When Solomon first began to serve as a supplier for British troops, he had never dreamed that it would come to this current state of affairs. Having once physically suffered under the French's earlier Indian policies, he empathized completely with those under attack. He had barely escaped the same atrocities. He knew well the blood baths and inhumane activities that accompanied an Indian at war. He had marched under threat of death before his rescue.

"My son, did your young man leave?"

"Yes, Nanna, he did. He has left for his lodging," Ezekiel answered his aunt. The gentle woman had become like a mother to him in the new world.

German=this font English=this font **French=this font** *Delaware=this font*

"Then to whom do you speak?"

"Just a prayer in the wind, Nanna. Now, what have you in your wonderful kitchen? I am starved."

"Ezekiel, you are always starved. How does your wife, Louise, ever keep you satisfied?"

Ezekiel's eyes twinkled. "Why ever, Nanna, do you ask such a personal question?"

"Ezekiel! I never—" His aunt blushed, before grabbing his arm and hauling him off to her kitchen.

Jeffries, Ewel, *A Short Biography of John Leeth, Giving a Brief Account of His Travels and Sufferings Among the Indians for Eighteen Years Together With His Religious Exercises From His Own Relations* **(Lancaster, Ohio: Gazette Office, 1891), as related by Thwaites, Ruben Gold, Editor. *A Short Biography of John Leeth with an account of his life among the Indians* **(New York: Benjamin Blom Inc., 1972). Closely paraphrased p. 30-31. Quotes p. 31 (Leeth never revealed who his employers were by name) author's choice.**

*Forsythe and Fogherty are sometimes interchanged in references when referring to this Inn. However, it appears that the Inn probably was named Fogherty and the managers were named Forsythe.

German=this font   English=this font   *French=this font*   *Delaware=this font*

Chapter 8   You Are Dead to Me!

Cooking [Coshocton], November 16, 1777

"Dr. Sir—As Capt. White Eyes is going to the fort, I will
not omit to acquaint you how matters are here with us.
Since my last we have been quiet & not any warriors have
passed by here except a small party of Mohickons & now 8
days ago, 14 Wyandotts & two white men with them who
come from Detroit; & as much as we know went to
Weelunk [Wheeling] John Montour being in their
company.

Some time ago, as we heard, 50 Frenchmen came over
the Lake to Cuyahoga, & gave the Delawares and Muncys
who live there the tomahawk, & desired them to go with
them to Ligonier. Capt. Pipe not being at home, they
consented, & 40 men went with the French, but Pipe met
them on the road, reproved the French for deceiving his
people in his absence, & told them that they were only
servants, & had no power to hand the tomahawk to them:
Nobody could force him neither to take it—whereupon
the greater part of the Indians turned back.

Capt. Killibuck & Pipe are gone to Detroit—upon what
business Capt. White Eyes can tell you better. They did
not desire me to write for them, so I suppose they did not
approve of what you proposed to them."

Rev. David Zeisberger, Moravian Missionary, to General Hand, American
Rebel Commander of Fort Pitt. Compiled from the Draper Manuscripts in the
Library of the Wisconsin Society and published at the charge of the
Wisconsin Society of the Sons of the American Revolution. *Frontier Defense
of the Upper Ohio, 1777-1778*, Edited by Reuben Gold Thwaites and Louise
Phelps Kellogg (Madison, WI: Wisconsin Historical Society, 1912), p. 164-
166.

Along the Ohio River, in a Wolf Delaware Village

"Mutti, Mutti, look at what Little Fox's Mutti gave to me." Henry
bounded proudly up to his mother as she strangled on an inner scream of
shock. Before her, her son filled with boyish pride jumped up and down
with total glee. Little Fox stood aside watching his friend and proud of his
mother's handiwork.

Henry's joyous face shone with total delight.

Had Eve's son told her that he had elected to follow Satan in all his ways, she could not have been more shocked than to see her son in buckskin breechclout and leggings. A wide braided band of sweet grass was tied about his upper forearm. He sported a new fringed vest and moccasins. God in heaven, he looked like a savage.

Margaret gasped her disapproval behind her.

"Henry!" Eve exclaimed. She longed to rip every shred of the clothing from his body and stomp on it, screaming. Grasping him roughly by the shoulder, she could not contain her intense hurt and anger. Peering down into his boyish face, she screamed, "Take those filthy clothes off, this very minute. Do you hear me?" Her voice had acquired a desperate shrill, a shrewish edge.

As Henry beheld the rage in his mother's face, he felt like a child slapped across the face. First, he was filled with humiliation, and then total defiance.

"Nein!" He screamed back in her face. He had spilled his pearls before her for her approval. She had thrown them with disdain back in his face. The revulsion in Henry's voice towards Eve caused her to release her grip. In that fraction of a second, Henry pulled away. "You can not make me!" Stung by her disapproval in the face of his absolute joy, he turned and ran, trying to hide his tears.

Little Fox, stunned by his friend's mother's strange and unreasonable outburst, ran after him.

Eve, Margaret, and little Mikie stood aghast.

Behind her, Stalking Wolf observed. "You have hurt the boy's pride."

"You want to steal my son!" Her unspoken fear, jealousy and hatred spread openly before Stalking Wolf for the first time.

"You make it easy. And I will," he said confidently as he turned from her, and disappeared as quickly as Henry had.

If Stalking Wolf had struck Eve down with his tomahawk, she could not have been more openly attacked. Her whole being shook. Henry had never sassed her or disobeyed her with such open hostility. Mikie, never having seen his Mutti in such a state, looked with fear at the woman before him, hardly recognizing his own mother.

Margaret grabbed her and hastily pulled her close. She clasped Eve tightly to her breast, holding the shaking woman tightly in her arms and restraining her from striking back or lashing out further.

"Pray for our Lord's guidance and mercy, Eve. Pray."

Eve did not struggle in Margaret's arms. She doubted if God cared anymore about any of them. How could He… given what happened to Adam Henry and to the others? How could He...given what was happening to her and Mikie? How could He…ever prevent what was happening to Henry?

German=this font   English=this font   *French=this font*   *Delaware=this font*

Wolf Delaware Village, Two Days Later

Hay studied the circle of braves before him.

"We need to set out for Fort Detroit. We have twenty-five prisoners. Cold will come soon."

"No."

"What do you mean, 'No'?"

"The women want the corn in."

"Since when do women rule?"

Stalking Wolf, who translated for the others, did not translate Hay's last words to the circle of men. His reluctance to do so surprised Major Hay.

"I think you need to say some other way," Stalking Wolf said after a long pause.

Blue Ice, who also had understood, glared at Hay, infuriated by this insult to his manhood and to the warriors who surrounded him.

"You do not like to eat in winter?" Blue Ice returned his question with a question.

Hay saw their resolve. The damned fool savages, he thought, they do not know how to fight. They refuse to go in spring when they plant or in late summer and early fall when they harvest. They refuse to fight during winter hunt. And now, the damned fools cannot leave the dry corn in the fields to harvest until they get back. Civilized men fought when their leaders ordered it, not when they damn well felt like it. What he had to tolerate in service to his Majesty and Hamilton exasperated him. Just once, he wished the Lieutenant Governor had to do his job. Just once!

Hay turned before his temper fully flared and walked out of the long cabin, away from the smoke and into the late fall air. As he expelled some of the pent-up air from within, his breath crystallized in the night glow of the cabins, forming a white cloud of vapor. Winter soon would be sweeping down, making their way harder. The damn prisoners were not dressed for that kind of journey. Hell, they had already lost two infants just getting here, and another woman had died from cold, wet and exposure, not that he missed her whining and complaining.

Hay failed to notice that more stars than usual could be seen this crystal cold night. The soft hoot of a sentinel confirmed his vigilance and was answered by another. Kicking a clump of dirt with his heel, sending a spray of dirt airborne, Hay stomped off from the commons area to relieve himself. He called out and identified his presence to the sentinels to avoid being shot.

The Next Day

A few miles away, a horse stood tethered. The steed patiently waited for its owner, munching contentedly on the mound of oats spilled onto the open ground before it. His owner had left him for most of the day. A few

German=this font   English=this font   *French=this font*   *Delaware=this font*

miles from the horse, a shadow pooled and lurked. Slipping high and low, it eddied about the base of tree trunks. Slithering, sliding, the shadow moved about the tree-lined fields. Many girdled trees hiding the shadow were dying. In good time, the men and women of this community would pull the roots and trunks to expand the rich fields. Young fruit trees grew in the bare sunny spots created when the canopy became free of leaves. The shadow circled the fields and evaluated each guard who stood about each field. It scrutinized the women and children working within the corn field. The shadow waited patiently for just the right moment.

Smoke in Eyes, Blue Ice's oldest son, stood attentively. Occasionally, he glanced at the women and children behind him as they pulled the corn from the dry stalks and piled them in the large woven baskets that sat at intervals. A festive atmosphere under the late fall sun radiated from those who labored below. Even as the sun began to drop and the shadows lengthened, the warmth still remained. The young warrior had a fusil loaded and folded in his arms. Turning his back to the field, he renewed his vigilance. From time to time behind him, a man would lift one of the heavy corn-filled baskets, shift the load onto his back, place the tump line across his forehead, carry the dry shucked harvest into the cluster of cabins that stood in the distance, empty it into the crib, and return with the empty basket to be refilled.

Eve, Anne and Sue Ellen worked closer and closer to the edge of the field near Blue Ice's son. Eve churned with inner turmoil as she watched her son and Little Fox. They scooted in and out amongst the rows playing tag and giggling. She realized that she did not dare to let her anger rise to the extent that it had the day before. Sullenly, she pulled corn from the stalks side-by-side with many of the other women prisoners and the able women of the Indian community. She realized fleetingly that everyone would have blisters and tiny cuts from the stiff dry husks. The gaping baskets gulped in the mottled cobs, like enormous, greedy, wide-mouthed birds.

But it was Henry who rubbed salt in her wounds. Every time she saw Henry in his new outfit, Eve felt an inner terror and foreboding. Horrible suspicions stung and needled her. Stalking Wolf might be correct. She might be driving her own son away.

Eve glanced for a moment at Margaret, who worked nearly a full field away. Margaret had tried to get out of the task today, endearing her to no one. She had bitterly complained to Hay that after all she was in his care, that she had come along willingly, and that he had promised to see her safely to Fort Detroit. She kept stressing that she was not a slave.

Eve realized that had she had similar alliances, she might have been tempted to do the same. Ever since she had spoken with White Corn Woman, Margaret seemed less accepting of Eve, looking for ways to distance herself from her. As a result, Margaret had chosen to work apart from them.

Anne worked beside her, singing softly. The rhythm of her hands and

German=this font   English=this font   *French=this font*   *Delaware=this font*

the rhythm of her voice dipped and became synchronized. Eve fell in with her easy rhythm.

"The sun, she feel real good today." Anne spoke to Eve, but Eve, so lost in her own thoughts, did not respond.

"What's the matter with you, Eve. Don't you feel that good sun? Life ain't too bad today. We could be out in the rain and cold a walking and a trucking their loads. We could be in de' sleet and the snow. This be not bad."

Eve smiled weakly at her. Of course, Anne was right. The sun did feel good. Her hands had mostly healed, thanks to the green salve, and had toughened considerably. She had to admit begrudgingly to herself that she barely felt the rough shucks of the corn and had only a few minor cuts so far. A few rows over, Sue Ellen was not so fortunate. Her bloodied hands stained the husks, but she worked without complaint. Younger than either Eve or Anne, her hands had not toughened to the full status of womanhood.

"Anne, you are right. The sun does feel good." At that moment, Henry ran as fast as a fox in a hunt. He barreled up behind Eve and grabbed her skirt, pulling it around him to hide himself from Little Fox, who followed in hot pursuit like a hound on a fresh scent. Henry sashayed back and forth, clutching her skirt. Surrounded by giggling boys, Eve had to smile. Their laughter awakened Mikie, who had drifted off as he had clung to his mother's back in her makeshift pouch. He shifted his weight with a squeal, spinning Eve momentarily and causing her to fall to one knee. Blue Ice's son looked over at the laughing women and giggling children, diverting his attention away from the woods.

For the first time in two days, Eve had to laugh aloud.

"Holtz-koph, dumkoph." Eve playfully cuffed Henry and gave him a quick hug and a playful swat on the bottom before freeing him to chase Little Fox down the row. Even if Henry dressed like a wild Indian, he was still her son and his laughter could always charm her. Turning about, Henry bayed like a hound, bounding after his foxy friend, scooting and zigzagging down the haphazard rows. Mikie struggled to get down and nearly tipped Eve over again.

"Best give that boy a run or you is never going to get this corn picked." Anne laughed too, fully understanding Mikie's desire to join them. For a moment, she too wanted to run with the children and to be utterly free from care. "No corn, no eat, you betcha'." Anne continued her work, resuming her working song.

Eve set Mikie down, leaving him to totter after his brother. What could happen with all the women and men about? If Mikie strayed too far, he would be sent back, given past experience. Blue Ice's boy would see that Mikie did not go in the woods. He often had brought him back to White Corn Woman's cabin when he ran off. Smoke in Eyes rarely threw the child in a heap at the door when doing so. The young warrior proved kinder than most, in that regard.

Eve stood, rolled her head in a circle to relieve the discomfort from

German=this font   English=this font   **French=this font**   *Delaware=this font*

carrying Mikie, and placed her hands in the small of her back to stretch before she reached for another corn stalk. Eve could hear the boys' laughter grow louder again as they ran towards her when she heard the first crack followed by a second telltale clicking sound. Immediately, she spun to throw her body over the buck-skinned child who ran towards her, cupping her body over the child and throwing them both to the ground. At the edge of her vision, she saw Blue Ice's boy fall. Anne spun and dropped. Within a split second, a second volley ripped through the corn between Eve and Anne, which narrowly missed Sue Ellen. Quickly on the heels of the second volley, a hand roughly grasped her by the arm and shoulder, pulling her toward the forest edge beside her. Looking over her shoulder, she saw a hatchet poised to strike the child beneath her.

Eve instantly recognized the figure before her. In that very same split second, her hand rose to ward off his attack. As her forearm painfully blocked the forceful stroke of the impending blow, she screamed. "Nein, Onkel!"

Immediately, his other hand fell from her. Just as quickly as the attacker had appeared, he melted into the brush adjacent to them, leaving a chorus of women and children screaming. Their cries of terror alerted the men in and about the field. In the chaos and pandemonium, another shot rang out at the parting shadow but to no avail. Beneath her, a screaming child fought to push her from above him. In that exact moment, Eve realized that it was not Henry beneath her, but Little Fox. She could see his face clearly for the first time.

Henry stood mute a few stalks away, his eyes sprung wide and full of terror. Mikie peeped out from beside him, a pale shadow.

Little Fox's mother, barreling full bore, reached Eve in the next moment. Instinctively, she began to scratch and claw to retrieve her son. Eve pushed her aside, thrusting Little Fox toward her. Rapidly, Eve began half crawling and half running to Blue Ice's son, who lay bleeding at the edge of the field.

"Jesus Christ. He's just a boy."

Eve heard Anne's curse behind her. Stumbling forward, she fell beside the fallen. Her hand reached out to the youth, who writhed with pain before her on a bed of broken cornstalks. His legs thrashed in response to the intensity of the pain. Eve's hand gentled the boy, who looked up at her in disbelief through a maze of hair. The untired fusil lay where it had flown from his arms beside her. In the distance, a voice sounded as she clasped her hand around the bleeding shoulder, stopping the spurting blood.

"You are dead to me." She heard the words clearly. They came to her like a clarion call out of darkness. She chose instead to move away from the words, to separate herself from their pain and from Onkel as well. Just as quickly, Jac distanced himself from her and blended into the increasing shadows and impending darkness.

Working purely from reflexive instinct, she applied just enough pressure to stop the flow of blood gushing forth from the boy's wound.

German=this font   English=this font   *French=this font*   *Delaware=this font*

Pulling a scrap of cloth from her apron pocket that she had earlier ripped to catch her expected menses, she put the clean wad of cloth over the wound and reapplied pressure. Setting back on her heels and using her other hand to touch the young man's face, she gently pushed the hair back from his sweaty face, freeing his eyes to engage hers. She could see his horrible agony reflected in his eyes that darted, rolled back in his head, and then stopped to focus deliberately on hers. He visually lept into the pool of Eve's dilated pupils so open and so unguarded. He knew instantly that somehow she felt responsible for all his pain, but he also sensed that she had never meant for this to happen to him.

Silence strikes more deeply than spoken words one freely hears and understands. His searing understanding caused Eve to look away into the shadows and then down at the ground with a deep sense of shame. He groaned. She felt him touch her cheek. In that touch, she could feel his growing apprehension and sense his stark recognition that men were coming. Their thundering strides pounded ever closer. The truths that hung between the youth and Eve tore at her soul, like a dog's unrelenting jaws shaking its prey between its teeth in a death grip, ripping and tearing deep, gashing wounds. Looking again into his eyes, she realized with him that now he must not show his pain to the men. Grimacing, he set his jaw, locked his teeth, closed his eyes to guard his soul, and grasped her arm with his other uninjured arm. The arm that he wrenched in his vice-tight grip was the same arm still rife with the pain of stopping her Uncle's killing blow to Little Fox. But Eve did not pull away. She set her teeth and welcomed the pain.

The smoky long house filled with elders and onlookers. In the far corner, a Midewiwin healer, one who had trained in the Order of Grand Medicine, worked with White Corn Woman to tend Smoke in Eyes' wound. Periodically, a small murmur came from the young man as the Midewiwin Medicine Man worked to extract the ball from the boy's shoulder. Smoke in Eyes welcomed White Corn Woman's chant that helped to cover the sounds of pain that he fought hard to suppress.

The elders focused on Little Fox. His mother sat thoroughly steeped in anger. She made no sound out of respect, but under the calm exterior she wanted to scream her anger for all to hear. Nothing fights like a mother for her child, and this mother proved no exception.

One of the elders held a staff with an eagle's head fastened at the top. Above and below his aged hand, eagle's talons clutched the staff. The man's hands resembled the eagle's talons. Thin with claw-like nails, stained with tobacco, age had yellowed the elder's nails to nearly the same hue as the dried eagle's talons. About mid-shaft, a cluster of eagle feathers and down hung from the staff. All were held by a decorative band of brightly colored porcupine quills. The downy feathers rose and fell with

German=this font   English=this font   **French=this font**   *Delaware=this font*

his words. Carvings of small animals spiraled up the wooden mace of spiritual power. Each animal held the tail of another in its mouth. In the elder's other hand, he held a single eagle feather.

"Tell us once more, Little Fox. What did you see? What did you hear? Do not speak quickly, little warrior." Seeing the terror still lurking in the child's eyes and fearing that the mother's hatred of the white ones might cloud his vision, the elder paused and then spoke very quietly to the child. He could sense that the child did not want to say anything to make his mother unhappy with him. But three lives balanced in truth's hand. Truth must be called upon to find justice. *"Hold this sacred eagle feather, so the creator hears your words clearly my son. The creator gives us eagle feathers so that we may speak the truth. Perhaps you should close your eyes. Let the grandfathers speak to you so that they can tell you what they saw. Let their spirits help you before you speak."*

Little Fox realized that what he said would be very important to the elders. He looked anxiously at his mother, but the touch of the eagle feather across his eyes pulled him back to the aged figure before him. He knew this old one. His eyes were set in deep wrinkles like White Corn Woman's.

"Close your eyes, Little Fox. Sit quietly. Listen to the grandfathers." The feather stroked the child's face in gentle arcs. Little Fox felt afraid to speak. What if what he said offended the elders? What if what he said offended his mother? He concentrated on the feather. The chant calmed him. The young boy began to sense a deeper mystery for which there can be no words. The feather gently stroked his face in a soft rhythm, blending with White Corn Woman's chant. He liked the touch of the feather. He drew comfort from White Corn Woman's voice and the softness of the feather. The feather touched him over and over, first one cheek, then another, then over his closed eyelids. He felt suspended, lifted away from the crowded room. Though his eyes were closed, he could see the corn field far below him. The sun warmed his back as he hovered over the field. The feather continued to stroke his face. The chant began to fade. He could hear his laughter. He could see Hanu and Mikie chasing someone. Who were they chasing? The feather touched his face like a whisper. Then he felt his hands lifted. The sacred feather was placed within his two hands. The great staff lightly touched his shoulder. The old one's hands cradled his hands.

"The grandfathers see Hanu and Mikie chasing me. They see me running toward the woman who makes colors. The thunderstick makes noise. They say that the woman hears something that I do not hear. She pulls me under her body and falls on me. They see me struggle. They know that I am fighting for breath and that I cannot breathe. She is heavy. The wind is gone from me." The child paused.

His mother began to reach out to touch him, but a vice grip to her shoulder by Stalking Wolf stopped her cold. Instantly, she withdrew her hand. Stalking Wolf released his sister.

German=this font   English=this font   **French=this font**   *Delaware=this font*

The child continued. *"They hear a second thunder and a mean spirit rips through the corn where I ran before. The dark white woman falls to the ground. The mean spirit goes between the dark white woman and the weak pale one with bloody hands. An evil shadow pulls on the woman who makes colors. We are being sucked into the wood shadows."*

Little Fox's mother began to open her mouth to speak to her son, but the piercing looks of the elders silenced her before her breath left her lips.

Little Fox felt himself slip under the woman. He no longer looked down at their bodies in the field from above with the grandfathers.

"I am looking up now, not down with the grandfathers. They say I can see better from there. I see a striped evil face. I see a dark tomahawk falling. Woman who makes colors screams at the evil one. She calls his name. Her arm stops the tomahawk. The evil one gets very angry. He pushes us away and joins the shadows. But I see his rifle across his back. I see his long rifle has two thunder holes."

Low murmurs broke into the space between the child's words. Startled, Little Fox's awareness brought him back into their presence. He looked dazed and not quite sure where he was. The old one's hands still surrounded his small hands. The eagle feather still nestled in their hands. Another old one beside the elder removed the sacred staff from where it touched Little Fox's shoulder. Little Fox looked to his mother, who looked with great pride back at him. Anger no longer filled her face. He smiled at her. He could tell that he had not disappointed her. The elder beamed his approval.

"Do you still desire the woman and her sons to die by fire, Singing Grass?"

Singing Grass answered, *"No, the woman who makes color saved my son."*

"But I do. She did not protect my son." Blue Ice's response cut through the smoky haze, shocking those who had heard and recognized the unexplained in the voice of the child in the moments before. The grandfathers seldom spoke to save an unadopted white one.

"But—I do not, father. And it is my blood that flows." The words cut deeper than his father's before him. Blue Ice turned towards the corner where his son lay injured on the brink of death. His life's blood still seeped from the long rifle's wound. He sat partially raised in the arms of White Corn Woman. *"She may be blood to this evil. The evil one came for her. She sent it away before more were harmed. She protected Little Fox. She gave comfort to me. She did not follow the evil. She does not understand why,"* Smoke In Eyes coughed before adding, *"because her vision is new."*

"How do you know this?" The elder who had retrieved his staff asked.

"Our eyes spoke. I dipped in her spirit."

The sound of rushing wind greeted those of the long house. After

German=this font   English=this font   **French=this font**   *Delaware=this font*

rattling the exterior bark walls, a downdraft nearly snuffed out the fire within. Sparks burst into the smoky air, igniting swirling sparks in the darkness. The fire replenished itself. Total stillness reigned.

After a long period of quiet, the old one spoke.

"Creator Spirit," the old one raised his staff, *"I am just a man and I do not understand. But I know that the grandfathers have spoken through their children. Since this woman protects and comforts our children, we must protect and comfort her children. She and her children will not die this time by our hands. Ahow."*

Resigned but angry, Blue Ice filed out quietly with the others from the long house, leaving the elders behind to chant for his motherless son. Twice now, Double Thunder had touched his life. Twice, he had been powerless to stop him.

White Corn Woman felt tired upon her return to her cabin. Smoke in Eyes finally slept. Dawn crept around the cabins and followed her in her door. The shaft of soft morning light gave the cabin a warm glow. She looked across at the two women who nested in her corner. The larger one huddled her children to her as usual. After surveying them for several minutes, she turned and left her cabin. Walking to Stalking Wolf's bark hut on the edge of the commons, she lifted the mat and entered. The warrior had heard her approach, recognized her foot fall, and sat upright in his skins as she entered.

"Grandmother?"

"Grandson."

"What brings you with the first light?"

"This grandmother asks little of you."

"This grandson would give more."

"You honor me with your ways. What more can a grandmother ask?"

"A grandmother can ask more."

"Woman who makes colors saved Little Fox."

"Did she save him? Or did she save her son?"

"Either way, your sister does not weep tonight. Your nephew sleeps soundly."

"You speak wisdom."

"Blue Ice has suffered much from Double Thunder."

"True."

"Blue Ice may seek to kill this woman or her children."

Stalking Wolf grunted a soft, affirming sound. Crossing his arms and clasping his elbows, inadvertently hugging some of his skins to him, he looked up at her once more.

"This grandmother asks you to protect her and her sons."

"The woman will not like this. I took her mate's spirit."

"You plan to collect bounty for his scalp?"

"The scalp disappeared with another's."

German=this font   English=this font   **French=this font**   *Delaware=this font*

A weary sigh escaped from White Corn Woman. Fatigue caused her to rock back and forth as she clung to her walking stick. She seemed to be caught in her own thoughts. Finally she spoke. *"You are not one who loses scalps. This woman senses that the grandfathers send omens that we do not understand. Does the trickster play?"*

"Maybe. I don't know. But will it not be strange for one of the people to protect a Rebel white woman?"

"My mother was a white woman."

"That is different. You are White Corn Woman."

His grandmother looked at him. Recognizing that her request might endanger him, but trusting the grandfathers and grandmothers to protect him, she spoke once more.

"Yes, and White Corn Woman asks you to protect the woman who makes colors."

"That will not be easy, grandmother." A bit of a roguish smile and a touch of the trickster himself crossed Stalking Wolf's face as he reluctantly accepted her request.

"Life's journey is never easy, my grandson." She smiled at him proudly. Turning away, the weary woman returned to her cabin. The day had begun well. If no fever or black and yellow ooze came, Smoke in Eyes would live. Her grandson, Stalking Wolf, and granddaughter, Singing Grass, still lived. Her great-grandson nestled by his mother. She prayed that Stalking Wolf would be protected by the grandfathers. She had lost so many young ones. She prayed that no more would be taken before their elder time.

German=this font   English=this font   **French=this font**   *Delaware=this font*

Chapter 9　Early December, 1777

"1777 Proclamation:　Detroit 24th of June.
By virtue of the power and authority given to me given by
his Excellency Sir Guy Carleton Knight of Bath,
Governor of the province of Quebec, General and
Commandant in chief, &c. &c. &c.

I do assure all such as are inclined to withdraw
themselves from the Tyranny and oppression of the rebel
committees, & take refuge in this Settlement, or any of
the Posts commanded by his Majesty's Officers, shall be
humanely treated, shall be lodged and victualled, and such
as come off in arms & shall use them in defence of his
Majesty against Rebels and Traytores, 'till the extinction
of this rebellion, shall receive pay adequate to their
former Stations in the rebel service, and all common men
who shall serve during that period, shall receive his
Majesty's bounty of two hundred acres of Land.　Given
under my hand & Seal.　God Save the King.　Henry
Hamilton, Lieut. Governor: and Superintendent."

Quoted in *Frontier Defense of the Upper Ohio, 1777-1778*, Edited by Reuben
Gold Thwaites and Louise Phelps Kellogg (Madison, WI: Wisconsin
Historical Society, 1912), p. 14. Compiled from the Draper Manuscripts in
the Library of the Wisconsin Society and published at the charge of the
Wisconsin Society of the Sons of the American Revolution.　The
Proclamation to be carried by Royal forces and to be left at battle sites
following raids.

Crossing through Ohio Territory

The cold rain left rivulets of hair down the edges of Eve's face.
Mikie's warm little body draped across her shoulders and back helped to
sustain her in the sleet and rain.　The hills and woods behind them now gave
way to a grassy plain.　The path beneath their treading feet quickly turned to
mud.

White Corn Woman had taken Eve's split and worn shoes as Eve left
her cabin.　In their place, she had given Eve moccasins stuffed with buffalo
wool and moss.　So although Eve's feet felt wet and cold, she blessed the

woman with every muddy step that she took. Through the leather soles, she could accurately assess the ground beneath her feet, sensing the slip and the slide before she would fall. All she had to do was see Margaret's feet as she stumbled ahead of her to recognize once more how extremely lucky she was. If she staggered like that, the weight of Mikie would long ago have left them both lying by the path.

A few people ahead of Margaret, an older woman fell for the fourth time. Her crying had become constant as the group of thirty-five struggled forward. The two prisoners ahead of Margaret had side-stepped her. Sobbing, crying, the nameless old woman grasped at Margaret's skirt. The older woman nearly toppled Margaret; but, before either Margaret or Eve could assist her, a brave pulled the woman gruffly away. To both women's utter consternation, the brave quickly dispatched the old one with one swift movement. He dropped his tomahawk and drew his scalping knife to remove her scalp. Stuffing the thatch of long, wet, straggly gray hair into the sleeve of his drop-shouldered linsey-woolsey shirt, he pulled the body from the path and threw it aside. Then he wiped his hands, his knife, and his tomahawk in the wet grass matter-of-factly, before replacing his knife to its scabbard and his tomahawk through the leather thong that he had tied snugly about his waist.

Eve could barely believe her eyes. Then the brave motioned the stunned Eve and Margaret to press on before leaving them to trudge to the front of the line. Margaret retched, spewed her stomach's contents to the side of the path, and picked up her pace once more.

Behind her, Eve could hear Anne's favorite epitaph, spoken under her breath. "Jesus Christ, that's two."

As Eve passed the broken form along the path, she squelched her revulsion and grabbed the end of the soaked shawl that clung to the chilling form. She needed it more than the old woman did. Jerking it away, she pulled twice to free it, but never broke stride. Mikie whimpered and shifted his weight. Eve compensated and wrapped the wet shawl quickly around her arm so that the trailing end would not trip her. Setting her jaw resolutely, she pushed on. Like everyone in the line, she recognized that to fall down could bring about one's certain doom.

Ahead of her, in spite of a lack of visibility, she could clearly make out Henry's hunched form dozing astride Stalking Wolf's shoulders near the head of the line. Henry's head bobbed in time with his conveyance. Then from before her, she heard Margaret's voice as Margaret began to softly intone the Lord's Prayer.

Eve mouthed the words silently in German rather than English, more from habit than commitment. She feared that her voice might awaken Mikie. Behind her, she could hear others softly join in. Each spoke in his own tongue. If nothing else, the words provided a cadence for their journey.

German=this font   English=this font   **French=this font**   *Delaware=this font*

Fort Bedford, Pennsylvania

"These children should earn their keep." Grossvater Emler's words gave no indication of any leeway. Ester Ana looked grave as they sat about her board. Children were to be seen, not heard. Eve's brood had finally learned never to speak about their grandfather's table. They ate whatever was given them. Molly and Jacob shared one trencher, George and Johannas another. Ester would tolerate no foolishness, making very sure not to give them too much, as they might become slovenly if indulged. She would unspoil them. Soon they would forget their parents' foolish ways.

Ester accepted that she must abide by her husband's decision as God's will and design. But, a small part of her felt reluctant to see the children part from one another, especially since the loss of their vater and the capture of their mutter and two tiny bruders. Her practical side would enjoy less work.

Brother Bergenfelder and her husband had agreed. If these children were coddled, they would slip into idleness. Idleness meant the children would turn from the Lord. Only sternness would save their souls and enable them to follow the true way.

None of the children looked up, but they could sense that things were about to change. They realized that they were powerless to do anything about events to come.

Grossvater balanced a row of peas upon his broad knife. Like dutiful soldiers, they rolled in a perfect line, as bidden, into his mouth. This act often could bring a smile to the younger boys' faces; but not today. Not one child smiled. None of them looked up from their trenchers. To a person, each felt like one of those little peas, dutifully in line, rolling into an abyss.

Grossvater poured the last of his steaming tea into his large deep porcelain saucer, swirled it, and then drank it noisily before wiping his mouth on his sleeve. His trencher and cup empty, he spoke once more.

"I know what is best for you." He prefaced his statement as if stating what he believed to be the fact would make it so. "These are hard times to place children. George, you will be bound to Conrad Samuel for the full four years. He has nothing but foolish women underfoot now and needs your help. He has consented to pay me your wage, since you would squander it foolishly. Jacob, now that you are twelve, you may be of some use to George Woods. He has consented to take you for room and board until you are worth more. His indentured man, Sill, is freed now and buying up the property from the family that left up the gap. Mary." He paused, stressing the use of Molly's given name. "Mary, since John Dibert's wife, Ene, has been ailing, the folks up that way could use an extra woman's hand. They cannot pay much more than a little grain, but at least they will take you." The disdain in his voice conveyed how little value he felt his granddaughter to be. "We have more than enough useless women in this house." He glanced at Jessie.

German=this font   English=this font   *French=this font*   *Delaware=this font*

"Johannas, unfortunately, you are worth nothing yet. So you will stay here to help your Grossmatter and me."

Tears welled up in Johannas's eyes. He glanced aside at Jacob, noting that tears filled his brother's eyes as well. In past times they were inseparable.

"Men do not show weakness, foolish boys. You may leave the table. I want no blubberpusses at this table."

"May we be excused?" Jacob knew to ask permission even if every fiber within him screamed at him to leave the room.

"You are excused," his grandfather responded.

Immediately, Jacob and Johannas excused themselves and bolted out the door.

"Do not slam the door." Ester intoned out of habit. Jacob caught the door just in time, pulled the door to, soundlessly, and latched it.

Molly and George remained. Molly pushed a bit of her food to Jacob's side. Her appetite had vanished.

"No foolishness, young woman. Mary, clean your trencher. God does not want us to waste his bounty." Her grandmother's eyes never missed any minor deed.

Molly filled her fork, chewed dutifully, swallowed, and tried not to gag.

Tante Jessie surveyed the table before her. She could barely believe the words spoken there. If only I were a man, she lamented silently to herself. She excused herself because she knew if she stayed one moment longer, she would explode. She wanted to go to her sister Barbara's home so badly. Inwardly, she imagined what it would be like to rant out loud about her parents' stupidity and their lack of compassion in her schwester's warm kitchen. Instead, not daring to disobey her vater's prior order, she chose not to walk over without his permission or protection. Seething, she had to admit reluctantly to herself that to do so would be totally foolish. Besides, where could she go if she rebelled? Who would take her in?

As Jessie stood, she squared her shoulders and back until she was ramrod straight. She grasped the chair back tightly to restrain any outburst.

A click of the door caused her to look up. The door opened abruptly. Jessie fully expected Johannas or Jacob to reappear, but instead her Onkel Jac's frame filled the door. Although in his early sixties, the man cut a striking figure, especially when he stood in his full hunting dress as he did now. Time had tempered him into steel to match the steely blue of his eyes. His wamus dripped from having ridden in the rain, the drops falling from the fringe onto the wooden floor. Unlike many long wamus hunting shirts, his skins were mottled in color and dark, smoked in irregular patterns. The broad cape collar bore no decorations or fur. His buckle turned inward toward his person so no light would reflect from the browned metal. Even his long rifle had been browned to curb reflection. While many hunters coveted white elk skins worked smooth and richly decorated, her uncle's wamus that he wore from spring to late fall blended

German=this font   English=this font   **French=this font**   *Delaware=this font*

with the shadows of the woods. He did have a totally white one, but she never saw him wear that one, unless the snow laid deep about them. He wore his fur leggings, the warmth turned inward, and on his feet, dark moccasins had been stitched to the leggings. He seldom wore his hunting gear in their presence. Jessie wondered why he entered the home so atypically today. His hunting hat full of water drained, forming a puddle by the door. Her mother quickly and quietly got up, grabbed a rag, and began to mop up.

George and Molly knew if either of them had made a mess like great-uncle's, their grandfather's rant could be heard to the end of the pasture. They remembered when Jacob had inadvertently spilled his tea. He had to lick it from the floor.

Jac snarled at them and waved his hat, sending a spray across part of the room.

"Leave this room! I need to speak to my bruder. You too, Ester. This is not for your woman ears. Molly, help your bruders in the barn."

Jac's firm dismissal of George and Molly left them scrambling for the door.

Ester turned to her husband, questioning Jac's order. She hoped that he would refute his brother about her presence. But instead, he brushed her aside with a curt nod of his head. Ester immediately joined Jessie to go to the small parlor.

"Shut the door!"

The door shut. Wordlessly, each picked up their knitting and stitching, seating themselves across from each other on the small rockers. Jessie, sensing that this might be a long stay, handed the throw from her chair to Ester. Then she pulled a second throw from another chair near her, and wrapped it around her legs. With the door closed, the chill would increase.

They could not hear the men's voices as they dropped to a low mumble. Occasionally, an expletive could be heard, but then the tempered voices would drop to inaudibility once more.

Outside the shuttered and papered window, Johannas had hunkered down in a sheltered dry spot out of the wind and rain. A steady stream of tears fell unchecked over his chubby, slightly freckled cheeks and spilled into the space created between his crossed legs and his folded arms. The spot soon would be as wet as his surroundings. The rise and fall of the inflections in the voices of his great-uncle and grandfather behind him left little impression on his own thoughts. The occasional expletive gave a secondary voice to vent his own feelings, allowing him for a moment to use words forbidden in his young vocabulary. But three words did penetrate the haze of his own anguish and pain...three words out of five that Johannas could swear he heard. "She is dead" not once, but twice, once from Onkel Jac and once from Opa. Choking back a sob, he stood shakily before running as fast as he could to the barn.

Johannas crashed through the small gate and tore in the side door to the makeshift shed that served as his grandfather's barn to hurl himself

German=this font   English=this font   ***French=this font***   *Delaware=this font*

headlong into George's arms. His short frame broke with huge heaving sobs as he clutched his older bruder, his only comfort.

George held his small brother, letting his small brother sob. Silently, Molly and Jacob looked on. Finally, the intensity of Johannas' sobs began to diminish. However, his desperate clutching hold on George did not release. George, realizing his parental role in this situation, lifted his brother into his arms. Backing up, he sat on a small barrel adjacent to the stalls. He cradled Johannas in his lap, holding the child tightly. Drawing closer to their sobbing brother, Molly crouched at their feet, Jacob moved behind her. They watched the smaller of them so wracked with sobs that they seemed to start at his toes and whip through his body. His arms encircled his big bruder's neck. His small boyish face nestled into the crook of George's broadening shoulders. In time, Molly reached out to him to push his wet hair away from his forehead. Her movement proved so typically like her mother's that Johannas responded as if touched by a firebrand. Molly hastily withdrew her hand.

"Mutti is dead," Johannas blurted out.

The three elder siblings stoically heard his words. No one moved except George, who tightened his hold about Jacob.

"How do you know this?" George asked gently after a few minutes.

"I overheard Onkel Jac." Johannas looked up at George. His tear-stained face had tiny dirt riverbanks and his freckles looked like rocks that diverted the channels of water. "I sat outside the window. I heard them both. First, Grossonkel. Then Opa." He sniffled and wiped his nose on his sleeve.

George said nothing. He pulled his brother to him, folding him in securely.

"We must be strong." George rocked Johannas in his arms, remembering how his own mother had once rocked him. "Remember Vati and Mutti would want us to be strong." He felt Jacob's hand on his shoulder and saw him lay his other hand on Johannas, who now lay quiet. Molly circled George's legs with one arm and laid her other hand on her smaller bruder's back.

As George felt the touch and security of his family about him, he spoke.

"We may be forced apart, but we will always be together. Do you understand?" He could feel Johannas nod in his shoulder. He could feel the affirming grasps of his brother Jacob and his sister Molly. "No one can truly separate us, unless we let them."

Later that night, Ester reached out to touch her husband.

"What will you tell the children?"

"Nothing."

"Nothing?"

"We will not speak of her again. She does not exist for us anymore."

"Surely, my husband…"

"You heard me, woman. She does not exist anymore. She will bring no more shame to this family."

"But the little ones..."

George Marc Emler turned on his side, his back like a cold stone wall. He began to snore.

Ester Ana lay still upon her back. She stared at the loft above her. The night seemed blacker somehow, and the children unusually quiet.

Outside, Jac kept watch.

Following the Great Path

The small circle of prisoners huddled together for warmth. Stalking Wolf set Henry down beside his mother and brother. He looked at the bedraggled woman, whose teeth chattered slightly as she reached for her son.

"Put your moccasins in your armpits," Stalking Wolf said, frowning at her.

"What?"

"You heard me. Put your moccasins in your armpits."

Eve looked at him, totally perplexed.

"They will be dry by morning, stupid woman." With that, Stalking Wolf set out to take his place as sentinel. He knew no one would attempt to escape tonight though, given the morning's earlier events.

Anne watched him go and pulled Mikie into her arms so that she and Eve might wedge the two boys between them. Sue Ellen covered Anne's back and her own shoulders with the nameless woman's shawl.

Earlier, Margaret had moved across the circle to edge closer to the Smythe couple. The Tory couple had garnered preferential treatment. Since Skelly's escape, Margaret needed to establish closer Tory ties. Besides, she had never been totally at ease with Eve's acceptance of Anne.

"Eve."

"Yes."

"Do you think Felix Skelly got away?" Sue Ellen whispered.

"I sure hope so. If he did not, he is liable to share Sander's fate," Eve answered.

"Sander's head shore did look horrible up on dat pole, poor man," Anne added. "It looked like he was still a screamin'."

"Did you know that there Skelly dropped nearly sixty feet from that there window into the mill pond?" An old man interjected his two cents worth into the woman's conversation as he nestled up behind Eve's back. Gender qualms squelched soundly as all packed together for warmth. "Still tied up, he was."

"Really, Biscoe?"

"Yup, he says, 'my maw's sick, and I gots to see her'. And then he ups and jump'd. Saw him crawl out and climb up on that old bank

German=this font   English=this font   *French=this font*   *Delaware=this font*

like my spaniel, Shep. Shake all over like a dog, he did. Then he just up'n melted into them there woods."

"He be damn lucky ifn't he don't die from dah cold. Dat's for sure." Anne added. "He's got no shoes."

The conversation paused as each reflected on the aftermath of Skelly's escape. Their captors obviously wanted to stop any future attempts by anyone else.

"Why'd you think they didn't finish off Master Smythe?" Anne asked. "At the last minute, they grabbed that other poor feller instead."

Biscoe answered. "Don't cha know, Anne. He and his wife is Tories. Major Hay done give them savages the word just in time, he did."

"Too bad that other poor man weren't no Torie," Sue Ellen added.

"It couldah' been me or you den," Biscoe answered ruefully.

Quiet ensued. Eve could feel Biscoe relax against her and a soft snore blanketed his wet, tired form. She and Anne cuddled close to the boys and Sue Ellen in turn.

"Eve."

"Yes."

"I shore do thank you for this shawl. Do you need it back for the boys?"

"No, Sue Ellen. You keep it. These boys got Anne and me." Eve felt herself drifting off. Then she roused herself to slip off her moccasins. One by one, she tucked each one in her armpits before pulling her legs up as close as she could and chucking her skirt about her bare, icy cold feet.

Anne, nearly asleep, groggily queried, "Wonder why that one keeps a helping you, Eve?"

"I do not know, Anne. I just do not know." Eve answered hesitatingly. She paused a long time before sharing her inner thoughts with Anne and Sue Ellen, a little surprised that she even spoke them aloud. "I think that he killed my Adam Henry."

"He did?" Sue Ellen and Anne responded together.

"Yes, I am convinced that he did. I think he wants to keep Lil' Henry."

"I shore hopes not." Sue Ellen offered her support.

"I wonder why? Seems like they got enough of their own to takes care of. No account for why they keep a grabbin' our boys and girls," Anne concluded.

No one spoke again. Sleep and exhaustion claimed them.

[Source for the characters Margaret Elder, Skelly, and unnamed English couple (here called Smythe) found in Replogle, Emma. *Indian Eve and Her Descendants* (1911. Bedford, PA: Reprinted by Messiah Lutheran Church, 1990), p. 23-31. Skelly's words quoted from this source.]

[The inspiration for Anne Wiley is primarily faithful to history in this novel. She is a combination of two black women, a freeborn black (unnamed) captured on horseback and Ann Wiley. The most extensive account of Ann Wiley may be found by Milo M. Quaife, "Detroit

German=this font   English=this font   *French=this font*   *Delaware=this font*

and George Rogers Clark, "*Indiana History Bulletin* (1928, Vol. 5), p.43-46. Also: Silas Farmer in *History of Detroit and Wayne County and Early Michigan, 1890* (Silas Farmer and Co. Republished by Gale Research, 1969), p. 173-174. Sue Ellen is a fictional character.]

Fort Detroit

A week had passed since Ezekiel Solomon had spoken with John Leeth. He planned to use the young man to his company's advantage. He would earn his pay and more. Everything fell perfectly in place.

Fogherty's tavern buzzed with Rangers playing cards and drinking. Off duty, they jockeyed for private stalls with the local serving wenches. Their laughter and revelry rippled through the main room.

John Leeth sat in one of the more quiet lower rooms. Inactivity and being cooped up inside brought no pleasure to him. After walking most of the day in the streets and after observing a hostile stare from DeJean, he had returned to the tavern to tuck himself in one of the rooms apart from the arrogant British for whom he had little tolerance. With no desire to deepen his misery with spirits, he sipped a cup of hot tea and gazed out at the rain which had begun to fall, making tiny curving trails down the wavy panes. Each day brought more cold and increasing dampness that chilled to the bone. Snow and sleet skittered across the crusted and frozen, mud-filled streets; but nothing stuck for long. Many within and without the fort were succumbing to flu and ague, Michigan's curse. Holding the cup to warm his hands and allowing the warm vapors to bathe his face, he silently lamented his condition and deplored his sad misfortune.

Initially, Leeth did not know what caused him to be aware of the two men speaking with his landlady, but his attention became riveted when he swore he heard his own name. Although they spoke quietly without trying to draw notice to themselves, the mention of one's own name has a way of reaching consciousness. Apparently, these men wanted to find him. But to what end, John wondered.

John saw his landlady, Ann Forsythe, discreetly pocket a coin before directing the two burly men to the upper floors. John smiled at her well-practiced maneuver. He watched her slyly as she feigned cleaning a table or two. Even as she worked, John sensed that she watched him. For some reason she did not want to draw attention to herself or to him. Joining in her silent conspiracy, he patiently waited until she could contact him. For John, the wait created a situation where curiosity and fear grew equally with each passing moment. Gradually, she worked her way down into the lower room.

"Do you think you need more tea, sir?"

"I don't think so," John answered. "It may be time to leave."

"No sir, I don't think one should go out on a nasty night like this. If I were you, sir, I'd tuck myself up to my room." A touch of brogue softened her speech. Ann Forsythe winked at John. "Take a bit of spirits, and call it a night."

German=this font   English=this font   *French=this font*   *Delaware=this font*

"You thinks so?" John smiled amiably. Curiosity gained an upper hand.

"Oh, I assure you, sir. That's what smart men do."

And with that, his landlady moved on to the next table, leaving John to debate when or whether to ascend the stairs.

John swallowed each remaining sip of tea with a sense of dread. He realized that sooner or later he was going to have to go up those steps. When his cup emptied, curiosity won out over fear.

"Mr. Leeth."

His landlady's voice caused him to jump. She had fresh towels looped over her arm. "Nearly forgot to give you one of these towels, sir. Shall we go up together? I have some for another room as well. Don't dry near as well on these damp days."

John stumbled to his feet, following his landlady up the stairs to his room. She spoke quietly to him as they climbed.

"Now don't you fret, sir. These men mean you no trouble. They're clever, and they'll cover ye well."

They opened his door to find the two gentlemen in question talking quietly. Seeing John, they shoved a chair at him, motioning to him to sit down. His landlady winked again at him and quickly left him, pushing his towel into his arms with a smile.

"Sit down, John." The larger of the two threw his hand in the air in a friendly manner. He exuded good humor. Stout, red haired, his face flushed from drinking wine, John realized that his impromptu Irish host had not waited for his arrival to begin toasting the cold night. His shorter companion, a bit more slender, also appeared slightly flushed from the fruit of the vine.

"Name's William Boslick," the stout one extended his hand. "And this here is James Cassidy, only we all calls 'im Jamie."

John shook their hands with reservation. They seemed friendly enough.

"Have a drink, John." The fellow named Jamie passed his port bottle to John.

John, recognizing a clear head might be to his advantage if a hasty escape was mandated, warily declined.

"Now come now, John, we're brothers of enterprise." He proffered the bottle again. John declined a second time, returning it to Boslick untouched. The companion took a hearty swig and passed it off to Jamie, who took more than his fair share.

"Now John, I 'spect you don't trust us a mite, but I tell yah laddie, you've got nothing to fear from either of us. We ha' been referred to you, we have. We hear yer a goot man."

John looked askance. His skepticism of his two guests was so obvious that both seemed perplexed for a minute how to overcome his resistance.

"Me don't thinks he trusts us yet, Jamie."

"Ye ehr the same lad that Hamilton and his henchmen are a danglin' aren't ye?"

German=this font   English=this font   *French=this font*   *Delaware=this font*

John crossed his arms, appraising the men before him with even more scrutiny. He rocked back on his chair, raising the front legs very slightly off the floor.

"What do you know about me and Hamilton?" John asked with a touch of annoyance in his voice.

"Have a drink, laddie." Boslick pushed the wine toward John again.

John had to grin; the man would not be denied. His smile disarmed him, for it was downright contagious. Rocking forward, he wiped the mouth, took a small swig, and handed it back. Try as he might to suppress it, the strength of the wine, compared to his earlier tea, elicited a cough. Boslick whacked John heartily across his back. "Now that's more like it," Boslick roared. Both men laughed jovially. Before John could blink, the wine had made another round and was being pushed back at him for a second go at it. He accepted this time without coughing.

"The lad wonders what we know'd about that English bastard, Hamilton. Well, we know'd that worms wouldn't wipe their slime on him if he were six foot under, and so ripe and rotten that he fairly begged for it. And we're damn proud to know a man that won't join him in his butchery. That we are."

"Aye, that we are," Jamie echoed.

"Won't give yeh a pass to Sandusky, will they? When all ye want to do is to be a free man and make an honest trade. Which is yer God given right, man."

"How do you know this?"

"Well, laddie, the less you know, the better sometimes. Just'ah realize, we mean you no harm. We've come to make an offer that just might interest a man of yer talents."

"No matter what, laddie, wither ye deal with us or no, don't give into that beast. That one's sure to foul your soul, he will."

"Aye, don't give into that bastard. There's no justice in hean' or hell if'n that one don't roast like the men and women who die at the stakes because he rum's up them savages. Whips up their hate he does. Damn him! And damn DeJean. What one canna' come up with, the other surely will," Boslick stated shaking his head.

"That's for damn sure," Jamie chimed in. "But, whatever you do, don't flee the Fort. His savage trackers will hound you to the death just'ah for spite."

"Aye, don't ye run. That's the wurst you can do."

"And sad it is, they're a both lining their pockets with the blood of innocents. Blood money, sure'n it tis." Jamie wiped the drips from his chin with the back of his hand before passing the wine again.

If their friendly manner had not disarmed John's mistrust, their full knowledge of him and his problems, as well as their openness, and their obvious and genuine hatred of Hamilton and DeJean completely won him over. He found himself among friends for the second time in a week; and again, when he least expected it.

German–this font   English=this font   *French=this font*   *Delaware=this font*

"You are brave to speak so loudly, gentlemen, with British only boards away. Have no fears, I'll not work for Indian Department. On that you can depend." John spoke again, somewhat thoughtfully, "Sometimes I fear that they have their ears to my wall, just waiting for something I say or do."

"Got ye a point in that, man." Boslick's voice lowered noticeably.

"Aye, why don't you move in tah our board'n house? Yer less likely to run afoul of the blokes. Besides, yer employer won't have no more to pay there than here," Jamie suggested.

"Sur'an, just be tellin' you employer that 'you do not like to board at the Tavern and that you had rather be at a private house,'"** Boslick added.

"Aye, 'preparation will be made for you to live with us.'"** Jamie settled the affair, assuming John's acceptance.

John reflected on what his two new friends offered. For the first time in weeks, he did not feel utterly alone. Instead, he felt joined to kindred spirits. He appreciated that the others did not want him to join Hamilton's henchmen. Their support, in what he thought was a lonely stand, felt like a healing salve on an open wound.

"I'll join you. But I must do nothin' to go against my employer. He's been right fair with me n' all."

"Dun."

"Yer word is good 'nough fer us." This time the second friendly whack that John received had more power from Boslick behind it. Like an overgrown bear cub, the large man truly did not fully recognize his own strength.

"Now, just what was it that you gentlemen had in mind for me to do?"

"Well, John, it's come to our attention that you speak Delaware and know a good bit more of the Indian tongue and sign."

"Some."

"Well, as long as yer stuck here, we just need'cha to walk about some, and listen. Spy, if you will, on the savages. If'n they have furs to sell, let us know and we'll make'm a better deal than DeJean without so much rum to cloud their minds in the end. And if'n your help gets us a seller, we'll pay you a finders fee...two to five dollars a day dependen' on what we can buy. And ye can count on that for as long as yer at ther Fort."

John reflected on what Boslick had said, when Jamie queried, "Is it a deal?"

"Deal."

As John extended his hand on it, he sensed more brains behind this arrangement than either of his two new friends exhibited. Even though he recognized that they were both very clever and capable men, John suspected that he knew to whom he really owed this opportunity. But he would go along with the ruse as though he did not know.

German=this font   English=this font   *French=this font*   *Delaware=this font*

John wondered if all Jewish merchants were this resourceful and enterprising. Most of all, he recognized that his employer's silent partner must be extremely cautious supporting him. To survive in these perilous times, John would have to be very careful too. In addition, he comprehended that his two greatest enemies, Hamilton and DeJean, were extremely wily, devious, and intelligent. Therefore, they must never be underestimated. He prayed that the training of his adopted Delaware father, Standing Bear, would keep him in good stead. Standing Bear taught him that the integrity in men must be read like the trail of a catamount. If one misunderstood where it led, the mistake could be fatal. At least now, John felt that he could earn his keep like a man. But most of all, he relished the challenge of silently fleecing DeJean and his hidden partners. If he could deprive the greasy weasel, DeJean, of even one pound, John would sleep a happier man.

[Leeth never names his employers or his associates in his narrative. A little author's license here. Leeth's two companions are well documented as Rebel sympathizers. Ezekial Solomon has been documented for his fair dealings and merchant work in many sources. The closely paraphrased dialogue and the intrigue in Forsythe's Tavern was inspired by dialogue from Leeth's narrative. p. 30 -33.] **Jeffries, Ewel, *A Short Biography of John Leeth, Giving a Brief Account of His Travels and Sufferings Among the Indians for Eighteen Years Together With His Religious Exercises From His Own Relations* (Lancaster, Ohio: Gazette Office, 1891), as related by Thwaites, Ruben Gold, Ed., *A Short Biography of John Leeth with an account of his life among the Indians* (New York: Benjamin Blom Inc., 1972).

Bedford, Pennsylvania

Jac passed the applejack to his brother. Even before recent events, both of them had markedly begun to show their years. Age and life had recently taken a very heavy toll on both men. The women and Johannas had turned in. The two older men sat smoking by the fire.

The heat of the hearth and the hot alcoholic buzz of applejack warmed their bodies and souls. Both found basking by the fire far more inviting than the prospect of stalking the cold woods, standing guard, or tending the barn.

Jac felt confident now that posting a guard was no longer necessary. He maintained that the savages would be too busy going on winter hunt or hiding under their blankets to pester them.

Resigned, Jac realized that the last outing had been his final major trek. His bones ached so much from having been in the wet and cold that he could barely walk when he awoke his first day back. With each day's passing, the effects of his attempt to free Eve and the boys impacted. His left knee, nearly doubled in size, throbbed with arthritic heat. Large bubbles of yellow-gray fluid built up beneath his skin. The right, favored with extra weight, soon joined suit. Jac found that it took nearly to midday to get the kinks out enough to walk with difficulty. The physical toll on

German=this font   English=this font   *French=this font*   Delaware=this font him had been far, far greater than he had ever anticipated. While hatred may have fueled his journey initially, hatred gave little ease to the increasing pain that struck viciously within days of his return. Only the applejack helped.

Applejack also freed their tongues. They could talk of important things, not just womanly or childish chatter.

"Did you hear the latest news from Point Pleasant?" Jac asked, tapping his long white clay pipe on his sole, then relighting it with a straw.

"No. But I tell you Jac, Tory or no, those folks will rue the day they run off Lord Dunmore. The man's earned nothing but my respect, war or no war. The man knew how to deal with those savages." He took a rather large swig from his stein and settled back.

"Cornplanter is dead. Looks like Dunmore finally got a little just revenge."

"Now that is refreshing news. One less of them to worry us."

"And that son of his, too—name's...Elinipso, Elinipsico—or something like that. Plus two other brown bastards. Hear tell, Matt Arbuckle's none too pleased since General Hand crawled all over him. Arbuckle had detained the old man because he could not be sure which way the old savage's Shawanese would align themselves with the British or the Virginian's. Guess Cornplanter had the gall to strut right into the fort and demand to speak to Arbuckle. Some claim Cornplanter came to warn the fort, but who can believe a savage anywise. Militia got their dander up. Rightly so. Some savages killed one of their own, right under their very noses. Hell, they were just across the river from the fort hunting up a bit of venison. Made the militia so damn mad, they shoved past Arbuckle and shot the arrogant brown bastards."

Jac paused and plied his tongue with a bit more applejack before continuing. "Damned if my knees were not so bad, George, I would go down there and lend those boys a hand. They got more guts than most of our Pennsylvania boys."

"Now Jac, that is not fair. You know that most of our good men got sent northeast." George's voice conveyed a deep sadness. He had been unable to protect his own. This crawled in his gut like a round worm nibbling at him from the inside out. He had even been unable to go with his brother. Maybe if he had been fit enough to go, they... At last to divert blame away from his own inabilities, he changed his focus. He spoke again to his brother after a long pause. "I guess you are right. Those damn Virginians have guts, all right, and more land surveyors than you can hatch mosquitoes on a warm spring night! If it keeps up, those Virginians will own half of Pennsylvania and all our Ohio territory while those Quaker idiots still debate what is to be done in Philly. Instead, they have set to entertaining that damned English General, Howe. Since Howe resigned his commission, he is just wintering over and waiting to be shipped home."

"Well, that is a Quaker for you. They will not defend their own city or stop their women from dancing with Howe and his boys."

German=this font   English=this font   *French=this font*   *Delaware=this font*

"Jac, now that the damn English have Philadelphia, what do they want to do with it? Useless effort, if you ask me. But I guess that it beats fighting Washington or those stinking Oneida Indians up in New York."

The fire crackled. Both men stared into the coals rather than at each other. The ravages of time proved less annoying that way.

"The Rebel Congress moved again."

"Where to this time?"

"After Philly, then Lancaster, now York, I hear."

"Creeping closer to Virginia."

"Yeh."

Both men sat quietly, lost in their own thoughts. Jac looked up at George, "I meant to ask you, did you give that stinking proclamation to Woods?"

"Yes, blood and all. Ripped it off Adam's face before anyone saw it."

"I tell you George, I have no love for English or Rebel, either one, but just where does that Gott damn Hamilton get off thinking that he can plaster our dead with an invite to join him and his hair buyers to murder more of our friends and neighbors for the mere price of two hundred acres of land?"

A knot exploded and sent a spray of sparks across the floor. Each man quickly stomped on any potential igniter. Jac automatically kicked the largest coal back into the hearth, wincing with pain after he had done so. His swollen knees strained his breeches, making them look like tightly packed sausages. Every button below the knee had been undone, but swelling demanded more give. A small tear had started. He rubbed his knees with the butt of his palms for some time.

"Wood had best keep that proclamation from any stinking loyalist's eyes. Just hope he can convince that quaking governor friend of his to get us some decently trained troops to protect our farms."

"You are right! Damn right, George. But what can we do? We just get the leavings of the barrel."

The blame cut like a two-edged sword. Both embittered men lifted their cups and stared into the coals of a waning fire. Silenced by their words, like many older increasingly powerless men, they knew all the answers, and some of them cut to the quick.

German=this font   English=this font   **French=this font**   *Delaware=this font*

Chapter 10   Sandusky and the Wyandots   Mid-December, 1777

"My son, the Great Spirit has seen fit that we should die together, and has sent you here to that end. It is his will and let us submit, it is all for the best."

Cornstalk to his son, Ellinipisco, as quoted by George P. Donehoo, Ed., "Dunmore's War— Pre-Revolutionary Events" *Pennsylvania, A History* (Volume I-IV New York, NY: Lewis Historical Publishing Inc., 1926), p. 959. Donehoo further relates that American Rebel Forces then shot Cornstalk, a Shawanese Chief, seven times, killed his son who never had time to stand, and proceeded to "hack to pieces" Chief Redhawk who "had hidden himself in the chimney."   Cornstalk and Redhawk had freely entered Fort Pitt <u>under a white flag of truce to warn Capt. Arbuckle about opposing forces</u>. When Arbuckle detained both men, Ellinipisco came out of concern for his father. Coincidentally, a soldier was slain by another Indian party, and all three men took the brunt of the militia anger.

South of Sandusky, Ohio Territory

The sleet had crusted on Anne's hair like a white, fluffy woolen cap, unlike Eve's and Sue Ellen's frozen waves that plastered to their faces held fast by crusts of ice. Mikie's little chin quivered and vibrated on Eve's wet shoulder as he clung to his mother's neck. He whimpered from time to time, sounding much like a beaten puppy.

As another ground sage ripped a chunk from Anne's leg, she swore softly under her breath. She looked over her shoulder at Eve and Sue Ellen, pointing out the vicious clump to them. The ground sages appeared so innocuous, but their tough, coral-like branches gave no quarter to the wet, cold flesh which could easily be torn. Between those and the dewberry vines that seemed specifically designed to trip up tired feet, the lower portions of the women's and men's cloth garments had become shredded over time. The dewberries skimmed over the surface of many of the meadows or higher humps in the swampy areas. They often grew in partnership with the long wiry canes of blackberry and raspberry, which would snake like living ropes beneath the women's skirts and petticoats, leaving long slashes on their legs and person. Sometimes these taller plants entangled the arms of the men and women as they waded through the underbrush, attempting to keep pace with the demands of their captors. As a result, any exposed skin became covered with mazes of tiny cuts and stabs from berry thorns. These wounds stung as if filled with hundreds of

115

microscopic bees—microscopic bees, who had stingers that imbedded themselves in every tiny valley of cut flesh.

Those who had leather leggings and skin wraps of course fared better, but few of the prisoners numbered among them. Biscoe stumbled behind the three women, a deep hacking cough his only comment.

Eve heard a sound, a sound totally unfamiliar to her. A whoosh, followed by crashes in repetitive falls, this sound pounded like a giant thrasher flailing an enormous bundle of grain and beating the ground in a cascade of power.

"What is that?" Eve finally asked as the sound grew closer and closer to them.

"The sweet water sea," Anne answered.

"What sea?"

"Sweet water sea, woman. Don't you be knowing that?"

"No."

"Why sweet water, Anne?"

"You can drink it."

"You mean there is a river or a stream. A sea is salty."

"Woman. Sometimes Dutchie, you don't know much." Anne felt a surge of pride. She loved to have a sense of one-upmanship on Eve. Their mutual fight to survive and the ensuing friendship had long ago given Anne license to tease her. She had come to admire her stout white companion, who melted away a little each day as she cared for her children and helped those about her. Both Anne and Sue Ellen had benefited from the additional share of food given to Eve by Stalking Wolf. Under the guise of feeding Henry, he made sure that the women were fed. Even Biscoe, who usually declined any offerings in favor of the women and children, occasionally benefited. Eve included Margaret if she returned to join the threesome and the children. Although Margaret no longer had anything for coughs or fever in her pockets, Eve freely shared whatever she had. She recognized that Margaret, like all of them, simply wanted to survive. So Eve understood when Margaret spent time between the Smythes, the Tory couple, and Eve's party depending on the amount of food. Eve would do the same, if necessary, to see that her boys survived.

"I swear if we do not stop soon, I will drop in my traces." Eve seldom complained, but the sleet had dipped her spirits to a new low.

"Want me to take Mikie for a bit? I be strong now."

Eve stopped and handed off Mikie to Anne. "I think it is my womanlies making me weaker. Third heavy day so far." In her former life, Eve would never have indicated anything about her menses to anyone. She kept her affairs privy only to herself and Adam Henry. Among the prisoners, she found herself utterly exposed in every way. No bodily functions could be hidden from her companions. Everyone knew your business down to the last grunt or awkward wipe. Sometimes the women would attempt to shield their sisters from view by circling about them as they defecated, but the Delaware and Mingo objected to that since it took

German=this font English=this font *French=this font* *Delaware=this font*

too much time and caused the line to break order. Since Skelly had escaped, their captors allowed them little or no privacy, for fear of another escapee.

However, of late, Eve noted that the Delaware gave her wide birth. For the last two days, Stalking Wolf did not approach her or bring Henry to her at night. Since he did not bring Henry, he brought no food either. She began to wonder if they had some repulsion to her or if the odor that she herself abhorred had been recognized.

Their captors seemed to sense odors just as well as their eyes could see, Eve had observed. Twice, small game had been discovered that way. Their party had not crossed any decent sized streams in the last three days, so the padded bits of petticoat that she had soiled were stuffed one upon another in her apron pocket. A small reddish brown stain on the outside of her pocket revealed their presence where it had soaked through her apron. She abhorred filth of this nature and at first had debated whether to throw away the soiled material or not. Finally, she decided that she could not do so because of the total lack of any extra cloth among the others. Besides, what would she do next time? If she kept tearing away at her petticoat and apron, she would soon find herself literally naked. So no matter how repugnant, she dutifully tucked each stiff, brown smelly parcel into her pocket. Perhaps she could wash them in Anne's freshwater sea, she mused. No way to boil them here like she had at home. The thought of home made a lump rise in her throat. She quickly tried to refocus on the path ahead.

They had trudged for about another hour when Anne spoke.

"Mikie sounds hungry, Eve. Got anything for him to chew or suck on?"

"Not really. I think this meat is spoiled." Eve pulled a small brown twisted bit of jerky-like fiber from her waist band. So far, she just could not bring herself to give it to Mikie or to throw it away. She tried not to think about food because when she did, she dreamed when she walked. Once, she swore that she saw schneckes flying though the air in front of her, dripping with warm butter and smelling of cinnamon, right out of the oven. When she opened her mouth to catch one between her teeth, her mouth watering; the whole image melted away like a snowflake on her tongue, leaving her with greater hunger than before and renewing horrible images from the beginning of her journey.

"I try not to think about food," she added, talking more to herself than to Anne.

"Ez you drying up Dutchie?"

"I fear so. Once my bleeds start, I usually wean my children for good. Not much there it seems after that."

"Well Eve, if'n this boy got no suckle, you'd best give that meat to me for him, spoiled or no." Anne reached back. Her hand cupped.

Reluctantly, Eve pressed the small twisted meat into Anne's outstretched hand. Anne passed it off to Mikie atop her shoulders, who tried to wrap his stiff fingers about it, only to have it slip from his tiny

German=this font   English=this font   *French=this font*   *Delaware=this font*

hands. He cried out softly as the bit of meat fell. Eve dropped to her knees, picked it from among the muddy foot print, wiped it off on the grass, rose to place it firmly in his hand, and wrapped his fingers about it.

Eve ignored a painful contraction in her lower abdomen. The cramp released. This had been a particularly painful period. Mikie, her primary concern, held her attention. Then, she realized how truly cold his fingers were as her hand surrounded his. No wonder he found it difficult to hold the meat.

"Hold fast, little one. Hold fast." She curled her hand about his until she felt his hand warm beneath hers enough that he was able to grasp the spoiled jerky. Mikie put the rotten meat to his mouth without any further hesitation. Saliva dripped off his tiny bluish chin, freezing in tiny lumps on his breast. Two long lamb's legs of green-yellow snot ran from his nose to his lip. Eve grasped the ooze gently between her first finger and her thumb, wiping it on what was left of her apron. Mikie frowned and turned his head from her. He hated to have his sore nose touched.

Eve, finding Mikie needed no further assistance, dropped back to walk almost but not quite beside Sue Ellen. Glancing at her pretty young friend, she grew shocked at the changed girl, who staggered intermittently, as they struggled to keep pace. Her fair skin had a ghastly gray pallor. Enormous circles under her eyes accented her dainty features, giving her a ghoulish look. Her pale, icy blue eyes, really her best feature, contrasted against the dark hollows that framed them.

Eve smiled at her. "You must not give up now, young woman. You just keep on walking. Anne and I are here for you, Sue Ellen. You must not give up. We are going to make it, girl. You just keep thinking on that."

Sue Ellen appeared partially dazed, but she managed a weak smile and nodded. She reached forward, extending her hand to Eve, who grasped it in her own. For a moment, they walked hand in hand. Then they dropped their hands to return to the favored cross-chest position of arms and hands to retain as much of their body warmth as humanly possible.

The crashing sounds increased in intensity. With the increase in sound came more wind. More wind, more cold, more wind, more penetrating cold built in progressive amounts. Another walker, well behind the women and Mr. Biscoe, fell and was clubbed, scalped, and left to die from exposure. No one reacted anymore. All were numbed from cold and horror.

When they crested a small ridge, Eve could see the water. She felt amazed by the sheer expanse of the horizon. The absence of an opposing shore surprised her. Anne rightly called it a sea. However, no pungent brine odors greeted her. Familiar with the ocean, she would have immediately recognized the smell. Instead, the breeze carried only hints of fresh, crisp spice-like odors that one associated with late fall foliage. The crashing sounds belonged to the long lines of white water that raced forward row, after row, after row. One after another they smashed

German=this font   English=this font   *French=this font*   *Delaware=this font*

themselves on the sandy shore and then ran willy-nilly like dozens of scurrying foamy-white baby chicks to hide beneath the next roaring wall of water.

"It's such a deep blue," Sue Ellen, reeling from exhaustion, breathed out in awe.

All twenty-three prisoners stood on the crest, coming to a stop as the waves broke onto the sandy ridge. The entire group, sodden though they were, stood quietly gaping at the long shoreline. A whoop from the rear and a push started them moving forward once more. In the distance, Eve noted the roof tops of a large cluster of cabins. Could that be a cross atop one building? A bubbling undercurrent of expectation rippled through the group. They hoped for a destination, a respite from the cold. A ship bobbed at anchor offshore. Its masts faded into a descending fog. Another lay haphazardly on its side. The toll of wave and wind had taken its seaworthiness away.

"Is it Fort Detroit?"

Biscoe coughed, clearing his throat. "No, Sue Ellen. That's the Erie's lake if my memory serves me. We might'n be near'n the Sandusky. We sure..." he burst into a racking spell of coughing. After clearing his throat, he hacked up a large gob of expectorant which he spewed into the mat of beach grass. He continued, "We sure walked fer' enough for it to be it." He cleared his throat, spitting again. "If'n it is, we'z in Wyandot country."

Suddenly, Eve doubled. An intense cramp folded her nearly in half. Stepping to the side of the path, she crouched in the tall grasses. She could feel her labial lips begin to separate, parting to release a large warm clot. As she extracted the semi-solid mass from her crotch, she knew that the very last internal physical presence of Adam Henry had deserted her. The unexpected realization ripped at her resolve to survive. For a fraction of a second, she flashed on a sunny morning, a stoop, a warm trickle down her leg—an unspoken prayer. She shuddered. A wrenching chill shook her.

Later, Eve would barely remember frantically digging a small hole at the base of a clump of frozen sedges. Her fingers stung and burned from the ravaging cold. The sharp, three-sided edges of the tough blades of sedge ripped her icy flesh. In that hellish, cold place, she tenderly laid the small bloody bundle to its final rest. As fellow prisoners and captors passed her by, no one interrupted her at her task. Eve barely comprehended their presence. She methodically cleaned herself. Then, patting some grass over the makeshift burial place one last time, she wiped her hands in a manner not unlike the brave who had earlier dispatched the nameless woman.

Eve rose to her feet, staggered momentarily, and caught up once more to Anne, Mikie, and Sue Ellen. She spoke no more that day.

Anne realized something profound had happened along the path and continued to carry Mikie, silencing him quickly if he called out to his mother. She and Sue Ellen respected Eve's silence. Neither woman

German=this font   English=this font   *French=this font*   *Delaware–this font* attempted to speak with her. Even Biscoe tried to muffle his coughs, so as not to intrude on her reverie.

Another set of very observant eyes noted Eve's behavior and knew that he had a difficult task in the village ahead. White Corn Woman had asked far too much of him, Stalking Wolf thought.

All the women and children huddled within a single cabin. For the first time in almost a week, they had a roof over their heads and buckskins to cover them while they slept. New lice and bedbugs were welcomed along with the warmth. Anne had finally gotten Mikie off to sleep. Sue Ellen, groggily wrapped in a hide beside Anne, cuddled close to her other side. Eve sat apart from everyone. Uncovered, she clasped her knees to her body. Having refused the dried corn bread that the others had greedily consumed, she rocked herself as if she were a child being comforted by its mother.

When the skin over the door pulled aside, a frowning Wyandot woman entered. All eyes, save Eve's, followed her as she walked directly up to Eve and crouched beside the distressed woman.

Eve pretended not to notice her. When the woman poked her thigh the third time, Eve glared at her. The woman shoved some leaves at her and then from beneath her tanned sleeve brought forth a small gourd. Going through the motions of drinking from the gourd, she extended it to Eve.

Eve shook her head no.

Again the woman went through the motions of drinking from the gourd and extended it to Eve a second time.

Again, Eve shook her head no.

When the Wyandot woman extended the gourd towards Eve a third time, Eve attempted to knock it from her hand. Frowning, the woman stood, said something in obvious anger, and exited.

Anne observed this. What was going on here?

A few minutes later, the skin lifted once more. This time, the Wyandot woman returned with a tall man. They walked up to Eve, who tried to ignore both of them. The boring gaze of Stalking Wolf demanded her attention. She acknowledged them, in spite of herself.

Every eye in the room observed them. Every conversation halted.

"You will drink, Hanu's Mutti." He did not speak loudly, but the words fell on Eve's ears as if he had shouted them. **"You have living sons who need you, selfish woman."**

The words slammed into Eve's inner self. The second blow of the day sent her emotionally reeling. Gott damn him, why must he be right? His words stung more than nettles. Why was this murdering savage always forcing her to address her weaknesses? Why?

Numbly, Eve accepted the gourd from the woman. Sipping a tiny bit of the bitter brew from within, she scrunched up her face and handed it back.

"All of it, woman."

German=this font   English=this font   *French=this font*   *Delaware=this font*

Eve raised the gourd and continued to drink the intensely bitter liquid until none remained.

"Why do you do this?" Eve asked, handing the empty gourd back to the woman who crouched beside her.

She searched Stalking Wolf's face for clues to his behavior.

He did not answer her. He stood quietly as he motioned to her to chew the leaves from the woman.

"Why?" Eve asked a second time. Juice escaped from the leaves, leaking out the right corner of her mouth and running down to her chin. She wiped it away with the back of her hand.

"Why?" She asked a third time. She touched his moccasin.

Finally, he answered with absolutely no inflection or emotion in his voice. "I get money for you when I sell you in Detroit. You must make up for the loss of your husband's scalp and the other one. You tell DeJean, so I get trade goods. If you dead, I have no proof of two scalps. The minister of justice believes white people, not Delaware." Turning on his heel, he left her.

The room of women perceived yet another facet of inhumanity.

The Wyandot beside Eve gave her another fistful of leaves. She feigned sleep and then made a wide awake expression, a yawn and a stretch, mimicking a waking person, and then she took Eve's hand to her mouth with the leaves. Looking at her questioningly, she rested back on her heels. Eve nodded affirmatively. Then the woman grabbed her own lower abdomen, kneading it like one did after childbirth. She pointed to Eve, motioning for her to knead her abdomen. Eve nodded affirmatively again. She should have thought of that earlier. Why had she forgotten? The woman was right. Eve should massage her fundus to slow her bleeding. Sensing that Eve understood, the woman left.

Immediately, Margaret Elder arose and came to Eve's side.

"What foul, heathen brew did she give you, Eve? If you place your finger in your throat, you can wretch it up. I will help you."

"No, Margaret." Eve stood up shakily, placing her extra leaves in her pocket beside the brown wads and steadying herself on Margaret's arm as she arose. "I do not think that they mean me harm."

"Well you have more faith in their godless medicines than I do, Eve," Margaret reprimanded, as she helped Eve over to the corner where Anne, the boy, and Sue Ellen lay. "You must pray to God that you are not poisoned." Helping Eve to sit down, she continued, "Major Hay says our journey soon will end. How I long for Fort Detroit. At least there, the British are civilized Christians. You might even find a barber or a doctor."

"Be careful of your desires, Margaret. In the end, they may not be anything that you can imagine," Eve said softly.

"Whatever could you mean?"

"Nothing Margaret. Nothing." Eve disengaged herself from

German=this font   English=this font   *French=this font*   *Delaware=this font*

Margaret's steadying hand and lay down beside Anne. A weak smile conveyed her thanks to Margaret.

Once Margaret had Eve settled, she crossed once more to rest by Mistress Smythe.

Eve's eyes had nearly closed from pain and exhaustion when she felt a soft touch on her arm. Sue Ellen's hand extended towards her with a crust of corn bread.

"I saved it fer you."

Eve nodded appreciatively. "Thank you, Sue Ellen." She said, accepting the dry crust to chew with the last of the leaves for the night.

Morning came with a shout and a loud pound on the side of the building. As usual, the abrupt John Montour, another of Hamilton's Indian Department's henchmen, proved that the British had little patience with the prisoners, especially children. He, like Jehu Hay, seemed absolutely driven to get back to Fort Detroit. The half-breed interpreter, in Eve's opinion, had inherited the worst traits from each of his parents. She steered clear of the angry man whenever possible. Biscoe claimed the man was Queen Esther's nephew. If indeed, Montour was related, it literally gave Eve the chills. Everyone in Pennsylvania had heard the tales of that Seneca mother's wrath after her son was murdered. A large rock, well greased with settler's brains, had become a memorial for the settlers that she had personally dispatched and confirmed a gory testament to her vengeful anger.

Though still dark, the women and children must be up and about their business quickly. Soon, they would head out again. Eve had cramped off and on through the night. Stirred from her slumber, she wondered if the medication had intensified her cramps. With the morning, she dutifully massaged her fundus, kneading, rolling, and squishing the flesh in her hands, taking the pain in stride. Chewing the leaves from her pocket, she recognized a growing need.

"Anne, will you watch the boy do his duty?"

Anne agreed. Sue Ellen steadied her as Eve arose.

Leaving the warmth of the cabin, Eve sought a place apart. A morning fog had settled about the cabins, giving them and the orchards about the cabins a monochromatic appearance. One could not even see the boat hulls in the morning fog, only the tip of one mast. The lap of the waves fell soundlessly on the shore. The exception to the pallor, two red fires glowed with large open trade kettles steaming over them. All else appeared colorless. Gray ghostly figures moved from time to time among the buildings. Stepping into the wooded area, Eve sensed that she was being watched. But, since no one stopped her, she selected a grassy knoll between two garden plots. Hunkering down, she expelled the last of the miscarriage.

Eve realized that her bleeding would probably wane after this act. Stacking another sticky brown bundle in her pocket, ripping off a bit more

German=this font   English=this font   *French=this font*   *Delaware=this font*

of her petticoat, folding it neatly and placing it within her labia, she cleansed herself as best she could with the wet grasses and returned to the cabin. As she walked toward it, the woman who had come to her the night before magically appeared by her side. Silently extending a refilled gourd to her, she indicated to Eve to swallow the bitter brew. When Eve returned the empty vessel, the woman handed her yet another handful of leaves before she melted into the morning fog amongst the cabins, disappearing as magically as she had initially appeared.

Unobserved, a tall figure watched them both and disappeared.

Inside the women's cabin, the women and children chattered with a sense of excitement. In their midst, a kettle of hot, sweet, meaty broth with bits of swollen hominy and small chunks of dried pumpkin steamed in the morning air. Short in the number of cups, each person took their turn to drink and to chew the bits of vegetable in their dip.

Mikie laughed. His laughter spread throughout the huddle of women and children like leavening, lifting their spirits. Eve smiled as she entered. How many days had it been since she had heard his musical chuckle? She stood at the doorway, observing the mass of women. Truly, they were her sisters, forced to become family. They were united by the terror and by the blood of their losses. To a person, they looked so wretched, so bedraggled. Yet here in the midst of a hellish journey, a warm night under cover, lice-infested deer hides for warmth, a bit of hot broth, and a child's sweet laugh gleamed like specks of silver mica amongst grains of sand. Eve stepped up to the pot for her share of hope.

As the group lined up once more to resume their trek, Anne cast a wary look at the sky. "Sure hope she don't rain or sleet again today."

Sue Ellen looked up and nodded in agreement. "Me too."

"I'll carry Mikie." Anne grabbed the boy and had snugged his legs around her strong lean neck before he even thought to protest. He clung to her like a fly on sticky paper, digging his fingers into her wooly hair. "You save your strength, Dutchie. You be needin' it later."

Anne's words proved prophetic.

Fort Detroit

"John, hey John." Above the milling crowd, a voice called repeatedly. "Leeth! Hey, John!" Jonas Schindler waved his hat, finally catching John's attention.

"What's all the excitement?" John grinned. In just over a week, Jonas and he had become fast friends. Jonas shared a room with him at Theresa Marie's boarding house. Forbidden as he was to leave, John found Jonas, a young silversmith, not only companionable, but a man who was not given to heavy drinking. This was an unexpected find among the traders who lived and played hard. Nor did Schindler indulge in some of the practical jokes that Boslick and Cassidy found continual delight in. Their

German=this font   English=this font   *French=this font*   *Delaware=this font*

room proved to be an island of sanity amongst some of the hard-drinking Irish and French traders who moved continuously in and out of Theresa Marie's establishment. Besides, Jonas enjoyed not having to share the bed, as his new friend preferred the floor and a blanket.

Jonas grasped his friend around the shoulder in a friendly manner, dragging him back behind a company store and towards the alley behind Fogherty's. "Come on—you can see it better from here. You have so much to learn, John Leeth. Those Delawares that you know have shielded you from civilized society." His good natured jest bubbled with double entendre. Throughout the streets, a buzz of excitement and anticipation ran up and down like the channels cut in the mud from the previous days' rains.

Neighbors called summons in French and English. Even the priest, Father Bocquet from Ste. Anne's Church, hobbled headlong out his door, clutching his long black robes above the top of his knobby knees to keep them free of the mud and moving as quickly as his strength and cane permitted.

At first, John expected something that would bring merriment. Had a late ship arrived with goods from Niagara? Had the *Welcome* returned to rejoin her sister ships, the *Felicity* and *Angelica*, with a load of furs from Fort Michilimackinac? Given the November storms, would it not be too late for that?

Jonas pointed to a group of Rangers struggling to pull the cannon out of the fort gates. One of them slipped in the icy mud. His clown-like pratfall brought wholesale delight to the growing crowd. Laughter roared as the Ranger tried to recover from his grimy dunking only to slip and fall a second time. This caused many of the French inhabitants to laugh and to slap their sides and thighs, hooting with absolute glee at his embarrassment. When a second man also fell on his backside, his feet above his head, the French among the crowd howled.

Suddenly, the crowd silenced. Hamilton appeared at the gate in full dress. One of two officers, directly behind him, hastily buttoned up his vest with his hat held tightly tucked under his arm. Two other officers, shortly behind the first three, ran forward, barking orders at those who hauled the cannon. Struggling to pivot the cannon so the barrel pointed to an empty space in the harbor, the swab man and the powder man readied their equipment for the order to load. Lagging behind, Lieutenant Governor Hamilton's day orderly toted a heavy chair for his superior. DeJean scurried up from his office to stand near the officers, as if his adjacent presence conferred a higher rank.

Then, John Leeth saw them. Later, he would not be sure if their weeping or their unusual body movements first caught his attention. Below them, the crowd lined each side of the road up to the fort gate.

But as the struggling group stumbled fully into view, the crowd centered its attention with deadly concentration. John took in a deep breath and clenched his fists. The memories of his own trek under the

German=this font English=this font *French=this font* *Delaware=this font*

guard of the Shawanese, his subsequent gauntlet run, and his sale to the Wyandot fully drenched his consciousness. But his hardship had come in summer, not winter. What he had experienced obviously did not compare for a moment to what he beheld.

Behind and adjacent to John and Jonas, another John stood watching with another coureurs de bois in the growing crowd.

"Sacra bleur," John Coutincinau wheezed between his teeth. The muscles of his temple expanded and contracted as his eyes narrowed to the disgusting sight before them, stilling his laughter. He crossed his arms across his chest to stifle a shiver of deep, deep revulsion. Though hardened by many years among the native peoples, this exceeded his realm of experience.

His friend mumbled an expletive underneath his breath as well.

Eighteen nearly naked women and children** staggered and stumbled in the muddy street. Blood streamed down their filthy legs** mixing with the slimy wet clay that sucked at their feet. Beaten and bruised, they were obviously starved, many drooping shadows of their former selves.

Alongside, a few braves prodded and shoved them forward.**

Ahead of the tortured captives, seven braves leapt and jumped for sheer joy. In one hand, each carried long poles with many small hairy hoops, dangling from their braided tethers, and decorated with feathers or occasional severed fingers. The scalps rose, fell, and twisted with the feathers in the cold December wind, like leaves on a blustery day. Occasionally, the fingers appeared to grasp onto the poles for dear life before, lifeless, they separated to grope the air once more. In the warrior's other hand, each brandished their musket or tomahawk, yelping and calling as they came into view.

Behind the group of tattered prisoners, other braves paraded. One held a young boy in buckskins on his shoulders, brandishing his tomahawk-pipe in one hand and his musket held high in the other. His screams joined in the triumphal chorus with his brothers. The child's hands clasped tightly, interlocked around the warrior's forehead. He bounced along happily, enjoying the view from the safety of his lofty perch.

Both Johns silently observed Hamilton sitting, laughing, and nonchalantly chatting with his men as the dreadfully mangled and emaciated prisoners trudged their way wearily forward. Hamilton monitored their approach, looking indirectly down the hill with cold disdain. DeJean could be seen counting the prisoners and recording their number with a charcoal stick on a small sheet, which he stuffed in his side pocket.

British Rangers pushed the crowd back to allow the bedraggled party to funnel towards the commons area and to reach the ceremonial pole, which would officially end their perilous journey with their captors. At that point, the British would assume full responsibility for the prisoners. Hamilton gave a signal for the cannon to be loaded. The wad, powder, and fuse in place, he haughtily signaled.

German=this font   English=this font   *French=this font*   *Delaware=this font*

The shout of "fire" preceded a deafening roar, at which point the Indians raised a horrendous shout to be echoed by every British soldier to a man, who waved their hats shrieking tremendous huzzahs.** The rest of the crowd observed the ceremony in silence. Occasionally, one could detect someone speaking an aside in the crowd, but only the Indians and the British screamed with glee as the men presented their trophy scalps to Hamilton, who quickly handed them off to subordinates.

"Dear God, they are 'like sheep to slaughter',"** John Leeth said, just loud enough for Jonas to hear. Rage fairly raised his hair.**

"Yes, my friend. Truly, we are civilized. Aren't we?"

"I've got to get out of here. If I don't, I'll stuff the governor's sneering smile up his pompous ass," John hissed. Jonas flashed a warning look at him. The crowd had ears. Disgusted, John turned and worked his way back through the observers.

John Coutincinau turned aside to let the two younger men pass.

As John Leeth and Jonas Schindler re-entered the alley, Leeth spoke again. "Those poor wretches. God help them."

"I could use a drink." Jonas answered.

"No drinks, for me. If I lose control, I'll kill the bloody British bastards... starting first with Hamilton."

Jonas evaluated John. He had seldom heard his friend swear. He generally spoke in a most civil manner. "Watch your tongue, John, or it'll be more than haven' no pass that'll be your trouble. Even the buildings in this town have ears."

Back in the crowd, John Coutincinau's attention felt drawn to one individual. She stood taller and prouder than any of those about her. Unlike the others, her head was held high. She had a small towhead crooked in one arm, sitting on her shoulder. Her other arm supported a hobbling, larger, haggard woman, who she supported with the help of another frailer woman. However, John suspected that in reality, she supported everyone.

In the crowd, another man stood silently watching. He had also noticed the tall dark one. When his master, James May, turned to leave, Pompey reluctantly went with him.

"You know, mon ami, I think we had best go trapping in the morning. I have no stomach for anymore of this. The rum and all is not worth it," Pierre Manseur observed.

"Wait. Pierre, regard the black one." John nudged his friend.

"Mais oui! That's a strong one, eh."

"Strong, yes. But look at her. Dat one, she is a dark pearl. A queen, dat one. She could make a man's loins sing."

Pierre elbowed his friend. *"The poor woman's damn near dead, filthy and covered with mud and blood, and you are thinking how to bed her. You are one strange fellow, John Coutincinau."*

"Oui, that I am, mon ami. That I am. You know, Pierre, I think

---

German=this font   English=this font   *French=this font*   *Delaware=this font*

Father Bocquet is trying to get my attention. You go ahead. I will join you later."

With that, the two Frenchmen separated, leaving the British to celebrate their glorious victory with their native allies. On the morrow, the two Frenchmen would leave for Arbor le Croche. They had ignored the call of the beaver too long. They would return come spring.

Jeffries, Ewel, *A Short Biography of John Leeth, Giving a Brief Account of His Travels and Sufferings Among the Indians for Eighteen Years Together With His Religious Exercises From His Own Relations* **(Lancaster, Ohio: Gazette Office, 1891) as related by Thwaites, Ruben Gold, Ed., *A Short Biography of John Leeth with an account of his life among the Indians* **(New York: Benjamin Blom Inc., 1972). Closely paraphrased description of the prisoners entry by Leeth on p. 33-34 Quotes p. 34. An unnamed young silversmith is mentioned by Leeth, author's license substituted the researched young silversmith, the very real Jonas Schindler. It is very apparent from Leeth's writings that he is essentially a gentle man, but his desire to murder Hamilton is very clear. He states:** *"To see those poor creatures dragged, like sheep to the slaughter along the British lines, caused my heart to shrink with throbbings, and my hair to raise with rage; if ever I committed murder in my heart, it was then, for if I had had an opportunity, and been supported with strength, I should certainly have killed the Governor, who seemed to take great delight in the exhibition."* **p. 34. We are totally indebted to John Leeth for his description of prisoners entering British Fort Detroit.**

German=this font   English=this font   ***French=this font***   *Delaware=this font*

Chapter 11   Late December 1777

"Staunton, 9th Dec. 1777

"...On my arrival at Fort Randolph the 18th. ult., I was much concerned to hear that Cornstalk, his son, the Red Hawk's son & another Indian had been murdered by the militia, tho' in close confinement in the garrison, more especially as the Cornstalk appeared to be the most active of his nation to promote peace....It would be vain for me to bring the perpetrators of this horrid act to justice at this time, therefore must comfort myself with giving your Exc. this detail..."

From a letter of Rebel Commander of Fort Pitt, General Edward Hand to Governor Patrick Henry as quoted in *Frontier Defense of the Upper Ohio, 1777-1778*, Edited by Reuben Gold Thwaites and Louise Phelps Kellogg (Madison, WI: Wisconsin Historical Society, 1912), p. 175-177. Compiled from the Draper Manuscripts in the Library of the Wisconsin Society and published at the charge of the Wisconsin Society of the Sons of the American Revolution.

At the Dibert Homestead, Bedford, Pennsylvania

Molly stood, satchel in hand, at the open door of the John Dibert residence. Older, more grayed over time, one section of the cabin still bore touches of charcoal where part of the original home had burned during two earlier raids. The cabin gave the appearance of a kind old woman who bore the marks of time but still emanated warmth.

Part of Molly felt extremely resentful to be a servant to breeds, and part of her remembered the warmth of Eve and Ene Dibert when Molly had staggered to their home after the Earnest raid. Those two parts battled simultaneously within her.

John stood with the youngest, Susannah, in his arms and the other four children huddled behind him. His mother, Mere Eve, busied herself about the hearth. The children peered at Molly, resembling a nest of baby owls. Ene lay ill, dozing quietly amongst her quilts.

Abruptly, Onkel Jac gave Molly a nudge from behind to allow him to enter the cabin as well. In one hand, he had a small flax wheel. In the other, a large cloth sack packed with tow from the Earnest attic. He limped over to the fireplace, setting the wheel in an area relatively free of clutter. Kicking a tiny corn-husk doll aside, he winced.

"Brought flax, so her hands will not be idle when you have no need of her." Jac plunked the flax wheel down with little ceremony and laid the tow along the side away from the fire. "When she has this spun all up, we will bring some more up." He spoke down to the Mere Eve and John as if they stood at least three foot shorter than he.

This prickled John's Huguenot pride. His eyes narrowed perceptively. Mere Eve, however, knew how to kill with kindness. So, laying a cautioning hand on her son's arm, she spoke up.

"Now, that is very thoughtful of you, Mister Emler. I do not know how much time the girl will have, but we appreciate you improving her state of industry." Her German halted in fits and starts, but she could be readily understood by Jac. She took Molly's small satchel from her and motioned to a new wooden hook on the wall. "You might put your shawl up there, Molly, on your hook. It is the new one." Then she handed off the satchel to David, who scooted up the ladder with it into the loft before she turned once more to Jac Emler.

"Will you have time for tea and a biscuit?"

Eve's hospitality in the face of his Palatine gruffness took Jac down a foot, but not nearly enough to associate with what he considered low-lifes. As Jac noted John's high cheekbones and the wiry hair on the youngest girl, his revulsion arose to anything that even hinted of savage blood.

"Thank you, I must be away." The 'thank you' smacked of artificial formality. He did not offer to see Molly at Christmastide. Nor did he offer to fetch her to see her brothers from time to time. Without so much as a whisper, a nod, or a fare-you-well, Jac Emler left Molly standing awkwardly.

Molly did not turn to wave good-bye to him, sensing that he had shaken off another problem, nothing more. She let her mother's oversized shawl, which hung much too heavily over her young shoulders, slip free. Lifting its cumbersome weight, she placed it on her hook and turned to face her employers.

"We speak mostly English and French in this house, Molly. My German is a mite halting so if you do not understand, please ask again." The German indeed buckled and bent awkwardly, but warmth hung on John's words. Susannah grinned and leaned forward, reaching out her tiny arms to Molly, who took her gladly.

Molly appreciated the breaking up of a horribly awkward moment. She delighted that she now had something for her hands to do. The softness of the young one's spiky hair surprised her. Molly instinctively nestled her chin into it, cuddling and enjoying the feel of a child once more. It reminded her so much of Mikie, although she tried very hard not to associate the two in her mind. Pain accompanied that association which might be too great for her to withstand.

"I speak a little English," Molly ventured.

"My God, son, look at her. What have they been feeding her?" Mere Eve spoke softly in French to John.

German=this font   English=this font   *French=this font*   *Delaware=this font*

"More likely what have they not fed her?" John glared once more after the departed figure.

"They would never deliberately starve her, son. She probably has been too heartsick to eat."

"We were just going to have tea." Mere Eve shifted to English, smiling broadly at Molly.

"Grandmere, we just—" before Elizabeth could say another word, Mere Eve's eye contact silenced the child and young Ene grasped her shoulder. "Wash up your hands, Elizabeth and Barbara. Molly, watch the little one while I get some biscuits and honey to go with our tea." Recognizing that David's curiosity probably had gotten the better of him, she hollered up to the loft, ***"David, now them things is Molly's, and they are not any of your affair."***

In moments, the healing laughter of children in a loving home began to envelope Molly, who continued to cuddle Susannah. Molly just could not let her go, nor Susannah, Molly. Like a new toy, Susannah delighted in twirling her tiny fingers in Molly's hair and investigating all of her various facial orifices. Up her nose, in her ears, gently deflected near her eyes, Molly's practiced manner deftly permitted curiosity without pain. As she drank her tea and welcomed the sweetness of the honey on her tongue, she did not notice that she ate the lion's share while trying to answer a dozen questions in makeshift English from her new younger charges. But John did.

Fort Detroit

Father Bocquet stood waiting patiently in Hamilton's office. At seventy-four, the Recollect priest bore many visible signs of hardship and a lifetime of service to his flock. As one of only four priests serving the British occupation area from Michilimackinac to the Mississippi, he fought constantly to support and to shepherd his French flock. However, in spite of his boast that his 'old hulk was still staunch',* his recent fall meant he needed a cane to steady himself, and his voice shook as his strength continued to fail him. Aided by Coutincinau's support and his ability to translate for him, Father Bocquet proved more than ready to approach the haughty Hamilton.

"Yes, Bocquet?" Hamilton, a rigid Anglican, could not bring himself to call the man 'Father' and utterly refused to extend this small courtesy. The omission of the priest's title served as one way to remind Bocquet of Hamilton and England's authority. Under the sixth Article of Capitulation after the surrender of Quebec proposed by de Ramesy, the inhabitants of Quebec, who were Roman Catholic, were allowed to exercise their

---

*As quoted by George Pare in *The Catholic Church in Detroit 1701-1888* (Detroit, MI: Gabriel Richard Press), p. 227.

German=this font   English=this font   ***French=this font***   *Delaware=this font*

religion. Hamilton followed this article begrudgingly. Hamilton's strong distaste for this churchman and his Church stuck out like erect porcupine quills, highly noticeable to those present.

"Tell him we have come to speak on the behalf of his new prisoners."

Coutincinau translated the statement.

"Ask him, whatever for? We are seeing to their needs."

"Asking the poor starved souls to stand in line while his Minister of Justice grills..." Father Bocquet paused and then selected a less offensive approach. *"No say—before the Minister investigates their place of capture and their family, we could address their needs tomorrow or the day after. Now, they appear very tired."* He paused a second time adding, *"John, be sure you have humble in your voice."*

Again Coutincinau translated the Father's concerns with tact.

"In good time, Bocquet. First things first. Everything is a matter of timing." Hamilton, even given his weak ability in French, began to feel that what was being translated did not necessarily match what he initially heard from the priest. Accents in the new world differed markedly from his training and made it harder for him to discern what was being said with absolute ease. He felt a little like Chaucer's Prioress, whose French resembled only the French spoken within the London suburbs and therefore proved useless to those who spoke proper Parisian French.

"He stalls, Father, saying this is not a good time. First things first, he says," Coutincinau translated. *"Their suffering is no issue to him."*

"Yes, to be assured, Gov. Hamilton. But perhaps you might get more information for the Crown if you consider their basic needs first. Indeed, they might speak more freely if less exhausted." Father Bocquet spoke deliberately, selecting his words very carefully. He could never be sure just how much Hamilton understood, since he knew the man knew something of French. *"Surely if you wish to continue to attract the Rebel defectors, your humane civilized treatment would not go unnoticed."*

When relayed in English, Hamilton saw that the old priest might, indeed, have a valid point. Hamilton looked up and gave the man his fullest attention for the first time since the aging priest and Coutincinau had entered the room.

"And what would he suggest?"

"My parish members could feed them." Bocquet instinctively knew this would appeal to Hamilton, as his prisoners would be no expense to the Indian Department for a few more days. *"And they could sleep on the church pews tonight and tomorrow. By Monday morning, their condition might be markedly improved to meet your needs."* Father Bocquet felt disgusted that he had to guise his remarks in such a fashion which did not appeal to man's humane instincts but rather to some

German=this font   English=this font   *French=this font*   *Delaware=this font*

baser cause. Given that Father Bocquet understood men, it seemed to be the only usable approach. The translation went smoothly. Coutincinau stressed the advantages well.

Hamilton swept the side of his face absentmindedly with the feathers of his writing quill, ruminating on the priest's suggestion. Deciding that it was not without merit, he selected a paper and wrote up the order for its implementation.

"Here, Coutincinau. Let the parish see to their needs. However, we will begin to take those most fit tomorrow to see DeJean."

Father Bocquet took the paper listening to Coutincinau's response.

"But tell him it is Sunday," Father Bocquet responded.

Coutincinau put the Father's response in the form of a question, short on the heels of Bocquet's response. "Will you still desire to see some of them even on Sunday?"

"That is workable. DeJean has less tasks on Sunday." Hamilton could care less if DeJean was forced to miss mass.

Hearing Hamilton's translation, Father Bocquet left the office before the winds of chance blew another direction. He would send John to the May's home. Mistress May had two large iron kettles suitable to heat water for baths and the metal hangers to hold them over a fire in the yard, the blessing and trappings of being the blacksmith's wife. May's big slave, Pompey, and John could easily fetch them down.

When Eve, Sue Ellen, and Anne were herded into Ste. Anne's Roman Catholic Church with the others, they looked around their surroundings with varying degrees of interest. Sue Ellen dropped to her knees in the aisle, crossing herself and giving way to tears. Anne looked about her at the beams, smoke-stained by candles that graced the sconces beside the Stations of the Cross. The main altar glistened in golden candlelight and shimmered in the light from the votive candles at each side altar. A small statue of the Blessed Virgin and a few other saints unknown to Anne and Eve looked on.

Father Bocquet slowly levered himself from pew to pew through the church amongst the women who stood or sat in small groups. Jean Baptiste Roucout, the parish schoolmaster, joined him to function as translator for those who spoke no French. Something said to the men that the women had heard too many shouts, too many orders bellowed, and that quietness would be more tolerable. When Jean Baptiste approached Anne, Eve, and Sue Ellen, who now held Mikie, he spoke in a soothing way.

"We welcome youz," the overtones of French glazed each word, "to our humble parish. The women of our Parish are going to bring items so you may bathe. Are any among you strong enough to carry water from the River to heat?"

"I be." Anne spoke up. Even though she ached to the bone, the thought of water to bathe renewed her strength. Warm water smacked of heaven on earth.

German=this font   English=this font   *French=this font*   *Delaware=this font*

"He asks your name, my child."

"I be Anne Wylie." She paused, "But you tell him, I be no child of his."

Immediately, Father Bocquet sensed her deep pride in herself and her people, even without the translation. "Tell her, Jean Baptiste, that God's children are my children," he answered, smiling as if the question had come phrased dozens of ways and hundreds of times before to him. Anne contained her surprise as Father Bocquet reached up and, without asking or seeking permission, blessed her forehead with a small sign of the cross and ascertained her temperature in one synchronized movement. Usually, she would have pulled herself away abruptly. This time, she did not. Then he turned her head by grasping her chin gently to check for bruises. Again to Anne's surprise, she did not pull away.

"Ask her why she has fewer bruises than many of her sisters?"

"Father Bocquet wants to know why you have fewer bruises than the others, good woman."

Anne smiled. "Tell him, I hit 'em back."

Taking both her hands in his, passing his thumbs tenderly over the rich brown surface, Father Bocquet observed even in the poor light that her knuckles were swollen, bruised and covered with small cuts. Her forearms had bruises and scrapes from warding off blows in the gauntlet runs.

Father Bocquet smiled, releasing her hands. *"Not one to turn the other cheek, eh Jean?"* His response did not hint any displeasure or condemnation, but rather, in fact, indicated respect.

The Father continued to function like a war surgeon, looking closely at the women before him. *"Ask this one if her child is ill."*

"Father wants to know is your baby ill?"

"No, he's fine. You tell the Father that he's just plumb tuckered and hungry. But I ain't his Mutti, she is." Sue Ellen nodded toward Eve, who held the edge of the pew, her knuckles white with effort to remain standing.

"You best sit down here." Father Bocquet guided Eve into the pew, pushing the kneeling board aside. *"Does she speak English?"* He looked to Anne and Sue Ellen more than directing his question to Eve, having noted Sue Ellen's use of Mutti.

"Does she speak only German?" Jean Baptiste asked.

"No, I speak English too." Eve, who had never met a priest in her life, evaluated the old weathered man in his long black gown, answering him directly before either woman responded. His manners appeared curious to her, but he did not look at all like the devil's spawn which had been her father's summary of the Roman priesthood.

"Good, it's easier. And you, my child, we saw you limping on your approach." Jean quickly translated for Father Bocquet, who extended his hand, blessed Eve, and felt her forehead. Fever raged. Observant, he noticed the bloody pocket staining the front of her apron and

German=this font   English=this font   *French=this font*   *Delaware=this font*

associated this with the paleness of her nails in the hands that draped over the pew ahead of her.

"Tell the Father Eve lost a baby." Sue Ellen blurted.

Eve's head snapped towards her. Simultaneously, a flash of guilt and anger floated across Eve's face like a leaf on a reflecting pool. She had not intended that information for this man.

Sue Ellen shifted the baby uncomfortably.

Eve felt ill at ease about hearing her problems aired so openly. Jean Baptiste, in turn, felt even more uncomfortable translating it for the aged priest. The flash of anger and guilt dissolved immediately, but the reaction had not escaped Father Bocquet's attentiveness.

"Tell this Eve, a woman of this parish, a metisse, has great skill in womanly things. She does not charge like Dr. Antron. Ask if her services would be acceptable. Be gentle, Jean. She is in pain both spiritually and bodily. Understand?"

Jean Baptiste nodded affirmatively.

"Father says, that in our parish, a metisse, has great skill in womanly things. She does not charge like Dr. Antron. He wants to know if you will accept her help?"

"A metisse?" The word sounded unfamiliar to Eve. She reached up to retrieve Mikie, settling him to her lap. She wiped the matted hair from his sleeping face, cuddling him close to her.

"She is Chippewa and French. We would not wish to bring either of you offense, my child, given your trials in recent days."

Eve's answer surprised even her. She had never tried to articulate her thoughts until that very moment. The words came directly and spontaneously. "Tell the Father not all Indians are cruel. I would be thankful for her help."

Sensing her reply from her demeanor, Father Bocquet quickly responded before he heard the translation. *"Tell her that God has blessed her with wisdom early in her life's journey. We will send word to fetch Martha."*

As Jean Baptiste began to translate the Father's response to Eve, Father Bocquet blessed Eve and Mikie. Giving a weary sigh, he turned to Sue Ellen.

"And your name, my child?" Jean Baptiste asked, after finishing Father's remarks to Eve.

Sue Ellen felt clammy and cold to the touch. Father took in the mazes of overlapping bruises on her face and arms, turning her face from side to side. The fair ones often took the blunt of the punishment in the gauntlets. She was typical.

Sue Ellen murmured a tiny portion of mass in response to his touch. Hearing the smatterings of an early faith, he laid his hand upon her head briefly, and in Latin intoned a blessing. She acknowledged this by crossing herself. When she lifted her stained face, two pale pink and blue trails ran from her eyes to her chin.

German=this font   English=this font   *French=this font*   *Delaware=this font*

"Thank you. God be with you, Father."

"And with you. You are most welcome, my child, for what little I can do." He answered her in a mix of Latin and French. *"Tell the one called Anne that she will find buckets and a yoke just outside the door."* Then Father Bocquet and Jean Baptiste moved on to another small group. Shaking his head sadly, Father Bocquet spoke an aside to Jean Baptiste. *"To think that they call them weak for they are but women."*

Jean Baptiste steadied his priest. He nodded, affirming his sad agreement to the Father's ironic understatement.

Sue Ellen started to follow Anne, when Anne stopped her. "You know you be as tired as the babe. You stay with Eve." Sue Ellen smiled as she pulled the tattered shawl away from her own shoulders. Sue Ellen placed it tenderly around Anne's shoulders. Anne tucked Sue Ellen's shawl into her shirt waist and slipped out into the wet and cold.

As Anne lifted the yoke to her shoulders, a deep baritone voice fairly purred to her, "Mon brown beauty, permit Coutincinau to help you." Anne cocked her head questioningly at the devilishly handsome man, who stood before her with his hands on his hips. Each word was overlaid with heavy French accents. His sexual warmth radiated from his smile, beginning at the top of his curly head and continuing down his stocky body to his feet spread provocatively before her. While she might have a half a head or more on him in height, Anne quickly realized that the short burly man before her exuded strength and virility. He obviously appeared quite taken with her.

"I don't need no help. I be strong," Anne growled. How the damn love-sick fool could even look at her totally perplexed her. Anne knew she looked absolutely wretched.

"Strong yes, brown beauty. Proud too. Of that Coutincinau has absolutely no doubt. Let me introduce myself. I am Jean Baptiste Coutincinau. But they call me John for short…which I assure you I am not." The last words accompanied a wave of his index finger in a no-no motion. Already, his mischievous nature revealed itself, for Coutincinau loved being a master of double entendre. And then, as if Anne had never refused his help, he gently removed the yoke from her shoulders. "Let me assist you or stay here with the women if you prefer." His smile left Anne with little doubt what she would elect to do. She walked with him down to the river and back, again and yet again, until both huge kettles were filled completely.

Pompey also watched the young negress with interest. She had not observed him bringing the kettles, nor had she been aware of his presence as she worked with Coutincinau. Anne only had eyes for the rugged Frenchman. Maybe next time she would notice him, he lamented silently. After all, he was much stronger and far taller than Coutincinau.

By evening's fall, the kettles that hung over the fires brimmed with hot water. The body heat of the prisoners had brought a certain degree of

German=this font   English=this font   *French=this font*   *Delaware=this font*

comfort to the interior of Ste. Anne's. The priest and his schoolmaster had discreetly disappeared. The women of the parish had left supplies before returning to their families. When the first steaming basin sat invitingly on the pew with a fresh brown orb of soap and a small towel, the women stood about it in absolute reverent silence. Sue Ellen broke the spell.

"Anne, you go first. You helped to brung up the most of it."

Mistress Smythe began to object. "But Sue Ellen, she is a..." She never finished her sentence. Censuring eyes to a person brought her up short. Even Margaret's eyes expressed disapproval.

Anne looked round the circle, before she shyly stepped forward. The women turned their backs to her, creating an illusion of privacy. Anne dipped her swollen hands into the warm water. For the very first time since her capture, she cried soundlessly. Her shoulders shook with her silent sobs. Rolling the hard ball of soap in her hands, she refused to wince at the small discomfort from the traces of lye. She slipped from her clothes. Ripping a small piece from her skirt, she bathed her privates and picked the lice free that nestled in the tight spring-like curls before squishing the nits in her fingers. She repeated the procedure for her armpits. Soaping her short cropped hair, she rubbed and rinsed it as hard as she could with the water that now began to ripple with bubbles over the surface before smearing her head and crotch with lard. Wiping her face, she sat on the bench and wiped down her arms and legs one at a time before drying each one. Then setting the basin on the ground, she put her cut, swollen feet into the lukewarm sudsy water. She winced and bit her tongue, so no sound escaped as she pulled the latest thorns from her torn feet. As she placed her feet in the basin for one final time, her deep audible sigh of pleasure freed the conversation about her.

"What yah doin' in there Anne?" Sue Ellen sing-songed her question, drawing giggles from those about her.

"You know you do not have to wash the little critters' backs, Anne."

"How much hide have you got left fer pity sakes?" The women took turns around the circle. Good humor cracked like a whip.

"That brown ain't all goonah' come off there, woman."

That one brought a deep chuckle from Anne.

"Save some soap for me, gal."

The girl within had not died. Occasional giggles and laughter flickered back and forth among the pews and around the bathing circles, like the candlelight that splayed in irregular changing patterns across the ceiling. Often, the laughter like the light would fade and then suddenly break forth in a whole new way. One by one, the women kept the three basins filled and emptied. The little ones submitted willingly to the warmth of a bath with a few smiles and giggles. The festivities ended as each woman bedded down, sharing the few blankets provided. No matter what the morning light would bring, soap and water had renewed their spirits. Fresh Johnny bread and a dab of beans invited a deep sleep.

German=this font   English=this font   *French=this font*   *Delaware=this font*

Martha, the metisse, had advised all of them to eat just a tiny bit so they would not be ill come morning. For most, this choice proved irrelevant. Their mouths had become entirely too sore to do otherwise. Teeth had loosened in their sockets. To swallow was difficult. Many simply held hot cups of slippery elm tea laced with sassafras in their hands, drawing the warmth within with tiny bird-like sips. The jellied brew brought comfort to stomachs deprived so long of adequate food. Martha also brought a strong willow tonic which she shared with those in need. Quickly, her midwifery skills addressed their needs.

The tonic reminded Eve of Eve Dibert's tea for Mikie. Eve drank her cup of half tonic and half tea slowly. She ignored the bitter aftertaste.

Sue Ellen paired with another waif-like young woman. They slept spoon fashion on two neighboring pews to share their blanket.

Anne, Eve and Mikie shared another blanket. They elected to sleep on the floor. The basin in the pew above their heads remained drained and empty, as drained and as empty as Eve. Where was her little Henry this night? Was he as warm as she? Would he think that she had deserted him? Would Stalking Wolf protect him? Would she ever get him back? She prayed Margaret's faith in the British justice system would prove true. She remembered the officer's wink at her when she told him that she preferred to stay behind with the Indians and both her sons rather than leave Henry behind alone.* The officer totally ignored her wishes, saying simply "'just come',"* as he pulled Mikie and her gruffly away to rejoin the others. Filled with many doubts and fears, Eve's attention drifted toward the votive candles that flickered at the front of the church. She listened to her friends' breathing and their restless snores as they slept about her. Hours passed before exhaustion silenced her repetitive questions.

In an inn near Fogherty's, John Coutincinau reflected on Anne's image before he drifted off to sleep. He remembered well the ripples of her muscles, the full breasts, the long lithe legs, the beautiful face and the smile that crackled around her eyes on their fourth trek to the river. Her laughter still rang in his ears after their eighth trek to the river. He had only to close his eyes, and he could see her deep brown eyes and the long lashes that dropped over them with a coquette's shyness. However, as she bent to lift the buckets to the yoke, she deliberately exposed a little more breast to his longing view. When he told her to watch for his return just before the ice left the river come spring, she looked at him as though he were truly crazy. When he pressed his last gold guinea into her hands as he left her, her eyes opened wide with total astonishment. He prayed that she would remember him come spring and that the gods of the beaver would bless him with many pelts, so he could dress her well upon his return. A beautiful, exotic woman such as Anne should have beautiful things, he

---

*Replogle, Emma. *Indian Eve and Her Descendants* (1911. Bedford, PA: Reprinted by Messiah Lutheran Church, 1990), p. 20.

German=this font   English=this font   *French=this font*   *Delaware=this font*

reasoned. The thoughts of her brought warmth to his loins, making him feel much like a foolish young man with vivid sensual dreams and an undisciplined body. He longed to hold her in his arms, reckoning that her passion could be as great as his own. His partner's teasing went unheeded. He knew that he would be dead on his feet carrying a full pack of winter supplies come the morning after working so hard this evening. But every moment of struggle would be worth it and more for just one moment with Anne. Trying at first to ignore his full erection, he debated and then disobeyed the good Father's admonitions against mortal sin. His dreams proved pleasant.

Minister of Justice Office   Fort Detroit, Sunday

Sue Ellen shifted her weight uneasily from one foot to another. She held her hands before her clasped low. Her eyes rarely looked up. A fire burned brightly in the fireplace but warmed her only slightly.

"Now, your given name."

"Sue Ellen."

"Your complete name." DeJean frowned up at her. Holding his quill, he made a large blot on his ledger. He wrinkled his forehead with displeasure and returned the quill to its holder. Taking powder, he sprinkled it on to the surface to absorb his ink spill; and then with his penknife, he neatly scraped it aside. He kept a neat ledger.

"Your complete name. Are you deaf, young woman?"

When Sue Ellen delayed in answering him, he looked very severely at her. "Woman, I need your family name so we can contact your family for the fees to release you."

"No...no family left...sir." She did not look up. "I gots no one tah pay fer me keep."

DeJean looked at her somewhat skeptically. There was something in her manner that somehow did not fully convince him. "Where did your family fight our forces?"

A touch of temper edged her response. "My family was ambushed working their fields near Frankstown."

DeJean entered, "Sue Ellen—Frankstown, Pennsylvania." He sensed that for some reason she would not or could not share her last name. "You will be a slop woman at Fogherty's. Your wages will be paid to me, to be credited to the crown after you pay for board and room." She might be a little pretty once she healed up, he thought. Maybe she could earn extras on the side there. He smiled at her with touches of lechery around his eyes.

He dismissed her with a wave of his hand. "Next."

"I be Anne Wylie. I ain't no slave. I be free." Anne stated her answer before the Minister of Justice, DeJean, asked his questions.

German=this font   English=this font   *French=this font*   *Delaware=this font*

DeJean lifted his eyebrows and then narrowed his eyes. Pinching the bridge of his nose to alleviate the strain, he answered disdainfully, "That may have been before your capture but not now. All of you are *esclaves* now. You belong in the crown's care."

Anne glared at him. Though unfamiliar with the meaning of the French word, she knew deep down the total connotation. Her capture had rendered her a slave, no matter what they called her. Her color would make it nearly impossible to re-establish her freeborn status. She knew in that very instant that the vermin that sat behind his desk playing the part of a so-called minister of justice represented only injustice. Loathing and contempt for him flooded her features.

DeJean flushed momentarily as a veritable tide of her disgust washed over him. His hide had thickened with his duties, but this one impacted him. He reviewed the list of possible employers, who might take prisoners. He remembered Abbot and Finchley's request for a strong back to load and reload supply ships for their store. This black bitch would be perfect. The last prisoner that he had sent up had lasted only six months before he fell and became totally useless. Maybe this one would last a little longer.

"You will work for Abbot and Finchley. Your salary will be paid to the crown to pay for your keep. You will stay at Yankee Hall if Finchley cannot provide bed and board. That is, but of course, unless you have a benefactor whom we can contact to secure your release." As DeJean spoke, the last statement dripped with rank condescension. Anne and he both knew that she had no one rich enough to pay for her. He relished rubbing it in her face like lye ashes. "The Ranger will take you up." His smile strained through his gray and blackened teeth.

"Next. Your name, please."

"My name is Margaret Elder, Mistress George Elder. I would like to bring to your attention that I expect protection as promised by Major Hay under the crown as one of His Majesty's subjects."

DeJean, if he was to have been dutifully impressed, showed no outward sign of it, which brought wrinkles of consternation to Margaret's features.

"Did you hear me, sir?"

"Yes, Mistress Elder."

Neither spoke for a short period.

"And who will pay for your keep and your release?"

"Pay?" If Margaret had taken a full blow to the gut, DeJean's question could not have hit her any harder.

"Major Hay promised me protection." This time Margaret protested but with considerably less authority in her voice.

"And I presume since you are standing here, Mistress Elder, that he gave you that protection. Now I repeat...who will pay for your keep?"

Margaret's shoulders drooped perceptively. She thought for a moment. Her husband George and her husband's family barely scratched out a living. Perhaps her father's and brother's, she considered. Then squaring her shoulders, she answered quietly. "The Cessna family of Cumberland Valley Township in Pennsylvania." Then she dropped her gaze to the floor.

"Do you know how to spell Cessna?"

"C, e, double s, n, a." Margaret answered.

"The officers' quarters has need of a cook, Mistress Elder. Can you cook?"

Margaret looked up. "Yes, Master DeJean, I can cook!" This time a little fire had returned to Margaret's composure.

DeJean wondered for a fleeting moment if she considered boiling him in a kettle over a fire.

"Until we receive the payment, you can begin to earn your keep with us. You will stay off the kitchen." Smiling one of his most sickeningly sweet smiles, he waved her aside.

When DeJean looked up next, he was dismayed to note that Stalking Wolf stood beside Eve. Eve waited her turn quietly. A veritable cyclone of thoughts whirled and ripped within, so she seemed detached and mentally apart from the office. However, Mikie's little head proved quite animated as he twisted and turned in his mother's arms to look over every detail in the small, well-appointed office. His curiosity, revived by food and a good night's rest, brought an alert quality to his eyes which contrasted totally with his mother's composure.

"You know, Stalking Wolf, we would prefer that you and your tribal members did not come into this office!"

Stalking Wolf nodded. "The visit is necessary."

"And just what do you deem so necessary?"

"This woman can tell you that we killed three of her men, but we only have one scalp."

"You know, Stalking Wolf, that the English have an old saying, 'finders keepers, losers weepers'."

Stalking Wolf glared. "Tell him woman!" Stalking Wolf pushed Eve none to gently.

"This man speaks the truth. He does not have two of the scalps from those he killed. He also has taken my other son." Eve juggled Mikie and readjusted his weight as he wriggled.

"And why do you not have the scalps to prove your kills, Stalking Wolf?"

Prodded again, Eve answered. "I hid them in the bureau." Then she paused and she continued looking at DeJean rather pointedly. "He has stolen my other son, Henry."

"And, I suppose, you expect extra credits for goods for your service to the Crown, Stalking Wolf?"

Stalking Wolf nodded affirmatively to the question that DeJean directed to him. Eve, ignored by DeJean, tapped her foot and frowned.

"What is your name, woman?" DeJean looked down at his ledger.

German=this font   English=this font   *French=this font*   *Delaware=this font*

"My name is Eve Earnest, wife of the late Henry Adam Earnest, whose scalp you may or may not elect to pay this man for."

DeJean's head raised.

"Woman, we do not pay for scalps. We urge humane treatment. If it were not so, you would not be here," he replied disdainfully. His bland reply hinted at a well-rehearsed response, one spoken on more than one occasion.

DeJean carefully inspected the woman who stood before him. Typical Germanic type, he decided. Sturdy, broad-hipped, broad shoulders, plain featured, high forehead, brown hair freshly braided and ringing her head, and given her accent, somewhat intelligent, for she obviously spoke two languages. She represented a fairly typical woman of her peasant class. He understood her English though it was heavily accented. Pale and obviously thinner than she had been in the past, her chemise hung in loose folds over her still ample breasts. DeJean slyly grinned as he imagined what it would be like to take both of his hands to encircle one of those soft mounds.

Eve scowled at his unspoken evaluation of her. Her foot tapped with greater frequency.

"The boy's name?" DeJean pointed at Michael.

"This son's name is Michael Earnest. My other son's name is Henry Earnest."

Eve watched with growing apprehension as she observed that the man put only one name in the ledger beside her name. Her foot stopped tapping.

"And where were you captured?"

"Near Dunnings Creek, north of Bedford, Pennsylvania with my two sons," she answered, but her voice sounded detached again and displaced, as if it came from another corner of the room.

"Who will pay your keep?"

Eve did not answer him. Her Onkel Jac's parting words kept intruding into her response, fighting with the two names on the ledger for her complete attention and silencing her reply. Although she could only read numbers not words, she saw clearly that only two names had been written down in what appeared to be a column of names.

"Woman, answer me. Who will pay for you?"

"Listen to me!" Eve's temper rose. "This man has my other son. He tomahawked my husband. Yes, I hid two of the scalps. So, he has stolen my other son in retaliation."

"Is the child in your arms your son?"

"Yes, of course."

"I see only one child, not two."

"Yes, but there are two sons...not just one! This...this," Eve gasped for air, "This savage has kidnapped one of my two sons!"

"Yes, I think I understand you, but your accent is very heavy. Now I ask you, one more time. Who will pay for your keep or your release?"

German=this font   English=this font   *French=this font*   *Delaware=this font*

Eve felt incredulous. This ridiculous little French quill-pusher had totally ignored her requests to have Lil' Henry returned. So much for British justice, she seethed. He acted as though Henry simply did not exist. Eve straightened her shoulders and looked at him squarely. Defiance and anger aligned her spine.

"Myself and my two sons could be paid for by my father, Eric Mens Emler, called George by the English from the country of Bedford in Pennsylvania."

"It is about time, Mistress Earnest. You have made others stand in line far too long." Pausing, he put a neat "4" beside her name. "As I see it, either your father or you will need to pay for four, one for you and your son and two for the goods that you state are due Stalking Wolf. You will work cleaning the Ranger's barracks and whatever chores this fort requires of you to pay for your board. You and your son will sleep in Yankee Hall. Other women sleep in those quarters and will assist you in caring for the child, so that your work is not impaired."

DeJean had reduced Eve to shocked silence, squelching her defiance completely. Stalking Wolf turned her and Mikie from DeJean's desk and led her out the door. For one fleeting moment, Stalking Wolf nearly regretted keeping Hanu. However, the thought of more rum, supplies, and his personal losses quickly snuffed any sympathy. As they walked past the queue, the others settled down quickly as Eve and Stalking Wolf passed. Something in Eve's countenance terrified them.

German=this font   English=this font   *French=this font*   *Delaware=this font*

Chapter 12   March 9, 1778   Following the Winter of Sevens

"The parties sent from hence have generally been successful, though the Indians have lost men enough to sharpen their resentment; they have brought in twenty-three prisoners alive, twenty of which they presented to me, and a hundred and twenty-nine scalps."

Lt. Governor Henry Hamilton reporting to Governor Guy Carleton in Quebec, January 15, 1778, as quoted by Silas Farmer, *History of Detroit and Wayne County* (Original publication 1884, republished in Salem, Massachusetts: Higgenson), p. 246.

Fort Detroit

John Leeth shuddered and shook violently. Cold, he donned his previously fever-dampened shirt from off the chair and hauled on his leggings as well before climbing back into the bed. He pulled a full mound of skins and blankets up to his chin. Shaking so hard that his teeth chattered, he struggled to fall back to sleep. Jonas Schindler watched him with mounting concern.

"Friend, I fear for you. Dis has been one hellish winter. I thought you were well past this. But good Lord man, look at you." Jonas took the small flask his landlady had earlier filled with stout tea and a touch of contraband brandy and tipped it to John's lips. "If I had known you were coming to this, we would have begged off that last drill this week."

"You, you kno-know that wou-wouldn't have worked, my ff-fff-friend." John's teeth chattered so hard he could barely speak. "Ham- Ham- Hamilton looks for any ex- ex- excuse to pen me up." Although Jonas feared contagion, he could not bear to leave his friend at a time like this. Overcome with concern more than fear, he touched his friend's forehead, finding it clammy and cool in stark contrast to his own warm hand.

A muffled rap sounded. Both men's heads snapped in direction of the door. Before Jonas could open it, William Boslick and his chum Jamie slipped inside. Boslick unwrapped his fist from the end of his scarf, which he had used to soften his knock. Outside, the morning light just pinkened the sky, heralding a bright day. No sooner had the door closed when drums began to beat, calling the militia to arms. Both men approached John Leeth as he struggled to right himself and to address the call.

"Bac' to yer sac, there John. Be Gosh and Pats, John, I've felt better dead herrings. What ails you, man?" Boslick's hand, in attempting to push John back in bed by pressing his forehead, retracted quickly.

"Jus' whar the 'ell do you think you ar' a goin' there, John?" Jamie countered. Ever the more observant of the two, he could see John was deathly ill. "Tis providence, I tell yah."

"I should go." John's chills had momentarily subsided as he struggled once more to sit up. "They're sounding the call to arms."

"Not today, John Leeth. Rumor is you'll be a draughted first. Your nam's on the top of the list. She is that, to go with the militia on the raids with Captain Hay. Yer' got the perfect excuse to stay ye here. Now doo it!" Boslick pressed on his shoulder. John, far too weak to make even the slightest resistance, settled resignedly back in his nest of blankets and fur. His teeth began to chatter once more after the exertion.

"We'll answer the call fer yah. Tell'm yer sick an' all," Jamie added. "I swear, tis providence, man. Stay here, John. Lay low and thank the Good Lord for his favors."

"Som-mme, some favors," John responded smiling weakly up at his friends.

With that, Boslick and Jamie stole out more quietly than when they had arrived. Leaving Jonas to catch up hurriedly, they all ran to answer the call to arms and to the compulsory drill.

John pulled the blanket up to his chin before turning on his side. Fear, fever, chill, and exhaustion in equal portions competed to be his masters now. Beaten, he succumbed into a troubled sleep.

Nearly two hours past midday, the door opened abruptly. The freshened air rushed to join the stale odors within the enclosed space.

John, too weak to leave the bed, had vomited on the floor beside him. In full fever, he had thrown the blanket and furs aside, lying nearly naked in the rope bed soaked with sweat and urine. His rumpled shirt and leggings lay amidst the vomit. The warm, sour odor tinged with rank ammonia made Jacob Schieffelin, Hamilton's secretary, immediately cover his nose and mouth with his handkerchief. Though the Lieutenant Governor felt thoroughly convinced that William Boslick and Jamie Cassidy had fabricated John Leeth's illness, this was no fabrication. No matter how skilled those lying rascals were, they simply did not have the pluck to stage this scenario.

The landlady, behind Schieffelin, still quaked from taking the brunt of his verbal tirade. Nothing would do until she had shown him the appropriate door and opened it. She stood silently in the hallway behind him.

German=this font   English=this font   *French=this font*   *Delaware=this font*

"Excuse me, woman. You are in my way." Schieffelin rudely shouldered past the woman, disappearing down the hall. He needed to return before the drills disbanded. Hamilton would be disappointed to learn the young man's current state of health. There was no lever here to press Leeth into service.

As the landlady reached to close the door, she could see the terrible misery of her young tenant. She devoutly hoped that his benefactor would not expect her to care for him. Latching the door, she descended the steps quickly and called to the houseboy. After she whispered her needs to the lad, he sped off down the street.

Anne Wylie had slipped away from Abbott and Finchley. The last load of furs for the afternoon had been carried down to the wharf. She knew that she could take just a moment or two to speak with Sue Ellen. Sue Ellen always saved the leftover crusts from her customer's plates until her pocket fairly bulged. Were it not for Sue Ellen, Anne would faint from hunger, since Anne often lacked for food. Her employers concentrated on output not input. They rejoiced that they had at last found someone who could work tirelessly for hours with little or no cost for victuals and who was hardy enough to stand sleeping among the packs and parcels in the unheated storeroom. DeJean's assessment of Anne to them had been accurate. Indeed, she was a strong one, an excellent beast of burden. In addition, she could navigate the muddy spring streets far better than a cart and horse. And, unlike the occasional mutt, she did not get sucked beneath the mud, either.

Sue Ellen's mistress, Ann Forsyth, knew that her comely blond charge indulged in a strange kind of charity. When Ann Forsyth noticed the tall black woman waiting in the alley across from the door as was her habit, she tried to signal Sue Ellen to tell her of the arrival of her friend. Ann Forsyth did not feel completely at ease about this situation. Sometimes, the proprietress felt that the less one involved one's self in the affairs of the prisoners, the better off one was.

Ever since Ann and her husband William had assumed the business affairs of Fogherty's, they had turned a fair profit for the owner. Ann Forsyth felt reasonably sure that Sue Ellen did not steal anything else from her employer. The loss of a few bread scraps decreased the amount of bread pudding to be served on the following week, but it had not been so much as to harm their profits. She had to admit that, strictly speaking, the bread really was not stolen as Sue Ellen had first asked for the right to withhold the scraps. In the end, the William and Ann Forsyth decided that they could afford to look the other way; even if it was for a negress. Mistress Forsyth tossed her head again in the direction of the door when she finally caught Sue Ellen's attention.

Sue Ellen quickly finished serving her table and ducked out the same door to share her cache of goodies with her friend.

"How you doin?"

"I doin fine, Sue Ellen. I doin fine." Anne gratefully took the bread

German=this font   English=this font   *French=this font*   *Delaware=this font*

scraps that Sue Ellen slipped to her and placed them in the hidden pocket that Eve had sewn from cloth remnants. The pocket fell neatly below the fullness of her hips. Little of its shape revealed itself, even when full. This insured that the stash could not be observed by either her employers or their snoop, Pierre. Anne obtained access through a very small slit several inches down from her waist tucked in a deep fold. This lower slit had been devised by Eve, so Anne's employer would be far less likely to notice the opening.

"Has he come by again?"

"Who?" Anne knew full well who the 'who' was that Sue Ellen referred to, but she refused to rise to the question.

"You know who. That big handsome buck of May's, who's been sniffing round the store like a hound after sweet meat."

"I keep tel'n you Sue Ellen, I ain't interested in that man, no how."

"But he's so handsome Anne, and big too. That one could keep even a tall woman like you warm. Gosh, he must be over six foot and a half again. And he dresses so fine." Sue Ellen sung Pompey's praises to the hilt, fairly dancing as she teased her friend.

"Look, if I told you once, I told you, I don't want to be attached to no slave man. No way, no how. You got that girl!" Anne's response showed some heat, but Sue Ellen plunged on. The sunny day had greatly enhanced her disposition.

"But, Anne, that man does writtin' and readin', and sounds so fine when he talks."

"Look, friend or no friend. You listen hard, gal. I! Be! Freeborn! You got that, woman? No child of mine is going to be born of a slave, not if I can help it. I die first!"

Seeing Anne's eyes catch fire and hearing the total conviction in her voice brought the point home, veritably slapping up Sue Ellen. Instantly deflated and taken aback by Anne's vehemence, Sue Ellen stepped back from her friend's stormy outburst.

"I'm sorry, Anne. I didn' mean no hatefulness. I just thought..." And she stopped mid-sentence as she saw a familiar figure approach them, his arms waving over his head. His back, loaded high with furs on circular frames, served as a furry halo behind his stocky figure.

"Mon Perle Noir, AAllo-oo-oo-ow."** John Coutincinau walked briskly towards the two women, who tried unsuccessfully not to draw attention to themselves. His voice carried down the street, like a loon call across the lake. The result—nearly every individual within a country mile heard his greeting and turned towards the women. "Remember me, No?"

In that very instant, Anne Wylie dissolved into a giggling coquette. She blushed through her deep rich color from head to toe. Her eyes instantly lost the fire of anger and conviction...and flared instead with awakening interest and the promise of passion. Dropping her gaze and then teasingly revealing her enormous black pupils through her lashes to John, she answered him. **"Oui,** I remember you, Jean Baptiste Coutincinau."

German=this font   English=this font   *French=this font*   *Delaware=this font*

"Ah, **Cheri**, I see you do." The distance between Anne, Sue Ellen and Coutincinau evaporated completely after his quick long strides. He filled his eyes with Anne, and she with him.

"John, this is my friend Sue Ellen," Anne stammered finally. "He helped me carry water at Ste. Anne's. Remember?"

John gave Sue Ellen a momentary glance, nodded, and then renewed his full gaze upon Anne.

Sue Ellen openly admired the stocky Frenchman. Even if he stood half a head shorter than Anne, the handsome, tanned, coureurs de bois would make any woman's heart beat faster. So, he was why Anne did not pay attention to Pompey.

"You wintered well. Your color ez much improved." He did not hesitate to turn her face from side to side and then touch her cheek with the back of his hand to spare her the rough side. She instinctively nestled against his hand as she flushed again. "No black and blue. Eh?"

"You too...." Anne dropped her lashes again in a flutter. Winter sun and exposure had tanned him a deep brown.

"I must trade these furs and then, my Anne, Coutincinau will find you and dine you...and..." his statement trailed off into a low sensual laugh. "Eh?" He raised one eyebrow, teasing her with his laugh and stroking her with searing glances filled with naked approval.

Across the street, Philip DeJean took notice of the threesome and made a mental note to stop by later to speak with Abbott or Finchley. Her employers just might be interested in knowing what else their wayward helper marketed on the streets. After all, he had recommended her to them. He reminded himself of his duty to see that Anne honored her contract completely.

James May also observed the threesome. He wondered momentarily if the tall one might be the woman that his slave, Pompey, had taken a fancy to. She would breed nicely. She looked strong enough. But she seemed to have little good sense in her choice of friends.

Each man resumed his business as Sue Ellen returned to her work. Coutincinau walked with Anne most of the way to Abbott and Finchley's warehouse before turning away to the trading area.

The woman and the child came more often, now that the sun had melted bare patches of muddy ground free from snow and ice along the shore. She would find a sun-warmed spot late in the day by the outer shed and allow the small boy to scavenge the shore. He would bring small stones, blue crab claws, empty clam shells, or fish vertebra picked clean by the persistent gulls which had recently returned. The child would gleefully lay his treasures before her on a small hanky that she perfunctorily provided and laid neatly on the freshly thawed ground.

Tchamaniked Joe watched her carefully. As he approached her, he noted her broad face streaked with fresh tears which she had smeared with the back of her callused hand, leaving a telltale yellowish-brown clay

German=this font   English=this font   **French=this font**   *Delaware=this font*

smudge behind. He observed over the winter that she had gained a little of her girth back, but her tattered clothes still hung loosely about her strong frame. She sat as usual, a piece of blanket hugged tightly about her and her arms protectively crossed across her breasts to conserve body heat. He spoke quietly, so as not to startle her as she gazed with sightless eyes into the dirt.

"*Animakwe...*" Tchamaniked Joe called softly to her in Chippewa.

Eve noticed his moccasins first and then looked up into a deeply weathered brown face. The man's eyes filled with black fire. She had sensed his presence even before he spoke and had noted that he had observed her many times before when she came with Mikie to the smaller boatyard near the base of the fort. In the past, the Indian man had kept a respectful distance from her while letting Mikie observe him at work. Sometimes he gave Mikie bits of birchbark or tiny animals that he had carved with his crooked knife and listened to his broken English and German prattle. He never spoke sharply to Mikie. Even his small yappy dog permitted Mikie to pet him and hunkered flat, tolerating Mikie's tiny curious fingers. Occasionally the mutt would even bestow his fondest favor to his young friend, an exposed and vulnerable tummy to rub. This gift of friendship inevitably brought a cascade of giggles from Mikie, who rarely laughed.

Whatever could this Indian want? Had Mikie caused a problem? Could the man not continue to leave her alone just as he had before?

Unlike the Delaware and the Shawnee, she noted this Indian did not have large ear loops cut free to hold silver objects, nor did he wear his hair as the Huron with a partially shaved head, centered with a roach of spiky tips decorated with feathers and tied with leather. Instead, he wrapped his hair and head in a cloth turban. Long locks of dark hair streaked with gray straggled over his shoulders where they escaped from beneath the turban. His overall appearance, in some ways, proved to be more English or European than Indian except for the puckered moccasins beaded with what appeared to be strawberries. He also had the typical high cheekbones, elongated face, and angular nose. Standing much taller than many Europeans, he towered over her, his muscular arms crossed. He held a crooked knife, the tool of his trade, which nestled in the bend of his elbow. A cleft in his cheek twitched.

"*Animakwe*, you cry, again?"

Eve touched the tear stains, realizing that they would not permit her to deny their presence. Her cheek was pulled smooth and taunt from the drying clay. She could not take her eyes off the knife, which curled and gleamed in the late golden sun light.

"Yes." To refuse to admit the truth seemed pointless, particularly since he obviously had seen her crying here before. Her 'yes,' however, had very icy overtones, instantly conveying her dislike of his intrusion. Her gaze, though direct, acknowledged her reservations about him and her fear of his manhood. After all, she was a woman, essentially alone. Mikie

German=this font   English=this font   *French=this font*   *Delaware=this font*

would be no help. Since having been at the fort, she had become far more wary of men.

"Your son will return." He spoke slowly. His voice conveyed certainty. His eyes, dark and bright, did not waver from hers. His gaze pulled her deep within, reminding her momentarily of someone else's eyes, someone she could not fully place at that moment.

Eve nearly gasped. She struggled not to betray any of her inner thoughts. Then, upbraiding herself for being so stupid for not having seen the obvious, she answered him in a detached manner.

"Yes, Mikie stays near and comes back."

"No. I mean your other son."

And before Eve could even think of how to respond to Tchamaniked Joe, he turned his back to her, walked back to his work area, resumed his work, and re-established the distance between them, but he left Eve flooded with a thousand questions.

Not the least among those questions...Who is this man? And why did he call her *Animakwe*?

Something else remained behind, which became even harder to fathom. A faint shaft of hope had pierced the hard icy shell around Eve, a shell which had protected her through the long winter but which had kept others at a distance. Even Mikie had been kept emotionally cold, well outside Eve's warmth. Even though she never mistreated him, Mikie, like everything else, was kept at a safe distance. Nothing before came this close to the center. Now, this shaft, that she barely acknowledged to herself, poked into her like a mini-arrow, hard, fast, and deeply imbedded. A cutting fear followed this faint promise of hope, causing Eve to abruptly end Mikie's outing, forcing him to cut short his pleasure. They returned early to Yankee Hall with Mikie's wailing protests ignored. She trudged wearily up the hill with one hand holding the hanky half full of treasures and grasping Mikie's hand firmly in the other.

Only once did Eve look back at the tall figure drawing his crooked knife over the thin cedar sheeting. The man did not look up; but she knew with absolute certainty that he sensed her gaze, and this added to her perplexity.

As Eve climbed the final hill, she turned up Ste. Anne's street and began to work her way up and over to the Citadel. Within, the oldest and most dilapidated barracks had been nicknamed Yankee Hall by the local people, for it now housed more Rebel prisoners than it had troops in its past. The dropping sun caught the west-facing windows along the street, turning them brilliant, golden orange. The deep ripples in the panes appeared azure blue. Still distracted by thoughts of the forward Indian man in the boatyard, Eve did not hear the gentleman's first call as she worked her way towards her quarters.

"Ho, good woman. Ho."

As the sound began to penetrate her consciousness, Eve tried to ignore

German=this font   English=this font   **French=this font**   *Delaware=this font*

it. Whore calls were common. Some fort men assumed that the women prisoners wanted to work off their debt to any and all comers. The French residents played sly about it, but the soldiers called brazenly.

"Ho, woman. Please, my good woman. Stop, please."

Eve looked up, still firmly holding Mikie's hand, for she had not allowed the child to buffalo her into carrying him. She frowned severely at the finely tailored, suited man standing before her. A handsome man with fine features, he sported a spotlessly white ruffled cravat with an unpretentious gold stud nestled within the folds surrounded by a woolen cape, now open to the increasing warmth.

"What do you want?" What was with the men today that they seemed to be laying for her at every turn, Eve wondered. She did not flirt, nor had she exposed her elbows and ankles. Her exasperation showed.

"Are you a prisoner?"

"I think my dress would indicate it to be so."

"You have been married?"

"Yes, this child is mine."

Mikie, more curious than hostile, looked the handsome man over with great interest as his Mutti fairly growled one response after another.

"I have a sick engage, who needs care. And ah...ah since you have knowledge of a man, it would not offend you to care for one, would it?" The man's intensity impressed her.

Eve sighed, laughed softly, and began to turn aside, but his hand gently restrained her.

"Please, could I hire you for the night? I...I will pay well." Immediately he sensed his faux pas. He took his hand away quickly. "Please, the young man is gravely ill. I meant no..." His palms raised in a gesture to further convey his honest intent. He stammered before he added a last attempt to set his final hook. "You have a kind face," he blurted with urgency. He realized he was like an angler playing a wily trout. Too much slack, she would shake his hook and be gone.

Eve hesitated.

"How much will you pay?" She felt shamed by her response, but if she could earn extra, maybe, just maybe, she could eventually buy their freedom in time, or maybe a new gown for Mikie, oh...but what was the use, DeJean would claim it, and with him there were no guarantees.

The gentleman smiled knowingly. "I will place one New York pound into your hand and no other."

Instantly, Eve realized that he would not pay her earnings to DeJean for her services.

"You can leave the child with my cousin's mother and me. We will feed him. He can sleep near our parlor fire. Nanna would delight in having another young charge."

Something about his speech and his manner, Eve found almost familiar but at the same instant quite different. An earnest quality to his voice, a sense of honesty, and an air of kindness hung about him like his heavy wool cape. His English had traces of a German accent; but then again, it sounded just a little strange.

Eve would never know why it seemed perfectly suitable to do what she did, but she permitted Mikie to accompany the man in complete confidence. Continuing to juggle Mikie's treasures in one hand, they walked with Mikie, hand-in-hand between them, to the boarding house. The gentleman pointed to his cousin's home across the way, where she could fetch Mikie in the morning. He explained to her which room belonged to his young engage. Before they and Mikie's treasures parted from her, he introduced himself as Ezekiel Solomon. He told her that he would inform Yankee Hall where she and her son could be found. She, in turn, told him only their first names, Eve and Mikie.

Mikie never looked back. Like his mother, he instinctively trusted the man as he babbled the man home.

When Eve entered John Leeth's door, she was appalled. Jonas may have been a fine silversmith, but he made a lousy nurse. She could see immediately that Jonas felt totally overwhelmed by his friend's illness and truly terrified about what was required to provide John's care.

Jonas quickly slipped out the door, relieved to leave the room at last. An obviously grateful landlady also had been primed for Eve's arrival. A bucket of steaming water, a softly scented soap, and a basin sat waiting for Eve with clean rags outside John's door.

Eve immediately assessed the situation. Fair, young, and filthy...Eve thought as she looked at the stricken man, with boyhood so recently behind him. Sinewy, lanky and tanned in places most white men were not, John Leeth proved to be as much a puzzle as his employer, Ezekiel Solomon. Pushing anything that looked even remotely clean aside, as well as blocking out memories of having cared for her young George in a similar fever, she set about cleaning the man and the room. The landlady removed the clothing Eve left in the hall and quickly took it to the wash shed behind her boarding house.

John Leeth skirted consciousness, ebbing in and out, expressing only momentary shyness as she washed his privates and all other surfaces. She reamed out his nose and ears. She decaked his eyes which had crusted shut with dried pus before greasing them gently with a touch of lard from an earlier crust of bread. She even scraped his teeth with a small stick and rinsed his mouth with cool water.

For a fleeting moment, John wondered if he were dead. Had someone come to prepare him for his grave blanket? Then, the dry heaves dispelled any doubts. Sadly, he still lived. Finally, tended and comfortable, he drifted off to sleep. His only awareness came as cool cloths on his forehead and chest were changed periodically during the long night, or with the sensation of blankets becoming heavy or light. The glow of the candle never extinguished. The soft light and nurturing touch held him fast.

German=this font   English=this font   **French=this font**   *Delaware=this font*

Wiping his lips with the back of his hand, the smell of rum and tobacco clung to his recently wetted lips. John Coutincinau studied the side of the two-story warehouse before him. Cursing under his breath, he evaluated the small set of doors set high to curtail petty thievery and to dispense goods from the loft by the ropes and pulleys which hung a few feet out from the yardarm. The rope tied off at the side of the building connected to the pulleys above. John would try to climb again, given the needs of his groins and the bravado of the rum. The first fall would not deter him. He might be drunk, but he still landed like a cat. Hell, why not try again! Capping his jug and tucking it into the folds of his shirt, John's arms, toughened by many long hours at the paddle, loosened the rope from above his head and began his slow hand over hand ascent to the doors. Foolhardy enough to hang by one arm, he slipped his long knife through the slit between the doors to lift the inner wooden latch, which freed the doors to swing open. Groomed by years of stalking game, the wily voyageur made his entrance with stealth. Closing the doors soundlessly behind him, repositioning the latch, he waited for his eyes to become accustomed to the darkness within the warehouse. He clutched an overhead timber while standing on a major cross beam.

Coutincinau heard her soft snore long before he saw her. In a corner, he found Anne coiled like a mouse in its burrow and tucked within a tiny fort made with barrels and lined with bags of flour. Splashes of moonlight from between the timbers shrunk by the previous winter's dryness spilled across her, caressing and accentuating her curled, curved form. Removing the jug of rum from his shirt, he set it on the ledge between the studs. Fuel for the return trip, he decided.

Anne slept hard after a day's work. Especially when her tummy was pleasantly full as it was now. Her pocket held half of the cache of bread crusts and her few treasures. A small beige clay jug near her head contained water to quench her thirst. No blanket, no bed, she kept warm by nestling close to the cloth sacks of flour and salt which she mounded around the edges of her nest.

In another corner, Coutincinau could hear a small animal, perhaps a rat, scavenging feed.

Coutincinau lowered himself down from a cross beam and dropped to the floor silently. He crawled carefully into Anne's nest. Immediately, his hand clamped over her mouth as he stretched beside her. She must not scream and betray his presence to any passerby. Anyway, other than perhaps a drunken highlander returning to the barracks from Fogherty's, few would be about this late. Besides, a woman's scream in the early morn rarely drew much notice in the fort. If a woman went about at this hour, the common consensus maintained that she deserved whatever she got for her foolishness.

Anne's eyes sprung open in alarm. She awoke fighting mad. In response, Coutincinau swung his leg and his hips across her tall thrashing form. Her heartbeat pounded aloud, audible to them both. Her chest

German=this font   English=this font   *French=this font*   *Delaware=this font*

heaved with fear. Only his very soft whispered wooing in French as his lips raked softly back and forth, back and forth, repeatedly over her ears quieted her terrified response. When he felt her smile break under his hand in recognition of his voice, Coutincinau slowly withdrew the temporary gag from his captive.

"You're drunk!" She whispered in a hoarse voice. But even in the darkness, Coutincinau realized her pleasure at his presence.

"Not too drunk, my ***noir perle***." He pressed his growing erection against the folds of her skirt and left no doubt of his intentions or his interest. Anne did not shy away for an instant. Instead, she snuggled her hips closer.

"How did you get in here?" Her whisper bordered on a moan.

"Up there, ***mon cheri.***" He motioned above to the loft doors. "No wall is too high to be with you***, mon Nancie.***"

"My name be Anne." A definite prickliness emerged to his last whisper. Angry, she turned her lips away from the close proximity of his.

Taking her chin gently in hand, Coutincinau turned her face to him and kissed Anne very tenderly on the lips. His thumb gently studied the fullness of her pout. He could feel her sigh rush by his fingers. Eagerly, his other hand had begun to explore her breasts.

"En my home country***, noir perle***, you would be ***Nancie.***" He sucked gently on her earlobe between words before nipping her neck softly with his teeth.

"Nan...cie?" Each syllable conveyed consent.

"Oui, mon Nancie. Mon noir perle. Mon Ann..nie." This time when he reclaimed her lips, he claimed his willing prize after a lonely winter. Coutincinau, always the skilled trapper, prevailed.

Before dawn, an odor assailed John Leeth, very faint, but it drew him like a moth through darkness to light. His lower lip sensed the tease of a spoon. Warm broth dribbled in his mouth and down his chin, only to be quickly and gently patted dry. He coughed. The spoon came again, and again. The life-giving fluid trickled in. Sipping gratefully, like a baby, he accepted the nourishment and even more the nurturing hand that brought it to his lips. By dawn, John Leeth had decided that it might be worthwhile to return to the living.

Jonas entered the room rested. He found his friend, though still wretchedly ill, faring far better than when he had left him. John's determined night-keeper made very sure Jonas knew what to do, going over everything twice and still a third time before she closed the door behind her. She promised Jonas that she would return to check on both of them following her work in the King's garden.

Eve felt surprisingly invigorated, despite her lack of sleep. She inhaled the cool morning air, stretched her arms lazily over her head, and set out for the Solomon's household. Ezekiel greeted her at the door, ushering her in quickly. A mixture of smells in the short entrance hall

German=this font   English=this font   ***French=this font***   *Delaware=this font*

filled her nostrils and caused her mouth to immediately fill with saliva. A bounding, clean Mikie greeted her just inside the door with a happy squeal and hauled her protesting into the kitchen, where he introduced her to Nanna.

"Mutti, see Nanna. Nanna cook. Sweet, Mutti, sweet Mutti." He vibrated with expectation, jumping back and forth between English and German. Excitedly, he danced about the kitchen, obviously well acquainted and comfortable under Nanna's relaxed smile. The twinkling maple sugar crystals on his cheek testified to a totally new experience for him at Fort Detroit. Eve stared at her giddy child. A tear welled up, unbidden.

"You have been most kind to him." Eve felt humbled by this unexpected warmth and kindness.

"Sit down. You have worked long this night. Ezekiel tells me that the young man's fever has broken, thanks to your fine care." At first, Eve in her fatigue and mild euphoria had not fully registered that she was spoken to in German. Though the inflection differed slightly from her own, she understood her perfectly.

"Yes, I believe so," Eve answered automatically in kind.

The warm liquid served in a perfect, beautiful, blue and white willow cup appeared too good to be real in Eve's hands. She sat motionless, holding the thin porcelain with its fanciful figures and strange houses nestled between strange windblown pine trees. She felt too unkempt to even dare to touch her lips to this beautiful Chinese porcelain. Her own mother owned a similar small teapot, which Ester protected like the crown jewels. Reluctant to drink the first sip for fear that it would suddenly vanish, Eve began to assess her surroundings, instead. The sideboard contained many pieces decorated with the wash of deep cobalt blue matching the cup. Silver candelabras and sconces winked her distorted image, which reflected on the polished curved surfaces. A large, deep tureen was turned on its side for viewing and had bright orange and yellow chrysanthemums imbedded in the clear glaze in the bottom. The lid helped to prop it in a secure position. Spotless whitewash brightened and lightened the surroundings. A real glass window let a flood of morning light fall on the rich walnut table before her. The table, graced with a fine linen scarf, was accented with gray and blue overshot on its border and begged for Eve's inquiring touch. However, Eve did not reach for it, despite her longing to do so; for she feared that she might mar it by her mere fingering of the cloth. Absolutely everything testified to an ample larder.

"Drink woman, I am sure you need it." Diminutive, with her thinning dark black hair streaked with gray pulled gently back from her face and stuffed under a round black cap, Nanna's features proved clearly defined. A narrow long nose and deep-set brown eyes accented with smile wrinkles matched the smile wrinkles about her mouth. Her gray linen day-dress was decorated only by a wide white mini-shawl accented with a tiny touch of hand lace which served as a collar of sorts, spilling in soft folds over the

German=this font   English=this font   *French=this font*   *Delaware=this font*

curve of her shoulders. Her apron testified to busy hands, as it was covered with stains from earlier work.

Eve realized that she had been distracted and perhaps rude. She smiled gratefully and brought the steaming liquid to her lips. Sweet spiced tea filled her mouth with wonder. She heard her loud smack as she relished the hints of allspice and cloves...and something slightly bitter and so different. What was it? "I taste spice, allspice and cloves...but the bitter?"

Nanna laughed. "You taste the dried bitter orange rind. Have you never had it?"

"No, but I have heard of them."

"Come now, drink. These buns are for you, too. Eat." Nanna grasped the warm plate with a napkin and thrust it closer to Eve. "Please, you have worked this whole night, while we slept."

"You did not sleep early this morning." Eve reached gratefully for the warm buttery bun as she acknowledged the maker of the healing broth that a manservant had delivered to her before dawn and now the raised buns. The scents of both mingled with the other scents of this kitchen.

The other woman smiled, nodded, acknowledged her role, and recognized another sister of the dawn who awoke early to grace her family in the ageless symmetry of womankind, a gift of caring. Wiping her hands on a small linen towel, she sat down on the other chair and no sooner having done so, Mikie scrambled up into her lap.

Eve, seeing their easy rapport, did not chastise him for his presumptuous familiarity. Then she saw it, nestled in the folds of the woman's ruffled neckline...a delicate silver necklace. At the apex of the necklace one found not the familiar or the expected cross but the Star of David. The two intersecting triangles cut into her vision. She looked quickly away. She would be impolite to stare. Of course, now the trace of familiarity as Ezekiel had spoken with her became abundantly clear. A memory tied to an over-talkative Philadelphia merchant on a rare outing with her father as a child. The six points also brought back momentarily another brief memory, her Vati and Onkel Jac's stormy tirades about the stinking Jews and their diabolical wickedness over many an evening fire. Reflecting only for a moment on this dark memory and also remembering Father Bocquet, she quickly recognized that the reality of real people thankfully conflicted with many of her schooled expectations. Good and evil abounded everywhere, among all peoples. She concluded that one needed to accept good wherever you found it, gratefully, and humbly. She bit into the sweet, rich cinnamon bun with relish and tried not to drool. She recognized that in that very instant, her cup runneth over.

On earth, heaven and hell keep close company. They can be less than a fraction of a heartbeat apart. No sooner had the taste of the bun touched her tongue and teeth when the cinnamon and butter unleashed a dark flood of Eve's inner awareness. Something deeply hidden broke. The earlier penetrating shaft of hope remained firmly imbedded. The compromised shell broke open violently.

German=this font   English=this font   *French=this font*   *Delaware=this font*

Eve emitted a low anguished scream. The scream sounded unearthly and like a wounded animal.

Ruth, seeing the woman's continence change from one of complete relaxed joy to pure abject horror, screamed for Ezekiel, who entered the kitchen on a dead run. Her alarm pierced the previous harmony. Ruth pushed the now frightened child into Ezekiel's arms and directed him with a flip of her head to remove the child and himself from the kitchen. As Ruth did so, Eve jumped to her feet and dropped the partially chewed bun from her mouth like a terrified creature. Eve pushed the beautiful cup away from her in a wild sweeping movement, spilling the contents across the table. The sweet tea rushed towards the gray and blue table scarf. The cup spun precariously. Eve gasped for air. Her hands clawed at her throat. She struggled to breathe. The surface seemed so far away. Her eyes glazed. She fought to return to light and air.

Throwing her linen towel to begin to absorb the tiny tide of tea, Ruth hastily grabbed the cup before it rolled to the floor.

Ruth grasped the stricken woman's hands and held them tight. Sensing the need for firmer control, Ruth backed Eve close to the adjacent wall, sandwiching Eve between herself and wedging Eve against the wall with her hips. Ruth struggled to restrain her. Grabbing the arms that broke free and that lashed blindly about her, Ruth shoved Eve firmly against the wall. Though a smaller woman, Ruth clung to the writhing wretch like a stick-tight burr with only sheer determination and will power to sustain her.

The horrible rush passed. Next, Eve's body became ridged and hard. Ruth recognized that this stiff pillar contained a raging tempest. She refused to release her. Instead, she continued to hold Eve fast. One hand at a time, Ruth began to move in soft comforting strokes up and down Eve's upper arms and shoulders...whispering, gentling, nurturing.

Beginning softly, continuously growing in intensity, deep wrenching sobs tore and eviscerated Eve. She clung to the strength that held her and wept. Her own strong frame shook as wave after wave of horror and sadness revisited her. This had come so untimely...so unbidden...so unexpected...so totally unwanted.

When finally the sobs began to come with gasps between and with far less violence, Ruth eased Eve gently into the chair, fetched the cup, and filled it with sweet tea for a second time.

"I am sorry. I am sorry. I am sorry." Eve hung her head in total shame. "I am so sorry. You are so kind. I am sorry."

"Shush, shush, shush now. Shush, shush, shush." Like mothers the world over, Ruth raised Eve's face with one hand and stroked the matted hair away from Eve's forehead and eyes. Her thumb expertly rubbed away the tears.

The softness of the shushing and the healing touch began to fill the void in Eve, who felt drained and wretchedly empty. Like a dropped egg, she had broken and splattered everything in sight.

German=this font   English=this font   *French=this font*   *Delaware=this font*

"It is alright, my dear. Now I must tell you, my buns have gotten me many reactions, even flowery flattery and a marriage proposal, but—well this one truly was the limit." The unexpected good humor laced with warmth helped Eve relax just a tiny bit and lessened her embarrassment.

Eve took a quick tentative look at the woman who crouched near her chair offering her tea. She saw not one trace of anger there...only compassion.

When Eve accepted the second cup of tea, Ruth rose. Wiping the table up quickly to remove the last hint of moisture, hanging the small towel to dry by the hearth, Ruth dried her hands on her apron and poured herself a cup of tea before she sat down across from Eve.

"Did I ruin your beautiful table scarf?"

"No, it is fine, my dear. The tea never reached it."

Ruth fingered the linen in response to Eve's concern, showing her the underside before she patted it neatly back into place.

"Now my dear, tell me why you think this happened."

"I do not know if I can."

"Try...I really think you need to do this."

"But..."

"No buts." She closed her eyes shaking her head thoughtfully. Reopening her eyes, she drew an invisible circle of protection about them. "You need to reconsider what happened here before it destroys you or your lovely boy. Now, I know you are exhausted, but that is not what happened here. Women are often exhausted and tired."

Eve looked up at Ruth, sheepishly wrinkling her nose and nodding in sad agreement.

"I do not think that I even know your name, Nanna." Eve began to realize that Nanna might be a family love name.

"My name is Ruth Solomon. Levi is my son and Ezekiel is my dear nephew. But, call me Nanna, if it is easier for you, most do. Do not sidestep. Let us not avoid this demon any longer. Let us speak about what happened here before it eats you alive."

Eve took a sip of tea. She took a deep breath. Tears began welling and spilling with a slow rhythm which matched her hesitant speech. She began to relate the joys of a warm October morning, her Adam Henry at the table, schneckes in the oven, the smell of cinnamon and buttery goodness, the laughter of dear friends, a foolish girl stuck in a dormer, and then the shear utter horrors that followed.

Ruth listened and soon her own tears fell in quiet cadence with the unbelievable words that marched before her ears and her heart.

Speaking in the comfort of her own language, Eve shared her story, her loss of family, her loss of Lil'Henry, as much to herself, as to the woman before her. The demon would never leave her, but at least Eve fully recognized its destructive power and could clip its horns.

Ezekiel wisely entertained the child as the hours passed. Much longer and he would need to send his cousin, Levi, up to the Citadel to tell them of

German=this font   English=this font   *French=this font*   *Delaware=this font*

Eve's whereabouts. Maybe a tiny lie would be needed to smooth over the rough spots.

The sounds of Levi, his wife and two young sons clamoring for Nanna as they entered the door brought Eve and Ruth abruptly back from the cold torturous trek to Fort Detroit and DeJean's subsequent inhumanity. Eve thanked her hostess quickly. Grabbing Mikie's arm, she hastily exited, murmuring an apology to the others present for staying too long and adding a hasty thank you for all their kindness. Mikie appeared bewildered and looked longingly at two potential playmates.

Levi watched the departing figures before turning to his Mother.

"Mother, are you taking in strays again?" Nothing in his manner spoke of any rebuke towards his mother or distaste towards the woman who had quickly skirted out the door, dragging her blond cherub behind her. Levi clasped his arm about Nanna's shoulder and smiled through unspoken pride as his sons scooted into the kitchen to grab something from the larder.

"No, Ezekiel made me do it," Ruth answered. Her eyes twinkled as she deftly deflected Levi and his wife's attention to the cinnamon buns in the kitchen. "See to your boys, or you both will miss out."

Ruth wondered if she would see Eve again. She knew that when people bared their souls to a complete stranger, that often they would turn away in shame from the person who so unexpectedly shared their pain. She hoped that this time would be different. The woman had depth. Besides, Ruth had totally enjoyed being immersed in her mother tongue. Unfortunately, the words had conveyed so much sadness, brutality, and terror.

Ezekiel watched Eve's parting figure, too. Suddenly, he realized that he had forgotten something that he had promised. "Oh my goodness, I did not pay her for her services."

"Good," Ruth responded. "That means we have an opportunity to see her once more. I like the woman. Please, bring her and the child again on another day." She turned to join the others in the kitchen, who playfully fought over the remaining cinnamon buns.

Ezekiel studied his aging aunt as she returned to the kitchen. His Nanna did not make friends easily here at the fort. But he knew that if his aunt held this woman to be of value, that he should make every effort to see that Eve and the child returned. His initial impression of the woman prisoner had been confirmed.

In the kitchen, only one buttery bun, with a small bite removed, would be quickly discarded. Frugality would not prevail this time. Ruth Solomon felt the bitter taste of tragic sadness must never touch anyone that she loved.

German=this font   English=this font   *French=this font*   *Delaware=this font*

Chapter 13   March 10, 1778   The Next Day

"...When it is considered how many people in the settlement have connections with the Americans, especially as an Indian, for a gallon of rum, will convey any letter of intelligence."

Lt. Governor Hamilton to General Frederick Haldimand complaining of Rebel spies January 15, 1778, as quoted by Silas Farmer, *History of Detroit and Wayne County* (Original publication 1884, republished in Salem, Massachusetts: Higgenson), p. 244.

"It is not people in arms that Indians will ever daringly attack, but the poor inoffensive families who fly to the deserts to be out of trouble, and who are inhumanely butchered, sparing neither women or children."

Lieutenant Governor Abbot at Detroit 1778 in an appeal to Guy Carleton in the home office of Quebec. As quoted by Nelson Vance Russell, "The Indian Policy of Henry Hamilton; A Re-evaluation," *The Canadian Historical Review, Volume 31* (1930), p. 25.

Fort Detroit

Anne stood with her back to the door as she straightened her gown and petticoat before she adjusted her torn chemise. Coutincinau had left prior to the awaking tempo of the streets, leaving her in a state of lassitude like a kitten bulging with milk, wanting only to lick its fur and nap.

Late morning, her employer's helper, Pierre, climbed the steps to enter her portion of the warehouse. Anne did not fully acknowledge his presence or the heaviness of his tread. When she turned at his final approach, open and unguarded, she was greeted with a vicious backhanded blow across her face that spun her against the neighboring barrels. All crashed, rolling to the floor. She had been caught totally off guard and unable to retaliate, although the stronger of the two. Raising her arm defensively, she tried to struggle to her feet. A second fist drove into the other side of her face and eye. Pain exploded. Half crouched, she spun wildly. The pocket slit, neatly hidden, caught on a barrel wire, ripping open her skirt and revealing the hidden pocket. The contraband contents fell, cascading to the floor. Half eaten bread crusts, scraps of cookies, and bits of jerky flew asunder, scattering in a myriad of directions. The unmistakable clink of a coin striking the wooden decking sounded. It flashed its golden sides, rolled across the floor, spun like a top, and dropped on its side to rest at the feet of Pierre.

"Uppity bitch. Lying slacker." He did not offer to help her as she attempted to rise. Slipping on water from her spilled jug, she fell again. Pierre stooped to pick up the coin. Turning the gold guinea over in his fingers, a slimy smile crossed his face before he closed his fist over the coin. "First, we hear that you are dallying in the streets and soliciting near the tavern. Now, we discover proof of your thievery. You filthy, black, lice-infested whore." He raised his hand to render another shattering blow, when his hand stopped mid-stroke.

"I presume, good sir, this poor woman has caused you a grievous wrong."

Pompey, one in a thousand and more who topped six-foot, held the man's arm in a vice-like grip. Stretching his arm to its full extension, he fairly lifted Pierre, whose slight build barely crested five foot four, off the floor. The traces of his Island accent played around his flawless English. His impeccably-tailored attire contrasted strikingly with the lower class Frenchman, whose linsey-woolsey garb smelled of rank perspiration. Unfortunately, neither Pierre nor his garments graced a wash tub on a regular basis.

The blood drained from Pierre's face. Fear replaced righteous wrath. Pierre knew Pompey. The man had the strength to kill him. Although the black man smiled, the smile insinuated the full desire to do just that and more. At first, Pierre paled; fearing the worst, but then he remembered his rightful place in life's order.

"Unhand me or I will tell your owner, black bastard." Pierre's threat trembled with his bobbing Adam's apple. His voice shook with fear.

"Tell his owner what, my good man?" James May stepped out of the shadows. "It appears we have interrupted a lover's spat, eh. Do you agree, Pompey?"

To have one of the town's richest leading citizens tell your employer that you and his lowly black had indulged in any liaison could terminate both of their employments. Employment to feed six hungry mouths and a shrewish wife could not be lost under these circumstances. Agnes would kill him.

Pompey dropped him unceremoniously and bent to assist Anne to her feet. Just as he did so, Finchley approached all three men and Anne.

"What happened here?" Finchley's port-reddened face flushed redder.

Suddenly, Pierre realized that he held the trump card. Though loath to part with it, he must play it now. Holding forth the gold piece, he dramatically opened his fist and handed the coin over to his employer. Better to give up the coin than his hide for this hand, he decided.

"I just found that this bitch stole this money."

"And what are these...?" Finchley kicked a few bread crusts across the room.

German=this font   English=this font   *French=this font*   *Delaware=this font*

"Other things she stole, sir."

"Is this true, Anne?"

Before Anne could spit the blood from her mouth to answer, Pierre jumped in again.

"It all was in her hidden pocket 'for she fell dat one."

From behind Finchley, May and Pompey glared at Pierre, but neither could help as the remains of the hidden pocket, now in full view, still contained a few telltale chunks of bread.

"Now Anne, after all we have provided for you, I am truly sickened by your immoral behavior. This is how you choose to thank us for our great generosity." Righteously indignant, Finchley felt embarrassed to be thrust in such a negative light before those he wished to impress. "When DeJean came to me, I protested that you surely would not do as he suggested. But now, what am I to think? How else could you ever come by this gold honestly?"

Atypically, Anne stood quiet. If she told them Coutincinau gave her the gold guinea, she and he might face even greater troubles. If she revealed Sue Ellen's role, her friend might suffer, too. She must remain silent.

"No answer?" Finchley frowned.

Time passed.

"Still no answer?"

Anne continued to stand mute.

"After all that we have provided to you as our Christian duty with charity?"

The silence continued.

"Now, I warn you in front of these good gentlemen! If there are any further irregularities, I shall be disposed to turn you over to the Minister of Justice." Finchley paused. He wanted to be very sure to emphasize his last point. "I think they can see what a compassionate man I am. I am giving you a second chance." He smiled and nodded his head to the men behind him. "But, there will be no next time, woman."

Her throbbing face began to swell. She decided resolutely that she absolutely would not cry before these bastards. She engaged Pompey's attention. Her brief eye contact conveyed her thanks. She understood fully that he and May could do no more to assist her. Anne must suffer alone.

"Now, gentlemen, how many hundred barrels of corn have you obtained from the Ottawa and Potawatomi of Lake Michigan?"

May and Pompey returned to the business at hand with Finchley. Pierre sneered with triumphant glee at Anne before disappearing in the shadows to join his employer.

Anne remained silent. Her eye would soon swell completely shut.

German=this font   English=this font   *French=this font*   *Delaware=this font*

In the weeks before, Eve had failed to notice the subtle changes around her. Besides the color changes, the buds of the apples and pears had doubled in size the last few weeks. The maples no longer teased her by dripping sap on her face, making her recall the sweet crystals that she had tasted when cleaning Mikie's face. She barely remembered looking up at the tiny brilliant-red, fuzzy flowers that tickled the pale blue sky. Sweet smelling fires about the fort in the outer wooded areas had disappeared. Sugaring season had finished. However, faint memories lingered, touching her like the caress of the perfumed smoke.

The severity of the long, hard winter clung between bare patches of ground. The snow crystals tinkled and winked as they melted away, sending tiny rivulets through the garden. Eve, though tired, seemed less burdened for the very first time. She felt a greater awareness and opened herself to the miracle of an early spring sun, a welcome change from cold and mist. Mikie toddled nearby as she hoed the earth before her, preparing it for the crop to come along with the other prisoners of Yankee Hall working in the King's plot. The pesky red osier shoots in the swampy areas gleamed in their bright crimson spring coats, and their catkins hung heavy with yellow pollen where uncut along the garden's edges. Pussy willows seemed to mew with joy to Eve, sporting thick, gray fur for the future nests of the hummingbirds which would soon arrive. Soft muted pinks and spring greens shimmered from within their gray downy covering. New songs also greeted Eve's ears as the latest avian arrivals tried to stake out their territory and attract a mate. Silvery-green poplar bark contrasted with the deep red of birches and the pure silver of maples. Warblers, flitting in the still bare branches, revealed flashes of yellow, black, and occasionally a rare blue.

Invigorated, she thrust the hoe deep into the thawing soil and threw the rock that she pulled from the cold gooey wetness of the clay loam, clanking it onto the nearest pile. Anne's working song came to mind, so Eve hummed.

Near the water, another's heart filled with song and a sense of spring.
"You have sung this entire day. No hang-over, mon ami?" Pierre Manseur elbowed his friend. *"You get yours, eh?"* he teased.

Coutincinau only grinned, but his unshaved face nearly broke in half in the process. He kept moving between the stack on the wharf and the wagon.

"She was worth it eh...all those cold lonesome nights with no squaws to warm you." Manseur tried to tease him into speaking. Instead, Coutincinau just grinned like a love-sick fool and sang on.

"What you do tonight, mon ami?"

Manseur, kicked a chunk of residual ice out of their path as they headed to the wharf for another heavy load.

"Then youze ez going with me to Fogherty's tonight eh?"
"No. Coutincinau ez going to buy a big bottle of rum, a leetle

German=this font   English=this font   *French=this font*   *Delaware=this font*

smoked fish, a leetle cloth, a leetle tobacco, and celebrate life, mon ami."

"Celebrate life?"

"Oui, oui. Celebrate life!" Coutincinau left absolutely no doubt what the celebration included. His voice rippled with sensuality and dripped with expectation.

Manseur stopped suddenly. A dark contrasting thought impaled him. Coutincinau stopped too when he realized that his friend no longer kept pace with him. He turned back to his friend who stood facing him. Manseur's face had filled with pathos.

"You be careful, mon ami." Manseur's tone changed abruptly to one of great seriousness and concern.

"Oui, I am always careful. You know dat," Coutincinau laughed, playfully jabbing at his friend's shoulder with his palm, knocking him off his stance momentarily.

"I am serious here, man. This could be bad. The stinking British are not like de French who can appreciate the affairs of the heart."

"You worry too much, mon ami. You forget no one ez more cunning and crafty...and better yet, stronger or quicker, than Coutincinau, the fox."

"Yah, well de fox best not be caught in the hen house, mon ami!" Manseur paused momentarily before adding under his breath, *"Especially with dat dark hen, no."*

Coutincinau just frowned, then cuffing at Manseur like a fellow kit in the pack, he put his arm around his friend's shoulders and turned them both back toward the water, laughing. Another stack of supplies on the wharves from Fort Niagara awaited their strong backs to carry it ashore. The off-season business after trapping had barely begun.

When Eve descended the hill towards town with the setting sun, she could see Anne trudging wearily below towards Abbott and Finchley's warehouse. Her head hung down. Her shoulders rounded over and sagged. Eve wondered momentarily if she had made a mistake. Anne always walked like a regal queen with a 'to hell with you' attitude, not like this at all. Even when carrying her heaviest loads, her back remained ramrod straight. Mikie squealed. Even at this distance, he recognized his friend. Eve released his hand so he could begin his usual toddling run towards her. This time, however, Anne did not return his squeal, run to meet him, and swing him up to her shoulders to run with him bouncing and laughing before returning him back to his mother with a crust of bread and a friendly pat or two. Instead, she turned quickly away, covering the side of her face with a raised arm before she melted into a side alley and disappeared. Perplexed, Mikie stood stock still, waiting for his mother to catch up again.

"Maybe she is just too tired to play tonight, Mikie. Come on." Eve

German=this font   English=this font   *French=this font*   *Delaware=this font*

extended her hand toward her son who latched onto her waggling fingers. "Come, come." Porridge waited them at the Citadel; and perhaps a portion of Johnny bread. She turned in the gateway to the cluster of buildings. She would have liked to have shared the events of her last two days with Anne, but not tonight, it seemed. Then, she remembered that she must stop by the young man's room. She had nearly forgotten. Leaving Mikie among the other children who clamored for porridge and telling a friend where she would be for an hour or so, she set out to return to the boarding house.

Eve rapped softly. Inside, she found Jonas feeding his friend, John. The Solomons' manservant had brought a fresh supply of broth.

"How is he doing?"

"Much better, mam."

"Do you need a break?"

"Oh mam, you're just back from the fields."

"It is all right. I can not stay the night...and by the looks, I will not need to. But I can spare you time to eat and drink a bit, if you do not tarry too long."

"Oh mam, that would be a blessing if you wouldn't mind."

Jonas beat a hasty retreat, promising to hurry back. Eve took over the spoon and the feeding duties.

The difference in touch of the spoon, the gentle tease of his lower lip, and the quick removal of any spill from his chin caused John to open his eyes and to look at his benefactress.

Eve smiled. "You have rejoined us."

John Leeth tipped his chin twice and then smiled back weakly. He coughed. She paused for him to recover and then to accept more broth. A soft, flat bread touched lightly with butter lay by the bowl.

"A bite?"

He shook his head positively. She ripped off a tiny chunk and popped it in his mouth like a mother to a baby bird. Too grateful to feel silly, John tried to manage it. Realizing that it might be too dry for him to swallow, Eve gave him a little broth to moisten it. He swallowed it. The next piece, she soaked in the spoon before she passed it on. His eye's brightened to convey his appreciation of her thoughtfulness. Ezekiel Solomon found them thus, when he entered the room after a quiet rap.

"Good evening, Eve. I thought I saw you come."

"Herr Solomon."

"Ezekiel, my good woman."

"Our charge has much improved." She noticed that this time he did not speak to her in English. John Leeth's eyes flickered at the exchange.

"Yes, he seems much improved. Death's door closes."

"Indeed, that appears to be so. He is a fine man, Eve. Too good to lose. The Lord blessed him by your presence." He pulled a small trunk from across the room and sat down beside them.

"John Leeth, may I introduce you to Eve."

John returned his second weak appreciative smile.

German=this font   English=this font   **French=this font**   *Delaware=this font*

"Eve Earnest." Eve responded.

"I owe you your fee for your fine services. In the rush this morning, it was inadvertently overlooked. I hope you realize that I never meant to leave you unpaid."

Eve smiled. "I did not imagine otherwise." Eve quite frankly had nearly forgotten the fee all together.

He sat watching her patiently feed John before he spoke again. "I saw one of your friends badly hurt today." He switched to English. "Do you know how she fares?"

Eve looked up in alarm.

"The tall black one that I often see you and your small son with on the streets."

Eve did not see a flicker of memory race across John Leeth's face as she faced Ezekiel.

"Anne?" Eve withdrew a full spoon from John's waiting mouth. His eyes darted back and forth, evaluating his two charitable friends with acute interest.

"What happened to Anne?"

"Her one eye is swollen badly shut. Her face is horribly covered with bruises and also swollen."

"Oh my goodness, how did that happen?" Eve said sadly as she finally spilled the full spoon into John's waiting mouth, remembering once more how her friend had turned unexpectedly from Mikie only a short time before.

"Someone must have struck her hard, repeatedly by the looks." He hesitated before adding further, "Truly, I felt sorry for her as she carried Finchley's goods today. It must have pained her terribly even to move, given her wounds. She walked with great discomfort."

Eve broke another piece of bread and soaked it for John. The sounds of the room amplified markedly for all present. She took the sopped food and placed it in John's open mouth before speaking to Ezekiel.

"No one should hit anyone that way, especially a woman."

Ezekiel did not answer her. He left her to her own thoughts.

"Who could I speak to on her behalf?" She asked.

Ezekiel shook his head thoughtfully. "DeJean is of no use. Maybe you could talk to Hamilton's secretary. He is German you know, a loyalist from Philadelphia. You might be able to speak with him if DeJean is not underfoot." He reflected again for a few minutes. "You will never gain any access to Hamilton, not for a Negro."

Eve glanced up again after spooning more nourishment to John and mopping up his chin. She knew better than to ask Solomon to go in her stead. He could be at as much of a disadvantage as Anne. She sighed with that sad realization.

"What is the secretary's name?" She asked with a sense of resignation. Someone had to speak up for Anne.

"Jacob, I believe. Jacob Schieffelin."

German=this font English=this font *French=this font* *Delaware=this font*

"He is his secretary?"

"Yes, and sort of a friend. Not that Hamilton makes many friends." He transferred a small cloth sack he carried back and forth from one hand to another before continuing, "Not even the women, young or old. Although, we do hear that Hamilton dances with a lot of young French belles at parties to keep up French alliances in the fort. You might approach Jehu Hay and Captain LaMothe, but neither would seem much help in my opinion. Now that Lernoult has taken Mompesson's position, he shows far less animosity to Hamilton, though I cannot see any change in cooperation with the military here at the fort. Hamilton and Lernoult go back a ways, I guess."

"Not Captain LaMothe or Hay, for sure. They have no love either for Anne or me."

"Well, I guess that leaves Schieffelin. He may be your best chance."

Jonas rapped, entered the room, and saw the two caretakers both looking very serious.

"Is John worse?"

"No, no, he is doing fine," Eve assured him, before removing the small napkin under John's chin. She wrapped the one small piece of leftover bread in the napkin and set it beside the empty broth bowl. "I will leave you to chamber him. Then, I think that he will sleep the night away, Jonas, and let you sleep, as well." She got up, stiff from hoeing, and excused herself, heading out with Ezekiel at her side.

"Nanna sent this for the boy," Ezekiel said, handing the cloth bag to Eve. He knew better than to even suggest for a moment anything for Eve. The woman had great pride. Both Nanna and Ezekiel realized it. She would only accept assistance for her child.

"Thank you. Tell..." Eve stopped. "Please convey my deep thanks to Mistress Solomon. Nanna I mean." She wanted Ezekiel to know which mistress she meant.

"Why not do that yourself?"

Eve's thoughts fleetingly returned to her early morning behavior.

"Nanna has been lamenting all day that none of us chat with her in good German like you do as we are all too busy with the English." Though not totally true, he knew that this would give Eve permission to return under the guise of doing them a favor. A woman like Eve did not like to be in debt to others without being able to give in return.

"Perhaps I could do that." She spoke politely, more to be agreeable than to agree.

"Bring the boy. My nephews long for playmates." Ezekiel reached in the pocket hidden within his cape. "Again, thank you for your kindness." Ezekiel pressed a sterling pound into her hand before turning to his cousin's home.

Eve watched him go. Then, she glanced up the street where Abbott and Finchley's warehouse stood. Standing for some time, Eve finally turned

German=this font   English=this font   *French=this font*   *Delaware=this font*

toward the Citadel. She uttered a heartfelt prayer that her friend would be safe this night. A prayer certainly would not hurt, although she still doubted that anyone heard them of late.

Darkness closed about her as she returned to Yankee Hall.

"Are you and your wife comfortable and settled now?" Lieutenant Governor Hamilton raised his brandy to his lips as Jacob Schieffelin, his secretary, replenished Lieutenant Governor Edward Abbott's brandy. Abbott and his wife, only days before, had returned from Vincennes to Fort Detroit. DeJean assigned them to a comfortable residence of an evicted Rebel sympathizer near the fort. The Abbott's would leave for Montreal as soon as favorable wind and weather permitted. For now, Hamilton and Abbott would suffer each other's company. Both men met the demands of their social and civil office. For, after all, one <u>must</u> be civil to the civilized.

Hamilton politely tried to cover the disgust that he felt for this man who had so mismanaged his duties at the other end of their territory as part of his power triad. The man had not raised one single Indian party to attack the western flank of the Rebels from the tribes along the Wabash. He had totally failed to support the Crown's orders or Hamilton's undertakings. Hamilton knew that Abbott had attempted to leave Vincennes in the fall, just shortly before Hamilton's letter arrived explaining the lack of crown financial support as demanded by Guy Carleton. Hamilton, disliked by many of the habitants in Detroit, resented deeply the reason that Abbott had remained in Vincennes. Abbott's relationship with the early French settlers included mutual respect, where as Hamilton's interactions varied with his view of their status and class or his need for their compliance. As a result, the local population of Vincennes had begged Abbott to stay and had even supported him with shares of their own meager supplies. Rumors relayed that the residents had even rebuilt portions of the fort at their own expense in an effort to keep Abbott at Fort Sackville in Vincennes. Together, they had faced one of the coldest winters in memory. But to no avail, Edward Abbott and his wife had decided to leave.

When Hamilton heard that the local priest, Gibault, had urged the Abbott and his wife to stay longer as well; Hamilton wondered if Abbott could have secret Catholic leanings. Why else would Gibault react that way? No doubt because Abbott had coddled them all, Hamilton concluded. Any fool could see that Abbott had continually been out-maneuvered by the Spanish, who drew the Indians of the Wabash to the north, crossing over the Mississippi to trade their pelts.

Hamilton would not miss the bleats and moans in Abbott's undermining letters to Lernoult, Carleton, and Rocheblave that continued to exaggerate the conditions on the frontier. Hopefully the crown would choose a better replacement this time round.

Major Jehu Hay rapped his pipe against his boot before taking a small stick from above the fireplace to ream out old tobacco and replenish it

German=this font   English=this font   **French=this font**   *Delaware=this font*

with new. He lit the pipe slowly. The sweet smoke circled his head like a wreath. He rejoined his seat near Captain Guillaume LaMothe.
LaMothe took great pride in his French heritage. Here, the Frenchman could be fully recognized in this circle of power, which he felt befitted his aristocratic lineage, not to mention his considerable military skills.

"Yes, we are quite comfortable. My wife extends her thanks to you and your staff. After our terrible thirty day journey through muck and mire, you have provided for our stay handsomely and with great courtesy. We are in your debt." His response was dictated by the veneer of manners and civility, covering the mutual disgust that Abbott felt towards Hamilton. The stories of the horror and slaughter that rippled across the frontiers from Pennsylvania through Kentucky gave him neither pride in British power nor their current policies of late. Had the home office forgotten so soon the atrocities of the French and Indian wars when the French enlisted the savage's services because they lacked French troops in New France to confront the English? The Seven Year War fought abroad in Africa, India, Europe, and on the high seas had cost them dearly, spreading their human resources to the breaking point. Daily, Abbott had heard new stories of treachery and mayhem which had filtered through the surrounding swamps of Vincennes like rain through lichens. He suspected that the Rebel sympathizers amplified some of the stories, but facts were facts. The faces of those who sought refuge in Vincennes spoke a sorry tale, even if they failed to open their mouths.

Abbott felt that just because Burgoyne suffered an ignoble defeat by an upstart bunch of rebellious hooligans and handed over six thousand prisoners to be sent home packing like dogs with tails between their legs was absolutely no excuse to loose the hounds of hell on the innocents.

"Virginia tobacco, Hay?" LaMothe tipped his French aristocratic nose into the sweet blue haze that wafted over his way.

Hay smirked, "Indeed, yes. As a matter of fact, my fellows liberated it on the last raid. We consider it as returning it to its rightful licensed owner, his majesty, King George." He nodded to his cohorts before inhaling another draw.

Abbott turned his head and coughed rather than revealing his feelings as laughter rippled around the rest of the room.

Hamilton swirled his brandy before sipping another mouthful. "Yes, Washington and his plantation cronies will certainly be upset when this whole fiasco is over, and they must again ship all their tobacco at a fair price to his majesty. That is, if they have plantations after the war. To King George." He raised his glass.

"Here, here." The group raised their glasses automatically as Jacob made the rounds again to replenish the source of their pleasure.

"Did you really retrieve a small boy today?" Hay asked his superior.

"Yes, the Mingo gave him up willingly."

"That is a change of heart."

"Yes, they are becoming more civilized in their conduct of war.

German=this font   English=this font   *French=this font*   *Delaware=this font*

One can see that our admonitions for mercy to noncombatants have not gone unheeded."

"Does the boy have family?" LaMothe asked.

"I doubt it. They traded in his father's scalp, as well," Hamilton informed him casually.

A shudder coursed through Abbott. He shifted uneasily in his chair.

"Too bad they do not think to ransom more of their prisoners themselves. The funds might be worth more than the goods they receive from the crown for scalps," LaMothe observed.

Hamilton frowned.

"No account for their ability to reason. Another example of their inferior savage minds," Hay reminded the group haughtily.

"Not that inferior, Major Hay. They are quick enough to pick up on the Rebels' bungling outrages. Believe me, Arbuckle and his ill-trained militia could not have murdered Cornstalk and his son at a better time. They have helped us immeasurably." Realizing he had a captive audience, Hamilton continued. He needed to air his ideas before others of like mind. He appreciated them after a long day confronting wave after wave of native speakers which he swore could talk any topic to death and with whom every word must be carefully chosen.

"Remember when that Rebel, Morgan, sent letters in December to the Delaware to tell them of Burgoyne's defeat saying that the King was too weak to protect them?"

Abbott, LaMothe, and Hay nodded in response.

"Well, they do not even pay attention to that now! Cornstalk's death eliminates one spiny thorn. He held a strong voice in the councils. The man visited General Hand in Rebel Philadelphia last fall to sue for peace, protection, and neutrality. Thank goodness he was rudely rebuffed by Hand." The Lieutenant Governor paused before he continued.

"The inept Rebels are their own worst enemy. Thanks to their collective stupidity, out of the three strong voices of dissent...we now have only White Eyes left. Thankfully, his reputation is being undercut by Cornstalk's death. And ironically, Cornstalk was not even a Delaware." Hamilton paused again and sipped once more. His mind strayed momentarily as he recognized silently his need of decent Delaware interpreters.

"Killbuck Jr. of the Turtle phantry and Captain Pipe of the Wolf should bring the Delaware firmly into our camp."

Hay agreed, nodding positively.

"Yes, we need to keep on drumming home that the Rebels say one thing and deceitfully do another," LaMothe added. "My scouts report that White Eyes has returned to Coshocton. But no one is really listening to him, especially since some of his chieftains are becoming religious to avoid the war."

"Religious?"

German=this font   English=this font   **French=this font**   *Delaware=this font*

"*Oui*, Welpachtachlechen has been baptized by the fool Rebel-spying Moravians, setting aside his leadership."

"All the better for us, as his flock scatters and realigns itself," Hay agreed.

"My thoughts exactly, Major." Brandy had increased the volume of his voice. Hamilton emphasized each word, pointing his index finger at Hay. "That is why I say that Lernoult's Rangers, our militia, and our savage allies should attack Fort Pitt this spring while the Rebels mill about in serious disarray. I am certain that the time to attack is now." Hamilton banged his closed fist down onto his other chair arm to emphasize his point. Brandy jumped out of his glass in the process, glazing the fine fabric of the chair.

Jacob hastily mopped up the splash.

"Then I," the latter vowel softened immediately. A hasty correction attempted to blend the sound. "Itha crown will control the Ohio country!" Hamilton added with his fist still clenched.

"Has the leadership sent orders to do this?" Abbott asked, full well knowing the answer. The leadership, other than their initial orders to Hamilton, had backed off from any other specific orders after the first suggestion to divert the Rebel's western edge. The office continued to pay Hamilton and DePeyster's outrageous bills at Fort Detroit and Fort Michilimackinac in tacit agreement, but they avoided full responsibility by refusing to put formal directives in writing. Since Abbott had not supplied tribal fighters, he had received nothing. Now the hounds unleashed had lives of their own. Many angry tribal parties attacked without the so-called supervisors, choosing their own targets. Random acts resulted in increased murdering and pillaging.

"You still have no new orders, *monsieur*?" LaMothe asked.

Hamilton glared at Abbott. Jehu Hay hastily stepped into the conversation when he observed Hamilton's reaction.

"You know Carleton. The man should be replaced. The head wound that he received on the Plains of Abraham obviously has addled his brains. He avoids responsibility like Gage of Philadelphia. Too busy dining and dancing with the local aristocrats, I fear. We will not miss either of them, I tell you. They do not dirty their hands fighting a man's war, so they will go home to play politics as usual."

"And while they are at it, perhaps, they can ship out DePeyster, too." LaMothe interjected following Hay's lead.

"Right so, good man. Bought his commission, that one did. Born in New York, he was. How do we know if we can really trust him?" Hay continued.

No one questioned Hay's logic. Only Abbott wondered at his choice of words given that he believed he had heard that Hay had hailed from Pennsylvania and Hamilton, like so many, bought his commission.

"Is it true? The rumor is that he has run up one rather untidy bill to dance the winter away up north and to pacify his greedy Ottawa

German=this font   English=this font   *French=this font*   *Delaware=this font*

and Chippewa," LaMothe agreed. "He is shelling out way too much. **No**?"

"Hurt feelings. His upper-lake captains from the Chippewa and Ottawa got thumped in New York along with Butler's Rangers. Burgoyne evidently treated them with open contempt, not the deference they expected. You know De Peyster. He claims that he cannot move until the ice leaves and that means any ice." Draining his brandy, Hay burped loudly. "He is an over-educated Swiss, that one," he added before wiping his mouth on his sleeve. The room remained quiet as Hay drew hard and puffed his pipe loudly to bring the sparks to life that nestled in the rich brown tobacco, wreathing his head again in smoke.

"How is Dodge doing?" LaMothe asked Hamilton, seizing a break in the conversation.

"Ah, what? Forgive me, I was distracted."

"The American spy you and DeJean put out in the prison ship?"

Jacob looked uncomfortable, his eyes widening a little. This subject should be best left unsaid in front of Abbott. Trying to catch LaMothe's attention discreetly, he shook his head, trying to indicate to LaMothe that he should drop the subject. LaMothe ignored the secretary's signal as his haughty demeanor came fully into play.

"Dodge..., the American spy. I heard that you had to call Dr. Antron in for him. Now would not that be a pity if he died in the line of duty," LaMothe continued, for LaMothe despised the Americans. He considered them crude and totally without the sense of proper deportment.

Abbott looked up with some surprise. Up until now, he had seemed distant to the patter of the room.

"Do you have a sick American officer prisoner?"

"No. Just a merchant Rebel spy," Hay corrected.

"Yes, but he is responding to care quite satisfactorily." Hamilton wanted the subject to drop. "He is currently at the citadel gaol with good care."

"Good." Abbott selected his words. "I believe if we continue to conduct our affairs with the Americans in a just manner, they will be less likely to go against King and country. You agree, do you not?"

A deafening silence hung in the air, like the haze of Hay's pipe.

Abbott had overstayed his welcome. Without a word, Hamilton decided that it was best to change the direction of the conversation again before Abbott heard too much more. A lull in the conversation resulted.

Abbott took his cue from the prolonged silence.

"I hope you will excuse me, but my wife would no doubt enjoy my company. I should not leave her alone in new surroundings." Abbott arose.

Hamilton nodded obligingly and waved him off. Jacob already had his outer coat and hat in-hand and stood waiting by the door.

"Again, my wife and I thank you for your hospitality."

The other men sensed that the circle had broken and prepared to leave.

German=this font   English=this font   *French=this font*   *Delaware=this font*

"I think I will turn in, too..." Hay dumped the last of his pipe in the coals as LaMothe joined him.

Once all the guests had left, Hamilton turned to Jacob.

"Jacob, get your writing desk. I think it high time that we write again about the need to attack Fort Pitt. Perhaps our January letter did not reach Carleton. Surely Montreal will listen. The outcome for success is so obvious with the Shawnee and Delaware support."

"Can we fully depend on that support? What of the demands of the bands today?"

"Demands?" Hamilton had attempted to forget the earlier confrontation in his office that day. Representatives from the Delaware, Shawnee, Wyandot and Mingo had confronted him. The bands boldly asserted that the British did not share the dangers with their men on the forays. Hamilton made a mental note to have Lernoult call the troops out in the morning to welcome the captive prisoners to be displayed. Ceremony and rum would go far to mend some of the frayed ends.

"I believe the vocal one, Stalking Wolf, fully asserted that if our Captains did not leave off their fat and lazy ways that they would not go forth to raid Wheeling and Kenhawa after their crops were planted."

"I know, I know." Hamilton's vain attempt to deflect their audacious demands ground on him. He absolutely hated to be reminded of his diplomatic failures.

"You were wise to release John Montour. I fear if you would have kept him in the Dungeon with the others, it would have caused even greater resistance among the Delaware. Even the Mingo and Shawnee seemed to support the Delaware in this." Jacob checked carefully to see if all of his secretarial kit was in order before he pulled his small writing table closer to the firelight.

Hamilton waited with some impatience. His crossed leg swung in increasing agitation. The rhythm kept pace with his mounting fury.

The forced release of John Montour had particularly stuck in Hamilton's craw. Montour, the Delaware breed, had once served as a Captain for successful raids in Pennsylvania last fall with Blue Ice and Stalking Wolf's parties. He had once been Hamilton's eyes and ears along the Wabash, attempting to build alliances in the west. But in January, the shifty devil had escaped from Fort Detroit to guide three Virginian prisoners nearly back to Fort Pitt. Had it not been for the superlative tracking skills of the party of Wyandot that Hamilton had sent on their veritable heels, Montour might have succeeded. The only consolation was that Hamilton had finally been able to implicate Dodge, who still lingered in his prison with the Virginians.

"With Montour's defection and Captain Eleople Chene's death, we badly need an interpreter for the Delaware. Stalking Wolf cannot be depended on." Jacob Schieffelin unknowingly had raised the total ire of his superior by his questioning and probing candor.

German=this font   English=this font   **French=this font**   *Delaware=this font*

"Jacob, enough!" Hamilton snapped. He silenced any further comment on the subject of John Montour. He paused. Regaining his composure, he spoke again, "Let us ready that letter to Carleton."

"Yes, Sir."

Jacob settled abruptly. He knew that he had overstepped his bounds.

"Cheri?" Coutincinau reached hesitantly to the crouched figure that whimpered in the dark, shying from his outstretched hand.

"Cheri?" He spoke tenderly.

"Go away."

"Did I hurt you?" He whispered.

"No, go away." Her voice sounded wretched.

"Mon perle noir, why?" He reached again only to have her roughly push his hand away.

"Go away. Leave me alone."

Coutincinau's manly pride asserted itself. He took responsibility for his actions, drunk or sober. Women who once tasted his favors rarely refused a second chance. This woman not only had tasted, she had drained him fully, repeatedly. He would not be put off easily. Her passion had equaled his passion.

Seeing that she was cornered between the barrels, he touched first her foot, cooing softly once more to her in French as he had the night before. The coldness of the iron at her ankle caused Coutincinau to withdraw his hand as if touched by a blacksmith's glowing iron.

"Le cochon, le cochon," Coutincinau hissed. "Your employer es a peeg." Touching the shackle, his hand followed the few rungs of chain to a lock and a large stone with a iron loop. At least she could move a little. Was this why she was so withdrawn?

Coutincinau returned his hand to her shackled limb. After her leg and thigh, he worked patiently up to her breasts. But as soon as he touched her chin, she pushed away his hand. Not one to give up, he returned to the iron clad foot to begin once more. Finally, after many tries, he held her curled form in his lap, cuddling her gently. He knew not to touch her face. He comforted her as she sobbed quietly in his arms. Her long form bent childlike, her face nestled into his broad shoulders surrounded by the scents of tobacco and honest sweat. No celebration of life on this night, he wisely reckoned. By midnight, he had learned the events of the previous day. Giving her rum to dull her pain, he eased her to sleep and left her early, far before dawn.

Finchley sent Pierre just before dawn to check up on Anne. The scoundrel reported back that she was quite alone in the warehouse and sleeping soundly.

On March 11, 1778, another day opened as over one hundred Wyandot, Mingo and Delaware approached Fort Detroit with prisoners and scalps. Phillip DeJean and Jacob Schieffelin chatted studiously over the tally books as the tribal representatives shared their exploits with Hamilton and Hay.

German=this font   English=this font   *French=this font*   *Delaware=this font*

"If this keeps up, we will be over the 8,000 pounds of black powder that we gave out last year."

"Do you think so, Minister DeJean?"

"I know so."

"Well, Quebec and the King want their savage allies."

"Then they will just have to pay the bills!"

Chapter 14   March 29-31, 1778

"Many war-parties bring in prisoners, and have shown a
humanity hitherto unpracticed among them. They never
fail of a gratuity on every proof of obedience they show in
sparing the lives of such as are incapable of defending
themselves."

"All parties going to war are exhorted to act with
humanity as the means of secure peace when His Majesty
shall be pleased to order the hatchet to be buried."

Excerpts from letters sent by Lt. Governor Henry Hamilton to his superiors in
the early spring of 1778 as quoted by Silas Farmer in *History of Detroit and
Wayne County and Early Michigan, 1890* (Silas Farmer and Co. Republished
by Gale Research, 1969), p. 246.

Fort Detroit

Anne balanced the eighty pound bundle of furs in the wooden saddle
strapped to her pack as the tump-line cut ridges in her forehead. Earlier
tracks of those who had hazarded the streets held water like makeshift
vessels. Packed clay became slippery mud. The mud sucked in one's feet,
reluctant to free them, which made any movement labored at best. Rain fell
in slanted opaque sheets. Oh, what she would not give for some of
Coutincinau's rum again to warm and sustain her. The very thought of it
caused her saliva to dilute the flood of water that coursed down her face,
running in her mouth. Unable to breathe through her nose, her mouth hung
open in the drenching rain. Gray fog drifted in and out of her mouth with
every labored breath. Hunger gnawed. Her wet clothes plastered to her
body. Trudging toward the warehouse, Anne struggled under her load. When
her feet slipped from side to side, causing her load to shift, she paused to
realign her burden.

Anne thought back to the harbor and Askin's sloop, the *Welcome*. The
ship brought part of the winter's bounty to be reloaded aboard the larger
boats to begin the trip to Niagara, to Montreal and finally to England. The
needs of commerce demanded loading and reloading at each portage along
the way as part of a complex process to insure that beavers graced the heads
of England's and Europe's fashionable. From freezing cold traps to mad
hatters poisoned by mercury, the gods of fashion held absolute sway.

Passing by Fogherty's Inn, the smell of hot-buttered rum, freshly baked
bread, and the thought of a hot beverage cruelly assaulted her. She avoided
Sue Ellen. She missed their alley chats and the gifts of bread scraps. One
thought drove her forward; the load must be unloaded. She must press on.
Fifteen more bundles waited for her at the wharf. Then, she could rest.
Although, the merchant devils ruled her days, the nights became her heaven.

Eve stood at the open door of the Citadel prisoner barracks. Unending shades of gray patterned the sky, day after day. Endless monotonous gray mixed with endless rain and penetrating mist. Holding a cloth out into the rivulet that streamed off the roof, she rinsed the towel and carefully worked her way back through the women and children to the small blanketed nest that held Mikie. Whimpering, he gratefully accepted the coolness when Eve placed the cold cloth across his shoulders and hot chest. Eve knew that she must keep him cool or he might go into another convulsion. The lessons learned from losing an earlier child had not been forgotten.

A malevolent odor hung about his burning, curled form. Eve took the black willow leaves and wild pin cherry bark that Sally Ainsee had given her and left them to soak in the broken porcelain cup with boiling water. She and Mikie had retrieved the small vessel one day near the shore. The handle gone, it sported a brown tea-soaked crack and three chips on the rim, but she found it useful as it could still hold liquid. By the time it cooled, Mikie would need another dose.

Few ventured out for wood today. The wet wood smoldered in the fireplace on the far wall and gave off little heat.

An occasional cough came from the Landlough's corner. Consumption, Eve feared. She thought she saw flecks of blood in the golden globs that dotted the floor near his bed roll. She devoutly wished that he would clean up after himself, but she forgave him, as he seemed much weaker of late. If she could just find a few scraps of soap thrown out the windows with the washbasin slop near the boarding house, she would wash it up proper. If only she could boil water on a larger scale. Some of her fellows literally wallowed in their own filth. She frowned. This constant grime depressed her. But crammed as they were with new folks coming and ransomed others going, cleanliness seemed an elusive dream. She had never been a spotless householder, but neither was she schmutzig or dirty.

Sitting at Mikie's feet, Eve pulled the bag of cloth scraps that Ezekiel Solomon had given her from Nana. Tucked inside, she found the tiny hand-carved spool of wood with thread wound about it. And, miracle of miracles, she had not dropped or lost the brass needle which ran through a brightly colored scrap. On days when she did not have to work in the King's garden or carry buckets of earth to reposition poles in the stockade, she delighted in fitting and sewing a few of the angles together. Although rarely more than three inches wide, the pieces began to come together as a crazy quilt of sorts. She would soon have a new gown for Mikie if she persevered. Her hands, toughened from labor, could not prevent an occasional poke, which Eve sucked until the blood stopped. She glanced sporadically in the dim light to assess Mikie's condition. The dry, hollow cough concerned her. Earlier, she had carefully inspected his stomach for the remembered red spots, but so far she had found none. The foul odor hung about him like a tiny ominous cloud and harkened her back to her

German=this font   English=this font   *French=this font*   *Delaware=this font*

childhood memories. She remembered too well the putrid smell that seemed to accompany every swallow and every breath. An odor so pervasive, she could not escape it. She wondered if she was just being foolish or if it could be what she feared.

Mikie whimpered again.

"Mutti, Mutti."

"I am here, Mikie. Sleep little one."

He coughed. A dry baying hound chased a phantom fox. Sitting up, he gasped between coughing spasms.

Eve lay her sewing aside and grasped the cooled cup. After his coughing subsided, she brought it to his fever-cracked lips, gently flicking off the hardened blood.

"Drink for Mutti."

Mikie grimaced, but he obediently gulped the cool bitter liquid.

A red pustule leered at Eve from the neck of his gown. When half of the liquid had been drunk, Eve laid the cup aside and carefully inspected her son's hot chest.

"Shumutzig krankheit...dirty sickness!" Eve said very quietly under her breath. She knew better than to utter the word aloud that filled her mind. Death lurked about Mikie. Perhaps he endangered others in the room. Holding her child to her, she rocked him. His hollow eyes flickered open and shut. The odor permeated her nose. She could taste it as she swallowed. The remembered announced itself with certainty. Her fears were realized. She felt absolutely certain; Mikie had the measles.

Jacob Schieffelin added another log. The flaring light flickered around the men's faces as they centered on a map spread on the table before them. The room had a fruity odor from the buttered slices of spiced currant bread on the sideboard. Lernoult, Hay and Hamilton rechecked the position of Fort Pitt in relationship to the Delaware towns mixed with the bothersome German, Moravian settlements.

"By mid-May, the Wyandot and the Shawnee will have their crops in place and will be free to raid again," Hay advised as he looked over the Ohio valley and mentally estimated the numbers that would be available. He knew stating the obvious would draw a glare from Hamilton, which it did.

"Lernoult, would your men lead our reluctant French and our eager merchant militia?" Hamilton asked, knowing the answer almost before the words were out of his mouth.

"We have no orders to leave the fort," Lernoult responded. "You know how many leaners there are. The west wall sags miserably from frost. It will take all my men and the prisoners weeks to right or replace those rotten posts." Sensing Hamilton's hidden disgust, he continued, "Besides, the high command wants us here to keep this port protected for the merchant trade and Captain Grant's ship building."

German=this font   English=this font   *French=this font*   *Delaware=this font*

"Trade will be up this year." Hay sought to change the subject. "Askin says that there will be nearly double the engages. With that many men, we should guarantee a maximum beaver harvest."

"And you say the Indians will not break free until May." Hamilton's words were clipped and precise. "Meanwhile our other dancer, DePeyster, prances about at Fort Michilimackinac, useless as usual. He can not leave the fort because of the weather, he says; but Askin can get his first load of furs down."

"I agree, DePeyster's not much help, but his man, Langlade, seems to be gathering tribes again. Perhaps they could assist you against Fort Pitt," Lernoult suggested, trying to point out a positive.

"Still no response from Carleton, after your January letter?" Hay asked.

"No word yet," Jacob answered when he knew Hamilton would not. He did not mention the second letter which he sent with LaMothe and his men.

"We need to be ready when they give permission to attack." Hamilton remained confident of his proposed plan.

"What do you suggest?" Hay asked.

"First, we can set up supply stations en route; so we can move quickly." Hamilton indicated sites on the map. "Here, here, and here."

"How do you suggest doing that?" Lernoult asked.

"Well, I know of one man who might take the first supplies for troops towards Sandusky for us. Has he recovered, Jacob, that Leeth fellow? You know the one I mean."

"He was still ill when I last called," Jacob replied as he took brandy-laced tea to help ward off a chill to each of the men.

"Is he the one who wanted a license to return to his employer's partner in Sandusky?" Hay asked.

"That is the one," Jacob answered.

"I think I saw him near his boarding house yesterday."

"Check on him in the morning, Jacob," Hamilton ordered casually, confident in his secretary's compliance.

"Can we even trust the French, especially now?" Lernoult asked.

"Why can we not trust them…especially now?" Hay hesitated before adding the last two words. He instantly surmised that he did not know something that the other three did. He frowned.

"We might as well tell him. The rebel rumor mill will be spilling it soon enough," Lernoult said as he pulled back from the table with cup in hand.

"Reliable sources have it that Benjamin Franklin is trying to make a deal with the French in Paris to sign on with the Americans," Hamilton relayed quietly. He drank a draught of tea before continuing. "King George may call this ***petite guerre***, the Presbyterian war; but lately the Pope himself seems to be sticking his nose into the mess."

"You cannot be bloody serious!" Hay responded in disbelief.

German=this font   English=this font   *French=this font*   *Delaware=this font*

Hamilton's eyes snapped open and revealed contempt and anger. Jacob leapt back. The intensity shocked him.

"I will not say it again." His intense glare could have parted hair. "This information should not leave this room. The merchant spy network will relay it soon enough." Hamilton continued, "One can not trust the lazy French Canadians as is now, even without this foul rumor."

"However, this could make more loyalists defect if nothing else will. Not many true Englishmen want to cozy up to the Catholics," Lernoult reasoned.

"First, the Spanish support on our western flank and now possibly the French. The Rebels must be crawling in bed with the Pope," Hay agreed.

An unexpected rap on the door brought all the men in the room to attention. Jacob opened the door to find a travel-worn, totally soaked, Sergeant John Turney.

"Lieutenant Governor, sir. Beggin' the late hour, sir."

"Come in, come in, good man. You are a glad sight." Hamilton rose to greet the young man. The others moved aside so Turney could approach the fire.

"You are safely returned." Hamilton extended his hands to clasp Turney's in welcome.

"Yes, sir. I came ashore first. Wait 'til you see the *Gage*, sir. She's a fine ship. Her fourteen guns will give those Rebels his Majesty's broadside. On that you can depend!"

Jacob pulled the wet cape from Turney's shoulders and laid it over the chair by his desk. After Turney released Hamilton's hands, he extended his arms toward the fire, gratefully accepting the warmth and rubbing his hands in the flickering light.

"I return with good news, sir."

"We could use some," Lernoult responded.

"I stopped in Niagara. Two day layover there."

"Then you saw Butler...?" Hamilton's voice betrayed his impatience.

"Yes, sir. He sends a wampum belt from the Six Nations." He paused, pulling the belt from his travel packet. In the firelight, they could see the fifteen white squares and the distinct initials of WJ at one end and the 1774 at the other. "Butler says it will make your tribes act as one man with one voice. He says it calls them to revenge and to support the King."

"Well, let us hope Butler is right. Sir William Johnson's name still holds magic for the tribes. We have only had a few troubles. I rather doubt if we will actually need it. So far they seem to 'continue to act with good temper, unanimity and success'"** "In point of fact, the Mingo even turned a young boy over to me a while back. They are becoming far more humane under our supervision." Hamilton took the wampum belt from Turney and looked at it carefully in the firelight. "Only

German=this font   English=this font   ***French=this font***   *Delaware=this font*

the tribes along the Wabash and White Eye's Delaware are not falling in line. They say that they prefer neutrality. At least they have not sided with the Rebels like the Oneida up Butler's way."

"Ah, but Butler has Joseph Brant with his Mohawks and his loyalist troops. The man is a treasure." One could hear a trace of lament in Hay's voice.

Jacob took the wampum and laid it gingerly across his desk.

"True," Lernoult added, "the Six Nations are not as strong as they once were. Besides, many have not joined the Rebels out of their fear of the Virginian's Longknives."

"The bumbling murderers in Pennsylvania helped too," Hay added.

"Do we have any news from Carleton?" Hamilton asked.

Turney did not answer.

"Do we have orders from Carleton?" Hamilton repeated.

"No, sir. Butler is frustrated too, sir."

Hamilton turned away. Beads of perspiration appeared on his forehead in the firelight as he grasped the back of the chair. His carotids swelled, pulsing with steady surges.

"No targets, no directions, no tactics?" Lernoult asked incredulously.

The fire crackled and whistled. Gas escaped from one log causing a spike of green and blue to color the fire. A prolonged stillness hung like the faint residue of smoke.

"No, sir." Turney broke the silence.

"Did Butler say when LaMothe and his men will be permitted to return?" Hay asked.

"No, sir. Could be as late as May some say."

Stevens, Paul Lawrence, *His Majesty's Savage Allies: British Policy and the Northern Indians During the Revolutionary War, The Carleton Years.* **1774-1778 XXIII p. 1580. A dissertation submitted to the Faculty of the Graduate School of the State University of New York, New York: Buffalo. Feb 1984. Turney's gift of the Johnson Belt and the reminder of the "inter-tribal coalition forged in September 1776," documented in this text p. 1579-1580.

Anne's water jug drained of its rummy contents laid on its side on the floor beside her. She sat with her legs straight before her. The shackle around her ankle held her in her place each night until Pierre came in the morning to free her. But while Anne could not exit, her lover could bring comfort to her. And he did.

Coutincinau blew the nipples of her breasts until they puckered tightly and then he nuzzled, her rubbing his rough stubbled chin across their hardened tips. Her head spun as she pushed him away playfully.

"You already got your fun." She blinked at him, trying to focus on his face which blurred in and out. "I just cold, Coutincinau." She pulled her arms across her bare breasts and shivered before drawing her chemise back into place. "I is so damn cold. I freezin'."

"More rum...?"

German=this font   English=this font   *French=this font*   *Delaware=this font*

"No, no." Anne shook her head in a vain attempt to straighten her vision and her jumbled mind.

"I hold you."

"No, nooo..." Anne's voice trailed off.

Coutincinau tried to pull her into his arms, but she pushed him away for a second time. His temporary warmth held no promise for her.

"No...I cold. I be cold all day."

"I make you fire."

"Your fire don't keep me warm all night." Anne giggled.

"No, woman, I make you real fire."

"You make fire?" Her speech and her mind sloshed and slurred.

"You don't think Coutincinau can make fire. I make fire anywhere," his rum bragged.

"No, no fire." The protest was diluted at best as reason flickered momentarily to the surface but then immediately dipped out of sight.

"I make you fire. You see." Staggering to his feet, Coutincinau broke off a few wooden pegs from the wall for fuel and gathered up two discarded slats from an old broken barrel that lay abandoned on the floor.

Too drunk to oppose, Anne watched as Coutincinau took his knife to shred the corners of some of the support posts nearest them. Before long a small pile of wood shavings mounded between them. Fuel awaited a spark.

"I make you warm. You see my ***noir beaute***. I make you warm." He slit a bundle near him and pulled one of the beaver hoops from it. Before Anne could protest or even whimper, the pelt, freed from its lacing, draped around her shoulders. The rich layers of hair and downy inner fluff cuddled her. She pulled it about her. The tag-alder hoop, quickly broken, waited its turn to be fuel. Why had she not thought of that, she wondered? A tiny little fire would not hurt. Surely one little hide would not be missed?

Then kneeling before her, Coutincinau took his flint and steel. Sparks sprayed into the dry wood. In moments, a small fire sprung to life to warm her ice cold hands.

Warmth brought a welcome lethargy. Cradling Anne in his arms, they circled the fire with their bodies catching the heat inside the hide. Coutincinau held her to him and exhaustion soaked with rum surrendered all their cares to the arms of Morpheus.

A faint smell of smoke greeted Pierre as he snuck in the door well before dawn. He had reported a wayward crust and a faint whiff of rum to Finchley yesterday. This had caused his employer to order him to make an earlier than normal check on his wayward esclave. The sight of the black bitch in the arms of her lover brought a broad smile to Pierre's bony face. If he ran for Finchley now, Coutincinau might be gone and only the black would bear his employer's wrath. He could see that the fire had burned down and a black charred floor spoke of a once potential danger. This would damn them both.

German=this font   English=this font   ***French=this font***   *Delaware=this font*

Somehow, Pierre must immobilize Coutincinau before he raised the alarm. Then he saw it; a shovel propped by the door in a thin shaft of pale morning light. The perfect solution awaited him. Although he suspected rum might give him a decided advantage, Pierre would not take any chances. Even now, Coutincinau's strength and agility could be real trouble.

Moving like a shadow, Pierre positioned himself very carefully and swung the shovel with a vengeance. Totally unprepared, the well-placed blow immediately cold-crocked Coutincinau. The shock of intrusion, the depth of a deep rum stupor, and post-coital sleep delayed Anne's first scream of shock. Pierre turned like a rabbit and scooted for the alarm triangle outside. Grasping the wrought iron striker, he began to clang the alarm triangle with every bit of might that he could muster.

Anne began to scream in earnest. A trickle of blood coursed down the side of Coutincinau's face. Shaking Coutincinau, she feared the worst. Was he dead? How could he get away? What's happening? What's ringing? Everything was happening at once. The noise, the infernal ringing, her head, nothing seemed to make sense. Placing her hands over her throbbing ears, she screamed.

Before Coutincinau could regain consciousness, a ring of partially clothed men had encircled the two culprits. Cocked fusils pointed directly at an attenuated Coutincinau and a stone quiet Anne. Only Anne's bloody shackle revealed her frantic efforts to pull free.

To add to the circus-like atmosphere, Pierre ran to the horse trough and brought bucket after bucket of icy water, dumping it half on Anne and half on the charred floor long after any faint ember remained. Struggling not to smile or look inordinately pleased, he suppressed a laugh as his employer confronted Anne and her lover.

"As soon as he puts out your odious arson attempt, Pierre will go directly to Phillip DeJean and post charges." Finchley's face flushed a horrible purple-red with anger. "Do you hear me, foul woman?"

Anne could hear him. So could others a block away as he bellowed at her.

"God, as my witness, I warned you!"

Finchley paced about Anne and Coutincinau's feet making a semicircle before he trumpeted at her again.

"Woman, after all my Christian charity and you repay me like this!" When Anne neither responded nor showed any emotion, Finchley turned his attention to Coutincinau. First, he kicked at Coutincinau's thighs. Finding the muscles unyielding, he kicked his ribs repeatedly. Coutincinau, who was bound and semi-conscious, moaned after each blow's impact.

Anne remained detached.

"We should have arrested you on the first round. Thief!! Ingrate!" Finchley continued to rant. He lowered his fusil to raise his other hand with a golden coin. "You see black whore, I kept this gold as

German=this font   English=this font   *French=this font*   *Delaware=this font*

proof." Finchley's parting words followed Anne and Coutincinau as they were half dragged by the others, limping and slipping their way to the gaol in the Citadel.

John Leeth drank his cold tea as his old partner sat beside his bed in the early morning light.

"Are you quite recovered now, John?" John Sterling asked.

"Yes, but I feign weakness to avoid the draft. Hamilton's henchmen will be out soon enough to devil the poor souls about the Ohio," Leeth answered. "They're sure to drag the militia with them."

"There is a rumor that's been relayed to me. Hamilton probably will need your services. This would be a good time to move our load to Sandusky. The boat, she is loaded, but I have left you a little room."

"A little room. For what?"

"Now lad, best you not be a know'n every thing." A partial smile crept across his employer's partner's face. Now that Sterling had returned, Solomon contacted Leeth rarely. Sterling's eyes wrinkled with merriment and his furry black eyebrows ruffled with humor. "Business has its ways."

"Well then, I'd best ask for a pass to leave again. Am I right?"

"Aye, lad. This is the best time to ask. And I wouldn't dally about it. Tis not wise to malinger now."

His partner stood, turned the chair about, and quietly closed the door behind him.

Leeth rose from his bed and began to pull his knee breeches in place, fastening the buttons at the knees. John Leeth truly dreaded facing Hamilton, but the desire to leave Fort Detroit proved stronger. Sometimes he wished that he had the strength of Moses to make the ground open up and swallow Hamilton and the filth about him like Korah and his men. But his wishes failed. The God that he learned of at his father's knee rarely intervened directly in the affairs of men, he concluded from his observations of life thus far.

Moving quickly, Leeth managed to be at the office before the guard had arrived after receiving his employer's orders.

Jacob ushered him in, relieved that he would not have to hazard the streets. Although the rain had stopped, the mud remained formidable.

Hamilton looked up as Leeth entered his office.

"I see you are returned to health." Hints of distrust skirted his words. "Leeth it is, is it not?"

"Yes, sir. John Leeth. And I am gaining strength, sir." John stood quietly, his hat in hand. He hoped that he had removed most of the mud from his moccasins on the blades by the door.

Hamilton, still in his silk banyan, reflected relaxed comfort. Steaming tea and fresh hot biscuits sat at his desk side. Jacob saw to it that he lacked for nothing upon awakening.

German=this font   English=this font   *French=this font*   *Delaware=this font*

"And what brings you out this early morning?" Hamilton asked. He enjoyed dangling the words before the man like a child teasing a cat with a bit of fluff on a string.

"Well, sir, as you know, I have been needin' to take goods to my employer's partner in Sandusky. His boat is loaded, and with your permission, I would accompany those goods to the Wyandot." John swatted the fluff but held his own.

"Goods to the Wyandot?"

"Yes, sir." John did not look away or down.

Hamilton did not answer for a moment before tossing the fluff once more.

"But do you not understand just the Delaware language?"

"Well, yes, but my employer's partner knows the Wyandot, sir," Leeth countered.

"Are you sure that your employer would not release you to work as interpreter for me?" Hamilton delighted in his game.

Leeth did not rise to his baiting. "I believe," Leeth paused, "we could be gone on the evening wind, with your permission."

Noting that Leeth had evaded his question, Hamilton opted for his other pressing need. "Would you have room to take some goods for my department?"**

"Well, sir, there's not much room, but perhaps we could snug it up a little." John Leeth joined the pretense, pretending to be unaware of any prior knowledge. "How much do you have, sir?" Even if Hamilton was not in cahoots with Sterling, someone behind the scenes was.

"Six barrels, four of flour, and two of pork. Perhaps a few small parcels." Hamilton's gaze riveted John. "Will you make room?"**

"Yes, if the provisions could be loaded today?"

"I think that could be arranged. I have a specific spot where I want these stored. You will see to it, if you receive a trade license and pass, I assume."

"Yes, sir."

Hamilton quickly signed a pass that Jacob had prepared for him in advance to use on such occasions. He also gave Leeth a small map which plotted the drop spot for his cache. Then, turning his back to John, he visibly dismissed him without saying a single word. Jacob, catching his cue quickly, showed John to the door, frowning at the muddy tracks.

The guard now having returned to his station immediately confronted John as he turned to exit Hamilton's office.

"Ah, I see you have a license. Now you must get yer certificate to leave the fort." The guard observed the flapping piece of paper in John's hand like a prearranged signal flag. "You need to see the Chief Justice. A certificate is necessary to make your license valid."**

"A what?"

"A certificate to allow you to leave the fort."

"Why?" John hoped his real feelings didn't show.

German=this font   English=this font   **French=this font**   *Delaware=this font*

"Them's the orders. Go see Justice DeJean." The guard smiled. "I don't make the orders, I just make sure they're followed."

John tried unsuccessfully to mask the frustration that he felt as he turned towards DeJean's Office. He shook his head in disbelief as he trudged in the outer door and waited in the hallway.

As usual, DeJean allowed all those who sought him out to cool their heels for a considerable time to impress them with his authority. In time, three others joined John in the hall. By the time John stood before DeJean's desk, it took every ounce of his self-control not to explode at the man that masqueraded as Chief of Justice.

"I understand I need to pay to obtain a certificate to leave the fort." John stated the obvious, knowing what was expected of him.

DeJean looked over Leeth's pass perfunctorily and then smiled the fullest smile possible before speaking.

"Yes, you will need bail of five-hundred-pounds sterling."**

The bail's staggering amount snuffed Leeth like a doused candle flame leaving a visible trail of smoke. Heat remained.

"Five—five hundred pounds?" Was the Justice daft?

"Yes, you will need bail of five hundred pounds. No bail, no certificate to use your pass to leave the Fort." DeJean fingered the paper still smiling to the fullest, showing off his snaggled teeth. "I will be happy to hold your pass until you return with the fee." On the surface DeJean's face looked cordial and pleasant like a reflecting pond. But if one hazarded to break that surface stillness, deep treachery would be found.**

John left the office with the words of DeJean wringing all reality out of his mind. When Finchley's man, Pierre, pressed by him to enter DeJean's office next, John barely noted his presence.

"The bastard sat there with a stinking grin, worse than a lowly skunk! I can't believe it!" John's composure dissolved completely before his old partner. "I cannot believe it!" He continued to storm, stomping about the Sterlings' parlor.

"Calm down lad. Calm down."

"Calm down. I don't have five hundred pounds sterling!"

"True lad, but they suspect I do. It is the price of doing business, lad. You do not think that Hamilton got that silky embroidered banyan on a mere Lieutenant Governor's salary, now do you laddie?" His employer's eyes twinkled for the second time that day. "Come now...." John Sterling attempted again to calm his man down.

His flames doused for the second time in less than an hour, John Leeth took a deep breath and sat down dejectedly.

"The cost of doing business...?" Leeth sat, lurching forward. His hands were clasped between his knees.

"Aye, the cost of doing business. Now simmer ye down. We will go back there 'n' wait for DeJean to give us audience. Believe me,

German=this font   English=this font   *French=this font*   *Delaware=this font*

your wait will be shorter this time. We will pay the bond, and you will be on your way by morning's light."

His partner proved right. John Leeth breathed in the crisp lake air. He rejoiced to leave the hell of Fort Detroit behind him. The clouds broke in irregular patterns allowing streaks of sunlight to fall on the rippled surface. Sun at last, free at last, John vowed never to return.**

**Jeffries, Ewel, *A Short Biography of John Leeth, Giving a Brief Account of His Travels and Sufferings Among the Indians for Eighteen Years Together With His Religious Exercises From His Own Relations* (Lancaster, Ohio: Gazette Office, 1891) as related by Thwaites, Ruben Gold, Ed., *A Short Biography of John Leeth with an account of his life among the Indians* (New York: Benjamin Blom Inc., 1972). Closely paraphrased on p. 33-35. In research materials, the charismatic James Sterling, a Detroit merchant, was selected as he was a perfect foil for Hamilton and figures well in the story of Anne and Coutincinau. As usual, John Leeth in his account does not name his employers or associates.

March 31, 1778   Fort Detroit

Morning brought an unexpected gift to Eve and Mikie. Solomon's man had dropped off a tiny container of dry ground corn dust to put on Mikie's red pustules and a small container of broth. Eve immediately recognized Nanna's handiwork for the ill when the odors wafted into the air. The warm scented cloud brought envious glances from those around her as she poured a small portion into her cup and held it to Mikie's hot lips. Bless the woman, Eve thought. However did she know we needed this so badly? Somehow she must repay the family for their kindness. But she had so little. What could she possibly do in return?

Across the room, a new hoarse cough joined the day noise. Was another child ill?

When Coutincinau finally regained full consciousness, he realized that he had company in his cell. The smell of urine and feces constituted his first clue. A cough and deep moan comprised the second. When his eyes adjusted to the diminished light, he saw an emaciated form beside him in the narrow cell. Though breathing and movement of any kind brought instant pain as reminders of earlier blows, Coutincinau edged his way closer to his companion.

"*Sacra bleu*, what did you do to deserve this, good man."

Dodge looked into the black and blue face of the handsome Frenchman and managed to summon a weak smile.

"I think they call it spying." The effort caused a prolonged moan and a coughing spell. When he finally stopped, Coutincinau assisted him to a sitting position. Both took great care not to spill the bucket which needed to be emptied of its foul contents. Catching his breath, Dodge appraised his companion.

"And you?"

German=this font   English=this font   *French=this font*   *Delaware=this font*

"The fire of love, **mon ami**." Coutincinau laughed and then clutched his sides from the resulting pain, **"le feu de amour."** The second time spoken barely above a whisper, Coutincinau did not laugh. He turned his head away so Dodge could not see the tears that welled up and threatened to spill over. Neither spoke again for a great while. Darkness fell about them as they both drifted into a painful sleep.

"Stop!" Eve raised her hand to halt Sue Ellen's approach.

Sue Ellen complied instantly. Her tear-streaked face drew in the scene before her. Eve had just rocked Mikie back to sleep in her cross-legged nesting position that Sue Ellen knew so well. But Eve's reluctance to let her approach puzzled her.

A shrewish woman a few blankets over quickly brought Sue Ellen up to date.

"The filthy German's pretty little festered son has the measles." The shrew, on a roll, continued, "Go ahead, get real close pretty one. You can have the cursed spots too."

Another hostile voice from Langlough's corner chimed in. "She has been with them Jews. That's what done it." He coughed and spat on the floor about him, leaving another blood speckled glob as if to agree with the speaker.

Eve just shook her head sadly, immediately conveying her feelings to Sue Ellen.

"I hav' more bad news, Eve." Sue Ellen spoke distinctly but not so loud that her voice would carry like Eve's informing neighbors.

"Anne's in the gaol's dungeon 'cross the way."

"Why in the name of heaven." Eve's reply sounded more like a heavy sigh. "Armes teufel (poor soul)".

Mikie moaned and Eve shifted him to give him greater comfort.

"They say that she and Coutincinau stole some pelts and stuff and that they tried to burn down Finchley's warehouse."

Eve looked up at Sue Ellen. Her forehead tightened and wrinkled the space between her eyebrows with questioning concern.

"That does not sound like anything those two would do. Are you sure?"

"It's all over Fogherty's. Everybody's buzzing about it."

"God help her. No one will believe good of her."

"Right about that. With them being poor an' all, that DeJean will really put them to the screws."

"What makes you think so?"

"Jonas says he heard that DeJean's been laying for Coutincinau. Don't know why he would despise another Frenchman so, him being French n'all. But that's what they say."

Eve noticed the tear trails on her friend's cheeks. "You've been crying."

"Yeah, some."

German=this font   English=this font   *French=this font*   *Delaware=this font*

"I wish you could come closer, but you had best keep your distance."

"Is he gonna die?" Sue Ellen nodded in the direction of Mikie.

"I do not think so." She caressed Mikie's forehead, pushing hair back from his face now spotted and reddish. "He is still drinking and peeing. I have strong hopes." Mikie's head hung back as he mouth breathed. "I do not hear any death rattles."

"That's good."

"You best go."

"Eve?"

"I know it hurts."

"Bye."

Eve watched sadly as Sue Ellen departed. Sue Ellen's shoulders looked as if she were carrying one of Anne's heaviest loads. Eve would have given anything just to put her arms about the girl to give them both comfort. She surveyed the room about her. All the frustration and sense of helplessness about Anne, Coutincinau, and Sue Ellen descended on her. In addition, she confronted Mikie and her own condition. Being called a filthy German added to the mix. Together these began to bubble as rage.

Some women drink, explode, implode, or nag when filled with rage…others clean. Eve cleaned. As soon as Mikie mended, she was going to do something about this sty. Her pig, Minnie, had lived better than this. Half the reason folks got sick, she surmised, was because they lived in this squalor. They must boil their clothes and blankets and scrub this flea and lice-infested hall. No longer would she accept these conditions as part of her imprisonment.

Eve's skin itched. She knew full well she had lice. She had noted the blood trails from the bed bugs. With no bath since the church, she stunk so bad she could hardly stand herself. Just like Mikie's festering pustules and stoked fever, the idea to clean had festered and now stoked up energy and gathered immense heat.

How had Nanna ever been so kind to them? How had Nanna ever held her to her breast?

When Mikie healed, the shrew and Langlough would be first on her list to face major changes, Eve concluded. Things were going to be different. The damned British might have the right to pen them up in here and make them work like bloody dogs, as they would say, but she and her fellows did not have to put up with this squalor. They could do something to change living in this hall.

A new Eve had been growing and healing under the filthy blankets during the long horrible winter. The strength of the old Eve had metamorphosed. Yankee Hall would never be the same while she was under its roof.

Chapter 15   April 1778, Justice Prevails?

"[first strike] **only one man, with some women and children was found...another woman was taken...and with difficulty saved; the remainder escaped...**[second strike]**...turned out to be four women and a boy, of whom one woman only was saved...In performing these great exploits...I had but one man—a captain wounded, and one drowned.**"

American General Edward Hand's written report to his commander concerning the activities of his 500 man strike force in February 1778. As quoted by Consul Willshire Butterfield in *History of the Girtys* (Robert Clark & Co. 1890 reprinted in Columbus, Ohio: Long's College Book Co., 1950), p. 48.

Fort Detroit

Pompey watched as the woman ahead of him allowed the child to range and then waggled her fingers from time to time to have him touch security and fetch a smile. The blonde's shaky toddle proved as irregular as his makeshift patched gown which caught the waning sunlight. He stumbled along and poked at a particularly interesting branch or treasure to be gathered up and placed in the other hand of the woman, as was his habit. The next time he touched the outstretched fingers, he raised his arms high over his head indicating his desire to be carried. Still somewhat winded from measles, Mikie gradually grew in strength each day, but he tired quickly. This time, his best smile failed. His mother refused. Her walk was labored but steady as she sought out the May's ribbon farm laid out like all the others, side-by-side, in parallel strips along the river. After a day of hauling buckets of mud for the palisade, she shook her head negatively, whereupon the youngster began to fuss.

"Would he permit me to carry him?" The deep baritone voice startled Eve, who turned to face the statuesque black. He walked stealthily, she noted. She had not realized his proximity to them as she had concentrated on Mikie's mini-excursions.

"Many children are frightened of me," he added.

Eve recognized him immediately. Somehow she associated him with her very first day at the fort, but those memories seemed unreliable at times. What serendipity! The manservant belonged to May.

"Yes, Pompey, he would delight if you carried him," and then she added with some shame, "but you may not wish to assist. You are clean. We have lice."

German=this font   English=this font   *French=this font*   *Delaware=this font*

"Thanks for the warning, madam." Pompey laughed good-naturedly as he swung a grinning Mikie into place. With no hesitation, Mikie soon straddled Pompey's thick strong neck just as he had Anne's so many times. Mikie's fingers at first played with the ruffles about his neck. Then, to Pompey's utter surprise, the child burrowed his short stubby fingers deep into Pompey's kinky hair and rubbed his cheek lovingly against the cropped hair as if renewing an old friendship before he giggled aloud with sheer delight. As they bobbed along down the road, Pompey steadied Mikie's back with one hand.

"Mutti, Mutti. Mikie high, high."

"Indeed you are my son."

"What brings you about, good woman. 'Tis late. Darkness falls soon."

"I wish to visit your master." Her response brought a momentary flush of pain to the man's face. Pompey looked away. They walked without speaking for some time. The only chatter or laughter came from Mikie.

"I am so sorry. Where are my manners?" Eve drew up short. She wiped her hands thoroughly on her apron to remove any residual mud. "My name is Eve, Eve Earnest." Eve extended her hand. The simple movement caught Pompey totally off guard.

Pompey paused momentarily, grasped her hand firmly just for a moment and then just as quickly dropped it. He looked around quickly, checking about to see if anyone could have possibly espied them.

Slightly embarrassed, Eve looked straight ahead. After a few steps, Pompey spoke.

"I knew your name, Mistress Earnest. Rumor has it...you are a troublemaker." A bit of license between slave and esclave permitted a freedom and openness not normally accepted. Eve instantly recognized the sparring good humor in his voice.

"Really?" Eve looked up at him, raising her eyebrows. Then her face broke into a full smile. Her eyes twinkling with good humor caused tiny wrinkles about her eyes to tighten.

"Really!" He grinned and chuckled. "How came you to know my name?"

"Pompey, everyone knows your name. You are hard to miss."

"Indeed, I guess I am."

They laughed at their mutual joke, relaxing any further tension between them.

"What rumors fly about me?"

"They call you the scrubbing demon."

"You jest." Eve began to laugh so hard that the tears welled up in her eyes. Goodness, it felt so good to laugh, she thought, as she wiped a tear from her cheek with the back of her hand.

"How did you get leave of the Citadel?"

"Captain Lernoult gave me permission to come."

"Mutti, Mutti, see birdies." Mikie squealed.

German=this font   English=this font   *French=this font*   *Delaware=this font*

Eve glanced up to see a small oak laden with in passenger pigeons in a nearby field. The tiny leaves, not much larger than the size of mouse ears, were totally hidden in feathered drapes as the birds cooed and chortled among the branches. As the males vied for their female's attention, smaller branches broke under their weight.

"Not a good place to land. Their noise will bring those who have nets," Pompey observed quietly before addressing Eve again. "Why do you need to see Master May?"

"I understand he owns the big kettles that we had at Ste. Anne's."

"Indeed, he does." Pompey suppressed an inclination to scratch his neck, deciding it was more the thought of lice and hoping that it was not a reality.

"We need to boil clothes and blankets."

"I understand."

"And take baths!" The latter said with such force and conviction that it left little doubt of Eve's full intent to make it happen.

"Do you think the others at Yankee Hall will go along with your plans?" Pompey's broad smile indicated his full appreciation of her feistiness.

"They will or they will sleep outdoors." Eve returned the grin just as broadly.

They walked quietly for a spell. Mikie, lulled by the gentle jogging motion and by the feathered chorister's evening songs, began to nod off.

"I understand you visit the black woman?"

Eve hesitated. Rumors really do get about, she decided.

"Yes, I visit Anne." Her eyes looked straight ahead.

"That is brave."

"No, not really," Eve answered thoughtfully, "She is our friend."

Nothing more needed to be said as they approached May's blacksmith shed.

The guard pushed Coutincinau into DeJean's office. Stumbling, Coutincinau caught himself just in time to prevent a humiliating fall, straightened himself to his fullest height as limited only by his bound hands behind him, and stood quietly erect.

"If you do not bolt, I will ask the guard to leave." DeJean spoke in French to Coutincinau.

"I will remain."

With a flick of his hand, DeJean dismissed the guard.

"But Sir, he is a prisoner. I should..."

"He will remain," DeJean interrupted him. "He is too weak to run far. Even you could catch him." DeJean rebuked the heavy-set soldier further. "Wait at the door. I will call you when he is to return to his cell."

The guard, though unconvinced, excused himself from their presence.

"Please be seated."

German=this font   English=this font   *French=this font*   *Delaware=this font*

"I prefer to stand." This position cost Coutincinau dearly, as his knees felt rubbery and his stance uncertain after so many days in the cramped cell with only watery oat-slop to sustain him. In the warm room, the smell of his stale perspiration and urine floated about him dehumanizing him further, but Coutincinau summoned his pride. He refused to cower before this man.

"You realize that Finchley has charged you with theft and arson."

"I was told this."

"You know the proof is irrefutable." DeJean evaluated Coutincinau to monitor his reaction. Seeing none, he continued.

"You also must realize that you and the black whore will most likely hang."

The words stung.

Coutincinau curbed a very strong impulse to kill DeJean with his bare hands, knowing that in his weakened and bound condition this excuse for a man sitting before him would delight in having the upper hand. No one would be happier to find a cause to inflict physical punishment. So, Coutincinau merely clenched his teeth first and then his hands into tight fists. His eyes narrowed slightly, but his gaze never faltered. The small wooden cane leaning against DeJean's desk had not gone unnoticed. Dodge bore the marks on his shoulders and face from the cane's blows. Coutincinau's ribs still remained tender from Finchley's flying booted feet. He desired no further physical contacts if they could be avoided. He stood mute.

"Did you hear me, Coutincinau? You and the wretched hussy will hang."

"I did not know that the __English__ crown gave you that much authority under the Quebec Act." Each word Coutincinau spoke distinctly, never once raising his voice.

To have a mere voyageur utter such a contemptible challenge caused DeJean to draw in a deep, deep breath. Red crept up slowly from under his collar, flowing onto his cheeks as he exhaled fully. His lips pursed. His eyes hardened with anger. His hand reached for the cane but stopped. Picking up his penknife instead, he passed his thumb ever so gently across the small curved blade that he used to scrape ink from parchment or paper. The edge left a tiny line of residual black ink on his skin's surface. Staring hard at the prisoner before him, he made tiny imaginary cuts to his palm and finally drew the knife repeatedly, like one sharpening a razor on a leather strop, back and forth across the back of his hand. On each return stroke, the dark hairs on the back of his hand struggled and wriggled to avoid being severed from their roots. A few failed to succeed, remaining instead on the shiny surface of the tiny blade. To have this lowly engage provoke DeJean into raising his voice would be completely beneath his station, he concluded.

Both men remained rigid. The knife and hand constituted the only

German=this font English=this font *French=this font* *Delaware=this font*

movement in the room. The rotating tips tapped on each turn. The sound from DeJean's penknife as it struck the edge of his writing table became like the ticking of a time piece in the intense lull. Tick, tick, tick emitted after each flip. With each turn, DeJean's fingers slid down the sides of the knife in a mock caress.

"And what do you think of your spy bunk-mate and his two Virginian friends?" DeJean spoke after a very long period of time.

"And why should you care?"

A flicker of venom crossed DeJean's eyes, like a blink of a nictitating membrane. One side of his mouth curved upward, for he could not fully mask his intense desire to grin. This time DeJean spoke as if coiled to strike. *"Perhaps if one could report the conversations of an American rebel spy among his fellows, one might be granted leniency."* DeJean paused. His tongue slicked his upper lip as if testing the air about him before thrusting it behind his lower teeth and causing his jaw to harden before he hissed, *"Perhaps a black slut might even be returned to her employer with only a public beating to show for her stupidity."*

Coutincinau drew a deep breath. Holding the breath within, he rocked ever so slightly up on to the balls of his feet but compensated quickly. His chin rose with defiant pride. His nostrils flared slightly as he slowly exhaled. He stood rightly accused, but to condemn a brother victim of the English crown or worse yet...still others...assaulted his French pride to the greatest depth imaginable.

For Coutincinau, to even deign to answer the unthinkable insulted him to the core.

The tapping penknife monitored the stillness. *"If you would consider hanging your cellmate, Dodge, I will even throw in an extra twenty pounds."*

DeJean's eyes never left Coutincinau's, nor Coutincinau's his. After minutes of ticking silence passed, DeJean spoke once more. *"Perhaps, if you listen carefully to your cell mate, Dodge, and the Virginian's and truly consider both you and your woman's fates, you will see fit to return to me."* Then he dropped the penknife, grabbed the cane, and whacked the cane sharply on the desk top to drive his point home. To his delight, Coutincinau jumped back one step. The jar as Coutincinau came down brought unsuppressed pain to the voyageur's features. As the guard burst through the door in response to the sound, DeJean expressed his amusement in the form of a thin, tight smile. He nodded to Coutincinau, savoring his power.

"This man desires to return to his cell with half rations." Setting the cane down behind his desk, he grasped his quill, and dipped it into the ink well. DeJean perfunctorily returned to his record-keeping as the guard shoved the prisoner from the room.

German=this font   English=this font   *French=this font*   *Delaware=this font*

Coshocton, Ohio

"Some days ago, a flock of birds that had come on from
the East lit at Goschochking [Coshocton], imposing a
song of theirs upon us, which song had nigh proved our
ruin! Should these birds, which upon leaving us, took
their flight toward Scioto, endeavor to impose a song on
you likewise, do not listen to them for they lie."

White Eyes to Shawanese as quoted by Consul Willshire Butterfield, 1890,
History of the Girtys (reprinted Columbus, Ohio: Long's College Book Co.,
1950), p. 60.

The village of Coshocton literally hummed with the business of
planting. Coshocton's ideal location on the Muskingum River, a tributary
of the Ohio, meant that the river's water nurtured their crops. The soil, a
gift from the movement of glaciers in earlier eons, held the promise of a
good crop. The Delaware of Killbuck and White Eyes, freed by their
choice of neutrality, focused their energies on the planting of corn, beans
and squash, known as the three sisters. Tradition held that as long as the
three sisters stayed with the people, they would live on and never die of
hunger.

Other men protected those who harvested spring greens instead of
raiding the settlements of Virginia, Kentucky, and Pennsylvania. Drying
racks hung heavy with fish soaking up the sun. The seasonal run had been
bountiful this year. Neat wooden cabins fringed by new green and an
occasional lilac stood amongst orchards full of swollen buds longing for
just enough warmth to burst open for the coming of the bees. Children
chased hoops with sticks slashing at the spinning orbs. Their squeals of joy
echoed in the dirt streets.

Everyone savored the emergence of spring, sprinkling the air with
laughter as they labored.

This location gave ease to the Delaware pushed inland from their
coastal homes as they were forced westward by the ever-pressing tide of
European migration. The Delaware, who sold land to William Penn, filled
the void left after the Erie's annihilation by the Six Nations, who came with
superior arms supplied by the British during the French and Indian War.
The Delaware remained in Ohio with the blessings of the Shawnee and the
Wyandot, who benefited as part of the Huron Confederacy.

The village of Coshocton had easy access to the Great Path, which
also connected with the Nachez and the Sante Fe Paths. As the Great Path
came through the passes of the Appalachians of Pennsylvania from the east,
it also connected to the Great Lakes Paths to the north and west. In
peaceful times, the community would have been a major trade center.
However, in times of war, the traffic included Rebel and British supporters

German=this font   English=this font   *French=this font*   *Delaware=this font*

alike. The Great Path funneled Hamilton's allies, who held the hatchet for His Majesty, King George, en route to their raids. When the raiders returned with prisoners and scalps, they retraced the Great Path. Likewise, when the rebellious upstarts from the east sought to attack Sandusky or Fort Detroit, they too would pass near or through Coshocton. Escapees fleeing captivity also sought solace there.

The Great Path provided all who passed access to Coshocton and the tribe's hospitality as they traveled. Coshocton fed Half King's arrogant Wyandot. The Wyandot harassed the Delaware women and taunted the younger Delaware men whom they considered too cowardly to fight. The Delaware even endured those, who killed their precious livestock. Coshocton also welcomed the Rebel representatives guided by Hand's troops from Fort Pitt and fed escaping rebels.

However, neutrality came at a high price. Suspicion and distrust by both adversaries centered here too.

A well-built, neatly dressed small man stepped briskly along the avenue between the homes. Familiar with the community, he strode with purpose. No cry of warning from the sentinels heralded his coming, only the laughter of children. His face, lined and weathered from repeated exposure to the sun's rays, meant that his exposed complexion nearly resembled the brown children who ran fearlessly to greet him and scampered about him. His infectious grin, the friendly ruffle of the hair to those who came near, and the grasping of his hands and arms by a few of the younger children spoke of their familiarity with the German Moravian teacher, who walked freely among them. Sixty plus years had diminished little of the vigor of the man.

White Eyes looked up from his chinking repairs, putting aside the small wooden bowl of mud to dry his hands in the dust before extending them to his friend. He waited patiently as the little ones melted away in deference to their elders. One small girl, whose large brown eyes nearly filled her round face, waited for one more ruffle of her hair before giggling and returning to her fellows.

"The creator gives us a good day, Brother Zeisburger."

"Indeed, we are most blessed this day."

"And does Gnadenhutten prepare for the crops, too?"

"Indeed, our Lord wants us not to waste a moment of His fine day."

"What brings you, brother?"

"I understand that Hamilton's Hazel has left you once more."

"Yes, we hope none of our dust clings to his feet," White Eyes chuckled.

"And what of McKee, Elliott, and Girty or the others? Have they left as well?"

"They go on to McKee's wife's people, the Shawnese. I fear the lies they told here will have no one to question them there."

"Have the lies finally settled here?"

White Eyes looked sadly about him. *"At first, I feared that Brother*

German=this font   English=this font   **French=this font**   *Delaware=this font*

Heckwelder could not convince the brothers that George Washington still lived, but finally the brothers believed him about the surrender of Burgoyne and the battles which still continue." He shook his head like one who seldom heard happy news, *"You know, Brother Zeisburger, when the backsettlers kill as they do and dishonor our neutrality, it is hard to keep our young men from going to war. Even when we send someone to warn them of raiding parties, they fire upon us. As we speak, Captain Pipe begs his men to return, rather than to take up arms and oppose the council.*

"Do your people still refuse to carry the new letters of Hamilton to Fort Pitt?"

"Yes, brother. But some of our young men badger the council to avenge Cornstalk. Others see the wisdom of not joining in this fight between parent and child. Sometimes when a parent and child fight and the battle ends, they embrace harder than before."

Zeisburger accepted his wise insight nodding in agreement.

"Our numbers grow here. The Mekoce of the Shawnese, Cornstalk's people, have joined us as he bid them do if he should die." White Eyes stopped momentarily before adding, *"They bring us strength at council."*

"I suspect their strength is needed with the many threats that your visitors shared."

"True, Brother Zeisburger. Many believe that the men, who the British did not hang for being rebels or export to England, have fled to the mountains and wait to seek revenge upon us. So many," he paused, *"so many of our brothers die each year that one wonders what we have done to have the creator permit this to happen."*

Zeisburger had no answer that made any sense for his friend or himself. So rather than be bombastic or simplistic, he remained silent. *"I have sent a letter to the Shawnese, warning them that these bad birds sing songs that lie. Let us hope that they hear my words of warning,"* White Eyes related after he realized that his friend had nothing to offer but his friendship.

Very softly after a quick perusal of the area, Zeisburger asked under his breath, *"Do you still have the wampum belt from Killbuck and Captain Pipe that Hamilton sent back with them?"*

White Eyes merely nodded in quiet response, casting an eye about as well. Wishing to change the subject, White Eyes drew Zeisburger's attention elsewhere.

"Come, Brother Zeisburger, let us take from the kettle. It is a poor man who can not stop to sup with his friends."

Smiling, he grasped Zeisburger about the shoulder and walked him to the tripod which hung its full kettle over hot embers. Stooping to remove a gourd from the stack, White Eyes dipped into the steaming fish porridge green with fresh potherbs. He took care not to dip too deep into the sediment of scales and bones, handing the very first serving to his friend

German=this font   English=this font   **French=this font**   *Delaware=this font*

before taking another gourd to fill. He motioned to the half log which lay by his cabin door on the sunward side of his home. Both men settled and sipped the hot rich maple-sweetened broth. Zeisburger appreciated the sweetened fish, an acquired taste for a European. He plucked the pieces from the mix to nibble on them independently and flipped a small set of fin bones into the grass. He knew that the crows joined by the late morning sun would quickly remove them before a day's passing.

"My brethren have come with a sorry tale. Brother Jung and I pray they are in error."

"What do you hear, my brother?"

"We hear that Colonel Hand of Fort Pitt and his militia attacked some of your people in late February and that they may have captured two women."

White Eyes took another sip of his broth. He did not answer directly. He stared down at ground between his feet.

David Zeisburger's concerned face never altered.

"What you hear is true brother. This tale brings many tears. Our Captain Pipe's brother fought bravely. He could not protect the women and children. He wounded one of their officers after they fired upon them. But before he could fire a second shot to protect the women, they shot him. They tomahawked him." White Eyes cradled the hot broth in his hands as if its heat would melt the ugliness away. *"They made sport in his blood."* His hands rubbed the sides of the gourd noggin. *"They scalped another old one. She died slowly with many cries that fell on ears that did not hear."* White Eyes paused. He drank from his gourd deeply before continuing.

Taciturn, Zeisburger waited for the rest to unfold.

"Captain Pipe's mother had one finger shot from her hand. She tried to send the Rebels on a wild goose chase saying ten other Braves were salting up the Mahoning River. She did this to help her daughter-in-law, Pipe's wife, and children escape into the forest. Sadly, four Munsee women and a young boy were there gathering herbs on the Mahoning River bank. They killed three of the women...and the child ...captured another, the young one."

Zeisburger sighed very heavily. He drained the last of his gourd before spitting a tiny bone into the sand. He rapped a few scales from the bottom by smacking the gourd against his thigh, rose, and returned the gourd to its place near the pot. Lost in thought as he did so, he slowly returned to his seat.

"And what of those that Hand's men captured? Are they dead, too?" Zeisburger asked with grave concern.

"No, they are here now."

"Here?" A touch of wonder edged Zeisburger's question.

"Yes, White Corn Woman has been called."

"Is she a women's healer?"

"You remember well, Brother."

German=this font   English=this font   *French=this font*   *Delaware=this font*

"Who sent the women back?"

"Morgan, the Rebel Indian Agent, sent them back to us. First he just sent messages. The man who brought messages grew sick and had to return midway. The second time, the man brought the women along."

"That was best."

White Eyes took time to respond. The words came at last but with difficulty. *"The Congress of the Rebels sent letters of apology for the death of Cornstalk. They seek Captain Pipe, Killbuck, and me to come to them at Fort Pitt."*

"In the name of…" Zeisburger stopped abruptly. He must not profane the name of the Lord. He shook his head in disgust. He remembered how Cornstalk and his sons found death under a flag of truce. He feared for his friend.

White Eyes continued, *"they sent the letters also to the Shawnee with the Girty, who has a Shawnee wife."* He paused. *"Nonhelma, Cornstalk's sister, has been sent by the Virginians."* Then his voice dropped perceptibly. *"Fort Pitt also sent us news that they will bring us goods."*

"They what?" Zeisburger stopped, appalled by the continuing travesty that spilled before his ears. The Rebels could not begin to match the British's lavish gifts. Washington's troops barely had enough to wear or to eat. The currency of the new Congress butted many a joke in any place of commerce. The solvency of the new government meant that most common folks preferred to do business in 'bucks', deer hides tanned and used as bartered currency. When White Eyes did not repeat his statement, Zeisburger asked, *"Have they told you the date they plan to send you goods?"*

"I believe McKee told us that the letter said, 'by and by'."

Zeisburger paused. *"Will Captain Pipe continue to refuse the hatchet?"*

"I cannot answer for him."

Both men sat peering into nothingness. Neither spoke as each sought to make some sense of the recent events.

"May I see Captain Pipe's mother? She fed the brothers and me well when last we visited her son."

At first, White Eyes hesitated. Then he spoke, his voice a little distant. *"Of course, White Corn Woman will be pleased to see you again, too."*

Silently the two men walked together to the house apart which stood nearest the young orchards. They became enveloped in the sweet sounds and smells about them. Surrounded by budding lilacs of white and deepest purple, Captain Pipe's mother's home reflected the pride the owner took in the cuttings carried from home to home over her lifetime. Snowdrops, wild blood root, and various trilliums bloomed side-by-side. Her skill in starting new plants had few rivals among the Delaware. Her varieties of beans and squash had always been the talk of every community in which she had lived. A slightly built young woman stood quietly at her door. The first thing that attracted the Moravian's attention was the paleness of her skin that peeped through the slits of her apparel. Her hair in the sun shone lighter on the ends and darker at its origin. David Zeisburger took note of her blue eyes, wondering how long she had been a Delaware captive. Those, however, were not questions one asked of one's host. She smiled shyly at the men's approach, calling softly to those within the darkness.

"Please, the women wish to make ready for your gaze." Her body language instantly conveyed that they should pause a respectable time before entering. Her Delaware tongue gave no hint of earlier German or English origins.

"You know the mud will not wait." White Eyes' discomfort became increasingly apparent as they stood. *"I should return to repairing my home, so there is time to dry before the next pounding rain."*

Zeisburger, sensing his friend's discomfort, nodded, freeing White Eyes to return to his earlier task.

Zeisburger scanned the orchard as he waited. He could hear the anxious tones of the women within as they readied to admit him. Perhaps something more than mud had pulled his friend away. He refocused his attention on the budded fruit trees. These apples and pears had been planted some years before his own orchards in Schoenbrunn and Gnadenhutten. These trees would have heavy yields this fall barring any unpredicted cold spell or infestation of pests. Aristotle's soil test had not failed in either of their mission's new communities. The rich loam favored a bountiful harvest. No wonder Britain, Massachusetts, Pennsylvania, and Virginia wished to lay claim to this choice farmland like rival dogs fighting for the same ripe bitch. Rarely would anyone go hungry here on such fertile land with water in abundance. However, working the fields could be truly dangerous. He knew the guards watched. Here just as in of Pennsylvania, New York, Kentucky, and Virginia, one constantly had to watch for raiding parties while planting or harvesting. No one, Indian or Rebel alike, planted without a ready musket and someone standing guard. In a far tree, he could just make out a young lad perched aloft. Other men stood stationed about the perimeter of the field. He shook his head in dismay when he heard White Corn Woman's call of admittance.

Pushing the brightly colored woven matt of reeds aside, he entered the dimly lit cabin which surprised Zeisburger. One candle shed light at the table. Usually on such a day, every window would be free of mats, permitting the light and wind to go at will within the walls.

"Sister." Zeisburger extended both hands to grasp White Corn Woman's extended hands. *"By God's Grace we meet once more. Sadly, these poor women are the reason."*

"Brother Zeisburger." White Corn Woman clasped his hands warmly. She appreciated that the holy man would come to show concern for the women.

The faint smell of putrefying flesh did not go unnoticed as Zeisburger

German=this font English=this font *French=this font* *Delaware=this font*

cast his eyes about the room. Soon his eyes adjusted to the diminished light. The young woman stood by another young woman, who lay on a mound of furs and mats with her face turned to the back wall. Apparently, the fair woman wanted to act as an additional barrier between Zeisburger and the recently released Munsee woman. The owner of the lovely cabin sat at the table. Her hands soaked in a decoction of herbs and lichens prepared for her. A dish of maggots waited to debride the wound. One particularly adventurous larva had escaped over the wooden bowl lip and set out hunching its way across the table. Zeisburger shuddered at the thought of the ancient remedy. But having seen cleaner wounds that appeared to heal easier, he uttered a silent prayer, hoping that his revulsion to these primitive practices would not show.

"How do your patients fare, sister?"

"I fare well, Brother Zeisburger." Light in the Morning spoke up sprightly before her caretaker could respond. *"What brings you away from your fields, you who find delight in putting his hands in the warm soil?"*

"The desire to see if a fellow planter will have the joy of the Creator's benevolence this spring brings me." He paused to look carefully at the wounded hand that blackened near the base of the missing appendage. A few tiny red streaks strayed to her wrist. One streak had ascended midway up the arm. Heat radiated from her warm flesh. He lifted her hand gently from the solution, turning it in the faint candlelight and then returned it to soak in the hot liquid. *"We heard that someone might have been injured and came to see if our help was needed."* He straightened up. *"But I see Corn Woman gives you good care."*

"Sister, I would not use your green salve, the Seneca oil, on this," Zeisburger said turning to White Corn Woman. His brow rippled with concern. *"We have observed that if there is blackness, the salve seems to make it worse."*

"We too have observed this, Brother Zeisburger. We will wrap her with slippery elm bark filled with drawing herbs, instead. We agree; the ooze that comes from Mother Earth's breast does not heal these black wounds."

"And your other patient?"

A mask of caution quickly covered White Corn Woman's face. In a sudden shift to English she said very softly and very distinctly, "This one...soul aches. Gentle be."

With apprehension growing, Zeisburger turned toward the Munsee woman. He knew instinctively that whatever his eyes beheld, his continence must not reflect what his eyes would see. He noted that White Corn Woman, who rarely if ever spoke English, felt moved to do so. Obviously, the others did not.

"Is she well enough to speak?" He asked of her young keeper as he approached the prone figure.

German=this font   English=this font   **French=this font**   *Delaware=this font*

The young woman nodded her head slowly, affirming his question. A swell of compassion arose in Zeisburger.

"She can speak," the pale one informed him.

"What is her name?"

"She is Sparkling Brook."

"Sparkling Brook, may I offer a prayer for you to the Creator to heal you?"

The woman did not stir. David Zeisburger waited patiently for her response.

None came.

"Perhaps I can speak to her for you," White Corn Woman said, standing at Zeisburger's shoulder.

"Sparkling Brook, a good man comes to see you. He is not one of the Brown Robes, but he is a man who listens to the Creator."

The woman lay very still. She curled like a wounded animal.

"Did you hear me? A good man comes to see you."

Still the young Munsee woman did not acknowledge their presence.

"Sister, you must turn to him. He will tell the truth to all he meets. His tongue does not split." White Corn Woman laid her hand softly on the mounded hip. Gently, she rubbed the woman's hip before her.

When the Munsee finally turned to Zeisburger, the sight that he had steeled himself for could not prevent him from clamping his mouth tightly shut to stop any stray sound or halt the tears that instantly filled his eyes as the injured woman said, *"Good brother, what brave will want me to wife now?"* The light shawl across her shoulders fell away.

Even in the dim light, one could see the horrific damage. Cut deeply in each cheek of the once handsome young woman, the letter 'w' glared as new scabbed scars. Her slashed chest, bared to the healing air without any cover, brought immediate awareness of her source of pain, emotionally and physically. One nipple had been severed completely. Remnants of crude stitching remained where the other breast had been reattached. Raw scars in the pale light indicated physical healing. Her few words, however, revealed the true depth of the emotional scaring.

"Brother Zeisburger, she says...'What brave will want me to wife now?'" White Corn Woman repeated Sparkling Brook's words as though Zeisburger had not understood them. But Zeisburger had. He responded quickly.

"Tell her, one who looks into her beautiful eyes and who sees the Creator God within her."

White Corn Woman relayed Zeisburger's response as he looked into the young Munsee's eyes. He did not look away.

"Tell this man, the true men will never look beyond my cheeks."

With that, the young Munsee woman turned her back to Zeisburger and the other women once more.

White Corn Woman conveyed the injured woman's last statement to Zeisburger, who apologized for his imposition, uttered a hasty prayer, and

German=this font   English=this font   ***French=this font***   *Delaware=this font*

awkwardly left the women to seek healing for himself amidst his garden plots. War, he decided, could eat the humanity from within mankind's soldiers like worms in the apple orchard, leaving a shiny outer shell and a few visible scars without, while corrupting and destroying the heart within. He would return another day to speak with White Eyes. Today the pain of the women silenced him. He must sing hymns on his return to Gnadenhutten. Perhaps this would help to mend his soul as he prayed for the souls of others and for this sad conflict to end.

Fort Detroit

The Contingents of Chickasaw and Cherokee had no sooner removed themselves after having sent representatives seeking protection from the Rebels and assistance from the British when another delegation of Mingo, Wyandot, Shawnee, and Delaware arrived. The campfires from one encampment barely cooled when yet another fire rekindled. Among them, the Delaware encampment set up far outside the gates of the fort and south on the shore of the Detroit River beyond the ribbon farms. The dogs and children taunted and circled a small group of new prisoners, who glanced apprehensively at the fort, which now came partially into view, as the fog lifted. The warriors and their woman, many still hung over with spirit waters from the night before, tried to quiet the children and to relight the morning fires.

Stalking Wolf, Sitting Rabbit, and Blue Ice had joined John Montour, who in full Delaware dress moved unnoticed among most of the Fort authorities. The guards and personnel rarely looked at native faces. Luckily for him, to the British, all Indians looked the same, as did the Red Coats to the Delaware and their associates. Montour had only to avoid the few who knew him. Freed as he was by the anger of his native brothers and their threatened refusal to take up the hatchet for Hamilton, Montour now turned his back on his earlier exploits with the British. No more would he take war parties into Pennsylvania. No more would he go to the Wabash Confederacy to ask them to carry the hatchet as Hamilton's representative.

"Look well into his face, my brothers. Ask him for your full rightful payment if you attack the settlements again this spring. Hamilton sends no red-coated brothers with you to fight. They shed no blood with you. Yet your blood is as red as their blood. Any land your bands capture should be yours by right of conquest when this conflict between white brothers ends." John Montour spoke sharply to the seated men. They tried to block his words, but the sense of them made inroads. Even in their hung-over state, they realized that the man was making sense. *"White Eyes would not settle for less than this with the Rebels to remain neutral. Why should you accept less than this with these English people when it is your blood that is shed....when it is your women and children who are attacked when they gather herbs or make sugar?"* To be compared to

German=this font English=this font **French=this font** *Delaware=this font*

White Eyes gave pause to the men before Montour. White Eyes, though respected as a skillful orator, failed in many eyes to gain respect as a great warrior, especially among these Delaware, who had chosen to fight.

"Montour, mostly the blood of the whites flows in your veins. Why do you think you are so smart?" Sitting Rabbit protested. He hated to shave the beaver too close. *"We get payment enough. My woman has more cloth than she needs and three iron pots. Who needs more? Except maybe more powder to hunt and much more rum to drink..."* He laughed.

"You settle cheap for your blood. I may be of mixed blood, but these bloods know when I am cheated."

That remark so inflamed Sitting Rabbit that he stood up and stomped off to relieve himself by a nearby tree. At just that precise moment, Hanu and Little Fox whipped around the lean-to and barreled into Sitting Rabbit, who sprayed himself.

All the men by the fire broke into raucous laughter. Sitting Rabbit, realizing that he was the butt of their merry response, raised his hand to backhand Hanu, who lay sprawled on the ground beside him.

"White mongrel!" But the blow never landed.

"Brother, your head pounds away all reason this morning. He is but a boy." Stalking Wolf released his grip and then as he pulled Hanu up from the ground, he gave him a playful swat. *"Get off with you, Hanu. You too, Little Fox. This is a man's talking circle."* His nephew, Little Fox, giggled. Both boys took off as quickly as they had come. This time Little Fox led the way.

Sitting Rabbit joined the group again, but since he could not take out his embarrassment on Hanu, he decided instead to take a verbal swipe at Stalking Wolf, whom he knew had developed a deep fondness for the boy.

"Why do you pamper the mongrel? His brother has golden hair, his mother light brown, and this one dark brown. One brother's eyes are blue. One brown. They are like stray mongrel dogs. One never can tell who belongs to a litter or who jumped the bitch."

For whatever reason, the words cut Stalking Wolf deeply. He knew as well as anyone in the circle that the White men were not at all like the true bloods, especially the Delaware or the Lenni Lenape as they called themselves. Once all tribes had called the Delaware the Grandfathers, a title they wore with pride. They were called upon to settle disputes. Like all the true men, the Great Spirit made them alike with the same brown eyes, the same warm brown skin, and the same noble features. In stories about their winter hearth since childhood, the elders taught that in the creative fires that baked all mankind, the true people were neither burned nor undercooked, but perfect in their Creator's eyes.

Stalking Wolf remembered the tall black one called Anne with her tight fuzzy hair, her broad nose, her sensual round rump and then Mikie, the blond child, whose hair surrounded his head like a golden wreath of light that day in the sunlit field by his cabin. Sitting Rabbit had spoken rightly.

German=this font   English=this font   *French=this font*   *Delaware=this font*

"Sitting Rabbit, you speak truth.   The white man is a mongrel, a dog of many colors, not like the true men. But Hanu soon will be our adopted brother, and then he will carry the blood of true men."

Having saved face, Sitting Rabbit relaxed. The fact that he was splashed would be tolerated and perhaps forgotten until the next drinking bout. His pride mended as Stalking Wolf had acknowledged his wisdom in front of the others.

John Montour recognized a perfect opportunity as the conversation lulled.

"In my blood flows the blood of the Seneca and Delaware. That blood can peer through the white blood to see lies more clearly. Sally Ainsee just as Queen Esther also has taught me much by example. Do you know what Brother Zeisburger read in the papers that you left behind on your raids? You know that though Zeisburger is white, the man speaks with a straight tongue."

The men, by their expressions, agreed with him. Like the white man, most were unable to read. But they had observed that those who could read the white man's written symbols carried more power. Unlike their own symbols, the white man's symbols were exact words. If a true man or a white man could read, the same words would be heard from reader to reader, unlike their talking symbols, which varied sometimes from shaman to shaman. But even then, they noticed that although the white men and the true men read aloud the exact same words, this did not mean the exact same thing to those who listened once the words filled the air. A great debate raged among the people about the written words. Were all white words lying words or were all those who spoke them liars?

Blue Ice spoke first. *"Hay said that the papers asked the loyal brothers to come to help their King and to fight with their real brothers."*

"That is a half truth, Blue Ice. But did he tell you what other words were on the white papers?"

Now all of the men gave Montour their undivided attention.

"Hamilton promised them 'his Majesty's bounty of two-hundred acres.'" The men looked puzzled. *"Our camp here fills one acre. Count your fingers and toes...ten times to count to two hundred. Imagine two hundred acres of the true people's land from the Ohio or Kentucky lands. This is the same land that Hamilton told you his Majesty has no wish to take from you. How can this be?"*

Then as quickly as John Montour had come, he melded into another camp, another talking circle, another group of men, leaving each group to ponder his message.

As the third hour of orations began, the constant round of deliberations from one visiting band to another wore on Hamilton like a too-tight heel in a short boot. He tired of their litany, the tiresome demands for more goods and more Redcoats to fight beside them. Their

German=this font   English=this font   ***French=this font***   *Delaware=this font*

repetitive requests blistered him. Lately, no matter how he tried to center his attention, once the verbose speakers began to speak, Hamilton's mind would begin to wander. Today he noted that the troublesome one, Stalking Wolf, sat in the Delaware delegation. Hamilton remembered too well Stalking Wolf's relayed comment from White Eyes, calling Hamilton's men lazy and fat on an earlier visit. He looked up as Stalking Wolf rose and began to speak.

"Brothers, you know the Grandfathers seek wisdom, truth and justice."

Translations in French, Shawnee, and Wyandot spread across the assemblage. Hamilton's mind began to wander. Here we go, he thought. I suppose this fool Delaware will speak for an hour or two.

"Since Lieutenant Governor Hamilton speaks for his Majesty and promises much to the loyalist brothers, who march with him against the rebellious brothers of the thirteen colonies, the Wolf Delaware think that the Delaware and their brother tribes should have the same promises or more since they are loyal too." As the translation rippled across the group, Hamilton suddenly found himself listening intently to Stalking Wolf's speech. Grunts of agreement returned from those who also listened. Staffs pounded on the ground, thumping accord.

"On the white papers, the loyalists who come are promised two hundred acres from his Majesty's bounty. Should we not...at the very least...receive those lands which we win back for the crown by right of conquest?" Stalking Wolf held one of the white papers in his hand, raising it high above his head and turning for all to see it. Jacob Schieffelin's neat script could be seen clearly even by Hamilton from his vantage point.

If Hamilton could have swallowed his Adam's apple at that precise moment, his neck would have been instantly hollow. Hamilton could see many brown eyes riveted on his person, and as the translation spread, the expectation of an answer from him clearly built. Everywhere, eyes, eyes, and more eyes centered on him. Hamilton stammered something barely coherent and something to the effect that he would have to check with his Majesty, King George, as to their reward before he beat an untimely and hasty retreat. He suggested to Hay as he left to get out double the usual portions of rum for those assembled.

As Hamilton stormed into his office, Jacob Schieffelin tried to suppress DeJean, who leapt to his feet and immediately began babbling to Hamilton about Coutincinau and the black whore. DeJean nipped at Hamilton's heels like an undisciplined pup with no letup.

Hamilton heard little of what was said. His mind twisted and spun. He wanted no additional problems from DeJean at that precise moment. He clearly had far greater challenges than this local rubbish confronting him.

Hamilton could see troubles with his plans to wrest the territories from the Spanish, dimming his chances for success with Lord George

German=this font   English=this font   *French=this font*   *Delaware=this font*

Germain and the English Parliament. He had noticed a drop in the lucrative fur trade that helped to sustain the English economy, with the lackluster Canadians increasingly trading with the Spanish. Damn the clannish Catholics! He tired of pussy-footing around the local French gentry, whom he must court and stroke constantly by attending every little ball, every little card game, and every little horse race. He grew increasingly furious that his home office failed to see the wisdom of taking over all trade on the Mississippi, blocking the supply of powder and supplies to the Rebel forces financed by the Spanish. He smarted because his requests for regulars to wipe out the weakly-posted Fort Pitt fell on deaf ears. He grew increasingly angry at the lack of clear orders from Carleton, which resulted in little or no support from Lernoult's troops. He seethed about the foul DePeyster at Fort Michilimackinac, who continued to run up enormous bills and who supplied few fighters. And when DePeyster did strike alliances, the warriors went to help Butler, Butler in Niagara, who consistently acted as if he outranked Hamilton.

Again and again, the greatness of Hamilton continued to be overlooked. Could they not see that he should be the top Indian Department supervisor? Fort Detroit should govern the heartlands, not Montreal. And meanwhile, Jehu Hay constantly informed Butler of Fort Detroit's activities. Increasingly, local traders slipped back and forth in spite of martial law that should curtail their business activities with the Rebel traders.

The Rebels continued to bring the contraband Rebel press to Sandusky and to the Fort. Hamilton felt grossly insulted to have heard the details of Burgoyne's fiasco from the Rebel press first, long before his home office finally reported the British leader's pathetic defeat. Worse yet, Hamilton must accept the further delay of LaMothe in Quebec, LaMothe who was by far his best militia and influential Indian leader.

And if that was not enough, on top of it all, Abbott sent pessimistic letters to Carleton, who appeared apathetic about this trifling **petite guerre** at best, to Germain, and to others in England, urging the cessation of the savage interventions, which ground Hamilton raw. On the other hand, the letters that Hamilton received back from Quebec questioned his finances and the costs of supplying the savages. These letters from underlings and nitpickers threatened to tie his purse strings just as they had with Abbott in Vincennes and Rocheblave in Kaskaskia, which meant that Hamilton must be enslaved to his own writing pad to put out one hot spot after another.

If only the sheepish Abbott had not left his post in an untimely fashion. Surely the crown would have paid off his personal debts that resulted from his leadership in Vincennes and Fort Sackville. The result...Rocheblave now bleated that they should send a stronger man to cope with manning his fort and to pacify the Weas and other tribes along the Wabash River. Then...then...then...the mouthy gall of those damn two-faced Delaware...his thoughts cascaded over him like a huge waterfall, thundering down.

German=this font   English=this font   **French=this font**   *Delaware=this font*

"In the name of God! DeJean! Handle them!" Hamilton roared. "I have far more important things to consider than some damn Frenchman poking his black wench in some foul warehouse. Deal with them! You are the Minister of Justice!" His hand ripped off his wig, throwing it onto the writing desk. Hamilton was saturated with anger, fatigue, and frustration. His hand raked his wet hair as he trembled violently with emotion.

As Hamilton disappeared into his sleeping room, he left DeJean and Schieffelin gaping. The door slammed violently behind him. The walls shook with the force. A small porcelain tobacco jar fell from the mantle, crashing onto the hearth. The pieces skittered in many directions across the floor much like the tribes, who left Fort Detroit the following morning, each to follow the direction of their own inclinations without supervision, each without coordinated targets, and each without the usual admonishment to spare the old, the women, and the children.

German=this font   English=this font   *French=this font*   *Delaware=this font*

Chapter 16   Justice Challenged, Early May, 1778

"Hazel went off again to conduct [McKee and his party] all safe through the [Indian] villages, having a letter and wampum for that purpose...Alexander McKee is a man of good character, and has great influence with the Shawanese; is well acquainted with the country, and probably can give some useful intelligence. He will probably reach this place {Fort Detroit} in a few days."

Lt. Governor Henry Hamilton to Sir Guy Carleton in Quebec, April 23, 1778 as quoted by Consul Willshire Butterfield, *History of the Girtys,* 1890 (reprinted Columbus, Ohio: Long's College Book Company, 1950), p. 60 -61.

Fort Detroit

Margaret Elder and Eve Earnest stood side-by-side at the edge of the cart lane to the south wharf. Since mending any divisions, both women actively sought out each other's company. Having walked from Pennsylvania on the initial trek together, whatever had separated them initially became lost in the common experience of unending labor for their captors, earning their ransoms, and sharing the mutual loss of their home, family, and friends.

Sometimes in the evenings, Nellie, Eve's loudmouth but increasingly thoughtful friend, would tend to Mikie and thus allow Eve to walk freely with Margaret. Lilacs abounded. The pears and apples bloomed, scenting the entire area with their pale, subtle fragrance. To be about in the balmy evening air soothed one's muscles and one's spirit, as well. Their walks gave them courage to face yet another exhausting day.

Eventually everyone, prisoner or inhabitant alike, migrated toward the King's docks or the merchant wharves. Watching the loading of the boats for the morning's sail helped Margaret and Eve to cope with their own fathomless desires to leave. Just being able to see the busy comings and goings before departures verified that other worlds coexisted outside their hateful drudgery.

For the town's inhabitants, the wharf side engendered wanderlust or brought a welcomed remembrance of their original homes in Quebec or Europe. The boats and their link with the so-called true civilization beckoned like a comely wench.

Besides, the wharf constituted the best sideshow in town, loading or unloading. Both women loved to people-watch and gossip as only servants can, servants who have ears and eyes, but who receive less notice than even the furniture in a room.

"Who is that?" Eve asked, knowing that Margaret's kitchen work at the barracks made her privy to more information than she.

"Which one are you talking about?"

"The one in shackles who limps. See him?" Eve nodded her head very slightly in the direction of the man who was propped between two burly redcoats. His escorts struggled with their prisoner's near dead weight. The result, their red faces blended with their coats and their auburn red hair in the late golden rays of sunshine. They struggled to put him aboard the dingy with little assistance from the heavily bearded and terribly weakened man. Behind him, two tall, rangy men in homespun, buckskins, and shackles climbed in at gunpoint urged on by another guard. The three prisoners would soon be put into the hold of the *Gage* with other goods destined for Niagara, Montreal, and then Quebec or beyond.

"You mean the bearded feller between the big Scots?

"Yes."

"Must be Dodge. They called Dr. Anton twice for him this week."

"I guess we are blessed after all. Sometimes I would truly hate to be a man."

"Sad story, that one, he once had a brisk trade with folks in New York and parts about."

"He did?"

"Yup, DeJean and Hamilton took away everything the man had, his house, his money, his trade goods, everything."

"Is he a spy or what?" Eve's attention focused on the man.

"Hmm, some say he is. Some say he is not." Margaret pulled a letter from her deep pocket and clutched it firmly in her hand, shielding it in her skirt from the view of others, including Eve. "I am not sure, but I think I heard the corporal say that they had Dodge in with that French friend of Anne's and two of those Virginians that they caught with John Montour."

"Oh, my." Just thinking of Anne brought pain to Eve's features, which changed to anger when she thought of John Montour.

"They cannot keep Dodge here any more since they released Montour."

"Montour. That no good, they should never have let him out." Eve remembered all too well the breed, who had captained Stalking Wolf, among others. She frankly did not care what prison Montour found himself in, just as long as someone penned up the scoundrel. She despised the man.

"Well he has been out awhile. They caught him with those three Virginians, who escaped in January."

"They what?" Eve questioned in disbelief.

German=this font   English=this font   *French=this font*   *Delaware=this font*

"Yup, he was taking them to Fort Pitt." Margaret looked about scanning the faces about the dock area. "That is what they say," she added, a little distracted.

"Are you sure?"

"I am sure. I overheard Hay sputtering about it to his brother-in-law, Reaume, the other morning when I scrubbed his floor. Seems Montour's ruffled Hamilton something fierce. Rumor has it that Hamilton trusted Montour to be his messenger to the Wabash savages. Hamilton sent him out there to deliberately rile up some more tribes."

"Well, whose side is Montour on, for heaven's sake?"

"I 'spect the only one who knows that is the good Lord himself, Eve."

A cart piled high with furs wobbled shakily toward Margaret and Eve, causing both of them to step back further from the roadway. The flick of the whip from the grinning driver, in theory to encourage the reluctant horse, just grazed Margaret's arm and ticked Eve's shoulder. Both women frowned at the driver, who they could tell swore at them under his breath. Once Finchley's cart had passed noisily by them, the women resumed their conversation.

"Savages raised quite a stink to get Montour out. Claimed they would not continue to carry the hatchet for Hamilton unless Montour was released."

"Honest, Margaret, how can you tell friend or foe in all this?"

"God knows, I do not know. Anyways, Dodge's old friends among the merchants evidently put up a royal fuss, too, after Montour got out," Margaret explained further.

"Well, I guess that explains why he is going to Quebec. Hamilton probably would rather he die there—out of sight," Eve concluded.

"How is Anne holding up?" Margaret asked, knowing Eve's strong feelings for her black friend. She failed to see what Eve possibly saw in the poor soul, but she never questioned that those feelings ran very deep.

"Each time I go to see that woman, I swear she is five pounds thinner."

"She is still losing weight?"

"Well...yes...no, I think so." Eve hesitated a little when she reflected. She did not know if she imagined it or not, but Anne's bodice did seem a mite tighter. A trace of uncertainty clung to her response. "Her color is a bit better of late. A little more blush to her cheeks. But I fear she is losing heart."

Margaret just shook her head sadly. "Too bad she did not have the good sense to stay away from that foul Frenchman." Margaret, ever the less tolerant of the two women, could not abide voyageurs. She considered them the devil's henchmen in **centure fléche**. She constantly scrutinized the boardwalks, watching for their brightly colored sashes and would cross the street even in deep mud to avoid their roving hands. Fresh

German=this font   English=this font   *French=this font*   *Delaware=this font*

from the trap lines or just off their ***maître carots***, the scoundrels delighted in randomly feeling up any free walking woman, particularly prisoners, whom they spotted easily in their patched and soiled attire. They pinched hard on these occasions, besides saying vile un-Christian things which even in French, Margaret recognized as lewd. In addition, if walking ahead of women, they delighted in turning around to urinate as they continued to walk backwards, laughing heartily at the shock in the women's faces behind them. They were definitely uncouth.

Margaret's eyes kept scanning the milling crowds in the street and dockside.

Eve realized that Margaret obviously sought someone in particular among the evening crowd.

"Another letter for George?"

Eve regretted her words almost as soon as she had said them. Margaret stiffened. Her gaze glazed reflecting the red rays. She coughed before clearing her throat and answered softly, "Yes, surely it does not hurt to try again."

Eve placed a sustaining hand on Margaret's shoulder. Eve could tell by the catch in Margaret's voice that her feisty friend was losing a little hope, too, with each day's passing. At least, she mused, Margaret had a husband that she loved waiting for her. Like Eve, Margaret worked hard scrubbing and cleaning for those little extras that made life bearable, a small round of soap, a bit of cloth, or as in Margaret's case, money to pay the rum fees for the letter carriers. Eve envied Margaret. Not that Eve could write, but even if she had known how to write, she knew down deep what the response would be. So rather than risk getting her hopes up, she chose not to even try to contact her father or uncle.

The women both knew that Lieutenant Governor Hamilton's office had told Margaret and many others that their families would be notified and invited to join them at Fort Detroit for safe passage to New York. But at the same time, every prisoner and certainly both women knew that the real desire of the British Indian Department was to collect the ransom to continue to finance their nefarious activities.

Having spied the Smythes, Margaret began to wave her arm back and forth to catch the couple's attention. The Smythe couple, dressed in new outfits, stood waiting to board the next dingy. This Tory couple, who also had made the trek with Margaret and Eve, had obviously reaped their rewards for their loyalty and now prepared to leave the frontier fort for British-held New York and better climes. Smythe, in return, would be a prison guard there to repay the British for their passage.

Eve hung back as Margaret worked her way through the milling observers and passengers. She simply felt no fondness for the Smythe and his wife.

Mistress Smythe kissed her rebel friend on each cheek and then discreetly received the letter from Margaret. When Eve observed that the Tory woman also accepted coins which Margaret hastily dug from her

German=this font   English=this font   *French=this font*   *Delaware=this font*

pocket, Eve shook her head in disgust and turned her back so as not to betray her feelings openly, which she knew plastered her face like whitewash on a dark wall.

Then, she saw him, waving his letter packet, trying to get the Captain's attention near the stacks of freight on the dock. For once, neither DeJean nor a single guard stood to bar her way. Eve realized quite suddenly that she just might get access to Jacob Schieffelin, Hamilton's Secretary. She watched him hand off his packet. Seeing that Margaret was fully engaged in conversation with the Smythe couple, Eve stealthily shadowed Schieffelin. After he finished speaking with the Captain, Eve fell in behind him as he walked up the hill to return to his office near the fort.

"May I speak with you, Herr Jacob Schieffelin?" She asked cautiously, at a time when no one walked near them.

Addressed in his mother tongue and by his full name, a curious Jacob Schieffelin stopped and turned to the woman, who had spoken so directly behind him. "You have the advantage of knowing my name. I do not know yours," he said, frowning at the stout, poorly dressed captive. Wide hips for easy birth, coiled braids, weather-reddened cheeks, rough hands, all revealed a working woman of some strength.

"My name is Eve Earnest." Eve did not extend her hand. She spoke quickly. She recognized that this brief opening for dialog between them was minute, leaving no time for foolish pleasantries. "I require your intercession in two matters. A Delaware, called *Stalking Wolf*, has kidnapped my son, Henry Earnest. I need your help. I know that Lieutenant Governor Hamilton rescues children. Recently he sent a boy to the Citadel. Also, I ask for mercy for a friend, Anne Wylie, who is in your gaol in the Citadel."

Jacob Schieffelin inwardly strived not to show any outward interest. His demeanor revealed little of the flood of thoughts that spilled over his mind. He mentally noted the names...Stalking Wolf, Henry Earnest and Eve Earnest. He ignored the reference to her friend as he delayed his answer.

"Can you help my friend Anne, the Negress? She is in the gaol. She is a good woman. I am sure she meant no harm. If—"

Jacob Schieffelin never let Eve finish. When he spoke, nothing in his inflection revealed his keen interest in any part of the woman's requests.

"We cannot help you. Please go about your business. Do not bother me again, woman." Curtly, he turned and continued up the hill.

Eve watched as Schieffelin's neatly attired figure disappeared in the evening shadows.

Stunned by his callous response, Eve turned hurriedly to rejoin Margaret. Neither woman should walk this late alone.

German=this font   English=this font   *French=this font*   *Delaware=this font*

Bedford, Pennsylvania

Eve Dibert looked skyward as a spring storm gathered itself up-mountain and slipped ever closer. Clouds obscured the top and had begun to spill down over the fresh green tree tops. A breeze dropped in suddenly, kicking up dust before it. Her son, John Dibert, squinted in an effort to keep the dirt out of his eyes. John, the leather rein wrapped around one shoulder as he nudged Mitsy into doing just one more row with the plow, sweated in the full sun, which would soon be extinguished by the building mounds of cumulus clouds.

Rumors flew rampantly in the Bedford and Westmoreland vicinity telling of more raids by Seneca and others from the northern Lakes. Both vigilant, John and Eve knew those rumors. The Dibert family had been victims of similar raids in 1737 and 1757. The widow empathized and feared more than most. John, who had narrowly missed death as a young man, strained to keep Mitsy in the proper furrow while keeping his eyes peeled for any unusual movement.

Mere Eve kept her vigilance. She listened alertly for any unreasonable silence from the birds who chorused about them as they sang their welcoming rain songs. Here on the mountain, they were late getting the corn planted. Seed increasingly proved harder to come by. Thankfully, John had finally been able to obtain some from Conrad Samuel after the May meeting. She remembered how she had badgered John to take Molly with him and his wife Ene down to be with the younger folks. **"Young folks need some sport, even in these times,"** she had told him. And after all, Molly had not seen her brothers since she had been dumped unceremoniously by her Uncle Jac.

Now Mere Eve wondered if she had been wise to pressure John so. For since the girl's return, Molly seemed more melancholy and snappy than before. John and Ene had also been rather closemouthed about the spring affair with little comment other than his Mere's venison mincemeat pie had been well received. Now Ene lay ill and even more responsibility had fallen on the young girl's shoulders.

A large raindrop plopped on her cheek.

"Ho, John, the storm is going to break o'r us."

"Mere, go back to the cabin. I will catch up."

"My son, you need another set of eyes and ears."

"Go on, Mere. I have just one more row." John waved her toward the cabin. **"No sense both of us getting soaking wet. Mitsy's restless anyway. She cannot go much longer."** He brought the mare back on course. **"I will be in shortly."**

Mere Eve turned reluctantly toward the cabin. As the wind picked up and the rain began to fall, she relished the increasing silence of her own steps in the wet grass and leaves. She loved the sounds of the woods and fields. The pizzicato of the raindrops on the new green leaves now nearly

German=this font   English=this font   *French=this font*   *Delaware=this font*

full size proved welcome music. A previously unnoticed stand of May Apples caught her eyes. She made a mental note to return in late June or July when the yellow fruit replaced the sweet smelling white flowers which nestled shyly beneath. Each white blossom snuggled beneath its own green umbrella. The wee apple-like fruit would make a fine jell. She considered the plant a little like life, beautiful above and hell to pay below the surface if pursued with cruel intent. She knew few plants which could be either a sweet jell or a killing poison, depending on how a person chose to use it.

Mere Eve's quiet approach as she came up behind Molly went unnoticed by Molly. Still some feet away, Mere Eve smiled as she observed her grandchildren dancing in the raindrops like butterflies around puddles after a dry spell. Spring had freed them from the necessity of playing in the cabin. The relief of warm rain had awakened their free spirits. Their giggles and laughter had drowned out early attempts by Molly to get them inside. Molly's repeated pleas fell like the pelting rain and washed off the children just as quickly. In a state of near bedlam, they jumped up and down, squished the mud between their toes, and then wiggled their bare toes in the shallow mud puddles to rinse them off. Their open mouths caught raindrops, which they swallowed like nectar as they darted about splashing in the puddles.

"Come now, we must go in," Molly called harshly. "You are getting all wet!" The children, in a state of jubilant ecstasy and playful anarchy, ignored her completely.

Frustration built rapidly, fueled in part by events of the recent past.

Mere Eve chuckled silently to herself as she approached. Only her shoulders shook to betray her good humor. The five children had Molly buffaloed again. David, their ringleader, had them in full revolt. They knew all too well that Molly's bark was worse than her bite; and like any group of children en masse, their collective power openly challenged Molly's young authority. Especially now, seeing their Grand'mere's approach and her face filled with amusement and open tolerance of their antics, they giggled in rebellion even louder.

All the strain of the prior week, combined with the open disobedience of the children, built to a flash point. Molly shifted in a lightning fast burst of light from victim to attacker. Unable to stand being ignored or to be taken lightly one more time, she stomped her foot defiantly, sending up a loop-shaped muddy splash, and hollered "Do you hear me, you stupid breeds?" She paused to let the words sink in. "Get in the house!"

Instantly, the children dropped in their tracks. In unison, their eyebrows raised. Little Susanna's hand flew to cover her mouth. David instinctively pulled Susanna protectively to him like any older brother called to shield a younger sibling. Young Ene, Lizzie, and Barbara grasped hands forming a picket fence. All their expressions filled with surprise and knowledge, for they knew their Grand'mere stood directly behind Molly. And what was more important, the children could see the complete change and the stark contrast of emotions in their Grand'mere's face.

German=this font   English=this font   *French=this font*   *Delaware=this font*

"Do you hear me?" Molly bellowed once more. Her volume increased threefold. Her arm fully extended, she pointed at the door, shaking her finger emphatically. The wind whipped about her. The rain began to mat wisps of her hair, which clung to her wet flushed face. "Get in that house, you stupid breeds! Do you hear me?"

"I am sure they do." Mere Eve's voice, low and direct, hit Molly from behind like a knee-buckling blow. "I certainly do." A distant clap of thunder rolled through the gap and added an exclamation point to Mere Eve's quiet words. Mere Eve wondered what crawled at the root of this horrible outburst by this beautiful child, which like the mayflower revealed itself with such poisonous intensity.

Molly's hand flew to cover her mouth. The children's wide-eyed expressions heaped more self-imposed guilt upon her. Riddled with shame, her own eyes filled instantly with searing tears. She could not bear to face Mere Eve. Obviously, the good woman had heard every horrible, hateful word she had said. Trapped in a net of her making, Molly bleated like a wounded rabbit and fled to the lean-to. Wrenching sobs built within her. She had failed one who had shown her nothing but kindness. She had grossly disparaged her benefactress by her hateful words. She felt as ugly and as hateful as those who had degraded her earlier that week. The self-knowledge devastated her.

"Grand'mere," Lizzie whined, ever the reporter, *"Molly called us 'stupid breeds'."* She restated the obvious in French to drive her point home.

"Yes, and we all might have pushed her to do that. No?" The girls cast their eyes down, recognizing suddenly their part in all the sadness. *"Now let us to the house and build de fire to dry you all before you catch your death of cold."* Grand'mere Eve put her arms about the older girls' shoulders turning them gently toward the open cabin door.

David, not willing to accept his portion of the blame, hung back. He protested with a touch of truthfulness. *"But Grand'mere, you tell us it is very bad to call people hateful names."*

"Yes, my grandson, but it also could be very bad not to follow Molly's orders. What if she had heard a raiding party...and you had ignored her?"

Chagrined, David finally had to acknowledge his part. As the oldest, his Grand'mere had expected more good sense from him.

Susanna to his rescue reached out to grab her hero's hand as they returned to the cabin. *"But Grand'mere, you like de rain, too?"* As youngest, she could say just about anything without strong rebuke, and she knew it.

"Yes, wee one, I liked de rain, too." Mere Eve smiled down at Susanna.

Barbara, ever the sensitive one, thought she detected a trace of deep hurt about her Grand'mere's eyes. *"Grand'mere, should I go get*

German=this font   English=this font   *French=this font*   *Delaware=this font*

Molly?" she asked, sensing something murkier than the water that swirled about their feet.

"No child, she needs to be alone for a spell." Grand'mere Eve walked a few steps before adding, *"Your Pere will see to her when he brings Mitsy in. Young Ene, run ahead and light a candle. Will you, child? Now let us get all of you dried off before you catch cold."*

Young Ene, usually as responsible and as sober as her sick mother, hurried to do her Grand'mere's bidding.

John Dibert finished the last row and flipped the reins back over Mitsy's yoke before pulling the plow free to retrieve at a later time. Then he tugged at Mitsy's halter to lead her in from the weather, stopping only to grab his long rifle from the dry side of the large oak that shaded the north side of the field. Walking briskly, the horse sensed his master's desire to be in from the rain, which now came in sheets. As the wind picked up; the horse perked up her ears. Both stepped up their pace. Soon horse and master ducked into the lean-to. They mutually appreciated the dry warmth within. John laid his musket up on a high ledge. The cold but steaming horse whinnied and shook from mane to tail, shivering off some of the rain from her coat. Mitsy stomped noisily as John dipped a precious portion of oats in appreciation of the horse's earlier efforts and placed it with the last of the dry timothy hay in the wooden feed trough, a well earned treat for his work partner, who usually was staked and left to forage on her own. Mitsy nuzzled John's chest, flaring her nostrils and snorting into his wet shirt. John returned her gesture of affection by stroking her wet mane back and by scratching her ears and under her halter. He turned to grab the brush to rub her down. He worked diligently down one side. Occasionally Mitsy rippled her hide under his hand as if to show her appreciation.

John had just begun the other side, when an unexpected whimper attracted his attention. Looking carefully, John could just make out Molly's form in the darkest corner, partially covered by hay.

Huddled in the shadows, shaking with silent sobs, curled like a wounded animal, Molly attempted to will herself to invisibility. She failed.

"Molly?"

Molly tried harder to melt deeper into shadows.

John started to put down the brush, but noting Molly's futile attempt to withdraw, he decided to settle one filly before starting up with another. He could not afford a sick horse, and the girl seemed in no hurry for his intervention.

"Well Mitsy girl, looks like we got a crying girl in de corner." The mare swung her head to gaze back at Molly, snorted, and then resumed eating. John continued to stroke and to brush his mare. His hands petted and soothed as he worked. The caring strokes had a comforting rhythm. Shaking his brush from time to time to expel the water, the arcs of liquid were flung into the rainy opening across from Molly, leaving the dry straw for Mitsy to bed down in. *"Now if dhat girl keeps a crying, she is*

German=this font   English=this font   *French=this font*   *Delaware=this font*

going to soak all your bedstraw, Mitsy." Mitsy snorted as if to answer affirmatively and stomped, shaking her back left flank. The thud of her hoof startled Molly, who jumped at the sound. **"Well, she is skittish, Mitsy. You made her jump. Yes, you did, girl."** He patted the mare's rump. Mitsy seemed to presume that her master and she were quite capable of conversation, snorted again, and whinnied softly in response to her master's voice.

The sounds of horse and master conversing back and forth brought memories of Molly's father, who also cared for his animals out of a sense of mutual respect. Molly wiped her waning tears on her sleeve and peeked up at John, who continued to stroke and brush his mare. He pretended not to notice her, concentrating on the horse and his currying. Finished, he hung the brush, wiped his hands on his damp shirt, and then hunkered down beside Molly.

"Now Molly, what's de matter, girl?" John spoke to her in English, the language that was better than his German. Lately the family and Molly had settled into English as a compromise, a midpoint between French and German that both could use to communicate.

"I am hateful." Molly blurted, before bursting into a whole new round of tears. Her whole body shook with the intensity of her conviction. She did not look up at him.

"Now, Molly. Nothin's so bad dhat one cannot ask forgiveness." Dropping to his knees, he reached into the shadow and drew her to him, flipping hay from her young shoulders. Just like he would do for any of his children, he pulled the child to him and allowed her to sob on his broad chest. "Now, now, it cannot be dhat bad."

"It is…it is." Molly gasped out between sobs. "It is." She gulped and snorted, wiping her running nose on her sleeve. "I am bad."

"Now shoosh, little one. Tell me what you did."

"I cannot…" Molly sniffled. "I just cannot."

"Yes, you can Molly. You ain't got'a mean bone anywhere, girl."

"Yes, I do." This time Molly's tone changed, and a faint hint of defiance crept in where once only despair had reigned.

"All right, so you do. Now, what did you do?" In response to her defiance, a fatherly tone entered John's voice as he ordered her to respond.

Molly sniffled and looked away. John gently turned her face toward him and repeated his question again. "What did you do, Molly?"

No escape. No excuses. John stopped any further evasion.

"I called…" she hesitated. "I called the children and Mere a name."

"What name?"

Her chin quivered as she pouted. Her face held firmly but gently, she could not avoid John's gaze.

"What name?"

"I called them…I called them…'stupid breeds,'" she blurted, finally.

She could feel the effect of her words, which jolted through John. His muscles tightened and stiffened. He willed himself to relax.

German=this font   English=this font   *French=this font*   *Delaware=this font*

"Why, Molly? Why...?" John asked trying to squelch any residual anger for her thoughtless action. "Why, Molly, dhat's not at all like you."

A very large tear welled up, rolled down her face, and warmed the side of John's finger. Almost as quick as he had asked, John began to suspect deep down that he knew at least part of the answer to his own question. Memories of the May gathering filled his mind. Molly's brother George had been too caught up in Lizzie's rapt gaze to pay any but scant attention to his sister, who had hungered for his attention. The young couple had disappeared down near the creek soon after John, Ene, and Molly's arrival, no doubt to spoon away from watching eyes. Jacob could not come; Mr. Wood's cow was too near to birthing. Her grandfather had not allowed her brother Johannas to attend, and on top of it all, most of the young folks had openly shunned her. When John had stopped to chat with her Aunt Jessie at the pie table, Molly had walked away from them. He had watched her over her Aunt's shoulder as Molly had tried to strike up a conversation with an old chum. When the young woman turned abruptly and walked away from Molly, Molly followed her. But her friend's brother had stopped her and had said something that caused Molly to turn flaming red before she slapped him, screaming, "Go to Michigan!!!"

The crack of her hand hitting the young man's face echoed through the picnic area like the report of a muzzle loader. Molly's profane curse damned the young man to hell as sure as Satan himself, stoking the fires with savage outrages and diseases, including ague, malaria, and raging fevers.

The response brought a profound hush over the assemblage, which turned simultaneously and centered their gazes on Molly. Brother Bergfelder sighed with theatrical resonance to express his marked disapproval. Her grandfather, standing nearby, frowned severely at her before walking over.

"Watch your profaning tongue, young woman." Then, puffing himself up, George Emler barked sharply, "Take this spoiled child from here, John. She is not worthy of our company."

Before him, he heard Molly's Aunt Jessie's very sharp intake of breath and a very low hissing whisper, "The bastard, how could he?" John knew enough German and its connotations to understand fully what she had said, and more especially, what Molly's Grandfather had implied.

John could see Ester look away from her granddaughter in shame. He could remember excusing himself courteously from Jessie before grasping Molly's shawl. He had walked with quiet dignity to Molly. Taking her arm, they left the May celebration wordlessly. Ene hurriedly caught up to them. No one spoke the whole way home about what had been said. John and Ene simply had respected her silence.

Now John realized that they should have spoken about the day's events. A fuse had been lit, had smoldered, and had exploded, causing deep wounds to everyone, including Molly, who seemed burned the most by her explosive outburst.

German=this font   English=this font   *French=this font*   *Delaware=this font*

Having tied the fuse to the right stick, John asked what seemed to him to be the only obvious question. The question should have been asked long before now.

"Molly, what did dhat young man say to you at de May day celebration?"

Molly gasped. She tried once more to turn away from John's insightful gaze and pushed with futility against his chest.

"What did he say, girl?"

She tried yet again, in vain, to pull away. However, John simply would not permit her to push him away. Instead, he pulled her more tightly to him and repeated, once more, softly in her ear.

"What did he say girl?

"He, he said—" Not having to look John full in the face, Molly stuttered and stopped.

"Molly, what did he say?" He held her even closer. Like swaddling about a baby, her restrained movement settled her.

"He asked me—he asked me if'n 'a half buck rode as good as a whole one'?"

Like his steaming mare, John knew instinctively what to do. John held her tight to him. His strong hands stroked her back, her head, and her neck. With each stroke like the arc of a curry brush, the hurt and the pain were rubbed away. She snuggled down secure in his arms and clung to his strength.

"Do not let dhat senseless hate crawl under your skin. Hate eats the heart away."

After John felt her nerve return, he stood and pulled her to stand. Gently, he wiped her face with the hem of his damp shirt, still warm from their embrace. She trembled as she stood before him. One thing remained to truly bother John. Molly did not seem so much anymore like John's child.

"Come girl, let us go in. Do not forget what I said. Nothing's so bad dhat you cannot ask forgiveness." John touched her cheek gently. His calloused hand curried Molly just as he had Mitsy before her. Like Mitsy, Molly inclined to his touch. He stopped abruptly, grabbed his gun from the ledge, and indicated by a nod to go inside the waiting cabin.

Molly raised her chin and returned a weak smile. She brushed off most of the straw from her garments. The smell of evening porridge and johnnycake wafted in the moist air.

The storm had ended, but the landscape had changed. Branches had blown down, broken by the force of the wind. The young trees would mend and strengthen with age. The old ones just bore deeper scars.

German=this font   English=this font   *French=this font*   *Delaware=this font*

Near Coshocton, Ohio

John Leeth sat for the first time in weeks at peace with the world about him. When Standing Bear sought him out and urged him to return to the true people, John did so with no hesitation. Just being able to be out on the trails again had healed him. Disgusted with both the Americans' and the British duplicities, he returned easily to the man who had raised him within a circle of respect and trust. John continued to work the trade routes in conjunction with his former employer. He would persevere if for no other reason than to show his appreciation and loyalty for his employer paying the bond for him. This was a very small price to leave the hell of Fort Detroit. His work, carrying supplies from trading post to trading post with ample shipments from Sandusky, promised to turn a nice profit for his employer and Alexander McCormick.

The decision to return to Standing Bear's village proved a wise one. This place satisfied a deep-seated need within John. Besides, he could stop at his father's home and enjoy his hospitality on each trading run. John's pack animals, loaded with trade goods, stood without guard or fear of pilfering. He passed in safety among the others, who respected the grandfathers. Life markedly improved for John Leeth, adopted son of Standing Bear and free trader.

Standing Bear shared his hearth again with open generosity. Today, the sagamite tasted especially delicious, so smoky, so filled with maple and corn-rich sweetness. The Lenape or Delaware, as the English called them, still made the best sagamite, in John's opinion. Among the scents of the smoke from the fire, there mingled the scents of herbs and basket materials, which hung from the rafters or pegs along the wall. Unlike the white settlers who often covered their walls with clothing to prove status and wealth, this cabin boasted dyed and woven mats, patterned ash baskets, and plant materials for medicine or fragrance.

Standing Bear's grandsons and two neighbor boys tumbled about the dirt cabin floor like unruly bear cubs. Their squeals and noisy laughter filled the room. John always marveled at the tolerance of the true men when it came to the antics of children. Censure would insure their children's obedience when needed. Often their behaviors were appreciated far more than he ever remembered as a child. His original father and mother's stern admonitions and stiff behavior patterns contrasted markedly when compared to this lenient household. He remembered his late father's frequent backhanded slaps and curses, mixed well with the scent of rum, a crying mother, and blackened cheeks or eyes.

Falling Water Woman busied about to make sure she met Standing Bear's and John's needs. Standing Bear teased her openly, but if one shared their cabin even for a day, one soon felt the mutual regard that they held for one another. The little touches, the warm glances, and the playful sparring of words illuminated their relationship.

German=this font   English=this font   *French=this font*   *Delaware=this font*

"Old Woman," Standing Bear called in mock anger, *"Herd out these noisy young ones, so I can speak with my son, John."*

Falling Water chuckled, reaching into a tiny sack of maple sugar bits to bribe the children to leave. She recognized the growing excitement in Standing Bear's voice. He anxiously wished to share his gift with his adopted son, alone. She rejoiced at the great joy her husband felt to have John home again. His happiness had made their life's journey together brighter amidst all the sadness. She wondered how John would accept his father's gift. One could never fully predict what the adopted ones would do. To save face, the father's or the son's, there would be no place for women at this fire. She must leave the men. But she remained confident that her husband would privately tell her of John's response that night when they shared their bear skin as the fire smoldered and the embers cooled.

Once quiet returned to the cabin, Standing Bear arose and took a small bit of tobacco and threw it into the fire. The aromatic tobacco smoke gave ample signal that Standing Bear had something significant to share with John, who was wise in the way of the true people. John waited expectantly.

"John," Standing Bear grinned proudly.

"Yes, my father."

"You know that I rejoice that you are my son and that you have returned once more to the true people."

"Yes, my father, I know."

"And I would do for you, as I would do for my own blood."

"Yes, my father. You have always honored me, as I hope to honor you."

"Good, because I have found you a wife!"

German=this font   English=this font   **French=this font**   *Delaware=this font*

Chapter 17   Late May 1778
Highs and Lows

"...the people of the frontier have been incessantly harassed by parties of Indians they have not been able to sow grain and at Kentucke will not have a morsel of bread by the middle of June. They have no clothing, nor do they expect any relief from Congress..."

Lieutenant Governor Henry Hamilton, relating the information he received from his captive, Daniel Boone in April 1778 to Gov. Guy Carleton on April 25, 1778 as quoted by Nelson Vance Russell, Ph.D in *The British Regime in Michigan and the Old Northwest, 1760-1796* (Northfield, Minnesota: Carleton College, 1939), p. 193.

Fort Detroit

Anne stood, her head bowed. She could not ignore her quaking kneecaps which betrayed her fear.

Philip DeJean knew instinctively that he had Anne Wylie exactly where he wanted her. Apparently her aversion to imprisonment in a cell had undermined her strength completely. The lioness had dissolved into a cowering kitten. Desperation and primitive survival instincts had kicked in, replacing the former bravado and arrogance. The state of her emotions stood out as surely as the hair that stood rigidly erect on the back of her neck. In short, Anne Wylie would do anything to live.

Absolutely anything!

While DeJean pondered how the mere confinement of her person could bring about such a profound change, he relished the power that he held over her. More power than he could exert over any local person or any of Lernoult's Rangers. Both had refused to perform the very task that he would now force her to commit. Like a huge hunting hound that had cornered an unprotected kitten, he salivated and drooled over the prospect before him. Once and for all he would silence that bastard Finchley and his bloody merchant friends. At the same time, he would show the local population, every man, every woman, and every child, the power of his office of justice. When he lunged into his demands, she never argued. She never protested. She never tried to bargain. She remained totally submissive. She acquiesced with a resigned nod. She emitted not a single murmur as DeJean set the day and time.

The woman appeared devoid of any outward reaction as she shuffled in her shackles. The guard returned her to the dehumanizing cell within the Citadel gaol.

When Eve brought an apple to Anne later that afternoon, she found Anne sitting back against the wall. Anne's knees were pulled up to her chest, her head bowed slightly forward and her face turned away from Eve.

Eve had scrubbed two extra floors to purchase the apple and pay the guard his usual fee to see her friend. The apple still felt cool and crisp from storage in a local root cellar over the winter. The hide had a few tiny wrinkles from winter's dehydration; but nonetheless, it was an apple that truly could make one's mouth water. Known as a *pomme caille*, a snow-apple deep red from skin to core, the apple brought great pride to the locals, who grew them and stored them to resurrect later to fetch the greatest price. She had bought two from Sally Ainsee that day, one for Mikie and one for Anne. She thought this very special treat might cheer her friend.

Eve abhorred seeing Anne like this. She did not know which was worse…her friend's previous rage and anger or her increasing stillness. No longer did Anne pace the cell like a caged mountain lioness. The small indented circle that she had worn into the floor from the firmness of her steps had not felt her heavy tread in a week or more.

Eve wondered at the disturbing changes she saw in her friend. Something different definitely plagued the woman, she feared. Something she did not comprehend.

"Anne…?"

Not a ripple of movement by her friend could Eve detect.

"Anne, I brought you an apple."

Anne did not stir. The soft rise and fall of her quiet breathing did not indicate either a sleeping or waking state.

"Anne, Mikie says hello. You should hear him. He speaks English more and more now. I fear he will lose his mother tongue." Usually any news of Mikie brought Anne around, but not today. Anne remained as before, rock hard, unmoved.

"Pompey brought the kettles down again. May said that we can keep them here 'til he needs them. He is sure that none of us is strong enough to truck'm elsewhere."

Anne made no response.

"May has accepted the women cleaning his house and shop and the men toting wood and tending charcoal in exchange."

Eve paused. She struggled for something, anything, to say to get Anne to respond.

"Smythe and his wife have left for Quebec. Margaret says they plan to resettle in Tory country, near New York City. Can you believe it? They charged poor Margaret to carry a letter back to George." Eve found herself chattering on. The lack of response from Anne puzzled Eve. Anne despised the Smythe couple. Usually Anne snarled at the mere mention of their name and made some disparaging comment.

Finally, resigned to her friend's silence, Eve began to sit down stiffly by the cell door of her friend. "Anne, I am going to sit here by your door a spell and be quiet. It seems you do not feel much like talking today."

"Don't bother! Just leave!" Anne's voice croaked raw and broke short.

Eve stopped, straightened, and looked in the small barred opening.

In all her visits, never had Anne ever asked her to leave. Never. Anne still did not look at her. Her head had not moved nor had her body changed from the exact position it held when Eve first arrived.

"Here is your apple. Maybe you will enjoy it later." Eve tried to hide the disappointment in her voice as she tossed the apple through the bars. The apple bounced and rolled across the floor before it stuck in the folds of Anne's torn skirt. Eve waited. The red apple nestled, unheeded.

Eve reluctantly gave up. "I will come another day."

"I doubt it." The words were spoken so softly that Eve could barely recognize or hear them. In fact, she wondered later if that was what Anne had said at all. Perplexed, Eve left her.

Morning—Two Days Later, Fort Detroit

Sue Ellen had first heard the wild rumors bandied about Fogherty's the day before, but she did not contact Eve. The inn proved busier than ever as it filled nightly with more and more Tories, soldiers, and paroled prisoners alike. Her employers, Ann and William Forsythe, kept her moving without letup. So although she might have shared the unbelievable rumor, she chose to fall into an exhausted sleep, instead of braving the late night streets to take a message to Eve.

Like an Irish jig, the tempo of the fort increased each day in the early summer. Outside the gates, more and more tribes arrived after planting to accept the gifts of His Majesty, to revel in drunkenness whenever the spirits permitted, and to gather up steam to raid the Pennsylvania and Virginia western flank once again. Egged on by Hamilton's Indian Department, they responded to the call to war in hopes of keeping their land and stopping the flow of western American migration. During the daylight hours, when the fort gate opened to them, they staggered and boasted to each other in the streets as they consumed the ample supply of rum. Occasionally, a new raiding party arrived with fresh prisoners and new scalps amid cannon fire salutes, drumming, and other public displays. Once paid, these warriors joined the din as they rushed to spend their earnings. Therefore, it fell to Nellie to break the news to Eve while she worked, as assigned, in the King's Garden.

When Eve looked up from hoeing, she could hear Nellie holler across the field as if she had a ship's foghorn placed to her mouth. No one in Yankee Hall could project sound quite like Nellie.

"Eve, Eve, yer negress friend is a hanging her Frenchman. Come quick. Come quick."

German=this font   English=this font   **French=this font**   *Delaware=this font*

Eve dropped the hoe.

"Eve, yer friend is hanging her Frenchman."

Instantly, Eve broke into a full run, sweeping Mikie up in her arms.

Nellie fell in alongside her, panting heavily from her run to fetch her friend. The wiry, raw boned, greasy-haired woman with high cheekbones epitomized the poor Appalachian Irish. She had struggled alongside her kin to eke out a living in the isolated back mountain hollows. Independent of spirit, she, like her kind, loved living apart from the towns, where they ate trout and venison convinced that they dined just like kings of England. The Irish and the borderland Scots had a long history of earlier conflicts, which meant that many of those sharing Celtic blood held the English kings in total contempt long before they harkened the shores of the new colonies. Her rugged toughness spelled survival, if any chance of it prevailed, no matter how slim.

In the distance, Eve could hear the sounds of mismatched horns, their discordant strains disrupting the countryside as they filtered into her consciousness. The earlier drums Eve had simply accepted as military posturing about the barracks, perhaps to herald more prisoners. Nellie's breathless chatter fell senselessly on her ears. "Hanging her Frenchman, hanging her Frenchman, hanging her Frenchman," became the only words that penetrated. Eve fell once only to have Nellie drag her to her feet and grasp a startled Mikie. They proceeded to dangle him between them while they continued their breakneck run to the fort with Mikie's feet dragging over the bumpy terrain.

The growing crowd milled ahead of them near Finchley's warehouse. The tempo of the drums increased. Eve's heart pounded in syncopation.

"Dear Gott, nein, nein," Eve muttered over and over in counter rhythm with her running feet. As they neared the site, Nellie pulled Eve into the crowd as they shouldered their way to the front of the spectators. There, under the bar, which once had helped Coutincinau to climb like Romeo to claim his love, a rope dangled in the morning sun. A cart stood with a horse snugly held by its bridle, a Redcoat on each side. On the cart, a new pine coffin lay horizontal and on that coffin lid stood John Coutincinau, his hands bound behind him. At the rear of the horse stood Anne, her torso humped in shame. Two drummers and two inane horn blowers made noise. The crowd continued to gather and eddy about them.

Soon Eve, Nellie, and Mikie stood numbly with the others to hear DeJean read the charges, first in English, and then in French. Across the circle, Eve could clearly see May and Pompey. Finchley and his fellow merchants stood smugly by the entrance of the warehouse.

All eyes riveted on the unfolding horror.

No one stepped forward to stop the travesty. Caught in a suspension of belief, the crowd, including soldiers, prisoners, local inhabitants, merchants, and voyagers alike, became entranced. They fixed all their attentions on the death loop.

The horse started a little as the schoolmaster, Jean Baptiste, helped

German=this font   English=this font   *French=this font*   *Delaware=this font*

Father Bocquet to stand on the cart beside Coutincinau. Baptiste remained on the ground to hold the good Father's legs securely as Bocquet offered the last words of comfort. The Recollect's soft intonations in Latin contrasted with the absurd drumming.

Coutincinau waved off the offer of a hood. His gaze never left the tragic figure of Anne, who stood with her head hung down before him. She held a riding crop at the ready to strike the horse before her, which would pull the cart away and drop Coutincinau to his doom.

Father Bocquet rendered his supplication asking quietly for Coutincinau to acknowledge his sins and to receive the blessings of Christ in his last moments. With holy oil, he sealed the Last Rites.

Upon completion of the Father's prayers, Jean Baptiste helped the old priest down from the cart. When Father Bocquet's feet were firmly planted once more, the priest turned and crossed himself, openly, deliberately. Other Catholics present crossed themselves in open recognition of their faith and with unspoken defiance of British Rule. They stood as quiet witnesses to the evil unfolding before them.

Eve found herself joining them in this simple gesture of faith and defiance. Nellie wrinkled her forehead and then, seeming to sense something a little beyond her depth of understanding and stronger than her prejudice, she followed Eve's lead and crossed herself, too, with her opposite free hand.

A latecomer touched Eve's shoulder.

Wordless, Eve put her other arm around Sue Ellen, whose eyes were open over-wide with the prospect of the coming event. Her black pupils erased her blue irises.

Mikie, as children often will in unusual situations, recognized his need to be extremely still. He held his mother's and Nellie's hands, never fussing once about his painful skinned knees after their breakneck run.

"Do you have any last words?"

Coutincinau, ever one to appreciate an audience even in this, his dying moment, looked over those assembled to fully engage their unflinching participation as they placed the noose about his neck. He smiled and nodded to Sue Ellen and Eve. He nodded to his trapping-mate, Pierre Manseur, as well. Then he turned his attention back to Anne.

"Anne, look up *moi perle noire*." His love for the woman saturated every word he spoke.

Anne continued to concentrate on her feet.

"Look up at him heartless bitch," Pierre Manseur cried out. He could restrain himself no longer in the presence of his friend. "*Mon Dieu*, he's dying for you, woman."

"No, no *mon ami*. My Anne is not the one to blame here." Coutincinau cast a disparaging glance at DeJean, whose face assumed a crueler visage.

An undercurrent rippled through the assemblage.

"Make it quick, thief," DeJean snarled.

German=this font   English=this font   *French=this font*   *Delaware=this font*

"Anne, look up," Coutincinau beseeched Anne. "My beauty. You were worth all dhis and more."

"Enough!" DeJean ordered. "Do it now!!!"

Anne did not look up. Instead, she raised the short riding whip to bring it down hard on the rump of the nervous horse as the handlers jumped back, freeing its bridle.

The crack of the whip, the roll of the wheels, the whinnying horse's heavy tread, and Coutincinau's last words overlaid each other.

"Anne, mi amour."

What followed definitely did not adhere to the script that DeJean had envisioned. An ill-placed knot would begin a string of truly tragic events, events caused by a failure of justice which centered in profound tragedy and in the abuse of power.

Quite simply, the grace and mercy of God failed to be with Coutincinau in the hour of his death.

Even though Coutincinau would have given anything to die with a trace of savoir-fare, he could not stifle the inhuman sounds that would gurgle forth repeatedly from his constricted throat. Neither could he attempt to stop the agonized twitching and flexing of his legs and body. Like a worm spinning a cocoon, he wriggled and contorted. The agony continued...and continued...and continued...until the audience, steeped in the utter unrelenting horror of it, began to whisper softly at first and then grew louder and louder. The once handsome Frenchman's facial features contorted. His eyes popped out grotesquely. The merely curious, among them women and children, began to flee the circle as the spectacle grew increasingly too ugly to stomach. Even those hardened by the normal daily cruelties of a very harsh existence grew angry in the face of the merciless display that unfolded before them. As for Finchley, he found himself brewing up another fury, wondering what would be the end effect of this event upon his business.

Eve, Nellie, and Sue Ellen, mutually bound by the spell of horror, made no attempt to leave. They faced the tragedy squarely. Strengthened by friendship and the bonds of the past, they simply could not leave Anne or Coutincinau. Eve clasped Mikie tight and pressed his face into her shoulder. Sue Ellen and Nellie, in turn, held her fast.

Cries began to be heard from many points around the circle. The men had had their gut full of it, too. Even Father Bocquet's weak voice could be heard pleading among them.

"In the name of God, shoot the poor Bastard."

"Mary, Mother of God, beseech your Son to have mercy. Hear our prayer for our brother."

"Dear Jesus."

"No man deserves this."

"Christ, all this for a God damn six pounds."

"God, Have mercy."

"What a night crock."

German=this font   English=this font   *French=this font*   *Delaware=this font*

Piercing the mumbled angry chorus, there issued a shrill banshee-like wail, "Coutincinau." Anne fell to her knees. Looking at Coutincinau for the very first time, she screamed as if her beating heart had ripped from her ribcage...torn by an invisible hand.

Silence came again to the sparser crowd, which had turned uglier with every moan and twitch before them. Anne's screeches continued to pierce the air.

"Forgive me. Forgive me," she screamed. "I didn't want to do this, my love. I didn't want to do this." Her words thrust between screams and sobs. "I jes'have to..." Her wails sliced between understandable words. "I has' to live. I has' to live. He said, I can live. He said..."

In total exasperation, DeJean lost his composure as his control of the diabolical farce, rich with injustice, became increasingly more inhumane.

"Silence, Bitch." DeJean's cane struck Anne across her breasts slicing deep. She bellowed from pain as the cane ripped through her gown and flesh.

In the infinitesimal moment of quiet that followed the echo of his smashing blow, the agony of Coutincinau became mixed with even more unimaginable gurgling, twitching, writhing, struggling, and wriggling. Everyone present realized that Coutincinau wanted to leap from his noose to strangle DeJean with his bare hands. While an elusive death toyed with Coutincinau, refusing to claim him, he twirled in the wind like the last oak leaf caught in a howling winter wind. The cord about his legs broke loose. His legs thrashed and lashed at the air. Urine flooded his breeches.

May turned and spoke something aside to Pompey, who stepped forward and grasped Coutincinau's flailing legs within his long, strong arms. Pompey gave one hard tug downward. Mercy came with the audible snap of Coutincinau's neck.

Pierre Manseur cried out pitifully and dropped to his knees, sobbing. The voyageur's great strength and heart broke with the sound of his friend's passing.

One great spasm, a release of any remaining bodily functions, and the soul escaped. The audience of onlookers, repulsed by the hellish sounds and odors, gasped and groaned in dismay.

Eve continued to hide Mikie's face in her shoulder as he struggled to follow the sounds before them.

Pompey turned. The stunned crowd stared. May stepped in behind Pompey. The sanity of their ribbon farm beckoned.

"Poor Bastard."

"God damn."

"Amen."

"Lord have mercy."

Coutincinau hung quietly for the very first time in the morning sun. The show over, the remaining crowd dispersed slowly. The horns and drums silenced. The motley musicians withdrew, ashamed to have been part of the fiasco. The sounds of Anne's pathetic screams and Mansuer's

German=this font   English=this font   *French=this font*   *Delaware=this font*

sobbing joined with Father Bocquet's prayer as a haunting refrain.

DeJean, however, saw one smiling face in the crowd...one smiling face to bring to his office before the day ended. One smiling face would be sure to accept payment to do his bidding. He would summon Finchley's Pierre as soon as the gaolers removed this screaming bitch out of public sight.

Anne continued to cry out her love for Coutincinau as the guards forcibly restrained her. Few harkened to her. Once she succeeded in breaking free only to be tackled just inches before she could reach Coutincinau's feet. As other guards lowered the body and freed Coutincinau from the noose, Father Bocquet kept a constant undertone of prayer. In moments, the soldiers stuffed Coutincinau unceremoniously into his coffin to begin his journey to the pauper's section and a waiting pit near Ste. Anne's Church cemetery. Father and Jean Baptiste followed prayerfully.

One man stood among the last to depart, alone and in stark dismay. Today, James Sterling had seen English justice trampled in the dust before him. He knew that if he did not flee this wretched new world, the hate that DeJean and men like Hamilton felt towards him could possibly result in another injustice just like this one. Only his wife and children would suffer, and he definitely had far more to lose than this poor bastard.

Resigned, he turned toward the wharf to book passage on the next outbound ship. He and his family must leave without delay. No amount of wealth, no amount of property, would be worth this risk. Askin would buy him out. Had he not offered the first time when Hamilton arrested him and had sent him to Quebec? Sadly, Sterling recognized that he simply could not count on Governor Guy Carleton to rescue him. He must leave this wretched city without delay.

To think that Sterling had once come to DeJean's defense sickened Sterling to the core. Sterling had been the first to sign a letter of support for DeJean years earlier. This brought him a sense of shame, as over time he had watched the disintegration of law and order under Hamilton's regime. First, they hung the furrier, Joseph Hecker, for killing his brother-in-law, Moran. The severity of the crime had dulled his perception of the punishment. Could Dodge's warnings have been right? Justice had most certainly failed here in Detroit. Sterling would speak with Carleton in Quebec upon his leaving. A Grand Jury must be called. Sterling would carry the details of this foul incident, a sorry excuse for English law, to any ear that would listen. Unfortunately, he had no choice. He must take his family home to England, where he hoped a modicum of sanity still prevailed. Perhaps someone, somewhere, who prided themselves in English law and justice, could see the travesty here today and take action against Hamilton and his henchman, DeJean. This time, he hoped that the local French population would not support DeJean. One thing Sterling knew with absolute certainty. He would not be duped again.

Eve and her friends stood quietly. They, too, were among the last to

German=this font   English=this font   *French=this font*   *Delaware=this font*

leave. Eve recognized Finchley's driver, the one who had ticked her with the whip at the wharf. His sniveling smile had changed little since their first encounter. He could only be Pierre, the same bastard who found her friend Anne and Coutincinau still warm in each others arms. Eve shuddered at the sight of him.

Simultaneously within Hamilton's Parlor

Lieutenant Governor Hamilton nodded to Jacob Schieffelin to spike their tea with a little brandy. Morning or no, this morning brought reason to celebrate. Even though he had dreaded the approaching June fire after Stalking Wolf's last affront in open council, Hamilton could not deny his incredible good fortune. A great gift had literally dropped in his lap.

An earlier letter had promised this possibility. Jehu Hay, Hazel, and three of the American defectors sat about him. Two of them came highly recommended by the late John Murry, or Lord Dunmore, as he was known during his British appointment in Virginia before the Bostonian's rebellion. Hamilton's secretary, Jacob, moved amongst the chatting men, serving them morning tea, buttery-rich shortbread, and scones filled with ham. Hamilton sat quietly and studied each man.

Hamilton focused first on the roughest and least polished, Simon Girty. Not put off by his base Irish background, Hamilton deliberately ignored the man's crude manners. They could be overlooked when one considered his considerable skills. Simon and his brothers had more knowledge of the Ohio tribes than any single family that had ever worked before for the crown. A true gift of providence, each brother had lived with separate tribes. When their stepfather had been unmercifully burned at the stake, they had been separated and adopted among three tribes to make up for the pain of other mothers, who had also lost their sons. Girty's mother and youngest brother were removed to still another tribe. Simon had been adopted as a Seneca, George by the Delaware, and James by the Shawanese. Only the oldest brother, Thomas, remained true to the American cause, making his home near Fort Pitt.

Simon Girty first served with Lord Dunmore as interpreter and had aspired to be a Captain with the Rebels. But just like his hard drinking, poorly educated, murdered father and stepfather, the occasionally loud and quarrelsome Simon never succeeded. The rejection had never set well. After having been part of the Squaw campaign, Simon got a belly full of many of the despicable backwoodsmen. He despised General Hand, whom he considered a sorry excuse for an officer, when Hand could not stop the atrocities toward women and children. In the end, convinced by Elliott of the eventual triumph of the British, who currently held New York and Philadelphia, he had defected with Elliott and the influential McKee. The Rebels, suspicious of his Tory leanings, had once jailed him, but Simon still had cleverly escaped to place McKee's letter where the British could

German=this font   English=this font   *French=this font*   *Delaware=this font*

find it in the hollow tree earlier last fall. His plan to turn himself back in to the Rebel jailer had worked well. The Rebels released him a short time later. As usual, the cocky Simon had used his Irish gift of Blarney to get himself back into the good graces of the Rebel forces.

But it was not just the Rebels that Simon had smooth-talked with his glib tongue. Hamilton discovered from Jehu Hay that Simon had gotten himself out of yet another ticklish situation. Simon had been captured by the Wyandot, Hamilton's staunch allies in Sandusky, when Simon was en route to Fort Detroit. After his adopted Seneca brothers had failed to convince the Wyandot to release Simon to them as their lost brother, Simon had saved himself. Speaking in fluent Seneca, he persuaded the angry Wyandot that he had been extremely ill-treated and even jailed by those in Fort Pitt for his allegiance to the King. He further convinced them that he longed now only to redeem himself by fighting for his Majesty, to fight for his brother Seneca, and to help stop the land grabbing Americans, who coveted all their tribal lands and who indiscriminately killed their women and children. He reiterated the lies that the Congress had dissolved and that many had been hung or exported. He stressed that the Rebels, who remained behind, would soon go on a killing spree to avenge their losses. His well-stated arguments proved so persuasive that the Wyandot released him on his own recognizance.

Unlike General Hand, Lieutenant Governor Hamilton recognized more in Simon than a lack of formal education and a propensity for undisciplined behavior when drinking. He valued a shrewd and skilled fighter when he saw one. Most of all, the astute Hamilton perceived a persuasive interpreter, one who could think very fast on his feet, a quality rarely found here on the fringes of civilization. Therefore, immediately upon his arrival, Hamilton insisted that Simon Girty join the payroll of Great Britain as a member of Hamilton's department. His brothers, George and James, quickly followed Simon's lead.

Hamilton smiled knowingly as Schieffelin shorted the amount of brandy in Girty's tea. His secretary intuitively acted as Hamilton would wish.

Second, Hamilton focused on Matthew Elliott. Elliott's voice rose in a heated but friendly debate with Hay about the trading potential in the coming year. Elliott stoutly maintained that the beaver population dropped each year from over-trapping, whereas Hay maintained that the beavers were just at a low end of a breeding cycle and would rebound shortly. Hamilton covered his intense dislike for Elliott with a thin veneer of professionalism. He felt that he could not trust the man any further than his gaze. He had arrested this complex man once before, packing him off to Quebec. From Quebec, Elliott had sailed to British-held New York, then on to British Philadelphia and returned again by way of Fort Pitt in league with the articulate McKee. Suspecting an opportunist, who could flip-flop in a heartbeat, Hamilton doubted if and when Elliott encountered a difficult situation whether he would be reliable. Hamilton felt sure that money

German=this font   English=this font   **French=this font**   *Delaware=this font*

talked louder than any allegiances for this man. Hamilton's distrust
initially began when Elliott sued for lost horses and trade goods upon his
first appearance in Fort Detroit. The trader had been so suspect that
Hamilton had arrested him as a Rebel spy. Elliott still continued to beat
this thin drum on his second admission to Fort Detroit. He pounded on
these self-same losses, returning again and again throughout their
conversations to plead for reimbursement for his losses to the allied
Wyandot and Mingo. While his stature and manner indicated that Elliott
might be a good fighter and possibly a fair interpreter, Hamilton refused to
hire him.

McKee, the prize in this litter of three defectors, intelligently
interacted with everyone in the room. His manner and his centered
authority screamed his leadership qualities. The wily man had been paroled
twice by the rebels. Feigning illness, McKee had thwarted the Rebel plan
to murder him when asked to appear before the Rebel congress on yet a
third occasion. The threesome had escaped Fort Pitt, just hours before
General Hand's men came to McKee's home to arrest them.
McKee had already proved invaluable with his early intelligence of the
American side. He constituted a jewel for the British Crown.

Hamilton sensed immediately that McKee could take over Hay's
position and accomplish far more with flair, freeing Hay for more patrols.
In fact, Hamilton had a strong feeling that even though he would replace
Hay with McKee, Hay would still maintain a good relationship with
McKee. McKee represented the kind of man that men liked and followed
gladly. Hamilton quickly decided that he would announce this defector's
captaincy tomorrow.

Hamilton, deep in introspection, barely heard Hay's question until Hay
repeated it for the third time.

"Governor, I say sir, what is the racket up the way? Do you hear
the noise?"

Hamilton, distracted, reined in his thoughts. "I believe..." he hesitated
for a few moments. He shook his head, trying to remember..."You know, I
think DeJean is punishing one of the locals. A petty affair, some
voyageur and his black wench." He waved the event away with a
distracted flip of his hand. Then, he shook his head thoughtfully before
taking out his snuff box, removing a tiny bit of snuff to place on the back
of his hand, sniffing it in, and then sneezing.

Jacob quickly handed him his lace hanky.

Hamilton sneezed again before adding, "Nothing of any
consequence, I assure you." Placing the hanky over his face, he
discreetly sniffed his nasal contents in and swallowed.

Girty masked his frown. He remained unimpressed by his high-
classed benefactor's mannerisms. He tried for the second time to get
Hamilton's fool secretary's attention to refill his tea, but the secretary
always seemed to have other business in the room. He liked that tea, given
that he seldom got brandy in any form. Girty settled instead for another

German=this font   English=this font   *French=this font*   *Delaware=this font*

scone. He shifted uneasily. He felt too closed in. He longed to get outside where he could breathe, maybe work his way down to Fogherty's for a rum or two. He felt a growing restlessness within the confines of the very close room. He tugged at his collar and tried to loosen the strangle-hold on his neck.

"Girty." This time Hamilton had to get the attention of another. "Girty."

"Yes, sir."

"Captain Hay tells me that your brother George will rejoin the Delaware encampment soon."

"Yes, sir."

"Jacob, will you see he has more tea." For a moment the uproar outside broke his concentration. "Excuse me, now where was I? Oh yes, Girty, it has come to my attention that a warrior named Stalking Wolf has a small boy which he forcibly removed from his mother, one of our prisoners here." He sniffled a little.

Hamilton monitored Girty's reaction. "You know how difficult this is for a child of five or six." Hamilton realized that the roughneck Girty would have empathy for the child.

Girty sat forward in his chair and stopped pulling at his collar.

"Stalking Wolf, shall we say, has been a fang in our flesh, so to speak," Hamilton continued. "I think if we could return this child to his mother, we might have a little more leverage with this man." He paused, "And save the boy."

"Do you know the child's name?"

"Yes, we believe it is Henry, Henry Earnest. They may call him Hanu. Do you think that you and your brother might resolve this problem? We are given to understand that the child currently stays in the Delaware encampment."

"Yes, Sir. We'll give it a go, sir."

"Good."

Jacob Schieffelin poured more tea and splashed a tad more brandy in it. Girty grinned approvingly.

Hamilton smiled.

The discordant noise without ceased. Morning continued with gracious civility in Hamilton's parlor.

That Evening

Eve threw a stone into the water. After she returned from the field, she always found a certain peace in the small boatyard at day's end. She watched the circles expand and ripple, one within another. When the late sun broke through in a hole creating a shaft of golden light like a beacon on the water, she wistfully wondered if Coutincinau flew in the light or where God had chosen to place him. He certainly had earned his wings. Life, filled with one senseless tragedy after another, daunted her.

German=this font   English=this font   *French=this font*   *Delaware=this font*

Yet here, by the water with the sounds of canoe building behind her, the delicate lapping of water, Mikie's laughter, and Teddy's playful barking, there resided a peacefulness that belied the daily rounds of horror that seemed to circle her, just like the ripples about the stone.

Mikie played near Tchamaniked Joe. The man's amazing tolerance for the child and his dog's gentle nature meant she could lose herself in reverie without fear for Mikie. She felt gutted again. Empty. She just could not reconcile the Anne that she knew and admired with what she had seen that morning. What in the name of God had driven her to do that wretched man's bidding? She threw another stone into the water and watched the circles expand.

"Would you like to speak about the loss of your friend?"

She looked quizzically up at Tchamaniked Joe. "I am sorry, what did you say?"

"I said…Would you like to speak about the loss of your friend?"

Eve always felt some sense of surprise when she spoke to Joe. His articulate nature somehow did not fit with her low expectations of him. Although his English had a heavy French accent, she usually could follow him. As spring had progressed, their familiarity with each other had grown. She welcomed his brief chats with her and found herself, if she could have admitted it, actually enjoying their encounters. Indians proved such a conundrum to her. Some, she found interesting, others she simply despised.

Joe said he was a Chippewa, if one followed the English name given to his tribe. On a prior occasion, he had explained this name for his people. He stated that he plainly preferred Anishinaabe, but he acknowledged that she might also hear Ojibwe if one Frenchified it. He conceded that if she used Anishinaabe, very few, if any, would understand her. His Chippewa tribe had joined the Ottawa also called Odawa, and the Potawatomi as part of the council of three fires in the Great Lakes region.

"May I sit, Madame Eve?"

"Oh, yes, of course. We invade your territory. You need no permission here when it is my son and I who impose on you." No matter how often Eve had tried to get him to drop the Madame, Joe persisted. Sometimes he called her '*Animakwe*', but lately he used Madame Eve. At least she had gotten him to shift to the more familiar Eve, not Earnest. When he realized that using Earnest brought painful memories, he ceased. Here in this place so far from her home, she preferred using Eve.

"You are not imposing. Besides, Teddy likes the boy's company."

Now that the weather warmed, Joe wore only a soft leather vest, breech cloth, and cloth-lined leggings tied at his knees with small fleche lacings. His well-tanned thighs and feet contrasted with his puckered moccasins. She especially liked his moccasins with their tiny, red-quill strawberry decorations. The colorful fruit on a man's moccasins and flowers in quill decoration on his vest appealed to the whimsical side of

German=this font   English=this font   *French=this font*   *Delaware=this font*

her nature. Adam Henry would have stormed over such a preposterous idea. Already, from having worked out in the sun and mild rain, Joe's skin browned and darkened. His upper arms and chest would soon match his weathered face, deeply cut with sun-wrinkles. His raven-like nose and long thin face had a raw strength about it.

Eve appreciated his hands most of all. She secretly loved watching him. Sometimes, she stood in awe of his creativity as the canoes magically formed from a flat piece of bark. She marveled how he could cut, fit, and bend the cedar to his every whim. Especially, she loved the tiny animals that he carved for Mikie.

Mikie's animals made him the envy of every child in Yankee Hall when he pulled them from their small leather pouch to line the tiny deer and other animals up to gallop across his covers on rainy days.

"Has your bark come yet from the North?" Eve asked, trying to change the subject, but Joe just chuckled at her attempt.

"My question first. I asked first, twice."

She smiled sadly, shaking her head. "It is hard. So much of it does not make any sense."

"Man's cruelty to man, that is a given. What else does not make sense to you?"

Eve never failed to be astounded by the man's take on things. His ideas slanted when compared to hers. She found it a complete wonder that they lived within such a short distance of each other but so far apart in their minds. She wondered just where he got some of his ideas. She thought over his question and then, after a moment or two of reflection, answered. Her voice sounded distant when she spoke.

"What does not make sense is that I thought I knew Anne. She loved Coutincinau. He loved her. He died loving her, even as she hung him. Why, in the name of God, would she ever do that?"

"Leave God out of this one, Eve. This is entirely mankind's doing. What thing do you remember meaning the very most to Anne? You traveled here with her. You struggled to survive with her. You faced death with her. What do you remember her saying or doing? These will point to her heart. Something meant far more to her than Coutincinau's love and life. Answer that and you may have your answer."

Teddy and Mikie came running. Mikie fell into his Mutti's arms, laughing. The dog, toot suite, behind him landed in the middle of the merry pile, dissolving all of them into merriment.

"Would you care for a bowl of soup, Madame Eve? I have extra to share."

The thought of a man preparing soup really set Eve back on her heels, diverting her away from their earlier conversation.

"You cook?"

"Either that or starve." Tchamaniked Joe stood, pulling Eve to her feet. When she winced, he looked concerned.

"Did I pull too roughly?"

"No, no, I fell earlier today with Nellie."

"Humph." This all purpose grunting sound Eve had come to understand as she had gotten to know Joe. The sound covered a veritable range of things from..."I understand, maybe, you do not say...or do not do that."

He really had not waited for her answer. But given that he was heading for his small bark shed that stood at the edge of the boat yard, Eve assumed that she should follow. Somehow, something told her that to refuse his offer of hospitality would also be taken as a refusal of his friendship. Since she valued one, she must accept the other. As she neared the shed, she could smell the soup, a strange mixture of smells but invitingly pleasant. Mikie danced on the end of her hand. The child had a dog-like nose when it came to food. Eve noticed a run of saliva already coursing down his chin in expectation.

With little ceremony, three small gourd shells were filled and handed to each with a small chunk of heavy coarse fry bread.

Eve savored the smoked fish and dried pea soup. The combination truly amazed her. The soup tasted wonderful. She quickly drained her portion with not even a word between herself and her host.

Joe watched her gobble down her portion with unabashed amusement. He had barely sipped his own soup, so caught up was he in watching his visitor's ravenous response.

His one eyebrow arched and with a bit of a smile that he could not hide, he asked, "Would you like another helping?"

Eve blushed like a young woman caught in a compromising situation. At this juncture, she could not suddenly pretend that she had a ladylike appetite. Absolutely nothing remained in her gourd. She had even wiped the gourd dry with her frybread.

Joe's countenance invited honesty over embarrassment, so she simply handed him her gourd, which he refilled with a slightly larger helping than on the first round. He handed her a second portion of bread, and they all continued to eat in silence.

A little more slowly this time, Eve savored her richly satisfying repast. As she came near to finishing the second helping, Eve looked up.

"I did not realize how hungry I was. You are most generous."

"My pleasure."

He watched her finish.

"By the way, in answer to your question. I hear the bark is beginning to separate. My supply should be here within the next moon."

"Moon?"

"Moon, we, Anishanabek, keep a calendar by the moon. Now it is the time of the Wabigonees Gieezis, the little flower moon. The bark usually separates during late Odehmeenon Gieezis, the strawberry moon." He tore another portion of bread for himself. Chewing on it, he rose and disappeared into his shed. In moments, he returned.

German=this font   English=this font   **French=this font**   *Delaware=this font*

"May the child have a touch of sweet?"

"Yes, he has eaten a good supper."

She polished off Mikie's leftover crust as Mikie reached to claim the small brown chunk of solid maple sugar.

Teddy had sat patiently awaiting his portion. The empty pot nearly devoid of soup now became his pleasure. His tail wagged in grateful appreciation. His appearance became quite comical as his head and one paw disappeared into the cooking pot.

As if anticipating Eve's unstated question, Joe said teasingly.

"I will wash the pot well, Madam Eve, before it is reused. I promise."

Eve looked up at him. She felt so cursedly transparent before this man. She swore sometimes he peeked in her mind and looked freely at her thoughts. This insight caused her to blush again.

Joe acknowledged her blush with a touch of his hand. He brushed her cheek with the back of his hand. His touch glided lightly over the soft down that covered her face like fine peach skin. Eve quizzically accepted his gentle touch.

The first evening cannon sounded. The spell broke. Hearing the cannon at the Fort, Eve pivoted anxiously towards the direction of the gate. More time had slipped by than she realized. She must leave.

Hastily excusing herself and her son, Eve and Mikie began their run towards the Fort. She heard Joe call out behind her.

"Madam Eve, follow the trails of your friend's heart, not just your head."

"I will!" She called back waving her hand to acknowledge his words.

"Thank you." She and Mikie had little time to lose.

That night as Eve drifted off to sleep, her stomach felt full and satisfied for the first time in many weeks. Clean and dry, Eve felt a momentary pang of guilt for feeling some happiness on this truly wretched day. She sensed an aura of warmth enfold her. Her imagination drifted. Was it Adam Henry's hands that she felt about her neck and shoulders, rubbing the tension away as he had so many times after she had woven for long periods? Ease and contentment surrounded her. Accepting her blessings with humility, she murmured "thank you" to the unseen and surrendered to a peaceful rest.

One Day Later

Margaret, Eve, Nellie, Mikie and Sue Ellen stood mute and dry eyed. They emulated Anne. They kept their heads up and remained just as quiet and dignified as Anne. After she nodded and smiled at them, she accepted the hood. The small ugly toad of a Frenchman, Pierre, struck the horse. Blessedly, the hangman's knot on this occasion had been placed correctly. Her suffering and agony proved shorter than Coutincinau's. While derogatory comments washed about them, the four women and child held

German=this font   English=this font   *French=this font*   *Delaware=this font*

fast as an island of support in an angry sea of jeering men and hostile women.

Sue Ellen spoke first. "What were her last words, Eve? Could you make them out?"

"We be free."

"We be free?" Margaret questioned. "Why would she say that? Did the poor fool think that she and Coutincinau were free?"

"No," Eve answered. She knew deep in her heart what Anne meant. Joe's admonition to listen to Anne's heart not just her reason pointed to the truth. Why had she failed to comprehend it earlier? She had seen all the signs including the tight bodice. She clutched Mikie's hand tightly. She smiled lovingly down at him, her child, her reason for being.

"Well, don't keep us hanging in suspense, Eve. What in the hell do you think she meant?" Nellie asked in her usual blunt and tactless way.

"I think that she meant that she..." Eve paused, "and their unborn were free." Leaving her friends speechless, she turned from them and began walking back to Yankee Hall with Mikie in hand. She could not summon the strength to see her friend taken down. The horrible emptiness had returned a hundred fold.

Pompey frowned as he overheard the women. He glared at Pierre, who still held the death-dealing crop in his hands.

A fair pause later, Eve heard Nellie growl far behind her. "Now just how in the hell did she know that?"

"You know, I think Eve may be right," Sue Ellen agreed softly, but Eve did not hear her finish as she said, "Anne loved Coutincinau. She really did. But for her, to be free for herself and her children was all she ever wanted. It makes sense somehow."

May and Pompey watched Finchley's man, Pierre, as he received his twenty pounds from DeJean.

Pierre returned the horse wagon to his employer and hurried towards Fogherty's Inn. He felt a need to order up a round of rum to celebrate his good fortune. Agnes and the brats did not need all of the money, Pierre reasoned. After all, a man deserved a round or two after a hard day's work.

As Eve walked down the street lined with pear trees covered with brown, spent blossoms, she offered a few silent prayers, including the hope that Anne could lie near her beloved Coutincinau. This prayer went unanswered. The establishment buried Anne in the unbeliever's cemetery. Anne had not been baptized a Roman Catholic.

German=this font   English=this font   *French=this font*   *Delaware=this font*

Dawn, the Next Day

Two deckhands from the *Welcome* found Finchley's employee, Pierre, floating face down in the water, drifting near the supports under the merchants' wharf. On the dock, his shoes were neatly placed side by side, each one filled with fifteen silver English pounds.

Later that morning, a delegation from Ste. Anne's informed Agnes, Pierre's wife, about his untimely death, the shoes, and the silver found ashore. Those who delivered the thirty pieces of silver and the tale of Pierre's demise to the new widow and his gaping children related that as the door closed they could hear Agnes in an absolute blood boil, swearing at Pierre's departed spirit. Before noon, the entire neighborhood about the hovel knew that Pierre's death had brought more money in the door that day than on any previous occasion.

Deemed an unfortunate accident, Pierre's final resting place lay next to Coutincinau in the pauper's section of Ste. Anne's cemetery. Both graves were unmarked.

Finchley needed to replace two of his employees. But this would be relatively simple, as more prisoners came with each passing day in the summer of 1778.

German=this font   English=this font   **French=this font**   *Delaware=this font*

Chapter 18   A Warm June in 1778 with New Wrinkles

"I cannot but praise the behavior of the Indian nations, who have taken hold of their Father's axe and who have acted as men. I hope you'll act the same part and not redden your axe with the blood of women and children. I speak to you who are men...Our intention is never to act against children, but against men."

Lieutenant Governor Henry Hamilton to a large council of Native Americans at Fort Detroit, June 1778. As quoted by Nelson Vance Russell in "The Indian Policy of Henry Hamilton," *The Canadian Historical Review* (Volume 31(11) 1930): p. 31.

Fort Detroit

Often humankind caught in the vice-like grip of death's stark reality, embarks in totally unexpected directions to seek the warmth of human touch. Skin against skin, rub against rub, face against face, genital against genital, absolutely nothing will suffice except the complete engagement of one human within and about another. Such is the drive to confirm life in the face of death, especially untimely or inhumane deaths...a drive stronger than lust. This can most clearly be seen when a birth in a family follows on the heels of the death of a loved one.

Eve left Mikie with Nellie that evening, saying that she wished to spend time with Sue Ellen. Only Sue Ellen suspected that Eve planned to rendezvous overnight with someone. She sensed this unspoken need within Eve. One simply did not speak of these things. Their friendship did not permit even raising the question. Sue Ellen simply accepted that her friend, who veritably radiated with heat, sought to put out the fire.

As part of her plan, Eve planned to go back to Sue Ellen's sleeping room if necessary. If rejected, Eve knew she would not want to return to the Citadel late. Eve had no desire to be subjected to a barrage of Nellie's questions, no matter how well-intentioned, or to the unwanted curiosity of the Citadel guards.

Sue Ellen, still reeling from the events of the last weeks herself, did not ask where Eve was going. She wondered fleetingly if Eve would meet with someone like Pierre Manseur. Both had spoken of his deep loss and his despair, so evident when he drank himself into a stupor at Fogherty's each night. She could not imagine for a moment that it was the kind Jewish merchant, who had hired Eve to care for his sick friend.

However, Eve selected neither Manseur, the French voyageur, nor Ezekiel Solomon, the kind merchant.

Eve had not seen Tchamaniked Joe since Anne's hanging, but something now drew her to him. She wondered if she had truly sensed the flash of his sensual side, or if she, like a misguided lady lightning bug, was honing in on the wrong signal light across a murky swamp. She really could not justify, even to herself, why she considered this course of action. She only sensed the growing conviction that she must. In the days leading up to tonight, she had debated with herself in horrible repetitive loops, asking herself over and over if she should approach this man, this Indian. He did not repel her like either Stalking Wolf or Blue Ice. She finally decided that something within the man himself drew her to him. She had wavered twice earlier, both times deciding at the last moment not to go. She feared rejection, but she finally elected to approach him. She had nothing to lose. At least if she went, she would know his response and not wonder. Knowing for certain seemed far more important than not knowing. In the end, her repulsion for his tribal affiliation faded and became completely lost in her pain and aching need. She considered no one else.

Eve walked resolutely towards the boatyard. The closer she came, the more she settled into a non-thinking daze, and the more her emotions expanded, consuming her entirely. As she approached Tchamaniked Joe, Teddy barked and ran up to her. Then the dog stopped as if pulled up short on an invisible leash, sat down, and simply stared at her quietly.

Tchamaniked Joe, putting the last lick to conform to his eye's desire on the gunwale, felt the force that emanated from her like white hot heat from a hemlock fueled forge long before he turned to face her. He had expected her. He did not know when she would come, but he knew she would come. He also knew they would weld like wrought iron, making a tight bond. He stood straight, his arms crossed. The crooked knife in his hand was placed in the exact position of their first meeting. He still looked dangerous to Eve.

Eve stopped at the distance of a body's length.

Joe could see waves of heat shimmering and distorting the air between them like full noon day sun over hot summer sand. Behind her, across the water, heat lightening flickered back and forth over the surface of the building clouds in the waning light. But nothing like the flickering heat that rippled through her hair in the light breeze. Stray locks slithered about her cheeks, parting the nearly invisible velvet of her face. She appeared luminescent in the fading light.

Some men have an instinctive sense of women, born out of love and respect for their kind. Tchamaniked Joe belonged to those chosen few. This instinct had altered his life so completely that it had brought him back to these very shores along the Great Lakes. Again, the love of women would impact on his life.

They stood facing each other. Only the unloving and the unfeeling would find it an insurmountable distance.

Joe wondered just how she would express her need. He knew exactly why she had come, but how would this woman of her culture ask? Asking

German=this font   English=this font   *French=this font*   *Delaware=this font*

was simpler among the people. At least it had been until the Black Robes came with their twisted celibacy and their concepts of carnal knowledge.

Eve had given great consideration to her coming. She knew what she would say. She knew how she would approach him. She pressed her arms stiffly at her sides. Within her sinister hand, she held something tightly. She devoutly wished that by some unholy chance, he would understand.

"I brought you something," she said awkwardly. Part of Eve wanted to break and run. The burning need held her fast.

"I see that." He looked as amused as he had the day that she had wolfed down his soup. His arms remained folded.

She extended her left arm, the hand palm down. Her fingers curled around a round object. Rotating her extended hand, she opened it flat. Nested in her palm, a nearly perfect **pomme caille** rested.

"You look hungry. Let us share it," he responded.

"You are most generous."

"My pleasure."

He extended his free hand in turn. She crossed the distance between them. She grasped his outstretched hand with her right hand as he led her to his bark shed at the yard's edge.

Teddy, a quiet sentinel, stayed seated.

The first rays of morning sun brought a dim awareness not only of Eve's surroundings but the sounds of a deep base snore. His arm still lay across her bare breasts as if to check her if she chose to depart while he slept. The rise and fall of his chest in sequence with his breathing lifted and dropped the hairless, tanned deer hide which lay loosely over them to ward off the morning chill. The low, narrow rope bed, more right for one than two, sagged deeply from their combined weight. She felt no shame, only a deep sense of relief. Under the blackened coals of the forge, glowing embers remained of the fire that had consumed them.

Eve allowed her eyes to focus on her surroundings. For a man, he is neat, she thought. The shed appeared far neater than Onkle Jac's cabin. Snowshoes hung on a far wall. Herbs, sage, tobacco, and sweetgrass hung suspended in pairs over the laced poles that held the sheets of bark and imparted a recognizable scent familiar to Eve. The scent imbedded in his pores. She acknowledged sheepishly that he smelled far better than she. Above her and to her left in the ceiling, a hole to draw the smoke remained open and permitted the light of sun, moon, and stars to enter.

A spider-like web within a hoop hung over the triangular opening where the corner of a well woven reed mat had been lifted to allow first light to enter. The still unlit candle, a small gourd filled with flowers plucked from the shore, the crooked knife, and the uncut apple sat on a small table next to one lone chair.

The chair, made not unlike the snowshoes, was laced with rawhide and hunched on four, strong hickory legs. This supported her clothes and his. Each article was folded neatly and laid alternately one upon another. The

German=this font   English=this font   *French=this font*   *Delaware=this font*

clothes had not been hastily removed but carefully peeled layer by layer.

A few shelves on another wall drew her attention. A small travel trunk sat on the highest shelf. A few black ash baskets with fitted lids trimmed in sweet grass filled the second. A quill, an ink well, two or three rolls of thin, tightly rolled birchbark, and three books neatly stacked lay on a third. Why would this man have books? How could he even afford books? Surely the man could not read. Indians did not read or write, or did they?

The high whine of mosquitoes sounded with the increasing warmth within the shed. The snoring ceased. Eve turned her face to Joe. Dark eyes fired. He caressed her, tracing the lines of her nose, her brows, her chin, and her lips. She warmed to his touch. She snuggled into his shoulder as he rolled over her. Let'um bite, she thought, as the soft hide slipped away to the floor.

Later, she gratefully accepted a cup of hot maple sweetened tea, a piece of apple, and the now familiar heavy bread as she sat on a log by the morning fire. The fish and net racks so common, the windmills in the distance, the sounds of lapping waves, all added to life along the shore. Gulls screamed and dipped in the morning breezes or bobbed like white corks in the water. Teddy still sat quietly. No one else had come.

"Will you be reported?"

"No, Nellie will cover for me."

"Can you trust her?"

"Can you trust anyone in these times? I cannot be sure." Eve spotted her reflection in the cup of liquid and smiled, amused at what she saw.

"You expected me," she said quietly.

"Yes."

"You continuously surprise me."

"I know."

"I must return now."

"Humph."

"I do not know if I will come back." The implication was clear.

"You will," he said matter-of-factly. He left her then to return to his work on the canoe.

Eve savored her tea, watching him appreciably. He looked good working in the early sun. For just a moment, the world seemed right. Reluctantly, she returned to the reality of her life. She headed up towards the King's Garden to resume her endless hoeing. However, morning sounds refreshed her. Her gait enlivened, she walked sprightly. Nellie and Mikie awaited her in the fields ahead.

That evening, Fogherty's hummed like a hive in full swarm. Sue Ellen, one of the worker bees, flitted from table-to-table holding the pewter tray filled with rum, fresh stores from Montreal and Quebec. The new

German=this font   English=this font   *French=this font*   *Delaware=this font*

shipment, the returning sailors, the voyageurs with a winter's harvest of money to spend, off-duty redcoats and a sundry of others filled every table. The inn swelled to capacity, which meant that Sue Ellen moved between the buzzing tables which leaned or swayed to permit her passage. All but one table complied. A particularly offensive group of malcontents deliberately jostled and groped her as she passed, hoping to make her spill her brew and rum. One man, in particular, grew louder and louder with each noggin that he imbibed. Unfortunately, his table stood alongside a well-used pathway from the kitchen.

John Leeth's friend, Jonas Schindler, the silversmith, watched Sue Ellen trying to dodge the rude man from his corner seat. He kindled disgust. Gossip flowed continuously in the fort. Jonas wondered if that crude man could be one of the American defectors spoken of in the latest round of rumors which bounced off the walls of the closely packed houses that peered out across narrow streets. Like the more cultured French, Jonas shared a low tolerance for disorderly rude Americans in general and drunken Irishmen in particular, no matter what their allegiance. He found it difficult to rank them in order of which characteristic he despised most.

"Hey there, freckle cheeks, when do we get service here?" Simon Girty, late in from his treks, had developed, in his opinion, a well deserved thirst. He had dropped his bundle with Hamilton and now used some of his reward to get uproariously drunk and hassle Sue Ellen in particular. On her next sashay by, he grabbed her arm firmly, yanked her roughly into his lap, and nuzzled the stubble of his beard into the cleavage of her bosom. He left a red whisker burn on her partially exposed breast. She pushed him away, bounded to her feet with a well practiced maneuver born of earlier experiences, and headed to the next table without spilling a drop.

Jonas wrinkled his forehead. His eyebrows drooped in the center.

"Loosen yer touch there, Simon?" One particularly unsavory bearded companion of Simon sniped.

"Roughed up her teattie, yah did." Another laughed in support.

"Jes wait'll next time. That bird won't fly." Spittle dripped down the side of his chin as the rum soaked every pore and cell, especially brain cells. Simon Girty, soddened to the gills, had lapsed into a stereotypical noisy and obnoxious drunk, mean and nearly stupid with rum.

On Sue Ellen's next pass, he belligerently swaggered to his feet, defiantly blocking her way. A square built Celt, he presented a formidable impasse.

Across the room, one table of guards from the Citadel observed the situation. However, none of them moved to assist Sue Ellen. They desired no trouble with any of Hamilton's bunch.

"Unhand her." Jonas spoke atypically loud for the quiet man. The volume even surprised him.

His voice carried the moment. Nearly all noise ceased. Only the soft clank of tankards returning to the tables could be heard.

"Who'n the hell do you think you are?" Simon jeered. He could

German=this font   English=this font   **French=this font**   *Delaware=this font*

barely stand, rocking back and forth, but he still held Sue Ellen and her tray captive.

Ever used to this type of scene, the burly owner, William Forsythe, and his wife, Ann, quickly moved in to divide and conquer. Antoine, their massive cook, instantly appeared in the kitchen doorway as back up.

"Now, let the little lady do her work." Forsythe casually removed Girty's hands, as if removing a toy from one spoiled child to give it to another as he handed Sue Ellen over to his wife.

Girty's meanness began to reach full boil. His wadded fist wound up to swing at Forsythe, when Jonas stepped up with a solid right hook that dropped the unsuspecting and disadvantaged drunkard to the floor. The resultant crash and Jonas's yelp of pain sounded, as he leapt up and down like water on a hot iron skillet. He shook his hand and arm wildly as pain shot up his arm. Girty's companions jumped to their feet. They fully intended to come to Simon's assistance, when they saw an impending Antoine. Not entirely stupid, they took to their heels, grabbing Simon by the shoulders and dragging their fallen companion out the door to make their hasty retreat.

Business resumed as noisily as before. Sue Ellen had a hero. The silversmith had a sprained hand. The Citadel guards chuckled about the Indian Department's new fighter and bought Schindler a drink. And Girty, Girty would have a sore jaw in the morning and a score to settle.

The Next Day, Fort Detroit

"Eve Earnest." A redcoat stood in the Yankee Hall door, calling over the sleepy inhabitants who had not awakened yet to the morning reveille. The trumpet had not sounded yet in the Citadel.

"Oh mein Gott," Eve wheezed, coming to a hasty stand as Mikie cried out a short yelp. He had been startled by his Mutti's quick leap to her feet. Someone must have talked, Eve decided, as she tried to straighten herself. She wrapped herself in a blanket and worked her way to the door, weaving among the sleeping circles and blanket piles.

"Are you Eve Earnest?"

"Yes, I am she."

"Bring your son and yourself to the Lieutenant Governor's office as quick as you can be presentable."

Eve watched the soldier disappear into the street. Dread filled her. She looked back at Nellie, who looked as alarmed as she. Wide eyed, Nellie shook her head no, speechless for a change. Others mirrored open questions, making interesting expressions and initiating an undercurrent of whispers about the large room. Even Langlough's hack registered that he was awake, too. Eve looked away from all the prying eyes. One must pay the fiddler, she admitted sadly as she re-threaded her earlier trail to fetch Mikie. She combed her hair quickly with her fingers, braided, and twisted

German=this font   English=this font   *French=this font*   *Delaware=this font*

her braids into place. After making their morning necessaries, she grasped Mikie's hand firmly; ready to face to what she feared must be certain doom. They trudged out of the Citadel. Reveille sounded behind them as they walked down the waking streets of the fort area.

When she reached Hamilton's office, the guard who had previously awakened her stood by the door. Eve responded weakly with a nod as he called within to announce her presence and admitted her to the short hallway that led to Hamilton's office. When Jacob Schieffelin opened the door a crack, he smiled. Eve, taken aback by his unexpected manner, smiled back more as a reaction to a stimulus than any feeling of genuine friendliness. But as the door opened wider so did her smile which broadened again and again until it filled her entire face, accompanied by an overflow of tears.

There on the round braided rug before the fireplace sat Lieutenant Governor Henry Hamilton, sitting cross-legged in his banyan, a turban wound about his head, playing with a tin of tiny lead soldiers, and with him sat another Henry...her Henry. Her Henry laughing, her Henry sitting, her Henry still dressed in his Indian garb...her Henry struggling to communicate with bits of broken English, mixed with German and laced with Delaware...her very own Henry. Henry Earnest, the son of Adam Henry Earnest and Eve Emler Earnest was here.

Mikie wiggled uncontrollably in her arms and squealed in recognition. Eve set him down shakily. Mikie took off lickety-split to his brother, who looked up for the first time. Little Henry's face filled with incredulous recognition.

"Mutti?" He said in disbelief. "Mikie?"

Young Henry stood very hesitantly, steadying himself with his hand on Hamilton's shoulder. Mikie groped for his other hand. He latched fast. Together, the brothers stood quietly, hand in hand.

"Go to your mother, young man." The haughty Jacob's usual secretarial snootiness had dissolved completely. A catch in his voice clearly revealed that he felt genuinely touched by this reunion of mother and child. Even the Lieutenant Governor looked away briefly to remove a tear that had come unbidden.

Eve's knees sagged in joy, as Schieffelin helped her regain her footing.

"Henry Earnest. Unser Gott has truly blessed us." And then she began to babble incoherently thank you, thank you, thank you, over and over. Both languages, English and German tumbled over each like dry beans turning in a crock. Tears falling in a cascade, she knelt down to be on Henry's level and opened her arms. She enfolded the two flying children into her embrace. Henry refused to let go of Mikie as his mother kissed his face over and over. She grasped Henry's cheeks between her hands in total joy. She pushed the hair from his face gruffly, again and again, as if to reassure herself that he was truly real. Then she clung to both her sons as never before.

Hamilton regained his composure. Agile as he was, he quickly

German=this font   English=this font   **French=this font**   *Delaware=this font*

assumed a more dignified manner, holding the box of metal soldiers behind him. Two telltale strays still marched on the rug confirming the earlier activity.

"Our new interpreters, Simon and George Girty, are responsible for your good fortune, woman. Perhaps if you see them about, you might thank them." Hamilton spoke formally, in a professional manner.

"Would you like a cup of tea before you return to work?" Schieffelin offered.

"Yes, we have a few things to discuss before you leave here," Hamilton added somewhat stiffly. He had sensed what his secretary had offered.

Over tea, Hamilton explained to Eve Henry's forced removal from the Delaware camp. The night before, Henry had been taken from a drunken Stalking Wolf, who had not sobered up enough yet to try to retrieve him. Stalking Wolf had been tricked into gambling Hanu away. Simon Girty and his brother George had deceived Stalking Wolf with a coin trick. The coin had been imbedded in a small glass bottom* by the glass blower, which magnified its size considerably, appealing to the warrior's greed. As soon as Stalking Wolf figured out the ruse, he might come in anger, Hamilton warned. Hamilton further explained that Eve would be working inside the Officer's quarters for a short time assisting Margaret Elder. In the coming days, after the ox roast and fire, the tribes encamped about the fort would be sent on new missions. Then he assured her that she and her children would be free to return to work the fields with more freedom of movement.

Mikie and Henry played with Hamilton's white metal soldiers on the rug as their elders talked. Henry, whose English understanding still lagged, could not understand the words. He looked up only once when he heard Stalking Wolf's name. Then, he returned to play and chattered with Mikie in German, who responded in broken German and English in return. Each nibbled on warm bread dripping with butter and bitter orange marmalade. Both noticed Jacob's scowl over their buttery crumbs as he tried to tidy up about them.

First, Eve took the boys to Fogherty's. A groggy Sue Ellen, awakened by Eve after her late night, wept with joy at the sight of both boys. Henry could not really understand what all the fuss was about but that did not mean that he would refuse the crust of brown bread that Sue Ellen took from her pocket for Mikie and him. He began to hide it in his leather pouch, when Eve frowned. He stopped and offered it to Eve. She smiled, shaking her head in refusal. Puzzled, he stuffed it away. His back turned, he shielded his activities from his mother and brother.

Following Hamilton's advice, Eve set out for the Officers Barracks in the old fort. Henry drank in the hubbub of a city and Fort Detroit on a busy morning. He moved in wonder at all the people and the homes about him.

German=this font   English=this font   *French=this font*   *Delaware=this font*

When he heard the drums and the cannon fire, he started. Dropping his mother's hand, he darted to hide behind a horse trough. Eve went to him, laughing. Mikie giggled and pointed at him. She explained his fears away but not his embarrassment. In prideful response, he assumed a false bravado and would not grasp his mother's hand. When she reached for his hand, he frowned at her and sidestepped away. Eve scowled at his behavior. What was going on here? Henry never acted like this before. She stopped. Looking intently at the child, she wondered why she had foolishly thought that he would not be touched as much by his experiences as she? She knew that she was not the same woman as when he last saw her. Both of them had changed in so many ways. She sighed. Would they be able to bridge the lost time? She knew she must be patient, but would she remember to be patient when the end of another exhausting day finished?

Upon entering Margaret's kitchen in the barracks, Margaret dropped to her knees in prayerful rejoicing and tears, an abundance of tears. Henry shook his head. So far, every woman that he encountered that he had known before burst into tears at the very sight of him. This one kept crying out hallelujah. He concluded that these white women acted like foolish crybabies, not brave like the women of the true people. He did, however, take advantage of the hearty bowl of porridge offered him with extra maple sugar and bacon grease. Afterwards, he slept most of the afternoon away in the warm loft tucked above and behind the kitchen fireplace, much to Mikie's dismay.

Over the days that followed, Margaret felt glad for an extra hand. More troops arrived daily from Niagara. Margaret quickly worked Eve into her busy schedule.

As they chatted over their daily workload, Eve explained all that Hamilton had related. Eve did not shirk work and fell easily into the routine. However, when Margaret caught Eve looking wistfully out the window, Margaret wondered why Eve would even miss the hard labor in the unrelenting sun or inclement weather in preference to kitchen work and scrubbing.

Time and life inevitably bring change. On the fourth day, the Delaware came to the fort wall. A group of women and children stood at the wall, calling and wailing.

"Hanu, Hanu," echoed over and over among their cries.*

Their voices resounded through the enclosed area. Soon whispers and then loud verbal questions began to fly within the fort and more especially Yankee Hall. Soldiers and prisoners alike wondered aloud about the calls by the Delaware. The tribal peoples remained outside the Fort and Citadel as a Fort policy. In Yankee Hall that night, a buzz filled the room.

"Who's Hanu?"

"How in the hell should I know?"

"Do you think it is the new one?"

"His name's Henry."

"Do they seek someone?"

German=this font   English=this font   **French=this font**   *Delaware=this font*

"Hanu, what is that?"

Henry knew when his name bandied around the room, but the English between clouded his understanding.

The fifth day, the Delaware contingent came once more. One small boy in particular yelled as loud as he could, louder than all the rest.

"Hanu. Hanu."

The first time, Henry had not heard them as he slept in the warmed fireplace loft where sounds were muffled at best. But the second time, on the fifth day, he did. Eve heard them, too, and watched her son's reaction as he moved stealthily toward the door to make an exit.

"Nein! Henry!" Her strongest mother tone rebuked him.

He scowled at his Mother. Defiance and anger filled his boyish face. He tried to dart for the door and stopped. Only Margaret stood in his way. Her petite frame attempted to fill the opening. Her arms spread wide to arrest him.

Evaluating her size quickly, he bolted and ran pell-mell into Margaret, who held him just long enough for Eve to retrieve him.

"Nein, Henry!" She plucked him back and set him sharply on the floor.

"I want to see Little Fox!" Henry stomped his foot.

"You must stay here."

"I want to see Little Fox!" He yelled at the top of his lungs. Mikie, thinking his brother had invented a new game, mimicked his brother, getting a quick swat for his efforts. His lip curled in anger in response.

Eve knelt before her older son. "No, Henry. You will stay here. If you do not, I fear I shall never see you again." Her eyes filled with tears, her manner so sincere and so sad that Henry, in spite of his own anger and pain, could see her pain. He quieted. Sulking, he crawled up into the loft. They did not see him for the rest of the day, but the calls continued outside the walls without letup.

The sixth day, the callers came again. The party of Delaware women, children and a man with a drum stationed themselves outside the Fort gate. The calls of Hanu formed a wailing chorus which interspersed between the beats of the drum. One of the guards, after an hour of this unrelenting din, stormed outside the gate and threatened to shoot them if they were not quiet.

The Delaware left.

While the drum had sounded, Henry paced the kitchen just as Anne had paced her cell. Margaret and Eve watched him closely, monitoring his every move, blessing the existence of only one exit door. The women always made sure that one of them remained stationed there to intercept him if Henry should choose to flee.

Hanu soon became part of the Fort gossip. The tale of the boy returned to his mother who provoked the Delaware to call for him daily spread quickly. Everyone remarked about the one Delaware woman and young boy, in particular, who called the longest and loudest for him. Everyone in Yankee Hall soon realized the identity of Hanu. Old, hacking

German=this font   English=this font   *French=this font*   *Delaware=this font*

Langlough, sensing someone weaker than he, began to tease Henry for being a little Indian boy. Nellie finally told him to shut his yap or she would see to it that he had breathed his last. Langlough complied quickly, knowing that Nellie could easily accomplish the task.

Eve continued to be embarrassed and worried as she monitored Henry's every move. The task wore on her as sleep deprivation and vigilance increased. Her mistrust of Henry grew each day. The realization came with a great deal of introspection and mounting fear for his safety.

On the seventh day, when the Delaware came again to drum and to call, Hamilton summoned some of the party to his office and George Girty to interpret.

In the end, the parties struck a hard bargain in the Delaware's favor. The Wolf Delaware from White River would receive five rations of rum per person, and Henry must return his Delaware clothes for the Delaware to cease their activities.

Hamilton smarted over the mounting costs for the child. He wondered if his effort against Stalking Wolf really merited the loss of rum stores so soon before the great fire.

That night, Eve could fight fatigue no longer. Henry lay pinned under her arm in his itchy new clothes. To Henry, the linsey-woolsey irritated his hide in more ways than one. Tears welled up and rolled from the corners of his eyes as he lay on his back, staring at the beamed interior. Like his clothing, the whole room felt unfriendly and over-large. The true people would not treat him like this. Among these people, a boy really did not count for much, he decided. He longed for Little Fox and for the feeling of easy closeness with his friend's mother. Most of all, he missed the freedom to run at will. When his Mutti turned on her side a few hours before first light, freeing him, Henry immediately knew that an opportunity had presented itself. So silent that mice did not know that he stirred, Henry carefully stood and stealthily slipped between the sleeping prisoners.

At the door, he paused, canvassing the empty center yard. The previous day, as they had returned from the kitchen, he had espied a hole that a dog had dug under one of the outer walls to reach his pack-mates. Not a single flicker of his eyes had he made to betray his future intent. The hole looked just big enough for a boy his size to exit. The dozing guard by the gate would not deter him, so Henry slipped across the compound and edged along the citadel wall. Looking about, Henry wriggled through the hole. Although the hole proved to be a tighter squeeze than he had anticipated, he struggled to pull himself through the opening. Many minutes passed before he reached the halfway point. He wriggled forward.

As Henry raised his head to scan the other side, he came face to face with a very strong warrior.

"Going somewhere?"

Henry nearly jumped out of his new clothes.

German=this font   English=this font   *French=this font*   *Delaware=this font*

Sensing by the child's mixed expression that the child did not fully comprehend English, the brave considered another language.

However, no matter the language, Henry knew he had been caught in the act of escaping. He studied the man who sat quietly adjacent to the opening. The Indian's hair straggled over his shoulders in the morning star light. No earrings or roach could Henry see. No gorget hung around his neck. In the pale light Henry could barely make out a simple vest, a breech-clout, no leggings, and a woolen trade blanket about the man's broad shoulders to ward of the morning chill. The stoic brave sat with his puckered moccasins still on his feet. His legs were crossed and loosely folded. He appeared to have been waiting patiently for Henry. A pile of wood chips lay scattered about him in the grass.

Henry immediately comprehended that the man had no intent to harm him, so he elected to try a smile and to evaluate the elder's response.

"I return to the true people," he said softly in Delaware to the man who beheld him, fully expecting his assistance. Henry reached out to him for a hand up.

The arms that fairly rippled with muscles did not move to assist Henry. The hands, lightly clasped, had something shiny and curved between them. A wood chip fluttered down. Whatever the man held was hard to discern in the near darkness.

"That would not be wise, small warrior." Although Henry thought he understood what the man said, his accent made the words very difficult to comprehend.

"Can you understand my words?"

Henry mulled over the words.

Henry nodded positively.

"How many summers are you?" The man asked Henry.

"I am six," Henry replied obediently. Lying on his stomach, feeling indignant, recognizing his disadvantage, the boy's anger and defiance once more began to surface.

"With trust, a boy of twelve summers can travel wherever he wills. But you must earn that trust. Do you understand, Hanu?"

The man did not lay a hand on him, but he forcibly nailed Henry in place by his words.

"No," Henry replied in his surliest manner.

"I think you do. Now understand this! If you try this again, I will find you. I will bring you back. Each and every time! Do you understand that?"

Henry glared up at the man before him. Raw strength radiated from the adult brave. Henry knew the man meant every word spoken. The brave obviously had the will and might to enforce it. He looked every bit as strong as Stalking Wolf and Blue Ice.

"Now return to Madame Eve *to build that trust."*

Henry felt as if he had had both ears soundly boxed. However, the man as before had not lifted a hand to him. The warrior just continued to sit quietly, never raising his voice, using a baritone whisper that only Henry could hear. Another wood chip fluttered down.

Henry never took his eyes off the man as he wriggled his body in reverse through the hole. He backed up like a crayfish into its lodge. Foiled, the child got quietly back to his feet, knocked off much of the dirt from his new clothes, and turned resignedly back to Yankee hall. He stopped only once to relieve himself against a neighboring building, before slipping through the door.

When Henry entered, he came face to face with Nellie, who frowned severely and pointed to his mother's area. He pointed to his crotch, but the woman did not respond in any positive way. She, in turn, pointed at the dirt which still clung to his knees. She obviously did not believe him. Returning as quietly as he left, he rejoined his family circle. Saddened, he curled next to his brother and drifted into an unhappy dream.

Late Morning

"It has come to my attention that you are shorting the silver content in your work," Lieutenant Governor Hamilton stated briefly, barely looking up from his desk at Jonas Schindler.

"No, sir, I would not do that!" Jonas responded forthrightly.

"But we have others who will testify to this fact," Hamilton added dryly.

"Well, sir, I do not understand why anyone would say anything like that about me. If I am not fair, I would lose all my business. No one would come. My reputation is everything." He stopped. He looked about the office, catching Jacob's eye helplessly and then refocused on Hamilton. "Please believe me, sir, I would never do a thing like that. Ask some of my best customers, John Askin, James May, and Ezekiel Solomon. They will tell you, sir, I am a man of my word."

"Well, we have proof otherwise, Jonas Schindler. This is the judgment of this office. The crown confiscates your business and all personal property. And since your dishonesty merits it, you will be drummed out of the Fort and of the Citadel to exit in the rear. You are not fit to leave by the main gate."

"But, sir, who are my accusers?"

"Dismissed." Hamilton terminated the interview.

"Captain Hay, see that this man is drummed from the Fort," Hamilton ordered.

Jonas Schindler felt like he had run smack dab into a stone wall at full gallop. He stumbled in disbelief from the Lieutenant Governor's office. A small column of drummers marched on either side as they noisily escorted him to the Citadel. As he passed Fogherty's, he swore that he saw Ann Forsythe wave her hanky until someone stepped in front of her. Others tried to avoid his eyes, turned their backs, or simply walked away.

German=this font   English=this font   *French=this font*   *Delaware=this font*

However, while Hamilton may have influenced or commanded much of the fort, he did not command the Citadel. That fact would be driven home painfully, much to Hamilton's dismay.

The events that followed consternated Hamilton before his peers. For when Jonas Schindler reached the Citadel, all of the guards, all of the drummers, and many of the prisoners were indeed lined up for his exit from the Citadel walls. Jonas instantly recognized the guards who had bought him rum at Fogherty's Inn. When he passed, quiet reigned. Not a single guard sounded a single drum within the Citadel. Eve, Margaret, the boys and anyone not otherwise engaged stood at silent attention as he passed. Instead of hostile faces, Jacob saw smiles, friendly waves, and even a few tears. At the outer gate, Sue Ellen stood waiting with Captain Lernoult. When Jonas approached, she walked boldly up to him.

"Thank you. I hope your hand heals." Shyly she recounted her thanks and then in a very quick and awkward movement, she stood on her tiptoes and quickly kissed her hero's cheek. Turning to Captain Lernoult, she received a round packet. She handed Schindler a small blanket roll. Within its folds, hard tack, a striking steel, flint, and a knife were neatly tucked. "Thank you. I am truly sorry to be the cause of yer misfortune."

Then, Sue Ellen backed up to stand aside the Captain, who shook Jonas Schindler's hand before the young silversmith exited at the rear entrance of the Citadel. The Captain palmed a few New York notes donated by his men into the man's hand, in the process.

Jonas Schindler never looked back. He headed west to Fort Sackville and Vincennes. Maybe the distant British fort would keep him out of the reach of Hamilton's wrath.

The news of the silent Citadel rubbed Hamilton's nose in his vague powers of command again. More gossip bounced off the hot narrow streets.

Author's note: Emma Replogle does not tell us how long Eve or Henry remained with the indigenous peoples, alone or separately. It is highly debatable which tribes captured her or Henry. Seneca, Delaware, Wyandot, and the tribes of the Great Lakes were all known to have conducted raiding parties during this period in the Pennsylvania area. This author elected to use the Delaware due to some interesting possibilities for plot formation. Emma Replogle does relate the poignant calling by those who had once held Henry and their demand for the return of his clothes. This is faithful to the first account found on page 21 of *Indian Eve and her Descendants.*

The embarrassment of Lieutenant Governor Henry Hamilton and the incident involving Jonas Schindler is alluded to in numerous sources as an example of Hamilton's governance problems and the lack of cooperation between his office and other British Troops stationed in Fort Detroit.

German=this font   English=this font   *French=this font*   *Delaware=this font*

Chapter 19 August 1778
A Hot Dry Summer

"You may well imagine how earnestly I look towards
Canada for Intelligence, instructions and orders. 'Tis
true the Indians continue to act with good temper,
unanimity & success, but to say the true, it is surprising,
considering the state of matters here, the coolness if not
disaffection of numbers, the reports of a French and
Spanish War, that the Indians are left to themselves, the
few [whites] I can possibly send out with them being too
inconsiderable to be mention....My authority has lately
been so cramped, that it will shortly have very little force
or influence."

* Lt. Gov. Henry Hamilton complaining to Lt. Gov. Hector T. Cramahe of
Quebec waiting on General Guy Carleton's replacement by Gen. Frederick
Haldimand.*

Governor Haldimand had already rejected Hamilton's plans to attack Fort Pitt
stating,

"I think no essential point would be gained by reducing it
[Fort Pitt]."**

Quoted by John D. Barnhart in *Henry Hamilton and George Rogers Clark in
the American Revolution* (Crawfordsville, IN: R. E. Banta, 1951) *p. 33-34,
** p. 32.

County of Bedford, Pennsylvania

A faint rustle of leaves caught David's attention. He thought that it
might have originated in the nearby thicket some piece away. The young
Dibert boy, ever on the alert, straightened up abruptly from his task of
cutting and stacking brush. The hoeing, having been done mostly by the
girls, left the menfolk time to clear an ever widening circle about their
home so that possible approaches by the Indians could be more easily
detected. His trained ears strained to decipher the sound. Could it be a
rattler? It had been so dry of late that the reptiles were coming down from
the mountains for life sustaining water. Of course, the cabin stood
between the venomous serpents and the creek. Just yesterday, Grand'mere
Eve had dispatched one with her hoe as the son of Satan sunned itself on
their stoop. On the other hand, was it a rabbit in the brush? He decided
that if it were, it sure would taste better than that rattler had. To reassure

himself, his eyes sought out his Pere. He observed him across the field just in earshot. When his eyes sought out his father, John straightened. John seemed to sense his son's attentiveness to something.

The rifle stood propped and waiting, close to John against the old oak.

David waved reassuringly, not wanting to give a false alarm. He had best check it out first.

His father continued to watch him, unconvinced. His son had sharp ears.

Another rustle came from the original source. And then, as if the sound had been strained by the wind, a thready voice drifted to David's ears. The voice reminded David of his father's voice when he whispered his name with his last goodnight touch before David drifted off to sleep.
"David...David..."

David's adrenaline kicked in. His heart beat wildly within his young chest.

"David, fetch tes Pere."

Instantly, David recognized the voice. Although he could not see him, only one man sounded like his Pere. Only one man could make the cabin ring with his songs and resound with his boisterous laughter. This could only be the man who tolerated David and his siblings crawling all over him like puppies on an old gentle hound. Who else would allow them to ride his back to foreign shores or to buck like a wild steed?

"Onkel Michel!" David began to charge the thicket.

"Arret!" The call to halt was followed immediately by a chest-splitting fit of coughing.

David came to an abrupt standstill. Behind him he could hear his father at a dead run, his hard footfalls pounding the ground.

"Duck, so I can shoot!"

"No, Pere, no, Pere!" David turned, waving his hands wildly over his head, for he could see his father literally barreling down on him. *"It is Onkel Michel! Pere!"* He waved his hands frantically. *"Do not shoot! Do not shoot!"*

Just as quickly, the cocked gun lowered, but the footfalls pounded ever closer, never once breaking their stride.

David turned to re-address his Onkel, who for some strange reason did not reveal himself.

"Onkel Michel? What is wrong?"

"Stay back...stay back. Please....David, stay back!"

The thicket shook with coughing.

David barely discerned the shadow of the crouched figure within.

The boy stood affixed. What was going on here? Onkel Michel always welcomed the children's flying hugs, lifting and whirling whoever arrived first in a swirl of welcome, only to drop and whirl the next until all stood dizzy with glee.

David felt his Pere's reassuring hand on his shoulder.

"Where is he, my son?"

German=this font   English=this font   *French=this font*   *Delaware=this font*

"There, there in the brush, see him Papa?" David used his baby name for his Pere, which he rarely used anymore. He pointed to the crouched man, who pulled himself to a shaky stand upon hearing his brother's welcome voice.

Another horrible coughing spell shook the man to the core. The silhouette, with arm outstretched to bar entrance to the thicket, shook with the violence of his lungs. The racking cough almost turned the coughing man inside out. Then the figure fell to his knees.

As John started forward, his son stopped him.

"No Papa, he says arret! Stay back!" David, even at his tender age, had learned well many harsh lessons of frontier life. First among them was not to come when told to stay.

When the coughing fit subsided, a long period of stillness followed, both John and David waited impatiently.

At last, his strength re-summoned, Michel spoke.

"Pox." The word brought on still more coughs.

"Mon Dieu!" John's voice now sounded as thready and as wheezy as his brother's. He turned grasping his son by the shoulders. *"Fetch your Grand'mere! Tell her to bring rum, blankets, and hot water."*

As David turned to run for the cabin, he heard his Pere admonish him to hurry. The entreaty proved unnecessary, for David could not think of slowing even for an instant.

"Grand'mere, Grand'mere."

David's screams caused all the women, young and old, to look up. Even little Susanna stopped instantly at her brother's noisy approach. He ran as if his shirttail flared with fire.

"What is wrong? Mon Dieu, not your father!" Mere Eve grabbed the gun beside her, preparing to defend the small fortress. She expertly cocked it.

"No! No!" David yelled, waving his arms frantically. Again David found himself in the unenviable position of backing down another loaded firearm. *"It is Onkel Michel."*

"Michel?" The word impacted Mere Eve immediately. She lowered the gun tentatively and shakily uncocked it. Was the boy daft? Did she hear him right? Then, more disturbing thoughts filled Mere Eve's mind. Could Michel be dead? Have they brought news? Is he injured? Worse yet, could he be crippled?

Molly grabbed Susanna as they watched the boy draw closer and closer.

Gasping, *"Onkel Michel,"* he caught a quick breath. *"In the bushes..."* David bent over, grasping both knees as he struggled to breathe after running so hard.

"Whatever are you talking about, child?"

"It is Onkel Michel," David gasped again. *"He has got the pox."*

Molly stiffened, clutching Susanna tighter to her. She did not know French well, but pox she understood. She shivered with apprehension.

German=this font   English=this font   *French=this font*   *Delaware=this font*

Ene, Elizabeth, young Ene and Barbara refrained from their carding and sorting, transfixed. No one made a sound or moved.

David, his small chest heaving, stood quieter now. His head still down, his arms still stiff, his hands clung to his knees.

His audience waited expectantly for him to catch his breath. They sensed that he had more to say.

When his breathing slowed, David stood uneasily and continued his tale of woe.

"He is really sick, Grand'Mere. He coughs terrible. Papa says to bring rum, blankets, and hot water." David, calmed, switched to English so that Molly would not feel left out.

"I will help," Molly ventured.

"No, you must not. Your job is here with Ene and the children. Do not let them follow, whatever you do." And then she touched her grandson's shoulder in a very loving way, "Including David."

David's head dropped immediately. His shoulders turned inward. Horribly deflated, he did not want the girls to see the tears that threatened.

Grand'mere gave his shoulder a soft shake before she released him. She wanted to give him a big hug, but she knew men, even young men, well enough that she would not embarrass him in front of the girls. Perhaps she would have the opportunity later, when they were alone after all things had passed, she thought. Then she raised her head as if to draw strength from the mountains, took a very deep breath, returned the gun to its former stand, and disappeared into the cabin.

As she departed from Ene, Molly and the children, Molly heard her say, "It was good of you to offer, Molly, but he is my son."

Fort Detroit

Henry ran through the field panting. A cloud of blackbirds rose before him, swirled, and then resettled in another section of the King's Garden. Stick in-hand, he turned to run again at the settled flock. He hated the task as much as he hated the canoe man. His mother, hoeing across the field, checked the corn hills for coon damage before walking over to wake Mikie. He napped at the edge of the field near a sassafras bush. In the hot sun, its mitten-like leaves drooped limply from dehydration. A cicada broke the hot simmering stillness. The insect's long cascading trill affirmed the summer's heat again and again. The air stifling, the humidity drenching, Eve wiped her forehead on the back of her forearm. Nellie stood, wilted. Were it not for her hoe, she could have crumpled on the spot.

"Sun's a killer today, Eve."

"Amen."

"Is it good for that boy to run so hard? Birds or no birds. Tain't worth it. If we don't get rain soon, twon't make no never mind anyway."

German=this font   English=this font   *French=this font*   *Delaware=this font*

Eve suddenly had a decidedly wicked thought.

"Nellie? Will you come with me and keep your mouth shut?"

"I reckon I can control my yap ifn' you can," Nellie barked back. She sensed her friend had something better in mind than the foul dusty garden.

"It will be just as easy to come back before twilight to finish. The dark comes later. Besides, the mosquitoes are not as bad since it is so dry."

Eve shook Mikie gently.

"Come Mikie, we go see Teddy."

No need to ask the child twice. He immediately jumped to his feet and grabbed his mother's hand.

Nellie caught up to her friend's side.

"Ho, Henry. Come."

Mikie tugged at his mother's hand impatiently. "Go see Teddy, Mutti."

Henry did not respond.

"Ho, Henry. Come in son."

Finally, catching her voice, he nodded and ran to join his mother and her friend. Beads of sweat coated his young forehead.

"Henry, we go see Teddy," Mikie hollered when Henry came within earshot.

"Aww, Mutti, do we hafta'?"

"Shush child!"

"Teddy? Who is Teddy?"

"Teddy is Mister Joe's dog." Mikie informed Nellie, before Eve could even answer.

"Joe? Joe, who?" Nellie asked.

Eve did not answer her question.

As they walked a path that Nellie found unfamiliar, Nellie observed that Eve knew the path well as she selected rights and lefts with ease. Nellie sensed that they were heading across the back of the fort to above the wharves.

"He is a big mean Indian," Henry answered Nellie when Eve did not. His English had improved enough to convey this concept.

"Henry, that is enough!" Eve grabbed his shoulder gruffly.

Nellie, quick to pick up, now really wondered where they were going.

As they broke into the clearing littered with stones, remnants of earlier kettle fires, bits of birchbark, and tangles of spruce roots and cedar shavings, Nellie began to look around with interest. She could make out the small bark shed. Two woven chairs sat at the fire's edge near the small lodging. One looked newer than the other. One completed canoe and another staked up with stones within spoke of continuing industry. Neatly piled rolls of birchbark and stacks of cedar and ash surrounded the building area. However, no fire burned today to heat water for bending ribs. The mini shipyard appeared deserted.

German=this font   English=this font   *French=this font*   *Delaware=this font*

Eve searched in vain for a dog and the man but could see neither one. Mikie began to look a little dejected.

A fresh, moist breeze swirled up off the Detroit River, refreshing the sweat-soaked workers and boys. Like a magnet, it drew them to the shore.

"Can I wade, Mutti?" Mikie, skipping backward, began to dance in anticipation while still clinging to his mother's hand. "Can I? Can I?"

"Of course, but do not go above your knees. You might catch cold."

"He don't look like he's catchen' cold," Nellie observed wryly.

Teddy's bark gave the women and children's position away.

Tchamaniked Joe, dressed only in his breech clout, smiled broadly at the women as he flipped his soaking wet hair back over his shoulders, sending a fine spray with it. Small droplets of water beaded over the surface of his browned body as he waded into shore. He rinsed his arms as he walked.

Mikie broke free and began to run as fast as he could, only to fall face flat into the water in front of Joe. Joe scooped up the child, who sputtered and laughed with glee. Teddy leapt up and down in the shallow water. Yipping, the tiny dog bounced with joy.

"Yes sir, injin or no, that'sa fine lookin' man," Nellie observed. Eve blushed. "Hell, woman, what you turning beet red for? You've seen a man before." Almost as quick as she said it, Nellie put everything together. "Well, I'll be damned!"

"Keep your mouth shut, please Nellie."

"Yap's shut. Damn lucky you saw him first." Nellie added approvingly. A second generation mountain gal, she had numbered Indians and Europeans alike numbered among her friends and enemies in war and in peace over the years. Her Uncle, a Scotch-Irish trader, and his squaw, Elsie, had lived up mountain from her as long as she could remember. So the guileless Nellie, though rough and tumble in some respects, could on occasion be more tolerant than most. That is, except when it came to Jews. But even there, Eve had softened her stance. During her short thirty years, during the troubles, Nellie had laid two husbands to rest and three children. Now like Eve, she found herself hostage to British power. In the end, Nellie learned to take comfort and joy where she found it. Loud, brash Nellie had proved to be as honest as they come. This quality Eve treasured most. Eve might not like where she stood with Nellie, but at least she knew.

"Will you ladies come in? It is far too hot to work," Joe invited still grinning and swishing Mikie in a circle around him. Although he did not understand the women's conversation given the distance, he read the body language.

"Sounds good to me," Nellie answered, before Eve could utter a sound. Quickly, she grasped her skirt from between her legs and hiked it up as high as she could, tucking it neatly over her front skirt band. Her ankles and knees daringly exposed, she pushed her sleeves up over her

German=this font   English=this font   *French=this font*   *Delaware=this font*

elbows like a whore advertising her wares. No need to invite her twice… she waded in without ceremony or modesty.

Eve stood awkwardly on the shore.

When Eve did not move, Henry got mad. Henry stomped in behind Nellie, disgusted with his mother's lagging spirit. His temper showed, but the temper became quickly quenched in the cool water. Immediately, the foursome fell to splashing and laughing.

"Spect I ought to introduce myself. Name's Nellie." Nellie cupped her hand, sending a wide arc of water which just missed Henry and Joe, soaking Mikie, who giggled and kicked his feet at her in a white froth.

"Name is Joe."

"Teddy's man," Nellie quipped, as she splashed Henry on the second round.

"Yes, Teddy's man." Joe, catching the double entendre, chuckled. He immediately liked the raw-boned woman.

Nellie grunted, seeing that he caught her meaning. Smart one too that one, she thought.

"Well, Eve, yer miss'n some fine water here," Nellie called ashore. She could not say a word more as Henry splashed her with Joe's assistance. "Why you little toad." She directed her attention to Henry, who stood giggling like a girl at her first dance. A mountain girl at heart, Nellie gave no quarter. Henry found himself thoroughly ducked and sputtering with laughter by Nellie before he could blink an eye. Nellie shook with raucous laughter, totally proud of her victory, only moments before Joe ducked her.

Shedding her embarrassment, Eve tucked her skirt and waded in boldly just as Nellie came up spitting and laughing. Although Eve's last clothed dip still haunted her, Eve would not miss out on the fun, propriety or no. Nellie was right. The water and the company were just fine, she thought just seconds before a waterfall of liquid descended on her followed by a cascade of laughter from friends and family.

"Now yer Mah and Mister Joe will make some soup and bring it up to us." Nellie walked up to the garden refreshed, a boy on each hand. A part of her envied the friend she left behind.

"Mutti should come with us," pouted Henry.

"Damn, boy, I sure wish you'd learn to speak English."

Nellie tugged the boy along who still continued to look back.

"She'll be along boy. She'll be along before you know it. Won't she?" The last two words were emphasized and just a tiny bit louder so his mother could hear them.

These were the last words that Eve heard before she turned to face Tchamaniked Joe. Like Nellie's, her skirt was nearly dry. They had laid them out on the shore earlier, sitting modestly in their petticoats to dry their underlayer. The children's clothes had hung on branches and dried quickly. While the children napped on one of Joe's blankets, the adults had chatted. Now, her hair neatly braided once more, Eve felt refreshed after their daring romp.

German=this font   English=this font   *French=this font*   *Delaware=this font*

"You should learn to swim."

"I do not think that I could do that in all this garb," Eve answered.

"Humph." He shook his head, wondering at her naiveté. "Swim as I do."

Eve caught her breath at his lewd suggestion.

Joe leaned forward. His nose tickled the arch of her ear and then lightly inhaled at the bend of her neck.

"You smell fresh like the lake."

Eve flushed.

"It is cooler in the shed." The back of his fingers lightly skimmed the edge of her jaw. His French accent sounded a little more pronounced.

She scanned him top to bottom appreciatively, noting an obvious physical change. "You think so? Looks hotter to me."

"Trust me. We will feel cooler, quickly."

She stood still, a touch of indecision holding her fast.

"Nellie is a good friend." Joe ran his hand up and down her forearm, his fingers skirting her elbow on the upper stroke teasing her under her sleeve ruffle.

"She is that." Even she could hear the breathiness in her voice.

Oh why not, she decided. The soup could wait a bit to get started; there would be time enough to lift a skirt.

Later that evening, the women headed in just before the last call. Mikie's arms hung sleepily over his mother's shoulders, his small butt in her clasped hands behind her back. His legs clung loosely to her waist.

Henry felt too tired to protest. He drug his mother's hoe in one hand and held Nellie's hand in the other as they trudged wearily along.

All would sleep well this night, but rest would come far later than first anticipated.

"I dang near died when I found out that man was to Paris. Can you beat that?"

"He continuously surprises me."

"It's a God's wonder he 'er got home again."

"I doubt if the Jesuits planned for that, Nellie. Sounds to me like they expected him to be a priest."

"That man weren't ne'er meant to be a priest," Nellie asserted.

Eve looked away smiling. "I agree," she said softly.

"Spect if you'n asked him, he'd write a letter home for you?"

"You know, Nellie, I never gave it a thought."

"You do want yer kin to know yer here, don't cha?"

"I expect they know I am here." Eve's voice sounded different, edgy. She had answered Nellie's question, but only after a very long pause.

Seeing Margaret ahead, frantically waving them in, both women sped up their approach.

Nellie sensed that Eve wished to clam-up now, so she did not ask another question. But she wondered all the more about her German friend. They had started out on the wrong foot, the two of them; but now she would

German=this font   English=this font   **French=this font**   *Delaware=this font*

sorely miss Eve's steadfast friendship. Nellie observed that Eve sure had a knack for choosing strange friends. Then Nellie chuckled a mite and accepted that she was probably as strange as any.

"We have been trying to find you all afternoon. We sent someone up to the garden," Margaret admonished them. "Where have you been?"

"What has happened?" Nellie asked without giving an explanation.

"We have whole new parcel of Germans. They brought them in this afternoon. Some of the women are pretty bad off."

Immediately, Eve shifted into another mode. Water would need to be fetched for the kettles. Soap must be found for bathing. Scraps of blankets and cleaner clothing gleaned from their meager stores. Combs rounded up to rout out the nits. They would need to assess the new prisoners' medical needs and purchase some willow leaves from Sally Ainsee for those in pain as well as selfheal for astringent for the inevitable cuts and scratches. The half-breed trader gave the prisoners the most honest exchange for basic goods. Often, Ainsee rounded up chores for them to do with the locals to work off their debts. As a result, while in constant debt to the trader, the prisoners were able to get supplies when needed. Martha, the metisse, who had assisted Eve when she came to the fort, would also need to be alerted if any woman had aborted or proved heavy with child.

"Have the men fetched water?"

"Well, we were waiting for you, Eve," Margaret said apologetically. "Nellie, can you get the men started fetching water?"

"Reckon I can." Nellie frowned slightly at Margaret. For a woman who could fight off injuns with a skillet while she walked the gauntlet, Margaret sure went soft asking the white menfolk to fetch and tote, Nellie thought. But then some folks would resent taking orders from someone with possible Tory leanings.

Nellie turned quickly toward Yankee Hall to get a group of men underway. Already, she could see the small circle of exhausted and filthy prisoners milling, standing, or sitting dazed in front of the Hall. A few complained loudly when those who obviously lived there would not admit them. But Nellie agreed with Eve's rule. Newcomers must not be admitted until they were cleaned up and deloused. Otherwise the whole floor would all be fighting the tiny varmints that inevitably infested every new armpit and crotch, and which quickly migrated from blanket to blanket.

"Yah, gotz to take a bath first," Nellie said in passing to a once stout Dutchman, whose clothes now draped over his thinner frame. "And yer clothes need boiled."

"And just who are you to tell me to endanger my life further by dipping myself in water and being naked?" The blustering man retorted.

"No bath, no floor. Simple as that."

"Well!"

"Sleep outside 'til you do!" Nellie added before she ducked inside to get the men and stronger women started.

German=this font   English=this font   *French=this font*   *Delaware=this font*

"Just whose foul rule is that?"

"It is our rules!" Eve answered in his tongue. "We voted on it. We will help feed you until you can earn your keep. You look strong enough; you can help tote water too."

"Good woman, where is your husband? Why does he permit you to be so uppity?" Insulted by a mere woman demanding his compliance, the Dutchman, though exhausted from his trials, sought to remind Eve of her subservient place in God's scheme. He did not know which angered him most, her directness or the thought that a woman should presume to vote on anything.

"His scalp is behind my bureau, and I expect they have buried the rest of him by now," she informed him in a matter-of-fact fashion, as she had to do for others from time to time. "Now if you will excuse me, get your buckets. You can follow the others down to the shore."

Eve ducked in, leaving the man with his mouth still open. While feeling appalled at her impudence, he had been brought to heel.

"Way to tell him, Eve. What 'er you said, yanked him up short," Nellie quipped, as she exited with Langlough and the others to fetch wood and water for the kettles.

"Who has soap they can share?" Eve called across the Hall. "Rum for wounds?"

A few more generous souls brought forward their scraps. Margaret brought forth a bottle of rum that she had tucked in the kitchen loft. Eve, quickly assessing the amount of soap and the number of new prisoners, realized that they were coming up short. Passing a groggy Mikie off to Fiona, the youngest and only surviving member of Nellie's brood, Eve went immediately to her blanket to fetch a few shillings from her bundle.

"Henry, you must go to Merchant Sally's and fetch soap. Tell her we have twenty-two new ones. Now, I want four soap and the usual medicines to start."

Henry stood quietly. Was his Mutti going to trust him to go all by himself?

"Now Henry, say back to me in English what you must fetch."

"Four soap and medicine," he said slowly and with some difficulty.

"How do you address her?"

"Madam Sally, my Mutti needs four soap and medicine."

"All in English Henry."

"Madam Sally, my mother needs four soap and medicine."

"And what else?"

"We have twenty-two new ones." He held up ten fingers twice and then two.

"That is much better. Be quick child." Eve pressed the shillings into his hand.

Henry felt a rush of pride. His Mutti trusted him to go to Sally Ainsee's shop. He must really be getting big.

Henry scooted by the mumbling Dutchman, who now had buckets in each hand for the first of dozens of trips to the shore.

"Where you going there youngin'?" The guard asked at the gate.

"My Mutti needs soap for the new prisoners."

"Oh, she does, does she?" The guard stepped aside to let him pass.

"Now you be back quick. You hear me, do not dally. It is getting late, boy."

Henry nodded in compliance and ran for Sally Ainsee's shop. He hoped the gruff tall lady would be there because sometimes she slipped him a bit of licorice. Like Nellie, the woman's bark hid her generous soul.

Henry quickly rounded the corner and bounded down the street. The Indians had been cleared from the streets due to the lateness of the hour. He clutched the shillings tightly in his hand. When he came to Sally's front door, he found the shop closed. Given the hour and the hotness of the day, the closure did not surprise Henry. So he quickly scooted to the back where his mother had gone on similar occasions with him when the hour proved late. As he approached the grape covered arbor that arched over the rear door, he could hear the voice of a man and woman within. He thought he recognized many words in the Delaware tongue. The man's voice had a familiar ring.

"My son, you risk much coming here. What if they catch you?"

"Your precious Hamilton and his crew? Not likely."

"Son, you know they are not precious to me. Trade is trade. War or no war."

Henry's footfall caused the conversation to abruptly end.

"Who goes there?"

Henry stood indecisively. How should he answer them? He remembered his Mutti's admonishment to speak English. What would they think if they knew that he understood them? Although he had to reach a little in memory, he thought that he understood their words.

"Who goes there? Answer up, or wear lead!" Sally stormed. Henry could hear the cock of a fusil.

"Madam Sally, Mutti sends Henry," Henry gasped.

The door opened a crack. The gun barrel, clearly evident, poked through the slot.

The dark glittering eyes looked over the rear stoop seeing only the child. The door opened.

"Get in here, boy!" Sally snarled. She yanked him by his small shoulder, pulling him hastily inside. With ease, she released her weapon.

To his great surprise, Henry saw John Montour, sitting in the darkest part of the room. He recognized the scout as Stalking Wolf's friend. Immediately, his eyes searched the room. Was Stalking Wolf here, too?

The door quickly clapped shut behind him.

"Now, what do you want, brat?"

Henry, stiffened by his realization, stood like a fort post.

"Speak, child, be quick about it. I do not have all night."

Henry remained silent with his eyes locked on Montour.

German=this font   English=this font   **French=this font**   *Delaware=this font*

"My Mutti wants four soap and medicine," he finally blurted after a pregnant pause. His speech, quickened by fear, had slurred.

Montour's eyes flashed. Montour wondered if the child recognized him.

"Say it in English, boy, slow like."

"He said four soap and medicine."

"Hell, I know what he said. I know Dutchie well enough, but we are trying to get him to speak English," Sally responded to Montour's translation.

Montour debated if he should tell his stepmother that the child possibly understood enough Delaware to have heard and understood them. His stepmother, Sally, had faunched enough that he had come, so he decided against it. Like his Seneca grandmother, his stepmother's wrath was no small thing to contend with when riled. He wished belatedly that he had spoken in the Seneca way, but he had spent so much time with the Delaware of late that his speech had fallen easily into the grandfather's tongue. His mother, Sally, spoke easily in both, so it had not been a consideration until this moment.

Henry studied each quickly and then very slowly in English he stated his need again. "Madam Sally, my mother needs four soap and medicine. We have..." But the words twenty-two just would not come in English, so Henry flashed two tens and a two in fingers.

"Ah twenty-two."

"Yes, mam."

Then Henry extended his hand to give her the four shillings, now sweat covered in his hand.

"Your mother's money?"

Henry nodded.

"That woman would give half her soul for the new ones, I swear." A softer side of Sally revealed itself in her next comment, a side that she preferred to submerge. "War is damn good for business, but hell for people."

"Come, Henry." She dragged the boy through the darkened hallway into the store front. Familiarity with her stores meant that in seconds, six round balls of soap and an assortment of bags were placed in another larger cloth bag for Henry to take to his Mother without the aid of light. Sally always made it a point to give things to Eve in cloth bags, for the scraps of cloth most always reappeared on some child's back. Slipping Henry two pieces of licorice, imparting a playful cuff and a reminder to share with Mikie, she ushered the child into the twilight.

John Montour heard the front door open and close. The bar slid snuggly back into place. His stepmother returned to the rear of the store, halting briefly to rearrange her wares. Again he debated whether he should mention the boy's past history with him. He decided to let sleeping dogs lie. Perhaps the child had not recognized him. Neither Montour's stepmother nor the boy's mother would be pleased if the boy had. Montour

German=this font   English=this font   **French=this font**   *Delaware=this font*

worried his stepmother enough coming here, without adding more to her fears. After the death of his own mother, Sally had raised him as her own until his father, Andrew, had thrown her aside. She had returned to her people, the Oneida, with only the children from her and Andrew's union. She had left the young John behind and a portion of her own heart with him. When the late Andrew Montour had passed away, his death had freed John to reestablish his prior relationship with Sally. John's service to Britain initially renewed this possibility. After his own Delaware mother's death following John's birth, his father, Andrew, never had settled into partnering with one woman again. The pain of his loss had hardened him. Despite her care of his young children, Sally's assertiveness and her taste for expensive wares had doomed their relationship from the start. As a result, Andrew, petitioned the Governor in Philadelphia to care for his twelve year old son and the other children from his first marriage, for he preferred a life unencumbered by permanent relationships. Given his great influence with the tribes of the Ohio, the government readily agreed. This arrangement meant that the multilingual Andrew would be totally dedicated to serve them in William Johnson's Indian department. A talented warrior and tracker, Andrew fought superbly during the French and Indian War, as well as leading British troops in Pontiac's war. A skilled arbitrator, he proved unrivaled at the treaty tables. Both General Edward Braddock and a young George Washington valued his services for the British Colonies. Through it all, no one collected the high bounty offered by the French for Andrew Montour's head.

Yes, his son had very big shoes to fill, but like his restless father, few of John's relationships were permanent. While he may have served with the British at the beginning of the Revolutionary War, he had strayed to the Rebel side. If Hamilton had not placated his native allies, John Montour would also have a price on his head.

As Sally entered the kitchen, John teased her, *"Hey, where is my licorice?"*

She laughed as she playfully cuffed him. *"Naughty children do not get treats!"* But even as she spoke, she started reaching for his favorite tin of cookies.

One of the last to tuck herself in, Eve returned to her place on the crowded, hall floor. The newcomers were washed and settled except for two stubborn ones, the water-carrying Dutchman, and a gruff old woman who refused to bathe.

Nellie sat by the door with Langlough to make sure the two stayed outdoors. The man's horrible cough would keep them both awake, for Langlough had overexerted himself that evening.

The prisoners' clothes hung on lines strung to dry outside. Naked and wrapped in blankets loaned by many across the floor, the newcomers slept fitfully, hoping to awake to dry clothes. Eve prayed for light dew and no rain. Some of those clothes would certainly need mending come morning,

German=this font   English=this font   *French=this font*   *Delaware=this font*

for they almost dissolved in the scrubbing. She thanked Sally silently for the bags, lots of useful patches there. The tie ribbons would mend frayed seams, although most could readily be taken in. Too soon for the newcomers to feel some sense of safety, she thought. They suffered from acute loss, the pain of disbelief, and wounds inflicted en route. Crying or occasional screaming broke out from time to time as they tossed and turned. Eve knew sadly that much of what they felt would not disappear. They would never feel totally safe again. Scars would cover the wounds, but she knew that these wounds ripped open easily. For some, only drunkenness would lessen their bitter memories. While many would elect to turn within or inversely lash out, still others would try to reach out in kindness to another to blunt the unrelenting pain. Some choices would prove more self-destructive than others. She decided that she had to keep reaching out to others, even when it hurt. If she did not, she feared for herself and her children.

Eve continued to allow her mind to drift as she acclimated to the new sounds in the Hall. Henry had been a mite strange upon his return from Sally's. Probably seeing the new prisoners brought back painful memories for him too. She admitted to herself that she would miss her blanket by morning. The thought of it caused her to shiver involuntarily. Her life here seemed to teeter on the edge of despair and happiness, dipping from one to the other like the diving terns who plunged from the heavens only to re-emerge from the water in full flight. Sometimes, the black-capped birds emerged with bounty in their beaks. Other times, they came up empty. Such seemed her lot as well.

A new cough sounded much like Langlough's across the room. Damn, another consumptive, she would lay odds on it. At last, she snuggled up to her boys, who curled to conform to her front and back, seeking heat. She reviewed the blessings of the day, felt once more the warmth of his tender touch, and drifted into a deep, exhausted sleep. Reveille would find her still tired.

August 8, 1778   Fort Detroit, Hamilton's Office

Lieutenant Governor Henry Hamilton's office boiled with quiet activity in response to the latest Virginian Longknives' assault. After a quick conference with his own department and the military officers, he had dismissed them to begin preparations. All left shocked by the news that in early July, Rebel forces from Virginia had captured the British Fort Gage or Kaskaskia as it was known by the French.

Hamilton took action immediately. A new threat had materialized. He faced two active fronts. The crude Virginians deviled him on his right flank and on his left at Fort Pitt. Hamilton remained convinced that the Virginians had the damned Spanish Catholics' assistance again. Hamilton's

German=this font   English=this font   *French=this font*   *Delaware=this font*

staff agreed that the challenge must be met with decisive force to save the interior Ohio country and the lands east of the Mississippi. The heartland was at stake. Kaskaskia centered their control of the Mississippi. The area must be retaken.

Now, not only must Hamilton maintain his alliances in Ohio and continue the diversion created by Indian attacks on his left Rebel flank, he had the possibility of even greater troubles on the right.

Consistent rumors persisted about the possibility of an American treaty with France, which meant the lukewarm French Canadians could shift their allegiance like the sands around a trapdoor spider's hole. Already, the Americans had only to step near a fort, and the sands drew them in without their even having to fire a single volley. Had not this Fort's inhabitants and other communities near them quickly sworn allegiance to Virginia? Almost immediately, Kaskaskia had espoused its desire to be part of Virginia with Cahokia and Prairie du Rocher clinging to its coat-tails. Worse yet, Lieutenant Governor Rocheblave, his lack luster counterpart, had been so damned inept that the Rebel troops had awakened his wife and him in their very beds at the conclusion of the attack.

Hamilton seethed as he thought of the incident. Daily the rumors increased about a spring attack on Fort Detroit by the Rebels. Any fool in Quebec or London could see that mandatory action was needed to protect the crown's best interests.

Hamilton paced about the room. In his thoughts, he considered the many impending threats, including Fort Pitt's forces against Detroit in his deliberations. He decided quickly that Elliott, McKee, and the Girty brothers could fend off that threat with the aid of his Majesty's friendly allies in Ohio. These men could be counted on. Their reconnaissance always proved reliable. Even McKee had exceeded his expectations. Simon Girty's party had just defeated and killed forty-two men of Colonel David Roger's Rebel forces in June along the Ohio, losing only a few lives in process. His five prisoners yielded an update of the Yankee's weaknesses. Now that George Girty had joined forces with Captain Lernoult, another capable brother could be counted on to assist in this endeavor with a strong voice among the Shawanese. These defectors proved each day to be a godsend.

Meanwhile, Jacob Schieffelin concentrated on re-copying the many letters that Hamilton had dictated in rapid succession.

Near the hearth, a rookie orderly from Lernoult's rangers quietly assumed Schieffelin's other duties as he dusted the mantel.

Frustrated and enraged, Hamilton suddenly swore aloud, startling both Jacob and the orderly. His voice momentarily silenced the solitary song of a cricket by the cold hearth. **"Damn that Gibault! The stinking priest no doubt influenced those communities in favor of rebels. Quebec's home church office be damned!"** To him, Gibault's Catholic superiors obviously had no influence on their rebellious priest, who regularly overstepped his order's explicit directives not to side with the Americans.

German=this font   English=this font   *French=this font*   *Delaware=this font*

Jacob glanced up at him briefly. He knew better than to speak, so he immediately resumed writing Fort St. Joseph and Fort Michilimackinac of their plans. Knowing of De Peyster's aversion to winter war activities in favor of dancing and partying, he wondered privately just how much help the man could truly muster to assist Hamilton.

The orderly, wisely and quietly, followed Jacob's suit.

Silent again, Hamilton mulled over his alternatives. There could be only one response to preserve the King's and God's interests. He did not care how Frederick Haldimand and his cronies replied from Quebec and Montreal.

Hamilton knew what would best serve the interests of the Crown. Deep within him, he tried to deny that this summons to glory could bring glory to him as well. Instead, he preferred to focus on his superior military training and his proven ability to command. Obviously, this meant that Hamilton could be the King's ideal man. When Hamilton compared himself to any enemy that the Rebels might send, he recognized his superlative education and intellectual abilities, his record as a proven diplomat, and his rational self-control and moderation. Indeed, Hamilton had been called by providence to be in the right place at the right time with the world's greatest power and wealth to back him. The poorly supplied, poorly trained, poorly educated Rebels would fail. Only a fool could fail to see this obvious truth.

Hamilton reflected again that Haldimand, his superior, had taken command since Carleton had beaten a hasty return to England. But Hamilton drew no pleasure from his appointment. Francois Louis Frederick Haldimand would no doubt fit in well with the damned French faction as the new Captain General and Governor in Chief of the Province of Quebec under Lord Germain. Thoroughly irked, Hamilton fumed about his new superior's privileges, as Haldimand reported directly to King George III. Unlike Hamilton, he did not have to contend with the whims of Parliament, the money office, or their lackeys in Quebec. Hamilton could not believe that, yet again, another non-British, a Swiss mercenary, for the love of God, had been promoted over him.

But down deep, Hamilton could not ignore his own true call to greatness. Like Drake, he would soften their real enemy, Spain, defeat the Americans, and allow the winds of a just Protestant God to blow both of them from the fertile center, leaving Fort Detroit as the hub of power in his wake. Just as England had earlier rid the new world of the French power, nothing, not even Frederick Haldimand, would deter Hamilton from achieving a great victory for the Crown.

The pounding of DeJean's cane on the hallway floor broke Hamilton's chain of thought. Earlier that day, Hamilton had voiced aloud to Jacob that from now on, no locals or prisoners were to work in his office. Jacob quickly complied. He, too, sensed Hamilton's fear that the plans for their upcoming invasion could be compromised without extreme caution. As a result, even DeJean found admittance to Hamilton's office a monumental

German=this font   English=this font   **French=this font**   *Delaware=this font*

struggle. But DeJean simply would not accept no for an answer or be turned aside.

"I must see the Lieutenant Governor. Let me in!" demanded Philip DeJean, Minister of Justice. As he tried to push the guard aside, he struck the man's hand with his cane for his effrontery. The guard drew him up short. Tall and commanding, the Scot blocked his way very effectively.

Hamilton quickly motioned to Jacob to cover his writing. His gaze also noted the maps spread openly on the small table which now had been moved in front of the fireplace. He pointed hastily at the maps, indicating his concern to the orderly. The orderly astutely surmised the map problem. Quickly, he shook out a linen cloth to cover the maps.

Schieffelin put his orders for goods from Quebec and Montreal neatly out of sight under fresh paper and covered other letters with a vellum packet so they were not visible.

When Hamilton waved off the guard, DeJean burst from the hallway into the room just after the linen settled neatly into place.

Hamilton wondered what had stirred up the new bridegroom this time? He had hoped that DeJean's recent liaison with Theotiste St. Cosme would keep his ferret-like minister of justice out of his hair for a while. Certainly, the new bride looked comely enough to garner the man's energies. Hamilton remembered her well from his few dances with her at the local balls. Given the prestige of her father, Pierre St. Cosme, DeJean, no doubt, would be inclined to treat her well to insure his place in the fort's French power structure. No one spoke of DeJean's recent loss of his first wife, Marie Louisa Augier, who appeared to have been quickly forgotten. Only his son and his namesake remained as a reminder of this first union.

"What is it, DeJean, that cannot wait another blessed moment?" Hamilton condescendingly asked.

"A grand jury!" DeJean gasped. "They may call a grand jury to investigate me." He took a deep breath before continuing. "The gossip is spreading about the fort like butter on hot bread. Everyone is soaking it up. My bride..."

Hamilton glared at the small wiry man, who obviously had not heard what Hamilton had known many days before. Charges had been drawn upon Hamilton as well, but, as usual, the self-centered oaf omitted that small detail. Hamilton interrupted DeJean. "Oh come now, DeJean, you must know how these things go. Believe me, with Haldimand being so new to his office and the current state of the war, he will have enough to keep him busy. He will not have time to worry about some fool arsonist voyageur and a Nancy's blanket capers."

DeJean quieted immediately when he observed his superior's apparently calm demeanor.

"Even if you were a bit heavy handed, good man, you simply followed my orders." Hamilton took a sip from a now cooled cup of tea and frowned. The orderly immediately took flight for a hotter cup of brew.

German=this font   English=this font   *French=this font*   *Delaware=this font*

"Too bad it was such a messy affair though. I would not choose to hang another for a while, if I were you." Hamilton sighed wearily. "Now if you do not mind, DeJean. We are busy here." He waved DeJean out casually.

No sooner had Hamilton uttered his last rebuff when a corporal tore in the door and reported briskly that Butler's July raids on Wyoming, Pennsylvania, had succeeded and that more prisoners would arrive at the fort in a few days.

DeJean backed out angrily. Damn the British with their holier than thou attitude. Hamilton better prove correct, he thought.

DeJean had to ask the French gentry of the Fort to back him a few years earlier during a prior irregularity. He had kissed hind-sides until his lips hurt to garner support. He did not need this now with his stuffy father-in-law already using his comely daughter as a lever to wheedle closer to British power. DeJean did not want to give the man anything else to wield over him.

As he left Hamilton's office, he deliberately swung his cane and painfully connected with the door guard's ankle.

"Yah French frog," the guard muttered under his breath.

DeJean smiled and headed home to collect dividends from the new wife. She cried a lot, but she entertained well enough that he did not have to frequent Fogherty's back rooms just yet. He popped a hard candy into his mouth, wincing slightly when he bit down on the wrong tooth.

German=this font   English=this font   *French=this font*   *Delaware=this font*

Chapter 20 September 1778, The Fourteenth Star

Sixth Article of Confederation

"And it is further agreed on between the contracting parties that, should it, in future, be found conducive to the mutual interest of both parties to invite any other tribe who have been friendly to the interest of the United States to join the present confederation and to form a State, whereof the Delaware nation shall be the head, and have a representative in Congress; provided nothing contained in this article be considered as conclusive until it meets with the approbation of Congress."

From a Manuscript of Col. George Morgan at Carnegie Library, Pittsburgh as quoted by George P. Donehoo, *Pennsylvania, A History* (New York: Lewis Historical Publishing, Inc., 1926), p. 985. "Witnessed by General Lachlan McIntosh, Col. Daniel Brodhead, Col. Wm. Crawford, Col. John Gibson, Major Arthur Graham, Capt. Joe L. Finley, John Campbell, John Stephenson, and Benjamin Mills. Signed by General Andrew Lewis, his brother, Thomas Lewis, White Eyes, the Pipe, and John Killbuck," p. 896.

"Since the preceding May, the Indians in his district had taken thirty-four prisoners, seventeen of which they had delivered up, and eighty-one scalps. Several prisoners that had been captured and adopted by the savages were not included in this number."

Michigan Pioneer Collections, Vol. IX, pp. 431, 476, 477. Lt. Governor Hamilton's written report to General Frederick Haldimand dated Sept 17, 1778, as quoted by Consul Wiltshire Butterfield, *History of the Girty's: Being a concise account of the Girty Brothers— Thomas, Simon, James and George, and of their half-brother, John Turner— * also of the part taken by them in Lord Dunmore's War, in the western border war of the Revolution, and in the Indian War of 1790-1795; with a recital of the Principal Events in the West during these wars, drawn from authentic sources largely original. (Cincinnati, Ohio: Robert Clark & Co., reprinted Columbus, Ohio: Long's College Book Co., 1950), p. 69.

Coshocton, Ohio

White Eyes returned to Coshocton with great pride. Just as once the Grandfathers of his tribe had entered into treaty with William Penn, he felt justified in what he had accomplished. Now he had insured his people their rightful place in the Ohio Valley on the Muskingum. Sovereignty would be unquestioned. All the strife with Killbuck and Captain Pipe would be ended. Certainly, the people could see the way of peace would clearly bring them greater benefits than joining the war parties of Hamilton and the King. White Eyes had put his reputation and his oration skills on the line with those assembled. He even offered to go to war and die if need be, if the council voted for war.

But in the end, his strength and his persuasive skills prevailed. White Eyes became the primary spokesman for the Delaware at Fort Pitt. He hammered out the Confederation articles, which recognized the true people's sovereignty and their rights as an independent nation. Now the Americans and the Delaware would aid each other and come to each other's defense. There would be justice for the Delaware, who would administer the law in their own courts. Killbuck had to eat crow; when to a man, the Americans had all signed the document.

White Eyes resigned himself to the failure of the Shawanese to come to treaty. The death of Cornstalk, his son Ellinipisco, and Redhawk had left them bitter and angry. Even though Cornstalk's people had come to live with the Delaware, as Cornstalk had directed them to do, some of the young ones still rebelled. Others from his people, ashamed to follow the peace road, still smarted from their loss to the Six Nations. They desired to carry the hatchet to regain their honor and hated being called women or Petticoats. Accepting favors from the Six Nations, Wyandot, Shawanese, and Cherokee made them feel like dogs taking scraps about the other tribal fires.

White Eyes despaired that good men like Blue Ice and Stalking Wolf had joined in the blood letting. While he understood their anger, White Eyes deplored that they could not see beyond their own pain. From his experience, White Eyes observed that every stroke against the Europeans came back tenfold.

White Eyes remembered hearing a Chippewa named Tchamaniked Joe at Grand Council. When he held the talking stick, Joe spoke of Europe's teeming cities across the whale's road. The young brave had been carried there by the Long Robes and had struggled to return to his home in the Lake region. He told of a few who had unimaginable wealth. However, he also reported that hordes of poor lived in hundreds of cities, great and small, in many countries, coming from many tribes and speaking many languages. These hordes could be sent to replace anyone who fell here at the hands of the true people. He said that the line of those who could come was endless. How could one possibly fight an enemy who had no end? Even now, the true people coveted the prisoners, adopting them to replace the others who had walked on. However, the true people's numbers still dwindled more and more with each passing moon.

So much unnecessary blood had been spilled. So many mothers had cried. These articles of Confederation would help his people to survive.

As the young ones and the dogs heralded the return of the council representatives, White Eyes held his head high. He greeted the children, who sought him with a warm loving touch, reaching out to each child to affirm life. The thought of the fourteenth star on the flag for his people and a voice of the true people in Congress for future generations gave him hope in these horrible times. They would rejoice this night in songs to the Creator and feast to celebrate their turn of good fortune. Just as in his ample orchards, the small saplings planted each spring would yield a great harvest in time. Today was a good day. Clasping the white paper in its white velum packet, he raised it high over his head and gave a jubilant cry that rang through the entire village of Coshocton.

Stalking Wolf sat quietly at the edge of his grandmother's night fire. The drumming sounds and the chanting of the singers' voices filtered through the wooden walls. He tuned it out.

When White Corn Woman entered her cabin, she studied the man before her, who appeared to be transported to another world. She busied herself with the last chores of the day.

"My grandson, where do you travel? What do your eyes see?"

"I see Hanu's smile. I feel the wet of his tears for his mother as he clung to me. I hear him laughing with Little Fox. I see him in my sister's arms healing her spirit."

"No shame for losing him after having drunk too much milk from the British breast?"

The pain of his wretched weakness struck home. Only a grandmother could speak of it and live. He considered striking her for her brashness. The momentary recognition of this desire slashed deeper than the initial blow of her words. What kind of man was he becoming?

White Corn Woman studied her favorite. She saw the flash of seething anger, the depth of his rage, and the resolute shame that followed. She had plunged a word-dagger deep into his heart. Would he be man enough to take the blow?

"You miss the child. He flows in your blood."

"Yes, I miss the child. You are right, my grandmother. I let the milk cloud my mind with all its chilling whiteness." To admit this fact aloud brought absolutely no comfort, only deeper shame at his weakness.

White Corn Woman knew that for a strong man to admit to any woman this love and to express his sadness at losing a small boy when he gambled as a mindless drunk took great inner strength. He had opened himself to pain again to love this child after his own great losses. Now, he permitted pain to re-enter once more.

White Corn Woman felt proud that this man she so treasured could admit his faults to her. She felt humbled by his love for her. A possibility hinted that he might yet turn his back on his self-destructive ways. So many good, true men had destroyed themselves sucking at the British teat.

She stopped the chores that she preformed more out of habit than need. Stiffly, she dropped to sit cross legged before him. The embers of an earlier fire flickered and crackled softly between them. She sat quietly, waiting for him to speak again.

German=this font   English=this font   *French=this font*   *Delaware=this font*

"I killed his father." He spoke slowly, searching for each word.

White Corn Woman waited. The fire crackled. One small ember rolled over another and flared.

"British say their rebellious children are our enemy. That Americans all seek to kill us," he stirred the fire thoughtfully. He paused between thoughts as he continued. *"That the Delaware must fight for the King, our father. They say we must go when they send us and where they send us. They direct us to kill only warriors, not women and children."*
A tiny shower of sparks shot up from his makeshift wooden poker.
"Hamilton says that White Eyes and the true people like him are not even worthy to be called weak women...that they are not warriors. He says that when the Delaware warn the Rebels of raiders, we are deceitful. We kill our relations when we do not help King George."

She said nothing.

"But does this not also make us their mindless children?"

She reasoned that he needed to hear his words aloud to make any sense of what ripped at his soul.

"Hanu's father was not a warrior." He stirred the fire slowly. *"He was a planter of seed."*

She listened attentively.

"I spared his girl child. She hid in nettles. She is like her mother, strong as true women." Before his eyes, he could clearly see the frightened child, her welted arms over her head, warding off the anticipated blows, her eyes filled with both defiance and fear. Something else also lurked in her eyes, something he could not fathom. Her words, "coon man," blended with those of the golden child in his memory.

The fire spit and snapped. A tiny issue of gas burned blue then green.

"Sometimes at night, I see that father's eyes." He took a small bundle of twigs, threw them on the fire. He continued very slowly.

"No hate."

His voice became very soft.

"Surprise."

He continued, barely audible. *"I smell his blood."* He paused, a catch in his voice when he continued. *"Sadness. Sadness, just like my own father's eyes the night my mother died of pox."*

The twigs caught.

"Sadness. Sadness like my mother, who was loathe to take leave of him...to walk on alone." He tossed back one small twig that had slid down on the ground between the stones.

"Hanu's mother heard this father's last words. She tried to hide his death from us to keep their pride."

The pain of recognizing the humanity of his enemy had impaled Stalking Wolf.

"This father sought only to protect his children. He did not hate us."

The brave stirred the coals again. He debated within whether to say

German=this font   English=this font   **French=this font**   *Delaware=this font*

another word. He had already shared far more than he had intended to, especially to a woman, especially to this woman for whom he felt a great love and a deep respect. But now that he had unfolded part of his pain, the rest followed.

"I have killed no others since that one."

The new flames flickered light across Stalking Wolf's face. For the first time, White Corn Woman saw old dry salt trails on his cheeks. Void of war paint, one could see faint pox scars in the light as it played across his cheeks. White Corn Woman remembered how she had put his hands in buckskin bags to keep him from scratching long ago, so the pox scars would not be deep. But he had deeper scars than these, deeper than she had initially realized.

"Others will soon notice how weak I am."

They sat silently for some time. Only the sounds of the crackling fire within and the drums from without surrounded them.

"You must know that the Americans lie. Those who hate will never let our star join with their stars," Stalking Wolf observed pessimistically, as the drum's meaning invaded his reason. He tried to avoid the truth that impacted on him by changing the subject.

"You probably speak truth, grandson."

"But you went to the fire to sing?"

"One must sing out with joy for hope whenever life permits."

He returned to the thoughts that tortured most.

"We are trapped between two great fires, Grandmother."

She agreed, nodding sadly.

They continued to stare into the fire. The drums stopped. They could barely hear White Eyes' voice as it rose in the night air to address his people, his faint voice blowing in the wind.

"Grandmother, what kind of warrior am I? Why does killing this man haunt me?"

"Perhaps you had no true hate for this enemy, my grandson. You may be called to be a man of peace...not war." She stopped before she spoke again. She must offer her opinion, even if it meant that he would leave her in anger.

"Stop hanging on the British breast. Go. Be with your sister and Little Fox at Gnadenhutten among those who live for peace. Tarry with them awhile. Consider their lessons that you may learn your true road. Once you walk both paths, you will wisely choose the way that the Creator desires. We do not all walk the same path, my grandson. Find your true path before you die an unhappy man."

Stalking Wolf rolled the idea around for a bit before he replied to his grandmother's challenge, *"but, what will Blue Ice and the others think?"*

"Does it matter? Is not this between you and the Creator?"

They watched the fire go cold as the village quieted.

German=this font   English=this font   **French=this font**   *Delaware=this font*

Up Gap, Bedford, Pennsylvania

The sound of the spade scraping across the rocks as it struck the shale in the soil grated hard on the profoundly weakened man who dug a hole for the woman he loved. No one else could do this task for him. No one else would face the risk of contagion. He would complete this burial if he had to crawl in the finished hole and die beside her from exhaustion. If he lived, no one else would care for him until he was free of contagion. He had told them to stay away, to return to the cabin.

In his mind, he re-played her coming a hundred times. She had stopped his mother a few yards before contact with him. One of the other returning prisoners must have gone by her home. How else would she have found out?

Alone, she had walked and then run all the way up the mountain to be with him. She panted from her laborious climb and demanded her right as his love to tend him. She reminded his mother that many lives depended on Mere Eve's skills. She maintained that if she should die caring for him that her loss to the community would be felt far less than Mere Eve's. She pointed out that it was Mere Eve who served as midwife in times of crisis. She insisted that no one knew the healing medicines in the surrounding gaps as well as Mere Eve. She argued that John and Ene's brood depended on her, especially now with Ene ill. She emphasized that Mere Eve's life remained too important to risk contagion.

In the end, her stubbornness prevailed, and she had carried the hot water, the blankets, and the rum to him. She sat them on the ground. Her face emblazoned with joy before she enfolded him in her arms.

"Michel, my love. Let me help you," she whispered in his ear as she clasped him to her.

She quickly improvised a lean-to with one of the precious blankets. From the stacks of nearby boughs, she stripped the leaves and cut straw for a bed. She bathed him. She held him. She restrained him when he dipped in and out of delirium. She rocked him in her arms, singing him to sleep. When painful crusts built up about his mouth, she put oil on them to soften them. When his tongue swelled, she rinsed his mouth with cool water. She cleaned and picked his nose. She warmed his body with her own when he shook with chills. She laid refreshing cloths dipped in the neighboring icy spring when his skin boiled. When his constipation finally subsided, she scrubbed him down like a mother would her tiny child. As the pustules ruptured, she ignored the sickening foul stench and cleansed them with rum, gently putting dry cornstarch on them to quiet the intense itch. She cut his nails short to curtail his scratching. She trimmed his hair to stubble to clean his scalp. When his scabs became dry, she buried his pox-stained garments and his old army blanket, replacing them with his brother's donated clothing. As Michel began to heal, she teased and giggled to cheer

German=this font   English=this font   **French=this font**   *Delaware=this font*

him as she spooned in the soups and broths that were left daily at the edge of the clearing. Her laughter like music, she delighted at the first fall rain, clinging to him in the night when the stars reappeared. Once again he could warm to her touch. Life had returned.

The following morning, she began to cough. Her strength failed rapidly as his slowly increased. He warmed her body with his own when she shook with chills. He laid cooling cloths when her skin boiled. He bathed her when necessary. Following the burning fever, the pustules erupted with fury. He tried not to cry when she became too weak to swallow the broth left for them. Her mouth and her throat had filled completely with the pox. The fetid discharge from her air passages choked her as she struggled to breathe. He held her in his lap, rocking her in his arms as she slipped away in a second raging fever, lost to delirium. Upon her passing, his mournful cry could be heard all the way to the cabin and echoed up and down the full length of the gap. The cry hung on the night wind like a wolf's lonesome howl for a lost mate. The women within the cabin wept openly at the sound. They knew their worst fears had come to pass. John cursed silently as he held David tightly to him.

A light rain misted the sweat of Michel's forehead. Each spade full mounded as the hours passed. At last he felt the hole respectable. He slid her slight figure, wrapped tightly in a pox blanket, into the waiting earth.

Wiping the sweat and mist from his eyes, Michel spoke quietly to the silent form before him. He leaned heavily on the spade for support.

"Jessie Emler. I thank you for saving my poor life. I will try to be worthy. I wish I had had the courage to stay and fight your Pere and Onkel Jac for your hand. Not run off to fight the British in this fool war. Forgive me for what I brought back to you, my love. Damn the British and their cursed prison-ships." He paused, his eyes dry. The depth of his loss still numbed him. **"Dear, sweet woman...the freedom I really wanted most...was just the freedom to love and to marry you."** The last words trailed off as he lifted the spade to return the earth from whence it came.

His brother, John, watched respectfully from the woods, trying to keep out of sight. He would check to see if Michel still lived tomorrow and leave porridge in the morning. He hoped that his brother would have both the strength and the desire to eat.

Fort Detroit

Some men did not have to wait to see Lieutenant Governor Hamilton, even in the dead of night. Jacob Schieffelin awakened Hamilton to come to his desk shortly after midnight. Quickly, the British spy related that the Priest Gibault had persuaded the people of Vincennes to join the Americans. Fort Sackville, which guarded the community of Vincennes, had surrendered in August without a shot being fired. Hamilton grew

German=this font   English=this font   *French=this font*   *Delaware=this font*

incensed at the grave news that a site one hundred eighty miles from Kaskaskia could fall merely on the strength of a priest's liaison. This contemptible challenge to the Crown and to God must not go unanswered. His gorge rose at the thought of Rocheblave being put in irons and confined to a pig pen. Even though he despised the late inept commander of Fort Gage, the barbaric nature of his enemy appalled him.

Hamilton recognized the ever-increasing threats against Fort Detroit. Girty's spying suggested that the Americans of Fort Pitt considered marching on Fort Detroit as well. Inwardly, he seethed that his plans for an earlier dismantling of Fort Pitt had been denied by the home office.

However, the western threat at this point definitely constituted the gravest danger. He silently damned the land-grubbing Virginians and Kentuckians. His Indian allies, assisted by McKee, Elliot, and the Girty brothers, could be depended on to hold the right flank. His left flank needed immediate attention. His forces must counterattack swiftly, for this spy also reported that the Rebel troops were thinly spread. He maintained that Rebel enlistments had expired. Many of the men headed home. Others simply deserted.

Many contradictory rumors also surfaced. These rumors maintained that the Long Knives were massed by the hundreds ready to strike northward. No matter, the Americans would not expect Hamilton's troops to head out now that their crops were being gathered for winter. The onset of cold weather on the heels of the harvest could work to Hamilton's advantage.

Hamilton did not return to his bed. By morning, the spy had helped him map out the best route to Fort Sackville and slipped out before the morning light.

Jacob Schieffelin brought more tea that morning as the sun rose red. Rain would follow. He wondered again at his good fortune to serve such a formidable leader.

Truly, Hamilton appeared tireless and invigorated by each challenge. His superior's only negative moment came when he swore about the incompetence of his fellow Lieutenant Governors, Sinclair and Abbott. Hamilton refused to mention Rocheblave's name, so utterly did the Lieutenant Governor hold him in contempt. Wondering aloud, he questioned once more the rationale of his government's home offices in Quebec and London. Fuming, Hamilton dictated a letter to Governor Haldimand, updating his plans and asking yet again for Haldimand to intercede in seeking additional help from DePeyster and his Lake Indians.

The confiscated boat from James Sterling, the *Felicity*, might be available to carry the letter packet before the weather set in. Now that Sterling had shipped out to England, his property share rightly belonged to the Crown. The ostracized merchant had stirred up no small tempest before he left. A grand jury concerning DeJean's duties as Justice convened shortly after Sterling's departure, for Sterling had instigated the Grand Jury inquiry. He supported his charge with letters from unnamed

German=this font   English=this font   *French=this font*   *Delaware=this font*

local individuals to document the horrors of Coutincinau's death under his Minister of Justice and Hamilton's direct authority.

In addition, Dodge had brazenly escaped from the prison below Quebec, causing gossip at the fort to sizzle like bacon.

Jacob Schieffelin also felt the increasing frustration of Hamilton for the French population's predilection to carry tales. This gossip hinted at the possibility of a French treaty with the Rebels. Little could be done. If Hamilton cracked down too hard; he might not get French support in his local Militias for the coming foray. Hamilton could not afford to lose anyone, not even the wishy-washy French.

Of course, not everyone in Fort Detroit was French. Hamilton could depend on a few British stalwarts such as Norman MacLeod.

Norman MacLeod waited in the hallway for over an hour before admittance to Lieutenant Governor Hamilton's office that morning. Occasionally, others who came after him shouldered by him, but he waited stoically. Volunteer militia knew their place in the scheme of things. Major Jehu Hay pushed rudely ahead of him, not just once, but twice. As Hamilton's second in command, the swaggering little man delighted in letting everyone know his status. Overbearing and condescending, he liked to remind everyone that their rank was beneath him. Mealy-mouthed, he capered when he could, especially when Hamilton's attentions were focused elsewhere.

While he waited, MacLeod paged through his experiences. An old hand at war, MacLeod, a seasoned British Veteran, had served in one capacity or another ever since he had been a strapping lad of sixteen. He had absolutely no love of anarchy or rebellion. The first time, he chose to be a loyal Hanoverian to help mop up the rebellion of 1745 by Stuart's followers, putting down his rebellious countrymen. He proved loyal to Great Britain, the King, and compliance to the law, but not necessarily in that order. In 1756, he had served as a member of the Black Watch as an ensign. After seeing service in Belgium and Holland, he had shipped with the 42nd Highlanders to fight the French in America. He never returned to his home in Scotland. After he had survived General Abercrombie's ridiculous bungling and the massacre of most of his Black Watch brethren by the French, he transferred to the 80th, Gage's Light Infantry. Quickly, he increased in rank to Captain Lieutenant. Proudly, MacLeod dressed in their atypical uniform of a short brown jacket and leggings. He joined many other Scots in this rapid deployment force, a force which took great pride in their ability to stealthily slip in and out of enemy lines and to fight in the manner of the frontier men and Indians.

Later, MacLeod joined the work of Sir William Johnson, the head of Indian Affairs for the colonies. William Johnson had been called Warraghiyagey, meaning "he who undertakes great things" or snidely, the King of the Mohawk, by those resented his prosperous landholdings. But no one doubted his handling of the British-American Indian Department, for he excelled in that capacity. Great Providence, MacLeod thought. Had

German=this font   English=this font   **French=this font**   *Delaware=this font*

it really been 1761 when he first met the man here in Detroit? After that meeting, MacLeod had worked in any capacity possible for the brilliant man. In turn, Sir William had accepted MacLeod's friendship, trusted in his integrity, and mentored him almost like he would a son. Both, like George Washington, were brothers in the Masonry. After Johnson's death in 1774, MacLeod sold his land in upstate New York, packed up his beautiful wife, Helen, and their daughter to stake what was left of his fortune on trading at Fort Detroit.

Only a fool could not sense the heady excitement that always preceded a major troop deployment. Any spy within fifty miles could recognize it, MacLeod acknowledged to himself, as he observed the steady stream of individuals in and out of the office. While part of MacLeod pulled at his traces, eager once more to test his mettle, another hated the very thought of leaving the comfort of his hearth and his dearest hearts to tramp about a wilderness at war again. He hated to admit to himself that at three shy of fifty, he could not expect to be as able as he once had been at soldiering. He knew the whimsical nature of death, the forces of weird at work. Only the young seemed oblivious of their mortality and could fight as if death and pain did not exist, a trait that commanders took full advantage of in war.

However, the choice in the end was not his. His volunteer militia, he laughed at the "volunteer" part, had been called to blaze trail for Hamilton's main assault force and to help the obviously ambitious man with his tons and tons of supplies to reach and to defeat the Americans at Vincennes on the Wabash. The volunteer militia must go.

The Military Commander, Lernoult, could spare no men. Instead, Lernoult's urgent panic drove him to build a new fort. He remained thoroughly convinced that the old one simply would not protect Detroit from the coming onslaught of Virginians.

When finally admitted to the office, MacLeod faced Captain Maisonville, Lieutenant Henry DuVernett, Lieutenant Jacob Schieffelin, Captain LaMothe, Major Jehu Hay, and Lieutenant Governor Henry Hamilton. Of the men assembled, he had little use for Hay, but he assumed that he would come to know the rest of the men better over time.

Lieutenant Governor Hamilton extended his hand to him.

"Captain MacLeod, please accept my apology for keeping you waiting. We have decided the route for your men and the pirogues to take. My carpenters assure me that these boats will all be repaired or reinforced to carry supplies. In addition, we will have built three additional ones for you and your militia to use." Scanning the men about him, Hamilton continued, "I assume you know everyone here."

"Yes, sir." The curt and quick response caught Hamilton's attention. The tall Scotsman's bearing suggested more than he had expected from the man. Grayed at the temples, lightning blue eyes under coal black brows and lashes, broad shouldered, he stood as tall as Hamilton and could easily match him eye-to-eye. Professionalism rang in his responses. However, one thing immediately struck Hamilton. He sensed that this man did not

German=this font   English=this font   *French=this font*   *Delaware=this font*

feel awed by either his rank or his class. For a fleeting moment, MacLeod reminded him of Coutincinau. Just like the Frenchman, MacLeod had obviously rubbed shoulders with too many Indians and too many Americans. What was there about this place that changed men so? What made them accept these harebrained ideas of equality? Why should they accept this simplistic philosophy of the Indians without question? Was Jacob Schieffelin correct in his evaluation of the man? His secretary maintained that MacLeod had valuable combat experience. While MacLeod's demeanor suggested the same, the man had yet to prove himself to Hamilton.

"I hear that you are familiar with the River Maumee."

"Yes, sir, I have done trading in that area."

"We understand that we can follow the river to here, where, between the junctions of the Sainte Mary and Saint Joe River, there is high ground. At this point, we must carry over to the Wabash. Initially, we will have some low water and white water conditions to cope with on the Wabash, but I have been assured that the journey will become easier as we progress down-river." Hamilton directed MacLeod's attention to the map drawn before them. "Do you have any questions?"

"No, sir."

"We assume you and your militia will be ready to commence by September twenty-fourth."

"Yes, sir." MacLeod did not have as much certainty as his voice tried to convey. Already, he recognized that many of his militia would do as little as mortally possible under the pretext of compliance. Unlike trained troops, the French Canadians always looked for an easy out. He had little real authority, so he would need to coddle them along or face their desertion. But as the appointed Mayor by Hamilton and leader of the Volunteer Militia garrison in the Fort, he must go. Besides, even if he could send another in his place, MacLeod admitted to himself that he would never do that under any circumstance. He would never shirk his duty. "Are my men on the payroll now, sir? I understand the other militias are starting a mite early to compensate for their packing. I thought since we would be first to leave, sir…" MacLeod's question hung dangerously.

"Yes, yes, of course. Major Hay, will you see to that?" Hamilton endorsed his request with absolutely no hesitation. One must be even-handed.

Hay frowned but nodded in agreement. As usual, he quickly complied with any order from Hamilton. But, he wondered, whose lips had flapped!

More pay for his troops might grease the wheels a little, MacLeod thought, as he focused again on the map before them. Obviously, the sneaky Hay had not informed the Lieutenant Governor that his men had already bellied up to the King's trough. Hay would bear watching.

German=this font   English=this font   *French=this font*   *Delaware=this font*

When MacLeod left Hamilton's office, he needed to speak first with Helen. Later, he would see if his friends Gregor MacGregor and Simon MacTavish would keep a watchful eye over her and the lass.

Helen. Dear God, how he had been blessed by her. She tied him to this new country like no other. He still found himself waking in the night, awed to be at her side. He would touch her gently, so as not to wake her, just to confirm once more his good fortune. No matter the hardship, as long as he had her, he remained truly blessed. There would only and ever be the one child, one sweet fruit from the union of their loins. He had nearly lost wife and child in the beginning. Had it not been for the care of Joseph Brant's sister, Molly, Sir William Johnson's consort, and Sir William's material and loving support during their time of travail, the end result would have been tragic. Would the MacLeod luck hold again through this? Just when the wheel of fate appeared to be on the up turn, this wicked spin changed the forces of weird.

Helen and his daughter, Jeannie, both looked up from their samplers as he entered. As usual, Helen knew without a word spoken that they would part soon. She tried desperately not to show any fear before Jeannie. Her chin quivered as he bent to press a brief kiss to her cheek. Her hands shook slightly. Her voice sounded underlaid with quiet apprehension.

"Jeannie, show your Father your French knots."

Jeannie intently wrinkled her forehead as she wrapped her needle, counting softly to herself, "A minute, Mommy, I am counting."

"Six, three, four, two, five."

"Fa—ther," Jeannie sputtered, "Do not mess my count!"

Ten-year-old Jeannie, the delight of Helen and Norman MacLeod, had, like her father, survived improbable odds. She had been a sickly baby. Sir William had once intervened, holding a commissary position open for many months with pay for MacLeod, because to move the sick child would have meant certain death. Now to see the hints of approaching puberty and the loveliness of her mother reborn momentarily took MacLeod's breath away.

That clinched it, they must make merry before he left, he insisted to himself, as he observed his daughter struggling to finish her knot. He would not depart from the young lass and her mother with only tears at the leaving. Better to have dancing and laughter as a last memory. Yet another thing to tell MacGregor and MacTavish, he decided. He would need their fiddles. He would speak of it tonight as he held Helen in his arms. He must try to reassure her yet one more time that he would be safe. Yes, music and merriment, and many a good stiff dram were in order. All he had to look forward to were shepherding bags of flour, toting firkins of butter, hauling a hundred or more bear skins, herding cattle and oxen to feed and to carry for Hamilton's men, and ferrying all the other sundry supplies, including carpenters and bakers through wet, cold, and inclement weather for many months under constant threat of attack. By God, he would at the very least go with a song on his lips and one dance with his Helen.

German=this font   English=this font   *French=this font*   *Delaware=this font*

MacLeod would not be the only one who made this decision at the Fort.

Eve slid in the mud, her feet squee-haw. The yoke slipped askew. She blessed Joe a thousand times for making her a yoke of her own. The yoke nearly fit her shoulders perfectly. The craftsmanship of the man's hands and the thoughtfulness that he expressed in a dozen small ways made the whole of the trials before her each day somehow more manageable. He even had made new spoons and dippers for Yankee Hall.

This amazed Eve, given that Joe had to put up with Major Hay's tirades concerning the extra canoes to go with the fleet of pirogues that Hamilton demanded readied in the coming weeks. If Hay had his way, Joe would never sleep. As it was, Joe and his expanded crew hardly had time to eat. Joe always seemed to appreciate the fresh biscuits, crusts, or breads that Eve provided him with Sue Ellen and Nanna's help. She realized that his time to cook for himself had diminished considerably.

Major Hay had even pitched an absolute purple fit when Joe had slipped away to be with his people near Saginaw Bay for a few days before MacLeod's projected departure. He insisted that every carpenter was needed to assist Hamilton's leaving. Tchamaniked Joe was no exception. Eve knew that Joe regularly took supplies and food to his family. He paid for these goods by working here at the Fort. Just as his family and friends up on the bay profited from his skills, so did she and the boys.

Joe could fashion nearly anything out of wood. Understandably, here at the Fort, he received the best pay for his remarkable abilities. Somehow the toad of a man, Hay, could not understand that Joe had family members and friends, who would be concerned if he was suddenly called to leave the Fort and to go to God knows where. Hay would not even tell Joe if he was to go or if he was not to go. Even a mindless one should have understood Joe's need to keep his family informed! If Eve could understand this, why in the name of heaven could not that miserable excuse for a man! But then she had despised Hay from the first time she clapped eyes on him en route to this wretched place. Nothing so far in her experience had redeemed him, not even for a moment.

In the end, Eve decided that Hay, and indeed most of the British, felt he had a God-given right to command people to go, to come, and to do whatever they thought best suited the Crown or their own rotten needs, if they felt that they ranked over you. Just as they had the right to command her to carry mud up and down this hill, a hundred stinking times a day, and to keep most of her pay for the privilege.

Ahead of her, Captain Lernoult squinted in the sun, making sure that the lines of the new fort agreed with his engineering plans. The speculation about the floor of Yankee Hall held that the officers expected a high and fancy Ranger fresh from Niagara, a Captain Henry Bird. Already folks debated as to how he might look or act. Would he have the right to order them around like Lernoult and Hay did? According to the gossip, Bird had had something to do with the planning of the new fort.

German=this font   English=this font   *French=this font*   *Delaware=this font*

Unlike the old fort that huddled near the river like an old woman, the new fort dominated the surroundings, strutting like a tall magnificent belle at the crest of the hill disdainfully overlooking the old. This hill also proved to be the same hill that Eve removed or replaced two buckets at a time, depending on the whims of their captors with others from Yankee Hall.

Most days, Hay and Lernoult huddled over the plans, no matter the weather. They drove their subordinates among the Rangers to dig the palisade placements deeper and wider, as if a devil dog chewed at their heels. The dirt that the troops removed, Eve and the others carried to another site. However, when rain caused runoff groves and banks to wash away, Eve would be called upon with the others to haul the sodden dirt back. She operated each day purely on the whims of need, dirt in and dirt out.

She waved to Nellie and Fiona across the way. They had also benefited from Joe's handiwork. The three women felt quite literally the envy of many within the hall. At night, their shoulders had a minimum of blisters and bruised spots from ill-fitting yokes. Most of Eve's floor-scrubbing money of late had gone for Seneca oil or Ashcu Shang's oil, as Sally Ainsee called it. The precious ointment helped to heal the three women. Like so many things, the price rose along with the numbers of blisters at the Fort. Nightly, Nellie and Fiona took turns with Eve to apply the healing miracle.

Eve looked up at the sky. She hoped that the weather would hold. Joe had invited them all up to the clearing tonight. Having finished his last canoe for MacLeod's militia, he wanted to celebrate. He told her to bring any good friends, who would not object to the company of savages or mixed bloods or to dancing and having a good time. Eve, Nellie, and Fiona had looked forward to this night for a week. Toby Langlough and Karl Wenzel, the stuffy and scrubbed Dutchman, who had lately warmed to their friendship, were among those who chose to join them.

Margaret acquiesced when she heard that there would be no liquor. She absolutely hated drunken Indians. Even Sue Ellen received permission from Ann Forsythe to attend. Eve, Nellie and she had purchased a bit of corn flour for extra Johnny cake. With the dried blueberries that Joe had given the women, the bread would be especially tasty. Mistress Forsythe said that Sue Ellen could bake it in the Inn's oven and use the special corn shaped wrought iron pans, which neatly turned out twelve cob-shaped buns. Margaret planned to bring her special rum-soaked pound cake. Eve checked first with Joe to see if this would be acceptable. Joe steadfastly refused to have any rum to drink at the festivities, so all the children would be welcomed warmly and not be harmed by fighting adults.

When Eve had gone to ask permission from Lernoult for all of them to attend, he had surprised her, telling her to have a good time and to be sure not to have any woman travel alone upon her return. He showed particular pleasure when he found out that a few of the men would be with the women at all times. He praised their wisdom, knowing that the women would be less disturbed by drunken revelers. He feared that with the impending

German=this font   English=this font   *French=this font*   *Delaware=this font*

forays from the Fort, too many displayed high spirits. He noted that their drunkenness had created more than enough problems for women who ventured about alone. Under no circumstances, he advised, should she or her friends travel singularly in the coming weeks. Lernoult did not specifically mention rape, but Eve knew of at least one woman who had been so tragically attacked. Rumors told of still another. The women prisoners constituted fair game. The skewed population of men to women created enough problems without this additional stress.

"Mistress Eve." Eve raised her head to the sound, finally realizing Lernoult called. When he saw that he had caught her attention, he continued, "Do you and the other ladies want to freshen a bit before your do?"

Astonished, Eve nearly staggered. She felt a little chagrined at all her earlier thoughts about the heartless British. "Yes, sir. That would be good, sir."

"Well, be careful all of you. You may leave after this load."

"Yee-haw." Eve could hear Nellie's take on the whole idea across the hill.

Eve waited for her last load of the day, grinning so hard her face nearly cracked the caked dust. Nanna would be amazed to see her so early to pick up the boys.

Later, Eve and her friends could hear the music long before they reached the clearing. When one of the Solomon boys rushed to grab Mikie and Henry away to join the other children by the food table, the women stood astounded. Mikie immediately responded to the music, bouncing in place. Fiddles, flutes, recorders, mouth harps, penny whistles, spoons, and any manner of instrument to strum or hum, homemade or otherwise, all joined in improvised or remembered tunes. The clearing overflowed with happy folk. Far more attended than any of Eve or her friends had expected. Amongst those laughing, talking or, dancing, Eve spotted the merchant, Sally Ainsee. She chatted animatedly with the good Father from Ste. Anne. Martha, the metisse healer, sported a fine new gingham dress. As she danced with her burly French husband, her laughter floated about her, enlivening the festivities.

Soon the newcomers' offerings joined with many others on the makeshift tables. Absolutely no one would go to bed hungry this night. Langlough immediately grabbed a big sweet bun and stood, stomping his foot in time as he enviously watched the couples, who spun before him. Just as quickly, the Dutchman, Wenzel asked Fiona to dance. With their arms loosely hung about each other's necks, they circled in the light provided by two or three small fires. Eve smiled. So that is what the old fool found so interesting about Eve and Nellie of late. Nellie frowned.

Eve froze. Right in the front of the musical merriment, Joe played a long wooden flute, one he obviously had made. The dark fruitwood fairly glowed in the firelight. He nodded to her, swinging the recorder-like flute in greeting to welcome her.

German=this font   English=this font   *French=this font*   *Delaware=this font*

"Well I'll be hog-tied," Nellie exclaimed. "That man of yers plays a flute, too?"

"He never ceases to amaze me."

"You're going to miss him, injun or no, if he has to go with Hamilton, Eve."

"I know." Eve almost choked on her words. "But he is here now. And so am I." She decided quickly what to do. "Come on, let us dance, Nellie." Grabbing Nellie, they entered the circle to dance before Eve burst into tears. Throwing back her head and laughing, she and Nellie whirled with the music late into the night. Even the light misty showers did not dampen their spirited revelry.

Chapter 21   The Great Leaving
First Week of October, 1778

After Hamilton reported that nearly 5,000 people in and near Fort Detroit depended on the British purse for support and after his entreaties to Tory loyalists to come to Ft. Detroit, General Haldimand replied as follows: **"I am of the opinion that driving these settlers back upon their brethren whom they would distress by an additional consumption of goods and provisions among them would prove a better measure for His Majesty's interest than inviting them to your post."**

[Haldimand further suggests that any Tories who did come to Fort Detroit should be part of the forces against their Rebellious countrymen], **"made to take arms,"** and **"exert themselves heartily."** Haldimand's chastisement of Hamilton for spiraling costs written August 6, 1778 as quoted by Silas Farmer in *History of Detroit and Wayne County and Early Michigan, 1890* (Silas Farmer and Co. Republished by Gale Research, 1969), p. 244.

"....Governor Haldimand rather justified and excused him [Lieutenant Governor Henry Hamilton] especially in the Coutincinau case; but the grand jury for the district of Montreal did not, and on Monday, September 17, 1778, they indicted Governor Hamilton for allowing DeJean to perpetuate such enormities...DeJean illegally acted as judge...and that then DeJean hanged her [Anne Wylie aka Nancy Wylie] also, and that without law or authority."

Silas Farmer's observation in *History of Detroit and Wayne County and Early Michigan, 1890* (Silas Farmer and Co. Republished by Gale Research, 1969), p. 173.

Fort Detroit

Rum amplified the voices in Fogherty's. The mix of sweat and moisture produced an echoing effect, which meant voices had a tendency to hang longer and run into or over each other. The excitement built as night proceeded.

Sue Ellen wove in and out among the tables with the heavy pewter tray filled to capacity. Fear, the yeast in every glass of brew, bubbled over, and ran down the edges of the crowd, seeping into every pore. The fearsome reputation of the Virginians spoken only in whisper, if spoken of at all, troubled those about to depart. These tales, originally enhanced as a fear device by the British in part to incite the Indians or to keep settlers from joining the Rebel side, returned to haunt the British command.

Ann Forsythe knew she had best keep the tallies building because tomorrow night the tavern would be considerably quieter. When MacLeod's militia left the fort in late September, the town had turned out to see the forty or so men off. Immediately, she and her husband had felt the impact on the Inn's till. But now, the toll would be higher with more lives touched with uncertainty and filled with foreboding. Additional troops would leave with the morning light. Day after day, since MacLeod and his men's departure on the twenty-fourth, a pall had settled on the fort. Many of the remaining men had a somber nature and introspective manner as they waited for the next parties' leaving. This and profit had moved Ann Forsythe to pursue an idea. She prevailed on Antoine, the cook, to write a new song for the pub as sort of a bon voyage for her loyal patrons.

Antoine had inherited a legacy of song from the coasts of Brittany in France. Blessed by his Celtic heritage, his voice touched the French and the Scots or Irish with equal ease. His songs were welcomed on many a cold evening. So the news of a new ballad had built an air of additional expectation which culminated when noggins and mugs began pounding on tables. A loud chorus demanded that Antoine take leave of his kitchen.

When Antoine laid his apron aside with a theatrical flair and took his fiddle into his lap, the crowd hushed with expectation.

"You know, good folks, a good ballad needs a good chorus, so you need to learn this so you can help me out."

Antoine strummed the simple jig-like chorus and had them hum along. Not once but thrice, he repeated the sequence of notes until he was sure that they had caught on to the melody. In the tradition of Border ballads, he began:

"Now here's the words, men. Let's try 'er out.

> Sing ye of Long Nancy
> And sing ye of her John
> Tho' she hung him high, oh
> He loved her as he died, oh"

On the fourth line, Sue Ellen nearly dropped her tray. She staggered against a table, catching her balance only moments before a crash of mugs and brew.

"I know you can all do better than that. We'd better sing it again 'til you have it down pat," Antoine playfully chided his unruly choristers. "Come now, try it again.

> Sing ye of Long Nancy
> And sing ye of her John
> Tho' she hung him high, oh
> He loved her as he died, oh"

German=this font   English=this font   *French=this font*   *Delaware=this font*

Ann Forsythe noticed the usual paleness of her serving wench go nearly gray-white. Her contrasting freckles nearly leapt from Sue Ellen's cheeks. For a brief moment, Ann Forsythe considered stopping Antoine. But as she scanned the many faces of her patrons, she could see that they already loved the direction that Antoine planned to take them. The crowd grew eager for the ballad to unfold. To stop Antoine might incite a small riot.

Sue Ellen's response did not go unnoticed by another. True evil lurked hidden among a sea of faces. Undetectable and unexpected, it observed and calculated its diabolical plans. Evil watched Sue Ellen's reaction and selected a victim. What a perfect time to punish one who befriended a Negro whore, a murderess. He would be gone with the morning's light with no one the wiser and with his victim the sadder. He savored the special gift that he intended to share like God's avenging angel. Who better to share his terrible curse with than this sinful serving wench?

"Now sing out men. I expect you to sing the chorus, good men, after every verse. Are you ready?" Antoine called for their gusto.

The clamor of voices and thumping cups gave heady assent. Antoine began—

> "John, he loved brown beavers
> Wild, sleek, wet, and warm.
> Free to hunt God's creatures
> A paddler strong of arm."

A raggedy chorus followed. Not always on key, but already the rowdy voices sought to lift the rafters.

> "Spied he the long tall Nancy
> And soon he sought her out.
> Wooed John the long, strong Nancy
> He quickly brought her 'bout."

The chorus grew more raucous. They began to build with assurance and volume as they delighted in the bawdy double entendre of his ballad.

> "John warmed her by his fire
> Held there his black pearl tight.
> But Pierre, the man for hire,
> Fetched men so late that night."

Now the chorus rang with approval and familiarity. Antoine belted out the next verse.

German=this font   English=this font   **French=this font**   *Delaware=this font*

"She bargained with the devil.
She hung her lover high.
She watched her lover swivel
And to her love did cry."

Sue Ellen crumpled into a chair near the corner that one man had vacated to sing the chorus on his feet. Tears cascaded down her face. The brutal death of Anne and Coutincinau came back to her so vividly that she gasped as if in pain. Her chest heaved rapidly, rising and falling.

Antoine had totally captivated his audience. With the last verses, he carried his ballad to a triumphant end. The crowd leapt to its feet to sing the chorus wildly between each verse.

"Don't bargain with the devil
Now listen to my lay
The devil's never civil
He'll hang you just for play.

For Dat Long Nancy and her John
They had a love so strong.
Tho' she hung him high-oh
He loved her 'til he died-oh."

"So—" Antoine held the note for a long time as the chorus rose to join him, nearly shouting the final refrain.

"Sing ye of Long Nancy
And sing ye of her John
Tho' she hung him high, oh
He loved her as he died, oh."

Whistles, huzzahs, stomping feet, pounding noggins, and screams of approval filled the air.

"Again, again, again..."

"Do 'er over."

"More. More."

The crowd fairly howled its pleasure until a piercing female wail rose with such intensity that it impaled the din.

A sudden stillness spread after the lamenting sound. Sue Ellen leapt to her feet and began to scream at the patrons, as if possessed by madness.

"What's the matter with you men? Have you no heart?"

Sue Ellen got no further as Ann Forsythe quickly pulled her from the impromptu center stage that she had created by her shrill entrance. Ann roughly shoved Sue Ellen through the kitchen door and into the nearest corner.

"What in the hell are you doing? Be quiet, for God's sake." She

German=this font   English=this font   **French=this font**   *Delaware=this font*

shook Sue Ellen hard by the shoulders. "Go to your room! Come back only if you can serve properly. This conduct will dock your pay for one week."

Sue Ellen pulled away from her employer. Her dressed ripped at the shoulder as she pushed Ann Forsythe away. She walked backwards, too stunned to believe her ears and too angry to speak.

Then turning abruptly, Sue Ellen fled into the night through the rear entrance.

As Antoine recovered his crowd and prepared to sing his new ballad for a second time, a dark figure also slipped into the blackness. Ann Forsythe stepped up to her serving wench's tray and kept the flow of spirits coming. She watched with joy the money going into the till late into the night.

A week later, another individual in the community would take offense at Antoine's new ballad. A stiff trumped up fine would prevent it from being sung again at Fogherty's. But not this night, on this night the spirited ballad rang in the rafters until the wee hours.

Tchamaniked Joe had departed two days before to make a last trip to Saginaw Bay before his departure with Hamilton's forces. However, he returned as she had hoped. Eve lay in his arms, looking into the star hole that occasionally cleared of rain and cloud. She could not sleep. She nearly cried with joy earlier when Nellie told her to climb the hill to the clearing before dark and not to come back if she found him there. They both hoped that he would be there alone, as he was under orders to leave come morning light. Neither could believe that he would leave without saying goodbye to Eve.

Nellie shrewdly measured men, and her yardstick found Joe dependable. She maintained that good men were so damn rare that you cornered them when they showed the slightest interest.

Joe would travel with Hamilton's entourage. Carpenters, bakers, and a blacksmith filled the support ranks. Someone had to fix boats, wagons, and cook the victuals on the long trek.

So many questions ripped through Eve's thoughts, repetitive and cycling. In addition, a thousand fears joined in the mix. She wanted to know more about him, but she had so little time to ask. She debated about things that she needed to tell him. She elected silence, instead. She realized that she had wasted precious time by not talking more with him. However, both of them had been so busy that during their brief moments alone, they had sought the solace of each others arms.

"Madame Eve. You do not sleep."

She could not speak of how much she would miss him. He had enough to consider without that type of annoying whining which would only precipitate her tears.

"My thoughts scatter, so full of questions. All a blur."

"Ask one, *Animakwe*?" He shifted her weight on his shoulder and

German=this font   English=this font   *French=this font*   *Delaware=this font*

pushed the hair back from her forehead. His eyes, in the starlight, gleamed like polished black onyx.

"Are you Roman Catholic?" The question when it popped out startled Eve. As just one of the minor questions that cycled through her thoughts, she had chosen it at random like one among lots. Questions like: Tell me about your family? What is your home like up on the Saginaw Bay? How long has it been since you returned from Paris? How did you ever finance your return passage? When did you find Teddy? Where did you learn to play the flute? Why do you call me Animakwe? All these questions tumbled about each other.

"If you mean Christian, I am not. Well, no, maybe I am. Do I have to make a choice one way or the other? Either...or. Neither really fits. Sometimes one can find something of value in each choice."

Not choosing either alternative had never occurred to Eve as a possibility. A third choice, perhaps, she considered, but could one accept part and not the whole? How utterly different than just either...or. A mix of the two confused her.

"I am sorry. I asked a silly question."

"No, not at all, especially since you knew that I have traveled far with the long Robes." He stroked her arm as he spoke to comfort her. "My turn, would it make a difference if I were...or were not?"

Eve mulled over his question for a moment and then snuggled into his shoulder.

"No, not really, I know you are a good man. I guess it really does not matter."

"Another question?"

She knew some women would ask a man if he loved her at a time like this, but to do this spoke blatantly to Eve of being shallow. Besides, part of her refused to risk asking him to make a choice. What meant most was simply being in his arms and hearing the timbre of his voice with his chest as a sounding board.

"What would you like to do when you return?"

"Humph."

She could tell that he thought this posed a better question. She waited for him to answer.

"Well, build another canoe. Make you laugh. See your boys at play—look at the lake in the morning. Visit my family..." His voice seemed to become increasingly distant as he spoke.

She sensed as he hesitated that he had other things that he wanted to say, but like her, he elected not to share his thoughts completely.

"Your turn."

"What?"

"Your question?"

"Oh, let's see..." He pulled her close, almost as if he returned from a great distance to her. "Do you want to go back to your home?"

German=this font   English=this font   *French=this font*   *Delaware=this font*

Eve's breath caught. In the year that had passed, she had been forced to live a lifetime and more. My God, what did she want? His arm nestled her closer. His nose softly stroked her cheek. He awaited her answer.

"I do not know, Joseph. I honestly do not know. When I am in your arms, I do not want to be anywhere else." She stopped and pulled herself closer to him, slipping one leg between his to make her point.

He noticed the use of his full Christian name.

"But I miss my family. My Mutter and Vater, my schwesters, my other children if they live," she continued.

His nose traced the side of her nose. "Make the easy choice now, Eve. The right path will always be clear when you need to walk it."

She made the easy choice.

For Eve, morning light dawned too soon.

"Remember, you and the boys are welcome here in my absence. Help yourself to any of the food stores. You know where they are. Sally Ainsee can send word to me if you have need." Joe's parting words considered the mundane things of life. He had accepted her parting gift, a small pot of Seneca oil, with an amused smile.

Joe touched the side of her face. His fingers very softly raked the fine, downy hairs which grew on her cheeks and which glowed as a fine aura in the early morning light. He would miss touching her softness.

"*Aakidewin.* Follow your heart." He translated the Anishinabemowin, the language of his people, for her. *"Baamaa pii ka-waab-min.* Until I see your face again." Then he turned abruptly from her without waiting for her reply.

Eve studied him as he departed. From a tump-line, a blanket covered roll of hide and birchbark hung low and across his broad back. His wooden flute peeked out in the middle of the bundle. A leather pouch with his crooked knife, his powder horn and a few strings of dried clams dangled loosely on leather thongs from his shoulder. A trade blanket was tossed loosely over his opposite shoulder. A musket, cradled in one hand, swung in rhythm with his long strides.

Joe never looked back.

Watching him leave, Eve realized for the first time that he must have left Teddy, his feisty canine friend, with his family.

Eve choked back her tears, wiped her cheek to remove any telltale traces, and began her lonely trek to the fort. Morning sun edged the trees back-lighting them with a golden glow to match the touch of fall colors which now struck in random, whimsical patterns among the predominating green. Reveille soon would sound with fewer birds to mix in the morning songs. A damp cold wind penetrated her clothing as though she wore nothing.

Eve decided as she walked that she had no heart to watch the men ship out. She simply could not observe them loading the last pirogues.

Captain Alexander Grant, the harbor Commandant, readied the sloop,

German=this font   English=this font   *French=this font*   *Delaware=this font*

Archangel. Fourteen tons of provisions and Hamilton's army would soon lift anchor to take Lieutenant Governor Hamilton and his men on the first leg of their journey.

For a time, Hamilton would have a cabin to keep him out of the inclement weather. Neither would he have to be party to the comical struggles to move the oxen on board, as they were reluctant sailors at best. The secondary crews and other men accompanied the *Archangel* in fifteen large open pirogues with various styles of canoes nestled between them. The pirogues, smaller and lighter vessels, had been built to carry a little less than a ton to a ton-and-a-half. They rocked and tossed more easily than the heavier and sturdier *Archangel.*

A monumental undertaking, men, oxen, horses, supplies, and boats, all assembled to reach the Maumee Rapids on the heels of Norman MacLeod's militia and the advance party. In the distance, faint streams of smoke from the last ox roast, once accompanied by savage drums and rum, smoldered. The tribal women, children, and old men stood quiet. The warriors had left by land at first light.

The fort would quiet quickly after the exit of so many men. The King's eighth regiment had reassigned thirty-two men. Lernoult supported Hamilton more in this undertaking than Mompesson ever would have. Haldimand's final orders still had not been received. With the arrival that morning of Captain Henry Bird and his rangers, Lernoult could afford to release a few of his men to Hamilton. Bird's battlewise men, dressed in green, had ample service working with men like Joseph Brant and contrasted markedly with the unseasoned red-coated troops of Fort Detroit, for few men stationed at the fort had fought in the Americas. Two more Detroit militia groups contributed seventeen men each; and with their accompaniment of officers, their numbers grew to forty-four men. LaMothe's company of forty-four men joined with many tribes in the area. Forty Ottawa, twenty Chippewa, four Wyandot, thirty Potawatomi and thirty Miami followed the King's men.

Before the day would end, Hamilton boasted deservedly that three hundred men accompanied his Indian department on Hamilton's great retaliation against Virginia's Rebel forces.

But for Eve, only one man of importance would leave the fort this morning, one whom she could not cheer on his way. How could one cheer for those who would be instrumental in helping to kill your own people? Her thoughts scattered. A whole year nearly spent. A year crammed with opposing events, joys, contradictions, and unexpected heartbreaks. Where would it end? Lost in her own thoughts, she barely realized that Pompey rushed toward her.

"Mistress Eve. Mistress Eve."

Never had she seen Pompey in such distress. The huge man shook with emotion. Even at a distance, she could see his deeply distraught features.

German=this font   English=this font   *French=this font*   *Delaware=this font*

"Mistress Eve."

"Pompey, what is it? Is it the boys?"

"Oh, no, mam, it is your friend. I dare not help her. They will say it was I."

"Goodness man, whatever are you talking about?"

"Your friend, your friend. I will tell you where to find her, but you must never say that it was I who found her."

"Of course, of course. Pompey, what are you talking about?"

She could tell that if he could, he would grasp her hands. But he knew that he dare not touch her. The obvious fear in this large man frightened Eve.

"It is your friend, Sue Ellen. Listen carefully. She is on the west side, in the shadows of the bastion along Citadel wall. I do not know what drew me to her, except, perhaps, the shape of the shadows. Go to her, good woman, I think she still lives."

Of course, you fool, she thought. She grew ashamed because it had taken her so long to trip to the cause of his intense fear. Many would instantly accuse the black slave to cover another's folly. As an esclave, she knew how blame shifted. She nodded and turned away from him to hastily follow his directions. Dread consumed her.

Sue Ellen's shadow did indeed protrude in an absurd way. Anyone with a sense of the terrain would wonder. The curious would check. In times of war, one became vigilant and more suspicious of one's surroundings, especially when each day daily rumors spoke of impending attacks and encroachments by the enemy.

Sue Ellen lay with her ripped apron, skirt, and petticoat above her head, her injured person bare for all to see. The violence of the attack sickened Eve. Slashes, bruises, and a pool of blood had soaked into the earth about her hips. Bruises almost in the form of large grotesque hands blotted her thighs. Eve muffled her outcry. She sank slowly to her knees and lifted the skirt from her unconscious friend's face.

Sue Ellen's face had not been spared in the vicious attack. Blood seeped from the corner of her mouth and from her cut lips. Eve suspected that Sue Ellen missed more than a few teeth. Her sweet freckled face, a maze of bruises, was filled with complementary blues and purples which contrasted with the fading golden morning light that reflected from the highest surfaces. Both eyes, already deepest blue-black, were swollen tightly shut from vicious blows.

"Sue Ellen...." Eve called softly to her injured friend.

Sue Ellen moaned, nothing more.

Eve immediately realized that she could not carry Sue Ellen by herself. If Eve cried out for help, she might garner a shot from a fidgety garrison guard responding only to the palatable tension which grew with each passing day at the fort. Eve tenderly pulled down Sue Ellen's petticoat and skirt. Crossing the ripped apron, she tucked the torn garments to begin to cover Sue Ellen's breasts and person with a modicum of modesty.

German=this font   English=this font   **French=this font**   *Delaware=this font*

Removing her own shawl, Eve tucked it gently under Sue Ellen's head, folding the ends across her chest.

"I will return, my friend."

Eve took to her feet and came to the gate just as reveille sounded. The guard snapped to attention as she neared. He frowned quizzically at her; but recognizing Eve, he allowed her to pass. Women occasionally returned in the early morning hours. Wise guards did not draw attention to them as they might have been company for a fellow officer.

Eve quickly ran for Yankee Hall. When she entered the hall, she immediately sought out Nellie. Nearly incoherent, she babbled to Nellie, who saw quickly the gravity of the situation. Eve was shaking so hard that Nellie directed four men to bring the largest blanket to carry Sue Ellen back to the Hall. Nellie agreed with Eve that Martha, the healer, must be fetched. Another woman took the boys aside. Fiona readied a clean area on which to bed-down Sue Ellen. Langlough went for Father Bocquet and Martha.

Nellie went on a dead run with the men, explaining to the guard as they ran why they needed him to help retrieve their friend. Nellie hoped that the presence of the red-coated guard among them would lessen their chances of being shot. To a person, Nellie and the men made as much of a racket as they could to draw attention to their presence. Never once did they want to give the impression of an enemy sneaking up on the position. Thankfully, no one on the wall fired upon them.

Eve ran for Lernoult's office to explain what had happened. By now Eve, who came on varying occasions for permissions, had established a mild rapport with the office personnel. The orderly, sensing the woman had unusual concerns, quickly admitted Eve to his superior's office.

Captain Lernoult looked up from his desk. The plans for Fort Lernoult were spread between him and Captain Henry Bird. New to the post, Bird immediately took offense to the woman's untimely entrance, but Lernoult, although he knew of Eve only in a superficial way as one of his carriers, sensed something had profoundly disturbed the woman. He laid a cautious hand on Bird's arm to restrain his outburst.

"What is it that brings you so hastily on this busy morning, Mistress Eve?"

"A prisoner has been raped, sir. We ask your permission to let us care for her at Yankee Hall." Eve knew no easy way to avoid the brutal truth or dress the ugly fact in pleasantries as she blurted out the situation in a direct manner.

"Where does she stay?"

"She works and boards at Fogherty's, sir."

"Her name?"

"Sue Ellen, sir."

"Should I have one of my men call for Dr. Anton? I do not believe that he left with Hamilton."

"No sir, we have fetched a midwife to assist us. And Father Bocquet, sir, as I fear she may need his words over her."

"Yes of course, you have my permission for her stay. You will advise me daily of her condition and progress. I assume you and your friends will join us on your work detail as soon as she is settled."

"Yes, sir. Thank you, sir."

As the woman left, Bird scowled.

"Are you not being a little too lenient in this matter, Lernoult?"

"Captain Bird, you have much to learn. May I remind you, these poor wretches were once our countrymen and women. We have plundered their homes, wrenched them from their families, and enslaved them to do our bidding. Surely, I can allow the woman and her friends an hour or two to care for a raped woman. Who, I might add, is also our prisoner and is under the Crown's dubious protection!"

Captain Bird re-evaluated Lernoult, who had rapidly grown in stature in his estimation. Prior to this time, he had dismissed the man as a mere alarmist and as a fool to build the new Fort. No longer did Bird think the man vainly sought the glory of naming the new fort after himself. Captain Bird revised his initial impression. Reproved correctly, he accepted his colleague's perceptions and moved back to the pressing task at hand.

Standing Bear's Village
near the Muskingum River

A restless John Leeth waited. He knew that the promised one would soon appear. He felt like a tiny songbird nestled between two cat paws.

Standing Bear and Falling Water Woman smiled knowingly at each other, fully aware and amused at their adopted son's discomfort. His parents knew that John Leeth had utterly no experience with women, European or Delaware. Leeth had always declined easy favors and feminine wiles. While Leeth might fearlessly take on a bear or cougar, put any animal away with easy dispatch, or track well; the female human presented an uncharted trail for him. Leeth did not dislike women or prefer the desires of the betweens. He simply had a fine nature which would not allow him to drop his pants for lustful satisfaction alone. His shyness, his industry, and his inexperience shielded him from exploration of these desires as surely as any device contrived by mankind.

When Stalking Wolf and White Corn Woman entered the cabin, Leeth's gaze dropped to the well swept earthen floor. Falling Water Woman suppressed a giggle, knowing that Leeth mistakenly had entertained the thought that the older woman was the woman to be considered. As Winter Hare, Sally Lowrey, modestly stepped in behind White Corn Woman just moments later, Leeth's eyes engaged ever so briefly with Sally's and then he, embarrassed, looked away.

Both parents noted a brief sweet smile when Leeth tried to straighten his shoulders to stand more erect.

German=this font   English=this font   **French=this font**   *Delaware=this font*

Out of Leeth's line of sight, Falling Water Woman's chest shook with a soft chuckle as Standing Bear introduced each of the visitors from Gnadenhutten to their son. One of the major hurdles in life for John Leeth now lay behind him. John Leeth had been formally introduced to Winter Hare, Sally Lowrey, an adopted Delaware like himself. Adopted when she was two, Winter Hare did not question her parents' arrangement.

Soon, all present sensed that Leeth also found pleasure with his parents' choice. The tall young woman became fairly luminescent in the warmth of Leeth's shy appreciation and repeated sly glances. His loving parents had chosen well for him.

October 9, 1778 At the Mouth of the Detroit River

Having survived his first night as a Commandant in charge of a large encampment, Hamilton reviewed in his mind the duties that he had attended. He hoped that his inexperience did not show to the men following his leadership. He missed the warmth of his wig, as he raked his fingers through his wet hair. Pickets and sentries were appointed. He worked out the order which secured the many pirogues and established parties to load and unload, as well as protect the many goods needed in the long trek ahead. The men protected all the baked biscuits with oil cloth. They stowed the many bags of flour under overturned canoes. Trusted guards were posted on the rum supply so no one absconded with the water of life.

The snow squall swirled about Hamilton's tent. Scratching on the tent in a token gesture to alert the inhabitants, Captain Alexander Grant entered, shaking the white corn snow from his shoulders before doffing his hat and batting it on his thigh. The minute balls bounced merrily across the tent floor. No one appreciated the early snow.

"We must not hold back."

"Does it look like this will let up?"

"Aye, I think so. The squall line is edged with blue now. It is just a matter of time. If the swells subside, we may be able to begin."

"How many miles do you estimate by a bird's flight?"

"My charts indicate we can expect about thirty five miles or more...closer to thirty-six."

"Well, I do not expect our opportunities will increase with the passage of time. We had best take to any advantage if the wind holds."

Noon came. The swells subsided. Hamilton briskly ordered his men to reload and depart.

Captain Grant had mixed feelings as he dealt with the driven man. On the plus side, the quicker Hamilton's expedition arrived at the mouth of the

German=this font   English=this font   *French=this font*   *Delaware=this font*

Maumee, the sooner Grant could return to his home port along the River Rouge near Fort Detroit to resume winter boat building and to share a warm fire. He envied no man this wretched march through the frigid water passage on the Maumee and Wabash Rivers. The portage in Indiana during winter weather would severely test the stamina of any man. The steady advance of winter could only guarantee the agony of each and every person. While Grant could see some sense in the venture, he hoped that Hamilton and his men had the pluck to pull it off. The operation demanded superlative leadership skills to command this ragtag group of militia and regulars, not to mention the savage allies. Grant paused only once to consider what pushed this commander not to wait for spring. For a fleeting moment, he wondered if Hamilton truly realized the distances involved from his main supplier to Vincennes. However, Grant's own duties occupied his attention so fully that these and any other questions quickly became forgotten in the task at hand.

October 10, 1778 In Search of the Maumee River

Blue Ice's head pounded as he walked. He did not relish following this fool English Father to Vincennes. He despised Stalking Wolf's unexpected choice to remain behind in Gnadenhutten. Blue Ice certainly did not relish the inevitable series of cold nights in damp impromptu lean-tos that he would face. He wondered if his Father's rum would help to warm them tonight. His tongue felt as though a thick rug lay upon it. Thirst plagued him. A touch of envy came with an incoming chill as he thought of a warm cabin and a hearty pot of venison stew that Stalking Wolf's sister would be sure to prepare. Although the advance party had prepared the trail well, even they could not stop the fall rains, snow, or the increasingly cold night temperatures.

Sitting Rabbit, his girth heaving from his exertion, kept up with Blue Ice, but at a cost.

"Who was that ugly woman you bedded last night?" Sitting Rabbit inquired with a slight pant between words. Trying anything he could think of to dispel his own misery, he instigated a conversation with the abnormally quiet Blue Ice. Perhaps a few juicy details could make the trail easier.

"No willing woman is ugly, especially in the dark."

"Yeah, she was willing, eh! I thought you were gifting Little Fox's mother, Singing Grass."

Sitting Rabbit thought he had heard a grunt, but he was not totally sure. Blue Ice did not answer him.

"I ask again, brother, who was the ugly one?"

"No wonder you had no one to warm your cock last night, Sitting

German=this font   English=this font   *French=this font*   *Delaware=this font*

Rabbit. One never speaks ill of a woman who laughs with you. " Blue Ice chided his lumbering friend. He pushed aside an overhanging branch heavy with an earlier rain. *"Her name is Sparkling Brook."*

Sitting Rabbit desired to know more about the woman with the strange scarred cheeks, who drank much and talked loudly. He still remembered her uncensored cries of climax that echoed around the fire, bothering the rest of the men, who slept alone. Proud women muffled their cries with modesty. This one talked boldly when she dove under the bear skin and drank rum naked in the firelight before seeking pleasure again from a drunken Blue Ice. Everyone heard her chide Blue Ice, who had needed extra assistance to pleasure her a third time in the night. In the firelight, Sitting Rabbit thought her breasts looked strange, but obviously his friend would not speak of this. No one could proudly admit to sleeping with such a disfigured woman.

"Does she also pleasure Logan?"

"Yes."

Sitting Rabbit waited for more of an answer, but receiving none, he took another tack.

"What do you know of Logan? Is he a Rebel lover?" If Sitting Rabbit could ask the right question, he knew a story would be sure to follow. Blue Ice collected stories like some men collected knives.

Blue Ice walked for some piece. Considering Sitting Rabbit's question, he felt himself responding as much out of boredom as any other reason. The tale would help the time pass.

"I heard this tale at one of the great fires two springs ago. Four springs ago, Logan once lived in peace with the whites. His father, Shikellamy and his father before him were friends of the English. His brother, John Petty Shickellmany and all his family and Logan's family lived near Yellow Creek across from Baker's camp. Logan's true name is Tah-gah-jute. In Iroquois, this means long eye lashes." Blue Ice jumped across a small stream, but Sitting Rabbit landed solid in the middle, soaking his moccasins.

Blue Ice continued after a small chuckle at his friend's misstep. *"I think that is a strange name for one who is so tall and gifted of tongue. Anyways, Logan took a white name. Many whites and many brothers came to visit him in his lodge. His hospitality was well known. His sister, rumors say, bore a child to one named Gibson, if the talk of the fire is true.*

"Even Brother Heckwelder and many others knew his lodge well. But the Rebellious ones came and slaughtered his family. The little ones, his brother, and the mothers...all scalped with no mercy." Blue Ice paused momentarily. He digressed, *"Lieutenant Governor Hamilton says we must spare the old ones, the women, and the children. I do not know why he says this. The English must be foolish. Why must we be weaker than our enemies?"* He hesitated briefly before resuming his initial tale. *"Logan would wonder as much if he were not so drunk. They say that*

German=this font English=this font **French=this font** *Delaware=this font*

Logan killed thirteen people...the same number as the two-faced ones killed. Then his scalping blade would cut no more. Now he stumbles and falls from the English rum day and night. His thirst never quits. He is of no use to anyone."

They walked a good piece more before Blue Ice finished his story. *"There is something strange though, my brother. Logan boasted that he killed thirteen for the thirteen who died. But many say that there were only twelve shining skulls around the fire stones. This is a puzzling mystery. Logan is not a stupid man. He knows how to count. Why would he kill thirteen and be satisfied if only twelve died about his fire? Maybe the Creator knows."*

The two walked on in silence, listening to the rain moisten the fall leaves and to the babble of others among their party.

Morning, October 11, 1778
At the Mouth of the Maumee

Much of the rain that had come with the howling wind shears just before midnight had begun to subside. Hamilton acknowledged to himself that the entire enterprise stood perilously close to the edge of death and failure in the last harrowing hours. He tried to shake off the memories of the water-swamped boats turned stern-to* struggling against banshee winds and huge rolling swells. The rigging screamed in their ears. Lines clapped and slapped the mast. The effort and exhaustion, as the men strained against the oars to fight their way ashore, nearly finished them. He wanted to forget how his eyes nearly popped from their sockets, straining to see the lanterns held ahead in one of the darkest nights that he had ever known.* Was this a promise of things to come?

Even after they waded ashore, the wind and rain gave no letup. Tents could not be pitched because either the howling wind or the mucky, 'oozy beach' * prevailed. Unable to build fires until an hour ago, a thankful Hamilton recognized that, providentially, they had missed the rocky shore, an area just prior to this landing area. He knew they would have 'inevitably perished' * to a man if they had gone ashore at that treacherous site. Although miserable, they rejoiced to be alive and intact. Not one man had been lost. Furthermore, his men had conducted themselves well. He heard few complaints. His small ration of rum had eased their pain and had not clouded their minds.

The miserable weather without tortured him nearly as much as the misery within. As if his trials were not enough, Monsieur de Celeron had deserted his post, traveling hundreds of miles to report to him this very morning of things Hamilton already knew. Furthermore, the rogue had exaggerated the number of the Rebel forces and their successes. His own man, the dependable Baby, had informed him earlier of the Rebel's progress. The mouthy fool, de Celeron, had obviously related tales of the

German=this font   English=this font   *French=this font*   *Delaware=this font*

Rebel take-overs en route from Fort Ouiatenon. He had left a verbal trail of lies that Hamilton would have to extinguish on the whole of his route.

The Wea, one of the independent groups of the Miami, continued to be uncertain enough in their support of the Crown as were others along the Wabash without this man's treacherous incompetence.

In his mind, Hamilton damned John Montour again. He wondered if Montour had already sided with the Rebel forces when Montour ventured along the Wabash to win allies for the Crown, long before his treachery with the escaping Virginians.

Hamilton tried to push back the gnawing petty problems of presiding over a Fort filled with untrustworthy French Canadians and traders who could trade sides in a heartbeat, oblivious of national pride or privilege. He swore that money must be a merchant's only true allegiance.

DeJean, his ridiculous excuse for a Minister of Justice, caused him more problems than not. The thought of a grand jury in session in Quebec possibly turning against Hamilton, creating even more testy situations with the home office in London, constantly nibbled at his thoughts like a mouse shredding a book to make a nest. No matter how he tried, thoughts of this injured his pride and made inroads into his thinking.

Hamilton recognized that the Rebel intelligence in the Fort constituted a tasteless joke. He felt angry at his inability to curtail the loss of information. Simultaneously, he grew fed up with the inefficient lag between correspondences. His commander, Haldimand, failed to respond to his nearly daily messages sent with as much expedition as he could muster. Now wind and weather could continue to plague the shipping of supplies and correspondence.

Hamilton confronted the risk of leaving the fort at a time when the latest intelligence from his interpreters described a potential threat from Fort Pitt against Fort Detroit. But the arrival of Captain Henry Bird, one of Butler's best, and fifty trained Rangers alleviated his concerns. He doubted if the undisciplined Americans could muster that much effort, anyway. Besides, he had not taken all the Militia. The damnable Frenchmen, who remained behind, would protect their own homes even if they could not be depended on for this adventure.

Alexander McKee, Simon Girty and his brothers, and Matthew Elliott continued to give the Crown good return for their pay. The Shawnees increasingly supported the Crown's efforts. More Delaware broke away daily to join the British. To reward them, Hamilton had made sure to send them more ammunition for their winter hunts and forays. Despite his distrust of Elliott, the man performed well.

If only Hamilton's exploits could shine so that he could begin to associate with those of rank and privilege. He had much more in common with men of education and skills than these coarse men with whom he must interact. But the Crown needed him here. He would excel here...where his potential for greatness would be fully realized. Whatever else, Hamilton recognized his strengths. Soon London would appreciate these qualities as

German=this font   English=this font   *French=this font*   *Delaware=this font*

well. This decisive endeavor would prove his abilities beyond any shadow of doubt.

* Hamilton's own description of the landing as quoted by Consul Wilshire Butterfield in *History of George Rogers Clark's Conquest of the Illinois and the Wabash Towns 1778 and 1779* (Boston: Gregg Press, 1972), p. 202.

Bedford, Pennsylvania

Michel sipped hot tea from the thick pottery mug. Healed but weak, he sat hunched over at his brother and mother's table. The children were put abed. Ene, John and Mere Eve allowed Michel to speak in his own good time. They had waited for days, now he seemed ripe to share.

Molly chose to allow them some semblance of privacy, but lay staring at the rafters hearing bits and pieces. She hoped that the smaller children slept and could not hear. Before Michel finished, she wished devoutly that she had not understood as much French as she did from the bits and pieces she overheard.

What Michel shared came in fits and starts. Jessie's recent loss made the horrors in past weeks paler, but nonetheless vivid.

First, Michel described for them the wretched prison ships barely afloat in the harbor, almost scuttled. A harbor filled with bloated and dismembered bodies.* How the ships tugged at their makeshift anchors or sagged, partially flooded, hanging on old sandbars, imprisoning hundreds and hundreds of men. There, in the lesser used harbors near British-held New York, prisoners, American men of the Continental Army, were crammed unmercifully into filthy, disease-infested quarters.* He relayed the struggles of these starving Rebels who elected leaders among them. How they had established times for prayer and rules of conduct.* He emphasized how the Americans came to appreciate the old timers, the ones who managed to survive the longest in the hellish prisons.*

Then, Michael related that they came to respect many of the retired British veterans, who had returned to British service and who served as some of their guards.* These retired veterans treated him and his fellow prisoners with some small degree of humanity. He contrasted this with the degrading treatment at the hands of Tory refugees, who also took their turns as guards.* Michel explained how the Tories taunted the prisoners and teased them about their lack of clothing. Clothing...such a precious commodity...constituted one of the Continental Armies greatest needs, third only to food and ammunition. He wondered aloud if the Continental Army would be known one day as the 'naked soldiers' of America.*

However, Michel broke down when he spoke of the dead...dead who were removed daily, sometimes as many as a dozen corpses a day.* How the toll, each and every day, weighed heavily on the men. How the bodies were crudely sewn in rag bags for disposal.* With a touch of shame, he

German=this font   English=this font   *French=this font*   *Delaware=this font*

explained how the men competed to serve on burial detail just to smell fresher air and to have a bit of exercise.* Even he had fought for a spot where an old splinter had sprung and allowed the air to eke in along the caulking seam in the hull. He wept as he confided that he prized his tiny whiff of air almost as much as life itself. Each night, he chose to sleep upright near that hole just to smell the comparatively fresh sea breezes instead of the sickening stench of diseased and dying prisoners, who moaned and suffered about him.

Michel realized that they were becoming numbed by his descriptions so he began to relate some of the more humorous events, albeit a dark humor. They soon laughed at the antics of Dame Grant,* an enterprising merchant woman who came to the boat each day with needles, soap and other desirables. Mere Eve, Ene, and John soon pictured this enormous woman with her tiny boat man, who would approach the prison boats each day with orders placed two days before. Dame Grant marketed her wares at a fair price, taking no guff from anyone, prisoner or guard alike. However, the sickness aboard finally became her undoing.* She died of fever just prior to Michel's release. No sooner had she passed, when an enterprising guard took her place as provider. However, his double-dealing and high prices quickly became apparent to the prisoners.*

Michel told of poisoned bread or rancid fat and biscuits riddled with worms.* He chuckled at the memory of the worm races. They laughed at the fools, who bet their rations on their favorites in hope of obtaining more food. He doubted if anyone about him could name their food.

Mere Eve smiled when he talked about the meat rations and the bizarre humor that surrounded these rations. Yes, the rotten meat had truly confounded the recipients.* Many jokes speculated whether the meat sprang from porpoise, dog, cat, rat, or horse. No one aboard really knew for sure.

Following his attempts to lighten his tale, Michel admitted that he truly hated the Scots, whom he considered the guards from hell.*

Michel told of one friend who had prized a special coat, only to have it stolen by a British nurse as he lay dying with the coat lay tucked under his head.* A near riot retrieved the coat to be given back to the dying man's family when they released prisoners later.*

"More tea, Mere?"

"Yes, of course, son. Of course." Eve quickly fetched the kettle.

*"We learned a strange thing there, Mere. I could not risk you all, but some of the old prisoners, who did not slip away with dysentery or the fevers, claimed it to be true."**

"What was that son?"

"The pox, they say if a man inoculates himself and does not catch it natural from one who is infected, you have a lighter case. You just rub some of the pus in a scratch. I saw one boy die yellow as a pumpkin after the self inoculation, but that is what old*

German=this font   English=this font   *French=this font*   *Delaware=this font*

*Bobby and some of the others maintained to be the God's truth."**

"Blessed be, son, you did not inoculate yourself did you?"

"No, Mere." Fighting for composure, Michel waited before he continued. *"I think the Brits gave me contaminated blankets. I think they wanted me to get sick coming home and to infect others."**

Mere Eve shook her head in disbelief. *"Saints in heaven, son. Even the British would not sink that low, would they?"*

"I think so, Mere. It is the only thing I can believe."

"Jesus, Peter and John," John cursed.

Mere Eve frowned at John.

"Well, Mere!"

"Do not 'well, Mere', me, John. You start a talking like that and you will slip in front of the children."

Ene nodded in assent.

John furled his brow, poured himself some more tea, and scraped nearly a half a teaspoon of sugar into it before his mother playfully slapped his hands.

The tension broke. John grinned, shook his head, and pretended to go for more sugar. His smile gave him away though. Mere Eve did not swat him a second time.

Mere Eve spoke.

"What will you do now, Michel? Surely, you will not go back to soldiering again."

"No. No. I have had a gut full, Mere. I have a mind to go down to New Orleans, some place warm. Visit our Onkel. Try to heal up a bit. But first, I have to go down to Emler's and tell them 'bout Jessie. It is my place." The last words trailed off drenched in sadness.

As the family sought to comfort each other, an animal dug and scratched near the clearing. Something smelled very intriguing, particularly rotten, and therefore quite pleasing to her canine sensibilities. The paws dug efficiently and soon the pointed snout could retrieve the corner of a woolen army blanket.

Tugging,

pulling,

digging,

pulling,

digging again,

the determined animal eventually wrenched the infected blanket and poorly buried clothes from the shallow site dug by Jessie. Pleased, the small fox dragged the smaller pieces to its lair, a bit of comfort for her and her young warm in the approaching winter. The heavier blanket proved too heavy to tow far. The fox left it adjacent to a deer run.

German=this font   English=this font   *French=this font*   *Delaware=this font*

Before the first morning light, another followed the way of the animals in soft moccasins that made no sounds on the damp, soft trail.

A silent runner,
                    alert and
                              observant,
                                        seized the unexpected opportunity. The brave scooped up the soiled woolen cloth. This blanket could warm a child, line one's leggings, or make a good saddle blanket, he decided as he disappeared into the night. What a find!

*Author's note. Jessie Emler is a fictional character. No historical account of these events happened to Michel Dibert. The events were inspired by accounts given by Continental prisoners in *American Prisoners of the Revolution* by Danske Dandridge (Charlottesville: Michie, 1911; republished by the Genealogical Publishing Company in 1967). A David Diber is listed among the American dead. Dandridge related a story of a man infecting his wife and child after being released and cared for by his wife. The descriptions of captivity in Wallabout, a bay near Long Island, were closely paraphrased to lend reality to this account. Old Bobby and Dame Grant, non-fiction persons, were also described in this source.

German=this font   English=this font   *French=this font*   *Delaware=this font*

Dear Readers,

One of the joys of research is being able to touch another's life. When I discovered that the sketches so often alluded to in Lieutenant Governor Henry Hamilton's journals and other texts actually existed and were here in the United States at the Houghton Library of Harvard University, I contacted them.

Thanks to the wonderful research department of Harvard University and their amazing Library Staff, MZW Ink was able to obtain photos of those sketches and to print them here for you to see. We selected six of those sketches. Harvard University has stipulated the following information be printed as part of the permission for their use in this publication.

1. State their call numbers: **pfMS Eng 509.2 (4)(7)(8)(11)(32)**
2. **By permission of the Houghton Library of Harvard University.**

The sketches include:

Pecane, a Native American of the Miami type (4)
A Native of the Jibboway (Ojibway) (7)
Shangress or Otcheek (8)
Ships at full sail (11)
Wooden Building and Forest 1784 (7)
View of the Wabash River (32)

We are deeply indebted to this institution for their patience and for their assistance to a small independent publisher.
Enjoy!

Pecan(e) Miami Chief

a Jibbowey Indian

A Jibboway Indian 1776-1778

Shangress or Otcheek

Ship at Full Sail

Wooden Buildings & Forest 1784

View of Wabash River

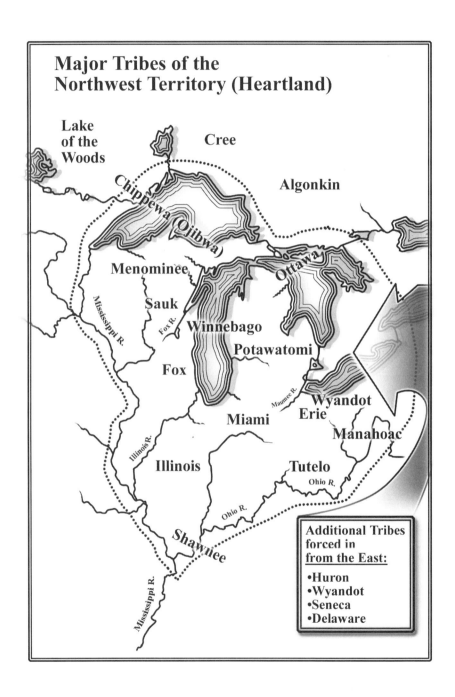

Major Tribes of the Northwest Territory (Heartland)

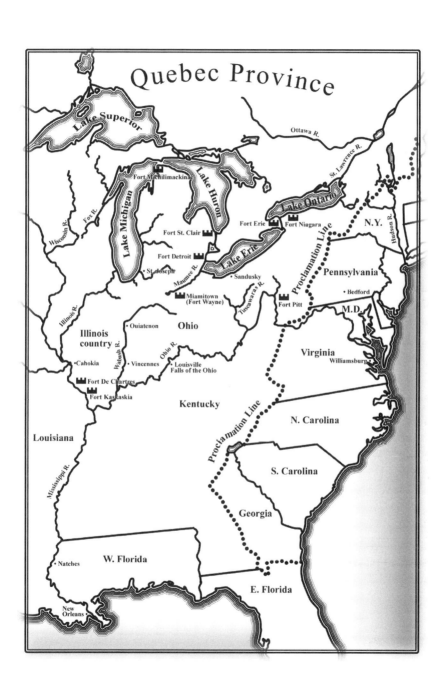

Fort Detroit

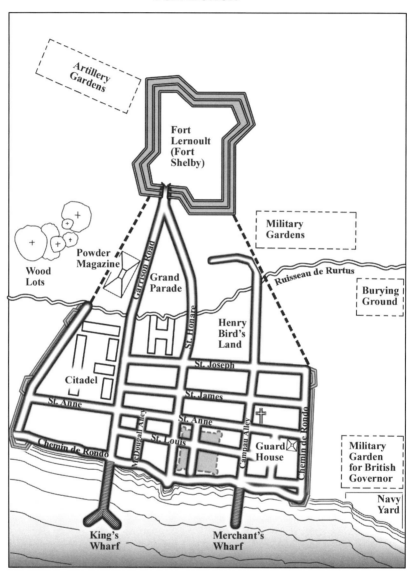

Based on a map drawn in 1796

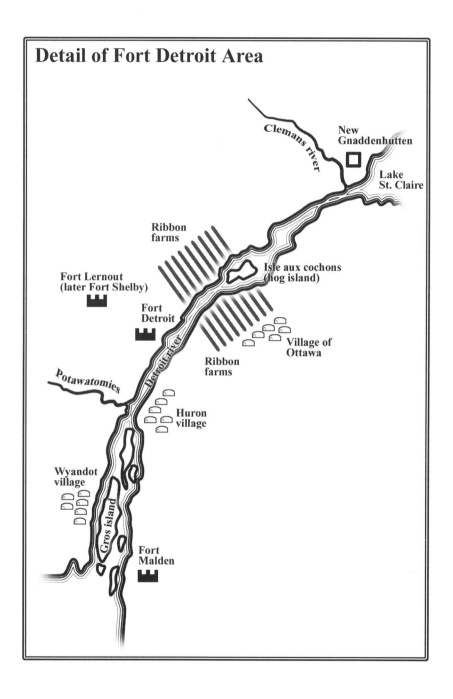

Detail of Fort Detroit Area

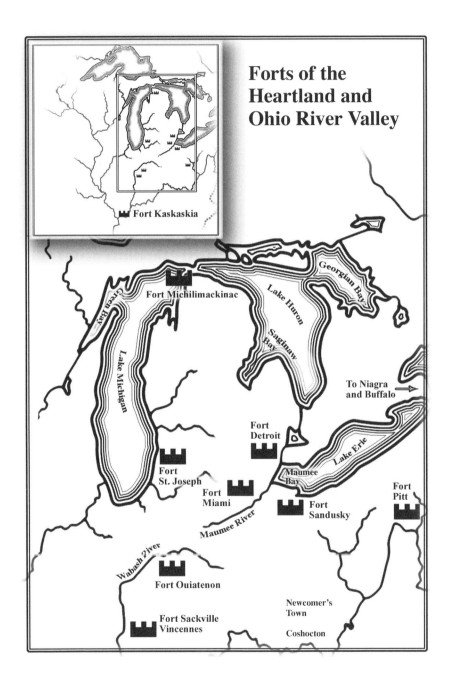

Forts of the
Heartland and
Ohio River Valley

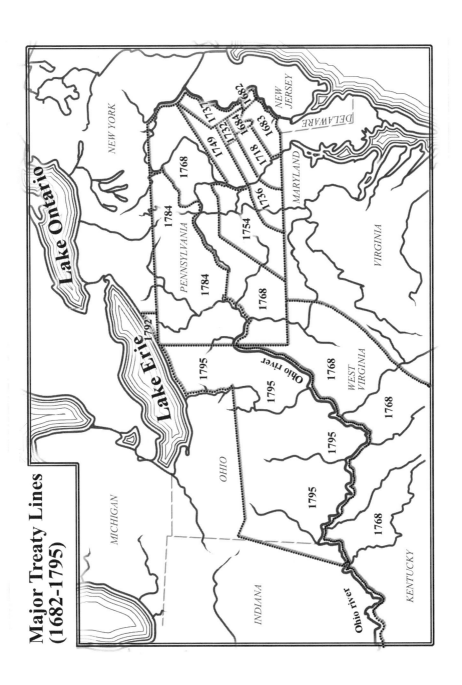

Major Treaty Lines (1682–1795)

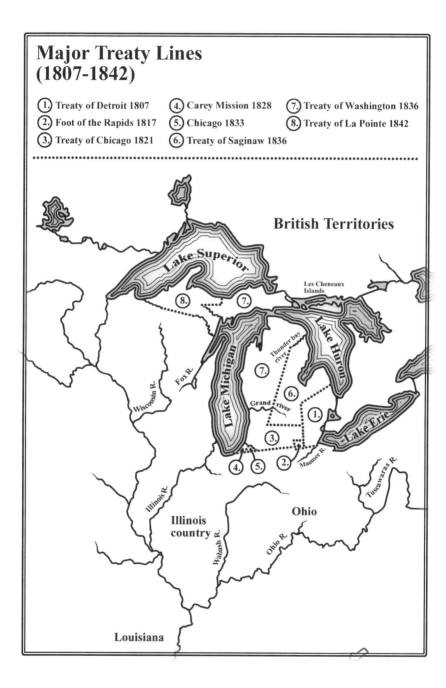

Major Treaty Lines (1807-1842)

1. Treaty of Detroit 1807
2. Foot of the Rapids 1817
3. Treaty of Chicago 1821
4. Carey Mission 1828
5. Chicago 1833
6. Treaty of Saginaw 1836
7. Treaty of Washington 1836
8. Treaty of La Pointe 1842

British Territories

Lake Superior

Les Cheneaux Islands

Lake Michigan

Lake Huron

Thunder bay river

Lake Erie

Wisconsin R.

Fox R.

Grand river

Maumee R.

Tuscarawas R.

Illinois R.

Illinois country

Wabash R.

Ohio

Ohio R.

Louisiana

Ancestors of Moira Zell "Pat" Dibert Wilson

Charles Frederic Debart D'Ibert Dibert (b.1660;d.1707)
John Dibert Debart (b.1685;m.1708;d.1732)
Magdalene Cartier Chartier (b.1661;d.1720)
Charles Christoper Dibert Deibert (b.1718;m.1736;d.1768)
Mary Seaworth (b.1687;d.1732)
Frederick E. Dibert (b.1750;m.1775;d.1826)
Eve Margaret Nei - Ney (b.1720;d.1757)
Michael Dibert (b.1793;m.1814;d.1874)
Madaline Steel (b.1770;d.1851)
Henry Dibert (b.1817;m.1840;d.1893)
Henry Adam Earnest (b.1740;m.1755;d.1777)
Henry Adam Earnest Jr. (b.1772;d.1857)
George Mark Imler (b.1705;m.1732;d.1788)
Eve (Indian Eve) Imler (?) (b.1734;d.1815) (Hillebartin)
Rudolph Schaber
EsterTheresia (Esther Anna) Schaber (b.1713)
Catharina Barbara
Susan Earnest (b.1795;d.1867)
David Miller
Margaret Miller (b.1766;d.1851)
Sarah Shoenfelt
David Henry Dibert (b.1852;d.1936)
William Bennett
Anthony Bennett (b.1776)
Nancy Jane Bennett (b.1809;d.1894)
George W. Espy
Nancy Espy (b.1785)
Mary Stewart
David Wilbur Dibert (b.1880;d.1920)
Susan Plummer (b.1851;d.1949)
Fred (aka Pat) Dibert (b.1913;d.1988)
Abraham L. Lingenfelter (b.1730;d.1813)
Jacob Lingenfelter (b.1762;d.1846)
Anna Barbara Stine (b.1732;d.1800)
George D. Lingenfelter (b.1808;m.1834;d.1892)
Margaret Neff (b.1768)
Thaddeus H or S. Lingenfelter (b.1848;d.1909)
Frederick Claar (b.1780;m.1800;d.1864)
Barbara Walter Claar (b.1816;d.1908)
Christina Walter (b.1780;d.1853)
Lucy Belle Lingenfelter (Dibert, Mauk) (b.1889;d.1964)
Margaret Susan Stine (b.1854)

(continued)

Ancestors of Moira Zell "Pat" Dibert Wilson (continued)

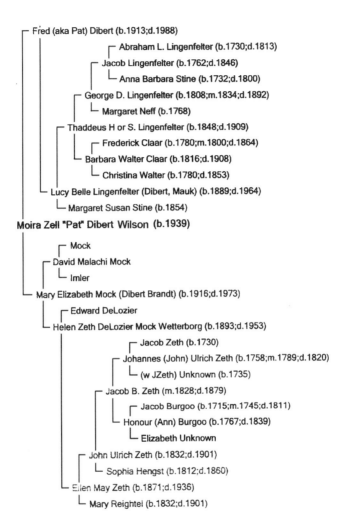

Fred (aka Pat) Dibert (b.1913;d.1988)
┌ Abraham L. Lingenfelter (b.1730;d.1813)
┌ Jacob Lingenfelter (b.1762;d.1846)
└ Anna Barbara Stine (b.1732;d.1800)
┌ George D. Lingenfelter (b.1808;m.1834;d.1892)
└ Margaret Neff (b.1768)
┌ Thaddeus H or S. Lingenfelter (b.1848;d.1909)
┌ Frederick Claar (b.1780;m.1800;d.1864)
└ Barbara Walter Claar (b.1816;d.1908)
└ Christina Walter (b.1780;d.1853)
└ Lucy Belle Lingenfelter (Dibert, Mauk) (b.1889;d.1964)
└ Margaret Susan Stine (b.1854)

Moira Zell "Pat" Dibert Wilson (b.1939)

┌ Mock
┌ David Malachi Mock
└ Imler
└ Mary Elizabeth Mock (Dibert Brandt) (b.1916;d.1973)
┌ Edward DeLozier
└ Helen Zeth DeLozier Mock Wetterborg (b.1893;d.1953)
┌ Jacob Zeth (b.1730)
┌ Johannes (John) Ulrich Zeth (b.1758;m.1789;d.1820)
└ (w JZeth) Unknown (b.1735)
┌ Jacob B. Zeth (m.1828;d.1879)
┌ Jacob Burgoo (b.1715;m.1745;d.1811)
└ Honour (Ann) Burgoo (b.1767;d.1839)
└ Elizabeth Unknown
┌ John Ulrich Zeth (b.1832;d.1901)
└ Sophia Hengst (b.1812;d.1860)
└ Ellen May Zeth (b.1871;d.1936)
└ Mary Reightel (b.1832;d.1901)

Family Tree as compiled by Roy Williams, Sr. based on current available information on the Web. Eve Earnest's maiden name increasingly reported as Hillebartin by other researchers.

Chapter 22   Mid to Late October
Among the Troops

Author's note: Nearly all events and facts in this chapter and subsequent chapters concerning the march to Vincennes are based on the personal journals or letters of Captain Norman MacLeod, Captain Joe Bowman, Colonel George Rogers Clark, and Lieutenant Governor Henry Hamilton.

> **"...it is evident that the said Philip Rochblave has done everything in his power to set the Indians against us. They are only too apt to accept of such offers. I am in hopes that his correspondence with them is entirely at an end, and wish that the executive power of Virginia may deal in the most severe terms with him, as no punishment can be too severe for the barbarity of his former proceedings."**

Captain Joe Bowman relating his experiences in the capture of Cahokia and Kaskaskia under the command of George Rogers Clark as quoted by William Hayden English, *Conquest of the Country Northwest of the River Ohio, 1778-1783 and Life of Gen. George Rogers Clark*, Vol. 1 (Indianapolis, IN: Bowen-Merrill Co., 1896), p. 194.

October 13,1778   At the Portage at Miami Town near Present Day Fort Wayne, Indiana

Francois Maisonville walked briskly along beside Captain Norman MacLeod. Boatbuilder and woodsman, this vital man moved with total confidence and self-assurance. American born, this Frenchman and member of the Detroit militia, survived with great skill. His easy humor was welcomed at any campfire. Unlike many of the English-types, he found MacLeod good company. He could be open with the man. Cloaking his thoughts in mannerly cover-ups proved unnecessary with Norman MacLeod.

"Well Captain. If you can't dazzle them, most try to bluff them with rum. You did neither."

"You approved."

"*Oui, monsieur*. I think it was adroit of you to show that the Americans can't protect their own. Good to point out the obvious, no? Your acknowledgement of the three scalps from their last raid, with more sure to come, showed that you recognized their abilities as warriors and their enemies' inability to stop their war parties.* The full boats coming will do the rest of it. Now they will finally know that the British mean what the say. Soon they will see Hamilton in dah flesh...that he is not a myth. Eh? He will make a good show and dance the dance."

"Yes, Francois, I think they now believe that he will fight beside them."

"The other point that you made about the Americans failing to give them lead and powder for the winter's hunt,* dhat was good. Better yet! The poor 'naked'* rebels who can not clothe themselves won't be able to clothe them."*

Maisonville grinned, raking his fingers through his jet black curly hair, curly hair for which he took great pride. His long locks hung loose about his shoulders.

"Hamilton, when he gets here, will really impress them. Hell, I will betcha dhat de Hamilton, he changes his uniform once every couple weeks. Maybe more, eh! Besides, I think he has half of Detroit's and Montreal's stores on them blame pirogues of his."

MacLeod chuckled at his friend's summary of his words. Good to know at least someone listened.

"I especially liked it when you told them that the Rebels were not asking for their help because they were afraid of the Miami. Very shrewd, Captain."

Then Maisonville clamped his hand on MacLeod's taller shoulder, as if to make sure that his seasoned companion heard him well. "But if I were you, sir, I would tread easier with the ones whose brains are soggy with a little rum and whose tongues run on. Sometimes they are the real troublemakers."

"Did my annoyance show that much?"

"*Oui*, it did. They're expecting Hamilton to supply them well with the milk of life. Certainly more than that last trader. When you said skilled warriors do not drink once they go to war and that you had set rum aside since you left Fort Detroit...eha...ah, that wore a bit thin."

MacLeod laughed. "I hear you, my good man." He chuckled again before he continued, "Maisonville, thank God, you came up with an excuse to leave. I think if I heard that one sloshed lad's account of his last raid for the fourth and fifth time, I would have been tempted to scalp him myself."

"Eh...ah," Maisonville nodded in agreement.

"I need you to take a report to Hamilton tomorrow. Can you do that?"

"But of course, Captain. You write it. I will make sure the Lieutenant Governor has it in his hands."

"We will need to administer the oaths of allegiance in the morning.* Will you help round up the locals?"

"*Oui*."

German=this font   English=this font   *French=this font*   *Delaware=this font*

"Really doubt their sincerity, especially some of them. But we will make sure it is more than lip service they give."

"Did you hear de Celeron say that there were two-hundred Virginians and two-hundred Frenchmen marching towards Fort Detroit by way of Chicago?*"

"Yes...I have heard him. Bobian heard him too."

"Well Captain, I doubt that they could round up two hundred Frenchmen to march on their brothers. In fact, I do not think you can get two hundred Frenchmen to march anywhere in same direction... anytime...anyhow. No?"

"Guard your tongue, Maisonville, but my intelligence tells me there are only forty Virginians at Vincennes,* and they do not plan to march anywhere either. I sent this on to Hamilton on the 11th and I have sent a few of my most trusted men ahead to check this out. I get little work out of this crew as it is, without fear to keep them in tow."

"Still having trouble with Nicholas Gowan?"

An exasperated sigh indicated MacLeod's only answer for a brief period. His head dropped, shaking with a sense of disbelief.

"That man will be late for his own funeral. He is sure to stop somewhere along the way."

"I thought you were just upset because he gave two of the King's best horses to his Indian friends for de winter hunt."

"That is only half of it. He makes one bloody portage or less a day! Anyone else could make two or three. Worse yet, he will tie up others while not doing his share. I truly want to strangle the man!"

"Patience, my good man. Patience. Scotsmen work far too hard, monsieur! And their curse is that they expect others to do it too!" Maisonville clamped his hand on MacLeod's shoulder once more in a gesture of warm good humor before turning away to his own tent.

Without the rays of sun to give warmth, the night frost hung on the air. Away from demands of the fire, both men sought the comfort of their bear skins. At least, at this time of the year, there would not be a chorus of flies and mosquitoes to annoy. Fall and the approaching winter had one true blessing...one would only have lice and bedbugs to contend with during the night. But MacLeod would not sleep this night through. An hour after MacLeod drifted off into a heavy slumber, Bobian fetched him for two more hours before a dwindling fire to hear another drunken rehash of earlier events.* MacLeod relented finally, giving the speakers an additional dram of rum to buy his leave before crawling once more between the welcome warmth of his bear skins.

*Norman MacLeod, *Detroit to Sackville, The Journal of Norman MacLeod. September 25-26, 1778 to January 12, 1779* (Detroit, MI : Wayne State University Press, 1978), p. 15-36.

German=this font   English=this font   *French=this font*   *Delaware=this font*

Mid-day, October 14, 1778, North of the Miami (Maumee) River, a Few Leagues from Lake Erie

Lieutenant Governor Hamilton looked across at the many crowded tents dotted over the fall-brown field. The encampment of so many allies nurtured his pride. More came daily to join his forces, forsaking their winter hunts. The Chippewa had hosted him and his officers to a bear roast last night. The Ottawa would host him this evening. A little one-upmanship among the lake tribes of the Three Fires, the Chippewa had one bear; the Ottawa had a she-bear and a cub.*

More good news than bad had come to Hamilton's attention since their precarious landing. Hamilton increasingly felt he had good reason to despise Monsieur de Celeron, a merchant appointed by Abbot to preside in his absence when the inept Abbot left his post in an untimely fashion. He feared the man could be a double agent. De Celeron had a wagging undisciplined tongue. Was he truly a terrified merchant, who spread tales at every turn of the River regarding the approach of the Virginia Long Knives, or did he work for the Americans by spreading a false fear? De Celeron, his Ottawa scouts reported, had hopped back and fourth across the river among the cabins of the Ottawa, like a 'bad bird'.*

An additional inconvenience resulted when Shroud, one of his lieutenants, accidentally shot himself in the leg. Unfortunately, the surgeon, Doctor McBeath would be needed to accompany the clumsy officer back to Fort Detroit. Luckily, the short distance insured that the surgeon would not fail to return. One must certainly keep a doctor just in case Hamilton or his men should need medical assistance.*

Hamilton preferred instead to consider the many good omens that he had found here at the foot of the Rapids on the banks of the Maumee. Even the size of the river had pleasantly impacted on him. On the maps, the Maumee had looked barely navigable. To his great relief, he found that the river was much larger than most of the River Thames in England. This river, like many in the new world, proved larger than any river he had encountered in any of the 'three kingdoms' of his homeland. Standing on the precipice of Rocher de Bout, Hamilton observed his men struggling to pole and to push the heavily laden boats about the huge twenty-five foot high rock which hung over the swirling waters. The river remained low despite the recent rains. Once past these rapids, he had been assured that the way would be smoother. The sounds of cracking wood and occasional oaths punctuated the cool day.

So far, for the most part, the depth of the Maumee had proved very navigable. One result, Captain Grant's delivery and departure on the sloop, *Archangel*, went smoothly. The fourteen tons of supplies were offloaded with few problems. After their harrowing night on the Great Lake and the thorough drenching only days before, the men's spirits were revived by an enjoyable meal of hot turkey. Some enterprising Huron, only six in number, had quickly harvested fifty wild turkeys.* Hamilton had given

German=this font   English=this font   **French=this font**   *Delaware=this font*

strict orders for his own men not to shoot the birds from the pirogues, as they might accidentally plug those who walked the shore.* Thankfully, these men conducted themselves with excellent deport. Correspondence from the MacLeod's party ahead of him brought increasingly good news. Sir William Johnson's Scot, MacLeod, proved himself more valuable each day. The man's skill with the tribes, having worked with Johnson's earlier Indian department and his military expertise, appeared evident in his reports. Unlike some of his wishy-washy French Canadians, this man could get things done. Though the brash Scot annoyed him on many occasions, Hamilton devoutly wished on this day that he had a hundred more like MacLeod.

As he walked, Hamilton could smell the odor of fresh-baked bread wafting in the autumn air from the twelve cabins.* The Ottawa squaws had generously shared their hearths and ovens with his bakers.* Across the river, he observed the earlier drenched powder and bread stores drying in the open sun. Looking skyward, he gratefully acknowledged the turquoise sky marred only by occasional multi-gray and white clouds. A clear sky called for frost.

Hamilton made a mental note to be sure that the milk of kindness did not flow too heavily as he traveled. Already, he could detect the savages' awe at the sheer amount of goods and the size of his vessels. These proved beyond any of their doubts the profundity of his majesties supplies. This image reinforced the bounty of the English compared to the poor upstart Bostonians, as the French called the Rebels. As he juggled to restrain the inter-tribal rivalries, petty turf wars rose again and yet again. Skillfully, Hamilton stressed that the tribes must recognize their common enemy, while he further convinced them that only the British could open the Mississippi to free trade and passage. This message carried the greatest weight, that and the promise that the King would be their supreme benefactor, meeting all their worldly needs and protecting them with his might.

Of course, Hamilton could always depend on the misconduct of the disorderly American militias, who continued to fuel the hatred of the tribes. The Rebel destruction of villages, plundering and looting of crops and property, and wanton destruction of lives, with little regard for those tribes who sought peace, or those who sought war, helped to bring more and more warriors to join the British cause. As a result, Hamilton's confidence grew with every passing day. He became increasingly certain that by the time he and his men reached Vincennes, he would amass an army that would put any rabble rounded up by the Americans to total shame. His forces would once more command the fort and the region for the King. Haldimand in Quebec and the London home office would relish his victory. The great heartland would return to the British fold.

Tired from the efforts of his unrelenting diplomacy, Hamilton turned wearily toward his own encampment. The tiny white tents stood in stark contrast to the earthen colored camps of the many tribes with their

German=this font   English=this font   **French=this font**   *Delaware=this font*

colorful feather staffs and banners blowing in the fall winds. Tonight, yet another council meeting would require his attendance.

*Barnhart, John D., Ed, *Henry Hamilton and George Rogers Clark in the American Revolution with the Unpublished Journal of Lieut. Gov. Henry Hamilton* (Crawfordsville, IN: R. E. Banta, 1951), p. 106-110.

Evening, October 14, 1778, About the Ottawa Fire

The 'mishinnawey'*, the appointed host and servant for the ceremonial meal, performed his tasks well. Hamilton tried not to let his mind drift as the native shaman, Macutte Wassong, invoked the blessings of the Great Spirit and sought to soothe the lesser ones. Although impressed by the reverence of the vermilion-painted Ottawa warriors, who sat in two long rows on either side of the fifteen-foot fire, the warmth and the lassitude of the event made inroads on Hamilton. He noted the similarity of customs between the Chippewa and Ottawa, since both were Anishinabeg. This meant that this evening's events would be nearly identical to the evening before, including sharing the head of the bear, a symbolic enemy, and the concluding war songs and war dance. As before, no women showed themselves during this ceremonial time. The old honored man, the mishinnawey, who presided over the large iron pot, began doling out the appropriate portions, reserving the choicest and fattest portions for those they wished to honor. He moved methodically from person to person.

Hamilton's stomach audibly growled in protest as he considered what would be his portion. Nearby, Hamilton could see the weapons of those assembled. The weapons of war, encircled around a pole, secured with a wampum belt and dusted well with red-ocher.

When a young warrior approached the mishinnawey, asking permission to speak before the assemblage, Hamilton took notice immediately. His attention focused sharply. Others paused to acknowledge the young warrior's presence.

The mishinnawey introduced the man as Neegik, the Otter. Hamilton recognized him immediately as the brother of Chamintawa, whom he had sent to see Gros Loup, the Miami chief. Gros Loup had conferred with the Rebels after their take over of the Fort Ouiatenon from the English.

The young warrior, with a sense of ceremony, stepped before the great fire to share his reconnaissance. Respectfully, he took great care not to step over any portion of the fire at any time.*

Hamilton became impressed again with the respect accorded each individual, regardless of age or rank. Once anyone held the speaker's position, he received quiet attention until he finished. Sometimes this meant that an old and windy elder or a drunken blow-hard vented at length. But each received his due. In many respects, Hamilton decided, this was far more civilized than the English Parliament.

German=this font English=this font *French=this font* *Delaware=this font*

Fired by a tiny jet of gas, a bright spark and ember struck the back of Neegik's leg. The young brave refused to acknowledge it. Stoically, he waited until it burned out on his flesh. All eyes centered on him. Then he spoke to those assembled. All waited with quiet anticipation. Immediately, the translator conveyed the man's words into English for Hamilton.

"I have spoken with Gros Loup, a Miami brother and chief from the West. He has seen the Long Knives and looked into their eyes. The Long Knives seek to capture Jean Baptist de Celeron." A few grunts affirmed his statement. "Before the Rebels called the elders and warriors together, they ripped the King's flag from the great staff before the Fort Ouiatenon. They filled it with rocks and threw it in the Wabash."*

Hay's face flushed with anger. His fists clenched tightly. But Hamilton, like the young warrior, refused to reveal any emotion.

"Then, they called us all together. They brought two wampum belts. One red. One green. They said we must choose. If we wished war...we must choose red. If we wished peace...we must choose green."*

A murmur of annoyance and anger rumbled through the assemblage like a rickety cart on a bumpy road.

"Old Tobacco said that they were horribly rude to bring two belts. 'What kind of people' crudely demands one to choose between two belts, between 'good and evil at one and the same time'?"* Neegik paused.

"One of our Potawatomie brothers became so angry that she kicked the belts. He threatened to attack the Rebels on the spot. But the old ones held her back from his temper by advising him to be wise on behalf of his wife and children."* This time a murmur of agreement rippled and shimmered around the fire like a wave of heat. Hamilton, from his experience with earlier translators, realized that some translators misunderstood the use of the feminine pronoun. The native speakers used a neuter pronoun unlike his more sophisticated English, so they failed to recognize the difference. He found this an amusing quirk in their language. Particularly when one realized that for his native allies to call a man, a woman or 'machicotte', a petticoat, constituted a major insult.*

Neegik waited for quiet to return before he continued. He knew how to pace his words and how to build to a climax. The insults made by the Rebels to the people would incite deep anger. He must reveal them now... insults which clearly exposed the viciousness and uncivilized nature of their enemy.

Neegik looked squarely at Hamilton as he continued. Steel reflected on steel.

"The Long Knives say that they will tread on any fire that is lit between here and Fort Detroit. If any barriers are built, they will tear them down and the splinters will wound anyone who stands in their way."*

German=this font   English=this font   **French=this font**   *Delaware=this font*

Neegik paused. "They will shut-up our father in a pen like a hog."*
Any insult which incorporated hogs constituted another major insult among
the people. Only to spit in a man's face or to bite off his nose remained
the 'penultimate indignity'.*

An audible hiss sounded. Hay inhaled sharply. Hamilton remained
stiff and unflinching.

"Once the hog is fattened, they will throw our Father in the River.
Then great forces will come to reinforce them from the Ohio River."*

Stillness reigned. One could have heard an owl fly. Even the fire
remained quiet.

Then laughter ignited like tiny flames of sparks in a pile of dry
tinder...first a small nervous laugh here...and then another flicker of
laughter there...followed by a chuckle here and a guffaw there.

One warrior summed it up finally to the satisfaction of all. "If they
can splinter all our barriers and stomp out all our fires all the way to
Fort Detroit, why do they need reinforcements?" *

Another added, "No Frenchman will march on Fort Detroit."*

Laughter dissolved the tension of the moment. Hamilton's translator
kept the pace of the dialogue skillfully. Hamilton joined uneasily in their
laughter. For a fleeting moment, he questioned his proposed task; but then
his composure instantly reasserted itself. The moment passed
entirely...willfully forgotten. After all, MacLeod's intelligence might be
correct. If it were, Hamilton's forces had an easy road ahead, while
impressing more and more tribes to heed his call to unity. They would
open the River Mississippi once more for British commerce. His
superlative diplomatic talents would be proved.

*Barnhart, John D., Ed. *Henry Hamilton and George Rogers Clark in the
American Revolution with the Unpublished Journal of Lieut. Gov. Henry Hamilton*
(Crawfordsville, IN: R. E. Banta, 1951), p. 110-112.

*Above the Rapids of the Miami,
in the Clearing near the River*

Tchamaniked Joe rammed the oakum into the open boat seam. He
disliked the odor of the tar and hemp mixture. While his fellow boat
carpenters would prefer that he use the caulking iron, he found the ax that
he had sharpened to a workable curve preferable. Perspiration stung his
eyes. He strained to see by the pale light of the lantern that burned
between him and Menard as they worked late into the night.

"What you think Chief. Wish yah had yer bear grease and pine
sap?"

Joe would not dignify the man's crude question with a retort, although
a few sharp replies whirled in his brain, begging to be voiced. The biggest

German=this font   English=this font   *French=this font*   *Delaware=this font*

crevice that he wanted to fill with grease and resin was the man's big mouth. He despised being called Chief in such a disdainful way. It was bad enough that he had to fetch and tote for men with half his skills or intelligence, without having to put up with their insults and their constant attempts to humiliate him. On the other hand, at least on this night, he did not stand chest-deep in the frigid river, cutting off branches that might cause holes in the flotilla of heavily laden pirogues.

Some of the men handled the boats ineptly. As a result, many of the canoes needed mending. He smiled to himself as he remembered how his manhood had shriveled and tucked within when submerged beneath the icy water. He wondered again to himself, what drove the European men to push themselves and their infernal devices? Why must they carry these ridiculously heavy loads to unrealistic places? They seemed bent on doing everything the hard way. Why not be more sensible and travel lightly? One could send pack horses with only the necessities. Joe could readily see another three full days of caulking, even if they worked nearly round the clock, especially given the recent toll on the boats from the rapids. Drawing a line from the catechism, Joe focused himself on the task before him. The rhythm of the chant lessened the monotony and his fatigue.

In the distance, the emerging sounds of drums indicated that the Ottawa war dance had begun. Joe fell into the comfort of the familiar beat, forgetting his earlier chant. He took up the later silently. No use alienating his work partner any more than he already did.

October 15 1778 at the Portage Site near Present Day Fort Wayne, Indiana

Maisonville paced about in Captain MacLeod's small tent. He hunched over, trying to avoid the ceiling at all costs for the rain that would follow his touch. The letters, all neatly wrapped in watertight skins and placed on the surface of his chest, caused his skin to itch under his shirt. They waited for yet another to join them.

"The nut, Pacane...how aptly named. Will he melt in the rain like de sugar, Mary, Mother..." Maisonville's voice trailed off before he had finished his oath. The impatience and anger of his second forced delay had clearly exasperated Maisonville. (Hamilton's sketch of Pacane in illustrations section)

A little deviltry edged the eyes of MacLeod as he looked up from his improvised desk. "Patience, Maisonville. Patience."

MacLeod continued writing more of Pacane's story and of the warrior's encounter with the Long Knives. Hamilton must be fully aware of MacLeod's suspicions about Old Tobacco and Young Tobacco. Rumors flew about the Tobaccos' selling large tracts along the Wabash to the American Wabash Company. MacLeod suspected that Tabaccos' groups

German=this font   English=this font   *French=this font*   *Delaware=this font*

were not squarely in the British camp, as thought previously. He knew that Maisonville had desired to leave yesterday, and again last night. But rather than irritate the head Chief of the Miami, Pacane, MacLeod had suffered him to wait. Maisonville could escort Pacane to Hamilton directly and thereby make a show-of-respect to the native leader. The reports proved consistent. A few Miami warriors recently reported that ahead, only twenty-five Long Knives remained to quarrel among themselves and to drink themselves into a stupor. This could be important intelligence. Hamilton would no doubt appreciate hearing it first hand. Already MacLeod had sent spies to Fort St. Joe and to the Wea to confirm the warrior's reconnaissance.

The Rebels continued to rile the tribesmen. Though apparently few in number, they proceeded from group to group along the Wabash with great brashness. Wild Beast had been roughed-up, for example, in a talking circle for saying that he did not believe the Virginians and that only their Father in Fort Detroit told the truth. This breach of native etiquette appalled the tribal assembly.

Narrowly, the Virginians had not been killed following the encounter. MacLeod wondered if the stupid fools had any sense of how close they had come to death. Daily, he felt that Providence had truly touched his life for the time he had spent with Sir William Johnson. Both as a father figure and as a mentor, few men on this continent understood or appreciated the native peoples as much as he. Years of shrewd observation and understanding had been passed on to those in his employ, and few more than MacLeod. At times like this, MacLeod devoutly wished that he could turn to his old friend and his Mohican consort, Molly Brant, for advice.

Norman MacLeod, *Detroit to Sackville, The Journal of Norman MacLeod. September 25-26, 1778 to January 12, 1779* (Detroit, MI: Wayne State University Press, 1978), p. 36-47.

Woodcock Valley near Coffey Run, Pennsylvania

George Elder and Richard Shirley trudged face-first into the biting November wind as they made their way through Coffey Run. Each thrust their bodies forward and kept their heads bent over to keep their eyes from watering. The sleet, without letup, pricked their faces. The bitter, penetrating wind meant that no amount of clothing could block the cold.

"How do you know that you can trust that man to take the money to free Margaret?" Shirley asked. "Hell, he's a breed. What's to say he won't be drunk for a week and take a roll in the hay?" Shirley spoke loudly as the sounds of wind howled about them. The scrunch of their steps on ice-crusted leaves made their passage noisier still.

"He brought Margaret's letter to her father. Cessna says he can

German=this font   English=this font   *French=this font*   *Delaware=this font*

be trusted." Elder struggled not to let his teeth chatter. "He said he traded with him before the troubles." Elder clasped the neck of his jacket tightly in his left fist in an effort to keep out the cold. His musket hung heavy in his right hand. His right side grew numb from cold and the weight of his fowling piece.

"Well, it's your father-in-law's money. But I don't think you can trust any of them that have had truck with the King's men."

Neither man considered themselves in danger. Neither doubted that the fall's faded warmth took with it the perils of an Indian summer attack. Neither man gave thought to the noise they made as they chatted and crunched their way home, crashing through the underbrush. Neither man heard the cock of the muskets as branches creaked and clicked about them. So, George Elder and his friend shared the fate of so many of the unlucky,* the unwary, or the hapless. Shot dead, his scalp and Shirley's would soon be stretched on anonymous willow hoops and arrive in Fort Detroit before Margaret Elder's ransom.

Replogle, Emma. *Indian Eve and Her Descendants* (1911. Bedford, PA: Reprinted by Messiah Lutheran Church, 1990), George Elder and Richard Shirley's story appears on p. 23.

German=this font   English=this font   *French=this font*   *Delaware=this font*

Chapter 23   November 1778
En Route to Justice

"The four nations of the Lakes—The Ottawas, Chippewas,
Hurons [Detroit Wyandots], and Pottawattamies—have
shown great attachment to his Majesty and Government.
The Shawanese, Mingoes and part of the Delawares have
been very active. They are stimulated as much by the late
incursion of the Virginians under Lord Dunmore and
their cruelties since as anything else. Some of them took
up the hatchet before they were asked; the rest upon
deliberation and in assurance of their being supported by
Government. And I must confess there never was known
an Indian war carried on with as little of their wanton
cruelty. Indeed, the sparing of the lives of prisoners, the
aged men, women and children, was insisted on from the
first; and they have paid great attention to it; and they
never went without some reward for their compliance."

Jehu Hay to Behm, September 1778 as quoted by Consul Wilshire Butterfield
in *History of George Roger Clark's Conquest of the Illinois and the Wabash
Towns 1778 and 1779*. (Boston: Gregg Press, 1972, original publishing date
1904), p. 168-169.

Fort Detroit

"Do you wish to carry it?" As usual, Nellie did not mince words.

"What?" Eve, distracted, tried to re-center her attention back to
Nellie, who had been babbling after she broke the news to her.

Nellie had been the only one Eve had told so far. She did not wait for
Eve to answer. Instead, she continued as before.

"I know two ways...the first less dangerous than the second. I
could put lye soap suds up mighty high. But the willow bolus is more
certain, unless you go to bleeding."

Eve evaluated what Nellie said from a vantage point that might have
been more than a hundred feet away rather than from their shoulder to
shoulder position. She felt as if she were somewhere else looking back on
herself and Nellie, measuring decisions from a point of detachment.

"It's much too late now to use Queen Ann's lace like we did for
Sue Ellen," Nellie observed wisely.

Eve had learned many years ago of the willow bolus, tightly wound
splinters of willow imbedded in God knows what, usually cow dung, that

sprang open inside the womb to instigate the abortion. She had seen firsthand a young woman bleed and then fade away with a horrid infection, dying a miserable, putrid death, her body swelling like a bloated toad. Eve would never deliberately put her life in harm's way; she had her two sons to consider. But abortion, as a choice for her, stood no chance of being sincerely considered in this instance. The danger of bearing another child could be danger enough, but one she met willingly. She had breached the curtain between life and death many times before. Besides, Eve had inwardly agreed to accept a child before she carried the apple to Joe. She barely acknowledged to herself that it had been her intent from their first sexual encounter.

Eve understood that Nellie considered her observations helpful, given the child would be a 'breed,' thus branding Mikie and Henry, and Eve as well. Nellie did not need to tell her how misplaced anger could be directed at those children of mixed blood, spilling onto other members of their families.

Eve had grown up with the Dibert's problems. She had observed that people could be so stupidly cruel. Unfortunately, she had to include her parents and some of her neighbors among that circle of intolerance. Smart folks recognized that the Dibert's family constituted good people, nothing more, nothing less. They had shared the burden of attacks just like their neighbors. Bloodlines made little difference to cruelty.

Eve accepted that there might be a time that she, too, could consider the abortion choice, Sue Ellen's being one. She shuddered at the thought of bearing a life that had been filtered through a heartless source of evil. The foul predator would surely have fouled and muddied any stream of life he passed on.

However, Eve felt a deep desire to preserve and to protect this flow of life that passed through Joe and her. From her simple view of the world, she believed that life did not suddenly materialize in a bright flash of magic, spontaneously generating. To her, only a fool believed the fairy tale where life zapped itself into being in a split second. Farming had revealed life to her in all its richness and sadness. She considered life a river. Sometimes one was privileged to continue a tributary, a branch that sustained the flow. No one could guarantee that the tributary would continue. Of course, one could choose to dam up the flow, like the celibate priests or nuns. Eve, on the other hand, had no desire to stop the flow. She paid the price willingly to be touched and to touch another in return, finding comfort in the union. Furthermore, she devoutly believed that the branch did not flow independent of the life before it or after it. But rather, life, not bound by time or person, became part of a miraculous whole. For Eve, one simply decided to be responsible for life's continuance...or not. She chose quite simply to be responsible.

Eve's affection for Joe meant to her that the promise of this child included a good man for a father when the time came. She felt that she had chosen well. Although she had not told Joe of this possibility upon his leaving, she already grew impatient for his return to share the good news. She just could not bear to burden him with any additional responsibilities when he left.

Finally, Eve interrupted Nellie mid-sentence. Poor Nellie did not realize that Eve had been lost in her own thoughts the whole time.

"Stop, Nellie. Stop, please. I know you mean well."

Nellie halted.

"Listen, Nellie. I want this baby! This heals me as nothing has in this whole rotten year. It feels so right to know that life can go on, despite the bastards who stalk and kill. I do not care which side you consider...Rebel. Indian. French. British. The whole lot of them! Mankind is all alike. There are good and bad among all of us." She stopped. "I once wished that I would not conceive another child of Adam Henry. I lost that one coming here, Nellie." Her voice choked up suddenly. Her eyes filled with tears. She shook her head as if trying to dispel a terrible memory. With effort, she continued. "Nellie, I just do not want to lose this one that is coming. Can you possibly understand how I feel?"

Nellie pondered her friend's words. Then she put her arm around Eve's waist. She gave her a sideways hug. "Yer a damn fine woman, Eve." Then she got a very sneaky grin. "How do yah think Margaret's goin' to take this news?"

Eve laughed aloud, throwing her arm around Nellie. "Oh, Nellie, that will be something to behold." She hugged her close, deliberately banging their hips together. "Nellie, you are a good friend. Thank you."

"And I'll just bet, woman, you never thought you'd live to say that," Nellie giggled, hugging her back and banging her hip in return.

The two women finished their tête-à-tête. They both relished the near privacy of a Sunday afternoon. Yankee Hall stood almost empty. Most everyone had gone to the horse race just outside of town. A good horse race took one's mind off the mud duties at the new fort. The boys napped near the fireplace, enjoying a break from the wet and cold.

Sue Ellen, still too weak to wait tables, slept fitfully. The two women noticed her stirring, poured water from the kettle, and took her a cup of hot tea.

As Eve knelt beside her, Sue Ellen's eyes flickered open.

Sue Ellen managed her usual weak, closemouthed smile in an attempt to cover her missing teeth. She struggled to come up to a sitting position and loosely wrapped her thin arms around her bunched skirt and her increasingly skinny legs. She felt some better now, although she had been having a touch of fever lately. Thankfully, no one else around her had caught it.

"Tea?" Eve extended the cup towards her.

"Thank you."

"Do you want a little sugar?" Nellie asked.

"No, this will be fine."

German=this font   English=this font   *French=this font*   *Delaware=this font*

Sue Ellen looked about. She appeared to be relieved as well to find herself pretty much alone in the Hall for a change. She looked around a second time and then she spoke very softly.

"I needs to ask you somethin'."

"Well what is it, Missy?" Nellie spoke in her usual brash manner.

"Shh-hh, I need to speak soft."

Nellie, no fool, settled quickly.

"What's botherin' you, girl? Don't be shy." Nellie covered Sue Ellen's knee with her hand and spoke softly. "You know'd us good. Don't shy-up on us."

Eve appreciated her brassy friend more each passing day. Whatever else one might think of her, Nellie could be kind to those she loved. When Nellie loved, she held nothing back, absolutely nothing. Sadly, if she hated, the feeling was twice as intense. Momentarily, Eve felt some sting yet from the remembered accusations that Nellie had made about her association with the Jews when Mikie had had the measles. Blessedly, no child in the hall had died from that cycle of illness. One poor woman miscarried about that same time, but that happened often in the way of things.

Sue Ellen looked around the room again. She noted who was where and the distances between. She observed that both of the boys slept.

"I gotz somethin' funny."

Eve looked concerned. "What is it, Sue Ellen?"

Sue Ellen again cased the room. "I got strange sores in my mouth."

"What are you talking about?" Nellie edged closer.

"Why do you think they are strange, Sue Ellen?" Eve asked, noting that Sue Ellen seemed spooked.

"They ain't sore, that's what. Ain't a sore supposed to be sore?"

Eve cocked her head. "Generally, I would say so."

"En' the hot tea don't bother them a bit. Not at all. They's jes' hard. I can feel the outer ridge with my tongue."

Nellie suddenly looked very concerned. "Do you think I could see them with my mirror?" She asked Sue Ellen.

"I don't know...I guess so." Sue Ellen pressed against her cheek with her tongue, bulging it out a ways. "I think you could see the one inside my cheek."

Eve watched as Nellie rummaged through her small basket of possessions and extracted the small three-cornered fragment of a mirror that she had found in the street one day. She had burnished the corners on a rock to round off their sharpness. It might have been seven years bad luck for another, but Nellie considered it a true find. She crawled back to where Sue Ellen sat.

"Now just where is it...?" Nellie took the cup from Sue Ellen and passed it back to Eve.

"There are two...one up near my gum and one on my cheek." She pushed her cheek out again. "I can feel them both with my tongue." Sue Ellen tipped her head back.

German=this font English=this font **French=this font** *Delaware=this font*

Angling the tiny mirror, Nellie reflected a ray of light within and looked carefully at the small raised chancre on the inside of Sue Ellen's cheek. The whitened edge was indeed raised. The center glistened an angry red. There did not appear to be any blood or ooze of pus. She could not see the one on the gum, but she took Sue Ellen's word for it.

Nellie rocked back on her heels. The next question that she asked pained her to the core to ask it. But she knew enough to ask the right question.

"Sue Ellen, I sure hates askin' you this, girl. I hates to, oh Lordy. But did that foul man..."

Eve could sense for the very first time since she had known Nellie that the woman was having a hard time trying to say what she desired to say. Beads of perspiration began to appear on the Nellie's forehead. This hard, tough woman, who never seemed to be flustered about anything and who could say well nigh anything to anybody, appeared visibly shaken.

Nellie glanced away, gathered her strength, and finished her question. She leaned very close to Sue Ellen as she did so. Eve barely heard her.

"...Did that foul man put his tally wag in yer mouth?"

Shock and revulsion impacted Eve like a slammed door upside her head. The cup rattled in her hand as she reeled from repulsion.

Sue Ellen fell forward, so no one could see her face. She reddened from her chest to her forehead. Shame cloaked her.

Nellie did not press her. She waited. Neither spoke for a very long time. When Nellie perceived the steady flow of tears which dripped from Sue Ellen's chin, she pulled Sue Ellen into her arms, rocking her just as Eve would rock the boys. They whispered very softly to each other. Then Nellie slowly released her.

Sue Ellen, completely debilitated by the question, rolled herself up into the smallest ball possible, and whimpered.

Nellie covered her tenderly with a blanket. She stroked her face, her hair, and patted her shoulders gently.

When the girl quieted, Nellie crept over to Eve. Nellie sat very hushed for a very long period. At last she spoke. "She bit the bastard hard," Nellie said under her breath. "That's why she lost her teeth."

Stunned, Eve could say nothing. What courage her young friend had in the face of such unthinkable evil.

When Nellie perceived that Sue Ellen had drifted off into another fitful sleep, she motioned to Eve to join her by the door where no one would hear them, including Sue Ellen.

"Damn him to hell. I hope he roasts on a slow spit," Nellie said softly as she looked out the door. Her face filled with undisguised hate and rage for the unknown rapist.

Eve waited. She had absolutely no idea how or why Nellie had proceeded or acted as she had. She only sensed that her friend understood something that she did not. Something had disturbed a woman that she thought was totally unflappable.

German=this font   English=this font   *French=this font*   *Delaware=this font*

"I sure as hell hope I'm wrong, Eve. I heard tell of this stuff when I was a young'n. My Daddy, he were a mighty tough man. He done cut the balls off a man once that he know'd spread it. I overheard him drunk and braggin' about it to his friends."

"What, for God's sake, are you talking about, Nellie?"

Nellie sighed. "We have got to take her down to see Dr. Anton. I sure hope it ain't so. But Eve, I know'd of only one sore that ain't sore...that's them French pox. She's been Frenchified."

Eve's soul felt ripped open again. The scab that had neatly formed over her many wounds had been torn. She sensed that this could be worse than death for her beautiful young friend. Words failed to come.

The two women stood staring vacantly out the door. They watched another group of storm clouds blow in off the lakes and shivered from cold that came from within. In the distance, they could hear the cheers for the latest horse race.

In Another Section of Fort Detroit

"Jeannie, Jeannie come quickly, child. There is a letter from your father. Come quickly."

Jeannie looked up from her swing. As usual, the Solomon boys were peering covetously over the small low fence wishing that they had a swing. Having no tree in their yard prevented their father from hanging one.

"Yes, Mama."

Jumping from the swing, Jeannie landed with both feet and sprinted unladylike to the door. Helen was tempted to reprove her for her behavior, but deferred, since it was she who admonished the child to hurry.

It took only moments for the adolescent girl to settle on her father's favorite foot stool, chin in both fists and eyes full of expectation.

My dearest Helen and beautiful Jeannie...

Already we tire of the rain. Early on, I had hoped to extend our progress in the moonlight but Messieurs Loren and Gowin correctly predicted wind and waves rise with the moon We satisfied ourselves instead by permitting a hunt for fresh game, so we need not exhaust our larder too soon. The following day, the 27th, we were becalmed resulting in a late arrival, near ten I recall. The following morning it poured until near noon. Then we had to battle head winds all the way to the next port. Rain again on the 29th, the deluge began so terribly early before we awoke and near to seven in the early evening before let up. Already the flour bags are soaked. The firkins of butter float about in our pirogues.

If it were not so tragic to see those tiny firkin ships adrift

German=this font   English=this font   *French=this font*   *Delaware=this font*

in our loaded dugouts, one could laugh heartily. So far we have lost nary a one. We will need those at the carry-overs to grease the cart wheels. We have none to spare.

But I am warm, dearest hearts, whenever my thoughts turn to you. I have but to think of your radiant smiles and my spirits lift.

Dear Helen, do remind MacGregor to watch for the shipment from Sandusky. That will help to put change in your pocket and provide well for you in my absence.

As ever, I remain your loving husband and Jeannie's adoring father.   Captain Norman MacLeod
this last day of September.

What MacLeod did not tell his wife and daughter at the time of his letter writing concerned the arrival of two Frenchmen, herding Isaac William's cattle to Sandusky on his way to Fort Detroit. The sounds of their cattle bells had first alerted the guards to the party, which included two of William's sons. On the 29th, they informed MacLeod that three thousand Virginia long-knives marched en route to Fort Vincennes as part of an attack force against Fort Detroit. Although the information proved fourth-handed, Lieutenant Governor Hamilton would be promptly alerted. These reports were touted to be accurate, according to the Frenchmen, who claimed that their source was a merchant named de Celeron.

At that time, MacLeod decided not to share that information for fear of terrifying his dear wife, Helen. The conflicting reports that he received daily disturbed him. This latter one could be far-fetched.

But far away in a cold tent, MacLeod offered up a silent prayer during the night that in doing his duty, his life would be spared. He admonished himself to address one day at a time on this four hundred mile mission for God and King, while a part of him chose to ignore what he felt might be an ambitious fool's folly to curry favor. The lag in time from message to viewer meant the news was late as usual and the conditions often far different than when the letter had been written.

Norman MacLeod, *Detroit to Sackville, the Journal of Norman MacLeod, Sept 25-26, 1778 to January 12, 1779* (Detroit, MI: Wayne State University Press, 1978), p. 3-8.

German=this font   English=this font   **French=this font**   *Delaware=this font*

En Route to Fort Laurens, November 10, 1778
West of Fort Pitt, North of Gnadenhutten
in Eastern Ohio, America's Newest Outpost

Whispers in the night between Virginian militiamen flowed just as quietly as did the darkened Tuscarawas River by the new site of Fort Laurens. Rebel forces had built the fort to protect their western edge, which incidentally included the Delaware tribes of the Ohio area, who expected protection from the British forces after their recent treaty. However, shadows often cover foul deeds.

"By'dee Christ, man, you stabbed the tawny bastard in the back."

"Aye, that I did. And I tell yah, every stroke of me knife felt good and right!" Youthful arrogance permeated each word.

"Captain McIntosh ain't goona like dis at all."

"Aye, White Eyes, he were paid to be our guide," a third voice added.

"He was a Colonel for Christ's sake," chimed a fourth.

"Colonel, be damned. Guide, yes. Guide to hell. Sure'n the tawny bastard would guide us right into ambushes. That he would. You all know that. Now he'll ne'r get the chance."

"I wouldn't scalp him if'n I were you."

"Yer choice, not mine. He'll feel real fine lining me ball pouch," the young militia man bragged.

"By'dee Christ, man."

Gnadenhutten, Ohio, Mid-November

Stalking Wolf spoke softly. He had no wish to wake Little Fox.

"My sister, why would the Rebels not relinquish Koquethagachton, White Eyes, to his family so that they could call upon the Great Spirit to guide him as he walked-on? Who will make offerings of tobacco and herbs so that his spirit may follow the smoke?"

"Sh-h-h. The brothers may hear you speak of heathen ways."

"What is wrong with you, my sister? You speak as if Delaware ways are shameful."

Singing Grass stopped weaving her basket. She pulled the last black ash lace tightly with her teeth before she spoke. *"Listen, my brother, you who still bears the scars of the sickness, White Eyes carried the killing pox. The good white brothers say he died from this. You would not wish Coshocton and its people to become ill again with the great sickness, would you?"*

Stalking Wolf pulled a straw from between his teeth, throwing it on the dirt floor of the neat cabin. The restlessness that sometimes plagued him brought him to his feet.

German=this font   English=this font   *French=this font*   *Delaware=this font*

"You need wood for the fire." Pulling a blanket from the wall peg, he left the cabin. The cold night air assaulted him. His breath in a dense white cloud contrasted with the cloudless, crystal clear night awash with light.

This night, stars could be touched. The spirit path marked a visible trail with many glowing footprints of those who crossed the heavens. Stalking Wolf gazed. How had the Delaware lost favor with the Great Spirit? Especially on nights like this, he felt confident that he could see the paths of the lost ones. Each year, the true people's numbers diminished. Even the new adopted ones could not stem the losses. In time, the night sky would be as bright as day with their many paths. What had happened for so much to come to pass? The Delaware had always been faithful stewards. He remembered his own grandfathers well. As a small boy, he had admired their faithfulness. His grandfathers always offered tobacco and said prayers when the sun arose each day. They worshipped, trusting their gods completely, but still the numbers of the white ones grew, bringing more sadness with each and every passing year. Were not the Delaware called to be the Grandfathers of all the tribes? Those called to carry the mantle of justice?

Armed with white man's guns, the Iroquois League had beaten the Delaware unmercifully, calling them cowards, women...petticoats. At least the Delaware had been spared the fate of the Erie. All the Erie walked among the stars, every last one. For the victors, the Iroquois confederacy had awarded the Erie ancestral lands to the Wyandot and other Hurons. Stalking Wolf had always considered it truly ironic that the great water would be named for the Erie, when none remained to walk its beautiful fruitful shores. He wondered how long his people would continue to walk the green paths of the Ohio Valley, especially now.

Stalking Wolf walked to the wood and brush piles deposited earlier by the women and smaller boys for the community. As he picked a fresh supply, he considered Isaac, who no longer answered easily to Glikhikan. As a long time friend and advisor to White Eyes, Isaac had wept openly at the loss of the great man. Lamenting the death of the great peacemaker, Isaac had openly expressed that perhaps the weaker Delaware would take up the hatchet and would accept the wampum belts from the English. He wondered aloud at what would happen to White Eyes' three sons. The white brothers had promised them an education in their finest schools. Issac feared for White Eyes' sons as this did not always help a boy to become a true man. Sometimes these men returned utterly useless, unable to hunt or support themselves.

Brother Zeisburger and Brother Heckwelder also expressed their fear that more Delaware would march with the British following in the ways of war.

Stalking Wolf had heard the rumors and wondered where the path to truth lay. He could tell that the Moravian missionaries considered it a perfect opportunity to explain the necessity to follow the ways of peace.

German=this font   English=this font   *French=this font*   *Delaware=this font*

He felt that the white brothers suggested in an oblique way that White Eyes had not truly followed the way of peace when he had accompanied the Rebel Troops. They almost suggested that perhaps White Eyes' life might have been spared had he followed the true path. This made little sense to Stalking Wolf, as it seemed to him that the smallpox came to all, white and true people alike, young or old, good or bad. The only real difference that he could see was that the white ones seemed to die less often than his own people.

As Stalking Wolf turned towards the cabin, he felt as if he floated upon an island of peace amid a sea of war. The thin parchment hides at his window glowed with the warm golden light of their late fire. Here, industry and plenty abounded. A bountiful harvest promised little hunger this winter. As he surveyed the work of his hands, he remembered when he had built the small cabin earlier in the fall for his sister and nephew. The Brothers had objected. They felt that his sister should continue to stay with the single women in their quarters, and he with the single men. The Brothers preferred to segregate the unmarried women and men. When Stalking Wolf told Isaac that if he could not have his own cabin with his sister and nephew, he would not stay; Isaac had prevailed upon the white Brothers. In the end, they begrudgingly granted him and Singing Grass the right to live apart. He wondered why these white brothers feared the mixing of the men and women so? Did they think he was so little of a man that he would take a woman against her will, even worse yet, his own sister? Had the lot not been in his favor, he realized that he would have been asked to leave.

Many things settled ill with him here. Stalking Wolf tired of the Brothers' continual effort to persuade him to take a new name and to become a new man in the Body of the Christ. He felt strange about surrendering his name. What was so wrong with his Delaware name? To be of the Wolf clan and to carry the name Wolf constituted a great honor. Their constant efforts to teach him German wore on his patience. A long list of dos and don'ts stipulated every approved activity and many disapproved activities. But he would honor his grandmother and stay the winter. Before entering the cabin, he took one last glance at the spirit path. What true path should he follow? What did the Great Spirit desire of him? Could Red Fawn Woman, his tall daughter, Willow, or his small son see him here on his lonely path? In that moment, he felt an unbearable thirst. He longed for the numbing effect of rum to ease that painful memory and admit him to the spirit world. Reluctantly pushing those thoughts aside, he re-entered the cabin.

German=this font   English=this font   *French=this font*   *Delaware=this font*

November 14, 1778   En Route to the Crossover near Fort Ouiatenon

Tchamaniked Joe guessed that nearly 14,000 pounds of goods had been carried on the land the day before to lighten their loads. Poling failed as the poles coated with ice with every thrust. His legs, sliced from having climbed into the icy water to lift and to push the pirogues through the water the day before, throbbed. The sharp broken pieces gashed a man's leg at any unguarded moment with only the feeling of intense burning before one grew wise to the oozing warmth of one's own blood escaping into the frigid water. He blessed Eve again for her thoughtfulness. When he had received the small pot of thick Seneca oil, he had felt quite amused by her gift. Now he marveled at her foresight. He still had one string of dried clams over his shoulder, so he felt no hunger. Three of the clams a day could keep him going, especially when he ate them with moistened bits of the pemmican made of smoked deer tallow, maple sugar, dried corn meal and dried fruit that he carried from his home. Both supplies dwindled of late. Perhaps he could trade his carved spoons or bowls for more from a kind woman when they reached Fort Ouiatenon.

The great father, Hamilton, must go on...snow, sleet, ice, no matter what, it seemed. Joe ached to the bone. His open canoe gave him little protection from the blowing winds and snow. Squinting, he could just see Hamilton's boat before the pirogue ahead. He knew instinctively that the man huddled down in a warm nest of bear skins with hot brandy as twenty or so men worked in the swirling water about his boat. Again today, the ice clung with every dip of the pole. The Lieutenant General would be lifted and poled, no matter the struggle, to continue his forward progress. And come the night, Joe and his now mostly quiet partner would clear the site for his tent before finally being allowed to find their own warmth and shelter.

Menard, his fellow carpenter, had fewer wisecracks of late. He, too, huddled in his bear skin as Joe skillfully guided their canoe through ice and projecting wood. Though Menard would never think to compliment Joe, he appreciated that their canoe magically mended in the night and proved to be drier than most.

Joe chuckled to himself at the thought of how the man tried to keep his wooden teeth from clattering. Finally, when the noise disturbed Menard to the limit of his own embarrassment, he removed his teeth and tucked them in his pouch. His face then caved in on itself and made him appear elfin-like as he curled deeper in his bear skin.

As Joe rocked his paddle from the hips and waist, moving their craft slowly amid the ice flows, he reflected on the words of Le Petit Gris, the Miami Chief. Last night, the Chief had spoken with much wisdom to the Miami and many others assembled. Joe wondered if the young bucks would heed his advice and guard their words and actions, so those of rival

German=this font   English=this font   *French=this font*   *Delaware=this font*

factions would not take offense. Give the devil his due, Hamilton kept the people working together. Joe hoped that Hamilton realized how much great men like Le Petit Gris helped him. Joe pushed away one rather sharp piece of ice, took note that Menard had dozed off again, and continued to wonder if the Chief's admonition not to run when the bullets dropped 'thick as drops of rain' would stick. Le Petite Gris, the Dappled Fawn, urged them 'to die well in this type of battle that the English Father preferred'.*

But, to die so stupidly continued to perplex Joe. He remembered reading about it when he had studied in Rome. White people, for whatever reason, felt valor meant simply to line up and to shoot at each other, step over the dead and shoot again. Over and over, until enough living remained on one side to claim a bloody victory. He noted that the weapons had changed over time, but the basic elements of their battles remained unchanged from the times of early Rome and Greece. He questioned momentarily the reason that the English wore bright red and the French, a brilliant blue. Why not do as his brothers? Was it not better to camouflage your body, advance with great stealth, attack with minimum loss, adopt the survivors, and then fade away quickly when finished. The whites must have an unending supply of people to waste them so foolishly, he decided. Then he laughed at himself for being silly enough to have such thoughts. His mind must be frozen.

*Barnhart, John D. Ed., *Henry Hamilton and George Rogers Clark in the American Revolution with the Unpublished Journal of Lieut. Gov. Henry Hamiltom* (Crawfordsville, IN: R. E. Banta, 1951), p. 120.

Late November, Fort Detroit

For the second time, the three women had come to him. After checking the swellings about her throat, Dr. Anton gently turned Sue Ellen's pale hands over in his larger ones.

In the service of the Crown, Dr. Anton utterly understood that his primary care responsibilities must be for the Fort's soldiers and sailors. But whenever he found a free moment, he served the local population as well. He felt that too few trained doctors resided here in the new world settlements not to do so.

Any feelings of superiority during his practice had been erased from the physician's personality. These traits were long shamed into non-existence as he strove to bring some comfort to the afflicted. His compassion grew when he observed the daily plight and courage of those he served, along with the stark realization of his own ability to genuinely aid so few of them as they suffered. The realization of his failings in so many instances humbled him. His kindness remained centered within a tough outer shell.

German=this font   English=this font   *French=this font*   *Delaware=this font*

Dr. Anton took great care not to touch the tiny eruptions that had just become faintly visible on Sue Ellen's palms. He asked her to lift her skirt and to bare her legs. Once she removed her stockings, he could look at the soles of her feet. He saw no sense in looking at her privates a second time, which would only humiliate her further. Truth would be revealed soon enough without that examination to confirm the second stage.

Sue Ellen blushed as her ankles came into his view. Her hands shook as she held her skirt to her knees modestly. On the soles of her small callused feet, he could see the eruptions emerging to the surface. Uneasy, not because of any training, he asked her to re-dress. Due to his own inner discomfort, he wiped his hands on a tiny half-soiled towel that he kept tied to the side of his office chair for just such occasions.

Eve and Nellie stood nearby. Silent and supportive, each waited to part, without a moment's hesitation, with the few coins saved from their heavy labors for his expertise.

"May I speak freely before your friends? Or would you prefer that we speak alone, my child?"

Wide-eyed, frightened, and trembling, Sue Ellen nodded affirmatively. She looked fleetingly at Eve and Nellie to draw on a little courage before returning her attention to Dr. Anton's grave face.

"Dear child, ye do have the pox still. Sad to say, yer friend, Nellie, is correct. It has come back."

Tears welled up around the room. Even Dr. Anton had to fight to restrain this reaction to his own words. She bloomed so pretty this one, so dainty, so like a pale spring lilac filled with the sweet scent of possibilities. Man's cruelty to others seemed unlimited to him sometimes. Bad enough that the poor child suffered sodomy, rape, and a vicious beating nearly to her death; he must share yet another horror with this sad young woman.

"I had truly hoped that the sores would leave you and not return. As I told you all earlier, sometimes they do. But now, I believe you are taking the pox within. From my experience, I believe you must be very careful not to touch others, since these new sores are coming on."

"And just how, in the name of Christ, will she do that?" Nellie blurted out.

"Well," the doctor rocked back on his chair, sighing as he did. He clasped his hands behind his softly curled and graying hair. His chair creaked as he leaned back. "We need to make gloves for her. And you must take great care that the children do not touch her now. She may be contagious, but probably only by directly touching the sores." He bit his lower lip absent mindedly for a moment and then he continued, "I do not think that she needs to wear a mask unless more sores come about her mouth. I believe that you can breathe freely about her. We really are not certain how this spreads." He reflected again and returned his clasped hands to between his knees. He gave them time to

German=this font   English=this font   *French=this font*   *Delaware=this font*

absorb his words fully. He leaned forward slightly. "However, I would keep her victuals and dishes separate."

Eve frowned.

"She won't be able to work at Fogherty's," Nellie realized aloud.

"You are quite correct, Nellie." Dr. Anton continued, "I have some mercury salve for the sores. Some mercury salts or arsenic that she can drink. But if she takes too much, she could become daffy or have convulsions."

"Sounds like the bloody cure is as bad as the damn French pox." Nellie voiced the obvious again. She felt driven to speak aloud in order to comprehend what she heard.

"That may be true, Mistress. These sores will go away in time too. And then she can be with others in most ways. But sadly, dear child, I fear this may not be the end of it." At this juncture, Dr. Anton slowly arose and stepped over to the bookshelf near his littered desk. "My colleague in London made these sketches for me from some of his pox patients there. He has noticed these effects among many of his patient's children." Shuffling through a stack of paper, he pulled three heavier sheets with brown curled edges from among the others. Across the surface, drawings of children covered the triptych.

"I find no pleasure to show these to you, young woman. But you must know that you must never have children, or the inflicted curse you have been given will most likely be visited upon them."

Simultaneously, the three women soughed. Their soft moans filled the office as Dr. Anton returned to his patient.

Holding the pictures up side-by-side before him, he directed their attention to strange jagged teeth, queer spade shaped heads with abnormally high sloped foreheads, nearly blind watery eyes, and thin misshapen limbs. Obviously, the children were dull. The gaping ulcerative lesions and the bulbous swellings on tiny babies and young children Mikie's age impacted upon the three women most severely. On some of the tiny wretches, one could hardly see the features of their small twisted faces, which were obliterated by ghastly sores. Sue Ellen stared at each of the drawings intently, cradling her lower face with both hands to prevent any outcry. No tears could come. Horror dried her ducts.

Eve and Nellie stood angrily rigid. Dr. Anton replaced the drawings to their former slot in the stack and returned to his chair.

"Young woman, you must know that there is not one among us who does not wish to clamp you to our breasts...to hold you close...to soothe your pain." But then Dr. Anton directed his attention fully to the two older women who stood before him. "But we must not!" His words stung. "We will be able to do this in due time.....but that time is not now. Do you both understand?"

Neither Eve nor Nellie answered him. Anger and helplessness silenced them. Eve touched her softly mounded abdomen. A small butterfly-like movement fluttered beneath the warmth of her hand.

German=this font English=this font *French=this font* *Delaware=this font*

Sue Ellen remained mute. She looked down at the floor.

Dr. Anton bent forward, his chair creaking.

"Do you all understand?"

Sue Ellen finally spoke as she raised her face and squared her shoulders. "Yes, I understand. I am like the leper in the Bible. I am unclean."

"Yes, my child."

When the women left the office, Dr. Anton refused to accept another payment. Instructing Sue Ellen carefully about the use of the mercury salve, he directed her to come twice a week for the next draught of mercury and arsenic salts. In that way, he felt that by observing her carefully, he could make sure to minimize any negative effects. He remembered as he watched them depart that he had depleted his Bismuth salts. His last pox patient, a burly coarse man, had needed them. He wondered if the spring supplies would bring more medication or if the need for more scalping knives and ammunition would demand the top priority again.

No one spoke as the women began their silent trek back to Yankee Hall.

Suddenly Sue Ellen pulled up short. Her friends had gone nearly six steps beyond her when they realized that she had dropped back.

"Sue Ellen...?" Eve could not even begin to frame a question.

"I must go to the Church of Ste. Anne." A note of quiet defiance revealed itself as she turned her back to Yankee Hall in the Citadel and headed deliberately down the street which led to the Church. Her friends fell into step behind her.

Nearly to the church's door, she stopped abruptly. Turning to face her two dear friends, she straightened her back once more. She exuded determination. "I cannot go with you. I would not harm Mikie or Henry—nor either of you—nor anyone." The last words came very softly. She resumed with more strength. "I pray I have not already brought you the contagion. You must understand. I can't bear to see any of you and not to touch you. Please my friends. Leave me here. I will ask the Father Bocquet what I must do."

"But, Sue Ellen..."

"Nellie, the Father will know what is best for me."

"But, Sue Ellen," Nellie protested yet a second time.

"Please go now before I lose my strength. Leave me!"

"I will make you gloves," Eve said softly to her parting figure as Sue Ellen turned to step through the open door into sanctuary.

"I know. You won't forget me. Nor will I, you."

"But, Bocquet doesn't speak English..." Nellie called after her. Her voice shook with the futility of it all.

"It won't matter," they heard faintly as she disappeared from their view.

And it did not.

German=this font   English=this font   *French=this font*   *Delaware=this font*

Chapter 24   Advent and More

"Memm: to have Powder, Rum &ca seized on the King's
Account."

*Hamilton, Henry, *Henry Hamilton and George Rogers Clark in the*
American Revolution with the Unpublished Journal of Gov. Henry Hamilton,
John D. Barnhart, Ed., (Crawfordsville, Indiana: R. E. Ranta, 1951). Quote
from Hamilton's journal p. 127, dated November 23, 1778…an important
order from Henry Hamilton.

November 29, 1778   British Encampment
Near Fort Ouiatenon, Indiana

Maisonville walked briskly aside MacLeod. Both men bent their
heads to deflect the latest shower of rain and snow which came nearly
head-on.

"Why all the damn secrecy?" MacLeod sputtered to Maisonville.
The Frenchman remained one of the few that he felt truly able to speak to
openly and honestly. "Does his royal realize that every trader and
engagé from here to the Illinois must surely know by now that we are
coming? We are hard to miss with all our tons of trappings."

As if to punctuate his comment, the six-pounder fired in the near
distance to impress the assembled natives. The cannon brigade aimed well
at the foot-square target, shattering it completely. The target's placement
stood at a remarkable distance away and convincingly proved to those
assembled that the King would indeed protect his savage allies, including
their families and their lands from the encroachment of his rebellious
children.

"Eh*, mon ami*, he's grilling Jean Baptiste now."

"Chapoton?"

"Oui."

"Good heavens, Maisonville. The man is no saint, but he and
Raimbault deal more fairly than most out here."

"Tell that to le General and his stinking friend, Hay." When
Maisonville nodded at the puddle ahead both men separated momentarily
and then rejoined on the other side.

"What do you think of Hay's latest?" He continued.

"What now?"

"The pot-licker has forbid anyone in the fort to trade with any
soldier or officer."

"You cannot be bloody serious."

"I'm serious."

"Patrick, Andrew, and John. That is exactly why Sir William Johnson wanted the military and the politicians to keep their stinking noses out of the native trade. They screw up every time with their greed and influence peddling. Traders, in the end, have to be honest or they destroy themselves. It all washes."

"What washes politicians and the military?"

"War, my friend. Insanely stupid wars!"

The warmth of Hamilton's well-heated tent did not extend to Jean Baptiste Chapoton. The animosity that he felt emanating from Lieutenant Governor Hamilton made him ill at ease. He looked nervously about the tent and tried to avoid eye contact with his superior. He clutched his trading license in his right hand, which hung stiffly at his side.

Every haughty cell in Hamilton's body hung front and center with open disdain for the Frenchman before him. His teeth clenched in anger. His jaw muscles tightened with the tension.

"Your license, if you please." Hamilton's forefinger tapped the desk before him three distinct times, indicating the place he wished Chapoton to place his well-worn document. He would not even do the trader the courtesy of extending his hand to receive it.

Chapoton placed it on the desk before the Lieutenant Governor. His arm quickly snapped back to his side. He flexed his fingers nervously, closing his fist and then flexing his fingers again.

Hamilton read the license carefully. "And just how do you justify going to the Illinois area when your license stops at Fort Sackville at Vincennes on the Wabash?"

Chapoton visibly blanched. "Governor, I work with Raimbault. Are we not free to go anywhere in his Majesty's territory?"

Hamilton glared. The ridiculous question deserved nothing but unconcealed contempt. To him, it constituted a mealy-mouthed excuse by this French vermin. In his eyes, this French trader represented just another example of the immoral animals that lurked at the fringes of society, like rats picking up the crumbs.* "Were you not there after the Rebel flag was raised?*"

"Well, yes, sir. I just informed you who is manning the forts there and at Vincennes. I hope the information of their numbers proves useful, sir."

"Interesting..." Hamilton paused. "Why did you not write earlier of their takeover?"

"My writing's middlin' to worse, sir." Chapoton hated to admit his lack of letters. Like many merchants he could cipher numbers with ease, keeping most book notes in his head for others to write down later. He could bluff to cover his poor skills most of the time, but not this time.

"You disgust me, Chapoton." Hamilton hardly needed to state the obvious in the heated tent, a tent warmed by candles and body heat.

German=this font   English=this font   *French=this font*   *Delaware=this font*

Chapoton broke out in a cold sweat.

Waving him from the tent, Chapoton's license remained with Hamilton.

Chapoton welcomed the warmth of the cold wet rain and sleet mixed with frigid air as he left the tent.

*Hamilton, Henry. *Henry Hamilton and George Rogers Clark in the American Revolution with the Unpublished Journal of Gov. Henry Hamilton,* John D. Barnhart, Ed. (Crawfordsville, Indiana: R. E. Ranta, 1951). Information paraphrased from Hamilton's journal p. 133-150.

November 30, 1778 Fort Detroit

Eve waited impatiently in the pew for the Father Bocquet. His schoolmaster, Jean Baptiste Roucout, had come to fetch her. Votive candles wove their mystery about her. Although not of this faith, she found a deep peace within these walls. This caused her again to wonder why her Vater had so despised these places as kin to the devil. The memories of her first nights within these walls flooded her consciousness. She could almost hear Anne's laughter echoing in the rafters and see the circle of women and children washing away the filth of their horrible journey. A warm invisible cloak settled about her shoulders. An unseen hand descended gently upon her head. For a moment or two, she bowed her head under the hand's weight. When the hand lifted, she raised her head. She observed the tiny Stations of the Cross nestled in the moving shadows which came to life in the flickering light. She recognized many of the events of Christ's life and remembered some of her earlier teachings.

Memories of her father's hearth as a child and his somber reading of verses at sundown contrasted with the laughter about her own hearth. She could hear young George struggling to read with Adam Henry's gentle guidance, often accompanied by giggles from his brothers and sister.

What had her Vater found so evil in these simple statues? The figure of Ste. Anne beside the altar before her had a countenance of acceptance as she sheltered a young Mary in the folds of her robes. The Holy Family in another alcove reminded her of more peaceful days when Adam Henry also had stood by her side. What would Adam Henry think of her? She carried not only another man's child, but a metis. Within her grew a promise of a child from one of the very peoples who had robbed the life of many of her countrymen and her own husband.

Her hands played absentmindedly with the gloves that she had fashioned for Sue Ellen. She had hastily grabbed the gloves as she left Yankee Hall with the schoolmaster, terrified that he brought more bad news.

When Father Bocquet and Roucout appeared near the side alter, Eve rose to her feet. The Father, with a hand of raised blessing indicated his desires of her, so she sat once more. Roucout steadied the staggering

German=this font   English=this font   *French=this font*   *Delaware=this font*

father, helping him into the pew to sit beside Eve. She could see age played no favorites with the good priest.

When the old priest's shaking hand fell where another's invisible hand touched only moments before, Eve accepted the blessing humbly. Father Bocquet knew instinctively that the woman before him had brought more than concern for her friend to God's house. He prayed silently that he could be an instrument of healing for her, even if she was not one of his parishioners. Over time, he had come to ignore the directive to only serve his own parishioners, following what he believed to be a higher dictate of service. He remembered this one well. The strength, the pain, the guilt so visible in her face when he first saw her still played around the edges of her being. Even if the bruises healed, the inner scars remained. Tragedy soared and circled about these prisoners like an eagle seeking a wounded prey.

His hand remained until he felt her begin to lift her head. He noted the shine on her cheeks, but her eyes cleared. Concern for her friend flooded her features.

"Father, how is my friend, Sue Ellen? Is she grave?"

The good Father spoke, his voice halting and unsteady. His schoolmaster dutifully related his words to Eve.

"Tell her that her friend, Sue Ellen, is well cared for."

"Father says your friend, Sue Ellen, has good care."

"She asked me to fetch you to tell you that you must not worry. Others who share her affliction care for her, so she brings harm to no one."

"Your friend wishes you not to worry. Others, who are as afflicted as she, care for her, so she harms no one."

Eve was taken-back by the Father's words. She never dreamed that others about her carried this cursed disease. She remained subdued. No one spoke for a time.

"I made her gloves. Can you take them to her?"

"But, of course." Roucout took them from Eve.

Uneasy, Eve fidgeted. "Ask the Father, schoolmaster, have her hands and feet healed yet?"

"Tell the woman, no, her friend still has the sores." Father Bocquet responded to the interpreted question. He saw no sense in telling her of the new gaping sores on her once beautiful face, poorly hidden behind a tattered veil. Nor did he tell her how Dr. Anton came to medicate Sue Ellen in the night, rather than have Sue Ellen bear the ridicule of being seen in public. He added as an afterthought, *"She has no pain."*

Eve nodded sadly at the translation.

"Ask the good woman, Roucout, if there is something that we may do to serve her spiritual needs?"

Roucout looked quizzically at the Father, but then almost asked the question as the priest directed.

"The Father asks; do you need a spiritual advisor?"

German=this font   English=this font   *French=this font*   *Delaware=this font*

Eve's brow wrinkled. She revealed her perplexed annoyance.

Father Bocquet put his hand on Roucout's sleeve. "Did you say what I truly said?" He sensed his words impacted poorly on Eve. Not at all as he thought they might.

"The Father wants me to restate his question. He fears I translated it wrong." Roucout paused for a long moment before he spoke again. "He wants to know, good woman, if he—no, we, could serve your spiritual needs?"

Eve replied after some thought. "Tell him I am not of his faith. I am a Lutheran. But if I could, I would like to come when the church is empty, if that is permitted."

Roucout more faithfully translated Eve's request this time.

Father Bocquet grinned broadly. ***"Tell her she is always welcome. This is God's house, but it is never empty."***

Roucout looked puzzled. ***"But Father...?"***

"Tell her exactly as I told you, Roucout. She will understand."

As Roucout relayed the Father's words, Eve returned his smile. He understands, she thought. He truly understands.

"Thank you both for your loving concern. Please tell Sue Ellen of our abiding love. My children miss her terribly. If she has needs, you have only to fetch Nellie or me."

The old priest nodded. No translation needed. Eve arose to leave after Father Bocquet made a small sign of the cross on her forehead. Roucout observed that she walked more erectly when she left the sanctuary than when first she came.

And so it became Eve's secret habit to enter the stillness of Ste. Anne's when her chores and church traffic permitted.

November 30, 1778 Saint Andrew's Day, At the British Encampment near Fort Ouiatenon, Indiana

The celebration of Scotland's patron Saint proved a welcome diversion for the militia and the officers. The translators and officers hoisted repeated toasts to the Queen, to the King, to the mission, and of course, incidentally, to Saint Andrew. All served as convenient excuses for their revelry. Earlier, Hamilton's voiced pleasure at their marksmanship practice helped to set the stage for the evening's mirth. MacLeod had astutely observed that his men needed to let off steam. The celebration had been his idea from the start.

After all, the troops had been sliced and slashed by floating ice over the last few days. On their muddy portage from the Miami to the headwaters of the Wabash, ridiculously heavy loads had been hauled and dragged over makeshift corduroy roads and through shallow streambeds.

German=this font   English=this font   *French=this font*   *Delaware=this font*

When that failed, they sometimes had to carry heavy loads over land themselves to lighten boats as the struggling oxen pulled the vessels on wooden carts that their carpenters had built and, just like the boats, endlessly repaired.

Before this Herculean effort, Hamilton's shrewd plan to dam water, to cause controlled floods, and to inch the heavy pirogues slowly forward on the seasonably low Miami had helped. But in the end, the men worked, more often than not, in chest deep, cold and freezing water.

With each passing day, the Wabash widened and deepened. The way became easier, but the cold became more intense. Snow and sleet increased daily with the rapid onset of winter.

MacLeod had invited anyone and everyone not on sentinel duty. Roasted turkeys; dried pumpkin sprinkled with maple sugar; thick bean, squash and venison soup swelled the stomachs of all. Shredded raccoon meat, served in its own rich fat, saturated the crevices in-between. All proved a refreshing change from the tasteless daily rations of stale bread, dried salted beef, hard biscuits, and potatoes. Mouth harps and raucous voices joined in familiar songs. Spoons and sticks struck up rhythms. One good natured lad removed his boot to drum on the sole. Laughter and friendly rabble-rousing reverberated about the cluster of fires. Men danced, linked arms, and spun to French, English, and Celtic pub songs. Even if one did not know the words, the melodies carried the day.

In the end, an opportunity to party brought huzzahs for MacLeod, who in return found a few extra drams of rum to warm their innards. But not everyone appreciated hoisting the diagonal cross or the company of common men, men with raised spirits.

As the evening progressed, MacLeod began to feel the effects of the rum. His longing for Helen, his desires to be by his own warm hearth, and his growing mistrust of Hamilton mixed with memories of campaigns won and campaigns lost.

"Should we rejoice or lament that neither the good Lieutenant Governor nor Hay could join us?" MacLeod lifted his pewter cup. MacLeod's exception to the Lieutenant Governor's slight was totally evident to those about his fire.

Maisonville lifted his own cup. "Here, here, good man. Let the fates decide which it is. 'Tis safer!"

Chapoton appreciated the camaraderie of those about him. He knew the reason that Hamilton and Hay had refused to come to the celebration lay fully at his feet. He admired MacLeod's courage to stand by him, for he had known the Scottish trader only casually at Fort Detroit. No wonder in Detroit, few ever spoke ill of the robust Scotsman. Chapoton understood how this man of integrity had garnered their respect.

A proud man, Chapoton did not want to bring shame to his family nor harm to his associates. He felt a growing inner fear. As chief trader at the Indiana fort, he already had made some good purchases for this trading season. He had accumulated promises for more. His reputation and the

German=this font   English=this font   *French=this font*   *Delaware=this font*

growing dependence of the tribes for manufactured goods bode well for him and his partner's future. He stood to lose a great deal if Hamilton cancelled his license. Already Hamilton had banned him from further trading at the fort.

Lieutenant DuVernett passed another round of rum to MacLeod and the others.

MacLeod bent forward, rolling his cup between his hands.

"I pray the man is not another Abercrombie." The memories of an earlier battle twenty years before, during which he had watched so many of his countrymen die at the foot of Fort Carillon's walls, came painfully to mind. The Fort would become known as Fort Ticonderoga over time, but the shame remained.

No one spoke. The defeat of the British forces there by the French still stung the British. Here about the fire, French and British sat side-by-side. Each man knew the outcome of that battle. To a man, they remembered how the destructive pride and the ineptness of the British commander had cost many Scottish lives, all seasoned fighters and officers of the 42nd Highlanders known as the Black Watch Brigade. General Sir James Abercrombie hid at the rear of his forces and endeared himself to no one, French or British. Cowards embarrass all men.

Maisonville decided instantly not to let his friend, MacLeod, continue his present course. Hamilton, no doubt, had ears about them and mouths that could carry tales.

"Eh, *mon ami*, did you not wear the brown and fight with Gage?" He clamped a hand on MacLeod's shoulder, his concern evident. "That man knew how to lead, did he not? Eh?"

Gage's Light Infantry had a reputation that shown brightly compared to Abercrombie's. The negative turned positive. Gage's men were renowned for their hit-and-run tactics, decisive victories, and their amazing ability to fight in both the European mode and just as aptly, if not better, in the Native manner of the new world. Many of the remaining Black Watch had joined Gage's command and distinguished themselves in his troop.

A flicker of pride crossed MacLeod's visage. His shoulders squared.

"Good man, that one." His brogue thickened by rum. "He made us wash our own bloody clothes, he did. If'n you can call them leggins, not breeches, clothes." Taking another swig from his cup, MacLeod continued, "But then I was a bit stronger, a bit younger, a bit more foolish, and to be sure, I had shapely legs."

A little nervous laughter about the fire joined MacLeod's. To a man, all rejoiced that Maisonville had changed topic.

German=this font   English=this font   **French=this font**   *Delaware=this font*

December 1, 1778, Fort Detroit

Margaret Elder stared across the almost vacant floor of Yankee Hall. Her back, turned toward Eve, set them apart just like the many makeshift curtains which divided the occupant's spaces in the hall. Mikie and Henry played with Mikie's wooden animals by the fireplace. Both boys were lost in their world of pretend.

"So you are telling me, Eve, you are with child."

"Yes."

"Expect whose is none of my business."

"Joseph, the canoe builder, is the father of this child. It will be obvious enough to discern once our child is born."

A curtain of stillness hung between them. Eve lay on her side on her blanket. The milky-tea that Margaret had brought sat untouched beside her on the floor. Eve felt too nauseous to drink it. Morning sickness had lingered far longer with this pregnancy and reappeared at unexpected intervals.

"Part of me wants to condemn you...to detest you for your behavior." Margaret turned slowly. "But, Eve, some nights I ache so for my George's arms about me. And I say, if I can just live one more day, maybe, just maybe, I can go home to my George to be with my family again. But you...you cannot go home to Adam Henry. He is gone. I understand that," Margaret paused, overcome with disgust, "But I do not think you should have done what you did. I do not think it is right. A heathen savage...Eve...why him of all..." She could not bring herself to say people. "Have you no shame?"

With that, Margaret spun on her heel and returned to her work in the barrack kitchen. She left Eve enveloped by her friend's scathing disappointment.

"Because he was the kindest man I knew," Eve answered almost inaudibly. Knowing the futility of her words, Eve realized that Margaret would never understand Eve's reason, no matter what Eve said.

Another wave of nausea struck. Eve sat up quickly, putting the chamber pot between her knees. She found the odor of her warm vomit mixed with stale urine repulsive. She retched again, going into a series of dry heaves.

Eve could stand it no longer. She called out to Mikie and Henry.

"Henry, go to Sally Ainsee. Tell her I cannot stop heaving. Ask her for medicine. Be sure you speak English. Tell her I will pay her this afternoon."

"Mee...go toooo!"

"No, Mikie. Just Henry. Mutti needs you." Eve heaved again. "Mutti is sick."

Mikie pouted, watching his brother's hasty departure.

As Henry slammed the merchant's door, Sally Ainsee looked up.

German=this font   English=this font   *French=this font*   *Delaware=this font*

Helen MacLeod stated her need again. "Is there no one here who can set up a loom? When will Nickerson come back? It has been over three months now."

"I suspect, Mistress MacLeod, he cannot get a trading license or maybe, heaven forbid, he has been waylaid. The Ohio country's mighty dangerous these days."

"Mistress Sally, my Mutti's a-heaving."

"Henry do not interrupt," Sally scolded. "At least this time he is interrupting in English." She tried to apologize for the boy's intrusion. Helen MacLeod, wife of the mayor and a Captain of the militia, brought respect to Sally's establishment. Unlike many of her customers, this one paid on time. Sally must give her undivided attention. Customers like this one brought others who had means.

Henry frowned. He tried to be mannerly, but the sounds of his mother's retching still rang in his ears.

Helen MacLeod smiled down at Henry. "You are the worried young lad. Do not fret child. I will be just a minute. I promise." Resuming, she turned again to Sally. "If I could just find someone to put the thread on my loom, I could put the woof in myself."

"My Mutti weaves."

"Hush, Henry. We have already heard that," Sally Ainsee growled.

Henry frowned harder. What was there about adults that they refused to listen to children?

"I am sorry for the lad. Where were we?" Helen shook off the distraction. Weave and heave jumped back and forth in her mind. "Oh...are you sure, Mistress Ainsee, that you do not know anyone who can string a loom?"

"My Mutti do dat," Henry blurted out again. His German accent thickly coated the words.

"Henry, enough!" Sally Ainsee snapped.

"Wait a minute, Mistress Ainsee, what did he say? He is hard to understand."

Trying not to show her exasperation, Sally Ainsee leaned over to Henry. "Say it again, Henry, only say it slow."

"My Mutti weave. She can fix a loom all by herself. She is better than my Opa." His young pride revealed itself in the set of his shoulders.

"Who is he talking about?" Helen MacLeod inquired.

"His mother, Eve, a prisoner. She lives at Yankee Hall. I suspect she is sick, given Henry's first interruption. But I do not think that she is a weaver. She probably just places the woof like you, mam. I doubt if she can set a loom. You know how children tend to exaggerate."

Henry, seeing that his words beat on deaf ears, dropped his head.

"Mrs. Ainsee, give the boy his medicine. I will walk him back." Helen MacLeod took Henry's hand, and his heart went with it. Such was Helen's effect on the male gender, young or old.

Although tempted to object, Sally Ainsee had absolutely no desire to

German=this font   English=this font   **French=this font**   *Delaware=this font*

rile her customer unnecessarily. If the foolish woman seemed bent on finding out the obvious, let her go to it.

As Henry and Helen MacLeod entered the hall, Eve retched again. Helen MacLeod had no doubt which direction to go or which blanket cubicle contained Henry's mother.

When Eve looked up, her untidy braids nearly plopped in the chamber pot. Her apron soiled, disheveled, she flushed with embarrassment as the well-dressed woman looked down at her. Mikie grinned up at the woman who held his brother's hand.

"Pretty lady." Mikie stated the obvious immediately.

"Let me help you, good woman. Then we will see if you can help me in return."

Eve gagged again. Helen immediately dropped to her knees to assist.

"Henry, get another pot. We must empty this one. This alone could make your mother ill." She wiped the damp hair back from Eve's wet clammy forehead. "My name is Helen MacLeod, and you are Eve."

Eve nodded. Another wave of nausea struck. She gratefully accepted Helen's gentle touch. What possibly could she do for this beautiful stranger? Who was this woman? Why had Henry brought her? Had Sally Ainsee sent her?

December 8, 1778 Nearing Vincennes Encamped Twelve Miles Below the River Vermillion

Earlier, Hamilton had ordered the pirogues to travel 'six, five or four abreast depending on the number in their division'*. Both the width of the Wabash and the flow worked in his war party's favor. Just as he had planned, the journey at the last proved easiest. He exalted in the growing number of warriors that he had been able to gather for his Majesty's endeavor. However, when snow fell thickly after the midday and a 'hard freeze'* set in, the weather began to impact heavily upon his military forces on the water and even more upon the warriors on shore, which numbered in excess of three hundred. His army of nearly five hundred stalled…just when Hamilton desired most to proceed. The tantalizing possibility of another victory without firing a single shot as they had at Fort Ouiatenon appealed to him.

Hamilton remembered how quickly the ninety cabins of Ouiatenon inhabitants had taken an oath to his Majesty. Hay led them as they renounced their weakness at having accepted the Virginian oath. A few of the more foolish residents maintained that they were drugged by the Virginia tobacco. However, Hamilton chose to ignore a tiny voice that whispered that these easy converts might be just as quick to renounce his Majesty's allegiance again in favor of the Virginians if the opportunity

German=this font   English=this font   *French=this font*   *Delaware=this font*

presented itself again. Instead, he blamed their foolish behavior on the influence of that contemptible priest, Gibault.

The differing nations, including the Potawatomi, Ottawa, and Chippewa from the Lakes, the Ouiatenon, Miami, Kickapoo, Wyandot, Shawnese and Huron, all suggested that Hamilton tarry to set up camp. In particular, the Ottawa Chief, Egushawa, prevailed on Hamilton to stop.

Hamilton did not want to offend Egushawa, whose authority included both Ottawa and Chippewa. Hamilton could always count on him and the Petite Gris. Like Petite Gris, known also as the Dappled Fawn, Egushawa's oration skills were remarkable. Having inherited the mantle as Pontiac's successor, he served the Crown well. As both war chief and civil chief, he commanded real power in the tribes that surrounded the Detroit area. Backed by the assistance of his fellow war chief, Naudowance, and the warrior, Flat Button, few ranked higher in esteem.

Hamilton inwardly fumed, but he honored his promise to Egushawa to permit their ceremonies before they attacked the fort. He recognized their need to sing to their bundles of relics or 'natte as the French called them'.* The tribes paraded their natte before them into battle and evidently had as much attachment to them as had the Crusaders for the containers of sacred bones or Church banners flown before them on their trips to the Holy Land. He felt dismayed to know, however, that if a warrior got ahead of the hallowed bundle that the warrior might put himself to death rather than be the cause of his own party's defeat. Hamilton believed that logic must rule and gave no truck with these superstitions. How stupid to have such deep seated fears of so many deities, he thought. An intelligent man made his own way by reason alone.

The melancholy sounds of the drums pounded unrelentingly. War chants, weaving between the tribal fires, knit the rivals into a single purpose, to join the English Father to defeat his rebellious children. When Hamilton publicly announced his intent to rescind Tobacco's recent sale of land to the Americans, the tribes roared their approval. Hamilton wet their axes with rum and rhetoric, so the cohesiveness of the otherwise warring factions increased. At last, their English Father had come to protect them from the Longknives.

While some chafed at being called his children, they readily accepted his bountiful supply of clothing and trade goods, which included powder and flint for the winter hunt. Ornamental pieces of silver, like the gorgets, replaced earlier French ones. About the ceremonial fires, only the Shawanese and the Huron remained skeptical of the Lake Indians' ancient incantations to their gods. However, they still attended the fires, as the food was plentiful. Not to do so might give offense.

When the interpreter, Isidor Chesne, shook the snow from his skin cap and brushed the snow from his winter moccasins and leggings, he called to the Lieutenant Governor within the warm, glowing tent.

"May I come in, sir? Chesne here."

"Advance."

German=this font   English=this font   *French=this font*   *Delaware=this font*

Once inside, Chesne removed his jacket and folded it over his arm so as not to overheat. He stood waiting for Hamilton's attention. His deeply lined and weathered face revealed possible metis parentage.

Hamilton acknowledged him, setting his writing aside. His hands fairly caressed the sides of his writing table as he did so. The brightly polished brass carrying-handles at the sides gleamed golden in the yellow lamplight. Hamilton truly loved fine things, this desk being one. He considered it a necessary trapping that officers of his rank were entitled to own and to use. Any thought of those who struggled to carry the heavy piece of furniture from campsite to campsite never really came into his consideration. After all, rank had privilege.

Major Jehu Hay lit a pipe and nodded to recognize Chesne.

"Sir, there's been a bad omen." Hamilton could see the man's obvious nervous demeanor.

Inwardly, Hamilton cursed at the willingness of so many among his troops to jump at the least superstition as if it revealed God's truth.

"What have you heard, Chesne?" This man always spoke slowly. There would be an eternity between each sentence for Hamilton. Hamilton, who spoke rapidly with great ease and thought at even a faster pace, barely tolerated this type of individual.

"Well, sir, the conjuror at the fire said he had a dream. Manitou spoke to him about you...sir." He paused for an extended period. "And me, sir."

Hamilton suspected what would come next almost before the poor quaking man before him spoke. The Lake peoples gave so much credence to dreams.

"And what did he say, Chesne?" Hamilton strove not to let the full extent of his impatience reveal itself. A fossil that Hamilton found in the last few days as he strolled and sketched near a rocky area once known as 'Le Navire, the ship,' lay beside a piece of coal found near their current campsite on the warm surface of his oiled walnut desk. (Hamilton's sketch of this site see *Maps & Illustrations* section, p. v)

To keep his mind busy as he waited on Chesne's halting words; he picked up the fossil and began to study it. Turning the imbedded seashell form in his hands, he wondered anew at its structure. He thought that he recognized it as the salt sea creature, 'corunus ammonius'. He had found the fragment in the remains of the huge rocky precipice which had fallen into the river during an earthquake last year. When he had suggested that there had been an earthquake, the area tribe had staunchly maintained that the gods of thunder and lightning had dislodged it instead. No logic of his could dissuade them otherwise. He momentarily despaired that he had had so little time to investigate the shoreline further, for he delighted in finding the tiny crystals which appeared there in abundance.

"Well, sir," Chesne droned. A small puddle had begun to form about him, caused by the melting snow from his outer clothing. "They say, sir, the Rebels will kill you and all the English... and they will imprison me.

German=this font   English=this font   *French=this font*   *Delaware=this font*

They say, sir, some French will die, but that Indians won't suffer much."

"Well, Chesne, take my word for this. We will have a triumphal victory. Accept my total assurance. Those within the fort will not likely attack their brethren. They will see the error of having taken a pledge to the Virginians. We know with absolute certainty that the Rebel forces are pitifully weak. Indeed, we have prevented their reconnaissance both into and out of the fort. Believe me; we have reliable information that will enable us to succeed decisively."

Chesne visibly relaxed. "Well, sir, I thought you ought to know."

"We will prevail, Chesne. I appreciate your concern. Depend on this. After our coming success, our inspired southern forces will join us in the early spring. With additional aid from the southern tribes, we will close this portion of the war against his Majesty's foes just as one would draw tightly shut the strings of a purse and crush its contents." His brimming confidence infected Chesne immediately. "Anything else?"

"No, sir!"

"Then you are dismissed."

Hay's hand covered a sneering grin as they watched the shaggy interpreter don his coat and take leave of the tent.

Hamilton just rolled his eyes and shook his head as the opening flap settled into place. He wished all his problems could be as easily resolved.

"Actually, Hay, I think our greatest problem when we succeed will be controlling our allies," Hamilton stated as he turned the fossil in his hands, catching the luminescence of the embedded pearly shell. "Many of these warriors will want to loot and plunder as part of their victory rites."

"Some of our militia are not above that either, sir."

"Agreed, but this will not be, will it?" Hamilton replaced the fossil with an authoritative rap, breaking off a small corner of the stone.

Hay knew immediately his superior's expectation of him.

Changing the subject abruptly, Hamilton continued, "I doubt that any of them will be willing to die for him and the other six or so rebels. Helm has little support among the fifty or so militia that they have enlisted. There will be little support to protect the incompetents who keep him company."

"Did you hear that the damned fool got locked out of his own fort?"

"You jest." Hamilton used Hay's pet expression mockingly.

"No, word has it that the nipper got tanked in town and that his own drunken guards would not admit him upon his return."

"And they call this an enemy?"

Both men simultaneously chuckled and moved in on the silver decanter of vintage brandy. Both filled with the certain knowledge that a true gentleman never over-imbibed.

German=this font   English=this font   **French=this font**   *Delaware=this font*

"Speaking of enemies, did you return the squaw I purchased to her brother?"

"Yes, it is done."

"Good, now if I can smooth over the rough edges, maybe we will settle one more inter-tribal dispute."

"And how was the Ouiatenon Chief's friendship offering last evening?"

Hamilton, as usual, revealed little of his private dealings. "'The lady followed her customs.'** My most difficult problem was convincing her to trade her silver French gorget for that of King George's."

"And why was that a problem?"

"Evidently, she had some fond attachment to the French one, expressing great reluctance to part with it."

"Did you succeed?"

"Yes. She honors his Majesty. She even garnered a few additional silver trinkets, as well, to insure her continuing allegiance." His lip turned up ever so slightly on the side of his face away from Hay. The positive remembrance of winning her over did little to eliminate the weighty necessity of tiptoeing between his allies, striving nearly every waking moment of every day not to offend anyone among their petty fiefdoms. He recognized that his diplomatic skills, for which he could take honest pride, had been honed to a new sharpness of late.

Hamilton envied his enemy, George Rogers Clark, in only one way. He believed that Clark's life was simple when compared to his own. The man seemed to dismiss all of the native alliances out of hand. One chief reported to him that Clark had emphatically stated that he and his troops had the ability to go it alone. He had absolutely no desire for their help, Clark had stated in council. They were to stay out of the conflict and go hunting...or prepare to die with the British.** But then Hamilton remembered his foolish, brash adversary must be barely in his mid-twenties. Not much of a threat there, he concluded.

Another group of voices chatted as they passed outside the Lieutenant Governor's tent. Matthew Elliott and Alexander McKee's intonations were immediately recognized by both men inside.

Hay shot to his feet and called out the flap.

"Ho, Elliott. What is the report from the surgeon?"

"Oh, he'll live. One less eye to be sure, but he'll live. The old Shawnee chief's only bitch is that he didn't lose his eye in battle as a true warrior should."*

"That is good news." Relief spoke in Hay's reply.

"Tell Elliott that we are going to renew the ban on shooting turkeys from the boats and by all parties along the shore tomorrow." Hamilton responded. He spoke loudly enough that Hay need not repeat his words.

"I sure as hell hope so. That damn ball went through the man's jacket next to him and whistled past my nose, a hellin'. His bloody eye still attached. A staring at me, it was."

German=this font   English=this font   *French=this font*   *Delaware=this font*

Hay shuddered at the mere thought of the event. He wondered if Elliott recognized Hamilton's voice.

"Half of those son's bitches get powder-drunk when game's so thick a'shore," McKee added.

"The order will go out." Hamilton's authority sounded finality and recognition.

"Night, sir." Elliott stammered, as he recognized his commander's voice.

"Goodnight, gentlemen."

Stillness returned.

The letter of the fifth containing the October eighth article from the *Quebec Gazette* lay on Hamilton's desk.*** But Hamilton turned in, leaving tomorrow to face the complications sure to arise from its contents. Best to sit on the *Gazette*'s news, he decided. They had enough problems without adding this one to the mix. Another busy morning would dawn soon enough.

*Hamilton, Henry, *Henry Hamilton and George Rogers Clark in the American Revolution with the Unpublished Journal of Gov. Henry Hamilton*, John D. Barnhart, Ed. (Crawfordsville, Indiana: R. E. Ranta, 1951) ** p. 135-136, *** p. 177. Other information paraphrased from the journal p. 133-150. The shooting incident* recorded by MacLeod, Norman, *Detroit to Sackville, the Journal of Norman MacLeod* (Detroit, MI: Wayne State University Press, 1978), p. 96.

December 18 1778   The Fall of Fort Patrick Henry and the Return of the British to Fort Sackville and Vincennes, Indiana

"I sent spies to find the certainty—the spies being taken prisoners I never got intelligence till they got within three miles of town....Excuse haste as the army is in sight. The army is in three hundred yards of village...You must think how I feel; not four men that I can really depend upon; but am determined to act brave—think of my condition. I know it is out of my power to defend the town, as not one of the militia will take arms, though before sight of the army no braver men. There is a flag at a small distance. I must conclude.   Your humble servant, Leo'd Helm. Must stop."

Captain Helm, American Revolutionary Forces letter as quoted by William Hayden English, Ed. in *Conquest of the Country Northwest of the River Ohio, 1778-1783 and Life of Gen. George Rogers Clark. Vol 1.* (Indianapolis, IN and Kansas City, MO: Bowen Merrill Company, 1896), p. 233. Letter removed from messenger when killed by British forces en route to George Rogers Clark.

German=this font   English=this font   *French=this font*   *Delaware=this font*

The American Captain, Leo Helm, surrendered his post to the British without a single shot. After Jehu Hay explained the number and depth of Hamilton's advancing forces, Helm had realistically faced the bitter recognition that the ridiculous militia, the same militia that Helm had sworn to serve Virginia in the days and weeks before, were totally useless. The reluctant militia men simply would not shoot at their brethren. Fort Patrick Henry had failed to protect Vincennes or itself. The name of the fort changed quickly. Fort Sackville had returned to British control. The following morning, Lieutenant Governor Henry Hamilton feared the worst as he approached the fort. The American flag still waved in the breeze and with it the promise of a brutal fight. However, Hamilton's initial fears quickly melted away to be replaced by heady pride as Hay breathlessly informed him of the breadth of the British victory. The prevention of looting had curtailed the British forces from quickly removing the offensive stars and stripes during the rapid British takeover.

By high noon, Lieutenant Governor Henry Hamilton stood in full dress in the esplanade, the flat area between the fort and the town. First, three volleys echoed off the decaying walls of the poorly maintained fort. Then, the six-pounder fired twenty-one rounds, one by one in succession as the town inhabitants waited to hear his speech of derision and disgust at their previous oath to the American forces. In the lull that followed, Hamilton stepped forward to give his magnanimous declaration of his Majesty's mercy to the wayward inhabitants if they would renounce any attachment to the rebels after their 'perfidious' conduct. He quickly pointed out that no blood had been spilled. But, he reserved a special amount of bile for those who still carried Abbott's commission on their person alongside that of the Rebel commissions.

Captain Leo Helm, the paroled American Captain, stood meekly at Hamilton's side. He listened as Hamilton derided the disloyal inhabitants. Helm had been freed to his own recognizance upon his promise not to contact any of the enemy. Earlier that morning, Helm showed his good faith when he informed Hamilton of the large barrel of spirits at the rear of his quarters…spirits to be immediately rescued from the 'smokey' supporters of the British. The few braves, who had entered through two cannon ports and who had created havoc as they stampeded the garrison's thirty-four horses out the gate, were quickly stopped.

Chaos proved short-lived. Hay succeeded to keep control with the assistance of the militia and strong admonishments from the tribal chieftains like Egushawa. The young bucks shrieked their disappointment, but the chieftain's authority held.

Captain MacLeod and J. Hunot waited impatiently for Hamilton to finish. MacLeod's Shawnee scout had just reported to him that two hundred rebels would attack the fort at dawn.

*Hamilton, Henry. *Henry Hamilton and George Rogers Clark in the American Revolution with the Unpublished Journal of Gov. Henry Hamilton*, John D. Barnhart, Ed. (Crawfordsville, Indiana: R. E. Ranta, 1951). Information paraphrased from the journal p. 133-150.

German=this font   English=this font   *French=this font*   *Delaware=this font*

December 19, 1778   Fort Sackville, Vincennes, Indiana

Two hundred and fifty inhabitants stood nervously awaiting their turn at the church to sign the oath of allegiance to his Majesty, King George, and to hand over their arms. Hamilton had the solemn oath drawn up in French just for the occasion. Admonishing them severely of the danger of perjuring themselves, he watched quietly as the captured town's people kissed the silver crucifix before the altar and then signed. He would later write a translation of their surrender statement in English in his journal.... "We whose names are here subscribed declare and acknowledge having taken the oath of fidelity to the Congress, that in so doing we have forgot our duty to God and Man, we implore the pardon of God, and hope from the goodness of our lawful Sovereign the King of Great Britain that he will accept our submission and take us again under his protection as good and faithful subjects, which we promise and swear before God and men we will here after become, in Witness whereof we sign our respective names, or set our customary Mark...this 19th day of December 1778...at the post of St. Vincennes."*

Hamilton would also relate his reeking distrust of their duplicitous nature in his journal. He recognized wearily that oaths of allegiance could be a farce when not written on one's heart and defended with one's own blood. In addition, he noted with satisfaction that he had rendered some of these weak men to tears.

MacLeod spat in the dust outside the church. He cleared his nose and spat again. He dared not speak aloud his thoughts. Fury built. He had left Helen's side for this fiasco. He tried to ignore it, but his astute business side had begun to size up the sheer cost of the venture. He was too much a Scot not to mentally count pennies or as in this case, hundreds of pounds. Having fought at Gage's side, he realized the Crown's cost had far exceeded the actual need to conquer this motley excuse for an enemy. Hell, ten of Gage's troops could have taken this whole damnable excuse for a fort, even less. Chagrined as well by his own failed warning of two hundred mythical Rebel troops coming from the Illinois, he realized that Hamilton would no longer value his reconnaissance either. The Shawnee had brought him a baseless rumor, no doubt as a Rebel diversion. In total fact, not one Virginian had presented himself at dawn, much less attacked. Well, at least MacLeod might be able to set up some trade deals so that something good would come out of this mess. Chapoton had given him some fine trading leads.

As MacLeod turned abruptly, he nearly flattened Maisonville, whom he caught in his arms. Both staggered momentarily.

"Eh ***mon ami***, is like getting all cocked for de woman, an' no place to shoot your wad, no?"

German=this font   English=this font   *French=this font*   *Delaware=this font*

For the first time in days, MacLeod laughed. His friend had stated it succinctly. Everything impacted. All the apprehension, all the expectation of death, all the drumming and ceremony, all the bone-chilling exhaustion and struggle just to arrive at this God-forsaken post after seventy-two days and six hundred miles hit him full force. The steel that infused one's spine in anticipation of military duty had built to a need for a climax. Instead, this so-called war represented an anticlimax.

"By God man! Ye have it right. Let's drink on that." The two friends, arm in arm, headed toward the village tavern.

In a darkened corner, Jonas Schindler, the ousted young silversmith from Fort Detroit and friend of John Leeth, sat quietly among the shadows, watching the British troops.

*Hamilton, Henry. *Henry Hamilton and George Rogers Clark in the American Revolution with the Unpublished Journal of Gov. Henry Hamilton,* John D. Barnhart, Ed. (Crawfordsville, Indiana: R. E. Ranta, 1951). Information paraphrased from the journal p. 149-151. Oath , p. 150-151.

December 24, 1778, Fort Sackville, Vincennes, Indiana

"You will be assisted by seven of LaMothe's men and Pierrot Chesne as interpreter. It is imperative that you cooperate with Egushawa and his braves. Do not let them go off half-cocked in their enthusiasm. Egushawa is one of our staunchest supporters and that may, in and of its self, create problems. Do you understand your orders?"

Lieutenant Governor Henry Hamilton patiently explained his directives to Lieutenant Jacob Schieffelin.

"Yes, sir. You can depend on me."

"As a major Great Lakes orator and war chief, we need to foster his feelings of importance and yet fully control him." Sensing that Schieffelin understood the delicacy of the situation, Hamilton rose, gathering his gloves and sword. "Now, if you will excuse me, I have to attend an Ouiatenon ceremony. They desire to remove locks of hair from our captured Virginians for their 'Natte'.* This is a minor concession. No pain to anyone is involved. Hopefully their superstitions will make them even braver in battle, so I see no reason not to cooperate."

"What about the captured Spanish Trader, Francis Vigo?"

"Well, that Piedmontese, Vigaud, is a Spanish citizen; so it will be necessary to grant him parole. However, we will keep a very close watch on him. It would not be wise to put him in lock-up. Agreed?"

"Agreed."

"Any more questions?"

German=this font   English=this font   *French=this font*   *Delaware=this font*

"No, sir."

"Well, Schieffelin, let us depart each to our respective duty."

When Hamilton started to pull the large package of vermilion from the sidebar, the red dust smeared one finger of his white gloves. Calling out to his dayman, he left the vermilion behind.

"Corporal, bring the vermilion."

"Who is the vermilion for?" Lieutenant Schieffelin asked as they exited.

"The Ouiatenon, Great Eyes."

An Ouiatenon brave and interpreter waited without to escort Hamilton and his aide to the ceremony. He had overheard both Schieffelin's parting question and Hamilton's response.

Assuming equality with the Lieutenant Governor, the warrior presumed to answer. He spoke with open candor as he fell into step beside Hamilton. "You do him honor. He and his family are well known for wearing vermilion about their mouths to terrify their enemies. They are 'eaters of men'....'You could not have made him a better present—whether the meat be green or stale, he can eat it'—"

Lieutenant Governor Hamilton started. He glared incredulously at the interpreter.

"Then it is time for him to learn that 'men with arms [are] proper objects of the warrior's resentment, that to lose the name of Barbarians, they must cease to act as Wolves—!'"* Hamilton rebutted. His indignation and fury were totally apparent to the warrior as the Lieutenant General's face colored as red as the vermilion without the aid of dye.

While Schieffelin had no disagreement with Hamilton's cutting retort, he felt a little incredulous that Hamilton could not see the dichotomy of his words and his gift. As their voices faded, Schieffelin faced his own hazardous balancing act, filled with a profound sense of duty and an intense desire to please his brilliant commander.

*Hamilton, Henry. *Henry Hamilton and George Rogers Clark in the American Revolution with the Unpublished Journal of Gov. Henry Hamilton,* John D. Barnhart, Ed. (Crawfordsville, Indiana: R. E. Ranta, 1951). Quote and information paraphrased from Hamilton's journal p. 155-156.

German=this font   English=this font   **French=this font**   *Delaware=this font*

Chapter 25   Twelve Days of Christmas and More   1778-1779

"One of the British Agents (Mons. de Celeron) residing at Oueaugh (Ouiatenon) about eighty leagues above St. Vincent (St. Vincennes), hurt our growing interest much. The Indians in that quarter being inclined to desert the British interest, but in some measure kept from their good intention by that person."

George Rogers Clark letter to friend and patron, George Mason of Gunston Hall, Virginia dated Louiville, Falls of Ohio, Nov 19, 1779 Quoted from: English, William Hyden, *Conquest of the Country Northwest of the River Ohio, 1778-1783 and the Life of Gen, George Rogers Clark, Vol I.* (Indianapolis, Indiana and Kansas City, Missouri: Bowen-Merrill Co., 1896), p. 427.

December 26, 1778   Bedford, Pennsylvania

Molly lay curled in a ball, her knees pulled up tightly under her flannel shift. The heated brick at her feet placed by her grandmother earlier had cooled. When her Onkel came to remove her from the Diberts' with even less ceremony than upon her arrival, she left hollow-eyed, hearing a chorus of whining and crying little ones behind her. Since her arrival, her Grossvater made her aware each day of the increased burden that she placed on him. She realized down deep though that Opa really did love her. Molly had learned a lot about loving at the Diberts' home. Though young in years, Molly recognized that the recent loss of her Tante Jessie pained Grossvater, her grandfather, deeply. Jessie's death was compounded by the loss of her Mutti and her two bruders. His inability to change the course of events battered him ceaselessly. Grossmutter, her grandmother, nearly overcome with her own grief, did all she could to help Molly, but asking two, who faced death within and without, to reach out freely and to emanate great warmth after such losses would mandate sainthood of mere mortals. Each dealt with sadness and anger in their own way.

But in the dead of night, Molly longed most to hear the sounds of sleeping children about her. Her Grossvater's hoarse snore sounded empty in comparison. Sometimes to cope with her loneliness, she would try to imagine each of their tiny faces in a row, mixing them in with Mikie and Henry's little faces. "Oh, Mutti, I miss you so. I miss you all. Why did you leave me?" A part of her realized that the answers to her quiet whispers to the night could never be answered. Molly wished that she could go back to her Vati's loft and erase everything that had begun there. A bitter-sweet memory flashed. Her mother's touch, her understanding, and her last words spoken to her..."You will survive, Molly. You will survive." These words nourished her. She slept at last.

December 28, 1778 Vincennes, Indiana
Outside Fort Sackville

Like a stoppered hornet's nest, MacLeod queued up with others to wait on Hamilton. Outside, the whole community also swarmed with anger. Captain Norman MacLeod seethed and his mind buzzed. His anger mounted over the news of a recent verbal order from Hay to receive a strict accounting of all 'liquor, drygoods and Tobacco in their possession.'*

Leaning against a wooden panel, MacLeod noted that the house that Hamilton had commandeered reflected his own good taste not to mention the prior owners, a local trader and his wife who had been asked to yield their home. The house functioned as the central hub of authority. Hamilton preferred to work outside the decaying fort and inside the village of Vincennes. The fort accommodations simply were not suitable.

MacLeod observed that today proved no exception as steady streams of scouts and interpreters came and went on raiding parties and reconnaissance. He remembered seeing Hazel with the young warrior, Kissingua, with letters for Hamilton's former secretary. Lieutenant Schieffelin had left days before accompanied by some of LaMothe's company. MacLeod respected Lieutenant Schieffelin. It never failed to amaze him that Hamilton would vest so much authority in Hay when Schieffelin showed far more loyalty and ability.

Trying in vain to check his rising temper, MacLeod attempted to focus on the events around him, but the annoying sting persisted.

An interpreter brushed by MacLeod, pushing him roughly aside to enter. A second exited, leaving MacLeod to wonder if the thirteen warriors milling around outside the residence would go on yet another raid under the interpreter's leadership.

The faint sounds of axes and shouts of a tree fall outside pressed in on him. The wood lot stood about a half a league from the village, not quite one and a half miles. The sound carried on this inclement day. He pitied the carpenters, who bore an especially heavy load of responsibility. They had been pressed into wood cutting, given that they no longer mended the pirogues and wagons. While yes, they were assisted by many of the regulars or the locals, who had refused to take the oath, most major tasks still fell to them. As MacLeod listened, he truly empathized with the poor blokes cutting firewood and timber for fort repairs in what had been the dreariest weather imaginable. Neither the Americans nor, sadly, the British before them had attempted to cope with the disrepair during their earlier occupations of the old French fort.

All day and well into the night these men labored. Even on Christmas

German=this font   English=this font   *French=this font*   *Delaware=this font*

Day, they gained no respite. Hamilton's make work scheme accomplished two goals. First, the fortress would be better able to withstand an attack by the Virginians if and when it ever came. Second, perhaps more importantly, the men had less time to drink.

Admitted, MacLeod skipped the small talk and protocol. He could not hold back.

"Sir, the word about is that Hay is to receive an account of all liquor and tobacco. Is this true?"

"Yes, and you are to include all drygoods, hunting supplies, arms and other marketable goods, as well." Hamilton glanced up briefly from writing a letter of explanation to Rocheblave about his plan to exchange him for the American, Captain Helm. The fact that Rocheblave had been shackled in irons like a mere commoner still choked his gorge. As much as Hamilton despised the lackluster man, Rocheblave held an office in his majesty's service. A gentleman deserved far better treatment by Clark's 'banditti'.**

"I assume, sir, that this does not apply to my barrels of taffia and my tobacco that I intend to trade at Fort Detroit!" The "my" had been stressed.

Hamilton frowned. Another petty trouble presented itself.

"MacLeod, the order applies to you the same as any other, no exceptions," Hamilton snapped. Responding to MacLeod's obvious ire, he continued, "'You are free to voice any complaint you may have to my two superiors. I am sure you know who they are. Since I am the sole authority at this time and in this place, that is my command. All is to be turned over to the crown! The road is well known to you if you have any complaints.'"*

"Well, if any person 'thought themselves aggrieved'; it is a 'very long road' indeed to wend! Would I at least be able to have one barrel?"*

The tall Scot's anger fairly ignited the air about him. Even Hamilton felt scorched.

Deciding to tread more lightly, Hamilton attempted another tack. Feigning politeness nearly to mockery, he responded, "I have denied Captain Maisonville one barrel. Surely you cannot expect me to grant you 'favor' or 'privilege' when I have refused another."*

"It is not a favor or a privilege to have what I ha' already paid for!"*

Seeing that Hamilton would not be budged, MacLeod withdrew immediately. Only his military training kept him from exploding. How in the name of St. Andrew could he ever find 'redress'? Norman MacLeod stood to lose up to four-hundred pounds, which cut the loyal Scotsman, a faithful steward, like a dirk to his heart. This abominable act constituted a hellish reward for his faithful service to the Crown.

German=this font   English=this font   *French=this font*   *Delaware=this font*

*MacLeod, Norman. *Detroit to Sackville, the Journal of Norman MacLeod* (Detroit, MI: Wayne State University Press, 1978). Paraphrased closely and some actual words from p. 118-121.

**Hamilton, Henry, *Henry Hamilton and George Rogers Clark in the American Revolution with the Unpublished Journal of Gov. Henry Hamilton,* John D. Barnhart, Ed. (Crawfordsville, Indiana: R. E. Ranta, 1951). Information paraphrased from the journal. "Banditti" from p. 185.

"Look out...All clear to west...tree down a comin'!" Menard hollered as he and Tchamaniked Joe stepped casually back from the trunk. The cracking sounds, as the sinews separated, increased in duration and frequency, signaling the drop. During winter, the sap-drained trees fell quickly with no leaves to retard their fall or cushion them when they crashed to the ground. Both men felt a bit smug as the tree landed with a swoosh, a bounce and a thump exactly where they had intended.

Menard and Tchamaniked Joe, well-matched for strength in spite of their height differences, had become a fair team on the two-man saw. Joe's tree savvy meant they had fewer misplaced falls. Rarely did the men have to jump back or run from a dangerous split. Menard's knowledge of come-a-longs and chains meant that the duo could snake more logs into the ramshackle fort or to the floating sawmill on any given day. Menard complained, of course, very vociferously that Joe worked too damn hard. Not given to drink, to spitting, or to smoking, Tchamaniked Joe took few breaks.

As they hewed side limbs off and tossed them aside, neither man spoke. Both instinctively sensed the other's moves.

"Miss yer family?"

"Yes."

"Me too."

A large limb required more than one swipe. Sweat joined the rain that ran down Menard's face.

"Do you have children?"

"Yes."

"How many children do yeh have?"

"Enough."

"Christ, Joe, don't you ever say more'n one word?"

"Yes." Joe's eyes fairly danced with good humor. He loved getting Menard's dander up. The man had grown under his hide like a shelf fungus on a birch. At first he had thought of him as a crude, mindless bastard. Despite his gruffness and swaggering ways, Joe had actually begun to like the man. Like Joe, Menard guarded his inner-self from those who would pry. Only, unlike Joe, this man did not make friends as easily.

"You smokey son-of-a-bitch. Yer pulling my chain again, aren't you?"

"Yup."

Menard chuckled. He never knew just what to believe about the man

German=this font   English=this font   *French=this font*   *Delaware=this font*

beside him. He had come to realize that this Indian knew far more than the rest of men about him. Like him, they did not expect much of Joe, especially being an Indian and all. His increasing knowledge of the strange man, that fate had randomly chosen for him as partner, made him feel special or somewhat lucky. He did not fully understand why. Once, Menard found Joe playing his flute, all melancholy. Twice, Menard had espied him sitting alone with a small book in a secluded area. Each time, Menard had taken great care not to spook Joe, who at the slightest sound would quickly hide the tiny leather covered volume in his loose fitting shirt. He wondered what in the hell the man read? Cripes, he couldn't read. How come Joe could read?

"Joe, don't tease now. What were you a read'n?"

Joe rose up quickly. At first, he wondered if he should just deny it.

"I see'd you readin'. I saw yer lips a movin'."

"Yes, I read."

"What?"

"Psalms."

"Would you read some to me?"

Joe cut four or five more limbs off with his ax while he debated his response to this totally unexpected request.

"Yes."

"I'd like that," Menard said.

"Do not tell the others."

"I won't. You know, my pap's pap could read."

Joe did not respond.

December 31, 1778   Fort Detroit

Jeannie giggled in one chair. Henry giggled in the other. The straight-backed wooden chairs stood approximately fifteen feet apart in the room mostly lit by the fireplace. Another dreary day gave little light through the wavy panes. An occasional one where the punty, or pontil as the French called it, had been removed leaving a bulls-eye caught the firelight in a red and navy swirl.

Both children served as weights to keep the chairs firmly in place while a mother on each side carefully counted and wound the yarn back and forth around one chair and back to the other, over and over. The elongated back posts on each side served as a makeshift warping frame. Eve instructed Helen how to keep the thread taut but not over-stretched to insure good tension.

Mikie, the entertainment for his captive audience, delighted in making silly faces between his legs while facing backwards. His little rear jiggled in the air as he bobbed up and down each time with a new funny face and as he peeked under his skirt. Sometimes a glimpse of more than two cheeks amused his viewers.

German=this font   English=this font   **French=this font**   *Delaware=this font*

Finally, Henry became so tickled over Mikie's performance that he fell off his chair and dissolved into a fit of laughter, mostly to show off to Jeannie. The empty chair, under tension, immediately toppled, spilling the half-wound yarn onto the braided rag rug. The two women glanced at each other, shaking their heads as they realized that these two lengths would need to be counted anew. But first, the chair must be carefully replaced on the tiny mark that they had made to keep the exact same distance before the tangle of yarns could be rewound. Another chair held a growing mound of chained-and-measured yarn waiting to be warped onto the waiting loom.

Eve wondered how Helen would respond to her son's laxness. But Helen's ready smile dismissed any fear.

"I think that the children have the sillies," Helen remarked. "Perhaps it is time for hot cider and shortbread."

"Ah, but do they deserve it?" Eve responded, winking at Helen before frowning at Henry.

"Please, Mutti. Please." Mikie fairly bounced beside her. "My fault. My fault."

Helen fluffed his golden curls. "Nobody's fault, Michael. Time for cookies. Come help me." Immediately, the towhead disappeared into the kitchen with Helen, leaving Eve to rewind the tangled yarn into balls again without his playfulness to cause additional problems.

"No, you don't, young man!" Eve caught Henry by his collar. "You need to help me hold this so we do not get any knots." Henry stopped mid-flight to the kitchen and dutifully turned to assist his mother.

"Mistress Earnest, how long have you been weaving?" Jeannie asked as she slipped one hand each into the loops on her chair-back before they spilled onto the floor to join the other tangled loops. An old hand at helping to wind skeins, she immediately recognized her task.

"Goodness," Eve reflected. "As far back as I can remember, I guess. My Vater taught me before my two brothers came along. I took to it more than they did."

"My Daddy only has me." Jeannie looked enviously at Henry. How she wished that she had a brother. Even if he were a pest, it might be nice to know she had her mother outnumbered with the help of a co-conspirator.

"I expect that makes you extra special to your father, does it not?" Eve noticed the fleeting look of envy quickly disappear as it merged into a proud grin. Eve had never really considered what it would be like to be the 'only' of anything.

"My Daddy is the head of the militia," Jeannie gushed proudly. "He went to Vincennes to rout the rebellious Americans."

"My Vati was a great farmer," Henry chimed in, not to be outdone.

"How come he did not come with you...?" Almost before the words left her mouth, she regretted having asked. Jeannie, like most young women in training, had learned to read faces and to evaluate responses. She detected Eve's pained expression when she quickly turned away. Sharp

German=this font   English=this font   *French=this font*   *Delaware=this font*

enough to recognize her error, she wished devoutly that she could withdraw her question.

Henry, however, having accepted his lot as perfectly normal and living as he did among so many others with similar problems, answered in a matter-of-fact manner. "He got scalped and murdered by Hamilton's Indians."

Jeannie's eyes widened. Her mouth dropped open abruptly. The realization that her Daddy at this very moment helped the very same Hamilton took her breath away. Sheltered from most adult conversations, she felt a flash of shame for the first time in her young life. She, like Eve, turned her head quickly aside.

Eve, even more experienced at reading reactions, changed the subject immediately, cutting off Henry before he added any gruesome details.

"Your mother and you must really miss your father. Do you have family or friends here to help you at the fort?"

"Yes, Mister MacGregor helps mother and me," Jeannie answered, but her voice betrayed her discomfort.

Mikie, jumping up and down like a jumping-man stick-toy, saved the day. His giggles and excitement over the treats to come instantly dispelled any gloom in the room. The warm cider, rich with scents of allspice and cinnamon, tickled the senses. With Helen and Eve focused on the warping and methods to weave it off, the children returned to play and to make-believe.

Jeannie, fascinated by Mikie's tiny wooden animals, galloped them about the hearth with the boys; for Mikie carried them everywhere, even to bed in a pouch tied to his wrist. The animals' antics in their pretend forest soon became interspersed with wild stories about Tchamaniked Joe, their maker, and his dog, Teddy.

The small loom sat patiently waiting by the fireplace, ready for woof to be woven in place as Helen showed Eve and the boys out shortly before dark.

As the door closed, Helen turned to face a child whose wadded-up face edged very close to tears. She could no longer hold them back.

"Mummy, Daddy would not kill a daddy farmer, would he?"

If her words had not signaled the child's wrenching concern, the use of her babyish Mummy revealed all Jeannie's pain in a single word.

Helen gathered her daughter to her. Holding her tightly, she held her fast.

"No my dearest, Jeannie. Your Father would not do that."

"But he is with that nasty Governor Hamilton. Henry says Hamilton's Indians killed his Daddy."

"Yes, my dearest. Sad things happen during war." Taking out the lace hanky that she carried between her breasts, she stroked the tears from her daughter's wet cheeks with the warm scented material. She both admired and feared for her daughter's worship of her father. "You know that your Father is a good man and a good soldier. Believe me, he

German=this font   English=this font   *French=this font*   *Delaware=this font*

would not be party to anything like that." Helen hoped that she was not lying to her daughter as she wiped a fresh tear away. In that moment, Helen confronted the horrors that surrounded her each and everyday in Fort Detroit. The distance between the victims and her life that she had so steadfastly maintained suddenly evaporated. Eve and her boys had brought the brutality of the times unbearably close.

Swaying Jeannie in her arms, Helen added, more to convince herself than Jeannie, "Governor Hamilton always rewards the Indians for captives. He does not want them to kill them either." But even as she spoke, Helen acknowledged the duplicity of her words and the duplicity of English war policy. She shuddered. Pulling Jeannie still closer to her, she held her daughter tightly. How would Jeannie accept the inhumanity of her own father? Could the child possibly understand that justice and soldiers can seldom march side-by-side when men make war?

January 1, 1779 Fort Sackville, Indiana

"That son-of-a-bitch! His damn Indians get rum and tobacco, but what do we get? Shit, that's what. Shit!" Menard's face flushed red. His fists clinched.

"What is in your craw now, Menard?" Tchamaniked Joe asked. He had scrounged a bit of paper and now sought out some pokeberries to make ink. Menard had caught up with him, hopping from high ground to high ground. All about them, the daily drenching rains filled every gully.

"Of course, you don't care. But they took down the billiards! Both tables! Precious little to do in this worthless Wabash ditch. And they took down the bloody billiards!" Menard raved. "Break my blessed back for that bunch of pompous brandy-sniffers. And what damn little pleasure a man has, they take away!" Menard flailed at a branch of tag alder, stripping off the tiny makeshift cones and catkins from the bare winter branch, sending the pieces splashing into the nearest puddle.

"And did you hear the other shit that Hamilton and his chief henchmen, Hay, are a pullin'?"

"No."

"Did you know that all three of the De Quindre Lieutenants from his stinking corps of interpreters got permission to return to Detroit?"

"Ummph." Joe signaled his attention as he bent to retrieve twelve precious deep purple pokeberries that clung fast to the wilted stalk.

"Well, a whole pack of others are a going back, too. The lucky bastards."

"More?"

"But here's the limit. That damn Hamilton says they don't get individual passes. Too much writing he says. Makes out one stinkin' list of them he does. Gives it to old Sergeant Burgois to escort them back. Doesn't that just slap a beaver's tail! For somebody who sits on his warm arse at that damn big desk of his all the day, he can't find the time to pen them passes. Then the sons-a-bitches won't let those returnin' take their own arms. They're given' them the worst of them guns that they took from the locals. One old broken gun for two people, he says!" Menard stripped another alder branch, sending cones and catkins flying. "Hell, what's a man to do, one aim and the other pull the trigger at some God damn rotten injun or Virginian itch'n to relieve you of your scalp?"

A look of amusement crossed Joe's face.

Menard, realizing the total impropriety of his last statement, added sheepishly, "I didn't mean you, Joe."

"I know."

January 3, 1779 Fort Sackville, Indiana

"Captain MacLeod, May I enter?"

"Enter."

The sight of the tall Native American in mostly European clothes with a wool turban wound about his long hair surprised MacLeod.

"And what may I do for you?" MacLeod wondered how the man even got inside the fort this early. Indians were not allowed in until after roll call and then only with an escort. His response, therefore, sounded curt.

"I am given to understand that you have members of your party heading to Fort Detroit today."

"Yes."

"Would you be kind enough to take a letter for me to the merchant woman, Sally Ainsee, sometimes called Willson?"

"Should I know you?" MacLeod still felt uncertainty about the man before him. Though his English had overtones of French, there were unmistakable Irish overtones as well. What a curious accent the man had. Why would this man of all people have letters?

"I am one of Hamilton's carpenters, sir." Though it grated on Joe a little to say sir, he felt that if he did not do something to show deference, he could fail his mission completely.

MacLeod's forehead wrinkled. Of course he was. MacLeod remembered Joe standing breast-deep in freezing water on more than one occasion and fixing the huge axle on Hamilton's second wagon during the portage on another. The poor bloke was one who endlessly chinked pirogues. "Forgive me. I did not recognize you momentarily." Picking up his own letter packet from the small makeshift desk behind him, he swore under his breath as he wiped water from the surface of the leather cover.

"Tent is a bit leaky, sir."

"Right, on that."

German=this font   English=this font   *French=this font*   *Delaware=this font*

"If I spot some leatherwood, you could use some additional cover."

MacLeod grinned. Tit for tat, not above a little honest bribery are you, he thought.

"So your chunky partner penned you a letter for your family, eh?" Untying the leather thong that closed his packet, he reached out to take Joe's letter. "I will put it in with my correspondence to my wife, Helen."

Joe did not answer the question, preferring to let MacLeod think what he would.

As MacLeod tucked it inside, he noticed that the letter, neatly folded, had Madam Sally Ainsee in broad French-styled script. That is curious, he observed as he closed the packet.

"As soon as I am free from today's work parties, I will gather the bark."

"I would appreciate that." Replacing the packet to the dry side of the desk, he turned to find that Joe had disappeared. Once assured that his footfalls fell some distance from the tent, MacLeod picked up the packet again. Curiosity his master, he opened the packet and investigated the letter. Opening it with care so as not to smudge the purple ink, he noticed the neat script in French. I wonder, he thought, who wrote this for him?

"George here, sir." MacLeod jumped like a kid caught with his hand in the maple sugar crock. He had not heard the second man's approach either.

"Enter."

The free-black waited respectfully while MacLeod replaced the letter.

"Ready to depart, George?"

"Yes, sir."

"I want you to carry these letters on your person. Make sure they do not get wet."

"I have another oiled leather pouch, sir, that will go over yours nicely. And I will hang it all from my neck, sir, under my shirt."

"You had better, my man. Your letter of introduction for my Helen is here, and I guarantee you, she will not let you in the door without it." A hint of good natured humor hung on MacLeod's words. "At least, she had better not!" The man before him, whom he had contracted for thirty-six pounds, New York, so far promised worth the cost. A compact man, raw-boned and strong for his size, already he had proved to be both temperate and industrious.

Not totally sure yet how to approach his new employer, George decided to go with facts and not his initial impression of the friendly good humor.

"Four pirogues by water, sir. Plumbfull of men, they are." He then paused. Something within said he should be honest with the man before him. "I think your commander's orders backfired."

"How so?"

"Well sir, he ordered them who were discharged to reside outside the fort in town. Ye know how costly that can be. Yesterday he had'um 'mount guard' and 'roll call' in their 'fatigues' thinking they'd choose to stay with the water risin' an all. Them men's all a leav' right now. There sure is a pa'cel of 'em."*

"You are going by land."

"I know, sir." His voice hinted at a faint note of resignation.

The English merchants who volunteered under MacLeod had purchased horses for their return trip. George would return with them.

"By the way, you will have a horse, George," MacLeod added.

"Oh, my." George's pleasure at this prospect, given that he thought he would walk or run the whole distance, changed his stance considerably. The small man veritably beamed. "Thank...you, sir!"

"God speed."

"Thank you, sir." He reached out to shake MacLeod's hand. "I'll be a watchin' over your letters sir. Yes, sir, you can depend on it, sir."

"Now be on your way." MacLeod pushed George gently out the door. He could tell his manservant had not expected this kindness. Additionally, MacLeod hated sticky departures.

MacLeod stood outside his tent watching George's back. Drizzle ran down his neck, but he did not feel the cold rain.

"Damn, I envy you, George. Would that I was in your stead," he said to no one in particular.

The image of Helen in his mind grew clearer.

*MacLeod, Norman, *Detroit to Sackville, the Journal of Norman MacLeod* (Detroit, MI: Wayne State University Press, 1978. Paraphrased closely and some actual words from p. 123.

January 6, 1779   Fort Detroit

Magically, two wooden boxes and a few cloth bags had appeared at the door of Yankee Hall. One box contained hard sugar candy carefully portioned in individual, tiny cloth sacks, each tied with a gray string surrounded by small trinkets and brightly colored ribbons. Children squealed and adults peered at the tiny treasures that filled the box from top to bottom. A box containing a large cloth bag of white wheat flour, a five-pound hard block of white sugar with a tiny bag of spices tied to it, and salt. A large sack of choice dark red snow apples, still cool from the root cellar, had been included as well.

The first hall resident that found the morning urgency of her bladder too much to deny had discovered it. Her cry of joy had awakened the whole room. Soon, wrapped in blankets and sleepy faces, they stood about the boxes.

"Mutti, mutti, who brought this?" Henry restrained himself admirably, waiting for the adults to portion out the gifts.

German=this font   English=this font   *French=this font*   *Delaware=this font*

Nellie answered Henry. "Oh, I spect it was one of the Three Wise Men, Henry."

"Gracious, the sugar will last us for five or six months, at least," one of the women observed.

"Does anybody know what these are?" Fiona asked, lifting a string of dried fruit up for those about her to see.

"I spect they're figs. I hear tell they are mighty tasty." Nydia, a woman who slept three blankets away from Eve and Nellie, responded.

"No kiddin'."

"They're pricey."

"How many is there?"

"Six."

"How do you eat 'em?" Fiona asked.

"Well, I hears the whole thing is good to eat. We can eat 'em like candy."

"I never saw one before," added another. "So that is what they look like."

"If we boil them a little to soften them first, we can use the water to make flavored bread," remarked still another. "Not nearly enough for figgy-puddin'."

The prospect of another day hauling frozen mud at the new fort melted. But Eve, and Eve alone, recognized the neatly tied loops of thread on each tiny sack of candy. She and Helen had removed those thrums during the warping session the day before. The thread from those thrums came not from one of the Three Wise Men, but one very generous and wise woman.

Each family or group returned to their blanket, dressing for the day. The figs were dropped in boiling water for a short period and divided among improvised family groups. The precious flavored water remained for the day cooks.

As Nellie, Fiona, Eve and her boys sat quietly, Toby Langlough carefully began to divide the hot fig. After the first cut in half, hot juice trickled over his finger. He licked it off sheepishly.

"Tis mighty tasty," he said apologetically as he smacked his lips.

From a blanket over, he heard someone remark.

"They sure are tough to cut!"

"Good thing I have a sharp knife." Langlough's pride in his honing ability asserted itself. He sharpened all the knives in Yankee Hall. This task gave him a little status and made him feel useful among the prisoners. "I do not think that I can cut it in six pieces though," he informed them.

"Well, then let's cut it into four pieces. Give one to each child. And Toby Langlough, since you're doin' a ruddy good job of divvying it up...you should have the last piece," Nellie decided decisively, knowing Eve would concur.

Langlough grinned guiltily but hastily grabbed his piece.

"Dis is good," Mikie grinned as the brown juice oozed up in the corner of his mouth, spilling over the edge. He quickly harvested it with his tongue.

"It's got see-eeds. It's got see-eeds."

"Well, Henry, why don't we plant a few and see what happens," Langlough volunteered. "We will dig a little dirt and put it in that broken bottle that you and I found a few days ago. I do not think we boiled them long enough to kill them."

"It is awful chewy and seedy, but good, Mom," Fiona concluded, sucking the juice from one finger.

Eve held one of the dark red snow apples in her hand, turning it over and over.

The **pomme caille** brought back so many memories, good and bad. Anne in her cell and Joe's gentle touch seemed but a whisper's length away.

"Wish Sue Ellen was here."

"Me too, Nellie. Me too." Eve held fast to the apple.

The services had filled and emptied when a small veiled figure entered the Church. She had used the side door normally reserved for Father Bocquet. Quickly checking to see if anyone had come for prayers and finding no one in the pews, the slight figure crossed herself. She knelt on the floor before the small wooden bench placed in front of the Holy family.

"Blessed Mother Mary, you told me to come."

"Oh, Blessed Mother." Prostrating herself, Sue Ellen reached out to the figures before her, resting her hands on the base of the statue.

"But I have no gift for you or the child."

"What do you mean...I am the gift?"

The candles within the sanctuary appeared to glow more brightly to the softly crying woman. "Thank you, Blessed Mother. I am unworthy."

"Hail Mary, full of grace..." Sue Ellen began the rosary.

A few hours later, Father Bocquet found Sue Ellen lying on the floor with her thin arms fully outstretched to each side, cross-like before the main altar. She appeared quite faint as he helped her to a pew. The two of them tottered together. Could it be? Was she truly smiling? Why does she not fear my sight of her? My touch? Bocquet's thoughts flickered like the rays of the votive lights. Stunned, his hand touched her cheek in awed belief as he realized for the very first time that the horrible sores had healed. Only faint scars remained on her freckled face, drawing her smiling mouth slightly askew.

Sue Ellen beamed. Her veil had been lifted.

German=this font   English=this font   *French=this font*   *Delaware=this font*

Chapter 26   Adventures and Mis-Adventures Beginning January 10 1779

"Mr. Hamilton, in the meantime, had sent a party of forty savages, headed by white men from St. Vincent, in order if possible, to take me prisoner, and gave such instructions for my treatment as did him no honor...I believe nothing here saved me but the instructions they had not to kill or the fear of being overpowered..."

George Rogers Clark letter to friend and patron, George Mason of Gunston Hall, Virginia dated Louisville, Falls of Ohio, November 19, 1779 which related events during this time period. Quoted from: English, William Hyden, *Conquest of the Country Northwest of the River Ohio, 1778-1783 and the Life of Gen, George Rogers Clark, Vol I* (Indianapolis, Indiana and Kansas City, Missouri: Bowen-Merrill Co., 1896), p. 430.

January 10, 1779   Fort Detroit

Dr. George Anton paced back and forth in front of Nellie and Eve. The tall grave man kept running his fingers through his hair and shaking his head.

"I called you dear women because you are her closest friends."

"Stop fret'n, Doctor. Come out with it," Nellie scolded gently.

"Well, it seems your good friend, Sue Ellen, has taken it in her foolish young head that she has had a vision. The poor child is absolutely delusional from the medications I have given her."

He paced back and forth. Both women recognized that he needed to organize his thoughts as much for himself as for them. "I will have to stop the medication or I fear I will totally unhinge the dear girl, but if I stop, the ravages may return."

"Is she healed now?" Eve asked.

"Yes, scarred, but healed. Typically, she is young and her wounds healed very quickly at the last."

Both women sat pondering the situation.

Finally Nellie spoke.

"Dr. Anton, does it hurt her to be a believin' she had a vision?"

Dr. Anton nearly staggered back under the impact of her question. He had never considered that as an option.

"Well, no, I suppose it would not hurt her."

"Then I 'pect, Doctor, you best let up and leave the Good Lord handle it from here on," Nellie advised. "Let's carry the cross next time if'n you're called."

The simple testament of faith by the woman before him astounded the reasoned man.

"You realize that I asked you both here to talk some sense into her." He ran his fingers through his hair once more, but he had become markedly relaxed. The change seemed obvious to both women as they observed him

"Well, if taint no harm believ'n, I see no sense to undo it. Besides, it may truly be a miracle. Do you agree, Eve?"

"I agree."

"Anything else you want us to know'd?"

"Well, no."

"Can we see her?" Nellie immediately asked.

"Can the children come?" Eve followed in rapid succession.

"Yes to both of your questions." Dr. Anton still marveled at the women before him. My God, they stick together, he thought, wondering if his own friends would stand by him in a similar situation. "I will contact her and tell her to contact you. That way she will feel more relaxed, I think. She can come to you when she is ready."

"We'd best go now. Need to get up to the new fort. They told us to help re-seat that east side. Washed out with the last rain, you know," Nellie informed him without any expectation of pity. She merely related a fact.

Dr. Anton shivered at the thought of his wife or daughter slogging about in the ice cold mud carrying pails of frozen dirt. As Eve turned, her profile, while mostly hidden by another skirt layered for warmth under her apron, revealed to Dr. Anton that she might be in her second trimester.

"When is the child due, Mistress Eve?"

"Late April, maybe May," Eve answered.

"Are you sure you should be out there at the fort?"

"Now that the morning sickness has let up, Doctor Anton, I have no troubles to speak of."

"Well, if you should take to spotting, you let me know. I will gladly write an excuse for you."

"That is kind, sir. Thank you."

"Will you need my services for the lying-in?"

"I expect not, sir. Martha said she would help."

"Is she the one that helped Sue Ellen initially?"

"Yes, sir."

"Thank you again, Dr. Anton." Nellie pumped his hand in her strong grip. "You tell that gal that there's some mighty big hugs await'n."

Eve had no heart to tell the doctor that the locals said that he lost too many babies to childbed fever, especially after all his kindness to Sue Ellen. But Martha had a far better record in the fort. Besides, Martha would not expect Eve to give birth lying down. Eve particularly wanted a woman with her this time, since her Adam Henry could not hold her in the birthing chair. Goodness, she would miss him at her delivery.

German=this font   English=this font   *French=this font*   *Delaware=this font*

The women left, chattering excitedly.

Dr. Anton still reeled from their insightful compassion.

January 10, 1779
Fort Sackville, Vincennes, Indiana

The men readied the forty-by-eighteen-foot rectangular trench dug in anticipation of the logs for the new barracks. Thirty feet away, Menard dropped a dirt bucket down to Tchamaniked Joe, who stood nearly mid-calf deep in water. With the water levels so high all about fort, the fort itself rose like an ancient castle in a mote. The well-digging crew had fervently hoped to find water before twenty feet. However, it appeared that twenty-five feet would be the actual case. Makeshift ladders enabled the diggers to climb up and down the tiered sides. Joe knew Menard's rheumatics could not bear as much standing in the cold water as he, so he volunteered for another hour's dig. Menard's grateful smile from topside conveyed his thanks.

The grumbles of some of the locals, especially the Bouchers, added to the mix of noise. They worked to square logs near them. Their steady patter of complaints mixed with the chopping sounds and with the raspy buzz of saws emanating from the saw pit.

When a major portion of the second tier oozed into the water beside Joe, he cursed quietly under his breath. Another ten or more bushels of wet earth moved to lay about his feet, bringing the water over his knees. Had the Major not been in earshot, he had a feeling that Menard would have roasted his ears with his choice epithets.

Beside the well, Major Jehu Hay peered down brimming with disapproval, as if Joe had single-handedly caused the landfall.

"Jehu!"

"Over here, Charles."

Charles Reaume, a member of Hay's wife's family, had finally caught up with Hay.

Joe gave a conniving grin to Menard, who knew that the Major's fury would be diverted for at least a few moments.

"Is that fool Rebel messenger going to live?" Hay asked.

"Probably, if he does not get pneumonia. I dare say at this point, if he knew, Lieutenant Clark would wish that the frozen fool were anywhere else but here, even dead. Believe me, definitely not here. Hamilton is totally ecstatic over his letter which Clark intended for Helm, our happy parolee."

"Really, how is that?"

"They have no suspicion that we have captured this fort. Jabbered on and on about De Peyster possibly sending forces down the Illinois in the spring. Clark even threatened the locals at his fort with burning their homes if they left for the Spanish side of the river."

German=this font   English=this font   ***French=this font***   *Delaware=this font*

Reaume saved the best gossip for last.

"And here is the coup de grace...they do not have powder, and they are sending two pirogues of taffia and flour here." He slapped Hay heartily on the shoulder. "Yup, right here! Can you beat that luck?"

Both Hay and Reaume fairly smacked their lips in anticipation.

The ignored workers, like all unnoticed eyes and ears, would dutifully pass the information on to their peers. And as usual, the officers would wonder where the leaks in their respective offices were and how the volunteer militia or other rabble knew what was going on nearly as well as they did.

Information paraphrased from the journal of MacLeod, Norman, *Detroit to Sackville, the Journal of Norman MacLeod* (Detroit, MI: Wayne State University Press, 1978), p. 127.

January 12, 1779
Fort Sackville, Vincennes, Indiana

"He does not believe me. I can see it in his eyes. He does not believe me," Lieutenant Jacob Schieffelin lamented to Captain MacLeod and Lieutenant Henry DuVernett.

MacLeod's tent proved the driest, thanks to Tchamaniked Joe's secondary tent of leatherwood bark on a willow frame which now covered the militia head's terribly worn and leaky tent. So, naturally, the men had congregated there in the pouring rain. The last wall for the new barrack would just have to wait another day.

"Take a bit of cheer, Jacob." MacLeod pulled a flask from amongst his bedding and poured an ample swig of it in his pewter mug.

Lieutenant Henry DuVernett looked sympathetically at Schieffelin, who had returned on one of the two pirogues owned by Jean L'Course, the merchant. L'Course and his men had apparently assisted Schieffelin in his hour of need.

However, Schieffelin returned in shame without the original party of men that he had led out in late December with explicit instructions from Hamilton. A party of seven of LaMothe's men had deserted him, taking his boat. In the sequence of events, Egushawa, the Ottawa and Chippewa chief, and his party of fifteen warriors and a Delaware had separated from his supervision and now scouted about on their own near Kaskaskia.

Hamilton's undisguised fury had so terrified Schieffelin that Jacob fairly shook remembering his superior's wrath.

"Sit down, man! Tell us what happened, for Christ's sake!" MacLeod ordered.

Schieffelin shook as he took the proffered cup. He took a deep swig. He stared at the empty doorway as though history replayed before him.

"We were camped at the mouth of the Wabash on the night of

German=this font   English=this font   *French=this font*   *Delaware=this font*

December 31. I did not trust that man L'Course. Cannot put a trunnel in it, but I had an uneasy feeling...what with all his constant prattle about how he is for our King. We expected more boats or pirogues from the Illinois, so I posted two sentries to be doubly alert and turned in for the night." Schieffelin took another sip, his teeth clicking against the side of the cup as he drank. "I was dry, thirsty, so I asked my man to bring me a draft of water before I turned in. No sooner had I swallowed it when my mouth tasted like bitter metal and my head spun. I swooned completely."*

Schieffelin studied the faces of the men about him and perceived no disbelief. He continued, "My last memory was falling pitch forward into my bed. I awoke about three in the morning, shaking from the cold. My head rung like a struck bell. I called out to my sentry." A look of sheer pain crossed Schieffelin's features. "No one." He took another sip, looking questionably at MacLeod. "Brandy?"

MacLeod nodded affirmatively. He figured his young friend needed the stronger spirit which had come from his personal flask. Obviously, he had been correct in his assessment. The poor lad had not noticed the type of spirits until now.

"So I called the Corporal. No answer. I stumbled into L'Course's camp and asked him if he saw my men and the boat leave.

"Of course that French..." he wanted to say bastard. But with Lieutenant DuVernett sitting across from him, he hesitated before continuing, "trader, L'Course denied hearing anyone leave or foreknowledge of any rumors before their departure. Instead, he says, 'you have only lost Seven men, there is seven more [of] my men. Command them; you'll find that they stand by you and So Shall I myself, oppose you who will. We will fight as long as we can for you and in behalf of your King——'"*

"But you still do not trust him?"

"Even though he helped you?"

Schieffelin surveyed both men, shaking his head negatively. "I really do not."

Information paraphrased closely from the journal of MacLeod, Norman, *Detroit to Sackville, the Journal of Norman MacLeod* **(Detroit, MI: Wayne State University Press, 1978). Words and paraphrase, p. 128-129. Actual quote: p. 129.**

January 14, 1779 Vincennes, Indiana

Lieutenant Governor Henry Hamilton finished his letter for Don Bernardo de Galvis. The two Spanish merchants waited in the anteroom. He felt approaching the Governor of New Orleans directly would be in the Crown's best interest at this juncture. Stressing the necessity of not supplying arms to the rebellious forces, Hamilton further warned the

German=this font   English=this font   *French=this font*   *Delaware=this font*

Governor that his Spanish officers along the Mississippi should not give aid or protection to the fleeing combatants or be willing to 'abide the consequences.' *   Satisfied that he had staunchly stated the Crown's strengths, he sealed the letter with hot wax. Grasping the other letter that he had prepared earlier for Captain Bloomer, the commander at Natchez, he placed them in two vellum folders. Straightening himself, he made sure his uniform was in perfect order before he returned to the anteroom.

Guillaume le Comte and Vigaud the Piedmontese, known simply as Vigo by many about the fort, jumped to their feet the instant Hamilton entered the room.

"Gentlemen, you know that your passports are contingent on delivery of these letters. Is that fully understood?"

"*Si, si, senor*, we understand *perfecto*," Vigo Francis answered.

Handing one packet to each, Hamilton curtly dismissed them with their passports and destination for their journey.

Major Jehu Hay brushed by them as they exited the office, stepping by three or four individuals waiting on the Lieutenant Governor.

"Where is Francis Vigo off to?" Hay asked as he entered the anteroom and followed Hamilton into his office.

"I have decided to contact the Spanish settlements directly, including the Spanish Governor in New Orleans. Since these two traders have no desire to be part of the conflict, I have directed them to act as neutral couriers to the Spanish. Hopefully, after their commandants become aware of the strength of our forces and that of our many allies, the Spanish will realize it would not be wise for them to leave their settlements west of the Mississippi."

"Brilliant move, Sir."

Hamilton sloughed off the compliment.

"What have you in mind?" Fatigue draped about the Commander.

"A celebration, sir. I think a little levity is in order. Our gracious Queen Charlotte seems a just reason. The barracks will be mostly finished. I suggest on the 18th we convene the Militia and hoist their colors. I have a brand new Union flag to complement the occasion. And then the officers can dine in the new barrack."*

Hamilton hesitated.

"It will give you a chance to see all the improvements, and it will uplift the men's spirits."

"All right, Major Hay. Say no more. See to it."

**Hamilton, Henry. *Henry Hamilton and George Rogers Clark in the American Revolution with the Unpublished Journal of Gov. Henry Hamilton,* John D. Barnhart, (Crawfordsville, Indiana: R. E. Ranta, 1951). Information paraphrased from Hamilton's journal. p. 163-164.
* quote p. 164.

German=this font   English=this font   *French=this font*   *Delaware=this font*

January 18, 1779
Fort Sackville, Vincennes, Indiana

Menard got through each day attached to a string of oaths. Even on this rare day off, he stood fuming. This time it was over the Bouchers' decision to pledge their allegiance to the Crown to get out of the hard work within the fort. The recalcitrant brothers had finally broken under the yoke of building barracks and powder magazines. Unlike many of the town's inhabitants, the Boucher brothers had initially refused to take the British oath of allegiance which meant they must serve on work details. However, the daily grind of exhausting, wet and cold work contrasted against the warm lassitude of their fellow townsmen, who had caved in. In the end, the three brothers had decided not to be heroes. The result placed an additional burden on the carpenters.

"Hell, Joe. If I take an oath to his majesty's arse, do you think that I could return to town and sit by a warm fire?" Menard cursed. "Better yet take me arse home."

Tchamaniked Joe stood beside him tallying the decreased numbers left in the three companies that stood at review in the mist before their colors. The numbers had dwindled remarkably over their month at the fort. Daily, discharged men returned to Fort Detroit. Like Menard, a bitter string of complaints strung them together.

Joe and Menard both recognized it was not just the volunteers leaving. Many of the campfires surrounding the Fort had also extinguished. On the few high spots left in the flooded area that totally surrounded them, fewer and fewer fires remained lit in the night.

Some tribes, under the guise of family responsibilities, feigned the need to appease hunger and return to the winter hunt. Hamilton heard their ready excuse that they could not be men growing fat around Hamilton's fires while their families grew thin.**

Others left with their interpreters for raiding parties or reconnaissance. However, each day fewer and fewer of them returned. The latest gossip said that even the well-respected Matthew Elliott had returned three days ago without his Shawnee brothers. Despite his urging, they would not proceed, for they feared that they had been discovered near the Falls of the Ohio. Instead, they left Elliott abruptly, stating that they must report back to their villages 'what was doing in Vincennes' rather than to stay with him.*

Still others begged leave to tell their tribes of the additional warriors needed to convene in the spring and to tell of the abundance of supplies by their English father, Hamilton. At the very same time, rumors widely reported that DeJean had already been sent back to Detroit for more supplies to fill a drained larder.

Joe jumped when Menard jabbed him in the ribs. He had been lost in thought.

German=this font   English=this font   *French=this font*   *Delaware=this font*

"Joe, look, the leatherwood shelter you put around MacLeod's tent is gone."

"Eh, Menard, you are right."

"How come, Joe? That kept the good Captain right dry."

Anderson, another carpenter, next to Menard stage whispered, "Hush up, you two. Captain LaMothe is a givin' us the evil eye." Then he added a morsel of gossip too juicy not to share. One worth the risk of being the butt of one of LaMothe's ranting sprees. "Didn't you hear that Hay ordered it pulled down? Said it was unprofessional. Not becoming an officer in his Majesty's service. That's what."

The royal salute almost drowned out his last words, but Menard thought he had whispered further, "And dat Scotsman, he got mighty damn mad."

The new quarters would be appreciated by the men. It was just too bad that they could not christen their own table with the officers. MacLeod felt uneasy when he saw the extent of the officers' spread before him. Ham, roast beef, turkey, and a large platter of roasted chickens centered the long table. Vegetables, pies and breads crowded around the plentiful meat dishes. MacLeod felt guilty given that boiled potatoes, salt pork, and dried beef would probably be the fare of his men after all their hard work, even if it did come with a double ration of rum.

Hay's chatter had already increased a notch in volume from the taffia that he had ingested. From time to time his laughter joined Hamilton's as Hamilton interacted with the Rebel prisoner, Helm. The commander obviously enjoyed the man's witty company. Lieutenant Henry DuVernett stood apart as well across the room, frowning. MacLeod, wrestling with the inconsistencies, decided to sally-up to the taffia barrel and give ease to his conscience. He assumed as he strode toward the barrel of low grade rum that it must be one of the confiscated barrels from the recent Rebel shipment.

However, MacLeod's first impression proved totally incorrect. An attempt had been made to erase the chalky scrawl. However, even partly obliterated, a man recognized his own name.

"Well, ifn' that would not make a banshee wail," MacLeod sputtered. I guess I get to drink a wee bit of me own barrel after all, he thought, as he extended his cup for a bit of ill-gotten goods. He made a mental note not to over imbibe, as he would never check his temper this night if he did.

*Hamilton, Henry, *Henry Hamilton and George Rogers Clark in the American Revolution with the Unpublished Journal of Gov. Henry Hamilton.* John D. Barnhart, Ed. (Crawfordsville, Indiana: R. E. Ranta, 1951). Information paraphrased from the journal p. 164-165. * quote p. 164. Closely paraphrased p. 166.

German=this font   English=this font   *French=this font*   *Delaware=this font*

January 18, 1779   Fort Detroit

"I need more thread for my loom, Mistress Ainsee. Do you think you could find some for me?" Helen MacLeod fingered the checkered gingham that Sally Ainsee had pulled down from her short stack of bolts. "I realize it is winter and all."

Sally Ainsee's usual supply had been markedly diminished by the impact of DeJean's recent buyout. Even though he had taken some of her less popular prints, the sale hurt her profits and depleted her stock. DeJean would never pay the full market price for Hamilton's Indian department. She had to accept less or take the chance of having the goods confiscated for the Crown with no remuneration at all.

"Mistress MacLeod, what are you doing with all your thread? Nickerson's not come by yet, and surely you and Jeannie can't be a knit'n it up that fast."

Helen MacLeod merely laughed.   "We warped the loom. It will be woven off right soon."

Sally Ainsee looked pleasantly surprised. "And how came you to do that?"

"Remember the lad, Henry?   Well, Mistress Ainsee, he bragged rightly. His mother, Eve, can set a loom with the best of them."

"Well, doesn't that beat all. By my mind, that's a sad waste to have her toten' mud."

"But it sure took some talking to get her to come."

"Oh, why is that?"

Sally Ainsee could tell that Helen MacLeod seemed reluctant to share at first. She never carried tales about anyone, even prisoners.

"Well, weaving is somehow tied to her late husband. She would not say how. She said she feared she would get too gloomy if she came. But you know, Mistress Ainsee, it seemed once her hands touched the threads, and she raked them with her fingers as she tied them fast, she looked as happy as I ever saw a woman. I had the feeling that she dearly envied me for weaving it off."

Sally Ainsee, never slow to recognize another opportunity, immediately considered a new enterprise. Astute, she constantly looked for ways to increase her capital. She still had that old log loom in the shed out back. An old man had traded it in for food and applejack one winter and then up and died on her before he could retrieve it. Sally, who had taken the loom only to save his pride in the first place, had no heart just to throw it away or to sell it off. Afterwards she had stuffed it in her cluttered stocking shed.

The woman was with child. Surely she could not work up at the new fort much longer. Maybe she might be better employed here to work off her debts. Yes, indeed, she might better work here. Even as Sally finalized the goods sale to Mistress MacLeod, Sally Ainsee planned where she might find space to set up the old man's loom.

German=this font   English=this font   *French=this font*   *Delaware=this font*

January 19, 1779 Fort Sackville, Vincennes, Indiana

Lieutenant Henry DuVernett and Captain Norman MacLeod bent over DuVernett's rough draft. The disgruntled Lieutenant had given up any pretense or desire to remain at Fort Sackville. He deeply regretted volunteering to leave his garrison and devoutly wished to return to his post in Detroit. Asking MacLeod to go over his written request that 'hinted at [the] Service being very disagreeable to him and his not being w[ell] or civilly used'*, he sought advice from one of the few men left that he respected. The calls and pounding of the carpenters without filtered in like the moisture through MacLeod's tent. Everyone had wet tasks this morning.

Information paraphrased closely from the journal MacLeod, Norman, *Detroit to Sackville, the Journal of Norman MacLeod* (Detroit, MI: Wayne State University Press, 1978), words and paraphrase, p. 131. Actual quote: p. 131.

January 20, 1779. Fort Sackville, Vincennes, Indiana

Lieutenant DuVernett would not be dissuaded to change his mind. Even when threatened, the Lieutenant firmly held his ground. Finally sensing the futility of reversing his Lieutenant's decision, Lieutenant Governor Hamilton recapitulated. "So it appears that you believe Major Hay is the 'chief cause' of your decision to leave us."* **

"Yes, sir, he lords it over the men. Believe me, sir, when I say that 'every officer and Soldier on the expedition hate[] and despise[] him.' " * Adding as an afterthought, "Captain LaMothe also interfered with the parade of my men."**

"Do you not recognize that this stand is 'not consistent with [your] voluntary offer'** to come under this command?"

Lieutenant DuVernett stood silent. He would not dignify the question with a response.

Knowing that DuVernett's service if 'detained against his inclination' would incite further defections, Hamilton decided to use his last resort, an apology.**

"I recognize that at times 'Major Hay [has]...'" Hamilton hated the awkwardness of this position, " 'not a method of gaining People's Good Will', for which 'I am sorry'." *

Hamilton neither had time to hear DuVernett's next response nor finish his sentence.

Lieutenant Jacob Schieffelin exploded through the door like a six-pound canon ball. His contorted face gleamed white-hot. The normally

German=this font   English=this font   *French=this font*   *Delaware=this font*

reserved Schieffelin shouted his dismay so loud that every room in the house registered his total dissatisfaction.

"If you think that I am going to work for a damn dollar a day at half pay, you can take this bloody commission and that stinking Major Hay back all the way to Montreal for all I care."

"Calm down, Jacob." The use of his given name harkened back to earlier times, times when Hamilton and Jacob Schieffelin had shared closer ties.

Immediately Lieutenant Jacob Schieffelin's fury damped down.

"I know he did it. He cut my pay, I know he did." The distraught man bordered on the brink of humiliating tears now that nothing but the smoke remained from his anger.

Hamilton moved to Jacob's side and touched his former secretary's shoulder in good faith. "Believe me, Jacob, 'whoever informed [you] of [your] pay being taken from [you] [has it] on poor authority.' Let me settle this misunderstanding once and for all." **

Hamilton at once called for his new secretary to draft his order that Schieffelin was to have his two-dollar per day pay reinstated. As Hamilton's current secretary completed his task, Hamilton and Schieffelin left the office together. In the adjacent room Lieutenant Henry DuVernett stood smiling, waiting for the Lieutenant Governor's return.

When Hamilton re-entered his office, he had no doubt concerning DuVernett's irrevocable decision.

"And that man is among your most loyal Lieutenants, sir. My discharge, sir."

Hamilton personally wrote the discharge and an order for DuVernett to accompany Matthew Elliott on his return through the southern Shawnee villages en route to Fort Detroit. They left early the following morning.

*Information paraphrased closely from the journal MacLeod, Norman, *Detroit to Sackville, the Journal of Norman MacLeod* (Detroit, MI: Wayne State University Press, 1978). Actual words, close paraphrases and quotes, p. 131- 133.

**Hamilton, Henry, *Henry Hamilton and George Rogers Clark in the American Revolution with the Unpublished Journal of Gov. Henry Hamilton.* John D. Barnhart, Ed. (Crawfordsville, Indiana: R.E. Ranta, 1951). Information closely paraphrased and quoted from Hamilton's journal p. 166- 167.

January 22, 1779   Fort Detroit

"Oh, Eve, Eve, I am a going home. I am going home." While she might have been angry and embarrassed by Eve's current pregnancy, Eve still remained Margaret Elder's strongest tie to her home, her family, and her beloved husband, George, in Pennsylvania. Filled with excitement and expectation, she turned to those closest to her and rushed over to Yankee Hall from the barracks' kitchen the first moment her duties permitted.

German=this font   English=this font   *French=this font*   *Delaware=this font*

Margaret Elder bounced up and down like an excited child, which was totally out of character for the reserved and pious Margaret. Absolutely giddy, she shared her heady news with Eve, Nellie and Fiona. "I have money for passage on a boat to Montreal and then to New York this spring. I have it all!"

All three women grinned back, fighting back any jealous urge in the face of their friend's joy. Too little good news entered the doors of Yankee Hall. Collectively, they had learned that one must learn to revel in anything that brings happiness to others because tragedies always gather sympathetic listeners while happiness garners few.

"I am going home! My ransom, my passage, and my fees, everything. Oh, however did my George manage this?" Margaret gushed.

"Well, he managed it plumb well by the sounds." Nellie verbally applauded Margaret's glad tidings. "That's mighty fine news, Margaret." Nellie found herself touching Margaret as if she had an unspoken need to confirm the reality of Margaret's happiness and rub some of her happiness off.

Usually Margaret stood apart, not given much to hugs and such, but not today. Soon the women locked their arms tightly about each other, congratulating Margaret for her good fortune. They joined her dancing about, laughing, and giggling. Margaret could not suppress the girl hidden in all women and the feeling proved contagious.

"Can I join in?" The four women turned simultaneously to greet Sue Ellen's shy request. Joyous tears immediately filled all their eyes. Even Toby Langlough across the room wiped away a tear before dissolving into a coughing spell. There, for the first time in over a month, stood Sue Ellen in a simple black dress. A small wooden cross hung from her waist on a finely braided rope. Her hair was neatly tucked beneath a plain black scarf.

The scars dimmed by their tears faded completely as their arms reached out to her.

"Hot damn, this is one mighty fine day," Nellie squealed, as she jerked Sue Ellen into the center of the four women, leaping the gulf between them, extinguishing the reluctance to touch with crushing finality. "One's a goin' home. One's back to stay."

Centered together, Margaret cried. "God be praised."

"Amen, and amen," Sue Ellen intoned while held fast in the arms of her friends.

January 22, 1779 Fort Sackville, Indiana

Hypolite Bolon slipped alongside Captain Norman MacLeod. Norman appeared not to notice his presence. "That damn 'impatient' Egushawa let the horse out of the barn," Bolon said quietly. "Clark knows we're here. We damn near caught him near Kaskaskia."

German=this font   English=this font   *French=this font*   *Delaware=this font*

Captain Norman MacLeod turned aside. All the pieces fell into place. Excusing himself, he went to his tent to record his thoughts in his journal.

*Information paraphrased closely from the journal MacLeod, Norman, *Detroit to Sackville, the Journal of Norman MacLeod* (Detroit, MI: Wayne State University Press, 1978). Close paraphrase, p. 133-134.

January 24, 1779   At a Campsite near Fort Sackville, Vincennes, Indiana

"Do you all know my wife's cousin? He works as carpenter for our English father, Hamilton."

Egushawa sat across from the young interpreter, Hypolite Bolon. Pierre and Isidore Chesne and the Delaware, Blue Ice, also joined the group about the fire. Tchamaniked Joe sat to Egushawa's left. Calamuti, nephew of Isidore, sat at Egushawa's right.

"Will you smoke, brother?" Blue Ice offered a clay pipe to Joe.

"No, it is not my habit. I think you all know me, save you." He scrutinized Blue Ice. He could tell that the Delaware, Blue Ice, found little to respect in carpentry by the way he withdrew the pipe and the open disdain on his face.

"This man makes a fine canoe. His paddles sing." Instantly, Egushawa's proud evaluation of Joe's skill brought a partial re-evaluation by Blue Ice. "He has traveled to the world of our French fathers and returned."

"Come, come, Egushawa. Enough of my foolish past. Let the memories sleep. What of your recent exploits?" Wisely, Joe deflected attention from himself to Egushawa. "The stories stampede about the Fort like many buffalo. Many say that you nearly caught the Virginian, Clark."**

"So you have heard already of our brave exploits." Egushawa cast a look of 'I told you so' in Isidore's direction. "And that one, he says...do not go! We hold back because this one says that we must not be seen by the farmers for we are strange Indians here. How foolish. Farmers do not know one Indian from another. Believe me, I know."** He drew deeply on his own pipe, sending a few smoke rings aloft for the raindrops to use as targets. "So we set a trap instead by the men's large trading canoe on the River near Kaskaskia and along the road. And because of this, we do not have Clark's scalp on our belts. Our trap never springs for Clark because he escapes our grasp on horseback in the depth of night.** How do we know the man was Clark? It is because of this brave one, Blue Ice. He went into the city of Kaskaskia. No one took notice of him because he is Delaware. They ask him questions, but he is wise and reveals nothing. He hears that Clark had just returned from Prairie de Rocher. So we know that it was he."

German=this font   English=this font   *French=this font*   *Delaware=this font*

Tchamaniked Joe sat quietly. He noticed the abbreviated shake of his head and the roll of Bolon's eyes followed by a brief glance to heaven for guidance.

"Will you stay this night, Joe? You can walk with me come morning light to the Huron Camp. Like the Wyandot, they talk of returning to their home camps until the spring. I must tell them that they should stay with our English Father until we 'see how matters turn out.' You wait, those ones will say that 'they do not let go of their father's hand', but as for me, I choose to stay. 'Others may do as they please*.'"

Pierre placed more wood on the roaring fire, recognizing that any letup meant that the chilling rain would prevail. He preferred to be wet and warm. He reasoned that this certainly beat being wet and cold. Tiny spirals of steam signaled the demise of each drop of rain and the dampness of the fuel.

"No, Egushawa, regretfully I must leave. Tell your shaman that I appreciate his strong medicine for my friend's chills. He shakes and sweats with fever, which is why I came. But your hospitality and fire truly tempt me to stay."

"Go then, but return soon. We see too little of you. *Baamaa pii.*"

"*Baamaa pii*...Until I see your face as well my brother."

Inwardly, Blue Ice smoldered as he considered how much English and French was spoken at the tribal fires. Here the brothers had spoken English. More and more the brothers opted to speak the white man's tongue rather than use their own when various tribes came together. Perhaps this made sure that no tribe was considered inferior because his language was not spoken, but did this give the English more power?

The rain had raised the water around the Fort by another foot, Joe observed as he worked his way back to the Fort. Indecision played with his thoughts. But when he arrived totally soaked and gave out the appropriate sentry call to re-enter the Fort, he had made up his mind.

MacLeod sat up abruptly. Startled, he nearly jumped out of his bearskin. A tall, rangy figure stood darkly silhouetted in his doorway. He had not heard the man enter, but he knew instinctively who it was.

"Carpenter Joe?"

"Go home to your Helen." Just as quietly as he came, Tchamaniked Joe vanished into the rainy night.

MacLeod settled back on his damp blanket, pulling the wet bearskin up to his nose. A large drop of water plopped on his forehead. Maybe the man is right. I am getting too old for this, he thought. But MacLeod knew down deep the real reason that he wanted to leave. Like Lieutenant DuVernett and so many, many others, he simply had a craw full of the whole wet fiasco. He had a duty to protect Helen and Jeannie, not this damn broken down fort in the middle of nowhere. For the first time in months, he felt the surge of his loins. "Behave laddy, we are not home yet," he said as he rolled on to his side and fell into a troubled sleep.

German=this font   English=this font   *French=this font*   *Delaware=this font*

*Hamilton, Henry, *Henry Hamilton and George Rogers Clark in the American Revolution with the Unpublished Journal of Gov. Henry Hamilton.* John D. Barnhart, Ed. (Crawfordsville, Indiana: R.E. Ranta, 1951). Information paraphrased from the journal p. 166-171.

**Information paraphrased closely from the journal MacLeod, Norman, *Detroit to Sackville, the Journal of Norman MacLeod,* (Detroit, MI: Wayne State University Press, 1978), p. 132-134.

January 27, 1779 Fort Sackville, Vincennes, Indiana

The sun burst through the cloud cover for the first time in days. Bright beams streamed favorably down on the soaked parade ground. Echoes of yesterday's long rallying speech to many tribes by Egushawa still clung to the trampled grasses like a morning's frost to be quickly sublimated by the morning's first rays. A new barrack waited to be raised and another to be covered with clapboards.

The Chippewa prepared to leave less one prisoner, a young man to replace a lost son stayed behind with Hamilton. They carried home more useless silver gorgets and trinkets instead. Steadfastly, Egushawa elected to remain with his young braves. The Wyandot had left earlier.

Three men packed their belongings, preparing for the long trip home. MacLeod surveyed the field and listened wistfully to the sounds of the carpenters at work. He could not make out Joe or his partner Menard in the crews. Ten pirogues waited for him and his companions. He prepared to join thirty of the local inhabitants who had been commandeered to return with the pirogues filled once more with more supplies purchased from the Miami. Shouldering his bedroll and grasping his Brown Bess, he joined Lieutenant St. Cosme and Charles Baubien.

"Has Maisonville returned yet with the defectors?" St. Cosme asked.

"Hell, if I know," Baubien replied.

"Enough, men, let us go home."

*Hamilton, Henry, *Henry Hamilton and George Rogers Clark in the American Revolution with the Unpublished Journal of Gov. Henry Hamilton.* John D. Barnhart, Ed. (Crawfordsville, Indiana: R.E. Ranta, 1951). Information paraphrased from the journal p. 170-171.

January 27, 1779 Fort Detroit

"Well, what do you think? Is it useable?"

Eve could not conceal her excitement from Sally Ainsee. "We need to make new string heddles. These are squee-hawed from storage.

German=this font   English=this font   *French=this font*   *Delaware=this font*

But that is easy done. I can put the boys to it." Her hands veritably caressed the hand-worn beams, smoothed and polished from repeated human touch, the mark of the hand, the mark of a working craftsman. "The reed is broken in two places but that is mostly at the ends. The middle is still good. It is wider than my one at home even without the ends." Barely had the words left her mouth, when a dark shadow crossed Eve's features.

Sally Ainsee grasped the woman's shoulders firmly between her two hands, giving her a gentle shake, as if to re-center her attention. "Woman, this may be your path home. If you can get this fool thing up and going, I'll do my damnedest to find what you need. I'll even try to get other looms. If you can train other women to string these infernal things and weave it off, I am absolutely certain the Frenchies will buy it up and at a damn good profit. I make a fair profit. You earn your freedom. I'll pay you by the piece for your time. You'll get some extra for trainin' and warpin'."

Eve reflected on Sally's words. She and the boys were barely getting by just paying their board and keep. The ugly number four put by her name by Philip DeJean for her ransom still smarted. Rarely could she put anything in her saving jug to go towards the ransom. And when she did save some, what little she had melted away for honest needs like Sue Ellen or Mikie's measles. The loom promised hope. "There is only one big problem as I see it, Mistress Ainsee."

"Hell, woman, call me Sally. What's the damn problem?"

"It takes four to seven spinners to keep one weaver really happy."

"Do you know how to spin?"

"Not well enough to make a warp. Weft I am okay with, but warp needs to be stronger and regular, otherwise the tension can be a real problem. Bad tension, bad quality. If I spin, I would not have time to weave."

"Well, like they say, if there's a will, there's a way."

She dropped her hands from Eve's shoulders and extended her right hand. "Deal?"

"Deal!"

As if the one within approved of the bargain struck between the two women, a mound raised and followed an invisible arc along the curve of Eve's abdomen before finishing the movement with a swift joyous kick.

When Eve flinched, Sally laughed. "You may have another wild boy there, Eve."

"Or a strong girl!"

Their laughter warmed a winter day.

German=this font English=this font **French=this font** *Delaware=this font*

Chapter 27
Flooding, Frenchmen, and Fury
Meet the Fates in February, 1779

"I sent off horsemen to St. Vincent to take a prisoner by which we might get intelligence, but found it impracticable on account of a the high waters; but in the height of our anxiety, on the evening of the 29th of January, 1779, Mr. Vigo, a Spanish merchant, arrived from St. Vincent, and was there the time of its being taken and gave me every intelligence that I could wish to have. Governor Hamilton's party consisted of about eight hundred when he took possession on the 17th day of December past. Finding the season too far spent for his intention against Kaskaskia, had sent nearly the whole of his Indians out in different parties to war, but to embody as soon as weather would permit and complete his design. He had also sent messengers to the southern Indians, five hundred of whom he expected to join him. Only eighty troops in garrison, our situation still appeared desperate. It was in this moment that I would have bound myself seven years a slave to have had five hundred troops."

George Rogers Clark letter to friend and patron, George Mason of Gunston Hall, Virginia dated Louisville, Falls of Ohio, November 19, 1779 relating events during this time period. Quoted from: English, William Hyden, *Conquest of the Country Northwest of the River Ohio, 1778-1783 and the Life of Gen. George Rogers Clark, Vol I.* (Indianapolis, Indiana and Kansas City, MO: Bowen-Merrill Co., 1896), p. 436.

February 2, 1779   Fort Detroit

"Listen up people, Eve's got something to share," Nellie announced to the crowd of folks that had gathered loosely about them.

"I suppose the Dutchy thinks we need another bath."

"Got a damn fixation on cleanliness that one."

"Cleanliness is next to Godliness, haven't you heard."

"Quiet! Buck! Hannah!" Nellie chided again. "Quiet everyone!!"

Langlough lay on his blanket and tried peeking through between the forest of legs and long skirts in front of his pallet. His recent coughing spell had subsided. He hid the bloody show in a rag under his blanket.

"Nellie, thank you." Eve paused, trying to get her furrows in a neat row. Could anyone get them to pull together? One simply could not find a more mismatched team. She recognized that she needed to reach the women. Her voice quavered a little as she began, but soon her enthusiasm took over.

"I have been talking to Sally Ainsee...and we think we could do some spinning, weaving, needlework, and knitting for folks here at the fort."

"Hell, ain't we got enough to do for the good folks at the fort now?"

"Hush up, Buck, let her finish."

"Mistress Ainsee feels that the French ladies and soldiers here would pay well for these items from her store, like warm socks, mittens, side runners and such."

"I could use some new socks." Buck loved an audience.

"She will pay us fairly by the piece." Eve caught their full attention for the first time. "Sally Ainsee has a loom and she is willing to get others. She will provide needles, cards, wheels, and such to get us started. But first, we need someone to spin warp. Is there any amongst you that can spin warp? It has to be reasonably fine and strong. Worsted would be best."

Maggie in the back row put up her hand shyly. "I used to pay my taxes with my linen warp. Spect I could do it again."

"Hot damn. Will you teach me?" Nellie asked.

Ugly little Maggie rarely spoke-up and rose to new importance. She nodded affirmatively as the center of attention. "Sure Nellie, I could teach you."

Now everyone in the room immediately understood why her lower lip seemed overly large. Her lip testified to years of spinning linen and the habit of moistening it between her lower lip and her gum before she wound it on the bobbin to set the twist. Eve looked at her with new knowledge and even greater appreciation.

"Would you teach me, too?" Fiona asked.

"Sure youngin'."

Already Eve saw a prideful change come over Maggie.

"I can spin." Hannah volunteered as Buck glared.

"Good. We have got a good start there. We will need others."

"I can card." The weakened voice from the vicinity of the floor surprised everyone. The legs and skirts parted to permit Langlough his space. "I used to card for my Ma." Then he looked down sadly. "I can still do that."

A wave of understanding encircled the room. Lately Toby Langlough had been able to do little else except lay on his pallet. This would give him a chance to contribute, to be a help and not to be a total burden.

" And baa, baa, baa, where in this blessed fort are you going to get sheep?" Buck cat-called.

"We may not need sheep. Mistress Ainsee will try to get us wool, but even if she fails, we can use other wool. Not to mention linen,

German=this font   English=this font   *French=this font*   *Anishinaabe=this font*

nettles or dogbane. There is plenty of dogbane that grows wild about here. Men, we will need brakes and scrunchers. Anyone who can carve, I need you to make spacers for the looms, shuttles, bobbins, combs and what not. The children can pull dogbane and nettles." For that fleeting moment, she remembered the lovely tools that Adam Henry had made for her. The joy of using them returned, mixed with sadness. "And collect the other wool," Eve added hastily, centering herself once more.

"Other wool? Next thing you know, she'll be shearing us."

"Shut up, Buck." Wenzel's put-down of Buck surprised Nellie and Eve both. A born skeptic and nay-sayer, was Wenzel changing his tune for a change? "Let her finish."

"Hell, who are you going to get to set up a loom? That takes skill and some pretty fancy counting, I hear tell. None of us here can do it that I know of." Even Wenzel could not silence Buck this time.

"My Mutti can," Henry proudly asserted, stepping into the circle of adults. Mikie giggled.

Laughter and group censure impacted on Buck for the third time, this time instigated by a child.

Buck, thrice rebuffed, huffed out of the room.

"Just what wool did you have in mind Eve?"

One of the most impish looks anyone ever saw crossed Eve's face. Her eyes twinkled. "If I tell you, we must keep it secret. The season for harvest will soon begin." The women drew close to hear her softly spoken words. Laughter and giggles skittered about the room while Wenzel broke into a deep belly laugh. Langlough felt left out until Mikie whispered it in his ear, and then he laughed, too, before dissolving into a coughing fit.

Early February, on Cold and Wretched Nights, En Route to Fort Patrick Henry aka Fort Sackville, Vincennes, Indiana

Complaints lessened as Clark's men, one by one, dropped off into a fitful slumber. Tied to trees, necessitated by the depth of the flood waters in and around them, they sagged like wet moths on the rough bark. Father Gibault's warm send-off and prayers for their protection were dimly remembered in the penetrating cold, cold that would reap a harvest of rheumatism and arthritis in the years to come.

Hate and revenge fueled the only fires permitted to keep their spirits alive. When that failed, the spirited songs and drumming of one of the youngest of the troop helped them slog on through icy water, chest deep and higher. These remarkable marksmen, common men, of Virginia, Pennsylvania and Kentucky were armed only with rifles. Rifles made

German=this font   English=this font   *French=this font*   *Anishinaabe=this font*

mostly by the skilled German gunsmiths of Pennsylvania and Virginia. Trusted rifles and powder horns were held high on cold stiff arms above their heads to keep their ammunition dry. These rifles proved renowned for their rifling. The spiral bores inside the barrels beat the British, Brown Bess musket hands down. In any head to head contest, the rifle won when it came to accuracy, a deadly improvement nourished by Yankee ingenuity and produced by skilled Yankee craftsmen. Where European war depended on the hail of bullets across a battlefield or at point-blank range, the guerilla tactics of the new world demanded accuracy and conservation of ammunition.

Once, these men took pride in themselves as providers of food and as traders of pelts. Necessity turned them into hunters of men.

These seasoned veterans, rough, woods wise, bitter, angry, and unbelievably committed, faced certain death. But these men also endeavored to live up to the hellish reputation that their own activities and others, including the British, had built for them as vicious Longknives. To a man, each had personally felt the brunt of Britain and Hamilton's diversionary plan. The memories of lost family, friends, and neighbors brutally murdered, wounded, or captured pushed them relentlessly forward.

Redemption and retribution lay just ahead in Vincennes.

Among them, no one questioned the leadership of George Rogers Clark. And no one, absolutely no one, detested the Lieutenant Governor Henry Hamilton any more than George Rogers Clark. Cocky, driven, ambitious and totally infected with the concept of liberty, George Rogers Clark branded Hamilton forever with the name, "Hamilton, the Hair Buyer," leaving generations to debate the validity. Side-by-side, he hung alongside his men, cold, wet, and just like his men…hungry.

February 18, 1779
Fort Sackville, Vincennes, Indiana

"Who in the hell ever thought we'd be fixing cow holes?"

Menard and Tchamaniked Joe worked on opposite sides of the boat. Menard pushed the oakum into the deepest crack. Joe replaced a sprung board broken free when the animal thrust its hoof through in desperation and retaliation for being hauled unceremoniously into the boat after nearly being swept away by an angry swirl of water and mud. The waters of the Wabash had flooded to such levels that the local inhabitants had needed to take boats out in an area encompassing a twenty-mile radius about the Fort to rescue their cattle. The cattle had been pushed out of their usual winter pastures by the rising waters, triggered by unseasonable warmth and unrelenting rain. Four hundred head of cattle and oxen had already drowned. The increasing stench nearly took one's breath away. The rest were severely threatened by the ever-raising flood levels. Lieutenant Governor Hamilton, realizing the gravity of the situation, had permitted some of his companies' pirogues to be enlisted in this endeavor. The end result was that the boats needed repaired before they could be used again.

"Quit bitchin' Menard. It is better than replacing the posts on the North East side."

"Humph." Menard copied Joe's usual grunt.

"Agreed?"

"Ah—greed."

For once, Joe and Menard had been cut some slack, since Menard still had not fully mended from his fevers.

"That's the most you've said in a week," Menard observed wryly. "What's up with you anyways?"

"What do you mean?"

"Joe, sometimes I feel like you ain't even here."

"Humph."

"There you go again. Clam'n up. You ain't even been reading much, either. That's not like you." Menard appeared thoughtful. "I likes it when you read, Joe."

Neither spoke for an extended period. Sensing that Joe would not explain what bothered him, Menard decided to change the topic. Maybe that would help, he reasoned. Besides, he usually did most of the talking for both of them while Joe listened.

"Did you hear that there prisoner that Hamilton bought, done up and deserted? Crazy name that one, William Williams. What kind of name is that?" From time to time, Menard would pause and when Joe did not respond, then he would take up where he had left off. "Took somebody with him he did. Everybody's suspicious. Some say that they saw him jawing with that man, Helm. Francis Maisonville's gone after them. Didn't get the last ones, doubt if he'll get these two, either."

"Shut up and work, Menard. My ears hurt."

Menard, like a reproved puppy, hung his head and shoved another piece of oakum in place, mumbling under his breath.

The unexpected being the norm this month, the peach blossoms**and the budding apples** about the village watched the human drama unfolding below as silent witnesses to triumph and tragedy.

**Hamilton, Henry, *Henry Hamilton and George Rogers Clark in the American Revolution with the Unpublished Journal of Gov. Henry Hamilton,* John D. Barnhart, Ed. (Crawfordsville, Indiana: R. E. Ranta, 1951). Information paraphrased from Hamilton's journal, quote p. 174-175.

February 18, 1799   Fort Detroit

In the stillness of Ste. Anne's, a slight figure sobbed in the corner of her family pew. Theotiste St. Cosme DeJean had never faced public humiliation like this, and only here did she feel safe from the censuring eyes. When she ventured out, she felt absolutely certain that every eye

German=this font   English=this font   *French=this font*   *Anishinaabe=this font*

glared knowingly at her, brutally aware of her husband's failings. She did not detect the approach of Sue Ellen, who sat down quietly beside her and waited for her to notice her presence.

The sobbing woman began to right herself, sensing warmth about her. "Sister, why do you weep?"

The calmness that emanated from Sue Ellen relaxed Theotiste. A small clean cloth appeared from a pocket hidden in the folds of Sue Ellen's skirt. Though unbidden, the scarred woman, dressed totally in black, gently wiped the tears from Theotiste's beautiful cheeks.

Contrary to her usual haughty manner with lesser people, Theotiste permitted this total stranger to touch her delicate features, actually welcoming it. She ignored the ugly rumors and felt no fear.

Theotiste DeJean recognized her immediately. Even in the pale light, the description of this strange figure fit perfectly with who and what she had imagined. All in keeping with the whole of what everyone had told her.

This could only be Sue Ellen.

The entire community recognized her by name and reputation. Rumors related that Sue Ellen would soon become a sister in the Nunnery of Montreal. She had been called by the Virgin and had accepted the call. Father and Mistress May had even found garments for her that would tell outwardly of her inward commitment. Some whispered that Sue Ellen helped Martha, the metisse, with the sick and poor, Indian or white alike. Skeptics just spoke of the strangeness of this colorless creature, who spoke in a soft quiet voice surrounded by a suspicious aura of humility. Still others recognized the telltale scars of the dread disease, the disease whispered about only in great secrecy, which no respectable person dared to utter aloud. They often mentioned the scars, for she wore her scars openly without shame or a veil to cover them. With each passing day, speculation devised endless reasons for these healed scars.

"I am shamed. Shamed. I will never be able to hold my head up. How could he possibly do this to me? To my family?" Theotiste blurted out.

"What shame could possibly be yours that our Christ could not heal?"

Theotiste protested. "You do not understand. He has left me all alone to face his disgrace. Everyone knows. The grand jury in Montreal has found my Philip and the Lieutenant Governor Hamilton guilty. Everyone knows. Simply everyone! Now all that horrible talk is starting up again about that wretched black bitch, Nancy, who hung her John." She sniffled and inhaled her runny nose's contents, swallowing it before wiping her damp face on the back of her gloved hand fastidiously.

"Mother Mary says your husband's sins will only fall upon your shoulders if you show no compassion for those whom your husband has wronged." Related with utmost sincerity, Sue Ellen's totally unexpected response brought Theotiste up short. But, Sue Ellen's next statement really struck harder, more insightfully, right where Theotiste least expected it. "The Blessed Mother Mary says you must pray for and forgive those who despitefully use you as her son, our Lord Jesus, taught. Even when your husband, Philip, takes you against your will or abuses your family's good name, you must forgive him and help him to seek redemption. She will give you strength to do this if you but ask."

Theotiste's sharp intake of breath became the only sound in the sanctuary that Sue Ellen heard as she arose, turned and left the young wife alone to make her own peace.

Right now, Sue Ellen recognized that she, too, must seek forgiveness. Yes, forgiveness for the surge of purely vindictive joy she felt for the very thing which brought another such deep pain. Vengeance should be the Lord's, she admonished herself. Perhaps Mother Mary could have her friends Anne and John intercede for her. A loving Father God would remember and understand.

Across town, a stunned merchant held a letter in her hand. A letter she had a premonition would not be anything she wanted to read. The new black hired man, George, had brought it in with the latest order of goods for Helen MacLeod.

Her hands shook slightly as she unfolded the letter. She recognized the neat script instantly. That man never wrote unless a critical demand necessitated it, like the time his boy fell fatally ill. Again she deplored that her own skills were so lacking. She struggled with great difficulty to sound out the French words.

The letter began: ***"Sally, I have a favor to ask and if the Creator is kind, you will never need to do as I request. But I had a dream Sally, and I fear..."***

She continued with effort to read the letter. Nicholas, her son and John's half-brother would have to help her with some of the words, but the gist of it was clear enough. When she finished, her hand holding the letter fell to her side. "Oh shit! Joe. Shit! Shit! Shit! God damn you Joe. You better not! You just better not!" Sally Ainsee slumped over her counter, "You better not leave me stuck with this God damned mess. I won't forgive you. Do you hear me?"

February 19, 1779 Near Fort Sackville, in the Camp of Egushawa

Egushawa felt surprised to see the wife's cousin again so soon, striding directly towards him with strong purpose in the early light as he returned from his morning walk.

"What brings you out before council meets?"

"A dream brings me."

German=this font   English=this font   ***French=this font***   *Anishinaabe=this font*

"What dream is that my brother?"

"I think my dream says that you and my brothers of the Lakes should leave this place."

"When did you have this dream, Joe?" Egushawa hated to tell Joseph that he was the sixth man who had come to him this week. He swore all the water about them had made many of them homesick.

"Shortly after the eclipse in month of Manido Geezisong, the Little Spirit Moon, or what the white men call December."

"Why have you waited until now to come to me with this?"

Joe pushed up a mound of mud with the side of his foot, crossed his arms, and spoke deliberately. *"As you know, the white world and the red world battle within me. Part of my thoughts say superstitious nonsense and part of my heart begs to listen. But I decided that it would be wise to come to you while the battle rages, and before it is won. If you stay, I must stay, for I will not leave my people again. But my heart says we should leave."*

"Have you had any more dreams since this one, Joe?"

"No. Only this one."

"Joe, many men have had dreams. You have heard some of them yourself. Foolish dreams, they melt away in the day's light on the dreamcatchers. But like you, my heart speaks to me, too. I made a promise to the English Father, Hamilton. My heart says that I cannot break my word! This is the true way. We will stay."

"Then I will stay. Ahow." Tchamaniked Joe turned and just as quickly as he came, he disappeared.

Egushawa wondered at the shadows that seemed to haunt Joe's face. The Holy Fathers never should have taken him away he thought. Now he is caught between two paths, between two fires.

February 21, 1779 Fort Sackville, Vincennes, Indiana

Governor Henry Hamilton could read the underlying hostility even before his interpreter translated the words. Egushawa had also lately come to join his frame of mind. Young Tobacco, nicknamed "the Gate" must not be trusted. Young Tobacco had openly declared in council his allegiance to the Americans a few days ago, but on this day Young Tobacco flip-flopped. First he had given a scalp to the old Delaware, now he was ranting again about the infallibility of his word.

Hamilton read the mounting anger beneath the formal manners of Egushawa. Finally the esteemed Chieftain rose politely to his feet.

"Young Tobacco...look about you." His arm swept the breadth of the circle which included Chippewa, Ottawa, Wyandot, Delaware, Miami, Ouiattanon, and Penakeshaw. " 'Be cautious of what [you] advance'

German=this font   English=this font   *French=this font*   *Anishinaabe=this font*

here. 'Remember well what promises [you make] in the presence of so many persons. In [the] future [do not] use your Tongue to call the Virginian [your] father. [Do] not speak from the lips outward, but from the heart.'"**

The threat delivered with great manners and authority reverberated about the fire. No one present misunderstood the intent.

Young Tobacco, heeding not, pleaded again with the circle to recognize that he had been baptized while very ill when young. He revered the 'divine being' too much to 'advance a falsehood.'**

"Maid, thou doth protest too much," Hamilton spoke under his breath as he remembered a line from a literate school chum who took great delight in womanizing. 'As [Tobacco] finished, a Messenger c[a]me to inform [Hamilton] that the two Miami and Huron, who set out [earlier] for the falls had returned with the scalp of a man whose rifle they brought in——'**

**Hamilton, Henry. *Henry Hamilton and George Rogers Clark in the American Revolution with the Unpublished Journal of Gov. Henry Hamilton.* John D. Barnhart, Ed. (Crawfordsville, Indiana: R.E. Ranta, 1951). Information paraphrased from Hamilton's journal as he quotes Egushewai [Egushawa]. p. 176. Final quotes also from Hamilton's journal p. 176.

February 22, 1779   The Councils Reconvene at Fort Sackville, Vincennes, Indiana

Lieutenant Governor Henry Hamilton felt like the coals in a blacksmith's forge licked by flames as the bellows compressed. He realized that if he continued to act as if he did not know, he could cause more collateral damage. But his unfortunate timing had not made his task any easier. Major Jehu Hay felt that his commander should continue to withhold the information, but in the end Hamilton decided to speak out. The time to take the heat had arrived.

As Hamilton patiently tried to explain the "rupture between the courts of Great Britain and France," he attempted to "soften" the "affect" of the new declaration of "war" between France and England on those who lived "so far inland."** Yes, his people were now at war with the French, and the French had sided with the Rebels, but he advised his allies strongly that they were to "behave to the French in this country as to brothers and fellow subjects, since tho' the French had for a while taken the part with the Rebels, they had on the [British] arrival declared their sorrow for their fault."** Hamilton stressed to them that the French had taken "a fresh oath to behave in the future as dutiful and faithful subjects" to their English Father.**

As Hamilton walked this narrow legalistic and moral thread, the Chieftains "appeared [] little struck at the news".** The more he tried to

German=this font   English=this font   *French=this font*   *Anishinaabe=this font*

explain and enlist their support, the more Hamilton had the distinct feeling that the news which had brought loud "rejoicing" along the Illinois River had already preceded his explanation.** Did those about him know that the Rebels had an alliance with the French, their previous fathers? Had he committed an error by not telling them? Now, the letter he had received at Fort Ouiatenon on the fifth of December which contained an article printed in the *Quebec Gazette* on the 8th of October had come back to plague him a hundred fold.**

As Hamilton and Hay returned to their new quarters, Hamilton noticed the completed North West Blockhouse. He made a note to finish hanging the gunports and the needed ironwork. The three-pounder sat in place waiting for the final supports to be placed.

"Have you any carpenter free who can forage for leatherwood bark? I understand that is the only one given to peeling now."

"Yes, there is Joe, the canoe maker. He knows his winter trees."

"Good, send him out in the morning, so we can narrow those gunport openings temporarily until we can make it permanent. The men are too visible up there."

"I will see to it." Hay left him to complete the task.

Hamilton threw his gloves down on the desk, removed his sword and yanked at his neck to loosen his uniform. He had no more settled in his seat, when he heard Francis Maisonville's voice without. Hamilton glanced at the clock. It neared three.

His aid attempted to hold him off, but relented quickly when Hamilton called out to admit him.

"What is it Maisonville?" His weariness hung openly like laundry on a line as he responded.

"Well Sir, my men and I captured two of four Virginians we spotted. Here's their letters, Sir." He plunked the pile of letters on Hamilton's desk.

Hamilton frowned when moisture rolled across the polished surface and plopped on the floor.

"Not much of interest from them that I read." Maisonville paced uneasily. "But that is not what worries me the most, sir." Maisonville stepped very close to the seated Hamilton whose hands had struck a pointed tent before him, nearly in an attitude of prayer. Hamilton's head bent slightly forward as he reflected on the council and on Maisonville's report. His chin rested on the tips of his fingers.

Standing very close to his commander, Maisonville bent forward from his waist. Lowering his voice markedly, he spoke quietly but distinctly in Hamilton's ear. "I 'spotted fourteen fires', sir 'on the East side of the Wabash, about four leagues below the fort.' I daren't 'expose' myself, sir. I couldn't get close enough 'to count them.' 'They must be Virginians, sir.'"**

Hamilton leapt to his feet, nearly colliding with Maisonville. He demanded his aid to fetch Captain Hay, Captain La Mothe and Lieutenant Schieffelin immediately.

The ancients had suddenly appeared. The Moirae, the three fates, stood within and without the gate. Clotho watched with interest, holding her distaff almost as a light on high after having spun the threads of life. Lachesi had appointed each thread neatly into its destined place and now Atropos waited patiently to cut some lives short.

**Hamilton, Henry, *Henry Hamilton and George Rogers Clark in the American Revolution with the Unpublished Journal of Gov. Henry Hamilton.* John D. Barnhart, Ed. (Crawfordsville, Indiana: R.E. Ranta, 1951). Information closely paraphrased from Hamilton's journal. p. 176-177. Quotes p. 176-177.

February 23, 1779 Vincennes, Indiana Early Morning

Whispers and huddled men crowded quietly around the letter-bearer. One of the Boucher brothers, who could read, shared the contents.

" 'To the Inhabitants of Post Vincennes:

Gentlemen— Being now within two miles of your village, with my army, determined to take your fort this night, and not willing to surprise you, I take this method to request such of you as are true citizens, and willing to enjoy the liberty I bring you, to remain still in your houses—and those, if any there be, that are friends to the king, shall instantly repair to the fort, and join the hair-buyer general, and fight like men. And if any such as do not got to the fort shall be discovered afterward, they may depend on severe punishment. On the contrary, those who are true friends to liberty may depend on being well treated; and I once more request them to keep out of the streets. For every one I find in arms on my arrival, I shall treat him as an enemy.   G. R. Clark.' "

No one repaired. The women of Vincennes prepared a much needed and hearty breakfast for George Roger Clark's troops. To assist in preparing the meal, a grinning silversmith, by the name of Jonas Schindler, gladly pitched in to help clean pans and carry the heavy pots since he had to stay off the streets anyway.

Within the Fort, Menard still smarted from Joe's rebuff. That man sure made strange of late, he thought. Hell, he would have helped him. If Joe was so damn hell bent on going by himself, then leave him to it. Returning to his tent disgruntled, something dark caught his attention lying in his bear skin. "What in the name of... is this?" Menard bent over and

German=this font   English=this font   *French=this font*   *Anishinaabe=this font*

picked up something terribly familiar. He turned the small leather book of Psalms slowly in his calloused hands. Opening to the title page, something new printed neatly in purple caught his attention. He recognized his name instantly for Joe had been teaching him to print it, so he would not have to hang his head and sign with an x any more for his pay. He had hoped that in time, he, too, would be able to read.

"To Menard, from Joe, In this year of our Lord, 1779—February 23."

But right now all that Menard sensed brought an unexplainable tightness in his gut. Why would Joe desert him? Why did he leave this? They were a team.

Quoted from: English, William Hyden. *Conquest of the Country Northwest of the River Ohio, 1778-1783 and the Life of Gen, George Rogers Clark, Vol I.* (Indianapolis, Indiana and Kansas City, MO: Bowen-Merrill Co., 1896), p. 309.

"I resolved to appear as daring as possible...the houses obstructed the forts observing us...I detached Lt. Bailey to attack the fort at a certain signal, and took possession of the strongest parts of the town with the main body. The garrison had so little suspicion of what was to happen that they did not believe the firing was from an enemy, until a man was wounded through the ports...a considerable number of British Indians made escape out of town....Kickepous and Penakeshaws...immediately armed themselves in our favor and marched to attack the fort. I thanked the chief [Young Tobacco] for his intended service, told him the ill consequence of our people being mingled in the dark and that they might lay in their quarters until light...In a few hours I found my prize sure, certain of taking every man that I could have wished for, being the whole of those that incited the Indians to war. All my past sufferings vanished; never was a man more happy. It wanted no encouragement from any officer to inflame our troops with a martial spirit. The knowledge of the person they attacked and the thoughts of their massacred friends was sufficient.
...Captain La Mothe [was] sent to intercept [us thinking us Kentucky spies]...I was convinced that they would make off to the Indians at daybreak if they could not join their friends...[so] I withdrew the troops a little from the garrison in order to give him an opportunity to get in, which much to his credit and my satisfaction I would rather it would receive that reinforcement than they should be at large amongst the savages."

German=this font   English=this font   *French=this font*   *Anishinaabe=this font*

George Rogers Clark's letter to friend and patron, George Mason of Gunston Hall, Virginia dated Louisville, Falls of Ohio, November 19, 1779 relating events during this time period. Quoted from: **English, William Hayden** *Conquest of the Country Northwest of the River Ohio, 1778-1783 and the Life of Gen, George Rogers Clark, Vol I.* (Indianapolis, Indiana and Kansas City, MO: Bowen-Merrill Co., 1896), p. 439-441.

February 23, 1779   Fort Detroit
After Breakfast, Early Morning

"My heart went out to that poor young woman," Sue Ellen related, surprising Nellie somewhat given that Sue Ellen probably was younger than Madam DeJean when she sounded as if she were much older than Nellie.

"Oh come on Sue Ellen, she's a climber. So now her fool foot has slipped a few rungs on the ladder because her husband's a slimy bastard." Nellie worked awkwardly at turning a heel with the yarn and needles supplied by Sally Ainsee. Her hands, stiffened by recent work, proved reluctant to take up prior habits. Her needles joined the soft chorus of clicks as many women and older girls about the room started and struggled with their projects.

"Well anyway, I feel sorry for her. She has to face the disgrace all alone. She's weak and hurt."

"Well you just go right ahead and feel sorry for her all you want to. I don't! So some stinkin' grand jury in Montreal finally owned up to the fact that DeJean shouldn't a killed Anne and John. What damn good does it do 'em now. They're both dead. And DeJean and Hamilton, spanked on their paddies. So what, for Christ's sake!"

"Where's Eve?" Sue Ellen saw the futility of changing Nellie's mind. She noticed Henry and Mikie playing with the new orphaned girl near the fireplace.

"Oh, she's put'n up the loom over at Ainsee's. They made a space in her storage room. It's going to be heated too, it is. Carpenters and masons puttin' in a fireplace on the back wall. Ain't that plush."

German=this font   English=this font   *French=this font*   *Anishinaabe=this font*

February 23, 1779 Noon
In a Tree Grove Just Outside Fort Sackville
Fifteen Ottawa and Two French Interpreters
Approach Headed by the Young Chief,
Macutte Mong

"Ho Joe! Join us. We'll help you carry your leatherwood back to the fort. You can enter in glory for a change." Macutte Mong loved to tease his distant cousin. Puffed and triumph from his raid, the young Ottawa chief bristled with pride. As if to second his response, his lead warrior shook the new scalps in the wind, whooping loudly as another pushed a prisoner forward. *"See we hunted well, and we have far more than leatherwood to show for it!"*

Tchamaniked Joe joined his brothers and his destiny.

February 23, 1779 Between Two and Three in the Afternoon in Fort Detroit.

When the door to the storage room blew open suddenly, both Sally Ainsee and Eve straightened up quickly from joining the last loom floor beam in place. Both women stared at the vacant doorway filled with the expectation of seeing someone.

A wooden mallet tied to a loom piece had served the women well as they pounded each member in place to be held firm with the neatly carved wedges; wedges found in a small muslin bag stained with mouse droppings. Gradually the tangled jigsaw puzzle of beams and supports took shape. Heady with their collective success, they exchanged smiles. Gazing out the open door, they both also experienced a flush of penetrating cold.

"That was weird," Sally Ainsee said as she handed the mallet off to Eve before stepping over a brace to close the door. "Look at it, would you. Not a whisper of wind is out there today. The trees aren't even moving."

Eve eased her back. This child grew heavier with each day

And then it happened. For a fleeting moment, she felt a soft feathery touch, a gentle stroking of her cheek, followed by a deep sense of warmth and cold simultaneously. Her hand flew up to the spot.

"Baamaa pii ka-waab-min. Until I see your face again."

Eve distinctly heard Joe's voice.

"What'd you say?" Sally turned about quite startled.

"I did not say anything."

"Yes, you did, I distinctly heard you. I didn't know you spoke the Anishanabek language."

German=this font   English=this font   *French=this font*   *Anishinaabe=this font*

"I do not!" Eve protested. And then inexplicably she began to shake.

Sally Ainsee looked hastily around the room with alarm. Then she went immediately to Eve. Standing within Eve's personal space, she peered at her penetratingly. "Eve, tell me what you felt. Did you hear anything? See anything?"

"Maybe it is the loom. So many memories." Eve tried to evade her questions, turning her face away.

Sally gently turned Eve's face to confront her.

"Eve, tell me what you felt—I know you felt it."

"You are going to think I am..." Eve did not want to admit to herself or to Sally that for a moment she felt that she was loosing her reason, her sense of reality.

"No. Trust me." Sally grasped Eve firmly. Holding her face between her hands, she repeated. "Tell me."

"I swear you will not believe me. I do not believe me."

Sally continued to hold her face firmly, but gently. Their gazes locked tightly. She would not permit Eve to turn away.

Something deep down brought Eve to the unexpected realization that Sally would believe her. Had she also experienced something strange moments ago?

"I know this sounds absolutely strange, but I swear I heard the voice of someone I love." She put her hand to her cheek once more. "I felt he touched me."

Sally released her grip. Instead she chose to rub Eve's shoulders understandingly. "My mother's people say that when those we love remember us with great feeling, they reach out to us. Joe has blessed you." But part of what Sally thought did not resemble the comforting words she spoke to Eve as she stroked her arms. There would be time enough to confirm her sad suspicions. No sense alarming the poor woman, not when she felt so flushed with success. Over and over Sally thought as she pulled Eve closer, God damn you, Joe. God damn you, Joe. I'll get you for this, I swear I will. Then, she felt his child move between them.

Eve clung to Sally. She had not expected comfort from this new friend. A nagging question began to formulate. How did Sally know it was Joe? Eve remembered the party in the clearing and wrote it off as an astute observation.

> **"Some time before, a party of warriors, sent by Mr. Hamilton against Kentucky [who] had taken two prisoners, was discovered by the Kickepues, who gave information of them. A party was immediately detached to meet them...I was highly pleased to see each party whooping, hallooing, and striking each other's breasts as they approached the open fields; each seemed to try to out do the other in the greatest signs of joy. The poor devils**

German=this font   English=this font   *French=this font*   *Anishinaabe=this font*

never discovered their mistake until too late for many of them to escape. Six of them were made prisoners, two of them scalped, and the rest wounded as we afterwards learned that one lived. I had now as fair an opportunity of making an impression on the Indians as I could have wished for—that of convincing them that Governor Hamilton could not give them that protection that he made them to believe he could; and in some measure to increase the Indians against him for not exerting himself to save their friends, ordered the prisoners to be tomahawked in the face of the garrison. It had the effect that I expected."

George Rogers Clark's letter to friend and patron, George Mason of Gunston Hall, Virginia dated Louisville, Falls of Ohio, November 19, 1779 relating events during this time period. Quoted from: English, William Hayden *Conquest of the Country Northwest of the River Ohio, 1778-1783 and the Life of Gen, George Rogers Clark, Vol I.* (Indianapolis, Indiana and Kansas City, MO: Bowen-Merrill Co., 1896), p. 442-443.

February 23, 1779 Late Afternoon, Fort Sackville, Vincennes, Indiana

The British garrison gaped in mute horror as one by one the prisoners fastened loosely in chairs or driven to their knees with ropes about their necks yielded their lives and scalps to the Rebel force before the Fort walls. Tchamaniked Joe led the ancient death song with the warriors before being brutally silenced. Blow after crushing blow fell until all who sang lay in pools of their own and their brother's blood.

Macutte Mong drew the Virginians' greatest wrath after he returned the tomahawk to his murderer with great dignity. His executioner, hands slippery with blood, had inadvertently dropped his weapon after the first glancing blow which had failed to dispatch his victim. This act of noble defiance in the face of death could not go unanswered, so Malcutte Mong bore the brunt of their collective anger. After two more blows failed to snuff his young life, the Virginians dragged the Ottawa chief by his neck to the river. After he was thrown and retrieved only to be thrown repeatedly again and again into the water, the young war chief at last unmercifully expired.

On his own parole, outside the fort and standing on the margin of the parade ground, Maisonville looked on in profound horror with other unarmed residents. Only Maisonville felt far more empathy for those who died as he shared a bloody vantage. Betrayed by family and friends, two sections of his scalp raised and bleeding from earlier blows had clotted now and had begun to dry. Freed at the very last moment by Clark's last minute reversal of intent and intercession, he stood outside the fort

German=this font   English=this font   *French=this font*   *Anishinaabe=this font*

watching the inhuman venting of revenging anger. He knew if not for the squeamish stomach of his own attacker, he too would have been dead.

Few would be spared as the bloody slaughter continued. The eighteen-year-old son of Pontiac by accident of birth would be saved when the Rebel Captain, McCarty, whose life had been spared by his father, Pontiac, interceded for him. In another rare instance, another father among Clark's troops stepped forward to raise Clark's gun just before firing to save his son, Sargeant Sancrainte. His father had barely recognized his son's heaven-sent plea for mercy before the final blow.* Only the familiar sound of his son's voice had saved him.* Sergeant Robert still openly sobbed his massive relief after his sister's tears and pleading had saved his life.

However, George Rogers Clark had been correct. Not one shot took down a single Virginian as the massacre transpired before the gates of the garrison. Not even a single shot of mercy rang out. The canons remained deathly still.

Initially, Hamilton refused meeting with Clark. Finally, accompanied by another British officer, he exited the gate to enter the parade ground soaked with blood.

Clark raised his hand. The mayhem paused. Exhilarated, he strode towards Hamilton, noting the guns within the fort had lifted for the very first time and focused on him. The cocking of the pieces, not lost on Clark, caused him to signal his sharpshooters to take aim at the positions of the British shooters before bending over a batteau partially full of water to wash some of the blood from his hands and to wipe the sweat from his forehead on his sleeve caused by his physical exertion.

"My canons are due momentarily. Surely you can see any effort to resist is an exercise in vanity."

"His Majesty's superior forces will staunchly defend our interests," Hamilton seethed. " 'My men [have] declared [that] they [will] die with arms in their hands rather than surrender at discretion.'"**

"All thirty-five or thirty-six of them?" Clark checkmated his foe completely. The kingpin was captured. Smug satisfaction reeked from George Rogers Clark. "Quit this folly. Surrender and trust to my generosity," he slyly added.

"'Sir, I shall abide the consequences for I never will take a step so disgraceful and unprecedented while I have ammunition and provision,'" Hamilton's pride asserted.

"'Then, you will be answerable for the lives lost by your obstinacy!'" Clark snapped, knowing exactly how many of his opponent's men were already wounded by his snipers' deadly accuracy.

"'My men have declared that they [will] die with arms in their hands then surrender at discretion.'"

"Sir, what good is it to spill more blood. Surely we can find a way to prevent more bloodshed." For the first time, Hamilton's companion spoke.

German=this font   English=this font   *French=this font*   *Anishinaabe=this font*

"Your companion is wise." Clark acknowledged Hamilton's man with a nod.

"I can only surrender if the terms are 'consist[ent] with my honor and duty.'" Hamilton backed down shakily. "We must prepare the articles. This will take time."

"A half an hour should be more than adequate..." Turning away from Hamilton's livid fury, George Rogers Clark rejoined his men.

**Hamilton, Henry, *Henry Hamilton and George Rogers Clark in the American Revolution with the Unpublished Journal of Gov. Henry Hamilton*. John D. Barnhart, Ed. (Crawfordsville, Indiana: R.E. Ranta, 1951). Information closely paraphrased from Hamilton's Journal. p. 182-184   quotes p. 182-184   *Validated also by George Rogers Clark letter to friend and patron, George Mason of Gunston Hall, Virginia dated Louisville, Falls of Ohio, Nov 19, 1779 relating events during this time period. Quoted from: English, William Hayden.

* *Conquest of the Country Northwest of the River Ohio, 1778-1783 and the Life of Gen, George Rogers Clark, Vol I.* (Indianapolis, Indiana and Kansas City, MO: Bowen-Merrill Co. 1896), p. 443.

Hamilton wrote: **"The Men were next called together and I convinced them that the King's service could not derive any advantage from holding out...the poltronnerie and treachery of our French Volunteers who made up half our number, with the certainty of the St. Vincennes men having joined Colol. Clark, and the miserable state of our wounded men, all conspired to make me adopt the disagreeable terms of capitulation...before the capitulation, was signed I had consulted with Major Hay on the practicability of getting of to the settlement of the Natchez on the Mississippi...but the treachery of our inmates and the necessity of leaving our wounded men behind made us relinquish this scheme...the mortification, disappointement and indignation I felt may possibly be conceived if all the considerations are taken together which suggested themselves in turn...being captives to an unprincipled motley Banditti and [] being by those very people who owed the preservation of their lives and property to us, and who had so lately at the foot of the altar called God to witness their sincerity and loyalty...."**

**Hamilton, Henry, *Henry Hamilton and George Rogers Clark in the American Revolution with the Unpublished Journal of Gov. Henry Hamilton*. John D. Barnhart, Ed. (Crawfordsville, Indiana: R.E. Ranta, 1951). Information closely paraphrased from Hamilton's journal. p. 184-186.

German=this font   English=this font   *French=this font*   *Delaware=this font*

Chapter 28   March Comes In
Like a Scotsman

"Colol. Clark told me allso some particulars of his
march which were very extraordinary—He had left the
Illinois when the Waters were out & had marched for 15
days successively, his people being exposed all that time
to the inconveniences of marching thro a flooded
Country—They set out without provision trusting
entirely to the Buffaloe or other game they might chance
to fall in with on their route—the greater part of his
people were half naked—His powder was all damaged
before he arrived in St. Vincennes—a nights frost must
have destroyed his whole party—

"Colol Clarkes having succeeded under such
circumstances illustrates the following remark made by
some author whose name I do not recollect// 'A Sanguine
temper forsees few difficulties and sometimes owes
success to a fortunate rashness which is esteemed by
shortsight people as taking Fortune in the willing
mood—tis true Fortune favors the bold, but the rash have
no pretensions to her favor—'"

**Hamilton, Henry, *Henry Hamilton and George Rogers Clark in the
American Revolution with the Unpublished Journal of Gov. Henry Hamilton.*
John D. Barnhart, Ed. (Crawfordsville, Indiana: R.E. Ranta, 1951). Quoted
from Hamilton's journal. p. 188-189.

March 3, 1779   Fort Detroit

"Daddy, Daddy, Daddy." Nothing quite plays for a father than the
squeals of a child full of joy to see him. Jeannie leapt into her father's
arms. He did not smell like her Daddy, but even though his sun and wind
burned face had cracked and peeled to the point of bleeding, nothing,
absolutely nothing held back the massive grin.

"My girl. My girl." Norman MacLeod closed his eyes tightly. He
nuzzled his whiskers into his daughter's neck bringing a cascade of giggles
and more squeals. He relished the smells, the feel of her, the velvety
softness of her hair, and the scent of fresh bread in the air.

This was his daughter.

This was flesh of his flesh bonded with and birthed by his loving
Helen.

This was his home.

Helen, wrist-deep kneading bread dough, heard the joy bouncing off the walls and reverberating through her home. Wiping her hands on a towel, she hurried to the parlor.

When Norman MacLeod's eyes could refocus from all the joy, he drank in the sight of his loving wife leaning with clear self-satisfaction against the door frame.

"Mummy, Daddy is home." Jeannie called out, assuming her mother still worked in the kitchen.

"Really now. How can you be sure? He does not look like your father to me."

"Yes Mother, it is Daddy. Can't you tell?" Jeannie sounded so serious, that immediately Helen gave up the tease.

"Of course Jeannie, I can tell. Welcome home Norman MacLeod. What kept you so long?"

"Now Helen, when am I going to get a big hug from you?"

"And what makes you think that you're going to get any hug from me when I can smell you all the way into the kitchen?" The look singed Norman all the way across the room. She emanated not the heat of anger but the heat of something far more satisfying and inviting. A promise issued silently between husband and wife. "And don't be bother'n me Norman MacLeod with your hugs until you have remedied the situation. I will start drawing water for you. Thank you!" With that, she turned towards the kitchen. A split second later, he spun her about. She dissolved into laughter and began her own cascade of giggles, struggling in his tickling grasp.

"Norman, Norman!" she laughed. "Quit that Norman!"

Her last joyous exclamation brought George charging in from outside.

"Mistress MacLeod, are you all right?"

"I will be when we get this stinking bear of a man scrubbed and clean again."

"Welcome home, Captain."

"Thank you George. Let's see to that bath Helen." He set her down on her feet again. Grasping both of his women about their shoulders, he headed to the kitchen. "How about some stout tea, wife. Ha' yah any shortbread?"

"George, get the tub from the shed," Helen instructed. "We have one filthy man here.

"Yes mam, right away."

"And yes, I have some shortbread."

When Norman MacLeod finally slipped between the blessedly clean and sweet smelling sheets, he found Helen's back turned to him. Had he chatted too long with Captain Lernoult about the building of the new fort? As he nuzzled her ear, he could feel the rapid beat of her heart. "Helen." His voice was a hoarse whisper, "There's a wee laddy that's missed you."

German=this font   English=this font   *French=this font*   *Delaware=this font*

She pretended to sleep.

"Helen?"

Gradually she allowed her curves to conform to his. "Norman MacLeod, that is not the wee lad, I remember. He has grown."

"Aye, Helen, aye Helen. I believe he has." Turning her to him, he began to kiss her.

"Norman, you still smell like a bear," was the last thing Helen whispered, laughing softly before Norman MacLeod thoroughly kissed his loving wife to quiet her.

Later that night as MacLeod nestled between his wife's beasts, his breathing evened out. Soon he began to snore as he dipped into an exhausted and satisfied slumber.

Helen held him fast, aware of the wetness on her breasts from his tears. She wondered if he could come to talk completely about this latest journey from her or if he would simply tuck it away like so many of his soldiering experiences. Realizing he slept deeply, she gently rolled his heaviness from her, but kept close enough to feel him breathe and to re-experience his warmth. Whatever this man would share or not, she would accept it just to remain by his side. She would be sore tomorrow, but that would ease. Next time, he would not be in such a hurry.

March 5-10, 1779   Fort Patrick Henry, Vincennes, Indiana

"I contented myself on that presumption having almost as many prisoners as I had men. Seeing the necessity of getting rid of many of the prisoners, not being able to guard them, not doubting but my good treatment to the volunteers and inhabitants of Detroit would promote my interests there, I discharged the greatest part of them that had not been with the Indian parties, on their taking the oath of neutrality. They went off huzzaing for the congress and declared thought they could not fight against Americans....As I after this had spies constant to and from Detroit, I learned they answered every purpose that I could have wished for by prejudicing their friends in favor of America."***

Menard looked up from repairing the wall displaced nearly an inch and a half by the explosion of the cannon cartridge. The damage resulted when the exuberant Americans' celebration blew two of their fellows to pieces and the face off of one of the King's gunners. The gunner's skin blown from face and arms had nearly blinded him in the process. Unlike one of the Frenchmen from town who had been blown over the wall to land ten

German=this font   English=this font   *French=this font*   *Delaware=this font*

feet below on his feet with a burst of laughter, the gunner continued to suffer with great courage.

Rumors had it that Dr. John McBeath had never been called on to accomplish so much for so many with so little for the wounded. Nearly a sixth of Hamilton's most dependable troops had fallen, struck by snipers' bullets. Folks said that the bullet hole in the doctor's pants reminded McBeath how close he had come to being wounded himself.

Unconsciously Menard's attention, drawn like a magnet, sought out the scalp of Joe. The third from the end, it hung on one of the many poles outside Hamilton's quarters to serve as a constant reminder of the Rebel carnage. Like heads on poles once proudly displayed on the London Bridge, they testified to a bloody victory. While every fiber of his being hated to look, another part equally as strong wanted to pay homage to his fallen friend. Menard remained convinced that Joe's friendship had saved him from certain death by refusing his help. He stopped working on the log work for a moment and gave silent reverent acknowledgement to his friend by touching the book of Psalms which hung about his neck. He kept the book tucked in a decorated leather pouch which he had taken from Joe's chilling corpse.

Menard still took some sad pleasure in remembering the burial of Joe. He had waded in and pushed the Rebels away from looting Joe's body, cursing loudly as he did. He had carried his friend away from the stunned Rebels, dug a presentable plot in the nearby grove where they had cut wood together, and placed a simple wooden cross above him. On it he carved "Jo" and dug-out a simple canoe with Joe's crooked knife. Hell, it was the least he could do.

The uproar on the street drew his attention. A jeering crowd ushered the new prisoners into the Fort.

As Philip DeJean staggered ahead of the armed party, Menard recognized him.

"Maybe there is some justice," Menard chuckled. Menard broke his self imposed silence for the first time in two days. He found untold satisfaction at this new prisoner, stumbling to join Hamilton and Hay in quarters. The Minister of Justice had few friends in Detroit, fewer still in Vincennes. Stories told about his brand of justice encircled many fires, white and red alike. His reputation preceded him even six hundred miles from home.

While Menard felt some satisfaction at DeJean's capture, Hamilton veritably exploded. Although DeJean had known that the Fort had fallen for a full twenty-four hours before his capture, DeJean, in a self-centered fog, had not destroyed valuable communications meant only for Hamilton's eyes. Now Clark's men had valuable information in addition to Hamilton's personal baggage, which Hamilton had ordered to be sent up with the shipments from the cache left with the Miami and which also had accompanied DeJean. Amongst this baggage came his officers and his 'personal clothing and private stores' not to mention his best wines. To

German=this font   English=this font   **French=this font**   *Delaware=this font*

Hamilton's utter dismay, the Rebel banditti immediately confiscated all of it.

While Hamilton felt justly furious when he found out that Hypolite Bolon had also turned his letters willingly over to Clark and his men, he simply could not reconcile DeJean's unfathomable stupidity. All the idiot could do was rave on and on about the guilty verdict by the Grand Jury in Montreal. His gross incompetence inflamed Hamilton so much, that had not Hay stepped quickly in front of the unwary, self-centered DeJean, Hamilton might have summarily decked him.

When Hamilton learned that his personal belongings had been confiscated by Clark as spoils of war, he steamed. When refused his own wine, he seethed. But the final straw resulted when Clark refused to give him advance notice concerning Hamilton's date to leave for Willamsburg, Virginia. Hamilton stormed and complained bitterly. How was he to know when he should have biscuits made for his journey without knowing his departure date?

Hamilton viewed each slight as one humiliating discourtesy after another. He reeled from this unbelievable treatment heaped upon an officer of his Majesty's service.

Recording the inhumanities to his person and to his men at length in his day journal, Hamilton ranted at DePeyster's failed support and recorded the names of the men who he thought may have led his northern allies to aid them. In event his journal should be taken, he omitted letters to encode their names. At this point, the daily rudeness of his captors seemed unending to him. Convinced that no inhumanity was beneath them, he heaped mounds of blame on those who he felt should be held accountable for all the recent failures. From pistol packing priests like Gibault to the duplicitous ungrateful French habitants including the traitorous men in his employ, only one person never took a full share of the blame in Hamilton's journal...George Henry Hamilton.

When Clark and his officers interrogated him daily and asked details concerning the activities of his Indian Department workers, Hamilton held the line. But one day, inflamed by Clark's refusal to give him some of his own wine yet again, he began to chide Clark for his inhumane treatment of his officers.

When Clark asked the names of his Indian department again, Hamilton snapped, **"Ask them yourself! 'They are present and [can] answer for themselves.'"**

Upon hearing this, Clark did so and hearing their affirmations his reaction proved instantaneous. Turning to the American Officer nearest him he instructed him gravely, **"Go to the smithie, I want irons for neck, hands, and feet for all these gentlemen."**

Seeing Hamilton's profound shock, Clark accepted his offer to speak apart. Stepping from main tent room into the ante area and out of the sight of their fellows, Clark waited impatiently for Hamilton to speak.

German=this font   English=this font   *French=this font*   *Delaware=this font*

Hamilton's voice shook with rising anger and fury, but he kept his speech low and controlled.

"Please explain the inhumane order that you have just made."

" 'I have taken a solemn resolution to make examples of all who [have] acted with the Indian's without exception.'"

Clark's cold calculated response increased Hamilton's shock.

" 'Whatever [your] resolution', I must remind you to 'remember' you have 'put [your] hand to the capitulation by which we were or ought to be secured from any act of violence.'"

"I have 'taken an oath and I am fixed on that resolution.'"

"'Then [you] must renounce all pretensions to the character of an Officer or a gentleman——"

'[Clark] smiled contemptuously.'

*** "I thought I made it clear earlier in St. Xavier's church, 'the cries of. the widows and the fatherless, on the frontiers, which [your staff] occasioned' requires me to obey 'the absolute commands of their authority, which I look[] upon to be next to divine'."

"In turn, 'I beg to remind you, that [this] is not a matter to trifle upon, that these Gentlemen [have] done no other than their duty in obeying orders I [have] given them. [I stand] responsible for their actions [.] Since my situation [has] reduced me so low as to ask a favor, I request [that you] put me in irons rather than them'."

Clark 'paid little attention'.

"'[Your] behavior [is] unaccountable....[given that] you permit me to carry a loaded pistol in my belt!'" Hamilton parried.

Clark opened the flap of the tent to expose the hair laden posts. Without a single word more to Hamilton, he returned to the room to speak with the other officers. There Clark showed them the treaty of alliance between France and America printed by the American Congress for dispersal amongst the many interested peoples of the heartland, who lived in and about what would eventually be called the Northwest Territory.**

Menard dipped his paddle deeply pushing his boat forward against the spring currents. Spring caressed the swollen river banks. Tiny yellow green leaflets contrasted with the dark red-greens of some of the emerging underbrush that stuck in bizarre directions out of the water. Spring songs on the wings of feathered migrations flitted from branch to branch. The birds were readily visible now in this time of emerging foliage. Floating logs and branches freed in the high waters scooted past Menard's bateau as they headed in the opposite direction downriver to Vincennes. He must watch carefully. Nothing would stop him now, he resolved. Great God, he was going home. Dipping his paddle deeply once more, he pictured Joe bending from the waist and hip, conserving his energy, and using his best leverage. Menard did his damnedest to emulate Joe's example. Everything spoke of life's renewal, of second chances...of hope.

Whereas when Lieutenant Governor Henry Hamilton departed from

German=this font   English=this font   *French=this font*   *Delaware=this font*

Vincennes, he felt further humiliation because so few of the men outside his department had come to see them off. In his journal, he stated sadly: "'Before our setting off I found that some of the Soldiers and others whom I had conceived a better opinion, had made their terms with Colol. Clark without saying anything to me....'" **

**Hamilton, Henry, *Henry Hamilton and George Rogers Clark in the American Revolution with the Unpublished Journal of Gov. Henry Hamilton.* John D. Barnhart, Ed. (Crawfordsville, Indiana: R.E. Ranta, 1951). Information paraphrased from Hamilton's journal. p. 187-188, p. 191. Quotes as indicated.

*** George Rogers Clark quoted from: English, William Hyden *Conquest of the Country Northwest of the River Ohio, 1778-1783 and the Life of Gen, George Rogers Clark, Vol I.* (Indianapolis, Indiana and Kansas City, MO: Bowen-Merrill Co., 1896), p. 341.

***George Rogers Clark's letter to friend and patron, George Mason of Gunston Hall, Virginia dated Louisville, Falls of Ohio, November 19, 1779 relating events during this time period. Quoted from: English, William Hyden. *Conquest of the Country Northwest of the River Ohio, 1778-1783 and the Life of Gen, George Rogers Clark, Vol I.* (Indianapolis, Indiana and Kansas City, MO: Bowen-Merrill Co., 1896), p. 444.

Mid-March 1779   Gnadenhutten, Ohio The Moravian Delaware Settlement

Strains of singing from the love feast for the wedding of John Leeth and his new wife, Winter Hare, Sally Lowrey, filtered through the trees. In a nearby creek, Blue Ice washed himself, beginning the cleansing to re-enter his civilian life. Having retrieved his promise to follow Egushawa and having taken leave of the war parties, he asked the Creator to wash him within to remove hatred and the stains of his enemy's blood. Only cleansed would he feel the right to return as a new man.

His sacred bundle held firmly in his hand, Blue Ice raised his voice in a chant as timeless as his people. New clothes lay waiting on the bank, old ones would be burned. The smoke would carry his prayers to the Creator. He thanked the Creator for his mercies to him in battle for the only wounds that he must cleanse and bandage were all spiritual.

For a time, Blue Ice would put aside war. He would carry the hatchet no more for the British. Still stung by their refusal to assist his brethren, his chant conveyed a mournful quality.

Perhaps the Virginians were right. This must be a time to stay out of the war between parent and child. To see the English Father and his army humbled in chains and begging for food and clothing sickened Blue Ice. The threat that the women and children of the people who continued to oppose the Rebels 'would be given to dogs to eat' whereas the 'nations who [kept] their words to [George Rogers Clark] would flourish and grow like the willow trees on the river banks, under the care and nourishment of their father, the big knives'* still rung in Blue Ice's ears.

German=this font   English=this font   *French=this font*   *Delaware=this font*

Little Fox first saw Blue Ice as he entered the circle of those listening to the married peoples' choir. Tugging on his mother's hand, he drew her attention to him.

Singing Grass's smile looked nearly as radiant as the brides. Stalking Wolf extended his arm in welcome to his friend before hugging him as a brother. Smoke in Eyes, now known as Peter, waited impatiently to clasp his father.

Standing Bear, his wife, Falling Water, and David Zeisburger looked on with approval on all who soon would partake of the ample wedding feast. Even in early spring, with the increased industry of the village and only a few American or British raids on their stored grain and livestock, they had wintered well. With their hidden supplies, the village could truly celebrate not only the wedding, but another returned son. Life held promise.

*George Rogers Clark letter to friend and patron, George Mason of Gunston Hall, Virginia dated Louisville, Falls of Ohio, November 19, 1779 relating events during this time period. Quoted from: English, William Hyden. *Conquest of the Country Northwest of the River Ohio, 1778-1783 and the Life of Gen, George Rogers Clark, Vol I.* (Indianapolis, Indiana and Kansas City, MO: Bowen-Merrill Co., 1896), p. 447.

Late-March, 1779   New Orleans

Michel Dibert peeked lackadaisically out the cut crystal window panes of his Uncle's door. He wondered if he would ever get used to the voices of street vendérs, to the plodding feet of horses, to the roll of the carriages, or to the cacophony of voices that accompanied a waking city. Those and the stale and smoky smells still seemed utterly strange for a man who had known only the creaking of wooden walls, the smells of a wood fire, and the sounds of birds upon waking. He knew that he would find his Onkel laboring over his books in the study. Michel still slept late each day in an effort to decrease his waking hours. His memories haunted him.

"Hear ye, I hear ye!" A town crier called for attention from the street, a clutch of papers under his arm. The singsong tonality caught Michel's attention, so he opened the door a crack for a better listen. First in French, then in Spanish, finally in English, the voice cried the news. The door had barely time to slam behind him when Michel burst into his Onkel's study. **"By the grace of God, George Rogers Clark has re-captured Fort Patrick Henry, and all Hamilton's damned Indian department! Can you believe it?"**

"I think this calls for my best Madeira. That is better news for a change!" Putting aside his books the older Dibert roared, **"Fetch the wine, my dear nephew. Fetch the wine! A toast to the Virginians!"**

German=this font   English=this font   *French=this font*   *Delaware=this font*

Late-March, 1779   Fort Detroit

"Hold his head still, Mikie."

Mikie's blond curls and cherub smile combined with Henry's ability to handle dogs and cats became the talk of Yankee Hall. The two of them had charmed their way into nearly every French household up and down Ste. Ann and St. Antoine streets. Soon even the most resistant of ladies turned her special pet over to the boys at weekly intervals to comb their shedding hair, making the owner's household cleaner and happier. What pleased the owners even more was that the dear boys took all the combings with them. Since the boys left no messes behind, they often received an additional small coin or cookie for their industry. Following their example, soon other youngsters at Yankee Hall followed their lead.

The men would not be outdone by the children. Wenzel and his friends slipped into the meadows at night. Livestock in the area appeared considerably neater and their coats shone in the few days of spring sun. Animals about the fort inexplicably lost their clumps of shed winter coats. Even rubbing posts stood clean. Other than one close call with May's cantankerous bull, the collections proceeded with few hitches.

Eve's 'anything moving that sheds' admonition meant nothing anywhere escaped a brush or comb if detected. Nearly as quick as the bags of fluff entered Yankee Hall, the industrious carders and spinners made it into yarn. The knitters made toques, socks and in some cases the fine cat and dog hair became finely-knitted lace shawls. Sally Ainsee, true to her word, found some wool. This was mixed with other more hairy fibers, carded and spun into lovely and varied threads. Toby Langlough prided himself on interesting combinations, perking up considerably. He coughed far less. A friendly competition developed among the women. The quality had begun to improve. The handmade items that Sally accepted became a desired item as more and more women about town sought something different, often far less expensive than the imported goods. Spared from the labor themselves, the good ladies of the fort found the touch of the helping hands most welcome. Men serving in the fort or from the boats kept a constant watch for the heavy oiled socks.

But it was the dogbane and nettle threads spun by Mattie, Nellie, Fiona, and Hannah that soon built up in quantity enough to weave runners that garnered the most attention. Finely set, edges straight, they disappeared from Ainsee's shelf nearly as quick as they could be carried from the weaving shed to the counter.

Eve wove and trained Agatha. Soon she was joined by others to be shuttle sallies, those who simply worked off the warp. Eve watched the loom work carefully, making sure to ensure uniform beat and consistency, helping her weavers to improve their craftsmanship.

The result, Eve counted her first coins carefully. She would be able to contribute to Sue Ellen's boat fare to Montreal and still start to build up

German=this font   English=this font   **French=this font**   *Delaware=this font*

her ransom money before the baby came. She sat cross-legged on her blanket, listening to the sounds of industry and the hum of the women whose voices revealed their increasing pride. Where once people fell exhausted into their pallets, silent after meals and work, Yankee Hall had a renewed spirit which increased their energy to face each day.

Each woman had brought skills that they had not fully appreciated until now. Collectively they could rely on each other's strengths. These skills had begun to build a road home.

Looking at her first few coins again, Eve wondered for a moment if that foul DeJean would now put a five by her name come summer. Fatigue overcame her for a spell. Taking advantage of a luxury she rarely had, she curled into a ball on her side and drifted off to sleep. Spring never had seemed closer. Outside, the lilac buds and pear buds swelled with promise. Inside, the new warmth of the late March afternoon sun combined with a gift of time while the boys were out combing. Eve had a rare treat, a pleasant, lazy afternoon nap.

Late that night Sally Ainsee crawled grumbling from beneath her mound of quilts. Just because one has a premonition, that does not mean it will come to pass. But she felt wary of any news that came by night messenger. When she allowed her stepson to slip into her quarters, she suspected the news he carried but prayed it would not be. John Montour kissed his stepmother's cheek in the French manner before setting his rifle in the rack above the door.

"You better have a good reason for risking your neck and mine to come here again," Sally growled.

Montour knew there were no teeth in it, only the threat of a bite. She would have gladly risked her life in a heartbeat to see him but her motherly concern for his life necessitated her response.

"I have much news. Your traders and you must be aware of the possible consequences."

"Come, I'll make tea."

"Spike it heavy Mother."

"That bad?"

"That good or that bad depending on what side you are on."

"Does one have to take sides or just survive these bloody bastards?"

A mother and son shared an ironic chuckle.

Pulling his wamus over his head and laying his powder horn beside it, Montour settled down to wait for tea. An imported English tea biscuit, his favorite, came from the black tin canister on a high shelf. The sugar block and knife pulled from another joined it on the table.

"Hamilton is in irons." Montour changed to English.

Sally dropped her fire tongs which clanged into the andirons as she straightened herself abruptly from stirring up the fire, nearly hitting her head on the overhanging fireplace mantle.

"You can't be bloody serious."

German=this font   English=this font   **French=this font**   *Delaware=this font*

"I am deadly serious. He, Hay, Maisonville, Schieffelin, DeJean, and bunch of others from his Indian department have an appointment to visit a jail in Williamsburg, Virginia. George Rogers Clark has booked their passage.

"Let me sit down here."

Sally pulled her chair up to the table. Leaning forward, she expressed her primary concern. "Will they attack Detroit?"

"If Clark has his way...I would say look for the Long Knives tomorrow morning. But the Pennsylvanian's suspicions of anything Virginian may hold sway." Montour leaned back, picking a chunk of biscuit out of his closely cropped whiskers; he stuffed the last of his first cookie in his mouth. "Frankly, I suspect Washington's buddy William Crawford will get the nod in Fort Pitt, not Clark to attack here. Patrick Henry and Washington do not always see eye to eye. Brodhead's sure to be in trouble before long."

"Is that good or bad for us?"

"Crawford's definitely more inept, but he's closer." He grabbed another biscuit. "It's a turkey shoot. God, I'm hungry Mom. Whatcha' got?"

"Eggs? Ham?"

"That'll be good."

"You have a two day head start on the news Mom, maybe less."

"That will hit this town like a prairie fire. Prices are going to skyrocket. I better buy up anything I can." She pulled down a black iron skillet, setting it on the table and then the ham that hung in the corner. "Many dead?"

"Egushawa's Lake tribes took the brunt of it. Clark's boys slaughtered a fair number of them to drive their point home at the beginning. Some pretty hellish tales comin' there, Mom. You don't want to hear them."

An involuntary shiver coursed down her spine.

"Rebel snipers took out a few regulars, mostly wounded I hear."

"My God who would have thought it? Last I heard Hamilton had over four-hundred braves in his service."

"Clark read him like a book, Mom. Hamilton talked a good talk, but he couldn't walk the walk he promised the tribes."

Sally glanced up, her face full of questions.

"Hamilton promised the tribes that he and his men would protect them. But when it came time to deliver, he and the garrison looked on and didn't make a single God damn move. Hell, Mom, the only time they aimed their guns when those men were being hacked to death in front of them was when his royal ass finally strolled out onto that blood soaked parade ground. They wouldn't even fire warning shots to warn Macutte Mong that they were walking into a trap. Those men danced into a hornets nest. Many of them fell dead on the ground before they ever knew what hit them. Why that damn Hamilton thought that the

German=this font   English=this font   *French=this font*   *Delaware=this font*

white flag that the French paraded out made any difference to George Rogers Clark, I will never know."

"What about the traders?"

"Well so far Clark has played up to the militia volunteers and such. He sent them packin' home, if they promise not to take up arms again against the Americans. I suspect they will show up here anytime, trying to stir up good will, downplaying the bloody side." Montour tore a chunk of johnny bread from the plate now before him. "I don't think interfering with trade is in his plan. The man's drunk on liberty. He wants the tribes to stay out of it, to stay neutral and to continue trading. But, I've got a gut feeling though that he's going to be like those damn Puritans in the east, who want religious freedom but that doesn't fit in their plan for anyone else but them. Besides, I think the tribes may fall for his line that the Americans don't desire or want their land, but in the end, mark my word, they will want it all. The Virginians don't go anywhere unless they pack up their surveyors first. My sources say Little Tobacco will be first in line to sell out."

Over eggs and ham, Sally Ainsee would sadly learn even more.

March 31, 1779   At the Falls
Near Present Day St. Louis

Hamilton shivered. The sounds of muskets, though lessened today, still resounded day and night as the revelry without celebrated their capture. The scene repeated itself in one small outpost after another. The sounds of joy confirmed to Hamilton, pop after pop, again and again, the utter contempt held for him on the frontier. He and his men were at great risk.** Their 'guardians' had little hunting success of late, therefore the prisoner's larder was nearly empty.**

The lack of adequate chinking in the log cabin meant the wind and the dampness from the dirt floor penetrated even more. Hamilton bit into the bread that he held in his hand. The lady baker had driven a hard bargain.** Only his personal quilt would satisfy her as payment for the bread.** His men ate quietly.

"Maisonville, you look peaked," Hay observed. "You should eat."

"I am all right."

Hamilton felt unsure as he heard Maisonville's hollow response. He knew that the ragged little girl, spitting in the Frenchman's face earlier today, had quite unnerved him. Maisonville had not expected this response when he gave the starving child a friendly pat and his last biscuit before Hamilton's unexpected and welcome purchase of bread.

Hamilton, Henry, *Henry Hamilton and George Rogers Clark in the American Revolution with the Unpublished Journal of Gov. Henry Hamilton.* **John D. Barnhart, Ed. (Crawfordsville, Indiana: R.E. Ranta, 1951). Information paraphrased from Hamilton's journal. p. 194.

German=this font   English=this font   *French=this font*   *Delaware=this font*

Early Morning after March 31, 1779 Fort Detroit In the Home of Norman MacLeod

"Norman MacLeod," Helen stood appalled at the sight of a drunken man who had spent most of the night at their kitchen table with only rum as his companion. MacLeod's eyes remained bloodshot from earlier anger and tears. No wonder his side of the bed had been so cold.

Captain Norman MacLeod looked up from his refilled cup. He sagged over the table like a soiled dishrag ready to mop up more liquid.

Seeing the tragic look and rum soaked despair, Helen pulled up to the table.

"Sure to God, man, you do not blame yourself for not being there?"

"No..." MacLeod slurred. "No, I blame that bloody bastard and Hay." He reached sheepishly for Helen's hand. "No mah' Helen, I will never regret coming back to you and our girl. My place is here. E'en more so, if Clark's boys attack us. It is all the damn good men that Hamilton has lost in all this. I do not know what drove the bastard out last fall like he had a bee up his ass. If they had just waited until spring, they might..." MacLeod stopped, placing his forehead in his hands, "Oh hell, Helen. What am I saying? They probably still would have beaten us, especially now with the French alliance. There are copies of the damn bloody thing all over town. Who in the hell can you trust?" He rubbed his eyes with the butt of his palms. "Just who in the hell can you trust? And after we gave our bloody lives up for the Rebels to protect them from the damnable French and their native allies? Why this? Why this?" The pains and sacrifices of the Seven Year War by the British still burned brightly in MacLeod's memory. The loss of his kinsmen, then and now, tore at his soul.

German=this font   English=this font   *French=this font*   *Delaware=this font*

Chapter 29   April 1780
Looking Homeward

"As we sat together this Evening the Colonel giving a loose to his military ardor said that he expected shortly to see the whole race of Indians extirpated, that for his part he would never spare Man, Woman or child of them on whom he could lay his hands—I represented to him the Indians having so far forgone their usual cruel habits as to have saved the lives of several of their captives and desired him to enquire of Henry the armourer who had been at Detroit and been witness to the treatment of Prisoners, which when the Colonel had done and received such answers as were indeed consistant with truth, Clarke turned to me and said, Sir I find I have been mistaken in your character and facts have been grosly misrepresented—On renewing his treats against the Indians. I warned him against exasperating a people who were so capable of ravaging the frontiers & being rendered implacable by severities at the same time I quoted Mr. Gay an authority for humanity being the proper companion to true courage "Cowards are cruel, but the brave" be appeard rather checkd "love mercy, and delight to save" and [he appeared] mortified."

**Hamilton, Henry, *Henry Hamilton and George Rogers Clark in the American Revolution with the Unpublished Journal of Gov. Henry Hamilton.* John D. Barnhart, Ed. (Crawfordsville, Indiana: R.E. Ranta, 1951). Conversation between Clark and Hamilton as related in Hamilton's Journal, p. 189.

April 1, 1779 Fort Detroit

Nellie and Agatha readied warp for the second loom as Sally Ainsee briskly entered the weaving shed.

"Nellie, will you hobble Eve's boys if they act up? I need her."

Nellie nodded.

"We'll be in my quarters," Sally said curtly.

Eve pulled away from the loom where she was helping Fiona place the weft. If the thread did not lie at a diagonal angle initially, it would pull in the edges or bulge-out, spoiling the straightness of the salvage. While Eve's little trick of doubling the number of threads in the last four dents of the reed helped, the proper laying of the weft, or woof as her Irish women called it, marked one of the final touches of quality.

"Now remember, Fiona, the thread has to be on a diagonal. In order to go over and under, the distance is greater than straight across. Snug, but not too tight, when you enter...high and loose when you leave the shed." Eve placed the thread correctly to illustrate her directives. She then pulled it out. "Now, you do it." Eve knew instinctively that unless her student attempted it herself, she would fail to master the instruction.

Once Fiona had done it twice correctly, Eve patted her shoulder with approval and joined Sally Ainsee. "Now keep it up. If you have any questions, ask Agatha," she added before making a quick inventory of the room to check-up on what her boys were doing.

"Now boys, behave for Nellie. Do you hear me?"

"Yes Mutti." Two devilish boys played at being angelic with a harmonizing chorus.

"What do you need, Sally?"

Sally did not answer but set out for her quarters. Eve struggled to keep up. As she walked between the shed and the store, she noted a small Indian pony. Typically, the saddle consisted of a tightly, woven matt of reeds with a pelt above. Only a small braided leather thong served as a bridle and reins. A tall solemn brave stood quietly by its side as if guarding it for an unseen rider.

Suddenly quite curious, Eve quickly surveyed Sally's room as she entered the warmth with a sense of expectation.

Sure enough, standing in the shadows stood a tall handsome woman. Staring, Eve tried not to be rude, but she felt quite taken with the statuesque woman. Like Annie Wylie and Helen MacLeod, the woman whose proud stance challenged her presence in the room fascinated her. Also like them, the Indian matron represented a fine example of her race. Her straight brown hair had dark chestnut highlights. One pure white strand accented the left side of her face. Her fiery eyes glowed blue-black like the blackest of birds. The woman wore a simple gray linsey-woolsey blouse over a leather skirt trimmed richly with fringe and quill decoration. Her leggings and puckered moccasins again spoke volumes of practical craftsmanship accented with matching quill embroidery. A rich fur cape with a silver clasp on the chair by the table had to be hers. The woman before her, unlike many of the squaws that Eve noticed frequently about the fort, could only be described as strikingly beautiful and richly adorned.

If ever Eve felt dowdy, she felt it now. Sweaty, hair disheveled, her face swollen, and waddling from her late stage of pregnancy, Eve felt the total antithesis of the woman before her.

"Sally, why must this bloated plain one be here?"

"Raven Wing, everything will be understood in good time. This plain one, as you call her, is named Eve. First, I must share some disturbing news with her. You will be patient."

"I have come in the name of friendship. I will do as you

request. But in this time of my grief, I have little patience. Do not presume too much from our friendship."
"Sit down, Raven Wing."
"No."
"Then be quiet."

Eve looked wonderingly from woman to woman as they verbally sparred amongst each other. Who was this woman? Why did she come here? How Eve devoutly wished she could understand what they said to each other. Her curiosity built.

Sally shrugged her shoulders with exasperation and turned to Eve. "Eve, will you please sit down?" She reached up on her shelf for her brandy that she kept for medicinal purposes and set it mid table.

Eve felt the other woman's keen interest as she dropped awkwardly into a chair.

"Eve, this is Raven Wing. You will learn more of each other directly." She mumbled curses under her breath as she roughly pulled the chair back. Sally, who rarely imbibed, opened her jug and poured two fingers of brandy in her cup, drank it down in one fluid gulp, replaced the cork with a sharp rap, and sat down. She did not offer any to either woman.

Eve looked first to one woman and then fleetingly at the other.

"Right now Eve, I have some damn sad news to share."

Before the words barely escaped Sally's mouth, Eve blurted, "Is Joe hurt? Is this why these people have come?"

"Joe is dead."

Eve turned dolomite white. Every ounce of color drained from her. Her face and body resembled the stone, hard, breakable, and crystalline. On the edge of shattering, she did not speak for a long time. She just sat there numbed by the bluntness of Sally's announcement.

Sally waited until Eve's mood settled and a trace of color returned.

Raven Wing moved closer to monitor the plain one's face. Though she spoke only a little English, she comprehended these words. She had clearly understood what Sally said to this woman called Eve. Why should this news impact upon this white one so?

"How did this come to be? Do you know?"

"It's damn ugly, Eve. But you might as well know the whole of it. Joe joined up with some of his brethren returning to Fort Sackville. The braves had returned from a raid. Joe had been gathering bark for Hamilton. Rebels captured them. George Rogers Clark and his Virginians proceeded to brutally butcher them before Hamilton's garrison whilst the British were holed up in the fort. Not one of the British bastards helped any of them. In the end, his scalp hung beside his brothers outside Hamilton's prison tent."

Darkness began to thread and alter the flat dolomite whiteness of Eve's complexion as her composure cracked and crazed like alabaster.

Eve took a deep breath before she spoke to the two women who waited patiently. "Is this Joe's sister?"

German=this font   English=this font   *French=this font*   *Anishinaabe=this font*

"Nope."

"Family?"

"In a manner of speaking."

Sally looked up at Raven Wing. ***"Now Raven Wing, will you do us all the courtesy of sitting down?***

Eve glanced up at Raven Wing. An unmistakable vacant space had appeared behind Eve's blue eyes that revealed a new haunted emptiness.

Raven Wing recognized loss's deep pain. Rebuked, she accepted the chair.

Now three women sat like the pillars of Stonehenge.

"You two are going to have to bear with me, I don't read all that well. ***Cause, Eve here does not speak French. And Raven Wing, you are not much good at English."*** Sally repeated her words in English to Eve. When Raven Wing frowned, she repeated her words again in Anishinabek. *"Would you prefer that I translate his words to Anishinaabe?"* Sally asked of Raven Wing.

Raven Wing's eyes dimmed perceptively. *"Yes, I would prefer my own tongue."*

"Eve, I know you've been gut ripped, but I got a letter here from Joe that he wants me to read. Now you brace up woman 'cause he wants you both to hear this together."

Then Sally turned to Raven Wing. *"The same goes for you too, sister. I can tell by your eyes that you understand perfectly well what I just said to her."*

Eve refocused on the two women before her, fighting desperately not to let her tears overflow.

"Did you know when he touched me?"

"I suspected it."

Raven Wing missed nothing in this brief exchange. Her eyes veritably blazed with intense interest.

"Now I'm going to translate this letter to you both. I expect you both to be quiet until I am finished. If you think this is easy, you got no head, nor heart. Can you do that?"

Each woman nodded mutely.

"I got this letter a few weeks ago." Sally unfolded the letter carefully, taking care not to break the brittle edges. She read with great difficulty. Even her son Nicholas's earlier assistance in sounding out each word would not help her now.

> ***"Sally, I have a favor to ask. If the Creator is kind, you will never need to do as I request. But I had a dream Sally. I fear I will not return. I believe Raven Wing and the Yankee Hall prisoner, Eve Earnest, must hear my last words to them—together. I beg you to do this, my good friend.***

My dearest ones forgive me. I never meant to deceive or to hurt either of you. This is not my way. I am a man of two worlds. Each of you touched a world within me.

I ask you both as loving mothers, when a new child comes—does your love die for the child before it? Does a good mother pick a favorite? No, as you know—a loving heart has no boundaries, just as with hate.

When you both freely offered the fruits of your great hearts, I could not refuse to eat.

Raven Wing, when we lost our youngest son to the white man's measles, we were filled with a great emptiness. For a time, coldness entered our lodge, but love brought warmth again.

Raven Wing, I ask you to look with compassion on Eve, who carries my child. Like us, she too has a torn heart with many open spaces. Help her discover the strength of our people so that your emptiness may also be filled. Teach her to walk with a high head when ugly hatred comes to her, to her two fine sons, and to the new metis child.

Eve, I ask you to look with compassion on Raven Wing. Her path is not unlike yours, but even harder to walk. Remember...strong women can draw great support from one another.

I plead with you both. Learn from each other so that you and our children may survive in this time of hatred.

Always I pledge to keep watch over you from about the Creator's great fire—where I believe all tribes will one day meet.

Tchamaniked Joe

Sally read the letter first in French, then repeated the words in Anishinabek and yet a third time in English. Sometimes the emotions caused her voice to crack and to break, causing her to pause. While, she struggled to regain her composure, Raven Wing and Eve waited silently, patiently. Once, Raven Wing reached out to touch Sally's hand in support just as did Eve. Their hands met. When Sally finished, both women's hands lay comfortingly over her hand.

No one moved after the last English word for a very long period of time.

Eve broke the silence. Withdrawing her hand, she squared her shoulders and lifted her quivering chin before she spoke.

German=this font   English=this font   *French=this font*   *Anishinaabe=this font*

"I need to know, Sally. Is Raven Wing the reason that Joe found the strength to return from France?"

Sally nodded affirmatively.

"Would you tell her, I am truly sorry for her losses?"

Eve staggered a little as she rose to leave the table just as a sobbing Mikie and a frustrated Nellie barged through the door.

Sally never got a chance to translate Eve's words. She could only breathe a heavy sigh of relief that the intruders had not entered a single moment sooner.

"Eve, Henry broke Mikie's deer. I cannot calm this child. He is throwing a hisser." Brutally aware suddenly that she may have waded into water over her head; Nellie flushed with embarrassment. "I'm sorry, I should'ave knocked."

"Yes, you should have." Sally growled.

"Mutti, mutti, Henry breaked my deer." Mikie's tear stained face still had traces of red from his temper tantrum. In his upturned dirty palm, the tiny broken wooden deer lay. Two legs pointed straight up. The other half lolled on its side.

But it was not Eve's calming hand that reached out to comfort Mikie. Raven Wing pushed the hair back from Mikie's hot angry face. Her thumbs gently brushed away his tears. Motioning for him to wait, she reached deep into a pouch which hung from a woven strap over her shoulder. She withdrew two small wooden deer, mirror images of the broken one in Henry's hand. She took the broken pieces gently from his hand and carefully put the two unbroken deer in Henry's hand.

"One, you. One brother. Yes?" Raven Wing's hands pantomimed with her halting words. She curled his tiny fingers tenderly around the two deer.

Mikie sniffled and then smiled ear to ear. Ever the flirt, still well schooled after fleecing the neighborhood, he responded immediately. "Thank you, pretty lady."

"I go. We meet...when knife not cut deep." Her halting English sounded clear enough to Eve. Nothing needed translation.

Raven Wing reverently put the tiny broken deer in her pouch. Then she straightened to her fullest height. A commanding woman, she looked at each of the women in the room. She nodded to each, turned, and picked up her cape.

Everyone watched her exit in absolute silence.

Even Nellie and Mikie deferred, backing up wordlessly.

Nellie whispered a few moments after the door closed behind Raven Wing, "Who's that?"

"Joe's widow," Eve answered simply before pulling Mikie into her arms. Mikie's small legs straddled her heavy abdomen as she returned to the weaving shed.

"Mutti, see deers from lady."

"Yes, Mikie. I see the deer."

"Aw shit. Can't anything ever come out right in this here world?" Nellie wheezed before walking quickly to catch up with her friend. She knew the shuttle would fly this day.

Sally watched the women leave and returned the brandy to its shelf.

April 15, 1779 Bedford, Pennsylvania

"Eric Mens Emler," Ester persisted using his full given name. "Please take the children to the spring outing in May. We should celebrate and lift the sadness a little. Surely you remember your young days."

Finally, Grossvater Emler fumed at Ester when his continued silence had been totally ignored and the question incessantly repeated. "Have you forgotten last year, woman? Remember what happened when the Diberts brought the child down? Do you wish to be embarrassed by her again?" But in the end, he relented. "All right, we go. It will be good to hoist a few with the men and to toast that damn Hairbuyer-Hamilton's capture."

Molly overheard them as she worked in the kitchen. Her stubbornness flowered fully as she replaced the pots noisily in their places.

"You can all go to Michigan for all I care. You can not make me go!" Molly whispered quietly to herself. Then she deliberately slammed the door behind her as she headed for the hen yard and her feeding chores.

April 26, 1779
Crossing the Cumberland Mountains

As the band of British prisoners and their guards entered Powell Valley, the stillness impacted. Before them, unattended cattle roamed and lowed softly as they grazed. No one talked openly of their suspicions, but they all knew that the owners probably had been dispatched by marauding Indians, no doubt formerly led by Hamilton's department. Even headless, the mayhem continued. The meat from a cow cut from the herd, however, became a welcome addition to the dwindling supply of parched Indian corn for all concerned.

Hamilton confronted the continuous dehumanization, exertion, and lack of food and provisions with courage. He struggled with the constant fording of rivers and creeks. His ankles ached, swelled, and bled from the forced marches in his shackles. The angry faces and the open hostility of the small communities continued to reveal the deep hatred that the inhabitants felt toward the British. Much of this hatred focused on the person of the Lieutenant Governor as he passed from settlement to settlement. Hamilton became increasingly aware that the colonists considered the British 'little better than savages.' Obviously, any good will that the British had engendered in the Seven Year War had been long

German=this font   English=this font   *French=this font*   *Anishinaabe=this font*

forgotten. No one remembered the lives lost earlier in defense of the colonies or the impact on the English home treasury. Could it be that after the British had employed the previous tactics of the French that the colonies were bonding as never before? The question plagued him. Hamilton continued to keep his diary, relating that Hamilton's party owed much to Colonel Bowman, for the American truly attempted to keep them from harm. When 'delayed against [their] will' in threatening areas, he had 'acted as a person above prejudice,'** Hamilton wrote. Like Clark before him, Bowman had prevented drunken hot heads, fueled with hate, from attacking Hamilton and his party.

Hamilton, though physically uncomfortable, fought against feeling despondent. In his sketches and drawings, he found a source of solace as he focused on the beauty of his surroundings. He recorded his experiences, citing the loveliness about him in his journal. He rarely mentioned the demeaning shackles, dwelling instead on the growing physical fitness of his party and relating their relative good health in the face of strenuous hardship.

Others coped less capably.

Maisonville become increasingly more despondent. The glaring hatred from those that he passed and the growing shame that he felt planted suicidal seeds.

DeJean bitched endlessly about everything, including his aching teeth.

Hamilton, Henry, *Henry Hamilton and George Rogers Clark in the American Revolution with the Unpublished Journal of Gov. Henry Hamilton.* John D. Barnhart, Ed. (Crawfordsville, Indiana: R.E. Ranta, 1951). Information paraphrased from Hamilton's Journal, p.194-196. Quotes p. 196.

The Last Week of April, 1779   Fort Detroit.

Nellie, Eve, and Fiona stood with the boys. Fiona, who had one free hand, shook her new hanky in the balmy breeze. Nellie sniffled into her sleeve.

"Good bye, good bye!" They called out when emotions permitted.

The boys chimed in with Fiona and the women from time to time as they jumped up and down with excitement. Swinging back and forth on the women's arms, the boys excitedly circled in and out among the women's skirts until Eve shook loose Henry's hand.

"Stop this Henry. You are stretching Mikie drum tight." No sooner had she spoken when Henry went dangerously close to the dock edge. "Henry! Stay away from the water!"

Henry grinned back in defiance. His mother could not run very fast of late and hardly constituted any real threat.

Mid-harbor, Margaret Elder and Sue Ellen sat side-by-side in the dingy that would take them out to the waiting boat at anchor. All their worldly goods were placed in two small blanket rolls and wedged between them on the seat. Margaret clutched the Bible given to her by the officers to her chest. Her eyes brimmed full of joyous tears. Sue Ellen sat transfixed in a state of bliss.

"Danged if I know'd where Sue Ellen got all that money for her to be goin' an all."

"Mama, some say she has a ben-e-factor," Fiona chirped, emphasizing each syllable. She liked using the fancy word.

"Maybe more than one," Eve added. "I was told that they took up a collection for her at the Church. But I would imagine because of all the threats and price increases, someone with more than most had to help out."

"Spec you'r right about that Eve."

When Eve winced a little, Nellie noticed.

"Eve, are you all right?"

"I am fine. I will stay until they are on the boat."

"Eve???"

"I am fine, Nellie. Do not fuss. You will rile the boys more than they are already."

They watched their friends climb aboard. The sailors pushed them ignominiously up the rope ladders into the ship and into the waiting arms of the men on deck.

Eve flinched again. Nearly doubling over, she straightened slowly. A trickle and then a tiny crooked stream zigzagged down her leg. The nitrous smell of amniotic waters, a smell familiar to Eve, greeted her nostrils. Eve shivered involuntarily. The sensation brought her back momentarily to a sunny cabin stoop on the banks of Dunnings Creek where she had pressed her petticoat to her leg to absorb a flow of semen. Blotting the liquid with her skirt, she straightened fully into the now.

Things had begun so simply so many mornings ago. What a blessing we do not know what life holds in store for us; she mused. Otherwise, we might give up too soon. She devoutly wished that Joe's advice would come true. Would she know which path to follow when the time came? Would it be an easy choice? Perhaps for now she must simply follow her heart as well as her head. Humbly accepting the promise of a new blessing in her life with every contraction, she turned toward Nellie.

"Nellie, will you take the boys up to the Hall? I am going to walk up to Martha's."

Nellie frowned at Eve. "Fiona can take the boys up to the hall. I will walk with you to Martha's."

Eve smiled sheepishly at the stalwart Nellie. "Only on one condition."

"What's that?"

"You have got to be quiet."

"You drive a hard bargain."

Eve winced a little.

"Are you sure you can make it?"

German=this font   English=this font   *French=this font*   *Anishinaabe=this font*

Eve laughed. "Do I have any choice?"

"Fiona, you take them boys up to the Hall. Henry, don't you give her any nonsense or I'll paddle your behind hard when I get back. Depend on it, young man!" She grabbed him roughly just as he skipped by her. "Boy, you're getting much too big to act like this. Your mother needs you to be a young man, not a spoiled brat. Straighten up and set an example for your brother, Mikie." She gave him a quick resounding swat before handing him gruffly over to Fiona.

Henry flushed with embarrassment. The swat barely stung, but his emerging male ego had been struck a harder blow. Quickly, he scanned the faces of those about him on the dock. Noting additional frowns from the strangers about him, he cooperated.

Giving Fiona a knowing glance, Nellie turned to catch up with Eve who started the climb up the long hill to the outskirts of town and Martha.

"I want to go with Mutti." Mikie called to his departing Mother and Nellie.

"Not this time, Mikie. She's about woman's business. She'll be back soon."

"Promise, Fiona?"

"I promise."

Near them a defaced squaw, without a nose and with scarred cheeks, observed the boat weighing anchor. Looking far more haggard than her true age, she stood quietly. A shawl hung loosely over her head so that her face hid within the shadows. She would miss the healing touch of Sue Ellen. Whoever could she turn to now? Who would listen? The coins from her last few tricks went into Father's tray for her friend. At least, in her own way, she had helped Sue Ellen leave this wretched place.

Across the street, Nanna Solomon watched the little drama. Taking her nephew, Ezekiel Solomon's arm, she nodded to him, indicating a desire to return home.

"Are you satisfied now? She is on the boat."

"Yes. Let us go home, Ezekiel."

"Too bad your friend and her boys cannot go."

"It is not her time, Ezekiel." Nanna clutched her nephew's arm, trying to ignore her own pain. "It is not her time." Her voice faded markedly when she repeated the phrase, for Nanna knew that like a ship's sail appearing on the far horizon, a heavy load would soon come to her homeport. Then she would have need of Eve. She could not ask her family…not for this. Nanna remained confident that Eve being Eve, Eve would come when called.

"Are you sure Nanna? Her time appears close to me."

"Enough Ezekiel, you know perfectly well what I mean," Nanna scolded, hugging her nephew's arm affectionately.

German=this font   English=this font   *French=this font*   *Anishinaabe=this font*

They walked steadily toward their home.

"Well, now that Hamilton is getting his comeuppance, I wonder who will take over his command." Nanna observed.

"We will know before long. You can be sure Haldimand knows of his capture," Ezekiel Solomon answered. "The real question could be...will it make any difference?"

"Probably not, my dear Ezekiel. Sadly, probably not. But let us hope that the change is for the better."

"One thing is sure."

"What is that?"

"No matter who wins this ugly war, history will have little good to say about Lieutenant Governor Henry Hamilton."

"I would not go so far as to say that, Ezekiel. Will it not depend on who writes the history?"

German=this font   English=this font   **French=this font**   *Anishinaabe=this font*

Characters of Revolutionary Fires, Volume I

(F) = fiction (NF) = non fiction in origin, researched and fictionalization only as needed to incorporate them in this historical tale using the life of a woman known as Indian Eve or Eve/Eva (Hillebartin/Imler) Earnest (Arnst) Samuels and the nine year period of her captivity as the connective thread. In lieu of an index, "Also" includes influential persons from quotes or those of historical importance and those mentioned in previous chapters.

Prologue:

William Wilson: (NF) An Indian Trader working out of Fort Pitt. One of the men chosen by George Morgan to take an invitation to the tribes west of the Ohio River to make peace with the Continental Congress at Fort Pitt in the fall of 1776.

George Morgan: (NF) a highly educated and wealthy man appointed by the Continental Congress appointee from Princeton, New Jersey. He was to work for the Rebels in the same capacity as the former, Sir William Johnson had for the British as the controller of Indian agencies.

John Montour: (NF) son of **Andrew Montour** (NF) and Delaware mother (daughter of a Delaware Chief) (NF), raised by **Sally Ainsee** (NF), a Oneida (second wife of Andrew Montour). Andrew Montour's (NF) mother, **Queen Catherine** (NF), and aunt, **Queen Esther** (NF),were Seneca Matriarchs. Queen Esther slaughtered many Pennsylvanians by bashing out their brains. After which time, she smeared their brains over a rock because her beloved son had been killed by renegade Americans when in theory her tribe was at peace. Andrew Montour, John's father was a flamboyant interpreter and guide for British Indian Department with **George Croghan** (NF) during the 1750s and 1760s. For a time, like his father before him, John Montour acted as guide and interpreter with British Forces under Lieutenant Governor Henry Hamilton and prior to that with the colony of Pennsylvania. Mid conflict he joined the rebellious Virginian and Pennsylvanian forces. It is sad that John Montour never kept a journal as he certainly is one of the most amazing and most controversial of early Americans. The entire Montour family would make a fantastic book.

White Eyes: (NF) A Delaware chief who consistently strove for peace and sided with the American Rebellion from the onset. His family sold land to the Penn family. See Chapter 13.

Lieutenant George Henry Hamilton: (NF) usually known as **Henry Hamilton** or the "**Hair Buyer**" as dubbed by **George Rogers Clark** (NF). A British appointee, he served as part of a Triad in civilian control of the Indian Department for the Province of Quebec under British Rule following the French and Indian War and during the Revolutionary War. He was born in Great Britain, educated in England, and initially brought to the Colonies with the military forces during the French and Indian War (1754-1763) or the Seven Year War as it is known in Britain. This war is considered by many to be a World War as it was fought in Europe, India, Africa, the West Indies, and North America. His distinguished service, class connections, and money allowed him to obtain this choice post. As the younger of two sons, Henry Hamilton had to gain status through ambition and skill not by inheritance. A great historical debate rages over whether he initiated the concept of Native American Raids against the rebellious Colonials.

Philip DeJean: (NF) Justice Minister, a civilian post, re-appointed by **Lieutenant Governor George Henry Hamilton** (NF), Roman Catholic, and a "habitant" of Fort Detroit. DeJean held similar posts before Lieutenant Governor Henry Hamilton took office. With the expansion of British power into the Heartland (the area west of the colonies extending to the Mississippi) in 1774, his authority and powers were not clear under the Quebec Act.

Sir Frederick Hamilton, Baron of Paisley, and Governor of Ulster: (NF) great grandfather of Henry Hamilton, of the linage of **Mary Queen of Scots** (NF). Scottish born, moved to Ireland where he amassed land and power.

Gustavas Hamilton: (NF) father of Henry Hamilton's father and grandfather to George Henry Hamilton.

Henry Hamilton: (NF) father of **George Henry Hamilton,** member of the Irish Parliament and collector for the port of Queenstown and third son of **Gustavas Hamilton (NF).**

Lord George Germain: (NF) **Lieutenant Governor Henry Hamilton's** (NF) superior in London, England. Germain was appointed by the British Parliament with direct access to **King George III** (NF) as the commander of the Province of Quebec and British Forces fighting the Rebels, rebellious American colonists.

Captain Mompesson: (NF) Military Commander of Fort Detroit in 1777 under the authority of **Lord Germain** (NF).

Major Jehu Hay: (NF) probably born in Chester, Pennsylvania, Appointed to the Indian Department under **Lieutenant Governor Henry Hamilton** (NF).

John Coutincinau: (NF) a coureur de bois or unlicensed independent trader, lightly fictionalized initially so events will correspond with time and activities concerning **Eve Emler (Imler) Earnest** (NF). Subsequent events between **John Coutincinau, Nancy (Anne) Wylie, Lieutenant Governor Henry Hamilton** and **Philip DeJean** are not fiction and follow the time line.

James Sterling: (NF) Captain of the Detroit Militia and British, charismatic, well liked, with a strong civilian following. He married **Angelique Cuillerier** (NF), a daughter of an Indian interpreter. Due to her connections and her ability to interpret, Sterling, although English, like many local French traders and French habitants had access to outstanding trade connections. Shrewd in business dealings, this couple wielded considerable influence in early Detroit. Sterling was atypical as the majority of British Traders distanced themselves from Native American or habitants in the province of Quebec.

Stalking Wolf: (F) a warrior of the Wolf band of Delaware. Many of his band sided with the British interests during the Revolutionary War in an effort to confront the Western expansion of the American settlers and traders and in response to the indiscriminate killing of tribal members. The Delaware nation had deep divisions of loyalty. Some Delaware sided with the American interests, some remained neutral living with the Moravian missionaries, and still others, as stated, sided with the British, who not incidentally had deeper pockets than the Americans. Historically, the Delaware sold land to **William Penn** (NF).

Jacques Duperon Baby, William Tucker, Pierre Drouillard, and Joseph Martin: All (NF) interpreters for the Indian Department under **Lieutenant Governor Henry Hamilton** (NF). These men probably accompanied the Native American (NA) allies on raids against the Colonial western flank.

Edward Abbott, Lieutenant Governor for the Indian Department: (NF) centered in Vincennes and **Mathew Johnson** (NF), Lieutenant Governor for the Indian Department, centered in KasKaskia (also NF) are the counterparts of Henry Hamilton in Fort Detroit. Mathew Johnson is the son of the late, **Sir William Johnson** (NF), the head of the Indian Department prior to the Revolutionary War for the colonies. Sir William Johnson's dealings made him a very rich man, so much so that he was occasionally referred to as the "King of the Mohawks." He was by in large much respected for his fair dealings and incisive knowledge of tribal ways. **Molly Brant** (NF), Mahican sister of **Joseph Brant** (NF) was Sir William Johnson's consort. Joseph Brant, her well educated and well traveled brother, proved to be one of the most capable British Officers in command of a Native and Tory force against the Rebels. Isabel Thompson Kelsay's book, ***Joseph Brant, 1743-1807; Man of Two Worlds*** should be considered a must read for those fascinated by this time period.

Sir Guy Carleton: (NF) under the direct command of **Lord Germain** (NF) and the Triad's immediate superior located in Montreal. Sir Carleton served as the civil and military governor of the Province of Quebec.

King George III of England: (NF) reigning monarch of England during the Revolutionary War. Third generation of an imported German Monarchy, George III, unlike his father or grandfather before him, was strongly nationalistic and desired to regain the power of royalty previously lost to the English Parliament.

Half King: (NF) one of the top chiefs of the Wyandot Indian tribe living near the Sandusky and Toledo areas in present day Ohio. This chief may have functioned more as a war chief than a civil chief. His status is not totally clear in research which is not surprising as, by in large, most historians did not understand that initially War Chiefs were in power only during conflict and were appointed by the civil chieftains. This concept was not fully understood by early historians or those dealing with Native Americans early in American history. Ironically, this very concept of civilian control over the military continues today as a corner stone of American law and part of our separation of powers in our democracy.

Tscendattong: (NF) principal civil chief of the Wyandot probably responsible for law and order within the tribe and preservation of tribal history.

Lieutenant Governor Hector Theophilus Cramahe: (NF) officer in the British Army, Civil Secretary to **Guy Carleton** (NF) and **Frederick Haldimand** (NF), served during Carleton's absence to England. He held this office from June 1771 to April. 1782. A man of moderation and a proponent of religious freedom, he garnered respect.

Chapter 1: Home on Dunnings Creek

Sir William Johnson: (NF) known as Warraghiyagey among the Six Nations (Iroquois League). Head of Indian Affairs for the British Crown prior to the Revolutionary War. Consort of **Mary Brant** (NF).

Eve (Emler, Imler, or Eva Catharina Hilpot, Eva Catharina Hillebartin): (NF + F) wife of **Adam Henry Earnest** (NF). In this publication she will be the daughter of **Eric Mens Emler** (NF) also known as **George Mark Imler** and **Ester (Esther) Ana Shaver** who immigrated from the Palatine area of Germany. Mother of **George, Jacob, Johannas, Mary (Molly), Henry** and **Michael Earnest** (all NF). To read a nonfiction account read: *Indian Eve and her Descendents* by Emma A.M. Replogle. The site of Eve Earnest Samuels grave is adjacent to the Messiah Lutheran Church in Bedford. Eve fed the builders of this early church upon her return to Bedford. **PLEASE NOTE:** This site badly needs funds to maintain the graveyard and site. The Cemetery Association would appreciate your donations. Please send them to: Messiah Church Cemetery Association, % P.O. Box 488, Osterburg, PA. 16667. Copies of the Replogle book can be obtained from this Church. Recent information suggests that Eve may not an Imler but rather a Hillpot, Hillebartin or Hillebart. The most important thing to remember is that she was a real person that either the Imler or the Hillebartin family would be very proud to claim her among their own.

Adam Henry Earnest: (NF) husband of **Eve Earnest** (NF). His gravesite and two unnamed individuals may be found adjacent to the rural roadway and marked with a historical marker in Bedford County, Pennsylvania.

George Earnest: (all NF) eldest son of **Adam Henry Earnest** and **Eve Earnest.**

Jacob Earnest: (all NF) second son of **Adam Henry Earnest** and **Eve Earnest.**

Johannas Earnest: (all NF) third son of **Adam Henry Earnest** and **Eve Earnest.**

Molly or Mary Earnest: (NF) only daughter of **Adam Henry Earnest (NF)** and **Eve Earnest** (NF + F).

Eve Dibert (Eve Margaret Nei Ney Dibert): (NF) + (F) called Mere Eve in this book. Widow of **Christopher Dibert** (NF), a French Huguenot of the Mannikin Colony, Virginia. **Christopher Dibert** had the dubious distinction of being the second generation of Dibert men to be massacred at the Dibert homestead located north of present day Bedford, Pennsylvania. **Frederick Dibert** (NF) and **Mary Seasworth** (NF) parents of Christopher also were massacred at this site. Their son, Christopher, (as a child) literally walked off his moccasins with his siblings to return to the Mannikin colony in Virginia following the first massacre. Eve Dibert's parentage is not clear, but there is some indication that both her family and the Dibert family like many early French had intermarried with local indigenous women. The Dibert men first arrived to the Mannikin colony in 1696. A dated stone indicates that the first Dibert family may have arrived in the Bedford area in 1710. Dates for Eve Dibert's death vary. She may have died prior to this fictional story.

Chloe: (NF) a freeborn black, owner or at least proprietress of an early Inn of Bedford, one of those places where **George Washington** stopped in history or in myth. She later worked as a cook for the Bedford Springs Inn and spa known in the early centuries for healing baths.

Brother Bergfelder: (F) a fictitious protestant lay-minister tending a far flung flock, probably Lutheran or Dutch Reformed. To the best of my knowledge there was not a "churched" congregation in Bedford in 1777.

Henry Earnest: (all NF) the fourth son of **Adam Henry Earnest** and **Eve Earnest.**

Michael Earnest: (NF) the fifth son of **Adam Henry Earnest** and **Eve Earnest**, last child of this union.

Jac Emler or Onkel Jac or "**Double Thunder**: (NF+F) this character is highly fictionalized for he is a composite of fact, fiction, and myth. Eric Mens Emler did have a brother named Jac. The stories that surround "Captain Jac" or "Black Jac" are nearly mythical in the Bedford area and have been incorporated into this portrayal of this very troubled man. His racist activities were typical of this time period. Double barreled rifles were unusual, but they did exist which suggested the title of "Double Thunder" (F) among the Native Americans that he preyed upon. Pictures and descriptions of a double barreled rifle may be found in *The Pennsylvania - Kentucky Rifle* by Henry J. Kauffman.

Tante Jessie or **Jessie Emler**: (F) fictional sister of **Eve Earnest** (NF + F).

Emily Reighard: (NF) sister of **Eve Earnest** (NF + F).

Mistress Conrad Samuels: (NF) first wife of **Conrad Samuels** (NF) and mother of **Lizzie (Elizabeth) Samuels** (NF) and **Deede Samuels** (NF).

Elizabeth Samuels (called Lizzie): (NF) daughter of **Conrad Samuels** (NF), future wife of **George Earnest** (NF), eldest son of **Eve Earnest Samuels** (NF + F) and **Adam Henry Earnest** (NF) see Vol. II.

Isaac and his son, Joseph (neighbors of **Adam Henry Earnest** (NF)): (NF)+(F) the only thing fictional is his name and his son's name. History never recorded who these two men were (although they lie buried aside Adam Henry Earnest). But his death and the death of his son with Adam Henry Earnest were dutifully recorded. These grave sites still may be seen in Bedford with an appropriate historical marker in place. The three men lay side by side on the soft slope facing Dunnings Creek.

Blackburns: (NF) neighbors of the Earnest and Emler families.

Garrett's: (NF) an Inn in the early Fort Bedford community.

Animals: (F) Minnie the breeding sow, Katie the cow, her calf, and Opa's bull Gregor.

John Heckwelder: (NF) a Moravian missionary to the Delaware. His writings and those of **David Zeisburger** (NF) would make fantastic additions to the canon of American Literature. They are rejected currently as they were originally written in German.

Cornstalk: (NF) Shawnee Leader, pro-American.

David Zeisburger: (NF) a Moravian missionary to the Delaware Indians.

George Washington: (NF) Commander and chief of the American Rebel Army under the command of the Continental Congress.

Chapter 2: Indian Summer Closes

Ethan Allen: (NF) A Revolutionary hero of the New England area.

Joseph (son of Isaac the neighbor of Adam Henry Earnest): (NF+F) fictitious in name only. History never recorded his name but he lies side by side with **Adam Henry Earnest** (NF) in death. See **Isaac** in Chapter 1.

Blue Ice: (F) Wolf Delaware and head of the initial raiding party of **Sitting Rabbit** (F) and **Standing Wolf** (F).

White Corn Woman: (F) grandmother of **Stalking Wolf** (F) inspired by women such as **Francis Slocum** (NF) and other white women who remained with Native Americans after their capture and a creek near Gnadenhutten called White Woman's Creek, so called from one **Mary Harris** (NF) who was also captured and stayed with the Native Americans of Ohio. Mary Harris offered hospitality to **Andrew Montour** (father of **John Montour**) in earlier days.

Sitting Rabbit: (F) a stout Wolf Delaware Scout with the raiding party of **Stalking Wolf** (F) and **Blue Ice** (F).

Also: **Eve Dibert, Adam Henry Earnest, Eve Earnest, Lil' Henry Earnest, Mikie Earnest, George Mark Emler (Eric Mens Emler which over time changed to Imler, Johannas Earnest, Jacob Earnest,** and **Mary (Molly) Earnest.**

Chapter 3: The Journey Begins

George Wood: (NF) a civilian leader in the Fort Bedford Community.

Lieutenant Jacob Schieffelin: (NF) initially the secretary of Henry Hamilton. He was of German heritage, but American born in Philadelphia, Pennsylvania. He was a loyalist and strong supporter of the British interests.

Jehu Hay: (NF) also known as the **Snipe**, a strong supporter of British policies during the Revolutionary War, a subordinate of **Lieutenant Governor Henry Hamilton** (NF), and who served as commander of raiding parties on the western flank early in the conflict. Fought in the takeover of Vincennes and was one of the last commanders of Fort Detroit under the British rule. He was probably born in Chester, Pennsylvania.

Also: **Mary (Molly) Earnest, Eve Earnest, Stalking Wolf, Eve Dibert, John Dibert, Michael (Mikie) Earnest, Lil' Henry Earnest, Sitting Rabbit, Blue Ice, Ester Emler, George Mark Emler, Jessie Emler,** *Angelica,* **a ship, Philip DeJean, Lieutenant Gov. Henry Hamilton, Governor Guy Carleton, and Captain Mompesson**

Chapter 4: Kittanning on the Allegheny

George Sill: (NF) an indentured servant living in Bedford.

John Dibert: (NF) third generation of Dibert men of Bedford, Pennsylvania. Husband of **Ene (or Eve) Ickes Dibert** (NF) and son of **Eve Margaret (Nei Ney) Dibert** (NF) and **Christopher Dibert** (NF). Grandson of **Frederick Dibert** (NF) and **Mary (Seasworth) Dibert** (NF).

Anne Wylie: (primarily NF) Anne Wylie is a composite of two characters, a spirited black-freeborn woman captured while riding and Anne Wylie, a woman of Fort Detroit. The activities between **John Coutincinau** (NF), Anne Wylie (NF), **Philip DeJean** (NF), **Lieutenant Governor Henry Hamilton** (NF) are well documented. Timeline shifted initially to correspond with **Eve Earnest** (NF + F) otherwise timeline is correct. Both of these black women were too fantastic to ignore and inspired this composite character.

Margaret Elder: (NF) wife of **George Elder** (NF) of Cessna, Pennsylvania.

Felix Skelly: (NF) friend and young neighbor of **Margaret Elder** (NF).

Deede Samuels: (NF) youngest daughter of **Conrad Samuels** (NF). Sister of **Elizabeth (Lizzie) Samuels** (NF).

Ene Ickes Dibert: (NF) wife of **John Dibert** (NF) and mother of **David** (NF), **Ene** (NF), **Elizabeth** (NF), **Barbara** (NF), and **Susannah** (NF).

Hanu: (NF) the name given by Native American captors to Lil Henry or **Henry Earnest** (NF).

Also: **Mary (Molly) Earnest, Stalking Wolf, Eve Dibert (Mere Eve), James Sterling, Sitting Rabbit, Blue Ice, George Mark Emler, Ester Emler, Philip DeJean, Jessie Emler, George Wood, Jac Emler, John Montour, Eve Earnest, Michael Earnest, Henry Earnest, Anne Wylie, Chloe, and John Dibert.**

Chapter 5: Allegheny and to the Ohio

Simon Girty: (NF) Rebel American soldier who defected to the British. He served with **Lord Dunmore** (NF). **Simon Girty** (NF) was adopted by Seneca. An observer of the infamous "Squaw Campaign." Brothers:

George Girty (NF) adopted by Delaware, **James Girty** (NF) adopted by Shawnee, **Thomas Girty** (NF) third and oldest brother, remained in Fort Pitt as a Rebel American.

Whig: Americans loyal to the rebellious American Continental Congress. Also refers to the liberal party of Great Britain who supported in part the American Rebellion and deplored the bloodshed of the Revolutionary War on both sides.

Also: **Lord Suffolk, Lord Chatham, Jacob Schieffelin, Sir Guy Carleton, Captain Mompesson, James Sterling, Lieutenant Governor Edward Abbott, Sitting Rabbit, Stalking Wolf, and Blue Ice, Eve Earnest, Henry, and Michel Earnest, Margaret Elder, Isaac and Joseph**, the neighbors of **Adam Henry Earnest.**

Chapter 6: About the Hearths

Lord Suffolk: (NF) a leading hawk in the British Parliament.

Lord Chatham: (NF) an outspoken opponent of British policies against the American colonies in the British Parliament, most particularly the use of Native Allies in the manner of the French during the Seven Year War i.e. French and Indian War.

Simon Girty: (NF) like **Benedict Arnold** (NF) this man's name was synonymous with treachery and being a traitor due to his defection to the British during the Revolutionary War. Like **Joseph Brant** (NF) in any raid, settlers would claim to have seen him as part of the war party, so like Joseph Brant many false sightings resulted.

Red Jacket (F): another member of the Wolf Delaware.

John Leeth (NF) adopted by the Delaware, his father was **Standing Stone** (NF) and **Falling Water Woman** (F). Orphaned son of a Scotsman of Leith County, Scotland and his mother was from Virginia. For his biography read *A Short Biography of John Leeth with an Account of his Life Among the Indians* by Ewel Jeffries.

Also: **Henry Earnest (Hanu), Eve Earnest, Mikie Earnest, Margaret Elder, Stalking Wolf, Blue Ice, White Corn Woman, Little Fox, Anne Wylie, Sue Ellen (unnamed), Major Jehu Hay, Lieutenant Governor Henry Hamilton, and Philip DeJean.**

Chapter 7: Letters and Pictures

Thomas Smith (NF) leading resident of Bedford, Pennsylvania.

President Wharton: (NF) President of the Commonwealth of Pennsylvania in 1777.

Ezekiel Solomon: (NF) a respected merchant and trader of Fort Michilimackinac and Fort Detroit. A member of the synagogue of Montreal. Ezekiel Solomon had endured Native American captivity before the Revolutionary War during Pontiac's Rebellion.

Fogherty's Tavern: (NF) this lively inn is sometimes referred to as **Forsythe's Inn**…**Ann Forsythe and William Forsythe** (both NF) managed the inn according to some research materials. Intrigue, spying, and drinking were common bedfellows here.

Ruth (Nanna) Solomon: (F) widowed Aunt of **Ezekiel Solomon** (NF).

Also: **George Wood, Jac Emler, George Emler, George Washington, George Sill, Eve Earnest, Margaret Elder, Adam Henry Earnest, Henry Earnest (Hanu), Mikie Earnest, George Earnest, and White Corn Woman.**

Chapter 8: You Are Dead to Me!:

Smoke in Eyes: (F) teenage son of **Blue Ice** and a young warrior.

Sue Ellen: (F) a fair young captive with a questionable past that is never revealed in Vol. 1. First heard when **Anne Wylie** (NF) and she approached the village.

Midewiwin Healer of the Order of the Grand Medicine Lodge: (NF) inspired. These men were dedicated to healing in the Native American society. Often cross tribal, these men were selected at an early age and initiated and taught the skills of their spiritual and healing society. Native American women probably had a counterpart society but little is recorded about them as they dealt with female medicine and birthing. The male society had degrees similar to Masonry.

Little Fox: (F) nephew of **Stalking Wolf** (F) and son of his sister, **Singing Grass** (F), a member of the Wolf Delaware, a great grandson of **White Corn Woman** (F).

Singing Grass: (F) mother of **Little Fox** (F) and sister of **Stalking Wolf** (F), granddaughter of **White Corn Woman** (F).

Also: **David Zeisberger, General Hand, Henry Earnest (Hanu), Margaret Elder, Eve Earnest, Mikie Earnest, Major Jehu Hay, Lieutenant Governor Henry Hamilton, Jac Emler (Double Thunder), Stalking Wolf, Anne Wylie, and Blue Ice.**

Chapter 9: Early December 1777

Sanders: (F) a fictional man who met the fate of many male prisoners.

Mister Biscoe: (F) an elderly gentleman captured with Eve.

Master and Mistress Smyth: (NF) (F name) inspired by the unnamed Tory couple mentioned in Emma A. M. Replogle's account of Indian Eve.

William Boslick (NF) and **James (Jamie) Cassidy**: (NF) men documented as Rebel sympathizers in Fort Detroit.

Lord Dunmore: (NF) aka **John Murry, Earl of Dunmore** and instigator of a war known as Dunmore's War in 1774 and known for his attacks against the Shawnee during which he took great pride in making "them [the Shawnee] sensible of their villainy and weakness," and believed that the Native Americans would never renew their attacks against the stronger white settlers due to his severe retaliation.

Cornplanter: (NF) father of **Ellinipisco,** major Shawanese Chief, who advocated peace with the Rebels and desired to remain neutral. See opening Chapter 11.

Ellinipsco: (NF) son of **Cornplanter**, a Shawanese Chief. See opening of Chapter 11.

Chief Redhawk: (NF) friend of **Cornplanter** and Shawanee Chief, as well. See opening of Chapter 11.

General William Howe: (NF) a British General who resigned his commission in 1777 and wintered over in Philadelphia before returning to England.

Captain Matthew Arbuckle: (NF) Rebel commander of Fort Pitt.

Also: **White Corn Woman, Sir Guy Carleton, Lieutenant Governor Henry Hamilton, Margaret Elder, Sue Ellen, Eve Earnest, Anne Wylie, Mikie Earnest, Henry Earnest, Ester Emler, George Emler, Conrad Samuel, Mary Earnest, George Earnest, Johannas Earnest, Jacob Earnest, Brother Bergfelder, George Woods, George Sill, Jessie Emler, Jac Emler, Barbara Emler Reighard, Stalking Wolf, the Smyth couple, Felix Skelly, Ezekiel Solomon, Philip DeJean, John Leeth, Ann Forsythe, General William Howe,** and **General Edward Hand.**

Chapter 10: Sandusky and the Wyandots, Mid December, 1777

Theresa Marie's (Boarding) house: (NF) a boarding house of Fort Detroit.

Jonas Schindler: (NF) this young silversmith has been documented as a resident of Detroit and like many locked ears with **Philip DeJean** (NF) and **Lieutenant Governor Henry Hamilton** (NF). **John Leeth** (NF) mentions his interaction with a young silversmith but does not name him.

The ***Welcome, Felicity*** and ***Angelica***: (NF) British merchant trade ships, confiscated for all practical purposes by the British for the War effort.

James May: (NF) blacksmith and outstanding merchant of Fort Detroit.

Pompey: (NF) black slave owned by **James May** (NF), educated by his former owners in the Caribbean.

Father Bocquet: (NF) a Recollect priest of the Roman Catholic Church serving Fort Detroit at Ste. Anne's Roman Catholic Church. This church and congregation still remain active in Detroit.

Pierre Mansour: (F) a coureur de bois or independent French trapper. and trader. A close friend of **John Coutincinau** (NF).

Also: **Cornstalk, Ellinipisco, Chief Redhawk, Captain Arbuckle, Anne Wylie, Eve Earnest, Sue Ellen, Mikie Earnest, Mister Biscoe, Henry Earnest (Hanu), Adam Henry Earnest, Felix Skelly, Stalking Wolf, White Corn Woman, Philip DeJean, John Montour, Queen Esther, John Leeth, Lieutenant Governor Henry Hamilton,** and **John Coutincinau.**

Chapter 11: Late December 1777

General Edward Hand: (NF) Rebel Commander of Fort Pitt (present day Pittsburgh, Pennsylvania). Fort Pitt will be commanded by both Pennsylvanian and Virginian commanders during the Revolutionary War. Many times there is no love lost between these two rebellious colonies and a dispute over this territory which to them included the Ohio territory. Oft times militia soldiers simply would not serve under a specific commander due to their state affiliation. Given that New England was once known as Upper Virginia and that Massachusetts also claimed the Ohio area, a rich farming and lumber area, residual hard feelings remained to fester and may have eventually been an underlying minor cause of the American Civil War.

Governor Patrick Henry: (NF) the governor of Virginia, commander of **George Rogers Clark** (NF), who does not always agree with **General George Washington,** commander of the Continental forces.

Toby Langlough: (F) a tuberculin infected gentleman, late in years living in the Citadel (ie Yankee Hall).

Susannah Dibert: (NF) youngest daughter of **John Dibert** (NF) and **Ene Ickes Dibert** (NF).

David Dibert: (all NF) eldest son of **John Dibert** and **Ene Ickes Dibert.**

Jean Baptiste Roucout: (NF) parish schoolmaster with the church of Ste. Anne of Fort Detroit.

Dr. George Anton: (NF) doctor for the Military of Fort Detroit who maintains a civilian practice on the side recognizing the lack of trained medical personnel in the area.

Martha: (F) a metisse, or half French and half Native American (Chippewa) woman who acts as a midwife for many people of the Fort Detroit area.

Abbott and Finchley (NF): one of the trading firms of Fort Detroit.

Also: **Mary Earnest, Eve Dibert (Mere Eve), Ene Dibert, John Dibert, Jac Emler, Mikie Earnest, Father Bocquet, John Coutincinau, Lieutenant Governor Henry Hamilton, Philip DeJean, Anne Wylie, Sue Ellen, Eve Earnest, Pompey, Mistress Smythe, Margaret Elder and her father's family, surname, Cessna, Stalking Wolf, Henry Earnest, and Eric Mens Emler.**

Chapter 12: March 9, 1778; Following the Winter of Sevens

William Forsythe: (NF) husband of **Ann Forsythe** (NF). Both managed **Fogherty's Inn** (NF) in Fort Detroit.

Tchamaniked Joe: (NF + F) meaning in Chippewa — "canoe maker" Joe. This character is inspired by an intelligent and talented man of the **Joseph Osogwin** (NF) family who was taken by Jesuits to France to become a priest. This man returned on his own against the wishes of the good Fathers to his homeland. He is dedicated to the **Osogwin**, **Shedawin**, and **Beaver** families who were well known in the Fort Michilimackinac and Fort Mackinac for their skillful canoe and boat building including the Mackinac boat and for being skilled pilots and licensed captains during a period when Native American Captains were not the norm. The Osogwin family continued as oral historians for the Chippewa and Ottawa after the father of **Chief Andrew J. Blackbird** (NF) initially appointed **Joseph Osogwin** (NF) prior to 1850. The Osogwin name is also spelled As-saw-gon. The Durant Roll lists these families. See also: ***Ogehmawahbee, Chippewa Warrior; And His Incredible Journey During the Time of Relocation*** retold by Mike Osogwin Jr. and Marianne Osogwin assisted by Moira Z. Wilson. Illustrated by Brian F. Wilson. It was also inspired by an unnamed Lakes Indian man (NF) who fearlessly confronted **George Rogers Clark** (NF) forces and who led the death song for his brethren at Fort Sackville i.e., Vincennes.

Teddy: (F) **Tchamaniked Joe's** (F) dog, brought with him from Ireland.

Levi Solomon: (NF) cousin of **Ezekiel Solomon** (NF). His mother is the **Ruth (Nanna) Solomon** (F). He is a merchant of Fort Detroit.

Also: John Leeth, William Boslick, James (Jamie) Cassidy, Abbott and Also continued: Finchley, Anne Wylie, Sue Ellen, Ann Forsyth, Pompey, John Coutincinau, Jacob Schieffelin, Lieutenant Governor Henry Hamilton, Philip DeJean, James May, Eve Earnest, Michael Earnest, Henry Earnest, Ezekiel Solomon, Ruth Solomon, and Jonas Schindler.

Chapter 13: The Next Day, March 10, 1778

General Frederick Haldimand (NF): **General Guy Carleton's** (NF) replacement. Head of British Forces for the Province of Quebec.

Pierre: (F) an employee of the Abbott and Finchley Warehouse.

Captain Guillaume LaMothe: (NF) a French habitant and one of the leaders of parties working for **Lieutenant Governor Henry Hamilton** (NF).

Richard Beringer Lernoult: (NF) builder of the new English fort (Fort Lernoult i.e. Fort Shelby) to replace deteriorated French fortification, Fort Pontchartrain (Fort Detroit). Initially the new English Fort was called Fort Lernoult. After American forces finally ousted the English years after the Revolutionary War Fort Lernoult became Fort Shelby. Lernoult served as Military Commander of Fort Detroit following **Captain Mompesson** (NF).

Philippe de Rastel Rocheblave: (NF) British Commandant of Fort Sackville, Vincennes, Indiana working with **Lieutenant Governor Henry Hamilton** (NF).

Father Pierre Gibault: (NF) a Roman Catholic Priest who sided with the American Forces (including **George Rogers Clark** (NF)) and who effectively guaranteed success for the Virginians in Vincennes and Kaskaskia.

Fort Sackville: (NF) the fort protecting Vincennes, IN aka **Fort Patrick Henry.**

General Edward Hand: (NF) American General of the Revolutionary Army stationed at Fort Pitt. Known rightly or wrongly for his questionable ability to command his militia forces during the infamous "Squaw Campaign."

Killbuck Jr. (NF) Delaware Chieftain and part of the Turtle phantry. Among those Delaware leaders who attempted to maintain neutrality and who was often thwarted in the process.

Captain Pipe: (NF) Delaware Chieftain of the Wolf phantry. Initially friendly to Rebel American's. Family members were involved in the "Squaw Campaign."

White Eyes (Koquenthagachton): (NF) Delaware Chieftain who sued for peace with the Americans. Signed Articles with the American side assuming that the Delaware (the Grandfathers) would be the spokesmen for the tribes of the heartland and assume the fourteenth star in the United States after the war. He most likely was murdered (some state that he died of smallpox) during the Revolutionary War while serving with American troops. After the war, the American government paid for formal education for his three sons at Princeton!

Welpachtachlechen: (NF): another Delaware Chieftain.

Colonel George Morgan: (NF) Rebel sympathizer and military person who aided the American cause by spreading information of Burgoyne's Defeat.

Arent Schuyler DePeyster: (NF): Eleventh Commander of Fort Detroit, former commander of Fort Michilimackinac.

Butler's Rangers: (NF) British forces under the control of **Lieutenant Colonel John Butler** (NF) out of British Fort Niagara and part if the British Indian Department, in command during the Wyoming massacre. Troops were well known for their fighting ability. He often worked in conjunction with **Joseph Brant** (NF). John Butler intensely hated Americans. **Walter Butler**, (NF) his son was captured and put in irons by Rebels in Albany, his wife and children were held as prisoners.

John Dodge: (NF): captured by **Lieutenant General Henry Hamilton** (NF). Eventually escaped from British prisons and gave some of the most damning testimony against Hamilton. Vol.II friendship to **John Montour** (NF) revealed.

Captain Eleople Chene: (NF) Delaware interpreter for **Lieutenant Governor Henry Hamilton**. Like many of the early French, his language skills and ties with the indigenous peoples through marriage and kinship made him extremely valuable to the British during the early stages of the Revolutionary War.

Also: **Lieutenant Governor Edward Abbott, Anne Wylie, James May, Pompey, Finchley of Abbott and Finchley, Philip DeJean, Pierre Manseur, John Coutincinau, Eve Earnest, Mikie Earnest, John Leeth, Jacob Schindler, Ezekiel Solomon, Jacob Schieffelin, Captain Jehu Hay, Lieutenant Governor Henry Hamilton, George Washington, King George III, Cornstalk, Ann Forsyth, Sue Ellen, Eve Earnest, Philip DeJean, Anne Wylie, General Guy Carleton, Stalking Wolf, John Montour, and Blue Ice.**

Chapter 14: March 29-31, 1778

John Askin: (NF) this astute Scotch-Irish trader had one Ottawa (Odawa) commonlaw wife from L'Arbor Croche and a second, **Marie Archange Barthe** (NF) at Fort Michilimackinac and later Fort Detroit. Shrewd and ambitious, having learned the importance of kinship in up-state New York trading, Askin soon amassed large property holdings and a thriving trading company in the Fort Michilimackinac area and Fort Detroit, the two major British Trading sites in the Great Lakes' heartland of Quebec referred to by the French as the Pays d'en Haut. Because Askin also owned ships and shipping interests in the Great Lakes, he was one of the major power brokers of his time.

Sally Ainsee: second wife of **Andrew Montour** (NF) and stepmother to **John Montour** (NF). An utterly amazing Oneida woman. Her name varies much in research. Her deeds included fighting for **Joseph Brant's** (NF) property rights and her own, also for assisting the Moravian refugees and her many business dealings as a successful woman merchant-trader. She accumulated many good properties and lived very well. Her expensive tastes have been referred to as a possible cause for her separation from Andrew Montour. She had many consorts after Montour. As a result she built kinship ties with the Delaware and Seneca in the East and affiliated tribes and the affiliation through kinship with her consorts' people in Northern Michigan near Fort Michilimackinac including Ottawa (Odawa) and Chippewa (Ojibway) peoples. She became a power major broker during this time period in Fort Detroit, and used her power, wealth, and influence to purchase land for the Moravians in what is now Mount Clemens. During this time period it was called New Gnadenhutten. She is the step-mother of **John Montour** (NF) (second wife of **Andrew Montour** (NF)). Andrew was the son of **Queen Catherine**, a sister to **Queen Esther**, a Seneca Matriarch well known in Pennsylvania for the slaughter of colonials following the death of her son when the Seneca were protected by treaty. Sally Ainsee also tried unsuccessfully to support the claims of **Joseph Brant** for money and lands due him after the Revolutionary War and fought many legal battles to secure her holdings on the Thames River in Ontario, Canada following the War of 1812.

Captain Charles Michel de Langlade (NF): French/Ottawa British supporter. Worked with **Ardent Schuyler DePeyster** (NF) to raise Ottawa troops to support the British cause.

Benjamin Franklin: (NF) the American Colonies Ambassador to France. Benjamin Franklin initially did not fully support the Rebel cause, but something he observed while in England brought him firmly to the Rebel side. He advocated speaking German as the common language for our country as it was close to English, easily learned, and spoken by many in our country already, but primarily because it would serve as a final rebuff to the English. Despite his brilliant arguments, the decision to use English as a common language won by one vote.

Sergeant John Turney: (NF) a British military messenger between Fort Detroit and Montreal.

The *Gage*: (NF) one of the largest British Warships on the Great Lakes boasting fourteen guns during the Revolutionary War.

Captain Alexander Grant: (NF) head of the naval forces in Fort Detroit and in charge of shipbuilding in the River Rouge area, west of Fort Detroit.

John Butler: (NF) British Military Commander of Fort Niagara, his forces were well known in the New England and New York areas for their raids on their western flank. His strong personality guaranteed that he and Lieutenant Governor Henry Hamilton would have an antagonistic relationship. Closer to Montreal, he could claim the ear of power in more ways than one. His greatest claim to fame included "Butler's Rangers," a well seasoned, highly effective strike force skilled in European and Native American fighting methods. See Butler's Rangers under Chapter 13.

Joseph Brant: (NF) one of the most interesting personalities of his time. Friend of **Sally Ainsee** (NF). British Commander of mixed European and Native American forces which was extremely unusual. College educated. World traveler. For the definitive work concerning this complex member of the Five Nations read Isabel Thompson Kelsay's *Joseph Brant, 1743 - 1807; Man of Two Worlds.*

Michel Dibert: (NF)+(F) brother of **John Dibert** (NF). Highly fictionized for the purposes of this book. Not historically accurate, but he did exist.

Also: **Anne Wylie, John Coutincinau, Sue Ellen, Eve Earnest, Mikie Earnest, Ruth Solomon, Toby Langlough, Jacob Schieffelin, Captain R. B. Lernoult, Lieutenant Governor Henry Hamilton, Arent DePeyster, John Leeth, Jacob Schindler, General Guy Carleton, Captain Guillaume LaMothe, Captain Jehu Hay, Jonas Schindler, King Gcrogc III, Sir Willam Johnson, White Eyes, Plerre (Abbott and Finchley's man). John Sterling, Philip DeJean, John Dodge, and "Nellie Mockler" as an unnamed shrew.**

Chapter 15: April 1778, Justice Prevails?

Nonhelma: (NF) sister of Shawnee Chief, **Cornstalk** (NF).

Light in the Morning: (NF) fiction in name only, mother of **Captain Pipe** (NF), injured in "Squaw Campaign."

Captain Pipe's Brother: (NF) killed protecting the women in the "Squaw Campaign."

Sparkling Brook: (NF + F) this character suggested by the young Munsee woman injured in the "Squaw Campaign."

Also: **General Edward Hand, Pompey, Eve Earnest, Mikie Earnest, James May, Anne Wylie, Philip DeJean, John Coutincinau, Finchley of Abbott and Finchley, White Eyes, Killbuck, King George III, Half King, David Zeisburger, George Washington, Captain Pipe, Alexander McKee, Simon Girty, Matthew Elliott, Cornstalk, George Morgan (Rebel), White Corn Woman, First encounter with unnamed captive Sally Lowrey i.e., Winter Hare see Chapter 21, Stalking Wolf, Blue Ice, Sitting Rabbit, John Montour, Hanu (Henry Earnest), Little Fox, Queen Esther, Jehu Hay, Lieutenant Governor Henry Hamilton, Jacob Schieffelin, Lord George Germain, Captain John Butler, Edward Abbott, Philippe de Rastel Rocheblave,** and **Sir Guy Carleton.**

Chapter 16: Justice Challenged, Early May 1778

Alexander McKee: (NF) an American defector who worked for the Indian Office under **Lieutenant General Henry Hamilton** (NF) and **Ardent Schuyler DePeyster** (NF).

Nellie Mockler: (F) a volatile Irish American captured like **Eve Earnest** (NF) with her lone daughter **Fiona** (F), she has buried many children and two husbands.

George Elder: (NF) husband of **Margaret Elder** (NF).

Mitsy: (F) **John Dibert's** (NF) horse.

Also: **Margaret Elder, Eve Earnest, Mikie Earnest, John Dodge, Dr. George Anton, Anne Wylie, John Coutincinau, John Montour, Stalking Wolf, Lieutenant Governor Henry Hamilton, Pierre of Abbott and Finchley, the Smythes, Jacob Schieffelin, Henry (Hanu)**

Earnest, Eve (Mere Eve) Dibert, John Dibert, Mary (Molly) Earnest, Ene Dibert (the mother), Conrad Samuel, Susanna Dibert, Ene Dibert (the younger), Elizabeth (Lizzie) Dibert, Barbara Dibert, David Dibert, Jessie Emler, Ester Emler, Eric Mens Emler (George Emler), John Leeth, Standing Bear, and Falling Water Woman.

Chapter 17, Late May, Highs and Lows

Hazel: (NF) well-known British message bearer and interpreter for **Lieutenant Governor Henry Hamilton's** (NF) Indian Department.

George Girty: (NF) brother of **Simon Girty** (NF). Fluent in Delaware.

James Girty: (NF) brother of **Simon Girty** (NF). Fluent in Shawanese.

Matthew Elliott: (NF) complex defector to the British side with Captain **Alexander McKee** (NF) a crafty Tory, he alluded capture by the Americans and Virginians of Fort Pitt. Probably, he functioned as a spy, long before his actual defection to Fort Detroit and the British forces.

Agnes: (F) shrewish wife of **Pierre** (F), the hired man working for **Abbott and Finchley** (NF).

Joseph Hecker: (NF) a man earlier executed by **Philip DeJean** (NF) for killing his brother-in-law, a man named **Moran** (NF).

Also: **Lieutenant Governor Henry Hamilton, Daniel Boone (NF), Governor Guy Carleton, Philip DeJean, Anne Wylie, Finchley of Abbott and Finchley, Eve Earnest, Mikie Earnest, Pompey, James May, the Smythes, Sue Ellen, Nellie Mockler, Jean Baptiste Roucout, Father Bouquet, John Coutincinau, Pierre Manseur, James Sterling, John Dodge, Stalking Wolf, Jehu Hay, Jacob Schieffelin, Lord Dunmore (John Murray), Simon Girty, General Hand, Henry Earnest (Hanu), Tchamaniked Joe, Teddy** and **Pierre, the employee of Finchley and Abbott.**

Chapter 18: A Warm June in 1778 with New Wrinkles

Antoine: (F) a man of Brittany, France with a love of Celtic music. This man could turn out a meal, a ballad, or a roughneck from **Fogherty's Inn** (NF), all in short order!

Also: **Lieutenant Governor Henry Hamilton, Eve Earnest, Mikie Earnest, Nellie Mockler, Sue Ellen, Pierre Manseur, Tchamaniked Joe, Anne Wylie, Teddy, John Leeth, Jonas Schindler, Simon Girty, William Forsythe, Ann Forsythe, Jacob Schieffelin, Henry (Hanu) Earnest, George Girty, Stalking Wolf, Margaret Elder, Toby Langlough, Little Fox, Blue Ice, James May, Ezekiel Solomon,** and **John Askin.**

Chapter 19: August 1778, A Hot Dry Summer

Elsie: (F) Native American wife of **Nellie Mockler**'s Uncle (all F).

Stuffy Dutchman: (F) **Karl Wenzel**, a male captive at Yankee Hall.

Colonel David Rogers: (NF) a leader and one of forty two Americans killed by **Simon Girty's** (NF) British and Native American raiding party in July or August 1778.

Theotiste St. Cosme: (NF) second wife of **Philip DeJean** (NF).

Pierre St. Cosme: (NF) early resident of Fort Detroit, a well established and respected French habitant.

Marie Louisa Augier: (NF) first wife of **Philip DeJean** (NF).

Also: **David Dibert, John Dibert, Eve Dibert (Mere Eve), Michel Dibert, Susanna Dibert, Mary (Molly) Earnest, Young Ene Dibert, Ene Dibert (the mother), Elizabeth Dibert, Henry Earnest, Mikie Earnest, Eve Earnest, Nellie Mockler, Teddy, Tchamaniked Joe, Margaret Elder, Sally Ainsee, Toby Langlough, Lieutenant Governor Henry Hamilton, John Montour, Stalking Wolf, Simon Girty, Matthew Elliott, Alexander McKee, Captain Lernoult, Jacob Schieffelin, Father Pierre Gibault, Arent DePeyster, Francois Louis Frederick Haldimand, Governor Guy Carleton, King George III,** and **Philip DeJean.**

Chapter 20: September 1778, The Fourteenth Star

Colonel George Morgan, General Lachlan McIntosh, Col. Daniel Brodhead, Colonel William Crawford, Captain John Gibson, Major Arthur Graham, Captain Joe L. Finley, John Campbell, John Stephenson, Benjamin Mills, General Andrew Lewis, Thomas Lewis,

White Eyes, the Pipe, and John Killbuck: (all NF) Signers of an Article of Confederation between the Delaware nation and individuals representing the American forces.

Major General James Abercromby: (NF) bungling British leader who watched his Scottish Highlanders brutally out maneuvered and killed by the French in the battle of Fort Ticonderoga (Known as Fort Carillon in New France) in 1756.

Captain Norman MacLeod: (NF) Mayor of Detroit, one if the Captains of the Militia, husband of **Helen MacLeod** (NF), and father of **Jeannie MacLeod** (NF). He served in many Military capacities before working with his mentor, **Sir William Johnston** (NF). If you have enjoyed this book, *Detroit to Fort Sackville, The Journal of Norman MacLeod* published by Wayne State University is a must read. His journal constitutes one of the jewels of the period and in my opinion should be included in American Literature Courses as part of the canon. He is an outstanding example of the Scottish forces sent to fight in and for America's colonies during the French and Indian War (Seven Year War).

Gregor MacGregor and Simon MacTavish: (NF) fellow merchants and friends of **Norman MacLeod** (NF).

Molly Brant: (NF) sister of **Joseph Brant** (NF) and consort of the late, **Sir William Johnson** (NF), who once headed the British Indian Office before the outbreak of the American Revolutionary War.

Captain Francois Maisonville: (NF) aka **Francis,** a habitant who worked as an interpreter for the Hamilton's department.

Lieutenant Henry DuVernett: (NF) a British military volunteer who served during Hamilton's march on Fort Sackville (Vincennes). Skilled and ambitious, the young military Lieutenant was on loan from **Captain Lernoult** (NF).

Captain LaMothe: (NF) French habitant who worked as an interpreter for Hamilton's department and Detroit Militia leader.

Also: **White Eyes, William Penn, Lieutenant Governor Henry Hamilton, King George III, Killbuck, Captain Pipe, Cornstalk, Ellinipisco, Redhawk, allusion to Tchmaniked Joe, Stalking Wolf, White Corn Woman, Little Fox, allusion to Mary (Molly) Earnest, Blue Ice, Eve Dibert (Mere Eve), Michel Dibert, John Dibert, David Dibert, Jessie Emler, allusion to Eric Mens Emler, Jac Emler, Jacob**

Schieffelin, Philippe Rocheblave, Matthew Elliott, Alexander McKee, the Girty Brothers, James Sterling, Philip DeJean, the *Felicity,* Arent DePeyster, Patrick Sinclair, Edward Abbott, Frederick Haldimand, Major Jehu Hay, John Coutincinau, Eve Earnest, Captain Lernoult, Captain Henry Bird, Fiona Mockler, Nellie Mockler, Sally Ainsee, Toby Langlough, Karl Wenzel, Martha, the matisse midwife and healer, Margaret Elder, Mikie and Henry Earnest, and the **Solomon children.**

Chapter 21: The Great Leaving, First Week of October, 1778

Captain Henry Bird: (NF) physically unattractive, a bit of a bantam rooster, but nonetheless an extremely talented builder, fighter, and commander of British troops.

Captain Alexander Grant: (NF) Naval Commander and Harbor Commander of Fort Detroit under the British, headquartered on the River Rouge where he commanded men and shipbuilders alike.

Archangel: (NF) Captain Grant's sloop during the Revolutionary War.

Standing Bear: (NF) Delaware adopted father of John Leeth.

Falling Water Woman: (F) wife of **Standing Bear** (NF). A Delaware mother who adopted **John Leeth** (NF).

Winter Hare: fictional name for **Sally Lowrey** (NF) white captive of the Delaware and wife of **John Leeth** (NF).

Sparkling Brook: (F) based on a beautiful young Maumee woman, scarred emotionally and physically in the infamous "Squaw Campaign." She represents many of the injured Native American women devastated by hate and hostility during the Revolutionary War.

Logan: Tah-gah-jute (Long Lashes): (NF) a former friend of the American Rebels and America under the British, his family and all its members, save one, were massacred by Americans. Like the Seneca, **Queen Esther** (aunt of **Andrew Montour** and great-aunt of **John Montour**—all NF), Logan exacted revenge by brutally killing thirteen Americans (some say more)…one for each lost family member. His last years were spent in an alcoholic stupor at British Fort Detroit as he sunk into complete bitterness and despair. Myth states that the one remaining member of his family (a child rumored to have been fathered by American

Colonel John Gibson (NF) and born of his murdered sister (NF)), was taken during the massacre and raised by an American military commander as his own. Logan's father was named **Shikellamy** (NF) and his brother, **John Petty Shickellmany** (NF). Both were slaughtered in the massacre. Many feel these inhumane acts helped to fuel part of the deep hatred which resulted in the torturous death of **George Washington**'s friend **Colonel William Crawford** (NF) after the Gnadenhutten Massacre. Logan may have been murdered by a remaining relative.

Monsieur Jean Baptist de Celeron: (NF) accused by **Lieutenant Governor Henry Hamilton** (NF) of being a rebel sympathizer and immediately on the outs because of his being an "interior habitant" or a leftover lazy and unscrupulous Frenchman from New France. De Celeron was also accused by **George Rogers Clark** (NF) for being a British sympathizer doing a great disservice to the Virginian and American interests among Wabash Indians.

Dame Grant: (NF) a very heavyset merchant woman who traded with American Revolutionary soldiers imprisoned on scuttled ships in the back harbors of New York.

Old Bobby: (NF) another American prisoner of the British, held in New York.

Also: **Governor Frederick Haldimand, Lieutenant Governor Henry Hamilton, Philip DeJean, Antoine, John Coutincinau, Anne Wylie, Ann Forsythe, Norman MacLeod, Sue Ellen, Tchamaniked Joe, Nellie Mockler, Sally Ainsee, Teddy, Captain Mompesson, Captain Lernoult, Pompey, Fiona Mockler, Martha, Toby Langlough, the metisse healer, Father Bouquet, John Leeth, Stalking Wolf, White Corn Woman, Blue Ice, Sitting Rabbit, Little Fox, Singing Grass, Sparkling Brook, Brother John Heckwelder, Alexander McKee, the Girty Brothers, Matthew Elliott, John Montour, Michel Dibert, Mere Eve Dibert, John Dibert, Ene Dibert, Jessie Emler,** and **Mary (Molly) Earnest.**

Chapter 22: Mid to Late October, Among the Troops

Captain Joe Bowman: (NF) Rebel leader from Virginia and friend of **George Rogers Clark** (NF).

Nicholas Gowan: (NF) a militia member from Detroit who created problems for **Norman MacLeod** (NF).

Charles Baubien or Bobian: (NF) an interpreter and leader amongst the British Forces out of Fort Detroit.

Captain and Dr. John McBeath: (NF) a military doctor who accompanied the British Forces. Though initially sent back to Fort Detroit with an injured soldier, he returned and continued to Vincennes. Nearly shot at Fort Sackville when George Rogers Clark's forces attacked. He heroically treated British casualties injured by American sharpshooters.

Lieutenant Shroud: (NF) a young British soldier who shot himself accidentally shortly after leaving Fort Detroit.

Neegik, the Otter: (NF) brother of **Chamintawa** (NF).

Gros Loup: (NF) Miami Chief

Young Tobacco: (NF) also called "The Gate" or "the Great Door of the Wabash." A Native American of the Piankashaw tribe who shifted allegiances during the Revolutionary War, a leader among the Wabash League. He and his father's position would be comparable to **Chief Pontiac** (NF) in the North.

Old Tobacco: (NF) father of **Young Tobacco** (NF).

Pacane, the Nut: (NF) Chief of the Miami. See Henry Hamilton's sketch.

Menard the Carpenter: (F) a fictional carpenter from Fort Detroit.

George Elder: (NF) husband of **Margaret Elder** (NF), son-in-law of **Cessna** (NF).

Richard Shirley: (NF) friend of **George Elder** (NF).

Also: **Norman MacLeod, George Rogers Clark, Lieutenant Governor Henry Hamilton, Phillipe Rocheblave, Francois Maisonville aka Francis, Monsieur Jean Baptist de Celeron, Edward Abbott, Frederick Haldimand, Jehu Hay,** and **Tchamaniked Joe.**

Chapter 23: November 1778, En Route to Justice

Isaac William and sons: (NF) traders allied with **Norman MacLeod** (NF).

Captain Lachland McIntosh: (NF) Rebel American serving with new American Indian Department. Guided by **White Eyes** (NF) shortly before his murder (as reported by **George Morgan** (NF)) and advanced into Indian Country with a false treaty which further alienated the tribes forced into the Ohio territory.

Isaac (Glikhikan): (NF) Delaware allied with the Moravian Missionaries, friend and advisor to **Chief White Eyes** (NF).

Red Fawn Woman: (F) dead wife of **Stalking Wolf** (F) and Mother of **Willow** (F) and a son (F), who also died from disease or violence during western expansion.

Le Petit Gris (The Dappled Fawn): (NF) Miami chieftain and orator for his nation.

Also: **Jehu Hay, Lord Dunmore, Nellie Mockler, Eve Earnest, Sue Ellen, Mikie Earnest, Henry Earnest, Adam Henry Earnest, Margaret Elder, Fiona Mockler, Menard, Tchamaniked Joe, Doctor John McBeath, Dr. George Anton, Jeannie MacLeod, Helen MacLeod, Norman MacLeod, Gregor MacGregor, Jean Baptist de Celeron, Lieutenant Governor Henry Hamilton, Chief White Eyes, Stalking Wolf, Little Fox, Singing Grass, Isaac (Glikhikan), David Zeisburger, John Heckwlder,** and **Father Bocquet.**

Chapter 24: Advent and More

Jean Baptiste Chapton: (NF) a French habitant trader near Illinois and suspect individual in the eyes of **Lieutenant Governor Henry Hamilton** (NF).

Raimbault: (NF) a fellow French Trader allied with **Jean Baptiste Chapton** (NF).

St. Andrew: (NF) Patron Saint of Scotland.

Egushawa: (NF) notable Chief Orator and War Chief for the Ottawa and Chippewa located in the area north of Detroit and near the Saginaw area.

Inheritor of **Chief Pontiac's** (NF) mantle of authority. Egushawa represented his people well, who farmed the Saginaw and Thumb areas of Michigan. These Chippewa bands would journey north at appropriate times to harvest whitefish, make pottery or hunt game in the Eastern Upper Peninsula and Upper Lower Michigan. Egushawa proved to be one of the most supportive of Native Allies for **Lieutenant Governor Henry Hamilton** (NF). However, after **George Roger Clark's** (NF) bloody opening and second winning of the Vincennes area at the very gates of Fort Sackville under the gaze of Lieutenant Governor Henry Hamilton, Egushawa advocated neutrality in the British-American conflict. With his support, **Sally Ainsee** (NF) purchased the Mount Clemens area for the Moravian and Delaware refugees, a property later purchased by **John Askin** (NF).

Chief Naudowance and Flat Button: (NF) war chief and top warrior under **Egushawa** (NF).

Isidor Chene: (NF) French habitant and interpreter for Lieutenant Governor Henry Hamilton's department.

Pierre Chesne: (NF) interpreter for the British Indian Department.

Le Navire: A ship like rock formation along the Wabash River. See the sketches of Henry Hamilton.

Captain Leonard Helm: (NF) Rebel Virginian commandant of Fort Sackville (Fort Patrick Henry) in the absence of **George Rogers Clark** (NF). He was easily defeated by **Lieutenant Governor Henry Hamilton** (NF) and became his prisoner prior to George Rogers Clark retaking the Fort.

J. Hunot: (NF) scout for **Norman MacLeod** (NF).

Francis Vigo (Vigaud the Piedmontese): (NF) a Spanish subject and trader working the Fort Vincennes area, a Piedmontese.

Great Eyes: (NF) an Ouiatenon (Wea) Chief presumably known for being an "eater of men" and a renowned warrior.

Also: **Francois Maisonville, Lieutenant Governor Henry Hamilton, Norman MacLeod, Lieutenant Henry DuVernett, Major General James Abercrombie, George Elder, Margaret Elder, Jehu Hay, Sir William Johnson, Eve Earnest, Sally Ainsee, Anne Wylie, allusion to George Emler, Adam Henry Earnest, Father Bouquet, Jean Baptiste**

Roucout, Sue Ellen, Dr. George Anton, Helen MacLeod, Major General Thomas, Gage, Old Tobacco, New Tobacco, King George III, George Rogers Clark, Matthew Elliott, Alexander McKee, Jonas Schindler, Captain LaMothe, and Lieutenant Jacob Schieffelin,

Chapter 25: Twelve Days of Christmas and more 1778-1779

George Mason: (NF) friend and patron of **George Rogers Clark** (NF).

Kissingua (NF) a young warrior who assisted the British and accompanied Hazel (NF) on expeditions.

Sargent Burgois: (NF) British Military officer who escorted militia members back to Detroit following the British Victory at Fort Sackville (Vincennes).

George: (NF) **Norman MacLeod** (NF) hired this free black in Fort Vincennes. The British released black slaves and indentured servants from their Rebel owners if they would serve the British side.

Three De Quindre Lieutenants: (NF) three French habitants who served with the British Indian Department under **Lieutenant Governor Henry Hamilton** (NF).
Nydia: (F) woman living in Yankee Hall.

Also: **George Rogers Clark, Mary Earnest (Molly), Mikie Earnest, Henry Earnest, Eve Earnest, Norman MacLeod, Sally Ainsee, George, Jehu Hay, Lieutenant Jacob Schieffelin, Captain LaMothe, Captain Leonard Helm, Phillipe Rocheblave, Lieutenant Governor Henry Hamilton, Captain Francois Maisonville, Menard the Carpenter, Tchamaniked Joe, Jeannie MacLeod, Helen MacLeod, Gregor MacGregor, Nellie Mockler, Fiona Mockler, Toby Langlough, Anne Wylie, Sue Ellen,** and **Father Bouquet.**

Chapter 26: Adventures and Mis-adventures Beginning January 10, 1779

Charles Reaume (NF): brother in law of **Jehu Hay** (NF).

Unnamed Rebel Messenger: (NF) an American carrying letters intended for **George Rogers Clark** concerning British troops near Vincennes who died.

The Bouchers: (NF) French habitant brothers residing in Vincennes. Initially they remained steadfast to the Rebel side before work projects discouraged their continued allegiance.

Jean L'Course: (NF) a French trader of questionable allegiance to the British in Vincennes.

Don Bernardo de Galvis: (NF) Spanish Governor of New Orleans during the Revolutionary War. His government supplied black powder and lead for American arms often extending large lines of credit and may have helped to assist Fort Pitt to stave off British attacks. Some maintain this powder supply also assisted George Washington's troops and were brought up the Mississippi to the Ohio River. This supply constitutes a major reason for **Lieutenant Governor Henry Hamilton's** (NF) desire to control the Mississippi.

Guillaume Le Comte: (NF) friend of **Vigaud the Piedmontese (Vigo Francis) (Francis Vigo)** (NF). These two men will prove to be major informants for **George Rogers Clark** (NF) and the American/Virginian Forces.

Captain Bloomer: (NF) a commander for the Spanish at Fort Natchez.

Anderson: (F) a fellow British militia member from Fort Detroit.

Nickerson: (F) an itinerant weaver who sold thread and helped to set up looms for women to weave off.

Hypolite Bolon: (NF) one of the interpreters for **Lieutenant Governor Henry Hamilton's** (NF) British Indian Department, a French habitant.

Pierre and Isidore Chesne: (NF) brothers and interpreters for **Lieutenant Governor Henry Hamilton's** (NF) British Indian Department, both French habitants.

Calamuti: (NF) nephew of **Isidore Chesne** (NF), probably a Native American.

Lieutenant St. Cosme: (NF) interpreter for **Lieutenant Governor Henry Hamilton's** (NF) British Indian Department and a French habitant.

Charles Baubien: (NF) interpreter for **Lieutenant Governor Henry Hamilton's** (NF) British Department and a French habitant.

Also: **George Rogers Clark, George Mason, Dr. George Anton, Eve Earnest, Nellie Mockler, Sue Ellen, Lieutenant Governor Henry Hamilton, Martha, the metisse midwife, Menard the Carpenter, Tchamaniked Joe, Major Jehu Hay, Lieutenant Henry DuVernett, Arent De Peyster, Captain LaMothe, Matthew Elliott, Captain Leonard Helm, Philip DeJean, Helen MacLeod, Sally Ainsee, Margaret Elder, George Elder, Egushawa, Blue Ice,** and **Captain Francis Maisonville.**

Chapter 27: Flooding, Frenchmen, and Fury Meet the Fates in February, 1779

Buck: (F) a prisoner of Fort Detroit living in the Yankee Hall.

Hannah: (F) a prisoner of Fort Detroit living in the Yankee Hall.

Maggie: (F) an unmarried spinster with a large lower lip living in the Yankee Hall.

William Williams: (NF) a young Rebel prisoner bought by **Lieutenant Governor Henry Hamilton** (NF) before he could be killed or adopted by one of his Native allies. The young man would escape and report to **George Rogers Clark** (NF).

Theotiste St. Cosme DeJean: (NF) second wife of Philip **DeJean** (NF), daughter of **Pierre St. Cosme** (NF) and **Catherine Barrios** (NF). A French habitant.

Nicholas Montour: (NF) son of **Andrew Montour** (NF) and **Sally (Montour) Ainsee** (NF), and half brother of **John Montour** (NF).

Lieutenant Bailey: (NF) a soldier under the command of **George Rogers Clark** (NF).

Macutte Mong: (NF) an Ottawa Chief killed by **George Rogers Clark** (NF) and his Virginian forces.

Captain McCarty: (NF) a Rebel Captain under the command of **George Rogers Clark** (NF) in Vincennes. In earlier battles before the Revolutionary War, **Chief Pontiac** (NF) had spared his life.

Chief Pontiac: (NF) an Ottawa war chieftain well known for his decisive attacks against the British beginning in 1761 at Fort Michilimackinac.

Originally promised by **Major Robert Rogers** (NF) and **George Crogan** (NF) after the surrender of Fort Detroit by the French to the British that the Ottawa would enjoy free trade under the British, the arrogant British alienated the Ottawa by treating them as a conquered people. **Pontiac's** unnamed son would be spared death at the hands of **George Rogers Clark** (NF) and his forces when **Captain McCarty** (NF) interceded for him at Vincennes.

Sergeant Sancrainte: (NF) son of one of **George Rogers Clark's** (NF) force. The son fought with the British under **Lieutenant Governor Henry Hamilton** (NF).

Sergeant Robert: (NF) a man under **Lieutenant Governor Henry Hamilton** (NF) whose death was prevented when **his sister** (a resident of Vincennes) (NF) pleaded and wept for his commuted sentence.

Also: **George Rogers Clark, George Mason, Francis Vigo, Eve Earnest, Nellie Mockler, Toby Langlough, Sally Ainsee, Karl Wenzel, Menard the Carpenter, Father Pierre Gibault, Tchamaniked Joe, Young Tobacco, Old Tobacco, the Boucher Brothers, Theotiste St. Cosme DeJean, Sue Ellen, Anne Wylie (Nancy), John Coutincinau, George, Egushawa, Lieutenant Governor Henry Hamilton, Major Jehu Hay, Captain Francois Maisonville aka Francis, Captain LaMothe, Lieutenant Jacob Schieffelin, Jonas Schindler, Henry Earnest, and Mikie Earnest.**

Chapter 28: March Comes in Like a Scotsman

Peter: (F) also known as **Smoke in Eyes** (F), son of **Blue Ice** (F), a young Delaware who will be converted to join the Moravian Delaware in Vol. II. See Chapter 8, Vol. I.

Patrick Henry: (NF) a brilliant and fiery orator lawyer in the assembly of Virginia, who boldly asserted that **King George III** (NF) was a tyrant, "I know not what course others may take; but as for me, give me liberty or give me death." Fort Sackville was renamed by the Virginia militia, Fort Patrick Henry.

Col. William Crawford: (NF) a close friend of **George Washington** (NF). Bombastic, he had been guided into the Ohio country by **Chief White Eyes** (NF) who was murdered during that outing. Detested, Crawford became a laughingstock to the Native American Tribes of Ohio area.

Col. Daniel Brodhead (later General): (NF) commandant of Fort Pitt who had complained to Washington about Crawford's poor leadership. Brodhead, however, would be challenged eventually by numerous Civilian complaints during his career for his cronyism and excessive lifestyle.

Agatha, Mattie, and Hannah: (F) other residents of Yankee Hall.

Also: **George Rogers Clark, Lieutenant Governor Henry Hamilton, Dr. John McBeath, Norman MacLeod Jeannie MacLeod, Helen MacLeod, George, Captain R. B. Lernoult, Menard the Carpenter, Tchamaniked Joe, Phillip DeJean, Hybolite Bolon, Major Jehu Hay, George Mason, John Leeth, Sally Lowrey (Winter Hare), Blue Ice, Egushawa, Little Fox, Singing Grass, Stalking Wolf, David Zeisburger, Standing Bear, Falling Water, Michel Dibert, his Uncle in New Orleans, Mikie Earnest, Henry Earnest, Karl Wenzel, Toby Langlough, James May, Sally Ainsee, Nellie Mockler, Fiona Mockler, Eve Earnest, John Montour, Macutte Mong,** and **Little Tobacco.**

Chapter 29: April 1780, Looking Homeward

Raven Wing: (F) Chippewa Matron and wife of **Tchamaniked Joe** (NF+F).

Col. Bowman: (NF) Rebel soldier put in command of the party which marched a chained **Lieutenant Governor Henry Hamilton** (NF) and his party to Williamsburg, Virginia. Bowman is known for his humane treatment.

Also: **Lieutenant Governor Henry Hamilton, George Rogers Clark, Nellie Mockler, Agatha, Sally Ainsee, Eve Earnest, Mikie Earnest, Henry Earnest, Fiona Mockler, Anne Wylie, Helen MacLeod, Nicholas Montour, Tchamaniked Joe, Eric Mens Emler (George), Ester Emler, Mary Earnest (Molly), Philip DeJean, Captain Francois Maisonville aka Francis, Margaret Elder, Sue Ellen, Fiona Mockler, Father Bocquet, Martha, the midwife, Sparkling Brook (unnamed) Ruth (Nanna) Solomon,** and **Ezekiel Solomon.**

Glossary

Aakidewin: Anishinaabe for "follow your heart"

Animakwe: German woman or Dutch woman in Ojibway (Chippewa or Anishinaabe) in part based on the French word for Germanic peoples, Allemand

Baamaa pii ka-waab-min: Anishanabek for "Until I see your face again"

Banyan: a long lounging shirt for men, it could be silk

Bastion: a fortified protrusion on a fort wall that allows the person on the wall to fire in several directions

Bateau: small boat

Breed: a racial slur focused on those who were part Native American

Brown Bess: British army flintlock musket with brown walnut stock, unrifled

Bruder: German for brother Bruderlein: affection term for brother

Bundling: An early dating custom where a young man and young women were placed side by side in bundling bags with a bundling board between them, and left all night in bed to become acquainted before marriage

Centure fleche: brightly colored, finger woven sashes, tied snuggly about the midriff of voyageurs, believed to give additional back support when carrying heavy loads on portages. Many voyageurs suffered from ruptured intestines due to the enormous amounts that they carried. These sashes were like a badge of office, woven with extreme patience, and great diligence during layovers. The patterns were very intricate and very colorful. Having attempted one, I assure you that it requires the patience of Job.

Chapbook: a small pamphlet or booklet often telling tales, ballads, or poems, sometimes a chapter at a time

Citadel: a fortress built on a high vantage spot. In Fort Detroit the Citadel became known as "Yankee Hall" due to the number of Rebel prisoners housed there during the Revolutionary War.

Consumption: an early word for a person suffering from Tuberculosis

Coureur de bois: woodsman or trapper, a woods runner

Crooked knife: a knife used by Native American canoe builders, often made from discarded files which was curved on the end and was pulled towards the user as a one handed draw knife to thin or smooth planking and wooden construction

Dram: a small drink of spirits

Draughted: drafted, earlier spelling of same

Esclave: a person used as a slave by the French, in some instances it was more like an indentured servant

Faunched (verb) or faunching (noun): this Appalachian word is one that I literally grew up with. My neighbor's family used it often. This refers to a state of agitation when just the slightest act or word will trigger a hot temper and a scorching rebuke. I have never found it in a dictionary. Perhaps it should be spelled fawnch or fonch.

Faus pas: an indiscreet remark or improper social action

Firkin: a small cask or quarter barrel to carry butter or liquids

Fusil: a light musket

Gaol: English for jail in the seventeen-hundreds

Gorget: worn by military forces as a protective armor at the vulnerable base of the throat made of stone or metal, sometimes worn as regalia by Native Americans.

Grossmutter: German for grandmother, intimate, Oma

Grossvater: German for grandfather, intimate, Opa

Hobble: tie two legs together to prevent an animal from straying

Huzzah: a hearty cheer of approval

Indentured servant: a party in agreement for another to work off a debt, for example, servitude for five years to pay ones passage to the new world, or for an apprenticeship. A legal contract was drawn up and had understandings for both parties involved.

Indian Eve: a name given to Eve Earnest Samuels which no doubt was a racial slur in her time, but for her descendents, it is a title accepted with pride

Indian summer: a time of fear when during the last hurrahs of fall, freed from harvesting, warrior could attack

League: a distance of about 3 miles or 5 kilometers

Le cochon: French for "the pig"

Mann: German for husband

Metis, Metisse, Metisses: a person of mixed descent, usually French and Native American, male, female, and plural given. Not politically correct today.

Mishinnawey: an appointed host, held in esteem by the Lakes tribes

Midewiwin medicine man: a respected shaman trained in the healing arts, completed in a series of degrees until he reaches the highest level of proficiency

Mon Dieu: "my God" in French

Mordant: verb: to impregnate wool with a metallic salt or compound to make it receptive to dye, noun: the metallic salt or compound used

Mutter or Mutti: German for Mother, Mutti intimate and affectionate

Nancy: a word used by the French for black women slaves also a synonym for Anne

Natte: a souvenir taken from battle used as a relic to insure victory in coming battles and paraded before raiding parties like a flag carried into battle

Noggin: a small drinking mug

Oakum: shredded rope used as caulking in boats

Onkel: German for Uncle

Onkle: French for Uncle

Pawl: the prong that engages the ratchet gear which holds tension on the warp when weaving and which secures the thread from moving forward. In sailing, it prevents the windlass or winch from recoiling

Pemmican: a cake of dried meat, berries, grains, and tallow

Perle noir: French for black pearl

Petite guerre: "a small war," the initial Rebellion by the Americans brought a loathing view of the war by the British initially considered as little more than a trifle.

Phantry: In early writings it may mean tribe or totem

Pirogues: canoes or open boats

Pomme caille: a deep red snow apple, flushed with red from skin to core which contrasts with the pure white interior, considered a winter apple because of its storing ability

Pontil (punty): a metal rod used in glass making which when broken from the molten surface leaves a telltale mark. Early window panes were globs of molten glass spun on the end of the pontil, leaving small waves and ripples in the surface and a rough spot where it was removed from the rod.

Regalia: distinctive or elaborate clothing or ornamentation

Roach: a brush cut strip of hair, waxed and often with ornamentation worn by the Huron, the rest of the scalp would be shaved clean

Schmierkase: dried cottage cheese, sometimes reconstituted in cream

Schmutzig krankheit: dirty sickness, German

Schnecke: snail shaped buns made with yeast, cinnamon, and nuts

Schnitz un knepp: apple, ham, and dumplings

Schwagerin: German for sister-in-law

Schwiegersohn: German for son-in-law

Schwieger Vater: German for father-in-law

Schwester: German for sister

Sinister hand: left hand

Sohn: German for son

Taffia: a cheap form of low grade rum distilled from low grade molasses or brown sugar

Tankard: a drinking vessel with single handle, often made of wooden staves and hooped as in barrel making

Tante: German for aunt

Tête-à-tête: a private conversation

Three sisters: corn, squash and beans, a Native American anecdote states, "as long as we have the three sisters, we shall never starve."

Thrums: the short leftover threads from warp after the warp has been completely woven as far as permissible

Tochter: German for daughter

Tow: the short stick-like fibers of waste linen which is left after the best fibers are retted, braked, and hackled (stems are rotted, broken, and combed over spikes)

Trencher: a hollowed-out wooden plate, often shared by more than one person

Tump-line: a leather strap put about the forehead to assist one in carrying heavy loads

Trunnel: A wooden nail, treenail which swells when wet, used in ship building

Unserr Gott: German for "our God"

Vater or Vati: German for father, intimate, Vati

Victuals: food

Wamus: A hip length hunting shirt, usually fringed and made of tanned leather

Warp: measured and tensioned thread on the loom to be woven, going from front to back of loom

Weft: or Woof (Scottish): threads woven in the warp, left to right